The Blushing Brides Quartet

An Earl for Ellen

A Marquis for Marianne

A Duke for Diana

A Captain for Clarissa

CATHERINE BILSON

CONTENTS

An Earl for Ellen

CATHERINE BILSON

CONTENTS

PROLOGUE

December, 1817

"I'm sorry, Miss Bentley." The land steward twisted his hat between his hands, an expression of genuine distress on his weathered face. "The living's been awarded, though, and the new vicar will be arriving soon to take up residence. You've two weeks to vacate the Vicarage."

Ellen Bentley clung to the door frame, hoping it would keep her upright as her knees threatened to give way. "My father was laid to rest just this morning, Mr Ellis, and as a female I was not even permitted to stand at his graveside to offer a proper farewell. I'd hoped to seek an audience with the Earl this week." A distant cousin, the Earl of Havers did not acknowledge their relationship, but she'd planned to ask him only for a letter of recommendation for employment, perhaps assistance to find a post somewhere as a governess or companion. It was evident, however, that the Earl had no intention of allowing her to impose upon their familial connection even that much. Mr Ellis was clearly acting on his employer's orders.

I am being thrown from the only home I have ever known, was all she could think.

"I'm right sorry, Miss Bentley." The steward twisted his hat again. In her state of shock, Ellen noticed minute details; the furrow of concern between the man's beetling brows, the mist hanging in the air from his quick breathing in the cold morning air, the way his twisting hands were damaging the hat's felt brim.

"I understand, Mr Ellis," she said quietly at last, and watched as he gave her a shallow bow before turning on his heel and retreating down the garden path.

The church bell tolled, clear in the frosty December air, and the tears Ellen had been holding back since her father's death from the influenza three days earlier, not even two weeks after her mother was laid to rest in the cold ground, finally flowed.

She sank to her knees there in the doorway of her home and bawled like a child.

What in the name of God was she going to do now?

CHAPTER ONE

Eight months later

Ellen was picking tomatoes from the vines in the garden when she heard a horse trotting along the lane, regular hoof beats punctuated by the sound of a man whistling a tune. He sounded jaunty, happy in the bright summer afternoon, and she found herself smiling, thinking that it was nice to hear someone sound so carefree.

The man came into view then, or rather his upper body did, as he rode along the lane that passed by the house. Spotting her over the hedge, he reined in his horse.

"Good afternoon, miss! Could you tell me if I am on the right road for Haverford Hall?"

"I'm afraid you just missed the turning, sir," Ellen said politely. "'Tis about a quarter mile back that way, on your left."

"Much obliged to you, miss!" He doffed his hat with another smile and she noticed how handsome he was, though his horse was a broken-down nag and his clothes looked worn. She smiled with a little tip of her head, but said nothing else, and he turned his horse about to ride on.

Pretty girl, Thomas thought, but he wasn't there to look at pretty girls. Riding up the long avenue lined by larch trees that led up to Haverford Hall, he paused for a moment to gaze in wonder at the building. His grandfather had described it to him many times, in loving detail, but Thomas had honestly thought the old man had been exaggerating, his memory not quite what it once was.

Now that he saw the Hall for the first time in person, Thomas realised that he had been doing his grandfather's memory a disservice, because the house was just as magnificent as he had always been told. Built of the local honey-coloured Cotswold stone, it glowed golden in the afternoon sun, windows all along the face of the building glinting in the light. He tried to count them and gave up at fifty; from his grandfather's tales he recalled the house had two large wings spreading out to the back as well, so trying to guess at the number of rooms by counting only the windows on the front elevation would grossly underestimate their number.

All this for one family, he thought, shaking his head and laughing quietly. He rattled around like a lone pea in a pod in the handsome house his grandfather had built in New York, but Haverford Hall must be ten times the size, and as far as he knew it was home to only two women. And a whole passel of servants, no doubt.

All of whom were now his responsibility.

Thomas sighed and pressed his weary horse to move on again; the nag nickered and flicked its ears at him. "Come on, you rotten beast," he muttered, but didn't have the heart to kick. The horse was probably nearly as old as he was, but it was the only one he'd been able to come by when the fine stallion he'd purchased in Bristol picked up a stone in his hoof and went lame ten miles from Haverford. Goliath had stumbled badly, startling Thomas who'd been riding along in a daze, and much to his embarrassment he'd fallen off.

Scrambling to his feet covered in dust, he'd groaned to see Goliath standing with one hoof held high off the ground and his noble head hanging low. "Not your fault, my fine fellow," he murmured to the stallion, searching his pockets for a tool to remove the stone. Goliath was too lame to ride, so Thomas led him on to the next village, where the blacksmith was happy to take care of him but could only provide this swaybacked old mare to carry Thomas on to his destination.

He debated dismounting and leading the horse; he was arriving in a poor enough state. He'd be lucky if he wasn't turned away at the front door as an impostor. Walking his horse wasn't likely to make much difference at this stage. He had to leave her at the bottom of the imposing steps leading up to the front door, but he was quite sure she didn't have the energy to run away anyway as he mounted the steps to knock on the huge double doors.

The door was opened by a very austere-looking and formidable butler, who looked down a nose Thomas thought a great deal more aristocratic than his own and said;

"Good afternoon, my lord. We have been expecting you."

Thomas opened his mouth to identify himself and shut it again with a snap, blinking. "I… beg your pardon?"

"You *are* Lord Havers, are you not?"

"Uhhh... yes?" He couldn't quite understand how they should be expecting him today. He had left the ship immediately upon docking amd headed directly here without stopping to send a message ahead, and it wasn't as though they could have known he would be aboard that particular ship anyway.

The butler inclined his head regally. "Welcome home, my lord. I am Allsopp." He had his hands firmly held behind his back, and Thomas had the distinct suspicion that shaking hands with servants was not at all the done thing, so he just nodded.

"Could you have someone attend to my horse, please, Allsopp... oh," he glanced around to see the mare already being led away by a groom. "She's not mine, actually, I had to leave my horse at the smithy in Alvescot when he went lame."

"I shall let Jenkins at the stables know, my lord," Allsopp intoned, standing back away from the door in an obvious signal for Thomas to enter.

"I can see my memory will be hard pressed to recall all your names," Thomas murmured, stepping inside the house and trying not to gawk at the huge hall, panelled in dark oak, tapestries taller than a man's height hanging from the walls.

"The Countess and Lady Louisa are in the blue withdrawing-room, sir. May I conduct you there?"

Glancing down at his dusty clothes, Thomas said "I think it might be best if I just freshen up first, don't you, Allsopp?"

The man didn't crack a smile, just inclined his head slightly and said "As you wish, sir. This way, please."

"Please tell me that you're not taking me to the chambers the last Earl occupied," it occurred to Thomas to say as they proceeded up the massive staircase that led up one side of the hall.

"But of course, sir," Allsopp said placidly.

"I'd... prefer not to. Not just yet." He already felt as though he was stepping into a dead man's shoes, not that it seemed he had much choice in the matter. He'd grown up listening to Gramps' tales of the earldom. And Gramps had indoctrinated Thomas in the beliefs that the Earl was responsible for his people, just as much as he would have been if he'd attended Eton with the sons of other aristocrats.

"As you wish, my lord," Allsopp said after a brief silence. "Several guest suites are always kept in a state of readiness, of course. Perhaps one of those will suffice?"

"Perfect," Thomas said gratefully, and Allsopp resumed ascending the stairs.

"The Cromwell Suite, I think, my lord. We will pass through the Long Gallery on the way."

He was going to need a full guided tour, Thomas could see, or he would be constantly lost. Allsopp led him into a room that seemed very nearly as large as the great hall below, and Thomas' jaw dropped.

"Now I see why you were so certain of my identity," he murmured, gazing up at his own likeness, repeated again and again.

Portraits lined the walls, and a goodly number of the gentlemen in the paintings were very obviously related to him. Dark brown hair, a strong chin and eyes of a shade somewhere between blue and grey were apparently Havers traits that held strong through generations.

Allsopp inclined his head again. "Indeed, sir." He seemed to hesitate before gesturing to one of the paintings, done in the style of half a century earlier. "That is your grandfather Lord Matthew, I believe. The younger child, on his mother's lap."

Startled, Thomas walked closer to inspect the painting. There were three children depicted with their elegantly dressed mother; a boy of about ten who would be Michael, Matthew's older brother, and a girl of about seven, which would make Matthew four in the painting. The children looked happy in the painting, the older boy standing behind his mother's chair with an open book in his hand, Matthew on her lap with a toy soldier in each hand and their sister sitting on a footstool with an orange cat sleeping in her lap.

"Is that Lady Eleanor?" Matthew had often talked of his sister. She had married beneath her station, to a local clergyman, but both her brothers had been too fond of her to try and deny her when she wished to follow her heart.

"The little girl with the cat? I believe so, my lord. The Countess or Lady Louisa would be able to tell you more about them."

With that it seemed he would have to be content, at least for now. Allsopp resumed his stately pace and Thomas followed along, watched every step of the way by the painted eyes of his ancestors.

The Cromwell Suite was rather more luxurious than the name implied, and Thomas looked about in approval as Allsopp showed him in, taking in the canopied, thickly mattressed bed, the elegantly made walnut furniture, the heavy velvet curtains at the windows. "Very suitable, thank you."

"I will have someone bring hot water directly, sir. Your luggage...?"

"My trunks should arrive from Bristol tomorrow." He smiled a little guiltily. "I'm afraid I was over-eager to see Haverford Hall and to meet my family. I do have a clean shirt and breeches in my saddlebags."

"Very good, my lord," and Allsopp withdrew, leaving him alone.

Going to the window to look out, Thomas found that he was at the rear of the house, or at least on the opposite side to where he had entered. He was looking down onto a sheltered courtyard, between the two rear wings of the house, immaculately manicured gardens separated by gravel walks. A gardener was carefully pruning roses.

Everything seemed very *orderly*, Thomas thought. He'd heard stories of Americans in similar situations to himself returning to England to find their ancestral estates in ruins, having to put their entrepreneurial skills to use to rescue the family fortunes, but Haverford Hall was a far cry from ruined. What would he even do, here? Presumably the estate business was all handled by a steward, and a very efficient one from what Thomas could see.

His musings were interrupted by a knock at the door. "Come in," he called, and smiled when a young man Thomas estimated to be a few years younger than himself entered and stood with his hands at his sides to offer a bow. "Hello."

"My lord. I'm Allsopp, my lord, I was your cousin Oliver's valet."

"Another Allsopp? Your father...?"

"My uncle." This Allsopp was capable of smiling, it seemed, anyway, a small grin lifting the corners of his mouth.

"It's going to confuse the dickens out of me; what's your first name?"

"Er, Kenneth, my lord, but really..."

"No buts. I shall call you Kenneth and you shall call me Thomas, because I'm already sick of being called *my lord* and I've only been on English soil since this morning."

Kenneth gaped at him. "That would be more than my job is worth, my lord!"

"Since I'm now your employer, I beg to differ." Thomas smiled at him. "Come now, it's a nice easy name. Thomas."

"... Sir?" Kenneth offered a compromise with a slightly panicked expression.

"I guess that'll do for now." Clearly he'd have to work on it. Kenneth might loosen up some when he became more comfortable with Thomas: he sincerely hoped the younger Allsopp wasn't going to be quite so stiff as his uncle.

Another knock on the door announced the arrival of two burly footmen with cans of steaming water, and another came in behind them bearing his saddlebags. Idly wondering just how many servants Haverford Hall actually maintained, Thomas shrugged out of his dusty coat and allowed Kenneth to take it from him. There was a mirror hanging above the dresser on the wall; one glance in it had Thomas wincing and relieved he had made the decision to wash up before meeting the countess and her daughter. He looked even worse than he had thought after his tumble from his horse. It was a good thing that the Havers blood apparently ran strong in his veins, or Allsopp would undoubtedly have turned him away at the door like the vagrant he resembled.

Half an hour later, freshly washed, with polished boots and almost all the dust brushed from his coat, Thomas asked Kenneth to show him to the blue withdrawing-room, and received his first lesson in what jobs belonged to who in the Haverford hierarchy. Kenneth was positively shocked.

"My uncle would have my hide, sir! If you would like to go somewhere in the house, I shall summon one of the footmen to conduct you until you find your way around, but to be presented to the Countess and Lady Louisa, that is my uncle's prerogative." He sent one of the footmen who had returned to collect the used wash water hurrying off with instructions to collect Allsopp at once.

"I'm going to make a lot of mistakes of this sort," Thomas said dismally as he waited. "Do you think everybody will just put it down to me being an uncouth American?"

"I'm sure they won't use the word *uncouth*, sir," Kenneth said, lips twitching very slightly, and Thomas decided that his valet did have a sense of humour, however well he might try to hide it.

"Not to my face, anyway."

"One hopes that they will not say anything so rude behind your back either, my lord," Allsopp said behind him, and Thomas almost jumped out of his skin.

"Good Lord, make a noise, man!"

"I shall endeavour to remember to do so in future, my lord."

"Does he *ever* smile?" Thomas mouthed to Kenneth as he left the room in Allsopp's imperious wake, sighing as the valet shook his head in response.

Allsopp led him back through the Long Gallery again, but turned in the opposite direction when they reached the top of the stairs, leading him into what Thomas was fairly sure was the eastern wing of the house. They proceeded past several closed doors before Allsopp came to a halt and knocked upon a door. Thomas admired the painting of a handsome bay horse hanging on the wall opposite the door, making a mental note of it as a landmark.

He didn't hear anything behind the door, but apparently Allsopp did, because he opened the door and stepped inside, intoning formally;

"The Earl of Havers."

That's me, Thomas thought with a sense of unreality coming over him. Entering the room, he stopped dead, his jaw falling open, as he came face to face with the most beautiful girl he had ever seen.

"Lady Havers, the Countess of Havers, and Lady Louisa Havers," Allsopp declared, startling Thomas and making him snap his jaw shut. He could barely drag his eyes from the vision of loveliness that had to be Lady Louisa long enough to give the countess a bow.

"It is lovely to meet you at last, my lord," the countess said formally, and Lady Louisa echoed her in a soft, musical voice.

It was an effort to keep his eyes on the older woman as Thomas said "Please, my lady, though we have never met, you are the only family I have and I am proud to claim you as such. I would be honoured if you would call me Thomas."

The countess was a handsome woman in late middle age; Thomas thought that she had once been a beauty to rival her daughter, though age had blurred the show-stopping nature of her good looks somewhat. Wearing an expensive-looking gown in pearl-grey silk trimmed with lavender ribbons, her fair hair drawn back beneath a lace cap, she curtsied to him, the gesture somehow regal and not deferential at all.

"That is very good of you, Thomas. Perhaps you would care to call me Aunt Clarice?"

"I should be delighted." He bowed again, beginning to feel a little foolish with all the bobbing up and down, but at least he could now turn to Louisa.

"I should like you to call me Louisa," she said in that softly musical voice, smiling at him.

"I am so happy to meet you both at last," he said truthfully, staring at Louisa. She blushed prettily under his scrutiny and followed her mother's lead in seating herself; the countess gestured to a chair and Thomas sat down too, feeling gauche and awkward beside their cultured, studied grace.

He really needed to stop staring, but Louisa was beyond beautiful, she was glorious, with thick golden curls framing a pale, finely-boned face, soft rosy lips and deep blue eyes giving her an almost doll-like prettiness. She was no cold porcelain figurine, though, not with that lush figure that looked as though it had been poured into a lavender silk gown, a band of lace at the neckline the only thing retaining her modesty.

If dresses like that were London fashion, then Thomas was all for it. He tried to remember Louisa's age; his uncle's letters had been brief and sporadic at best, and had stopped entirely after Gramps died five years ago. Surely she was old enough to be out in society, though. He wondered why she wasn't married; but perhaps she had been just due to start a London Season when her father died. Recalled to his duty, he said;

"I must offer my most sincere condolences for the loss of the Earl and Lord Oliver. I was deeply grieved to hear of their deaths; I hope you will believe that I was perfectly content in my life in America and never for a moment coveted the earldom."

The countess inclined her head. "Thank you, Thomas. That is kind of you to say. You look very much like a Havers, I must say; Allsopp said that you saw the Long Gallery?"

"Yes, Aunt Clarice, I did, and I do hope that you or my cousin will have time to tell me who all those handsome fellows and beautiful ladies were, one day soon."

They both smiled at that. "You will have to have your own likeness taken," Louisa said.

"I suppose so." It hadn't even occurred to him.

"Sir Thomas Lawrence is a very fine painter; he recently completed a portrait of Louisa which hangs now in the music room," the countess offered. "Perhaps you could commission him to take your likeness."

"Perhaps, but after painting Louisa, surely all the rest of us mere mortals must look as ugly as mules to his eyes," Thomas said.

Louisa blushed again and looked down at her lap. Busy staring at her, Thomas didn't notice the countess's satisfied smile.

CHAPTER TWO

"I BELIEVE I HAVE some news that may be of interest to you, my dear," Mr Bledsloe announced at dinner, two evenings after Ellen had seen the stranger riding along the lane.

"Well, do not keep us in suspense!" his wife Demelza cried, setting down her fork. "Tell us all, Mr Bledsloe, and quickly, if you please!" She smiled at Ellen, inviting her to rejoice in the juicy gossip which was no doubt about to be imparted. Ellen smiled weakly in reply, not wishing to offend, but her Mama had abhorred gossip and passed her dislike on to Ellen. As a parson's wife, Mrs Bentley had come by a goodly amount of secrets, but she had always said that words had the power to be harmful.

"Sticks and stones may indeed break your bones, but words most certainly do have the power to hurt as well," Mama had told Ellen. "People trust me with their secrets, and I will not betray that trust."

Mr Bledsloe paused importantly, and then declared "The Earl of Havers has arrived at Haverford Hall."

Ellen relaxed; that was surely not a secret that could hurt anyone. The whole village had been on tenterhooks for months, wondering when or even if the American cousin would come to claim his title. As eager as Demelza for information, she hushed her friend, who was squealing with excitement and fanning herself.

"When did he arrive, Mr Bledsloe? Have you seen him?"

"Apparently, he came to the Hall the day before yesterday. The butcher's apprentice is walking out with one of the downstairs maids at the Hall and he saw her on her half-day yesterday; she said that the Hall's servants are all abuzz about it."

"Oh," Ellen said, surprised, "I think I saw him, perhaps, riding along the lane. He asked directions to Haverford Hall."

"Then you *spoke* to him, not *saw* him, you silly clunch! Was he handsome?" Demelza leaned forward eagerly.

Ellen blushed, thinking that she had indeed been struck by the good looks of the man who had asked her for directions. "I am sure I could not say," she said demurely. "I only saw him briefly, riding his horse. He spoke to me over the garden hedge. I do not even know if it was the Earl; it might have been a servant, perhaps, who came with him. He was riding an old hack of a horse, and his coat did not look as expensive as those that the old Earl or Lord Oliver used to wear."

"I shall go up to the Hall and seek an audience with him tomorrow," Mr Bledsloe said importantly. "I have some papers the old Earl entrusted to me. I shall mention you to him then, Ellen."

She said nothing, just quietly carried on eating her dinner. She was nothing to the new Earl; a distant, penniless cousin. He was obliged to do nothing at all for her, and considering the attitude of every member of the aristocracy she had ever met, was likely to consider her of no more importance than the dirt on his shoe... that is, of absolutely no importance and to be scraped off at the earliest opportunity.

Once Mr Bledsloe had confirmed that the Earl had no interest in her, she would begin tomorrow to look more seriously for paid work. She would ask Mr Bledsloe for his newspapers and begin writing letters applying for situations as a governess or companion. It was time to earn her keep. Demelza was a dear friend who had come to Ellen's rescue in those ghastly days after her father's funeral when she had nowhere else to go, insisting that Ellen must come to stay with the Bledsloes for as long as she wished, but Ellen was conscious she was living on her friend's charity. The situation could not continue for ever.

Eating his breakfast and managing to miss his mouth with his fork more often than not because he couldn't stop gazing at Lady Louisa, demurely nibbling on a buttered scone, Thomas was startled when the butler announced that he had a visitor.

"Who is it?" Thomas asked, discarding his napkin and rising, almost relieved for an excuse to stop making a fool of himself. He'd already smeared jam over his chin twice.

"The local solicitor, Mr Bledsloe," Allsopp intoned formally.

"He can have no business with you, Thomas dear," the countess said dismissively. "My husband conducted all his legal matters through our London solicitors, of course. Send him away, Allsopp."

"No, I'll see him, Aunt Clarice. He is a neighbour, after all."

Lady Havers blinked at him, apparently quite bemused. "I do not know how things are done in America, Thomas, but here neighbours are other members of the gentry, not *solicitors*."

The scorn in her voice made Thomas blink. Gently, he said "In America, neighbours are the folks who live close by and who we see regularly, ma'am. No matter what their station in life." Turning away, he said "Lead the way, Allsopp. To... uh..." He hadn't the faintest idea where one received visitors of any rank at all.

"The study, my lord." Allsopp actually cracked a little smile. "This way, if you please."

"I actually think I can find the study," Thomas said cheerfully to Allsopp as they left the small dining room where he'd leaned the family customarily ate breakfast. "It's down that corridor and just past the really short suit of armour, right?"

"Correct, my lord." Allsopp didn't smile again, but Thomas was sure the butler was beginning to unbend. He'd get a chuckle from the man yet.

"And Mr Bledsloe, what can you tell me about him?"

"He is very well-respected in the local area, my lord." Allsopp paused before saying "It's not my place to contradict the Countess, of course, but Mr Bledsloe and the Earl met regularly. The Earl was also the local magistrate, you see, so they consulted regularly on legal matters. And the Bledsloe house is just past the end of the southern avenue approaching the Hall."

"Then he *is* a neighbour," Thomas said triumphantly. "Very good, Allsopp. Would it be appropriate to have coffee sent in?"

"Certainly, my lord. I shall have it brought in shortly."

"Thank you." Thomas smiled as Allsopp looked faintly startled; the servants were definitely not used to being thanked, but Thomas had no intention of changing his habits of courtesy now that he happened to have a title tacked onto his name. Opening the study door, he entered the room with a ready smile.

"Mr Bledsloe! I am delighted to meet you, sir."

The solicitor was a stout man in early middle age, his hair thinning. He jumped to his feet as Thomas entered, his expression quite shocked at Thomas' friendly greeting. Bowing, he stuttered "Uh, very good of you, my lord, very good indeed. I'm honoured that you'd see me."

"Nonsense, we're neighbours, and please call me Havers," Thomas said affably. He was trying for a charm offensive; if he could catch the man by surprise at the beginning of their acquaintance, perhaps he could convince him that all the bowing and scraping really wasn't necessary. He was already thoroughly sick of it.

"Uh, yes, my l-Havers," Bledsloe said, his eyes wide and a little shocked. "Honoured." He accepted Thomas's offered hand and shook.

"Good, that's settled. Do sit down." Instead of rounding the huge desk and sitting imposingly behind it, Thomas caught up another chair and sat down near Bledsloe. "It's very good of you to call. I'm delighted to start meeting my new neighbours."

"Neighbours? Why, yes... I suppose we are."

"Allsopp tells me that you live at the end of the southern avenue, which must surely make you one of our closest neighbours, since the northern approach is three times as long, I'm told."

"Not quite at the end, my l-Havers. A little further along the road towards Colesbourne. In fact, I believe you may have spoken to a young lady in my garden the day you arrived, asking directions?"

"The girl in the grey bonnet! A relative of yours?" Thomas nodded, remembering the girl and her smile, the friendly way she had spoken to him.

"A friend of my wife, actually; she is staying with us for a while, since the loss of her parents. They both passed in the same tragic manner as your uncle and cousin. For which losses, please allow me to extend my condolences."

"Thank you," Thomas said with a nod. "That must have been difficult, for a young girl to lose her parents both at the same time. I suffered the same loss, but I was not old enough to remember their passing; my grandfather raised me."

"That would be Lord Matthew?"

"That's right. He raised me on tales of Haverford." Thomas smiled, looking around the study, which still bore his uncle's imprint in every piece of imposingly made furniture, the choices of books on the shelves. "I'm afraid the images my imagination produced did not do it justice, though."

"Indeed." Mr Bledsloe paused, and then said, seemingly choosing his words with some delicacy, "Did Lord Matthew ever speak of his sister?"

"Lady Eleanor? Frequently! I think he missed her most of all when he emigrated, and she sounded a delight; I am sorry I never had the chance to meet her. They wrote letters until her death, I believe, but that was before I was born. In fact, perhaps you can tell me - I know she married, but did she have children? I have not yet had the chance to ask my aunt about other living relatives I may have, indeed I am just getting used to having *any*!"

"Quite understandable, my lord. And yes, Lady Eleanor did have a daughter. In fact, if I may?" Bledsloe gestured to a bookshelf behind the desk, and Thomas nodded, watching curiously as the man stood and pulled down a large, old-looking book richly bound in gold-embossed green leather.

"This is the Havers family bible," Bledsloe told him. "The fourth Earl, that was the previous Earl's father, of course, and your grandfather's older brother, kept it updated until his death not quite twenty years ago."

Thomas nodded in understanding as Bledsloe laid the book on the desk and carefully opened it to the back pages, showing a family tree written out in several different hands.

"Ah, this will be useful when I am trying to keep straight who is who in the portraits in the Long Gallery," Thomas murmured thoughtfully, leaning forward to look.

"Here, you see," Bledsloe pointed. "The fourth Earl and his siblings, Matthew and Eleanor."

A line led down from Matthew to *Ellis (b. 1767, m. 1789, d.1792)*. Written beneath his name was *Julia Henry, (d.1792)* and another line led down from there to *Thomas (b. 1790)*.

"You can, of course, write *6th Earl Havers* in beside your name now," Bledsloe noted.

"Perhaps another day." Everything in Thomas rebelled against that, right now. Maybe he'd leave it to a descendant who didn't feel like a complete impostor. He looked across the family tree and realised that he would also have to write in the date of death for Michael and Oliver.

No, he wasn't ready to deal with that right now either. He moved his finger back to Eleanor's name, and down from there.

"She had two daughters... oh, one died young, how sad." Five years old, Miss Sarah Ripley had been. Looking at the dates, he realised that must have been the same year Gramps had left for America. Had little Sarah died before or after his departure? What a terrible year that must have been for Eleanor.

"Yes, but Miss Laura survived to adulthood. She married a Bristol merchant, and they had a daughter, Susan. On a visit to her relatives here in Haverford, Miss Susan fell in love with the local curate and they married. Following the wedding, the fourth Earl bestowed the living on Mr Bentley, so that his relative Susan should be sure of a comfortable life."

Thomas listened with interest as Bledsloe told him about the family he had never known. Following the line written in a spidery hand in the back of the old bible, he came to *Ellen (b. 1798)*. The same year as Louisa on the other branch of the family tree, he noted.

"Did the fifth Earl keep the family tree updated?" he asked.

"He wrote in your grandfather's date of death, so I assume so. So far as I know, there were no other records that required noting during his stewardship of the title."

"So Ellen is still alive?"

"Ellen is the young lady I told you about, Havers. Susan Bentley was her mother."

Thomas fairly gaped at him, eyes flying back to the family tree. In all the myriad branches, so far as he could see, there were only three Havers descendants living; himself, Louisa, and Ellen. "Why is she staying with your wife, then, and not here with her family?" he demanded indignantly.

Bledsloe hesitated, and then said delicately "While the fourth earl considered Lady Eleanor's descendants to be family and bestowed the living on Mr Bentley to ensure that Miss Susan should be taken care of when she married him, the fifth earl did not."

Thomas sat back and looked at the other man. "You're saying that the previous earl--hang it, I'm just going to call him my uncle--did not acknowledge Susan and Ellen Bentley as relations?"

"May I speak frankly?"

"Please do, because I have the feeling that I'm missing something here. From what I see here, we hardly *have* any family." Thomas waved his hand over the book. "Why would my uncle not acknowledge the perfectly respectable wife of a clergyman, and her daughter, as members of the family?"

"Because your uncle was a penny-pinching petty tyrant who never did a thing unless he thought it benefited him." Bledsloe looked half-defiant, half-afraid as he said the words.

A knock on the door interrupted them, a maid bringing in a tray with a steaming pot of coffee. Thomas poured a cup for Bledsloe and one for himself, grateful for the interruption since it gave him time to gather his thoughts.

"What provision was made for Ellen when her parents died?" Thomas enquired.

"She inherited savings of some one hundred and seventy pounds," Bledsloe said. "Though her grandfather was quite a successful merchant in Bristol, he married again after his first wife died and had two sons, who inherited his wealth. The living was quickly awarded to another man when Mr Bentley died; signing those papers was one of your uncle's last acts, as it happens." Bledsloe looked down, bit his lip. "Ellen intends to seek a position as a governess, or companion. We asked her to stay on with us at least until your arrival; she has been helping my wife with the children. While we cannot afford to pay her a proper wage, she eats with the family and Demelza treats her like a sister."

Like an unpaid governess, you mean, Thomas thought a little unkindly, but he suspected that Bledsloe's guilt over the matter was the reason why the solicitor had approached him now.

"It seems entirely unfair that my cousin should be forced to make a living for herself in this way," he said aloud. "She is twenty, by the date here?"

"Indeed."

"Should she like to marry? If there is a suitor in the wings for her, I would happily provide a dowry."

"The only suitor who has ever asked for her is the new parson," Bledsloe said. "He seemed to think that she should be grateful for an opportunity to stay in her old home, though it meant she would also have to be his unpaid housekeeper and warm his bed. Since he is some five and fifty years old, however, I advised Ellen against it. She did seriously consider it, though. She does not wish to be a burden upon anyone."

"I am already thinking that I do not like the new parson," Thomas said after a moment of stunned silence. "What is his name?"

"Mr Brownlee. He has already found another wife, a daughter of one of your tenant farmers who was quite happy to accept his offer."

Shaking his head, Thomas considered his options. The easiest thing to do would be to settle some money on Ellen, but then what? Where would she live? She would need to find a companion of her own, to lend her countenance. Would she even want that, or accept the money?

"I believe that I should like to meet Ellen," he said finally, after taking a long sip of his coffee. "We spoke only briefly when she gave me directions to the Hall, but she seemed quite charming. She is my cousin no less than Lady Louisa, and I should like to know her."

"Very good, Havers." Bledsloe gave him an approving nod. "When would be convenient for you?"

"No time like the present, Gramps always used to say. May I walk back with you?"

"It would be my pleasure."

CHAPTER THREE

It was a very pleasant walk along the avenue between the larch trees. Thomas found himself whistling again, enjoying the weather.

"Is it always this pleasant here in September?" he asked.

"Not always, this is a very fine late summer," Bledsloe said. "October rains will start soon enough, and the nights start drawing in. How is the climate in New York, Havers? I have heard that the winters can be very bitter."

"Indeed, with heavy snowfall at times," Thomas agreed. "Summers are unbearably hot, too; I was not sorry to leave in May, before the weather became too hot. I understand the English climate to be milder all around."

They talked about the weather, about the harvests, and about the work Bledsloe had done with the previous earl as they walked. Bledsloe said that another local landowner, Sir Edward Kingsley, had been appointed magistrate after the earl's demise, for which Thomas was grateful; he would have quite enough on his plate without needing to worry about enforcing the law in the area as well!

At last they came to the end of the half-mile-long avenue and Bledsloe turned towards the house Thomas had passed the other day. He remembered thinking it looked quite a nice property, on an acre or so of grounds with a large kitchen garden to one side, where he had spied Ellen picking fruit. Bledsloe pushed open the wooden gate and they walked up to the front door.

"Demelza will likely carry on a little bit," Bledsloe said in an undertone. "Don't mind her nonsense. She likes to fuss, that's all."

Seeing the smile on the man's face, Thomas thought that he seemed very fond of his wife despite any fussing. At least Ellen was in a home where she need not fear importuning by the master of the house, a very real danger if she should indeed go into service as a governess or companion.

"Demelza? I have brought a visitor to meet you, my dear," Bledsloe said, leading Thomas into a parlour where a pretty woman of about thirty years of age sat with two children, both listening intently as their mother read to them. "Boys, stand up and give your best bows, now. This is the Earl of Havers. My lord, my wife and my two sons, Jacob and Jason."

The boys were twins, he saw, of about seven years or so, quite identical in their blue-eyed, fair-haired, freckled little faces, open-mouthed with awe at the sight of a real live earl there in their parlour.

Demelza Bledsloe gave a little shriek and dropped her book. "John! Oh, my lord!" she curtsied a little frantically. "I never... oh my goodness!"

"Please, do not be put out, Mrs Bledsloe," Thomas turned on the charm offensive again, stepping forward to lift her hand and kiss it. "I do beg your pardon for my dropping in on you unannounced, but when your husband was good enough to pay a call upon me I decided that I simply could not wait to return it--and to meet my relative, who I understand is your very dear friend."

"Yes, where is Ellen, my dear?" John asked.

"Oh, she is in the morning-room," Demelza fluttered a little, settled down as Thomas smiled reassuringly at her. "She found a notice in yesterday's newspaper with a position she thought might suit, said that she wished to write an application letter--I did tell her to wait until after John had spoken with you, my lord, but she was so certain you would not be interested in even meeting such a distant relative..."

"On the contrary, ma'am, I am most interested in meeting Miss Bentley. So far as I know, I only have two living blood relatives, Miss Bentley and Lady Louisa. I am not of a mind to snub one of them for any reason."

"That is very good to hear; I knew it must be so! I heard that Americans have quite a different way of thinking than we English, well, to the aristocracy at least. Please, my lord, do not let me keep you; the boys have not yet finished their geography lesson. Perhaps we shall all come and have tea together in the morning-room shortly?"

Thomas allowed that sounded very pleasant, smiled at the twins whose faces had turned immediately downcast at the mention of the temporarily abandoned lesson. Emboldened by his smile, one of them--he had no idea which--blurted "Have you ever seen a Red Indian, m'lord?"

"Perhaps if your mother tells me that you have paid close attention for the remainder of your lesson, I will tell you when we take tea," Thomas bent down to whisper, and was rewarded with a pair of beaming smiles.

Cute little devils, he thought, taking a polite leave of Mrs Bledsloe and following her husband from the room. He'd not thought seriously yet about taking a wife and setting up a nursery--he was only twenty-eight!--but he supposed that he must now view it as his duty to do so, and as soon as possible. The earldom needed an heir.

The next door along the small hallway stood open, into a room of similar size to the parlour, an oval table to seat eight or so in the centre of it. Ellen sat at the table, papers spread out before her and a quill pen held in her hand.

"Ellen?" Bledsloe said. She looked up, her eyes widening at the sight of Thomas entering the room behind him.

"Oh!" Startled, she set down her pen, rose to her feet and made a graceful curtsy.

"The Earl of Havers, pray allow me to present Miss Ellen Bentley," Bledsloe said formally, and then with a smile, "your cousin."

"It is quite a distant connection, my lord," Ellen rushed to say.

"I know exactly how distant, Miss Bentley; your great-grandmother was my grandfather's dear sister. He told me many stories of Lady Eleanor, and I am delighted to meet her descendant." Thomas bowed, giving Ellen a reassuring smile. She looked troubled, her brow furrowed.

"I'll just step to the kitchen and ask Betsy to see about that tea," Bledsloe said, "let you two get acquainted." Leaving the room, he left the door standing wide open and Ellen and Thomas staring at each other in silence.

She was prettier than he'd thought with that ugly grey bonnet obscuring her hair, Thomas realised, though the plain dark grey gown she wore did nothing for her. She was still in mourning for her parents, of course, but then so was Lady Louisa for her father, and she had managed to find a gown that flattered her.

As soon as he thought it, Thomas mentally kicked himself for such insensitivity. Louisa had an unlimited budget and probably a seamstress dedicated to her wardrobe, whereas Ellen had only a paltry legacy. Undoubtedly she was making do with whatever she had, seeking to preserve her small funds for her future.

"Won't you sit down, my lord?" Ellen said eventually, taking a seat herself. Thomas sat down, still taking her in. She looked thin, although Bledsloe had said she ate with the family. There were hollows in her pale cheeks and shadows beneath her eyes, a dark chocolate colour quite unlike his own blue-grey. Her hair was darker than his, almost black, though the sunlight pouring in through the window behind her brought out some mahogany-red glints in it. He saw little resemblance in her features to either his own or Louisa, and wondered if she took after her Havers grandmother at all, or whether her looks favoured a different part of her family. Certainly, he could not immediately recall anyone in the Long Gallery's portraits who Ellen might confidently be said to resemble.

"Bledsloe told me something of your situation," Thomas said awkwardly after a moment of silence. Ellen was just sitting in silence, her hands folded in her lap, not looking at him, apparently waiting for him to make conversation. Or, he thought, issue edicts, as she might have expected the previous earl to do. "I am very sorry to hear of the loss of your parents."

"I am sorry for your loss too, my lord."

He blinked in confusion.

"The Earl and Lord Oliver?" she prompted.

"Oh, I see. I never knew them, I'm afraid. My grandfather corresponded with them to some extent while he was still alive, but since his death five years ago I heard not a word until a representative from my uncle's London solicitor contacted me in New York."

"I see," Ellen said colourlessly, and there was another brief silence before she said "Do you have other family, back in America?"

"No, my parents died when I was very young. A fire. Gramps raised me."

She nodded silently, and Thomas wondered where the friendly, smiling girl he had seen in the garden just two days ago had gone. *She didn't know who I was then*, he realised in a flash of enlightenment. *She's afraid of me, of how my actions may upset her little world.*

"May I call you Ellen?" Thomas asked, trying to make his voice as quiet and gentle as he could. "And I should like it if you will call me Thomas, if you will. I have only three living relatives in this whole world, and you are one of them."

Wide eyes lifted to his face, and he noticed lighter amber glints in the dark chocolate of her eyes. She said nothing for a long moment before finally saying "I do not want to appear disrespectful in front of others, but I suppose if we are in private conversation, as we are now, I could call you Thomas."

"There, that wasn't so hard, was it?"

She smiled at last in response to his teasing tone. "Not so hard. I have never had a cousin before."

That raised his eyebrows. "Of course you do. Lady Louisa..."

"I have seen Lady Louisa every Sunday at church since we were both old enough to attend and I am quite sure she has no idea what my name is."

Thomas sat back, studied her thoughtfully.

Ellen looked down at her hands, biting her lip guiltily. "I should probably not have said that," she murmured.

It had been decidedly snippy, Thomas thought. Very much at odds with the mild, demure girl Ellen was obviously seeking to present herself as. She had a fiery side, though she obviously sought to keep it well hidden.

"No, you have every right to be resentful. I can hardly believe the way the family has treated you myself. That changes now."

Her eyes were still wary as she looked at him. "What do you mean?"

"What do you want, Ellen?" he asked her.

"Excuse me?" Startled, she blinked at him.

"What do *you* want? To do with your life, I mean? What are your dreams, what would you do if you could do anything at all?"

She hesitated, staring at him. "I... don't know. Nobody ever asked me that question before. I don't think it's a question that many girls are asked, really. We are expected to want nothing more than to be a wife and mother to some man..."

"That's not what you want?"

"Maybe." A tinge of colour touched her pale cheeks. "I haven't ever met a man who made me want those things."

"Fair enough." Thomas steepled his fingers, tapped his fingertips together thoughtfully. "Do I take it, then, that becoming a governess or a schoolteacher, or companion to some wealthy lady, is not in fact your life's ultimate dream?"

"It is not. Until this meeting, though, I thought it was the only future that might possibly be open to me!"

"Are you happy here?" he asked, seeing that she seemed a little more relaxed and easy with him.

"Here?" She looked puzzled. "In Haverford? I have never known anywhere else."

"Staying with your friends, I mean. Mr and Mrs Bledsloe."

"Oh, I see... well, Demelza has been so very kind. I had nowhere else to go after Mr Ellis told me I had two weeks to vacate the Vicarage."

Arrested, Thomas blinked. "Wait. What, Mr Ellis, the land steward?"

"That's right."

"My uncle's steward... ordered you out of your home? Within days of your parents' deaths?"

"The very day of Papa's funeral. Mama died two weeks before... she was not very strong, and once she died I think Papa just gave up the will to live." Ellen blinked back tears, remembering those awful weeks. She had fallen ill first, and was just recovering when Mama caught the illness. Exhausted and still recovering herself, Ellen did her best to nurse her mother, but to no avail.

"I'm so sorry," Thomas said. "I can't believe Ellis took that upon himself." He was furious. How dare the man? It was most certainly not his place.

"Oh, Thomas." She gave him a world-weary look. "Mr Ellis would never have taken any such action without the direction of the Earl. I had already moved here by the time I heard that the Earl himself had caught the influenza and fallen ill."

Thomas buried his head in his hands, feeling utterly ashamed of his late relative. "Dear Lord, how could he be so cruel? To you, to a young female relative, all alone in the world?"

Ellen had no answer for him. She had asked herself that question many times, how a man who called himself Christian, who attended church, could behave in such a way.

"I think you should come and live at the Hall." Thomas dropped his hands from his face to look at her again. She gaped at him in utmost astonishment.

"I... do not think that the Countess would care for that very much."

"Since it is not her house, I do not particularly care what she thinks," Thomas said sharply. "Do not tell me that *she* could not have done anything for you, even if her husband was the veriest miser! I saw the household accounts yesterday. A single month's worth of her pin money could have purchased you a cottage of your own outright!"

He seemed quite outraged on her behalf. There was really nothing Ellen could say; she just sat looking at him, hands folded in her lap.

"I am below the age of majority," she finally offered hesitantly. "I suppose... technically, as my closest relative, you are my legal guardian."

"Am I?"

"We could ask John. He is a solicitor, after all, I am sure he could advise on the legality of the matter." Ellen gave him a little smile. "Thomas, truly, I am grateful that you want to do something for me. I don't really want to be a governess or a companion. I suppose I had always hoped I would find some nice gentleman farmer or perhaps a curate who liked me well enough to offer for me."

"If that's what you wish, Ellen, I will see that you are introduced to every gentleman farmer and curate in England until you find the one who can make you happy," he promised.

She actually giggled at such a ridiculous statement, hand flying up to cover her mouth, her eyes sparkling. "I am sure it would not take so very many!"

Delighted to have made her laugh, Thomas smiled broadly at her. "Is it settled, then? You will come to live at the Hall... with your family?"

She nibbled on her lower lip, considering it. "I think that you should speak with the countess first," she said carefully at last. "While you are of course correct that it is your house, I do not wish to be the cause of contention between you and your family."

"If I do, will you prepare to remove to the Hall within the next few days?"

She nodded at last. "I will. And Thomas... thank you."

Reaching across the table, he took her hand between both of his and pressed it gently. "We are *family*, Ellen. That means something to me, and I should have wished to see you comfortable even if I had not inherited the title. My grandfather made himself quite the fortune in the Americas, you know."

"Did he?" Ellen looked genuinely interested. "I should very much like to hear about your grandfather."

"He was a character, to be sure. I'd be delighted to tell you some of his stories. He was your relative too, after all."

Footsteps at the door made Thomas let go of her hands and look around; the twins came darting in, their mother behind them and John Bledsloe on their heels with a tray in his hands.

Any serious conversation had to be cut short as the boys promptly annexed Thomas and bombarded him with questions about America. Laughing, he attempted to answer them as best he could while Demelza poured tea and handed around a plate of biscuits.

Walking back up to the Hall an hour later, it occurred to Thomas that he had not enjoyed himself so much in a very long time. Ellen had relaxed further with her friends in the room, and he had enjoyed hearing her merry giggle ring out at the twins' antics. The two boys were obviously very fond of her, and she of them. After a little while, Bledsloe had quietly asked Thomas to step out, and the two men adjourned to a small study to converse privately.

Thomas began to whistle again as he walked, feeling good about himself and the actions he'd taken that morning. Bledsloe had indicated his appreciation that Thomas wished to bring Ellen into the bosom of the Havers family.

"We shall be sorry to lose her, I know Demelza quite relies upon her, but it is not fair to Ellen. She is a good, sweet girl and she deserves the opportunity to make something of her life. I must say, Havers, I am very glad that you are not of the same mind as your late relative in this matter."

Thomas was honestly ashamed that a relation of his could have treated a blameless young woman so shabbily. Ellen clearly had no great expectations, but his uncle could have made her life comfortable with barely any inconvenience to himself. Why, a dowry of a few hundred pounds would have had every gentleman farmer and curate in the county queueing up to court Ellen!

Merely dowering her did not feel like enough to Thomas now that he had met Ellen, though. Doing so would push her down that narrow path into marriage, and he wondered if she even wanted that. As she had said, women were rarely asked what they wanted from life, it was merely *expected* of them that they would want to be wives and mothers.

Ellen deserved a chance to discover what she really wanted to be in life, and by God, Thomas was going to give it to her.

CHAPTER FOUR

"YOU WANT TO *WHAT*?" Clarice's voice rose shrilly as she stared at Thomas, her eyes wide with incredulity.

"I want our cousin to come and live here at Haverford Hall." He kept his voice even, glancing sideways at Louisa as he spoke. She was sitting with a piece of embroidery in her hands, but had not placed a stitch since he began speaking. Her face was as still and cool as a marble statue; he could not read what she was thinking.

"She is a *vicar's daughter,*" Clarice exclaimed.

"She is *my cousin.*"

They stared at each other in a silent battle of wills, Clarice every inch the noblewoman. Thomas finally broke the deadlock by saying;

"I am not asking your permission, Aunt Clarice. Should you find that you are unable to reside beneath the same roof as Miss Bentley, you have life rights to the Dower House as stipulated in your marriage settlements, I believe."

Clarice's mouth opened with shock. Louisa made a small sound, and when Thomas looked back at her, he found that she had laid down her embroidery and was looking at him directly.

"Of course that will not be necessary, Thomas," she said in her soft voice, smiling sweetly at him. "I am delighted by the opportunity to get to know Miss Bentley. As you say, she is my cousin too. We shall be pleased to welcome her to the Hall, will we not, Mama?"

Relieved that Louisa was on his side, and pleased by her compassion and eagerness to meet Ellen, Thomas nodded happily at her. She returned her attention to her embroidery, a little smile playing about her lips, becoming colour in her cheeks.

My God, she is so beautiful.

Lost in gazing at Louisa, Thomas barely noticed Clarice's put-upon sigh, and her eventual remark of "Fine, then. If you *must.*"

Clarice's reaction once Thomas had left the room revealed her true feelings, however. She rose from her chair and stalked up and down, swishing her skirts about and scowling. "I cannot believe he means to foist off this girl upon us!" she cried, plainly enraged at having been thwarted.

"He is American, Mama," Louisa placidly set another stitch. "I understand they have very different ideas about the lower classes, indeed they do not seem to think that there *are* any lower classes."

"Utter nonsense," Clarice harrumphed. "There is a natural order to things. Bringing Miss Bentley to live here indeed! Whatever will he do next? The sooner he comes to his senses and marries you, the better."

"These things cannot be rushed, Mama," Louisa snipped a trailing end of thread neatly. "You told me that. Slowly, softly, so that he does not know he is in the trap until it is already closed. He is already sniffing about, ready to take the bait."

"Must you speak in those crass hunting terms, Louisa? You sound positively bloodthirsty." Clarice wrinkled her nose with distaste. "Be very sure that you do not allow Thomas to know you have a ruthless side until you have his ring upon your finger, my dear."

"Never fear, Mama. I have things well in hand. Miss Bentley will be no obstacle to our plans, I assure you." She held up her needlework, turning it this way and that to examine the tiny, precise stitches she had set. The quality of the work was undeniable, but an observer might have queried the subject matter. Far from stitching some beautiful design of flowers or butterflies, Louisa's needle had picked out a gory hunting scene, foxes tearing at the throat of a downed stag, scarlet drops of blood spattering the green undergrowth of the background.

Mollified and reassured by her daughter's calmness, Clarice sighed and took a seat again. "Very well, dear. For your sake I shall try to pretend I am pleased by the girl's presence."

"I do not think that you need to go that far, Mama. Let me befriend her while you act as though you tolerate her merely because Thomas has ordered it. She will want a friend and she will soon be willing to do anything I ask, never fear."

"And then what?"

"Why, then I find some suitor to marry her and take her off our hands." Louisa shrugged. "Thomas can dower her with a few hundred pounds or so, and we will have minor squires crawling all over her in eagerness to be connected to the Havers family."

"Hm." Clarice looked thoughtful at that. "I suppose she might even be useful, that way. I shall have a think about who might be suitable."

"As you say, Mama." Louisa picked up her handiwork and resumed stitching, the very image of a well-bred lady filling her time... as she added more blood to the hunting scene in her image.

For the second time in the space of a year Ellen found herself uprooted, but this time she was moving up in the world. She had never been closer to Haverford Hall than seeing it in the distance when walking up Wyck Beacon; the previous Earl had not exactly been the type to welcome the residents of the village to his home. It truly was quite magnificent, she thought as she walked up the avenue, Demelza beside her holding her hand, John slightly ahead of them.

Thomas had sent a baggage cart to collect her belongings and invited the Bledsloes to accompany her to tea, doubtless hoping that their presence might help ease her transition to residing at the Hall. He had stopped by almost every day during the previous week, assuring her that the countess and Lady Louisa were eager to welcome her to the Hall, asking when she could be ready to move. His enthusiasm was irresistible, and Ellen found herself quite excited about what the future might now hold for her.

As they approached the Hall, however, Ellen found herself holding tighter to Demelza's hand.

"Just remember, you belong here," Demelza said in an undertone as they walked up to the great doors. "You were named for Lady Eleanor, your great-grandmother, who was born under this very roof. You have every right to be here."

Sucking in a deep breath, Ellen squeezed one more time before letting go of her friend's hand. She would not be seen clinging on like a child to her nursemaid.

The door opened almost immediately upon John's knock to reveal a formally-garbed, stern-faced butler. Ellen knew who he was, of course; the Allsopp family had been in Haverford as long as the noble family they served, and she had seen Allsopp in church on many occasions.

"Good afternoon, Mr Bledsloe, Mrs Bledsloe," Allsopp intoned, and then to Ellen's surprise, he bowed to her. "A very great pleasure to have you here at last, Miss Bentley."

Was Allsopp *smiling*? Stunned, Ellen mumbled something unintelligible in response. She hadn't even thought the poker-faced butler knew *how* to smile.

"The family are gathered in the Oriental sitting-room," Allsopp informed them. "Please, allow me to escort you there."

Another shock; Ellen would have thought that task might be delegated to a footman, but apparently they--*she*--was considered a significant enough guest to merit Allsopp's personal attention.

Thomas fairly leaped to his feet as the party entered the sitting-room, beaming a smile. "Here you are!"

"Havers." Bledsloe shook his hand in greeting, bowed formally to the countess and Lady Louisa, who were rising to their feet. "Lady Havers, Lady Louisa."

"Mr Bledsloe." Clarice nodded regally at him. "I do not recall that your wife has ever been presented to me."

Demelza was not in the least overawed. "We have seen each other many times in church, your ladyship," she said rather dryly, dipping into a curtsy that was just barely low enough to show respect to a peeress.

Clarice's smile looked as though it had been painted on, but she said nothing else as John presented Demelza to her and Louisa. Louisa at least seemed more friendly, saying;

"A pleasure to make your acquaintance, Mrs Bledsloe."

"As it is yours, Lady Louisa."

Ellen hung back, biting on her lip, but Thomas would have none of it. Seizing her hand, he placed it on his arm and led her forward.

"I know you will wish to join me in welcoming Ellen to our home, Aunt."

"Of course." Clarice inclined her head graciously. "Though, Thomas dear, you really must remember to call her Miss Bentley when we are in company. Really, are all Americans so informal?"

"Most of them are considerably less formal than I, Aunt Clarice," Thomas replied with a chuckle. "Consider the advantages, though; any error in address I may make will not reflect badly upon you. Indeed, you can commiserate with the offended party while informing them that I am merely an ignorant American!"

There was a distinct bite to his words; Clarice, far from accepting the rebuke, merely sniffed. "You *are* an Earl. The number of those who could rightfully be offended by any informality in your address are few in number. I was merely thinking of Miss Bentley's reputation. Over-familiarity in address must be avoided for her sake, lest assumptions be made."

Louisa tittered behind her hand, and Thomas, who had been about to ask what kind of *assumptions* Clarice could mean, closed his mouth. A young lady's reputation was all-important, and in England the rules of etiquette were even stricter than in America, he had already worked that out.

"Yes, Aunt Clarice," he said penitently at last.

Ellen had not said a word since entering the room. She took advantage of the silence that fell now to curtsy and say quietly;

"I am honoured to make your acquaintance, Your Ladyship."

Clarice inclined her head regally, before tilting her head to the side and considering Ellen thoughtfully. "You have a little of the Havers colouring, though not the eyes. And the Havers nose."

Ellen's hand rose instinctively to touch the feature remarked upon, before she lowered it again. "So I have been told."

"I have only seen a portrait of your great-grandmother Lady Eleanor as a child," Thomas put in, "but perhaps there is a picture of her in later life, somewhere in the collection?"

"You are quite correct, cousin," Louisa said, smiling sweetly at Ellen. "It is in the music room on the ground floor. Cousin Ellen, I must say that you resemble her quite strongly. Except for the eyes, of course."

Ellen smiled back, relieved that the other girl seemed disposed to be friendly. "I should be pleased to see it, if you would care to show me, Lady Louisa."

"Not right now, dear, we are going to have tea. Sit here by me, if you please," Clarice said, her tone making it clear that she was giving an order. Thomas frowned at his aunt, but Ellen made no objection, merely taking the indicated seat with a smile on her face and every indication of being honoured at Clarice showing her attention.

"How are you enjoying Gloucestershire, my lord?" Demelza enquired then. "You are aware, perhaps, that the Cotswolds are considered one of the greatest beauties of England? Is there anything to compare to them in America?"

Thomas smiled, turning to her. "The area is indeed very beautiful, and quite different to what I am used to. America is vast and very diverse in landscape, though I regret to say I have not travelled so much of the country as I should like. I did go once with my grandfather to see the great waterfall at Niagara, which was quite the most spectacular sight I have ever seen."

"I saw a drawing of the falls once," Ellen said, a little surprisingly. "Is it not where Bonaparte's brother honeymooned with his first wife?"

Everyone in the room stared at her. Ellen's cheeks coloured. "Sometimes Papa used to show me the newspapers and discuss things with me," she mumbled.

"Ladies of *quality* do not read the *newspapers*, dear," Clarice said patronisingly.

Thomas saw Ellen's eyes flash with rebellion for an instant before she lowered them to her hands, clasped in her lap. He immediately made a silent promise to himself to see to it that Ellen had the opportunity to peruse the newspapers whenever she wished, and to discuss them with him, too. She probably had a far greater understanding of current affairs in England then he did.

"Is it true that mountains of ice float in the ocean?" Demelza changed the subject gracefully.

"I have heard so, but did not see them on my voyage to England. Of course, I was lucky enough to be making the crossing at the height of summer; winter crossings are much more perilous, I understand," Thomas turned to her with a smile.

After the tea, at which Thomas and Demelza carried the conversation with little input from the others, John and Demelza took their leave and Clarice summoned a maid to show Ellen to her room while Thomas escorted John and Demelza out.

"Susan will be your personal maid, Miss Bentley," Clarice said, gesturing to the girl sunk in so low a curtsy her knees almost touched the floor. "She has been well trained as a lady's maid. I trust you will find her to your satisfaction."

"I had not expected such generosity as to have a maid assigned to me at all, my lady," Ellen said. "Indeed, it is entirely unnecessary. I am quite accustomed to making shift for myself."

Louisa tittered a little behind her hand; Clarice merely elevated her head a little higher. "That would be quite unsuitable," was all she said, and the conversation was at an end.

CHAPTER FIVE

HAVERFORD HALL WAS A maze, Ellen discovered as she followed Susan along apparently interminable corridors and up and down several short flights of stairs. She knew that the Hall had been built in several stages, the earliest part dating back to the fourteenth century and subsequent owners adding onto it until it reached its present size. From the outside, the house looked reasonably consistent; three sides of a square all built from golden Cotswold stone. Inside, it was something of a muddle, at least once one left the reception rooms at the front of the house.

"I believe I may need a map, Susan," she said in an attempt at humour as they finally reached her new room. Or *rooms*, as she soon discovered when Susan opened the door to show her inside; she had a private sitting-room, a dressing-room and a bedroom beyond that, all furnished far more luxuriously than any room she had ever occupied in her life. She looked about in awe, wondering how she would ever get used to such comforts.

"You'll soon find your way about, Miss Bentley," Susan said shyly. "Besides, I've a bed in your dressing-room; I can take you anywhere you want to go until you have your bearings."

Grateful for the consideration, Ellen nodded. Susan had already unpacked her belongings, she could see; hung her few gowns in one of the closets. They looked meagre and pathetic in the large space, and that was only one of the closets.

A knock on the door to the sitting-room made Ellen turn; she was half-way over to open it herself when Susan rushed past her, wide-eyed with panic.

"Oh no, Miss Bentley, you must let me get that!"

Apparently, she was not supposed to do anything for herself. Ellen found herself wondering just what exactly she *was* supposed to do as Susan opened the door to reveal Thomas standing outside.

"Do you like the rooms?" Thomas asked as soon as Susan admitted him. "I think Aunt Clarice would have put you up in the attics with the kitchen-maids if she could, but Louisa suggested this guest suite. They call it the Yellow Room."

Ellen could see why; the furniture was all upholstered in a soft shade of golden yellow, which matched the fittings on the bed and the curtains at the window. Fortunately, whoever had selected the decorations had an eye for subtlety and had not gone too overboard with the colour; the rugs on the floor were dark blue, which set the golden yellow off beautifully.

"They are very pretty rooms, I thank you," she said honestly. "Far grander than what I was expecting. I do not doubt that even the servants' rooms in the attics are quite comfortable."

"Not so much as I would like," Thomas said, rather unexpectedly. "I inspected them this morning. I will not have my staff living in meagre conditions while I wallow in luxury; I will be ordering several new beds and chairs, and I intend to instruct the housekeeper to ensure that extra blankets are available for anybody who asks for them, and sufficient wood and coal for all the fireplaces are to be provided too. I have been cold, New York is bitter in the wintertime, and I would not have anyone suffer that if I can prevent it."

Susan gave Thomas a look that was near-worshipful. "That is very good of you, my lord," she said timidly. "I shared one of those rooms with my sister Agnes until her ladyship said I was to move in here and do for Miss Bentley. I was right worried about her being cold this winter."

"Nobody at Haverford Hall will go cold this winter, and that is a promise," Thomas said firmly. "Nor in Haverford village, if I have my way. Ellen, it strikes me that as the vicar's daughter you very likely know all the residents and their needs far better than my aunt does."

"I doubt Lady Havers knows anyone with any *needs*," Ellen said unguardedly, before clapping a hand over her mouth. "I beg your pardon. I should not have said that," she mumbled through her fingers, her cheeks bright red.

"Why not? It's almost certainly true. Aunt Clarice does her very best to only associate with the upper echelons of society; I have known her barely a week and that much is quite obvious. Neither she nor Lady Louisa have ever visited the tenants, charitably or otherwise, I understand from the housekeeper, and I have to say that I do not approve. It does not fit with the stories Gramps used to tell me about the responsibilities of the earldom; he told me he regularly used to escort his mother and his sister about on their visits."

"I should like to hear about that," Ellen said eagerly. She glanced at Susan, who took her cue.

"Could I ring for some refreshments for you, Miss Bentley, m'lord?"

"We just had tea, thank you... what is your name?"

"Susan, m'lord," she gave him a deeply respectful curtsy.

"Perhaps you might just sit over there by the door, which we shall leave open? To give Lord Havers and myself countenance if anyone should happen by," Ellen suggested. Seeing Thomas' puzzled frown, she realised that he didn't understand why she'd made the request. "We cannot speak in private in a room with a closed door," she advised him gently. "Even though we are cousins and I am technically your ward."

"I see."

She wasn't sure that he did. Considering what she suspected of Lady Louisa's motives towards him, she wasn't too sure that his aunt and his other cousin could be relied upon to ensure he understood all the other rules of English polite society, either.

"You would escape censure, but my reputation could be irretrievably damaged," Ellen warned. "You should never allow yourself to be alone with any unmarried female, Thomas, lest you find yourself confronted by an angry father bound and determined on making you marry her. I don't have one of those," her smile was sad, "so I would just be ruined. As relations we have a little more leeway than most, but you should bear in mind that there are plenty of ladies who would seek to entrap you into marriage. You are wealthy, titled, young and handsome. Avoid being alone anywhere."

"Lest a young lady suddenly join me, and we be found together mere moments later by an enraged father?" Thomas understood what Ellen was getting at. Shaking his head at the idea of such manipulation, he smiled suddenly. "You and I shall have to shield each other; you can protect me from marriage-minded misses and I can protect you from the young men who will no doubt swarm about you!"

Ellen blinked. "What young men?"

"When we go to London, of course."

"London?" She stared at him in incredulity. "What do you mean, when *we* go to London?"

Thomas opened and closed his mouth several times, finally taking on a rather sheepish expression. "In all the kerfuffle of getting you moved here, I have just realized that I have neglected to apprise you of the plans my aunt has been making," he said. "The Little Season is under way at the present time, and she thinks that now would be a good time for me to get my feet wet in the deep waters of London society. The household will remove to the Havers townhouse in Belgravia in ten days' time."

Ellen was silent for a little while, considering. It was clear that her options were limited; she supposed that if she made enough fuss, she might be permitted to stay with John and Demelza while the others went to London, but if she were being honest, she had always dreamed of seeing the capital.

"We are still in mourning," she said at last, knowing it for a feeble excuse.

"True, but it has been more than half a year. Aunt Clarice and Louisa have set aside their blacks and greys for violet and lavender; you could do the same." He gave her an encouraging smile. "You would look charming in lavender."

She laughed, thinking of the contents of her wardrobe. Every dress she had was one that she had made over, either from one of her mother's or one of her own. Most of them were black, dyed from their original colours when she entered mourning. The others were carefully saved awaiting the day when she would put it off. There was nothing lavender or violet among them. Nor could she borrow anything from Louisa or Lady Havers, even if they would lend it to her; she was taller by a handsbreath than either of them, and any of their gowns on her would show far too much ankle.

"What is funny?" Thomas gave her a quizzical look.

"I have nothing suitable to be seen in London, cousin. My gowns mark me as the poor relation here; there, it will be assumed I am a servant attached to your household." She gave him a direct look. "You know very well I am penniless, so what is your plan?"

"You and I will both need new wardrobes," Thomas replied, apparently unconcerned. "Fashions are slightly different in London than New York, I believe, and I do not wish to appear the unlettered colonial. Aunt Clarice and Louisa are already making plans to order new gowns for themselves; all bills will be sent to me. I have no doubt that Aunt Clarice will be happy to advise you as to what you should order."

Ellen did not feel nearly so certain of that, but once again, she supposed that she had little choice. *Consider it an adventure,* she told herself. *How many times did you daydream of going to London, of seeing places you have only read about in books and newspapers?*

"I must say that I am looking forward to seeing London very much," Thomas said, unconsciously echoing her thoughts. "I have read so much about it!"

Bracing herself with thoughts of the adventure to come, all the new places she would see, Ellen smiled at him determinedly. "So am I, Thomas. Tell me, what do you wish to see first?"

CHAPTER SIX

Ellen could hardly believe the amount of baggage Lady Clarice seemed to think was necessary to remove the household to London for a few weeks. Trunk after trunk was packed and loaded onto a veritable procession of baggage carts, despite both Clarice and Louisa continually discussing the entire new wardrobes they planned to order for themselves once they reached the city.

Thomas actually came out and said what Ellen was thinking, when he cast an appalled eye over the mountain of trunks already strapped to one of the carts.

"What are you planning to do with all these things, Aunt? You have enough clothes packed here to wear three different outfits every day in London; shall I take it then that you do not plan to visit the modistes after all?"

Clarice looked down her long nose at him and sniffed dismissively. "You know nothing about London fashions, Thomas, nor of what is required to ensure that our family remains in the first circles of society."

"True," Thomas admitted with a sigh. "Very well, Aunt Clarice. Do as you see fit."

"I shall." Turning her head away from him, she called "Careful with that band-box, man! My favourite hat is in it!"

"Yes, your ladyship," the hapless footman she was addressing replied.

"Come," Ellen touched Thomas's arm. "Will you walk with me, Cousin?"

"Indeed, I believe a walk would be just the thing right now." Thomas shook his head. "All this... I packed my clothes and moved *continents* on a few days' notice, with no expectation of ever returning to my old home. Everything I absolutely, positively could not live without fit into just two trunks."

Ellen said nothing as they walked along one of the curving paths that led through the Hall's famous rose garden. All her belongings, treasured or otherwise, hadn't filled the single trunk she had borrowed from Demelza to transport them to the

Hall. She could not ever imagine owning as many beautiful gowns as Louisa and Clarice possessed, never mind desiring more.

"Are you looking forward to London?" Thomas asked. "To having some new gowns and meeting new people?"

"I do not particularly care for new gowns," Ellen said, "though Lady Havers insists that I must have them, and I will accept her advice on the matter. I would not for the world bring shame upon the family, even though I am in truth a poor relation."

"You are *not* a poor relation," Thomas said firmly. "You are one of the only living members of the Havers family."

"The poorest one."

"For now." He smiled mysteriously and would say no more, even when Ellen pressed him. They had become quite friendly in the few days she had resided at the Hall. It transpired that they both liked to rise early in the morning, and regularly encountered each other in the breakfast room. Thomas had surprised her on the very first day by asking if she would like to see the library; Ellen agreed eagerly and was delighted when he oh-so-casually pointed out a table in the large room and remarked that the newspapers were always left there once he had done perusing them.

"Allsopp has instructions not to dispose of them for seven days," Thomas noted, "just in case I should think of something I would wish to review, of course."

"Of course," Ellen echoed in wonder, looking around the library. She had never imagined that so many books could even exist, never mind be kept all in one room. There had to be thousands of volumes on the oaken shelves.

Following her gaze, Thomas said "It appears that the previous Earl was an inveterate reader. Much of the collection was added during his lifetime, I understand. You are welcome to borrow any book which takes your fancy, Ellen."

He had no idea of the magnitude of the gift he had just given her, Ellen knew. She could not adequately express her gratitude, but she tried, stumbling over her words until Thomas took her hand in his and pressed his fingers on it lightly.

"Haverford Hall is your home now, Ellen. This is your library as much as mine. You have no need to thank me."

She knew he was wrong about that, but he would not hear her exclamations, only shaking his head and saying that he would leave her to look about at her leisure.

Every morning since then, they had breakfasted together and Thomas took the time to ask her what she was reading, and discuss it with her. He was well-read,

Ellen had discovered; apparently he had attended the American university of Harvard, which Americans considered just as good as Oxford or Cambridge. Nor was he dismissive of her opinions just because of her gender, which was a first for her. Even her father had occasionally told her that she could not possibly understand something simply because she was female.

Ellen hoped that they would be able to continue their morning routine in London. "Does the London house have a library?" she thought to ask as she and Thomas turned about on their walk to return to the Hall.

"I should be very surprised if it does not, though perhaps it may not be quite as extensive as the one here at the Hall. Consider, though, the opportunities London offers for shopping! I have no doubt that there will be plenty of bookshops; if we find the library at the townhouse inadequate, we shall have plenty of opportunity to improve it."

Ellen smiled at his enthusiasm. "You shall be too busy, surely, joining gentleman's clubs and giving speeches in the House of Lords."

"How shall I contribute sensibly in the House of Lords if I do not read the news and talk it over with you, Ellen?" Thomas laughed at her. "I am not too sure that English gentlemen will be interested in socialising with an uncouth American, besides."

He was nervous, Ellen realised with incredulity. "Of course they will," she said robustly, "all of the neighbouring gentry who have come to meet you have been very friendly."

Haverford Hall had been positively swarmed with everyone who could think of a good excuse to call, all eager to meet and curry favour with the new Earl. Thomas had insisted on presenting Ellen to everyone as well, even though many of them already knew her and looked askance at Thomas presenting her as his cousin, equally with Lady Louisa. None of them wanted to offend Thomas, though, so they were all polite, at least publicly, though she had seen a few sneers directed her way when Thomas' attention was elsewhere.

"The baggage carts are ready to depart, my lord, with your approval," Allsopp met them on their re-entry into the Hall.

"Of course, if everything my aunt wants has been packed," Thomas nodded his agreement. The carts were being sent ahead so that everything would be already in London when they arrived; the family would not depart until the following morning and planned to spend two days travelling. Lady Clarice had already arranged for them to spend their nights with noble families who resided along their route. There would be no roadside inns for the Havers family; when Thomas had asked what inns they should contact to reserve rooms to break their journey, he had thought Clarice might faint from horror.

"An inn!" she had shrieked. "With the common folk... and vermin... and who knows what ghastly food we would be served! Over my dead body would I let my Louisa set foot in such a place!"

Ellen was not particularly looking forward to spending two days in a carriage in company with Lady Clarice and Lady Louisa. Thomas had already announced his intention to ride his stallion for most of the journey, at least so long as the weather remained clement and she envied him the option. Peering up at the sky as they entered the Hall, Ellen sent up a silent prayer for rain. Thomas' presence in the carriage would make the journey a great deal more bearable. Clarice and Louisa did not criticise her directly, but she always felt as though she was being judged and found wanting when their cool blue eyes fell upon her.

On the other hand, the thought of sitting in the carriage watching Thomas and Louisa making calf eyes at each other didn't hold all that much appeal, either.

She walked down to the village that afternoon to visit John and Demelza, to farewell them before her trip. A footman and her maid escorted her and waited to walk her back; despite Ellen's laughing protests that she had been walking alone all over Haverford since she was let off leading strings, on this matter Thomas had sided with Lady Clarice, who threw up her hands in horror at the thought. So Ellen just did her best to pretend that the two servants weren't there, walking ahead and humming softly under her breath, enjoying the crispness of the air on the pleasant September day.

"Ellen!" Demelza exclaimed over her with all her customary warmth, but her sharp eyes quickly spotted that something was bothering her younger friend. Deflecting her children with promises of cake in half an hour if they would play quietly until then, she drew Ellen into the parlour and closed the door. "Darling girl, what's the matter?"

Ellen tried to protest that everything was fine, but she crumbled under the pressure of Demelza's genuine, gentle concern, and ended up confessing all her fears and worries about going to London.

"... and I just *know* that everyone will look at me and see me for the poor country cousin I am," Ellen ran down finally, and Demelza rose and took her in a warm, comforting embrace.

"They will see you for the charming, caring, beautiful young woman that you are," she reassured. "You will be a hit in London, Ellen; I don't doubt that you will come back engaged to a duke or someone else terribly important who has recognised you as a treasure beyond compare."

Ellen laughed through the lump in her throat. "I don't think I'd make a very good duchess."

"You would be magnificent," Demelza said loyally. "You *will* be magnificent. Promise that you will write and tell me all about it?"

"I shall write so often you will spend all your allowance on paying for the postage and write back begging me to stop." Ellen had to hold back tears as Demelza hugged her close.

"Never," Demelza promised. "John would never grudge me your letters, dearest. You shall write as much as you wish, and I will write back, though our dull lives will be of little interest."

"Oh, never say so," Ellen smiled through her teary eyes. "Your recounting of the boys' antics will keep me greatly entertained, I am sure!"

A crash in the next room made them both wince. "Talking of which," Demelza said with a sigh, "I knew it was too good to be true."

"Come, they are eager for their cake, and you have reassured me." Ellen smiled bravely, and her friend took her hand, squeezed it.

"You will be fine, dearest. Just be yourself, and you will soon make friends."

Ellen could only hope Demelza was correct.

CHAPTER SEVEN

HAVERS HOUSE IN LONDON was just as opulent as Haverford Hall, though thankfully not on quite such a grand scale. Susan had thankfully been permitted to accompany her, so Ellen did not feel entirely friendless, and the Havers House staff turned out to be just as kind and welcoming as those at the Hall – at least when not under the sharp eyes of Lady Clarice. Nobody dared so much as crack a smile if she was looking.

It was evident that Clarice and Louisa would, if permitted, have ignored Ellen and left her in her room when they went out, but Thomas made his expectations more than clear. Ellen was to be provided a new, fashionable wardrobe, and she was to accompany Clarice and Louisa to any events to which they were invited.

"We cannot accept any invitations for a week at least, in that case," Clarice had sniffed in disgust, "for Ellen has not a single thing fit to be seen in, and I will not have her shame the family. It will take the modiste a week at least to put together a new outfit or two!"

"Nobody will have anything ready-made which could be provided sooner?" Thomas asked.

"Ready-made! Rejected by other ladies as being of inferior quality or not up to the latest fashions, you mean!" Clarice's voice rose to a shriek.

"Ah. Very well. In that case." Thomas cast Ellen a slightly hunted look, and she smiled into her teacup. "Of course, we defer to your expertise, Aunt Clarice."

"Indeed, you must." Clarice harrumphed, ruffled feathers obviously settling. "We shall be off to the modiste first thing tomorrow. And it is not just new gowns, you know; we must have shoes and gloves and hats and... perhaps some jewels?"

Thomas opened his mouth, and closed it again, and Ellen wondered what he had been about to say. He pursed his lips and nodded. "I will attend to the jewels. Some simple things, Ellen?"

"Yes, please," she said gratefully. "I am still in half-mourning, after all."

"Which is such a bore," Louisa put in. "Even though lavender suits me, I am so thoroughly tired of it."

"Three more months, dearest, and you may have all the bright colours you wish. Perhaps we shall look into placing some orders now," Clarice said thoughtfully.

"Certainly not, the fashions will have changed in three months, Mother!" Louisa cried in disgust. Then her eyes narrowed. "Though perhaps we might purchase some of the best quality fabrics and put them by for later."

"An excellent idea," Clarice approved. "Then nobody else will have them!"

Thomas met Ellen's eyes again, and she could see he was stifling laughter. She hid her own smile behind her cup again, though it faded when she thought that at least Thomas could escape Clarice and Louisa's snobbiness whenever he wished, whereas she was trapped and at the mercy of their whims.

"What did you not say?" she asked Thomas quietly as the pair of them left the dining room. "When Aunt Clarice said I'd need jewels."

"Ah." He gave her a rueful glance. "I was about to say something which might have caused quite an eruption, and thought better of it. Even though it is something to which I believe you are entitled... I don't think Aunt Clarice would see it that way."

"You're being mysterious, Thomas, tell me!" She pinched his arm lightly, and he laughed.

"I was going to suggest she open up the Havers jewel box to share some of them with you. As the Countess, it appeared my uncle gave her custody of it without restriction, and I can hardly ask her to hand it back when I have no *new* Countess to give it to."

"Of course. I quite understand, and I'm sure everything in there would be too grand for me. I have a string of pearls from Mama I like very much and would prefer to wear anyway." She lifted her chin proudly. "I don't need you to buy me anything."

"Perhaps not," he said, his tone gentle, "but I am pleased to do it, Ellen, and as I've said before, I believe it to be no less than you are owed by the earldom. Wear your mother's pearls... and I'll buy you some earbobs and a bracelet or two and perhaps a brooch to go with them."

If it had been anyone else, her pride would never have permitted her to accept, but this was Thomas, and he was, already, quite the best friend she had ever had. He was kind, thoughtful and gentle, considerate of everyone's feelings, whether they be members of his family or the lowliest servant at Haverford Hall.

Ellen didn't think even her parents, loving though they had been, had listened so intently whenever she spoke. Thomas listened as though there was nobody else in the world he'd rather be talking to. As though her opinions mattered, as though *she* mattered. They'd had long conversations about Haverford and its residents; he claimed she was by far the best source of information he could have, and she allowed that might not be too far from the truth. Louisa and Clarice had barely deigned to acknowledge anyone from the village, whereas Ellen had interacted with all of them at church, and most of them had come to seek advice from one or other of her parents at some time. Ellen knew them, knew their needs and concerns, their lives and troubles. Knew who was related and who was feuding and who was both, and in most cases, the stories behind their feuds too.

Even though Thomas had only been at Haverford Hall for a matter of days, he'd already begun putting plans into action. Men were being called on to work, to replace rotting thatch and fix crumbling walls on tenants' cottages which hadn't seen maintenance in a generation.

John had stopped by a time or two to discuss legal matters, and mentioned quietly to Ellen that nobody in the village could have a bad word to say about Thomas. And he'd left John with authority to deal with all minor matters which might arise while the family was in London, so nobody need suffer while waiting for letters to be sent back and forth.

"You are so very kind, Thomas," she said softly, "and I would love some earbobs."

"And bracelets, and a brooch. Maybe a hairpin or two." He grinned at her unrepentantly, and she could not help but laugh.

"Considering how many gowns Aunt Clarice claims I must have, all of which you will be paying for, I suppose a hairpin or two will not make much difference to your pocketbook!"

"My pocketbook can withstand whatever expenditure you can possibly make. I promise it."

Ellen stood on a box with the modiste pinning fabric about her for the fifth – or was it the sixth? – day gown Clarice insisted she needed. And this was after three ball gowns had been ordered, plus a riding habit, three walking gowns, and more underpinnings than she could wear in a month.

"Miss looks very well in this colour," the modiste murmured, "though 'tis a shame you are still in half-mourning. I have a lovely yellow muslin which will be beautiful on you after you are out of mourning."

"Yellow is my favourite colour," Louisa said pettishly. "We cannot both be wearing it. I don't like pink. You can wear pink, Ellen."

Ellen blinked. Looked at the row of fabric bolts set to one side, all of which Louisa had reserved for herself, for when she was out of mourning. Blues, greens, orange and yes, yellow, but there was no reason why they should ever both be wearing it at the same time, unless Ellen was allowed to wear nothing *but* yellow.

"I like pink," she said quietly.

It wasn't worth fighting over. She did like pink. She wasn't ready to wear it yet, and she wasn't sure that three more months would be enough for her to feel ready to come out of mourning, either, but she was fairly sure Clarice wasn't going to give her much choice in the matter.

"Well, if you can really have the first gowns delivered on Friday, we shall be able to accept an invitation I've received for Saturday evening," Clarice was saying to the modiste, looking pleased.

"Of course, my lady. If it was Miss Bentley's gowns alone, I could have one delivered tomorrow..."

"No, no," Clarice said hastily. "I will not have Miss Bentley in a new gown while Lady Louisa is in one of last season's creations, that would not do at all, you must see that!"

"Whatever you say, my lady," the modiste curtsied, but Ellen saw the slight sneer as she bent her head. "Spoiled," the woman muttered as she disappeared behind a curtain into the back of the shop, too quietly for Clarice or Louisa to overhear.

Ellen did not disagree. She could only imagine the tantrum which might have ensued if a new gown had been delivered for Ellen while Louisa yet had none. For every item Clarice had insisted Ellen would require, Louisa had demanded two for herself.

"What is the event to which we are invited on Saturday, Aunt Clarice?" Ellen inquired once they were finally back in the carriage, though they were not going home as yet, with a visit to the milliner's to occur first.

"Just a small party with friends," Clarice said with a little sniff, pinning Ellen with a hard stare. "I will need to see how you conduct yourself in a small gathering before we dare expose you to the *Ton* at large, my girl. If you must needs have etiquette and dancing lessons so you will not disgrace us, so be it."

There was little Ellen could say to that. She knew how to dance, or thought she did, having attended several assemblies and a private ball or two since she turned eighteen, but whether or not she might pass muster among the Ton remained to be seen.

"I will try not to disgrace you, Aunt Clarice," she said quietly. "And of course, if you think I require further instruction, I will do my best to learn quickly."

"You're meek, and obedient, at least," Clarice said with another sniff. "I daresay I might be able to find you a husband who wants a quiet wife. A widower with some children to raise, perhaps."

"Oh yes," Louisa said with a scornful laugh, "I should not want a man who already has children. Ellen may have all those suitors she pleases!"

"What if you should fall in love with someone who has children already, Cousin Louisa?" Ellen asked curiously. "Should you not change your mind then?"

Louisa stared at her as though Ellen had suddenly begun speaking in Greek. "Love?" she cried disdainfully. "What has *love* to do with anything? What utter nonsense you talk! Just keep your mouth shut, Ellen, or everyone will think you a simpleton and even the widowers will not bother with you!"

Crushed, Ellen subsided, not daring to say anything more. She leaned against the side of the coach and watched the London scenery pass by, Demelza's words once again echoing in her mind.

"You will be fine, dearest. Just be yourself, and you will soon make friends."

"I hope so," she whispered, very quietly. "I do hope so."

CHAPTER EIGHT

Two weeks later

Demelza's words came back to Ellen once again as she looked around the crowded ballroom, and she smiled ruefully. Her friend had never even been to London, had no idea of the ways of high society. Beauty, wealth and connections were the only coin the *Ton* recognised, and Ellen had none of the first two and little of the last. The first night wearing one of her new gowns, she had truly felt like a princess as she entered the ballroom just a step behind Louisa.

By the end of the night, however, the scales had well and truly fallen from her eyes. Thomas was the only man who had asked Ellen to dance while Louisa was constantly surrounded by a crowd of gentlemen three deep clamouring for her attention. None of them had given Ellen more than a second glance.

Tonight marked the third ball she had attended as part of the Havers family, and she had still only ever danced duty dances with Thomas.

Sipping on a cup of punch she had been forced to ask a footman to procure for her, it occurred to Ellen that she was, in fact, a confirmed wallflower. Relegated to the fringes of the room where matrons sat on uncomfortable chairs and gossiped about the gathered throng, she might as well have been invisible.

With a quiet sigh, Ellen found a seat for herself. Her new dancing slippers pinched her toes and she was glad to sit down and ease her feet.

"Hello," a friendly voice said, and she looked to her left, her eyes widening as she took in the beauty of the woman sitting beside her. Around the same age as Ellen herself, she guessed, the lady wore a gown in the first stare of fashion, a choker of impossibly large diamonds around her slender throat, a mass of deep red curls artfully arranged atop her head.

"Er, hello," Ellen stuttered, a little awe-struck by the lady's beauty. Why in the world was someone who looked like *that* sitting alone at the side of the room engaging complete strangers in conversation? She should be on the dance floor, being fawned over by a horde of swains even larger than Louisa's.

A handsome young gentleman paused in front of them, making the lady an impeccable bow. "Might I implore you for a dance, Lady Creighton?"

The lady's smile vanished instantly. "Thank you, I do not care to dance," she said, not meeting his eyes.

"May I fetch you something? A glass of punch?"

"I thank you, no." Deliberately, Lady Creighton lifted her fan, snapped it open and turned her head to the side, looking at Ellen and hiding her face from the gentleman. He bowed, his expression melancholy, before backing away.

"Did you know him?" Ellen asked impulsively.

"Only slightly," Lady Creighton said with a sigh, lowering her fan and checking that the gentleman had truly left them alone. Her foot was tapping along to the music, Ellen saw.

"But you did not wish to dance with him?" Curiosity roused, Ellen quite realised that she was being rude, but she couldn't help herself.

"I am not permitted to dance with anyone except my husband," Lady Creighton said with another sigh, "nor to converse with any gentleman when I am not in his presence."

Ellen's eyes widened with shock. "I... see," she said at last, thinking that the lady's husband must be very jealous.

"So I find events like this dreadfully tedious, since generally after the first dance my husband abandons me to my own devices and heads for the card room."

Lady Creighton was lonely, Ellen realised. She offered her a friendly smile. "He does not object to your conversing with other ladies, though?"

"Fortunately, no. I am Marianne, by the way."

"Ellen Bentley... Lady Creighton?"

"Countess of Creighton, for my sins." Marianne's smile was weary. "It is a pleasure to make your acquaintance, Miss Bentley. You do not dance tonight?"

"I did dance," Ellen said a little defensively. "The second dance, with my cousin, the Earl of Havers."

"How nice."

"…And since then, nobody has asked me," Ellen confessed. "I'm a wallflower, I'm afraid."

"Which is quite ridiculous, for you're very pretty, and cousin to an Earl."

"The poor relation, I'm afraid," Ellen smiled her thanks for the compliment, but she couldn't quite hide her hurt. Thomas had promised, after all, that she would be treated equally to the rest of the Havers family. She could hardly blame him for the way other people treated her, though, and how was he to know? He was from America, and no more familiar with London society and its unspoken rules than she.

Marianne tilted her head curiously. "What difference does that make?"

"I'm sorry, but I don't understand what you mean."

"Allow me to share a story with you," Marianne said. "Once upon a time, there was a gentleman with an unfortunate habit of losing at the card tables. Without particular connections of his own, he had entrée into the higher circles of society through his wife's family."

Spellbound and wondering who the gentleman in the story was, Ellen listened in silence.

"One day, the gentleman sat down to a game of cards at his club which was particularly ill-fated. By the end of it, he had lost every possession he ever owned and his opponents held notes of debt he could never hope to meet. He was a pauper. Desperate, he approached the only connection he had who might offer him aid in his time of need; his late wife's cousin, the Earl of Creighton." Marianne's lovely face was emotionless as she continued. "The gentleman had only one thing left to offer the Earl; his eighteen-year-old daughter, accounted a very pretty girl by all who saw her. Indeed, her first London season was turning out a smashing success. Miss Abingdon was courted by quite a number of eligible gentlemen, all of whom were willing to overlook her lack of dowry and her father's well-known habits. Their suits all came to naught, however, when Mr Abingdon accepted the Earl of Creighton's offer for her."

Marianne's expression was remote as she finished her little story. Ellen did not quite know what to say. Miss Abingdon was evidently Marianne herself.

"So, you see," Marianne said after a few moments of silence, "wealth and connections are not required in order to catch a husband, even one among the wealthiest and most highly titled in the land. There are plenty of gentlemen out there with their own fortunes, in charge of their own destinies, and I cannot at all comprehend why some of them are not looking at you and seeing a lovely young woman who would make some lucky gentleman a fine wife."

Put like that, Ellen supposed it was a little odd that nobody at all approached her. There were plenty of plainer girls than she, of no greater wealth and in many cases lesser family, who regularly appeared on the dance floor on the arms of eligible young men.

"Even Miss Brightling dances more than you, and she is afflicted with eyes that cross, protruding teeth and an insatiable appetite for sweets which has given her a girth similar to that of a horse," Marianne said, accurately if a little cruelly. "Why does Lady Havers not introduce you to some of the young men buzzing about her daughter? There would not be enough dances for Lady Louisa to give them one each if this ball lasted until tomorrow night."

"I suppose... maybe Lady Havers does not want me distracting from Louisa's limelight?" Ellen said uncertainly. Although she was not sure why Louisa apparently needed suitors at all; her play for Thomas had been both obvious and apparently successful. Thomas stood glowering jealously at Louisa's group even now. Poor Thomas; every time Louisa smiled at one of her swains he looked most distressed. Ellen wished that she might say or do something to comfort him.

"The Earl needs to stop pining after Lady Louisa and start making acquaintances of his own social circle," Marianne said. "I'm afraid that I may not speak to him to effect introductions, but there are some ladies I might introduce *you* to, if you would be willing? They have relatives near to your cousin's age who are upstanding young men."

The slightly wistful tone in Marianne's voice made Ellen wonder if the young men in question had been among her suitors before she was married off to Creighton. Grateful for her condescension, though, Ellen said honestly that she should be delighted to make any new acquaintances.

"Excellent. Do come with me." Rising gracefully to her feet, Marianne led Ellen along the wall to where a group of older society matrons were gathered. "Lady Jersey, Lady Sale, Mrs Peabody. May I introduce Miss Ellen Bentley to your notice? She is a cousin of the new Earl of Havers."

"An American?" Lady Sale said sharply. She had a long, narrow nose, and a way of looking down it that made Ellen feel very small.

"No, my lady, I was born and raised in Haverford," Ellen dipped a curtsy. "I am quite a distant cousin," she said with devastating honesty, "my great-grandmother was sister to the Earl's grandfather."

"Quite close enough," Lady Jersey said with a hearty chuckle. "*My* great-grandmother was mistress to one of our former monarchs, and my family has never quite managed to live down the scandal!"

"Sally!" Lady Sale shook her head, but a smile curved her thin lips upward as Mrs Peabody let out a high, girlish giggle.

A little shocked, Ellen blushed, saw that Marianne was blushing too. Lady Jersey was examining her now with a critical eye.

"You're here with Clarice, I suppose?"

"Lady Havers, yes, my lady," Ellen nodded.

"Never did like her. Why isn't she introducing you about, hm? Worried you'll be competition for her daughter, Laura is it?"

"Lady Louisa," Mrs Peabody corrected her.

Lady Jersey waved a plump, beringed hand carelessly in the other woman's direction. "Yes, yes, Lady Louisa, we all know the type. Diamond of the first water and all that. Why didn't she find a husband in her first two seasons, hm?"

"Holding out for a bigger fish," Lady Sale said knowledgeably.

The other ladies hummed in agreement before all looking back at Ellen, beady eyes assessing her gown and carriage, the way her hair was dressed. The quiet loveliness of her features.

"You did well to bring her to us, Lady Creighton," Lady Jersey nodded to Marianne.

"I hoped. My situation means that I cannot be of much use, but you ladies... well, you were very kind to me at my debut."

"You quite broke poor Tristan's heart when you married Creighton, my dear," Lady Sale said, "but I never blamed you. *We* know what kind of man your father was."

Looking past them, Marianne paled suddenly. "Excuse me," she said hastily, and walked briskly away to join a gentleman who had just entered the ballroom.

"Poor girl," Lady Sale and Mrs Peabody said almost in unison while Lady Jersey was not nearly so restrained.

"Wasted!" she snapped.

"Is that Lord Creighton?" Ellen asked shyly, a little horrified. The earl, if it were he, had to be at least seventy years old if not more, almost entirely bald, his face deeply wrinkled. He was a big man, though, tall and still powerfully built despite his age, and as Marianne hastened to his side he put out a large hand and clamped it tightly around her wrist, almost dragging her from the room.

"Unfortunately, yes," Lady Jersey said, "and if Clarice has her way, you'll probably end up married off to someone just as awful. Let us see to thwarting her plans, my dears. Regrettably, Almack's is closed until the Season proper or I should provide you with vouchers, but Town is not entirely devoid of suitable prospects at this time of year." She gave Ellen a warm smile, raking her from head to foot with sharp eyes. "At least Clarice has seen fit to outfit you properly, although lavender isn't quite your colour. Why are you still in mourning, if the previous earl was such a distant cousin?"

"My parents both passed away last December," Ellen said, once again having to swallow the painful lump in her throat. She did not think that she would ever stop missing them.

"Oh, you poor dear!" Mrs Peabody said sympathetically. "I must introduce you to my godson. Now where is that boy..."

"Edmund is far too young to be looking for a wife, Agatha," Lady Jersey said firmly. "Nice boy, but still at Oxford," she informed Ellen. "You need a man already set up; I take it you don't have your heart set on a title or one of England's great fortunes?"

"Just a simple home of my own and a man with a kind heart," Ellen said. "I grew up in the parsonage at Haverford, my lady; my expectations are humble."

"Humble, indeed!" Lady Sale gave her an approving look and the other two nodded. "Well, perhaps we can do a little better than that. Would you have any objections to a military man? The Wares' second son is in the Navy and has lately received promotion to a captaincy and his own ship..." without waiting for Ellen's reply, she waved to a sturdy young man in uniform and soon recruited him to dance the next set with her.

While Mr Ware was pleasant enough, he did not seem particularly interested in making more than polite conversation. Ellen was nevertheless pleased to dance at all, and grateful to the ladies for their condescension. Upon the conclusion of the set, Mr Ware returned her to her new benefactresses, where Ellen was surprised to find that they already had another partner awaiting her. Lord Bellmere was duly introduced, politely enquired as to whether she was engaged for the dance, and upon hearing that she was not, escorted her to the line of couples.

Beginning to enjoy herself despite the new dancing slippers still pinching her toes, Ellen smiled at Lord Bellmere when he asked how she was enjoying London.

"Oh, a good deal, my lord! Though I have not as yet had an opportunity to go to the British Museum; I am hoping that my cousin will be able to arrange a visit for us soon. I am very eager to see the famous marbles which Lord Elgin brought back from Athens."

Lord Bellmere, a softly-spoken gentleman in his early forties who had not particularly objected when his cousin Lady Sale caught his attention and insisted he danced with a country nobody, found himself intrigued. In his experience, the Elgin Marbles and the British Museum were not generally the attractions which young ladies found of particular interest on their first visit to London.

"I have a friend who is on the board of the Museum," he offered. "While the public opening times are a sad crush, it is possible to obtain tickets to more exclusive viewings. I could see if my friend might be able to assist...?"

Ellen's smile was quite radiant as the dance brought them back together to clasp hands and bow. "Why, Lord Bellmere, that is a most generous offer! Thank you so much!"

Miss Bentley was very pretty when she smiled like that, Lord Bellmere thought, deciding that he would pay a call on his friend on the morrow. And that he owed his cousin Lady Sale a thank-you, for bringing Miss Bentley to his attention. No dowry to speak of, Lady Sale had said, but he was more than comfortably off and had no need of a wealthy wife. A pretty one with a brain between her ears, someone who would not bore him to tears in conversation, would suit him very well.

"Might I call upon you, Miss Bentley?" he enquired.

A pretty colour flushed Ellen's cheeks as the dance ended and they bowed to each other. "That would be very pleasant, Lord Bellmere."

CHAPTER NINE

Partnering the pretty wife of another young Earl he had lately been introduced to in the dancing, Thomas was surprised to see Ellen join the set with a gentleman he did not know. Ellen looked happy, smiling and talking animatedly with her partner, and the gentleman seemed equally taken with her.

"Pardon me, Lady Hallam," Thomas said, "but do you see the couple three down from us in the set, the beautiful dark-haired lady in the lavender dress with the green sash..."

"I see them, but I do not know her, if you are angling for an introduction," Lady Hallam said with a cheerful laugh.

"That is my cousin Miss Bentley, ma'am. I was just wondering if you knew her partner?"

"Ah! Indeed, I do, that is Lord Bellmere. One of the Duke of Northumberland's grandsons; there are a whole collection of them, and though he's a long way from the ducal coronet he has a baronetcy from his mother and a very nice estate near Warwick, I believe." She cast another look at the pair as the dance took them around to face Ellen and her partner. "Your cousin seems to have caught his fancy. He's a very respectable gentleman, I assure you. No scandals or black sheep in that family."

The news should have pleased Thomas, but he found himself frowning as he saw Ellen smiling widely at her partner again. What was the man saying, to make her look so pleased? He had not thought Ellen the type to fall for empty flattery. At the end of the dance, he hastily returned an amused Lady Hallam to her husband and set off in search of Ellen, finding her just as the next dance started.

"El-Miss Bentley," he said.

"Cousin," she offered him a pretty curtsy and a smile. "I pray you will excuse me; Major Trevithick has just engaged me for this dance."

The very tall, very thin redheaded gentleman on whose arm Ellen's gloved hand daintily rested, gave him a polite bow. There was little Thomas could do but smile and nod, though he found himself frowning after Ellen as she and her partner joined the forming set.

"So you're Havers," a voice said behind him, and he turned to find himself the focus of several pairs of beady eyes.

"At your service," he bowed, unsure of the protocol. They had not been formally introduced, but then one of the ladies had addressed him, and from their jewels and gowns these were the kind of highly-ranked ladies who could sneer at convention all they pleased. Bellmere was standing with them, he noticed, and the baronet stepped forward.

"I'm Bellmere, my lord; I just had the pleasure of a dance with your charming cousin Miss Bentley."

"Yes," Thomas said, deciding quite irrationally that he did not like the shape of the other man's eyebrows. Recognising that he was being slightly ridiculous, he forced himself to smile and be polite as Bellmere introduced Lady Jersey, Lady Sale and Mrs Peabody. Having read the newspapers diligently since his arrival in England, and not merely the political pages but the society ones as well, he recognised the names as some of the leaders of the *Ton*. Apparently they had taken a liking to Ellen, because no sooner had they been introduced than they started telling him--not asking, but telling--that they intended to take her on and see her well married.

"Ellen--ah, Miss Bentley--is my ward, yes," he answered a question from Lady Sale, "but she is in the charge of my aunt the Countess."

"Clarice has her hands full with Lady Louisa and her army of suitors," Lady Jersey said with a sniff, "whereas here we are, three bored dowagers with not a single girl between us to bring out this season. Lady Havers hasn't had a minute to introduce Miss Bentley to anyone, Havers--do you mind if I call you Havers?"

"Would it matter if I did?"

"Not in the least, dear boy." She smiled at him. "You may be American, but clearly you're not a fool."

There wasn't much he could say to that, so he just bowed politely. Clearly Lady Jersey was a law unto herself.

"Thank you for your attentions to my cousin, milady. I will assume that you have her best interests at heart."

"Don't worry about a thing, Havers," Lady Jersey waved a hand weighed down with gem-studded rings. "We'll have her married off in no time."

Thomas found that he could not feel as enthused about that idea as Lady Jersey and her friends seemed to be. "I will have to approve any serious suitors for her hand, of course," he said stiffly, "and I trust that you will not introduce her to any gentlemen who are unsuitable."

Lady Jersey gave him a penetrating look, but it was Mrs Peabody who asked;

"And do you have any particular criteria for suitability, my lord?"

Lord Bellmere hadn't made himself scarce, Thomas noted, and was listening avidly to the conversation.

"No gamblers, or heavy drinkers," Thomas said, trying to think of a good reason to exclude Bellmere apart from his detestable eyebrows. His age, that had to count against him. "A gentleman with his own property, but not too high in the instep; Miss Bentley's father was a parson and she was raised quite simply."

"Pshaw," Lady Sale said sharply, "my father was a parson too, and I managed perfectly well when I married Sale."

"The *Marquess* of Sale," Mrs Peabody murmured, for Thomas' edification.

"Your pardon, my lady, I meant no offence." He offered the marchioness a deep bow, and she sniffed, looking slightly mollified.

From the corner of his eye, Thomas caught a glimpse of Ellen and her tall partner in the dance. The man's red coat, clashing with his hair, gave him another idea.

"While I have the utmost respect for the courage of England's brave soldiers, I am not sure that I should care to see Miss Bentley married to a military man, either. The necessities of military service must needs keep them apart, and happiness in a marriage is difficult to achieve in such cases." He carefully didn't look at Lord Bellmere as he added one final recommendation. "Finally, I should prefer Ellen to marry a man reasonably close to her own age."

"Well, we shall take all those things into account, Havers," Lady Jersey said, sharp eyes boring into him. "For the most part, they are not unreasonable things to want for your cousin. I note that you did not mention her preference, though. Are we to take that into account and deny her if she discovers a partiality, for example, for naval captains?"

Thomas had the uneasy feeling that she was teasing him, though he could not discern precisely how. "Miss Bentley's happiness is my first concern," he said.

"Of course."

Lady Jersey was definitely laughing in her sleeve about him, and Lady Sale and Mrs Peabody looked quite unaccountably amused as well. Bellmere was eyeing him in a peculiar way, almost as though sizing him up.

Deciding that retreat, in this case, would be well-advised, Thomas politely excused himself and made his way back across the room, glimpsing Ellen and her partner again on the way. Ellen was smiling again, that happy, bright smile he had only ever glimpsed a few times, usually in the library at Haverford when she discussed a particularly interesting book with him.

Was Ellen truly enjoying the ball so much? Thomas could not say that he was; so far, the people he had met had been dull, sycophantic or both, for the most part. The three older ladies he had just met were by far the most interesting encounters of the night.

"I say, Havers," a hand caught at his sleeve and he paused, recognising Viscount Danbury, a gentleman around his own age who he had met earlier in the week. Two other young men were with Danbury, smiling at him in welcome.

"Danbury," Thomas acknowledged. He had the distinct suspicion that the other man's only interest in him was because of his relationship to Lady Louisa; Danbury had been very quick to trade on their brief acquaintance to claim an introduction and a place on Louisa's dance card.

"We've done our duty to the elders and are off to Boodle's; would you care to accompany us? My younger brother Alexander, by the way, and our friend Mr Penn."

Thomas had been in London long enough to know that Boodle's was a gentleman's club, popular among the younger set while the older gentlemen preferred White's or Brooks, depending on their political leanings for the most part. At least they hadn't said Watier's, he mused; the infamous gamester's club was no place he cared to visit.

"Why not," he decided. When the alternative was to spend the evening here watching Ellen dance and smile with an apparently interminable series of partners presented by Lady Jersey and her cronies, spending an evening with some friendly young men of his own age sounded really quite interesting. "Pardon me a few moments while I let my aunt know I am leaving; I can send my carriage back for her later."

"No need for that, I've my own," Danbury said cheerfully. "We'll await you in the foyer."

"Yes, yes, off you go," Lady Havers said when Thomas approached her to mention he was going to leave with some other young gentlemen. "You've done your duty to Louisa. I shall take her home when she wearies of dancing and we shall see you tomorrow."

"And Ellen."

"Excuse me?" Lady Havers blinked at him.

"Ellen. Miss Bentley, Aunt Clarice!"

"Oh, yes, of course… where is she? Sitting down with the other wallflowers?" Lady Havers spared a glance towards the side of the room. "No matter, I shall have a servant locate her when we are ready to depart."

"She is dancing; with a Major Trevithick at present, I believe."

That got Clarice's attention; her head snapped around and she stared at him. "Who introduced her to him?" she asked, her tone disbelieving. "He's one of the Earl of Exeter's sons!"

"Lady Jersey did, I believe," Thomas said, finding a perverse pleasure in the way Clarice gaped at him. "Although it might possibly have been Lady Sale, I am not sure."

"Those two interfering old biddies!" Clarice's fair expression darkened to puce. She took a deep breath, though, and forced a smile. "Well, I daresay Ellen will enjoy herself for the evening, if they have taken a momentary interest in her. They will tire of her soon enough and toss her aside."

"Indeed. I shall depend upon you, Aunt Clarice, to determine whether those they introduce her to are suitable gentlemen for Ellen to associate with. A Lord Bellmere has already asked if he may call…"

"Bellmere!" Clarice's eyes fairly popped at that. "He's one of the wealthiest men in England! I tried all last season to find someone to introduce Louisa to him!"

"Well," Thomas said, "now Ellen can make the introduction for you."

For a moment he thought Clarice might slap his face, she looked so angry. He really should not prod at her so, but her unkindness to Ellen was beginning to grate on him. Making her a polite bow, he excused himself and departed to find Danbury and his cronies.

CHAPTER TEN

THE GANGLING MAJOR WAS just escorting Ellen back to the older ladies when she spied Thomas taking his leave of their hosts. He caught her eye across the room and for a moment she thought he was going to turn away without acknowledging her, but he did nod briefly before turning away and exiting the ballroom.

"Thank you so much for asking me to dance, Major Trevithick," Ellen said. "I enjoyed our dance very much."

"I did too." The major flushed, a look rather unbecoming with his red hair, and ducked his head awkwardly. "Might I call upon you, Miss Bentley?"

"I am sure that would be acceptable," Ellen said, wondering what strange magic was about tonight, that *two* most eligible gentlemen had expressed a desire to get to know her better. "Lady Havers accepts callers on Tuesday and Friday afternoons."

"I shall look forward to it greatly," Trevithick said, "and perhaps the next time we find ourselves at the same ball, you would be so kind as to reserve me the supper dance?"

That was a singular honour indeed; Ellen's own cheeks flushed as she curtsied and said she should be delighted. The dowagers, listening avidly, beamed at her with approval and, once the major had excused himself, bombarded her with questions, demanding to know what they had talked about. Ellen hardly knew how to answer their questions; she had not thought that they talked of anything unusual. The major seemed quite shy, so after dancing a few moments in silence she had asked him if he had read any interesting books recently, hoping desperately that he was a gentleman who enjoyed reading.

"He said that he had recently re-read *Don Quixote,*" Ellen told the ladies, "and I asked if he read it in translation or the original Spanish, and which translation, because I have lately read Mr Motteux's version, and rather prefer it to Mr Shelton's."

There was a brief and rather stunned silence, and then Lady Jersey laughed quite loudly. "You'll do, my girl. You'll do."

Ellen hadn't the faintest idea what Lady Jersey found so amusing. She smiled a little shyly, curtsied again and said "Perhaps it was an inappropriate conversation for me to have with a gentleman, but I am afraid I panicked a little because the major was so quiet."

"Well, some will disparagingly call you a bluestocking for it," Lady Sale said, "but let me assure you, Miss Bentley, any man worth his salt will prefer a young lady who demonstrates that she has something more than fluff between her ears."

"Oh, most certainly," Lady Jersey agreed. "A man who does not value your intelligence is not worthy of your time, my dear. Do not let anyone tell you otherwise. I despise young ladies who pretend to be something they are not to try to appeal to gentlemen, silly creatures. Getting to the altar under false pretences will not a happy marriage make."

"Who is going to the altar?" a new voice said, and Ellen felt her shoulders tighten. She forced a smile to her lips and stepped aside deferentially to allow Lady Havers to join the group.

"Nobody I know, at present," Lady Jersey said cheerfully. "About time you got your girl married off though, Clarice. Can't bring any of her suitors up to scratch, hm?"

"I'll have you know that Louisa received several offers last season," Clarice snapped.

"Oh, so she's *picky*," Lady Jersey said in enlightened tones.

Clarice's face turned red. Afraid that a full-scale confrontation was brewing, and she would be forbidden to associate with the dowagers, Ellen said hastily "Aunt Clarice, I just saw Thomas, I mean Lord Havers, leaving the ball."

"Oh, don't worry about him, girl," Clarice shook her head. "He's off to sow his wild oats with some of his young friends, I daresay."

Ellen knew full well what *wild oats* referred to and she felt a knot of unhappiness lodge in her chest. Still, she made herself smile and nod. "Will we be leaving soon?" she asked, realising that she was beginning to feel very tired. It must be long past midnight, and she had not managed to break her habit of rising early in the mornings, though Clarice and Louisa were never seen until past noon.

"In a little while," Clarice looked about with a discerning eye. "Most of the eligible gentlemen have had their fill for the night and are departing. Louisa is engaged for this dance, I believe, and then I think we shall depart. Our hostess has allowed her servants to serve the wine a little too liberally and a few of the guests are becoming rowdy." She wrinkled her nose in aristocratic distaste as a young lady ran past, hotly pursued by a much older gentleman.

Ellen was shocked too, and determined that she would not accept any more dances that evening, though Mrs Peabody suggested the son of a friend who happened to be passing. "Thank you, but I have danced far more than I am accustomed to this evening," she said with a shy smile. "I should be most honoured to make your friend's acquaintance on another occasion, though."

Mrs Peabody beamed at her, and Ellen thought privately that she seemed to be a perpetually cheerful lady. She was also dressed by far the most opulently of the three dowagers, which was really saying something since all of them were in the first stare of fashion. Ellen knew little of jewels, but the multiple long strands of large, creamy pearls draped around Mrs Peabody's neck and the diamond bracelets on her wrists seemed to bespeak extreme wealth.

Louisa danced past just then on the arm of a short, rotund young man with several chins wobbling above his shirt points, and Lady Jersey snorted loudly.

"Don't think your girl will suit Ormiston, Clarice. She's not fond enough of her food!"

All three of the Dauntless Dowagers, as Ellen mentally christened them, cackled merrily at Lady Jersey's remark, and Clarice turned red again. Ellen bit back laughter too, knowing she would pay for it later if she permitted herself to be amused at Louisa's expense.

"Good evening, ladies," Clarice said frostily. "We will await the end of the dance by the stairs, Ellen." Her hand locked around Ellen's wrist like a manacle and she set off briskly, towing Ellen behind her. With no opportunity to do anything else, Ellen had to settle for bowing her head to the dowagers and saying a quick thank you for their kindnesses. They smiled benignly on her in return, so she was reassured they did not take offence at her rapid departure in Clarice's wake.

The carriage ride back to the Havers townhouse seemed endless to a weary Ellen, obliged to sit and listen to Louisa chattering excitedly about how many gentlemen had asked her to dance, and how highly titled they were. Her last partner had been a duke, about whom Clarice was particularly enthused, despite Lady Jersey's remarks.

Both the Havers ladies ignored Ellen's existence, which she had become entirely used to. They made every effort to include her in front of Thomas, Louisa going so far as to pretend they were bosom friends, but as soon as Thomas left the room the masks of civility came down.

In truth, Ellen didn't care. She had known Clarice and Louisa her entire life, had known of her relationship to them, and they had treated her as a nobody. It had taken a direct order from Thomas to even get them to acknowledge her existence, but she was quite certain they would be perfectly happy for her to disappear back into obscurity as soon as possible.

They were but a few minutes from the townhouse when Clarice at last turned her attention upon Ellen.

"And you, miss, what have you to say for yourself?"

Startled, Ellen dragged her attention away from her pensive study of the quiet, dark streets passing by outside the coach's window. "I beg your pardon, Aunt Clarice?"

"It was not well done of you at all to impose yourself upon your betters, Ellen. Why ever did you bring yourself to the notice of Lady Jersey and her friends?"

"I did not, ma'am. I was sitting quietly at the side of the room when a lady sitting in a nearby chair spoke to me. She was the one who made the introductions."

"And who was this lady?" Clarice said sharply.

"The Countess of Creighton, ma'am."

Louisa gasped at that, and Clarice's lips tightened further. "I see," she said coldly.

"Is there some reason I should not have spoken to the Countess, ma'am? She seemed perfectly respectable, and Lady Jersey and Lady Sale greeted her warmly ..."

"Yes," Clarice said, "she is quite respectable. I suppose there is no reason you should have known, but Creighton was talking with my late husband about a potential alliance with Louisa some years ago – before Louisa was formally out, of course, but for an alliance such as that, a Season would have been forgone. He pulled back quite unexpectedly and the next thing we knew, his engagement to Miss Abingdon, as she was then, was announced."

"Well," Ellen said frankly, "I think you had a lucky escape, Cousin Louisa."

"How so?" Louisa looked quite startled.

"Lady Creighton does not seem happy in her marriage. It seems the Earl is very jealous; he does not permit her to dance with other men, nor even to speak with them if he is not present."

Louisa looked shocked at Ellen's revelations, looking to her mother as though asking for confirmation. Clarice shrugged a little pettishly.

"How should I have known he would behave so? Perhaps he is that way with Lady Creighton with just cause."

Both girls looked at her in confusion. Clarice pursed her lips before leaning forward and saying "Perhaps he has good reason to be jealous."

"Well, Lady Creighton is quite remarkably beautiful," Ellen said. "No doubt she will always attract attention."

Clarice sighed impatiently. "Perhaps she encourages it. Perhaps she *likes* the attention. Perhaps she even disrespects her marriage vows. It is not for us to question why the Earl of Creighton chooses to keep a close watch on his wife."

"Well," Louisa said pettishly, "I am very glad I didn't marry him after all, then. I shall certainly not give up dancing and having a good time when I marry."

Thomas would never ask you to, Ellen thought, turning her head away. *I only hope that I may find someone who will permit me my small enjoyments, too.*

CHAPTER ELEVEN

Despite the lateness of the hour, Ellen could not sleep. She lay in bed gazing at the ceiling, her room well-lit by the moonlight flooding in through the open curtains. London was never quiet, and even at this hour in the exclusive streets of Belgravia she could hear the hooves of horses and the wheels of carriages outside, though more infrequently than during the daytime.

Was one of those carriages carrying Thomas home? Would he even return home? Perhaps he would spend the night at the club, with his new friends. How nice it must be, to be able to make friends and go with them on a whim, to enjoy oneself without having to answer to anyone else! Ellen had thought Lady Creighton might be a friend she could talk to, but Clarice's disapproval meant she would not be able to spend time with the lady openly. There would be no visits or outings to the shops, away from Clarice's eagle eye and Louisa's unconcealed sneers.

It was too warm in her room; with a sigh, Ellen flipped her pillow over, seeking coolness. Within five minutes her head felt hot again, though, and she sat up impatiently. She would go to the kitchen and seek a cup of milk from the pantry. Perhaps that might help her rest.

She tugged her robe on over her plain flannel nightgown. Even though her room was warm, there had been a fire blazing in there all evening to make it so, and the rest of the house would likely be quite cool. Pushing her feet into slippers, she opened her door and crept quietly to the head of the stairs.

Ellen was almost at the foot, her hand on the newel post, when the front door suddenly swung open. She froze, mouth open on a half-shriek, even though intellectually she knew Thomas must be the one coming in.

"Ellen!" Thomas seemed, if anything, more startled than she when he saw her. Placing a hand over his heart, he closed the front door, shaking his head. "You gave me a start. Whatever are you doing out of bed at this hour?"

"I could ask the same of you," she replied, feeling inexplicably argumentative. "Why is it only men who may go out to have a good time, and young ladies cannot even go to the kitchen for a cup of hot milk without being questioned?"

Typical for Thomas, he chuckled good-naturedly and came forward to offer her his arm. "A cup of hot milk sounds just the thing. Do you think we might find some bread and cheese as well? I'm starving."

Unable to stay annoyed with him, Ellen smiled. "What, do they not feed you at those fine gentlemens' clubs?"

"They have dining-rooms, I believe, but I did not see them. The gentlemen I went there with preferred to drink and gamble."

"And you?" He did not smell of strong drink, though the woodsy aroma of cigars was rising to her nose as they walked to the kitchen.

"They have very good brandy and port," Thomas admitted, "but gambling when one is in his cups is a good way to get parted from one's money. I have seen too many good men make such mistakes in America, and have no wish to fall into the same trap myself."

The kitchen was quiet, the stove banked. Ellen set her candle down on the table and headed unerringly for the pantry.

"How did you know where to find everything?" Thomas asked curiously when she set a cup of milk, half a loaf of bread, a chunk of cheese and a pat of butter wrapped in muslin in front of him.

Ellen hesitated before she took a plate from the dresser and set that down too. "Please don't tell Aunt Clarice?"

"Your secrets are safe with me, always." He smiled warmly at her, and she smiled back.

"Well, Aunt Clarice and cousin Louisa always sleep in, and sometimes I feel a little bored in the mornings, if you are gone to meet with your man of business. I asked Susan to show me the servants' areas of the house. I know about the improvements you wish to make to the servants' quarters at Haverford Hall," she continued in a babbling rush when Thomas said nothing, "but you have been dreadfully busy since we came to London and I thought you might not have had time to observe here and see if there is anything that needs to be done... I am so sorry if I have overstepped my place..."

Chuckling gently and shaking his head, Thomas held up a hand to stop her. "Ellen. Ellen! Thank you."

"Really? You don't mind?"

"I'm grateful. You must tell me what you've observed. It's obvious Aunt Clarice does not think of such things, and neither did my uncle, or the servants at Haverford would not be so ill-served. Why would things be any different here? It was something I hoped to look at in the next week or two, certainly before the cold weather begins in earnest, but I am more than happy to have your advice on the matter."

Pleased by his approval, Ellen blushed a little, casting her eyes down to the scarred, pitted surface of the scrubbed pine table. "Well--I think things are a little better here than at Haverford, in some ways. Perhaps because the house butler is not quite so intimidatingly severe as Allsopp, and for the most part the house is largely unstaffed while the family is not in residence."

Not understanding, Thomas frowned. "I don't see why that would make a difference, Ellen?"

"I talked with Dolly, the under-housekeeper," Ellen admitted. "She was just lately promoted from upstairs maid, and she talked to me about how last winter, for example, because the family did not visit, the servants were able to share all the blankets among just a few of them, rather than having to divide them between a full complement. Mr. Henry, the butler, had no objection if the blanket cupboard in the servants' area was empty, you see."

"I see," Thomas said, nodding. "This winter will be different though, won't it? Since we now have a houseful."

"Quite. And while the household budget has been increased to account for the meals the family eats, the kitchen budget for the servants has not, even though they have twice as many mouths to feed." Animated by the subject, Ellen leaned across the table to enumerate the points she wished to make, unaware that with every word she spoke, Thomas became more and more entranced by her passion.

She was, Thomas thought, quite magnificent as the words poured forth, her anger over the injustice and inequities suffered by the lower classes animating her usually still features and making her suddenly, spectacularly beautiful. She was right, too, in every point she made, and he made a mental note to have her present when he spoke with his steward, in case he forgot anything she had said.

Ellen deserved, he realised, to be mistress of a great estate. She would do far better at the task than Louisa, supposedly bred and raised for such a purpose, or any of the brainless Society misses who had been thrust under his nose thus far. How many of them would even think of the comfort of the servants who saw to their every wish? Even his aunt, herself the daughter of an earl and the mistress of a great estate for many years, did not adequately do so.

With every day Thomas spent in England, he found himself more disillusioned with the members of those who were supposedly his equals. The young men of his own age he had spent the evening with, while pleasant enough, thought of little beyond their own pleasures and pastimes, and the women seemed to speak of nothing but fashion and gossip. He had already decided not to take up the membership at Boodle's he had been offered, but to seek admittance to Brooks or White's instead, where the more serious business seemed to take place.

The truth was, he considered as he watched Ellen talk, her eyes flashing in the candlelight as she spoke, her hands moving gracefully with her animation and excitement, Ellen was the only person he had met since his arrival in England with whom he really felt he had significant interests in common.

Seeming to finally notice his intent scrutiny, Ellen stopped mid-sentence before dropping her gaze and blushing. "I am so sorry, here I am rattling on and you must be exhausted!"

"Not at all," Thomas said firmly. "I am just thinking, though, that I may not remember tomorrow--later today, that is--everything you are saying. Can I ask you to attend the meeting I have scheduled with my steward at two this afternoon? He can take notes and we can discuss how best to address the issues you have observed."

Ellen looked delighted to be asked, but she wrinkled her nose and tapped her fingertip on her lower lip. "We are supposed to be at home to callers this afternoon--though I daresay Aunt Clarice and Louisa will hardly notice if I am not present. I am sure I can slip away."

"Absolutely," Thomas agreed. "I shall see you at two, then. Now off to bed with you, and get some rest." He tempered the order with a warm smile, and she flashed one of her own in return.

"Good night, Thomas," her voice floated across the darkened kitchen as she left him alone, and for a long time Thomas sat in silence, lost in thought.

CHAPTER TWELVE

As Ellen had expected, even before the clock struck two, Mr. Henry was admitting the first of a stream of gentlemen callers eager to pay court to Louisa. None of them gave her a second glance, and when she quietly whispered a request to be excused to her aunt a few minutes later, Clarice didn't even look at her before waving her hand in dismissal.

The study door stood open, and Thomas looked up with a smile of welcome when she hesitated outside, wondering if she should knock. "Ellen! Come on in. Please, allow me to introduce my steward, Mr. Gallagher."

Ellen froze for a moment, unsure whether she should curtsy. The steward offered a deep bow, she decided not, and settled for a little dip of her head. "A pleasure to make your acquaintance, sir."

"The honour is mine, Miss Bentley. Please, Lord Havers has been telling me that you have assessed the servants' quarters here and have some recommendations?"

Pleased by the businesslike way he addressed her, Ellen accepted the chair Thomas held for her to sit, and soon the three of them had their heads together over a thick sheaf of papers, Mr. Gallagher taking copious notes.

"Excuse me, my lord," Mr. Henry interrupted them about a quarter hour later. "Lady Havers is requesting Miss Bentley's presence in the Chinese Drawing Room."

Thomas looked up with a frown. "Why?" he asked bluntly.

Mr. Henry coughed delicately. "Two of the callers who are lately arrived, are here specifically to see Miss Bentley, my lord." He paused. "They have brought flowers."

Thomas was on his feet before he knew what he was about. "Gentlemen callers for Ellen--I mean Miss Bentley? Who are they?" he rapped out.

It was only after he had spoken that it occurred to him, he did not care a whit who had come to call for Louisa.

"Lord Bellmere and Major Trevithick, my lord," Mr. Henry answered him with a hint of something in his expression that might have been approval. The staff appreciated his concern for Ellen's welfare, he supposed; after all, she showed concern for theirs. They would want to see her happy and well settled.

"I shall escort you, Ellen," Thomas decided. "I think we've left Gallagher enough to be going on with for now, hm?"

"Indeed, my lord, I shall get to work straight away," the steward agreed.

"Shall we?" Thomas invited, offering his arm for Ellen. She looked at him queerly.

"I thought you did not care for Aunt Clarice's At Homes?" she queried softly as they left the study.

"I wished for a break," he fibbed smoothly, "and some of Cook's delicious lemon tarts, which I happen to know she made this morning. And, of course, to meet your suitors, Ellen."

"They are not my suitors," Ellen said at once, too quickly for Thomas' liking.

The lady doth protest too much, he thought as he watched the blush colour her cheeks. Did she already have a preference for one of the gentlemen, after a single evening in his company? Silently, he cursed himself for leaving the ball last night. Clearly, one or other of the two men had taken the opportunity to get to know Ellen, and had made a favourable impression.

The Chinese Drawing Room was packed to capacity, it seemed, as Mr. Henry opened the door for them with a bow. Faces turned in their direction, mostly gentlemen though a few had brought their mothers and sisters along. Several female faces brightened notably at the sight of Thomas, but he ignored them all, watching with narrowed eyes as two gentlemen approached with broad smiles.

"Cousin, pray allow me to introduce Lord Bellmere and Major Trevithick," Ellen made the introductions. "My cousin, Lord Havers."

Both men bowed with the perfect amount of deference to a peer of his rank, but it was more than clear that their interest was fixed upon Ellen. Neither of them seemed a brainless fribble blithering out fulsome compliments, either, rather to Thomas' irritation. Indeed, both seemed intelligent, thoughtful gentlemen of exactly the sort he would rather like to know better... if they weren't making calf eyes at Ellen.

"I met with my cousin on the board of the Museum this morning," Bellmere was telling Ellen genially. "The Museum is closed to the general public until noon on Mondays and Tuesdays, so if an early morning outing would be acceptable, I should be delighted to escort you to see the Elgin Marbles."

Ellen looked quite delighted too, though she very properly said "I should have to seek Lady Havers' permission, of course, and arrange for a chaperone..."

"No need to bother Aunt Clarice," Thomas said jovially. "I should like to see the Marbles too. I can chaperone you."

"Perhaps we might make a party of it," Major Trevithick said, and Thomas thought he would have to watch out for the military man. Likely a master of strategy, Trevithick could well sneak into Ellen's favour right under both his and Bellmere's noses.

"Did you say a party? Are we giving a party, cousin?" Louisa called from across the room, obviously put out that they were having a conversation of which she was not the central focus.

Left with no choice but to include Louisa, Thomas took a few reluctant steps closer to inform her of Lord Bellmere's proposed outing to the Museum. He was astonished when Louisa claimed a great interest in being one of the party, but did not take long to discern her reasoning. Lord Bellmere was reputed to be one of the wealthiest men in England, after all, and Louisa was piqued that the baronet had not chosen to join the ranks of her suitors, but instead expressed an interest in Ellen.

With Louisa's avowal of interest, suddenly all her suitors expressed a great desire to view Lord Elgin's famous acquisitions too, and Bellmere acquired a distinctly aggrieved look, though he was gentleman enough to promise they might all attend.

Thomas caught a slight smirk playing around Major Trevithick's lips as Bellmere was drawn inexorably into the circle around Louisa. Turning away as though disinterested, the major picked up a book lying on a side table and asked Ellen a question about it which Thomas did not hear, as he was addressed at that moment by an older lady seeking to bring her daughter to his notice.

Louisa's tinkling laugh rang out, and Thomas glanced across to see her lay a hand on Bellmere's sleeve, smiling coyly up at him.

It hit him then, all of a sudden.

He did not care in the slightest who Louisa smiled at or flirted with, despite having been briefly bowled over by her beauty. He cared very much, though, that Ellen had her head bowed over a book with Major Trevithick, a small smile playing about her soft lips.

Jealousy was an entirely new emotion for Thomas, and he found he did not care for the feeling at all. *He* wanted to be the only one favoured with Ellen's smiles.

In the centre of a crowded drawing-room was probably the worst possible place for his true feelings to suddenly become clear, Thomas realised, but there was nothing he could do about the fact that his entire world had just turned topsy-turvy.

Clarice was looking at him strangely, coming across to intercept the persistent woman with the daughter and remove Thomas to Louisa's side, which she obviously felt was his proper place. Clarice was going to be disappointed, Thomas thought dimly, but he knew now he could never marry Louisa, even if her feelings for him were what Clarice claimed. His minor infatuation with her beauty was as nothing compared to what he felt for Ellen.

Love. He whispered the word silently, inside the vaults of his own mind, and knew it for an immutable, timeless truth. He loved Ellen; loved everything about her, from her intelligent, curious mind to her kindness and empathy for others. Best of all, she would be the kind of Countess he had imagined ever since his grandfather's stories of Haverford Hall when he was a child; a gracious lady of the manor, always aware of the needs of her people.

Ellen glanced up from the book just then, looking around the room until her gaze settled on Thomas. At once she smiled, more widely than the slight smile she had given the major. Thomas smiled back, wishing everyone else in the room to perdition so he could tell Ellen how he felt--but no, he must not rush this. She had not the slightest idea, he thought, and he had thus far encouraged her to treat him as a trusted older brother. What a fool he was! He should have recognised her sterling qualities earlier, realised that his delight in her company was far more than mere friendship. Now he would have to fight off other suitors for her hand, all while convincing Ellen his intentions were genuine... and somehow not allowing Clarice or Louisa to figure out what he was about, lest they sabotage his suit.

At that moment, Thomas rather wished he could plead a headache and quit the room. But no; he would not leave the field to Trevithick and Bellmere, who had slipped from Louisa's court back to Ellen's side, insinuating himself into her conversation with the major.

The At Home seemed to last forever. Thomas was sure a half-hour was considered the polite maximum of time to spend at such things before taking one's leave, and indeed most of Louisa's court seemed to drift in and out, though there was always a constant circle around her. Neither Lord Bellmere nor Major Trevithick showed any inclination to depart, however, eyeing one another like a pair of wary cats. Ellen did not seem to favour either of them above the other, which was some comfort at least to Thomas. She merely seemed delighted to have someone willing to make intelligent conversation with her.

Clarice watched from across the room with sharp eyes as Thomas remained at Ellen's side, and no sooner had the last of their guests finally departed than she was ordering the two girls upstairs to dress for dinner and catching Thomas' arm.

"You must not hover so over Ellen, nephew. Louisa felt quite neglected! It was very ill-done of Ellen to monopolise Lord Bellmere and Major Trevithick, too!"

"Ellen is in her first season, ma'am," Thomas said reasonably. "While Louisa is in her third, quite comfortable handling a horde of enthusiastic swains. I did not observe her to be forlorn. Quite the opposite, actually." Louisa had laughed often and loudly, though Thomas caught her sneaking regular looks at their little grouping. "If anything distressed her, it was undoubtedly that she was not the centre of everyone's attention, for once."

"Thomas!" Clarice affected shock. "That is unkind!"

"It is the truth," Thomas said curtly. "Two dukes, a marquess and any number of earls, barons and heirs danced attendance on your daughter this afternoon, Aunt Clarice. Louisa should not grudge Ellen a pair of suitors who are discerning enough to see her good qualities."

Clarice's mouth flattened to a thin line. "Good qualities?" she said scornfully. "She is a parson's daughter with little in the way of manners and no looks to recommend her! You waste your time and diminish the family name with your recognition of her!"

Shocked, Thomas stared at her. "Ellen Bentley is my relative by blood," he said, his tone quiet but with a dangerous edge to it. "She has more right to my time, and to the family name, than you do. Indeed, I have no doubt that she will--*would* make a far better Countess than you have ever been!"

His slip of the tongue did not go unnoticed. Eyes narrowed, Clarice spat out "Oh, I see how it is. The hussy has seduced you, right underneath Louisa's nose!"

"That will be quite enough," Thomas said, surprising himself with the snap in his voice. "You will keep a civil tongue in your head when you speak of Ellen, or you will find yourself no longer welcome beneath my roof."

If looks could kill, he would no doubt have been struck dead on the spot. "Upstart American," Clarice hissed. "You understand nothing of class and society!"

"I understand I want nothing to do with any society which cannot recognise the superior qualities of an intelligent young woman with a kind heart, merely because she is three generations removed from an earldom rather than one!"

They were both breathing fast, voices raised. Clarice looked away first, though, when she saw Thomas clearly had no intention of backing down.

"I am only thinking of Louisa's future," she muttered.

"As you should," Thomas said, gentling his tone. "There are, however, many eligible suitors for Louisa's hand. This is her third season, Aunt, and I do not doubt that she has been just as overwhelmed with suitors throughout the previous two. What is she waiting for?"

Clarice hesitated before sighing heavily. "I do not know," she admitted. "She seems to delight in having every man at her feet; if she chooses one, I think she fears the others will all abandon her."

"That is rather the point of a marriage," Thomas said, not unkindly. "I should not want a wife who wanted to be surrounded and adored by other suitors."

"Of course not."

Clarice's head was down, and Thomas realised his aunt was deeply distressed about something. Gently, he took her arm and guided her to a chaise, pressing her to take a seat.

"Is there something you want to tell me, Aunt?" he asked gently.

There were tears on her cheeks when she looked up at him. "Perhaps we spoiled her," Clarice said, her voice cracking. "Yet I too was a little spoiled by my parents, and I am sure I was not so awful as Louisa can be when she does not get her way. I saw her face when Lord Bellmere left her to return to Ellen, and you followed; someone will pay for that, Thomas."

"What do you mean?" He really didn't understand.

Clarice hesitated before the words spilled from her in a rush. "She is my daughter, the only child I have left, but God help me, she terrifies me! She stabbed a maid once with a pair of scissors; the poor girl almost bled to death, Havers had to pay her off..."

Thomas' jaw dropped. He could scarcely believe what his aunt was saying. "Louisa *stabbed* a maid?" he said faintly as Clarice sobbed.

"There was so much blood," Clarice sniffled. "And Louisa seemed so calm, just stabbing her again and again, saying that Nellie had made eyes at Mr Danvers while she was carrying in the tea tray."

"Christ!" Thomas was appalled. There was something seriously wrong with Louisa, that was obvious. He'd thought Clarice's efforts to satisfy Louisa's every whim were just those of a mother over-indulging a spoiled daughter, but now he realised Clarice was terrified of the consequences should Louisa feel she was not receiving her due.

"Oh, dear God. *Ellen*."

He was on his feet without conscious thought, running for the door, sprinting across the hall to take the stairs three at a time, shouting Ellen's name.

Behind him, he heard Clarice call his name, but he ignored her entirely, too focused on getting to Ellen as quickly as possible. Just in case. Surely Louisa wouldn't hurt her, but...

He ran faster.

CHAPTER THIRTEEN

"WHAT A DELIGHTFUL AFTERNOON!" Louisa exclaimed as they walked up the stairs together. "Did you enjoy yourself, Ellen?"

"I did, yes," Ellen agreed.

"Were you surprised to receive callers yourself? You looked surprised, when you entered the parlour to see Major Trevithick and Lord Bellmere."

"I was," Ellen admitted. "Though both of them asked at the ball last night if they might call on me, I confess I did not truly expect them to do so, and certainly not so soon."

Louisa hummed to herself and nodded. "Come into my room so we can talk further," she invited as they reached her door. "I've had two seasons already, and my fair share of importunate suitors. There are things you should know."

Her last words were delivered with a tone and expression of dire warning. Concerned, Ellen immediately followed Louisa into her room, where Louisa's maid looked up in consternation from her task of laying out clean clothes on the bed.

"M'lady?"

'Leave us," Louisa said, waving a hand towards the door. "I'll ring when I need you."

"Very good, m'lady!" The girl scurried quickly from the room, closing the door behind her.

Louisa wandered over to the bed, hummed thoughtfully as she inspected the gown laid out there, and turned away, crossing the room to an elegant writing-desk by the window.

Uncertain what she should do, Ellen stood close to the door, waiting for Louisa to speak, or invite her to a chair. After a couple of minutes of silence, though, she spoke first.

"What sort of things do you think I should know, cousin?"

Louisa did not speak for another full minute, toying with an ornate silver letter-opener on her desk, before finally turning and looking at Ellen. "Which of them will you choose?" she asked.

Confused, Ellen blinked. "Excuse me?"

"Major Trevithick, or Lord Bellmere. Which will you choose? You are unlikely to find any other suitors, you know. Best for you to accept one of them quickly, before they come to realise you are not truly of our station. Look how Thomas hovered close when you spoke with them today, terrified you would say or do something to embarrass the Havers name."

Horrified, Ellen took a step back as Louisa approached her. "Really?" Her voice shook. "I did not think..."

Louisa sneered. "Why else would he leave my side, for *you*?"

Ellen's head drooped forward. She had no answer for that question; Thomas' admiration for Louisa had been evident from the first time she saw them together. With a crowd of rival suitors in the room, surely Thomas would not have left Louisa's side unless he saw a clear duty to do so.

"So I ask again, which shall it be, Trevithick or Bellmere?" Louisa pressed.

"I barely know either of them! Why do you demand I choose now? Surely it is not so urgent!" She could not possibly make a decision of such magnitude on such a slight acquaintance, Ellen thought with a surge of anger.

Louisa's beautiful face twisted with a sudden rage. "I was willing to allow you *one*," she said, her voice a low, harsh snarl. "Mama said I must let you have one. You're being greedy, Ellen." She changed to a high, almost sing-song voice. "Choose, Ellen, you have to choose!"

Louisa was making no sense, and acting very strangely. Suddenly frightened, Ellen took another step back, towards the door.

A clawlike hand locked around her wrist. "You have to choose, Ellen. You're being naughty."

"Let go of me," Ellen said, trying to keep her tone steady even though panic gripped at her insides, making her knees tremble. "You're hurting my wrist. Thomas will be angry with you for hurting me."

Louisa tilted her head to one side, and a dreadful rictus of a grin spread across her beautiful face. "I know your *seeeeeecret*," she said, drawing the word out. "So foolish, to think Thomas would ever look at you. Such a silly, naive little girl."

Ellen swallowed. "Let go of me," she said again, but it was becoming harder to speak calmly. Louisa's grip was tight, and despite her fragile appearance, the other girl was terrifyingly strong. "You're not well, Louisa." Indeed, she was beginning to fear that her cousin was not entirely sane. There was a strange light in Louisa's blue–grey eyes that spoke of madness.

"Enough!" Louisa shouted suddenly. "You won't *listen*!"

Ellen gasped as Louisa's other hand came up between them, silver flashing as she brought the letter-opener from her writing-desk to Ellen's throat.

"Louisa, don't," she croaked, suddenly petrified.

"You won't *listen*, so I have to make you be *quiet*," Louisa crooned. Cold metal traced over Ellen's skin, pressing lightly at first, and then harder. Frightened to breathe, wondering just how sharp the letter-opener was, Ellen stood stock still.

"I knew you'd ruin everything from the moment Thomas insisted you come to live at the Hall. You should have married some yeoman farmer and stayed in the country. Then I wouldn't have to do *this*."

Louisa was going to kill her, Ellen realised incredulously. She was insane, and she was actually going to kill Ellen.

Some ancient instinct of self-defence kicked in as Louisa drew back her arm, and Ellen jumped back, her free hand coming up to try and fend Louisa off. The other girl was still holding onto her wrist, though, and Ellen couldn't get loose. Her heel caught on the edge of one of the floor rugs and she tripped, falling backwards. Landing with a thud, she finally managed to get out a scream as Louisa came down atop her, malevolence written all over her beautiful features as she stabbed the knife down.

Unable to escape, it was all Ellen could do to try and swipe Louisa's arm aside with her own. Instead of piercing her heart, the knife caught her forearm instead, driving clean between the delicate bones of her wrist and piercing deep into the floorboards with the force of the thrust.

Ellen screamed with shock at the excruciating pain, pinned to the floor by the knife through her arm.

"Damn you!" Louisa shouted, yanking at the knife, but it was stuck fast. Ellen screamed again, agonised, as the knife shifted slightly inside her arm. "Damn you, just *die*!" Letting go of the knife, she put her hands around Ellen's neck and squeezed.

"Ellen!" Thomas roared her name, cursing his legs for not carrying him faster as he took the stairs three at a time, suddenly absolutely certain that Ellen was in mortal danger. "*Ellen!*" He flung her bedroom door open without bothering to knock, startling her poor maid. "Where is she, Susan?"

Susan just shook her head, staring at him with wide eyes, and Thomas spun on his heel. If Ellen hadn't made it to her room, she must have gone into Louisa's for some reason. Louisa had lured her in, undoubtedly, and Ellen, in her innocence of Louisa's true nature, had trusted her.

The sight which greeted him as he flung Louisa's door wide would stay with him forever; Ellen on her back on the floor, blood spreading in a wide pool from her arm, pinned to the floorboards by a gleaming silver knife. Louisa knelt atop her still form, her hands around Ellen's throat.

Ellen's face was blue.

Louisa looked up at him, her mouth opening, but what she would have said would have to remain unknown. Thomas had never in his life struck a woman, but he didn't think twice before grabbing Louisa by the shoulders and throwing her bodily across the room.

Falling to his knees beside Ellen's still body, Thomas cried out her name in utter despair.

"Thomas," Clarice said from the doorway, and then as she took in the scene, "Oh, dear God in Heaven."

"It is all her fault!" Louisa cried from across the room, where she had fallen when Thomas flung her off Ellen. "She would not choose!"

"What have you done?" Clarice cried, utterly distraught. "Oh, Louisa, what have you *done*?"

"My lord?"

Thomas glanced up to find his valet Kenneth at the head of a crowd of servants, all with shocked expressions on their faces.

"Send for a doctor," he ordered, "and take her," he pointed a shaking finger at Louisa, "and lock her up somewhere until I can find a magistrate."

Clarice set up a terrible wail, but Thomas had no time for her. The danger of Louisa dealt with at least temporarily, he turned his attention back to Ellen. She was terribly still, but the blue colour was fading slightly from her face, giving him hope that she might yet live. Leaning down close to her face, he turned his head to the side, hoping to feel her breath upon his cheek.

There; the faintest whisper of air! "She lives," he gasped in relief.

"Miss Ellen!" Susan shrieked as she pushed her way through the crowd of shocked, whispering servants and fell to her knees on the other side of Ellen's body. "Oh, Miss Ellen! Whatever *happened*?"

Thomas couldn't answer her, only shaking his head as Kenneth manhandled a strangely silent Louisa from the room with the aid of a burly footman. He could hear Mr Henry issuing orders, sending several footmen running to find a doctor as fast as possible, but everything seemed very far away as he knelt beside Ellen's still form, his hand placed gently against her pale cheek.

"M'lord," he looked up as Susan spoke loudly. The maid was pale, but her hands were steady as she reached out to him imploringly. "M'lord... if we wait until the doctor gets here, it might be too late."

Thomas frowned, not sure what she meant, at least until she pointed to the steadily spreading pool of blood beneath Ellen's arm.

"We have to stop the bleeding, m'lord, or she might bleed to death before they find a doctor." Reaching behind her to untie the strings of her apron, Susan nodded at him. "I can bandage her arm with this, for now, if you will pull out the knife."

Thomas felt queasy at the mere idea, but Susan was quite right, and at least Ellen seemed to be unconscious, so hopefully she would feel no pain. Taking a deep breath, he grasped the hilt of the knife, trying not to think about the force with which Louisa must have stabbed Ellen, to have the knife go right through her arm and jam in the floor.

Not wanting to wiggle the knife about and maybe do more damage, he gave it a single, sharp yank with all his might. The knife popped free and he threw it aside, unable to bear touching it for a moment longer than necessary.

"Hold this," Susan said, handing him one of the apron strings. Grateful that she seemed to know what to do, Thomas obeyed, watching as she wrapped the folded cloth tightly around Ellen's arm, covering both cuts. Tying the strings off once she had finished, Susan sat back on her heels and bit her lip nervously. "Perhaps you should move her to the bed, m'lord?"

"Not in here." Thomas didn't want Ellen to wake up in Louisa's room. "Her own room." A little colour was returning to Ellen's pale cheeks, though he could see purpling bruises springing up on her throat. Gently, he gathered her in his arms, giving Susan a grateful smile when she carefully lifted Ellen's injured arm and placed her hand across her stomach. The maid hurried ahead of him, urging other shocked servants out of their way and holding doors open wide, pulling back the covers on Ellen's bed as Thomas prepared to lay her down.

"Thank you," Thomas said as Susan removed Ellen's shoes. He should leave, he supposed, particularly as the housekeeper came bustling in then with several more maids, but he couldn't bear to let Ellen out of his sight.

"Anything for Miss Bentley, m'lord. She's been right kind to me." Susan sniffled slightly, but Thomas did not comment on the tears rolling down her cheeks.

"She'll be fine," he said bracingly, as much to himself as Susan. "She's strong. And we'll take good care of her, won't we?"

"The best, m'lord," Susan said fervently. "The very best."

CHAPTER FOURTEEN

THE DOCTOR SEEMED TO take forever to come. The housekeeper tried to shoo Thomas out, but he refused to leave Ellen's side, afraid she might perish if for even a moment he took his eyes from the faint rise and fall of her chest. The white apron bandage wrapped tightly around her arm was slowly turning crimson with blood. How much had she already lost? How much *could* a person lose, and live? Would the doctor be able to close the wounds properly? Sitting beside Ellen on her bed, her hand clasped in his, Thomas bowed his head and prayed that Ellen would recover.

"The doctor is here, m'lord," Mr Henry said from the doorway, and Thomas lifted his head to see a small, grey-haired man wearing a slightly threadbare suit and thick glasses.

"Doctor Smithee, at your service, m'lord."

Thomas appreciated that the doctor didn't waste time bowing and scraping, but came briskly forward, stopping at the bedside and eyeing him. "It's probably best if you leave the room, m'lord. No doubt your staff can amply assist me."

"I'm not going anywhere," Thomas said firmly. "Miss Bentley is my ward, and my responsibility." And the guilt was his too, he acknowledged privately; he would always blame himself for not pressing Clarice earlier, discovering Louisa's predilection for violence. He'd trusted blindly and put Ellen in danger because of it.

Dr Smithee seemed to accept his pronouncement and moved around to the other side of the bed, displacing Susan who stood wringing her hands while the doctor examined Ellen's neck, humming quietly under his breath. Someone had obviously informed him of the situation before showing him into the room, for which Thomas was grateful.

"Nasty," Smithee said finally, "but the bruising is not so severe as to put her life at risk, I believe. Cool compresses of water and witch hazel will be beneficial."

The housekeeper sent a maid scurrying from the room at once, and the doctor turned his attention to Ellen's arm.

"Quick thinking, to bandage it so tightly," he said approvingly. "Your handiwork, m'lord?"

"I cannot take credit; it was Miss Bentley's maid, Susan, who suggested we stop the bleeding and used her apron as a bandage," Thomas nodded towards Susan, who blushed and ducked her head.

"Good work, girl. I don't suppose you'd be interested in a career change? Good nurses with common sense like yours are hard to find."

Susan looked quite startled, but shook her head emphatically. "I'm happy being a ladies' maid, sir," she said shyly. "I shouldn't want to leave Miss Bentley, besides."

"No doubt she will be glad of your service. Now, let's have a look here. A narrow blade, hm?" The doctor peered closely at the wound on the upper side of Ellen's arm as he uncovered it.

"It was a letter-opener, I believe," Thomas said bleakly, thinking even as he spoke that Louisa must have secretly sharpened the blade, making sure she always had a lethal weapon on hand. Whatever was he do with her? Perhaps he should ask the good doctor's advice, after Ellen had been taken care of.

By the time Dr Smithee had finished putting several stitches in each side of Ellen's arm, the other maid had returned with a basin of clean water mixed with witch hazel. The doctor took one of the clean cloths the maid proffered and soaked it in the water, squeezing it out before placing it carefully across the bruises on Ellen's throat.

"Change the cloth every half hour," the doctor instructed Susan. "Now, let us see if we cannot bring Miss Bentley back to her senses, hm?" Removing a small vial from his bag, he uncapped it and held it under Ellen's nose.

The strong scent of sal ammoniac made Thomas' eyes water, and it seemed to work even on Ellen in her unconscious state, because her eyelids fluttered and she coughed.

"Ellen," Thomas said urgently, squeezing her hand. "Ellen! Open your eyes, dearest."

Her eyelids fluttered again, and he realised inconsequentially that he had never noticed how long and dark her lashes were, a thick fan brushing the paleness of her cheek.

"Tho-Thomas?" she whispered thickly, before coughing again. "Uh." She tried to lift her hand towards her throat, but he squeezed her fingers gently.

"Don't try to talk, dearest. Your throat is very bruised." Gazing at her, he tried to smile reassuringly as she opened her eyes fully at last, looking directly at him, though their brown colour seemed dull, glazed over with pain.

"I feel so tired," Ellen whispered, and her lashes drifted down again. Panicking, Thomas looked at the doctor, who nodded reassuringly.

"After blood loss like that, she will be weary for some time. Beef tea every day will soon see her right, though of course you must watch carefully for infection."

Thomas listened carefully as the doctor spoke, outlining what must be done for Ellen's care. He promised to attend every day to check on her until she was entirely recovered from her ordeal, too.

"I wonder if I might speak to you regarding the, ah, perpetrator?" Thomas said quietly as Dr Smithee began to pack his things away in his bag again. He did not wish to leave Ellen, but gently laid her hand down and eased off the bed, moving over to the window and beckoning the doctor to join him.

"I take it someone told you who attacked Ellen?" Thomas asked softly.

"Indeed." The doctor peered at him over his spectacles. "Forgive me for saying so, my lord, but it sounds as though Lady Louisa may be somewhat, ah, *disturbed*."

"I trust we can rely on your discretion in the matter? I will make it worth your while."

Dr Smithee looked properly horrified. "Of course, my lord! My patients' confidentiality is of the utmost importance!"

He wouldn't be a doctor to the aristocracy otherwise, Thomas supposed. Word would soon spread of his inability to keep secrets.

"That's good," he said aloud. "My aunt has made me aware that this is not Lady Louisa's first episode of violence. She came horrifyingly close to killing Miss Bentley today, and it is obvious to me that she must be withdrawn from society and treated for her illness. I was wondering if you had any recommendations?"

Smithee squinted a little and sucked on his teeth. "I understand you are an American, my lord--have you perhaps heard of the Bethlem Hospital?"

"Bedlam, you mean? I have, but surely such a remedy is entirely unsuitable for a young lady such as my cousin, however disturbed her mind!" Thomas had read of the infamous hospital for the insane in the newspapers, and indeed going to tour the facility had been suggested to him, though he could think of nothing more grotesque.

"Indeed, I should never recommend such a place. Bethlem is the most famous, but there are several treatment facilities for those of unsound mind, both in London and in the countryside. A friend of mine I attended medical school with is the senior doctor in residence at a small facility on the Isle of Wight. They accept only a few patients from the upper classes at a time, who are looked after very well, of course. Perhaps I should write him a letter and enquire whether they might have a vacancy?"

"Thank you," Thomas said gratefully. "We shall be leaving London as soon as Ellen--Miss Bentley, that is--is fit to travel, and I should hope to have somewhere to take Lady Louisa before that."

Ellen coughed from the bed, and Thomas turned away from the doctor immediately, eager to return to her. Though he knew Louisa would have to be dealt with--and he would have to talk seriously with Clarice, too--right now, he couldn't bear to be away from Ellen's side.

Susan, however, seemed to have other ideas. Intercepting him before he reached the bed, the maid curtsied deferentially before saying "Begging your pardon, m'lord, but we need to make Miss Bentley comfortable."

Thomas frowned, looking at Ellen reclining against her pillows. She looked perfectly comfortable to him.

"Get that dress off her and settle her into bed," Susan said more bluntly, and he nodded, finally understanding. Ellen's dress was blood-spattered and stained, and she would surely be distressed if she woke to find herself still wearing it.

"I should go and check on my aunt, and ensure Lady Louisa is safely confined," Thomas suggested, and Susan gave him an approving nod and another curtsy before turning her attention solely to attending to Ellen's needs.

Ellen woke with a throbbing ache in her arm and a desperate thirst. Coughing hurt, a great deal, until a strong arm behind her shoulders pushed her up to a sitting position and a glass was held to her lips.

Water dribbled into her mouth, soothing and cool, flavoured lightly with honey and lemon. She swallowed, coughed, sipped a little more.

"Easy," Thomas' voice said quietly into her ear. "Drink slowly."

"Thomas?" Exhausted by the effort of drinking, she whispered his name as her head rolled back against his shoulder. An unseen hand took the glass away, and

Thomas guided her gently to lie down again. "What happened?" Her voice was a thin thread, every word a huge effort to push out.

"Louisa attacked you."

All at once, Ellen remembered. Her whole body stiffened, her eyes flying wide open as she jerked, trying to sit up.

"It's all right," Thomas soothed, gently pressing her back down. "She can't hurt you. You're quite safe."

It really hurt too much to speak, but Ellen lifted her arm to look at the bandage swathing her arm. She hadn't imagined it, then, the dreadful pain as Louisa's knife stabbed through her flesh.

"Ellen," Thomas said, and she raised her eyes to look at him. He sat close beside the bed in a chair, his coat cast aside, shirtsleeves rolled up to reveal strong forearms. He looked haggard, and for the first time she could recall, there was no smile on his handsome face for her. "Oh Ellen, I'm so sorry."

She shook her head at him, forced out a few words. "Not your fault."

"Clarice confessed Louisa has been violent before. She attacked a maid, once; stabbed her with a pair of scissors for supposedly making eyes at one of her suitors. She seems to need to be the centre of attention, and once Clarice admitted that, I realised her jealousy towards you might have turned more sinister."

How could he ever have known Louisa might snap like that, though? Ellen shook her head at him again, reaching out to touch his cheek as his head lowered, though she winced as she moved her arm.

"*Not* your fault," she whispered again.

"You'll never have to see her again. I promise you that. Mr Gallagher is looking into a hospital for the disturbed of mind, which the doctor who saw you suggested."

"Not Bedlam!" Ellen's eyes widened again, as she thought with horror of all she'd read of that place. There would be no help for Louisa there, only abuse and further descent into madness, and despite what Louisa had done, Ellen would not wish that on her.

"No, not Bedlam. A place on the Isle of Wight, I understand. A country house, a place where Louisa can rest and be treated for whatever sickness of the mind makes her act so."

Silent, Ellen watched Thomas. *He must be devastated*, she thought. "And when she is better?" she whispered finally. "Will you marry her?"

Thomas' head snapped up, his expression pure shock. "Marry Louisa?" he exclaimed. "Good God, no! How could Louisa ever be permitted to marry *anyone*? What if she had *children*, Ellen?"

"You think the madness might be passed on?"

"That, or she might be a danger to them herself! I could never forgive myself if she harmed a child, knowing I had it in my power to ensure she would never have the chance. No," Thomas shook his head. "Should any man ask to marry Louisa, I would be compelled to tell them the truth."

No man would marry Louisa then, Ellen knew. Or if one did, it would be solely for her dowry, and he would likely do something awful like shut her up in Bedlam. At least in refusing her the chance to marry, Thomas protected her from that.

"I'm so sorry," she whispered. "You must be devastated. I know you loved her."

CHAPTER FIFTEEN

THOMAS BLINKED IN SURPRISE as Ellen whispered her sympathetic words, her delicate hand outstretched to touch lightly on his wrist.

"You think I'm in love with *Louisa*," he said, in dawning realisation. "I am most assuredly not, Ellen."

Her sidelong look expressed cynicism at his denial.

"Really! Yes, I was somewhat blinded by her beauty at first, but it did not take me long to recognise she and I have absolutely no interests in common. Every time we try to talk, it ends in uncomfortable silence as I run out of things to say to her."

Ellen's lips twitched. She did not think she had ever even seen Thomas reduced to an uncomfortable silence; he never seemed to have any issues talking to *her*.

Seeing her amusement, Thomas lifted her hand to his lips, pressing a kiss against the back of it gently. "It has taken me a quite unconscionably long time, however, to realise I have already met the only woman with whom I *can* imagine spending the rest of my life in perfect harmony and contentment."

Ellen's brow furrowed as she obviously wondered who he meant, causing Thomas to shake his head and laugh. She was too modest.

"You, Ellen," he said gently. "I mean you."

Her eyes widened, lips parting with shock. She did not attempt to speak, though, so he ploughed valiantly on, hoping desperately that she would not reject him without thinking it over, at least.

"From our very first meeting, I was struck by your kindness and your good nature; the way you treat others, especially servants, sets an example I wish more would follow. It is to my shame that I did not comprehend until now, when two other men saw at first sight your eminent good qualities and immediately desired to court you, just how empty my life would be if you married another. I love you, Ellen. I cannot imagine living my life without seeing you every day, without talking to you about the issues which trouble me, sharing with you my triumphs and tragedies."

Ellen's eyes welled with tears as she gazed at him, but still she did not speak. Thomas stumbled on.

"When I saw you lying on the floor with blood everywhere, my heart stopped. I would have done anything in that moment, given even my own life, for you to just look at me and smile."

She smiled at him as a tear trickled down her cheek. Reaching to stroke it away gently, he begged "Forgive me for being slow to come to the understanding there is nobody else I could possibly love." Hesitating briefly, he plunged on. "This may be the most inopportune moment I could possibly have chosen but... I love you quite desperately, you see, and if I do not ask you to marry me now, I may never pluck up the courage."

Ellen could scarcely believe what Thomas was saying. It was every wistful daydream she ever had, all coming true at once. The only problem was that she could barely make a sound.

"Ask me again once I can speak," she whispered through happy tears, "so that I may fully express all the joy I feel at this moment."

At once, Thomas' expression of trepidation changed to pure joy, and he lifted her hand to his mouth again and lavished kisses upon it. "Dearest love," he said, over and over again, "my dearest, darling Ellen!"

She still wondered if she was in some sort of fever dream, but if it truly was a dream, she would be quite happy never to awaken. Thomas took out his handkerchief and dried her wet face before leaning in to press a respectful kiss on her cheek. Which did more than anything else to convince her it was real; surely if it was a dream, he would have been a little less respectful and addressed her lips, as she had daydreamed of so many times.

It was only then, when Thomas stood up and said she should rest, that he had to speak with Clarice, that Ellen realised they had never been alone. Susan had been sitting on a stool at the end of the bed the whole time.

"Are you hungry, Miss? The doctor recommended beef broth for you and I have some warm here, if you think you could sip a little," Susan said, as Thomas departed the room.

Blushing furiously, Ellen nodded.

Susan smiled shyly at her as she came to stand at her side. "It isn't my place to say, really, Miss, but congratulations," the maid said, smiling broadly. "You and m'lord will be very happy together, I am sure! All the staff will be overjoyed to hear the news you are to be their new mistress!"

That was something she hadn't even considered; in marrying Thomas, she would become the new Countess of Havers, which was a rather nerve-wracking proposition. She was reassured, however, that Thomas would not wish her to ape Clarice, with her haughty ways and dismissal of those who did not share her exalted rank.

Susan helped Ellen sip warm beef broth from a small cup with a spout, until at last she shook her head, indicating she could drink no more.

"The doctor left some laudanum for you," Susan said, "he said you should have a drop tonight to help you sleep, with the pain in your arm."

Ellen did not care much for laudanum, since she had seen the effects of overindulgence more than once in her work assisting her mother in parish duties. Considering the pain in her arm and her throat, though, she nodded acceptance. Poppy-induced oblivion would be welcome just now.

The bitter taste lingered on her tongue, but she soon found herself drifting off, numbness overwhelming her and washing away the pain. She was on the edge of sleep when Thomas sat down beside the bed again.

"Thomas," she whispered his name, fumbling for his hand. Warm, strong fingers wrapped around hers.

"I'm here. Sleep, Ellen. You're safe, I promise."

She wanted to stay awake, to look on his dear, beloved face, but the poppy had her deep in its thrall. Her eyelids were so heavy. They drifted closed to the sound of Thomas humming a soft, soothing lullaby.

Ellen woke screaming, or trying to, hoarse croaks all that emitted from her bruised throat. Thomas was there at once, strong arms folding around her as he spoke, assuring her she was safe.

Leaning against Thomas' strong chest, Ellen remembered the other reason why she did not care for laudanum. Her mother had given it to her when she was ten or so and had an infected tooth. The nightmares had woken her screaming five times that horrible night. What she had dreamed, she could not say; nameless horrors with sharp teeth and tearing claws teased the edges of her consciousness.

"It's all right," Thomas was whispering, stroking her hair, and she realised he had moved to sit on the edge of the bed, the better to comfort her. Daringly, she put her arm about his waist and leaned in closer, feeling to her amazement the way he placed tender kisses against her hair and brow.

The room was quite dark, lit only by the faint glow of the banked fire and a single candlestick on her dresser.

"What time is it?" she whispered finally.

"Sometime after midnight. I sent Susan to get some sleep; do you need anything?"

She shook her head against his chest. "It was just a nightmare." Her eyelids were already beginning to droop again.

"Sleep," Thomas told her softly. "You're quite safe, I promise." He kissed her hair again and drew her gently down to lie among the pillows. Comforted by his warmth, Ellen snuggled close to him and let herself drift off again.

"My lord, the doctor is here."

Susan's voice woke Ellen from slumber; she was warm and comfortable, and quite disinclined to move. Unfortunately, her bed seemed to have other ideas, as it shifted beneath her.

"What the... oh." Opening her eyes, she discovered it was not her bed which was moving, but Thomas, upon whose chest she was currently reclining. He shot her a sheepish smile as he laid her back gently against the pillows, and she looked around the room, face flaming. Only Susan appeared to be witness to their very compromising situation, though, and the maid stood with face averted, firmly not looking at them.

"I'll just go and make myself presentable," Thomas told Susan quietly as she passed. "I'll wait outside; please call me in once the doctor has completed his examination."

Ellen was, for the first time, grateful for her sore throat, because it meant she had an excellent excuse not to try and explain away the unexplainable. Susan appeared quite happy to pretend she had seen nothing untoward, in any case, as she bustled about tidying the room and helping Ellen to sit up, re-brushing her hair and pulling it back into a loose braid.

"There you go, Miss." Susan gave her a warm smile, patting her hand lightly. "I'll bring the doctor in now, shall I?"

Ellen didn't remember meeting Doctor Smithee the previous evening, but his quiet manner inspired confidence, and she lay back to allow him to inspect her throat with gentle fingers. He did not unwrap the bandage about her arm, but asked her how it was feeling and listened gravely to her whispered answer.

"Unless you begin to feel heat in it, or start running a fever, I think we shall leave that to itself for a few days yet," he said finally. "The witch hazel compresses are doing their job to minimise the bruising on your throat, which frankly was my most immediate concern. Severe swelling there might restrict your breathing. Keep them up for two more days at least," he instructed Susan, who nodded quick acceptance of the order.

"My voice?" Ellen whispered. She could barely get a sound out; even attempting to shout produced nothing more than a faint croak, and a painful one at that.

"Patience, my dear." Doctor Smithee twinkled at her. "Nasty bruises take a few days to heal, don't they? Well, in a few days I believe you will find your voice beginning to return. Plenty of soothing tea to drink and soup to eat until you feel able to take something firmer. I believe you should be your own best guide, as regards your return to health; I have no doubt Lord Havers will be keeping a close eye to ensure you do not do too much, at any rate."

Ellen smiled shyly and ducked her head at the mention of Thomas' name, and the doctor nodded, stepping back.

"Indeed, I have no doubt his Lordship is waiting outside the door at this very moment, agitating to be let back in so he may quiz me as to the progress of your recovery. Admit him, if you would, my good woman," he addressed Susan, who hurried to the door to do his bidding.

CHAPTER SIXTEEN

Once Doctor Smithee departed, Thomas lost no time in settling back down on the bed beside Ellen again, drawing her into his arms. With a shy glance at Susan, who studiously ignored them, Ellen settled her head on his chest. She had questions to ask, but for now, it felt so good just to be held close and safe in Thomas' arms.

Finally, she whispered "What happens now?"

"For us?" Thomas asked, brushing a gentle kiss over her brow.

"Louisa, Clarice, too." Though she had wracked her brain, Ellen could see no way out of the current situation without some sort of scandal enveloping the family, one Thomas did not deserve.

"Ah. Yes. Well, I have sent off an inquiry to the hospital the good doctor told me about on the Isle of Wight, and I hope to hear back from them in a few days. Should they be able to accept Louisa for treatment, I will have to escort her there. Clarice has expressed a desire to remain close to her daughter, so she will accompany us and I will find her a house, set her up with some servants and the like."

Ellen squeezed his hand, glad of his consideration, but questions still remained. What would people say if Louisa and Clarice just up and vanished in the middle of the Little Season?

"As to what story we should put about, I had a thought on that subject I wished to run by you," Thomas said, almost as though he had read her mind. "Obviously, letting it be known that Louisa is dangerously insane is... not ideal."

She snorted at the understatement, though it made her cough.

"So I thought we could tell people she ran away with a footman."

Ellen choked. Wide-eyed, she stared at Thomas, who chuckled at her reaction. He was absolutely serious, she realised as he spoke again.

"Clarice, obviously, will choose to retire from society in shame. She intends to live secluded on the Isle of Wight anyway, and anyone who might recognise her or Louisa while visiting relatives of their own at the asylum is unlikely to speak out, for reasons of their own secrecy."

Though the idea seemed wild at first, Ellen soon saw the sense in it. She touched her throat, though, and looked at Thomas with questioning eyes.

"Yes, we shall have to remain in seclusion until your throat has healed," Thomas agreed, "though a case of the influenza would explain both the doctor's visits and our absence from Society for a few days at least. Easy enough to have Mr Henry tell anyone who calls that you, Clarice and I are all afflicted, and for Louisa to 'take advantage' of our illnesses to 'run away' with her lover."

It was actually a very clever plan, Ellen thought as she ran through some of the issues in her mind. While it would certainly be a scandal, Louisa would hardly be the first heiress to disgrace herself with a lover from the servant classes, and Clarice retiring from society would be a perfectly natural reaction to her daughter's fall from grace.

"The servants?" she asked hoarsely, glancing across at where Susan was now sitting by the window quietly sewing.

"Have no wish to see the Havers family as a whole disgraced by the madness of one member. You have endeared yourself to them greatly, Ellen; you should have heard the celebrating below stairs when Susan told them our news. I believe I have been congratulated by almost every member of the staff on my excellent choice of bride."

She blushed at the compliment and cast her eyes down shyly. Thomas waited patiently for her to look back at him, at which point he took the opportunity to steal a kiss.

Ellen was even redder when he moved back, and he chuckled warmly. "You have to marry me now, anyway. You are hopelessly compromised, not that anyone who knows would ever breathe a word of it."

She expressed her opinion of his poor humour with a light slap to his arm. Thomas smiled before continuing.

"And we have the perfect ally to help us sell the story. Your new friend Lady Jersey."

Ellen gave him a wide-eyed look of dread. Lady Jersey's reputation as a gossip was unparalleled; if she didn't buy the story, they were doomed. She would undoubtedly dig until she uncovered the truth, and she had the resources and the contacts to root it out.

On the other hand, Lady Jersey had shown no particular liking for Louisa, or Clarice. If Ellen and Thomas offered her a salacious piece of gossip--delivered with suitable regret, of course, for a situation that could not be helped and a scandal that could not be hidden--why would she look any further?

“You seem to have thought it all through very well,” Ellen whispered at last.

“It is merely the bones of a plan, Ellen, and one I would not even think of executing without talking it over with you first. You know well that from the very first, I have valued your counsel above all others. Doing this without your approval is unthinkable.”

Ellen reached up to touch his face in gentle wonder. He’d obviously had his valet shave him while the doctor attended her, for his cheek was smooth, her fingertips skating lightly over his skin.

“I love you, Thomas,” she whispered.

The expression on Thomas’ face was one of pure joy and adoration as he pulled her closer and kissed her again, this time until she thought she might swoon from sheer delight.

“Ahem,” Susan said eventually, and Thomas let Ellen go with a quiet laugh.

“Do not fear, Susan, I do not intend to ravish Ellen before we have said our vows in a church.”

“I would never doubt you, my lord,” Susan replied, a thread of laughter in her voice.

“Excellent, Susan. Excellent. I believe you deserve a promotion for your loyal service, in fact; how does being the Countess of Havers’ personal maid sound to you?”

“As long as it is the future countess and not the present one, I shall be delighted and honoured, my lord,” Susan said gravely.

Laughing hurt too much, so Ellen swallowed it down and rested her head against Thomas’ shoulder again. Her eyelids felt heavy, and she realised sleep was approaching once more.

“Sleep,” Thomas whispered, kissing her cheek tenderly. “I will have more news once you wake up again. For now, I need you to rest, regain your strength. I will need your wise counsel when you wake, if we are to pull this off.”

The plan to remove Louisa and Clarice to the Isle of Wight went off without a hitch. Thomas had his secretary write polite refusals to all invitations they received, explaining that influenza had laid them all low, and the staff told anyone who asked the same. Doctor Smithee's regular visits to the house only confirmed the fact in everyone's minds.

Clarice came to see Ellen once before their departure. "I'm sorry," was all she managed to say, through tears streaming down her cheeks. "I hope you and Thomas will be happy together, truly." She could not look at Ellen directly as she spoke.

"I hope Louisa finds peace," was all Ellen could think of to say. She pitied Clarice deeply, but the older woman's decisions made to protect her daughter had almost caused Ellen's demise, and even with Ellen's forgiving nature she could not find it in herself to entirely absolve Clarice of guilt.

Thomas had to escort Clarice and Louisa to their destination, of course. They slipped out of London in a closed carriage, one without the family crest emblazoned on it, late one night. Still weak and easily exhausted, Thomas made Ellen promise to remain in bed until he returned, charging the servants with her welfare. He hated leaving her, but there was nothing for it; she was not well enough to travel and he had to see Clarice and Louisa settled. Letters sent ahead to arrange Louisa's residency at the psychiatric hospital and have a house arranged for Clarice would, he hoped, minimise the amount of time he would need to spend on the island.

Doctor Smithee had prescribed herbs and teas which they had been using to keep Louisa calm ever since her attack on Ellen, and she spent the journey in a quiet, dreamlike haze. Once or twice she murmured something about 'a honeymoon by the seaside' and Thomas realised she thought they were married, or soon to be so. Not wishing to disrupt her calm state of mind, he said nothing to contradict her, but made sure to keep his distance, riding alongside the carriage rather than in it for most of the journey.

The hospital was in a large, elegantly appointed country house close to the centre of the island. Considering the fees they charged to enrol patients, the property *should* be well maintained, Thomas considered, and was pleased to note the exceptional cleanliness of every room. While the residents were permitted to mingle with each other, they did so only under supervision, and no resident was allowed to roam alone outside or to leave the estate's grounds under any circumstances.

"You should go," Clarice told Thomas quietly as Louisa inspected the large, well-appointed suite set aside for her personal use. Her 'maid' was a specially trained nurse, a large, no-nonsense countrywoman with a thick Hampshire accent who was well aware of Louisa's occasional violent proclivities, and, she assured Thomas privately, well-equipped to handle them.

"You have not seen your house yet," Thomas protested, turning to look at his aunt.

"I'll not leave Louisa here alone yet. Her rage when you leave will be ugly to witness; I may be able to calm her somewhat. Once she is settled here, I'll have the carriage take me to the house. You have been more than kind, Thomas, giving me my own carriage and buying a house and arranging all... this."

Clarice seemed a different woman, Thomas thought. Yet, what would she have done to conceal Louisa's terrible secret, if she had been able? Her silence almost cost Ellen's life, and he could not, would not trust her. He had already assigned a man to ensure neither she nor Louisa would ever find passage back to the mainland without his express authority.

With a last look at Louisa, examining a delicate writing-desk fully fitted out for her with papers, pens and ink--though any letters she sent would never reach their destination, unless it was to him--Thomas nodded.

"Take care, Clarice. If there is anything you ever need--anything at all--I pray you will let me know at once."

She did not offer an embrace, only inclined her head regally and said a single word.

"Goodbye."

CHAPTER SEVENTEEN

THOMAS DID NOT HIDE his return to London. Supposedly, he was arriving back after a frantic attempt to intercept Louisa before reaching Scotland with her lowborn lover, after all. Late that day, a closed carriage would depart the house, and he would tell anyone who asked that Clarice was in it, leaving to be with her daughter as they settled in an undisclosed location.

For now, all he could think of was Ellen, as he handed the reins of his tired horse to a groom who wished him a good day. Taking the steps to the house two at a time, he strode past the smiling Mr Henry and headed for the interior stairs.

"Not that way, my lord!" Mr Henry called after him.

"I beg your pardon?" Thomas paused, one foot on the bottom step.

"In the parlour, my lord." Mr Henry gestured. "I daresay you don't need me to present you?"

The butler was talking to thin air.

Ellen looked up from her book as the parlour door opened. A second later the book fell unheeded to the floor as she leaped to her feet, and a second after that she was rushing into Thomas' arms, heedless of any audience who might observe them.

"Ellen," he kept saying as he rained kisses on her face, "my Ellen, how I've missed you!"

Ellen could find no words, too choked with emotion to speak. She clung tightly to Thomas and closed her eyes, revelling in the solid strength of him as he held her close.

"You should not be out of bed," Thomas said finally, pulling back to hold her at arm's length, his palms cupped over her shoulders.

Ellen laughed. The sound was husky yet, but she could speak and make herself heard. Although the bruises on her throat were still livid with colour, they were green and yellow rather than black and purple, clearly ageing and fading away. "I have been pampered and waited on hand and foot ever since you left, Thomas. Today is the first day Susan has even permitted me to leave my room, and that only because I protested I would run mad if I did not see something other than those four walls."

Hearing her speak, sounding almost like her old self, Thomas smiled in relief. He still led her back to the comfortable fireside chair she had been occupying, though, settling her down in it and seating himself on the footstool, keeping her hands held in his.

"Obviously you are on the mend. Has Doctor Smithee been attentive?"

"Here every day at least once, sometimes twice." Ellen smiled at him, pulling one of her hands free and reaching to touch his cheek. "How are you, Thomas?"

"I'm not the one who was injured."

"No, but you have still had a long journey, and I have no doubt settling Louisa and Clarice did not go entirely smoothly. So I ask again; how are you?"

He stared into her eyes for a long moment before bowing his head and laying it in her lap. "Did I do the right thing, Ellen?"

"It was the only thing you could do," she replied at once, stroking her fingers through his hair tenderly. "I have thought on it a great deal, since you left; I have had little else to do other than think, and no matter how many different possibilities I considered, none of them ended any better than the path you chose."

Thomas sighed deeply, nodding slowly against her lap. "I know. I have had a good deal of time to think too, and I could not think of anything else either. Short of shipping Louisa off somewhere even more remote and locking her in a cottage in the Highlands or something where there is no chance of her ever being seen again by someone who might possibly recognise her..."

"Which would be too cruel a fate, even for her," Ellen said quietly as he trailed off.

"Even if it were not, I believe Clarice would have insisted on going with her, and that would most definitely have been unfair." Thomas lifted his head to look at her. "I know she was unkind to you, Ellen, but she is, after all, family."

"And neither you nor I have so many family members that we are willing to let any of them suffer unnecessarily."

"Exactly." Taking her hand, he pressed a kiss to her fingers. "To tell the truth, my joy in loving you is so all-encompassing, I cannot consider anything which might make anyone in the least distressed."

For a long moment they sat lost in each other's eyes, so glad to be reunited all worldly cares fell away. At last, though, Thomas shook himself and addressed the most pressing item on his mind.

"I tasked Gallagher with obtaining a special licence when I sent him back to town, and if he is half as efficient as I think him to be, it will even now be lying on my desk. Forgive me if it is your dream to have a magnificent wedding at Haverford attended by half the county, but I think it best for us to marry as quickly and quietly as possible, and then to depart London immediately."

"I have no such yearnings, and I quite agree that is the best plan," Ellen said at once. "So long as you are the bridegroom, I find I care not for any other details as to when and where."

Thomas looked delighted by her sentiment, and kissed her hands again. "Have you a gown with a high collar which would conceal your bruises? If so, we might be able to invite a few close friends to witness the nuptials."

Ellen considered that. While she had not been in London long enough to make many friends, she thought she would like to invite Lady Creighton, who had been so kind to her, and the three older ladies who wished to take her under their wing. She felt quite sure they would all be pleased for her to marry Thomas, who they had seemed to look upon with some favour despite his American birth.

Thomas left her briefly to go to his study, where he found both his steward and the special licence the faithful man had efficiently procured. Gallagher was more than happy to go out at once and find an amenable parson to perform the ceremony as soon as possible.

"I have been thinking," Ellen told Thomas as the pair of them ate dinner together that evening, sitting in Ellen's sitting-room with Susan sewing quietly in the corner, "that I should pay a call on Lady Jersey."

Thomas stopped with his soup spoon suspended in mid-air, eyed her uncertainly. "Would it not be better to write to her once we have left London?"

"Except that I should like to invite her to attend the wedding." The ceremony was set for three days' hence, in a small church close by.

Thomas set the spoon down with a sigh. "Well. It was always part of the plan to tell her the public version of events to spread, was it not? I daresay if we do so in person, we will be that much more believable."

Ellen nodded in agreement. "I should like to call on Lady Creighton, too," she said. "She was very kind to me, and indeed, without her interference we might not even be sitting here now. It was her insistence that I not be a wallflower which led me to dance with Lord Bellmere and Major Trevithick, after all."

Thomas narrowed his eyes at her. "Which caused me to realise my own idiocy in not noticing your utter perfection from the very first moment. Indeed, your reproach is valid."

She laughed at him in return. "Do not dare to be jealous, Thomas. Neither of them had any chance of winning my heart, I promise you. It has long been yours."

They gazed at each other until Susan coughed from the corner. "That soup will taste far better while it's hot, m'lord, Miss Bentley," she said in gentle reproach.

"You see, I am well cared for." Ellen smiled at her maid and picked up her spoon again. "Susan has coddled me like a hen with one chick in your absence."

"Good," Thomas said emphatically.

Choosing to change the subject, and given a new one because of Susan's gentle reminder, Ellen remarked on the gossip already beginning to circulate. "The servants have begun spreading the requested story, whispering of Louisa's departure and disgrace with a fictional member of their number." Shaking her head, Ellen said "It's a sad indictment of her behaviour towards them, that they are positively eager to begin crowing of her downfall."

"Let them enjoy their revenge, Ellen. Who knows how many servants Louisa had dismissed, or even hurt more seriously, like that maid Clarice told me about? Frankly, I think we should just be thankful they are not trumpeting the truth of her madness all over London."

"They would not," Ellen denied firmly.

"I happen to agree, mainly because you have endeared yourself so greatly to them, both here and at Haverford Hall!"

They paid a call on Lady Jersey the following morning, Ellen's still-bruised throat well covered by a lacy shawl wrapped high, the huskiness of her voice explained away by the lingering effects of influenza.

The countess asked a few probing questions about Louisa, and Thomas and Ellen answered carefully, their story well-rehearsed. They both expressed regret at their cousin's disgrace, shock at her abrupt departure.

"I had not the slightest idea she planned anything of the sort, I assure you," Ellen told the countess. "I do know Lady Havers was pressing Louisa to settle on one of her suitors; perhaps that prompted her to take her chance when we were all ill abed with influenza."

"Foolish chit." Lady Jersey shook her head. "Well, it is certainly a scandal, but I do not believe it shall touch you particularly. Especially since you plan to marry so soon. You sly thing, Miss Bentley, you gave no hint of that at all!" She tapped Ellen's hand with her fan, chuckling to herself.

Ellen blushed, glanced sideways at Thomas, who grinned at her in return. "In my defence, my lady, I had no idea Thomas returned my affections until after Louisa's disgrace came to light. Emotions were running high at that time."

"No doubt, no doubt." Lady Jersey seemed highly amused. "Well, it is a charming outcome for the pair of you, to be certain, though I quite understand why you feel it necessary to marry quickly and return to the country." Waving a languid hand, she declared "I shall make sure the new Countess of Havers can move in society without any hint of scandal attaching to her from her cousin's foolishness. You leave *that* to *me*."

"We defer to your expertise, of course, Lady Jersey," Thomas said, amused.

"I knew you were a smart young man, Havers, despite hailing from the colonies. You'll do well enough, I dare say."

Ellen stifled a little giggle as Lady Jersey accepted the compliment imperiously. She could only count herself lucky that the formidable lady was disposed to believe their story.

"You will come to the wedding, won't you, Lady Jersey?" she asked hopefully.

"I would not miss it, dear girl, and I shall bring Eliza Sale and Charlotte Peabody with me, and anyone else I can scoop up."

"Oh, thank you," Ellen said gratefully. "We will not have time to call upon everyone who I should have wished to invite, though we go from here to the Creighton townhouse. I should very much like to invite Lady Creighton to attend."

"Good luck with that; her husband does not permit her to accept many invitations. Only those events he wishes to attend." Lady Jersey favoured Ellen with a smile. "She deserves a friend, though, so I hope you will persist. Flatter Creighton's vanity and hopefully he will allow you some small friendship with his wife."

"I'll try my best," Ellen vowed.

"As will I. I look forward to meeting this friend of yours," Thomas noted as they left the palatial Jersey townhouse. "She's the one who introduced you to Lady Jersey and her friends, is she not?"

"Indeed, but you must promise not to be stunned by her beauty when you meet her. I should take it very ill, but I promise you, her husband would take it worse, and he takes out his temper on poor Marianne. Turn your charm upon him instead, Thomas, if you will?"

"Anything for you, my love."

Despite her teasing words, Ellen really did feel a little nervous about how Thomas would react on meeting Marianne. Beyond a single startled blink, however, he showed no reaction to the stunning redhead's looks, only telling her how pleased he was to meet her and thanking her for her kindness to Ellen, before excusing himself to seek out Lord Creighton.

"You look so very happy, Ellen," Marianne came straight to the point as she poured Ellen tea in a delicate Sèvres cup. "I suspected from the outset that you had a tendre for Lord Havers, and I am very glad he has the good sense to see you for the treasure you are."

"Thank you."

"Though I am very sorry to hear about your cousin's disgrace."

Ellen blinked, startled by the remark. "Where did you hear about Louisa?" she asked, stalling for time.

"Servants talk." Marianne gave her a small smile. "I cannot say that Lady Louisa and I were ever friends... but I hope she is happy with her footman."

"Really?" Startled again, Ellen set down her cup. That was not a reaction she had expected from anyone in society.

"Long ago, there was someone..." Marianne lowered her voice. "A soldier. If he had asked me to run away with him, I would have, without a second thought, and considered everything I gave up well lost for love. So yes, I hope your cousin is happy with her choice."

"She is safe and well, that much I know. And Thomas would never let anything bad happen to her, nor let her go hungry or be ill-treated." Ellen stuck to half-truths, and Marianne seemed happy enough to accept them. It was tempting to confide in Marianne completely, but Ellen did not dare. She and Thomas had agreed; it was a secret the two of them must keep close, forever.

CHAPTER EIGHTEEN

THE DAY OF THE wedding dawned dull and raining, though Susan claimed it would clear up later. Refusing to let the weather sour her mood, Ellen smiled and insisted it would not matter if it rained all day. She had no doubt Mr Henry would have arranged things so that no guest would risk so much as a single raindrop touching their hair or clothing.

"Perhaps, but your shoes would be all over mud, miss!" Susan muttered direly. "Come, into your bath and let's get your hair washed and drying in front of the fire. Betty will be bringing your breakfast up directly."

Smiling as her maid took charge, Ellen slipped into the prepared bath and relaxed in the warm water as Susan massaged flakes of Castile soap into her hair before washing it out with apple cider vinegar and a rosemary and lavender rinse.

"I wonder if Thomas is being fussed over as much as I?" she murmured as Susan helped her dry off and slip on a robe.

"I've no doubt he is having a bath, miss. There were a great many jugs of water being warmed by fireplaces all over the house this morning." Susan squeezed water from Ellen's hair with a linen cloth before taking a comb and carefully beginning to separate the strands, using a little lavender oil on her fingers to smooth out tangles. "Though for sure his hair will be quicker for Kenneth to dry!"

For some reason, Ellen found that ridiculously funny. Giggling, she picked up the cup of chocolate Betty had brought with her breakfast tray to take a sip.

"'Tis good to hear you laughing on your wedding day, miss," Susan said. "And look—the rain has stopped!"

"So it has," Ellen agreed, peering out of the window.

"Happy is the bride the sun shines upon," Susan quoted the old saying.

"Perhaps, but my parents were the happiest couple I know and Mama always said it snowed on their wedding day. And it certainly poured with rain the day Demelza and John married, and they are very happy too, so I will not put stock in miserable wedding days having anything to do with unhappy marriages," Ellen declared firmly.

"Very wise too, I dare say," Susan agreed. "Won't you eat something, miss?"

Ellen smiled wryly. Of course her sharp-eyed maid had noticed Ellen had not chosen anything from the tempting array on the tray. "My stomach is in knots, with nerves," she confessed.

"Just think of it like every other wedding your father, God rest his soul, officiated over the years," Susan suggested. "I dare say you've seen more weddings than anyone else in this house!"

That was quite true, Ellen mused as she allowed Susan to coax her into eating a slice of toast spread with butter and honey. Her father always said he loved nothing better than conducting a wedding, seeing a loving couple joined together in matrimony in God's house... unless it was the baptisms which often followed, sometimes a little less than nine months later, though her father would never comment no matter how short the time between wedding and birth.

Her parents would have liked Thomas, she thought, very much. She could imagine he and her father having long debates over what they read in the newspapers, her mother recruiting Thomas into helping with one of her projects to improve the lot of the poorest villagers.

A tear trickled from her eye, and she blotted it away. "I am just thinking of Mama and Papa," she replied to Susan's concerned query. "I wish they were here."

"Of course you do, miss. No doubt they'll be watching over you from heaven, though," Susan said stoutly, and Ellen nodded.

"No doubt," she agreed quietly. No doubt the old Earl would be rolling over in his grave, too, if he could see his upstart American heir marrying the impoverished parson's daughter he had never deigned to acknowledge as his relation, but she did not voice that thought aloud.

The servants had filled the little church with foliage, purchasing all the hothouse blooms they could find with Thomas' purse opened for the purpose, and adding beautifully woven wreaths of greenery. The sweet scent of the blossoms filled Ellen's nose as she took a deep breath before stepping over the threshold of the church.

Smiling faces greeted her, the servants at the back of the church and a surprising number of higher society at the front as she walked up the aisle. Lady Jersey, in a position of honour in the front row, was positively beaming, Lady Sale and Mrs Peabody beside her looking just as pleased to see Ellen married. Marianne Creighton was directly behind them, her older husband at her side looking less than pleased with the occasion, but Marianne's smile was bright. Ellen thought she would be sure to write Marianne very often. Lady Creighton seemed very much in need of a friend.

At last, she reached the end of the seemingly interminable walk to where Thomas awaited her before the altar, a broad grin on his face. Seeing how joyous he looked soothed the butterflies in Ellen's stomach and she smiled happily back at him, the last of her worries falling away.

Together, she thought as she placed her hand in Thomas's and the curate began intoning the words to the marriage ceremony, they would deal with whatever trials and tribulations might come their way. They might well set the Ton on its ear with their new-fangled ideas and determination that the common folk should be treated just the same as the aristocracy, but Ellen found she did not care in the slightest what the spoiled scions of the upper class might think of them, and she knew Thomas did not either.

"I love you," Thomas mouthed as the curate droned on.

"I love you too," Ellen mouthed back.

"If any man here knows any reason why this couple should not be joined together in holy matrimony," the curate said, frowning at them both, "let him speak now, or forever hold his peace."

For a wild moment, Ellen half-expected Louisa to leap from behind one of the pews, knife in hand, and she flinched slightly. Thomas tightened his grasp on her hand, concern entering his expression, but she shook her head and smiled at him again.

The church was absolutely quiet. Thomas smiled reassuringly back at Ellen, perhaps guessing something of what she was thinking, and the curate began the ceremony again, this time preparing them to speak their vows.

"I now pronounce you to be man and wife in the sight of God," the curate ended at last. "My lords, ladies and gentlemen, the Earl and Countess of Havers."

"My lady," Thomas said with a smile, and Ellen laughed delightedly.

"Your lady indeed, my lord!"

Uncaring in the least whether they scandalised their audience, Thomas drew her close to place a lingering kiss on her lips. A few tuts sounded from the most traditional, but almost all the congregation beamed at the happy couple, glad to see Ellen find happiness with her Earl at last.

The End

I hope you enjoyed reading Ellen and Thomas' story. Don't forget to read on to enjoy for *A Marquis For Marianne*, Book 2 in the series... you didn't think I was going to leave poor Marianne Creighton to suffer with that awful husband forever, did you?

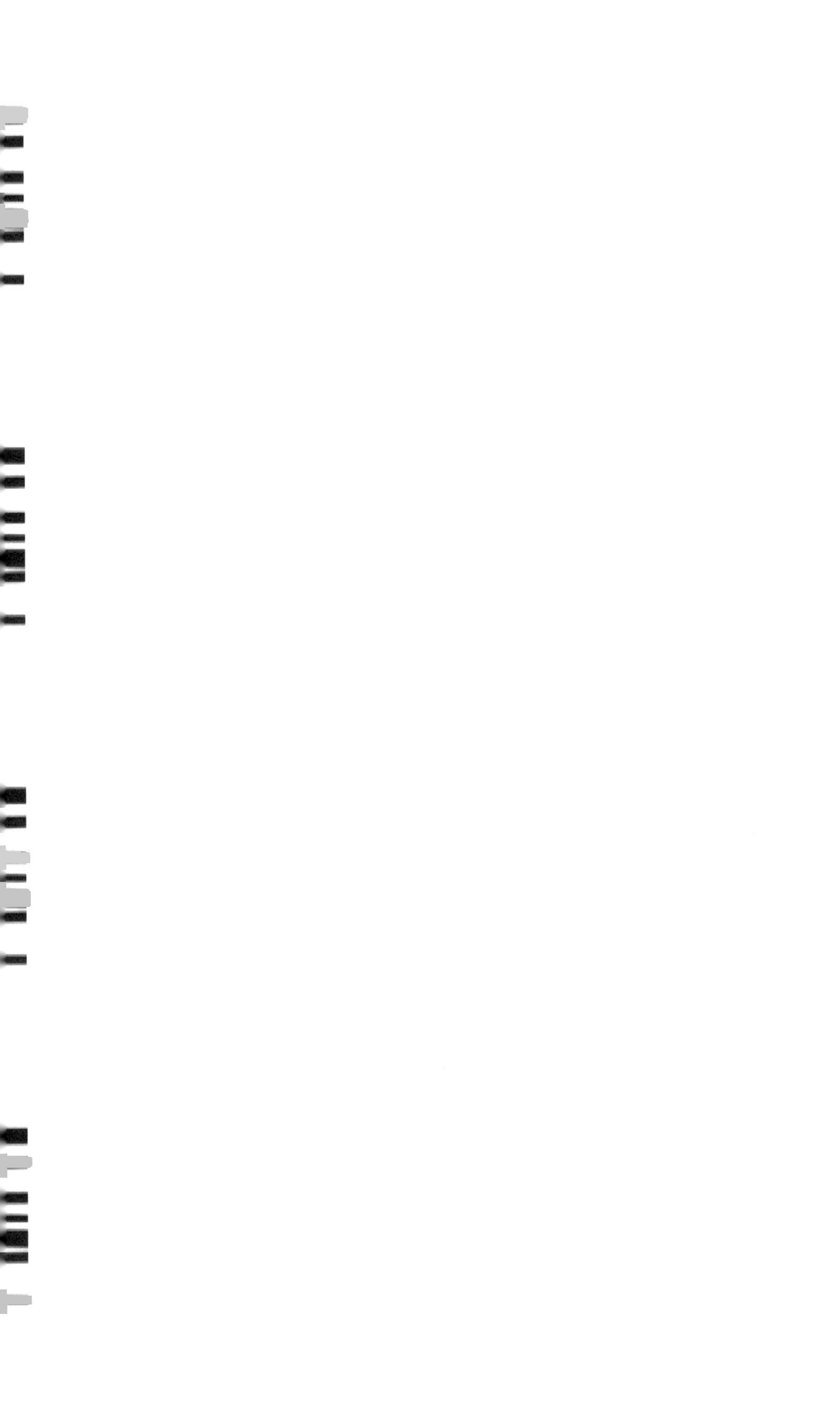

A Marquis for Marianne

CATHERINE BILSON

CONTENTS

PROLOGUE

A Private Ball at Temple Grove Manor, near Cambridge, March, 1810

"YOUR MOST PERSISTENT SUITOR is back, Miss Abingdon."

Marianne permitted only a slight smile to touch her lips as Amelia Temple spoke. The other girl's tone held just the slightest hint of jealousy, as the tall young man approaching the pair was easily the handsomest in the room -- especially in a lieutenant's scarlet regimentals.

"I've been acquainted with Mr. Rotherhithe since we were both children, Miss Temple," Marianne attempted to defray Amelia's envy. "We are friends; that is all." The lie almost scalded her tongue, but it would not do for whispers of her true attachment to Alexander Rotherhithe to reach her father's ears. Or, God forbid, *his* father's or grandfather's ears.

"Miss Abingdon." Alexander bowed very correctly, his dark brown eyes warm as he straightened to gaze upon her face. "Dare I hope you have a space remaining on your dance card for me?"

Without a word, Marianne slipped the ribbon holding the tiny booklet from about her wrist and offered it to him. His lips quirked minutely as he examined the card before lifting the equally tiny pencil attached and jotted his initials down in the single space remaining. She had saved that precious space by dint of avoiding as many potential dance partners as possible, no easy feat when you were lauded as the greatest beauty of the Season.

"I shall consider myself exceptionally fortunate, Miss Abingdon. Until our dance, then." He bowed once again and left them alone.

Amelia sighed wistfully as she watched the lieutenant depart and muttered, "I wish he'd asked *me* to dance."

"Since your card is full already, it would do you no good if he had," Marianne pointed out dryly. "As the daughter of the house, your dances have all been reserved since the house party began!"

"True, but still, he could have asked," Amelia sighed again before linking her arm through Marianne's. "I hear the orchestra tuning up. We should go into the ballroom; the first set will begin shortly."

Marianne did not care in the slightest for the first set, or any set other than the one she would dance with Alexander. Nevertheless, she painted a false smile on her lips and allowed herself to be led onto the floor.

He hated every man who dared approach her.

She was his, had always been his. Ever since he'd laid eyes on her years ago, her auburn-haired perfection had drawn him like a moth to a flame. Every other girl paled into boring insignificance beside her spectacular, eye-catching beauty.

She was too young then, of course, but now she was a woman grown. Eighteen years old and ripe for the plucking, a peach just ready to drop into his waiting hand. Especially considering her father, who was even now gambling away the last of his late wife's money at the gaming tables.

Taking a sip of his brandy, he watched with narrowed eyes as a tall young sprig in a scarlet coat claimed her hand for a dance. How dare that upstart touch what was his!

Soon, nobody would be allowed to dance with her but him.

Very soon.

"It's terribly warm in here," Marianne said as the musicians struck the first chords. "Would you mind terribly if we sat out the dance? I think perhaps I should get some air."

"Of course," Alexander said with a secret little smile, promptly escorting her from the floor. "I would not for a moment have you distress yourself for the sake of a mere dance, Miss Abingdon. Pray, retire to refresh yourself."

"Thank you for your understanding, Lieutenant." Marianne curtseyed gracefully before making her way out of the room.

Once out of the ballroom, she did not turn left to ascend the stairs to the retiring rooms. Instead, she turned to the right and opened a door mostly concealed behind a large potted plant, a door which led to the servants' quarters. Lifting her skirts in her hands, she rushed along the narrow, poorly lit corridor as fast as she could in her dancing slippers, hoping desperately nobody was coming the other way. She was lucky, though, and reached her next destination without seeing another soul.

A second door let out below the terrace immediately outside the ballroom, and she stepped out onto the raked gravel, careful not to let her feet make a sound. Directly above her head she could hear voices, people talking and laughing, cigar smoke drifting upwards as some gentleman indulged in the cool night air.

A hand curled around her elbow, and she bit back a gasp. Relaxing at once, she followed the insistent tug of that strong hand, tiptoeing on the loud gravel until they were around the side of the house and walking on grass, moving further away from the lighted windows and the noise until everything became dark and quiet.

"Marianne," he said her name gruffly once they were free to speak without fear of being overheard.

She sobbed his name in return, throwing herself against him. "Oh, Alexander! You came!"

"Nothing could have kept me away." He caught her in strong arms, bending down to kiss her upturned lips.

"Not even your grandfather?" Marianne whispered when he broke the kiss.

"It turns out that joining the army has had a remarkably freeing effect. My commanding officer is a great deal less strict than dear Grandpapa."

She could not see his wry smile in the darkness, but she could hear it in his voice. Smiling herself, she rested her head against his chest, heedless to the disarray of her curls. His warm hand came up to rest at the back of her neck and for a long moment they remained thus, in a close and loving embrace.

"I wish I could ask you to come away with me now," Alexander murmured, "but my regiment is bound for Spain next week. Even if we were to marry, I have no safe haven to provide you."

"It doesn't matter," Marianne said fiercely. "Just promise me you'll be careful, Alex? Promise you'll come back to me?"

They both knew there were no guarantees in war. Both of them had lost family and friends to the war against the French: Marianne, her only brother; Alexander, two uncles and his best friend from his school days.

Still, Alexander promised her, and he meant every word. "If God grants that I survive, I will come back to you, Marianne. There is no force on earth which will stop me coming for you, if you will but wait for me."

His words had the solemnity of a marriage vow, and in his mind they were exactly that. In that moment, he pledged himself to the girl who he had known all his life. The girl who had been his childhood companion in numerous escapades. The girl who had been his shoulder to cry on when his baby sister died of fever, just as he had returned the favour a year later when her mother drowned in a tragic accident. The girl who he loved above all others. And always would.

"I will wait for you," Marianne pledged in return, reaching up to place her hands on his cheeks, and though he could not see her eyes, in his mind they glowed blue as the summer sky, bright with her love. "I will *always* wait for you."

He watched the young officer return to the ballroom from the terrace, his smile a great deal too self-satisfied for a man who'd lost out on dancing with the most beautiful girl at the ball. Moments later, Marianne walked back in through the main doors, smiling just as happily.

Two pairs of eyes met and secret glances were exchanged before both looked away, feigning gaiety while mingling with the other partygoers.

He downed the last of his brandy.

It was time to make his move.

CHAPTER ONE

The townhouse of the Earl of Havers, London, November, 1818

"He's dead."

Marianne stared in disbelief.

"Lady Creighton?"

Behind her, the whispers began: *"Poor thing." "She's in shock." "So sudden."*

"Lady Creighton, I think you'd best sit down."

A strong hand touched her elbow, guided her away from her husband's body. Out of the room entirely, to a smaller, empty parlour and a couch where she was pressed to sit down.

"Marianne," her friend Ellen said, taking a seat beside her, looking and sounding desperately concerned. "Are you all right? Please, say something. Should we fetch a doctor?"

"I think it's rather too late for that," Marianne said and then had to suppress a totally inappropriate giggle. "My husband is dead."

"Thomas," Ellen said, and her husband of less than a day immediately moved to her side. "A drink, do you think?"

"Brandy," the Earl of Havers agreed. Within moments he knelt by the couch, pressing a glass into Marianne's hand, which she only then realised was shaking. "Drink it, Lady Creighton. You've had a terrible shock."

"I'm so sorry," she said. "At your wedding party..."

"Don't you dare apologise!" Ellen almost pushed the glass to her lips, forcing her to take a sip. The brandy burned all the way down her throat.

"Lady Creighton," Thomas said, and she couldn't stop her flinch. He paused and began again, "Forgive me for being familiar - Marianne. Will you allow me to handle things regarding the disposition of your husb- I mean, Lord Creighton's body? I assume he should be returned to his estate?"

"Yes."

She should say more, Marianne realised when the pair of them just stared at her. Thomas was an American, only lately come to England when he'd inherited his title. Though Ellen was possibly the only person she could truly call a friend, her friend was the daughter of a country parson, with no knowledge of society.

"It's near Durham," she managed to get out. "I - perhaps Lord Creighton's valet would be able to give you some useful information."

"Yes," Thomas agreed with some relief. "Yes, of course. I'm sure he will. I'll get right to it, then." He exchanged a glance with Ellen which somehow conveyed a great deal, before leaving the room and closing the door behind him with a soft click.

"Drink the rest of this," Ellen said quietly, urging the glass back to Marianne's lips, "and then I'm going to ring for my maid. You remember Susan? She's terribly efficient. We'll get you up to your room and then you can rest. You've had a terrible shock."

Yes, Marianne thought, letting Ellen coax her into drinking the rest of the brandy. *It is indeed shocking when your husband suffers an apoplectic fit while reproaching you for smiling at the man your friend married just yesterday, dropping dead at your feet.*

She must keep herself together, lest Ellen think she had run mad. So she called upon years of training, years of controlling even her slightest expression, to rein her emotions in. It was not until hours later, when she had finally convinced Ellen and her terrifyingly efficient maid that she was perfectly fine and only wished to be alone, that she could finally allow her feelings to show.

Standing at the window of her bedroom, in the magnificent suite she had been allotted as one of the guests of honour at Ellen's wedding, she watched as the carriage bearing a hastily-procured casket containing her late husband's earthly remains rolled away from the house and down the long avenue of larch trees, bare now of leaves. She would have to follow, of course, and remain at Creighton Hall for the foreseeable future, at least until her period of mourning had ended.

But now, for the first time in more years than she cared to remember, Marianne was *free*.

She had thought she would laugh, in this moment.

The tears surprised her; she had thought there were no more tears left to weep. Years of pain and suffering, loneliness and fear, had dried them all up. Yet the view of the receding carriage blurred, fat drops raced down her cheeks, and Marianne Creighton fell to her knees and wept in sheer, unadulterated relief.

CHAPTER TWO

Brooks' Gentlemen's Club, London, November, 1819

"YOU LOOK BORED TO tears, Glenkellie."

"Give it a few years, Havers." Alexander Rotherhithe, Marquis of Glenkellie, looked up from the news sheet he had been perusing without really taking in any of the information. "Everything in London will bore you to tears, too."

The young Earl of Havers laughed, taking the free seat at Alex's table without waiting to be invited. Which was probably why Alex liked the American; it wasn't so much that he had no idea of the niceties of behaviour, but more that he thought they were utter nonsense and refused to abide by them. The seat was free, and Thomas wanted to sit down. Why wait for Alex to ask, just because he happened to possess a loftier title?

Setting the news sheet down, Alex smiled at Thomas. They had only met a few months ago, when Thomas brought his new wife down to London for the Little Season, but hit it off right away. Alex was tired of sycophants and toadies, of those too intimidated by his wealth and title to want to get to know the real him. Thomas' cheerful disregard for protocol was a breath of fresh air.

"Drink?" Alex suggested, gesturing to an attentive waiter.

"I'll have what you're having." Thomas nodded to his cup on the table.

"Coffee? Sure you wouldn't like anything stronger?"

"I've promised to take Ellen to a ball tonight. If I start in on anything stronger now, I'll not see it through until four, or whatever ridiculous hour these things finish." Thomas grimaced. "I'm looking forward to heading back to Herefordshire and going to bed before midnight, for once!"

Alex had to laugh. "You're such a provincial, Havers."

"Says the man whose estate comprises much of the remotest parts of Scotland," Thomas shot back dryly.

"Why do you think I'm in London? Nothing up there but cranky crofters and sheep. Castle Glenkellie is only tolerable for a month or two in the summer, and barely that. Were it not entailed, I'd sell the lot and live here year-round."

The words were empty, and Thomas' sharp-eyed stare let Alex know he wasn't fooled. The truth was: Alex loved his home no matter the time of year. He simply couldn't bear it when his mother was in residence, as she was at the moment. God willing, she'd take it into their heads to tour Greece or Italy or some such place soon, and he'd be able to go home without fear of her producing a bride for him out of thin air.

Thomas' coffee arrived, and he sat back in his chair, relaxing as he took a sip of the hot, fragrant brew. "Rather you than me," he said, and it took Alex a moment to realise Thomas was talking about living in London. "In fact, we're heading home earlier than we planned. As much as Ellen has enjoyed our visit this time around, she wants to be home in plenty of time for Christmas. In fact, she plans to host a house party, and she has charged me with extending an invitation to you."

Surprised, Alex paused with his own coffee cup an inch or so from his lips. While he had met the lovely young Countess of Havers on several occasions and even stood up with her at a few dances, they'd had little chance to get to know each other. "Why?" he asked bluntly, lowering the cup.

Thomas looked amused. "Because she knows you and I have struck up a friendship, Glenkellie. Ellen has made plenty of friends among the ladies -- both married and single -- and has invited a number of them, but none of their attached husbands, brothers, or fathers are people I would call a close friend. You, on the other hand, are. She asked if I should like to invite you, I said I would, and she wrote out an invitation." Slipping a cream-coloured envelope from his pocket, he placed it on the table between them. "Should you fancy an escape from the delights of London for a few days without journeying to the frozen wastes of the north, we would be delighted to have you."

Touched, nonetheless Alexander affected disinterest as he picked up the envelope, broke the seal, and perused the brief invitation written in the Countess of Havers' own hand. Ellen had been raised a country parson's daughter, and her handwriting bore none of the flourishes and curlicues the daughters of the aristocracy were wont to affect; it was plain, neat, and very readable.

"How kind," Alexander murmured distantly. "Perhaps I will join you for a few days. It might be diverting."

Thomas smirked into his coffee, and Alex knew he hadn't fooled the American in the slightest. The truth was, he'd already received and rejected more than a dozen invitations to Christmas house parties, many of them at homes both more magnificent and more conveniently situated to London than Havers Hall, a good three days' journey away in Herefordshire, near the Welsh border.

All those invitations, however, had been extended by families with marriageable daughters looking to snag a marquis to hang on their family tree. Thomas and Ellen had no such ulterior motive. No, they had invited him quite simply for the pleasure of his company, and therefore he made up his mind then and there to accept the offer.

"Has Lady Havers invited many single ladies?" he asked in a last-ditch effort to talk himself out of it.

"Only a couple, I believe, and they're rather of the bluestocking variety who definitely wouldn't be likely to set their caps for you, never fear. There's also a widowed friend of hers who we hope to persuade to come."

"Ah, merry widows. Those I appreciate." Alex grinned wickedly.

Thomas shook his head, laughing in his good-natured way. "Don't play the rake with me, Glenkellie, I've seen you roll your eyes when ladies of the demi-rep make eyes at you. You've no more interest in them than I do, and have not even the good reason of a wife you adore!"

"You haven't known me all that long, Havers. For the right bird of paradise, I can be very accommodating indeed."

"I don't think Lady Creighton will be falling into your arms, charming as I'm sure you can be if you make the effort," Thomas said dryly.

Alex froze in the act of setting down his coffee cup. "Lady Creighton? The... former countess?"

Thomas' brow wrinkled. "Correct, though I think she's technically still a countess. Ellen says 'Marianne, Lady Creighton' is the correct address now, however. Since she's not the mother of the current earl, she's not a dowager." He looked exasperated. "Have I the right of that, or do I need to consult Debrett's again? I swear, the whole English system of titles and honorifics has the most abstruse rules; it's worse than conjugating Latin verb tenses! Sometimes I think Lady Jersey just makes them up as she goes along."

Alex burst out laughing, entertained as always by Thomas' irreverent wit. "It's quite possible you're correct," he said between guffaws, "but it's almost certainly not the done thing to talk about it!"

Thomas grinned unrepentantly. "Oh, I don't know. I'm sure Lady Jersey would be highly entertained if she found out I'd said it!"

"Only because she likes your wife so much." His chuckles subsiding, Alex picked up his coffee cup and drained the last of it. "Very well, Havers. Please tell Lady Havers I shall be delighted to accept your invitation to spend the Christmas season with you at Havers Hall."

"You can tell her yourself," Thomas said, finishing off his own coffee. "She also told me to invite you to dinner tonight, if you're not otherwise engaged."

"Well, I'd planned to dine here, but the chance to spend an evening being amused by you and charmed by your lovely lady is far too tempting to pass up."

"Excellent, we'll see you around seven, then? I must take my leave, I'm sorry. Tomorrow is our first wedding anniversary and I have to stop by Garrard's to collect Ellen's gift."

"Until this evening, then." Alex nodded in farewell and watched as Thomas collected his hat and coat and left the club, speaking cheerfully to several gentlemen as he passed.

Havers was possibly the most likable man he'd ever met, Alex mused, and he wondered whatever he had done to attract as a friend a man who could befriend literally anyone.

Lifting one hand, he fingered the long, livid scar down his cheek, where a Frenchman's bayonet had nearly skewered him at Waterloo. The tip of the blade had missed his eye by less than a quarter inch, scraping downwards and flaying his cheek to the bone, ripping a long gash all the way to his chin. The infection afterwards had nearly cost Alex his life.

The jagged scar, still red almost four years later, was ugly enough that several young women of less than robust constitutions had been sickened by it. One had even swooned from the horror. He hadn't yet met one who could look him in the eyes and not stare at his scar with a horrified fascination, riveted by its ugliness.

Alexander Rotherhithe was no longer the perfectly handsome young man a diamond of the Ton had sworn her heart to. The scar pulled as he smiled tightly, hitching one corner of his mouth up into a grimace.

Marianne Abingdon hadn't waited for him as she had promised. She hadn't even done him the courtesy of sending him a letter, telling him she'd chosen another. The first he'd known of her betrayal was when a brother officer had wordlessly handed him a copy of a month-old newspaper, folded open to the announcements of marriages, and the bottom had fallen out of his world.

Alex remembered little of the next few months. He'd drowned his sorrows in liquor, whenever he could find any, and in leading suicidal charges in every damned battle across the Iberian Peninsula. Or so it seemed later, when he'd finally come out of his haze to realise he'd been promoted (twice!) and decorated with more medals and mentions in dispatches than any one soldier should earn in a lifetime of war, never mind only two years of it.

How he'd escaped death; he had no idea. But somehow he had. Because of it he'd drawn around him a cadre of devoted soldiers who had convinced themselves he was some sort of god of war -- unbeatable on the battlefield.

An officer who could inspire that sort of loyalty was far too valuable to the War Office to have anywhere else but on the battlefield. Even during Bonaparte's exile on Elba, Alex hadn't been permitted to return to England. Only when he was finally -- shockingly -- wounded at Waterloo, proving himself mortal after all, was he allowed to leave the field. He recuperated in Brussels, and as soon as he was fit to sit a horse, he was set to be sent straight back out again to mop up stray pockets of French resistance.

Perhaps he'd have carried on fighting England's wars until he grew old and grey or a bullet proved he was only mortal in the most final way possible, but for a freak accident of succession. Once fourth in line to the marquisate, he'd suddenly become the heir apparent when his uncle, cousin and father were all killed in a flood which swept away their hunting party as they descended a narrow gully.

His grandfather had summoned Alex home peremptorily, and not even the lords at the War Office were inclined to deny the old man his only living heir -- no matter how useful a soldier.

Packed onto a ship bound for Inverness with no ceremony at all, Alex had arrived home barely in time to bid farewell to his grandfather. Broken-hearted by the death of both his sons and the grandson he'd raised from birth to be his successor, Duncan Rotherhithe had cast one disparaging look over Alex and declared, "You'll have to do, I suppose," before drawing his final breath.

He'd been living down to his grandfather's expectations ever since.

CHAPTER THREE

Creighton Hall, Cumbria, Early December, 1819

"ANOTHER LETTER FOR YOU, Aunt Marianne." Her nephew Arthur, the new Earl of Creighton, passed the letter to her from the stack a footman had just delivered to the breakfast table on a silver salver.

"Thank you," Marianne said sedately, taking the letter and putting it into her pocket.

"You will not read it now?" Her successor as Countess, Lavinia, peered at her from watery blue eyes. *Curiosity sharpens her already thin face, making her look rather like a ferret,* Marianne thought whimsically.

"It is only from my friend Ellen," she disclaimed quietly, lifting her cup to take a sip of tea. "No doubt full of inane gossip from Herefordshire."

"You do exchange a lot of letters with her," Arthur said peevishly. "The postage costs a pretty penny."

Marianne took a deep, unseen breath to suppress her immediate urge to make a sharp retort. "She is a faithful correspondent," she answered after a moment, "but an excellent contact to maintain, nonetheless. With Lady Diana to make her debut next Season, I feel it is imperative to keep my Society friendships alive."

"Yes," Lavinia said quickly with a sharp glance at her husband, "yes, of course, you must maintain the friendship, Marianne. The Countess of Havers will be an invaluable friend to have when Diana makes her bows, Arthur."

Marianne hid her smile behind her cup as Arthur sighed and acquiesced to Lavinia's demand. The new Earl had been raised on a very limited allowance and still liked to pinch a penny until it squeaked. Without expectation of inheriting the title since his uncle had been most determined to sire an heir, neither Arthur nor Lavinia had ever even been to London. They knew nobody and would be dependent on Marianne to make their introductions when their eldest daughter was presented.

Marianne had no intention of informing them Ellen had far fewer friends among the London set than Marianne herself. With Ellen as her only regular correspondent, she would lie without compunction to keep her friendship alive.

After all, so very much had already been taken from her.

Much later that day, as she walked back to the small cottage grandiosely named the Creighton Estate Dower House, Marianne slipped the letter from her pocket and broke the seal. She had hoped to escape earlier, but Lavinia required her to be available at all times to assist with her five children -- four of whom were daughters who Lavinia desperately wanted to marry well.

Marianne's father died penniless shortly after her marriage, which left her with no family who might assist her and entirely dependent on Arthur and Lavinia. Since she had never had a dowry and her widow's jointure was almost non-existent, Marianne had no choice but to essentially act as an unpaid finishing school teacher to the four girls, teaching them the social graces they had not learned so far. By the time she led them through a reading in French, given each a half-hour piano lesson and a group singing class, helped them with their needlework, and supervised Diana's efforts at pouring tea, it was late afternoon and Marianne was desperate for some time to herself, even if it was only an hour before she must return to take dinner with the family.

Still in the habit of penny-pinching, Arthur saw no reason to employ a cook for Marianne's use when she could perfectly well take meals with them. It was only grudgingly that he permitted a chambermaid to come over from the main house to clean the cottage and lay the fires and a man to spend an hour or so every other day carrying firewood and water.

"You might as well live in the house with us," Arthur had said when he and Lavinia had first moved in with their children. "Take a room with the girls. No sense opening up the Dower House just for you, is there?"

Lavinia had proved a surprising ally when Marianne insisted she needed her own space. Marianne suspected it was because Lavinia liked to escape over to visit her now and then, taking a break from her noisy, demanding family. Lavinia always brought some biscuits and they would share a quiet cup of tea before returning to the chaos of the main house.

Marianne doubted she and Lavinia would ever be friends - it had to be hard on the new Countess, to have a predecessor ten years her junior still hanging around - and Lavinia was certainly not above using Marianne's dependence on them for her own ends. Still, Marianne would not say she was unhappy.

Not as unhappy as she had been, anyway, even if she no longer wore bright, expensive silk gowns and drank champagne at the most exclusive events in London. Now she wore heavy gowns in the black or grey of mourning, despite her official period ending a month past. Since her husband had preferred to reside in London for most of the year, she had nothing else to wear which was suitable for Creighton's cold winters, and with six dozen gowns in her wardrobe already Arthur would not spend another penny on clothing for her.

Perhaps I should try and sell some of my old gowns, Marianne mused, *or exchange them for some plainer, warmer ones.* Certainly she would not need as many as once she had, even when they repaired to London for Diana's Season.

At least then she would see Ellen again, and the thought warmed her. Settling down in her comfortable chair near the fire in her tiny parlour, she unfolded her letter and began to read.

"You look remarkably pleased with yourself, Aunt Marianne," Arthur remarked as soon as she entered the parlour before dinner.

"I have received an invitation to visit my friend, Lady Havers," Marianne said. "I have already advised her of Diana's upcoming debut, and she proposes that I travel to Haverford to visit with her for a couple of weeks over Christmas and then accompany them on to London to rejoin you in time for the start of the Season."

Arthur had been sipping on a glass of wine; he lowered it now and stared at her, his brow furrowing. "Why would you do that?" he asked, apparently genuinely befuddled.

"Visit with Lady Havers?" Confused in turn, Marianne stared back. "She is my friend, Arthur, and I am very much looking forward to seeing her again. Though we would see her in London, of course, I will be much tied up with Diana..."

"No," Arthur shook his head. "I think there has been some misunderstanding, Aunt Marianne. You're not coming to London."

"What?" Marianne blinked, astonished.

Lavinia did not meet Marianne's eyes when she spoke. "You have done us the very great service of writing letters of introduction to everyone we will need to know, but you need not accompany us yourself. Indeed, it would be much better for you to remain here with the other girls, focusing on their education and their futures."

"Better for whom?" Marianne enquired, then nodded as enlightenment dawned. "Ah... for Diana, of course. You do not want me to be a distraction to any potential suitors, I daresay."

"You flatter yourself." Arthur's expression turned puce. "You're a penniless widow. What possible attraction could you have for the sort of gentlemen who would court an earl's daughter?"

"I have never cared for false modesty," Marianne informed him, "so I will merely say that even when I was an earl's wife, there were never any shortage of gentlemen who should have been courting earls' daughters who preferred to seek my company instead. Though I was never permitted to so much as smile in their direction, much less dance with them."

She saw exactly how it was, and in truth, she could not blame Arthur and Lavinia. Diana was a pretty enough girl and pleasant-natured in a quiet way, but in a room with Marianne she would pale into the background, and they all knew it.

"Very well," Marianne said after a few moments of taut silence. "If I am not to join you in London, so be it. May I at least visit with my friend beforehand and return here when they depart for London?"

"No," Arthur said, and she knew he would not be moved. He stared at her, his lips thinned. "I will not permit it."

"How fortunate, then, that you are not my husband, or my father or brother, and therefore are not in a position of authority to permit or deny me anything!" Marianne's temper flared. She had thought she was done with being controlled by men when Creighton died. She would not tolerate it from a man not even related to her by blood!

"Perhaps not." Arthur's smile was unpleasant. "But I will certainly not permit your use of *our* carriage to travel, and as for money..."

"Arthur," Lavinia said quietly. "Enough."

It's probably a good thing Lavinia stepped in, Marianne thought as she turned and stormed from the parlour, her fists clenched at her sides. *If Arthur had said one more word about my complete lack of funds, I would have slapped him, and goodness knows where that would have ended.*

In the hallway, she almost collided with Diana and her next-in-age sister Clarissa, who both jumped out of her way with startled gasps. She did not even stop to acknowledge them, striding straight back out through the side door she always used and down the short path to her cottage.

I've traded in one prison for another, she thought, stamping her feet as she strode back and forth in her small bedroom. She was still not free to live her life as she chose, and she very likely never would be.

By the following morning, her stomach was grumbling, but Marianne could not bring herself to go up to the house for breakfast and pretend nothing had happened the night prior. She had spent a sleepless night tossing and turning, trying to find a way out of her dilemma and failing. It all came down to money: something of which she had none and no way to get any.

Even if she could find a position as a paid governess or companion, that would be better than working for free for Arthur and Lavinia. But who would hire her? It wasn't as though she had any references. While there might be some rich merchant families who would hire her for the sheer novelty of having a countess work for them, she shied away from the notion. How would she even go about finding such a position, anyway? She had not the faintest idea how such things were done.

A knock at the front door surprised her, and she sighed and went to answer it. She had few visitors, and Lavinia never knocked.

It was a surprise to find Diana and Clarissa on the doorstep, both looking at her with worried eyes. Clarissa held out a small package wrapped in a linen napkin. "Good morning, Aunt Marianne. We - we thought you might be hungry."

She was not too proud, Marianne discovered, to accept the offering. Inside there was a half loaf of fresh bread, a chunk of cheese, and several slices of ham. "Thank you," she managed past a lump in her throat. "That's very kind of you, girls. Would you like to come in?"

Neither of the girls had ever been inside the cottage, and they stepped in shyly, looking about with wide eyes. She gestured them into her tiny parlour, and they sat down together on the little couch, shoulders almost touching.

"Will you excuse me a moment?" She didn't wait for their acquiescence before heading for the kitchen.

When she returned after gulping down a few mouthfuls of the bread, a chunk of cheese, and a slice of ham, she felt a great deal more composed. Taking her usual chair by the fire, she considered the sisters.

There was only a little more than a year between the two girls in age, Marianne knew, and they were very close. Clarissa had more than once expressed distress over Diana's going to London for the upcoming Season, but Marianne had always assumed -- incorrectly, she now realised -- the whole family would be going. Clarissa being left behind would be upsetting for both girls, and not helpful for Diana's nerves at all.

"Thank you for bringing me something to eat," Marianne said finally when neither of the girls seemed inclined to break the silence. "I appreciate your thoughtfulness."

Diana looked at Clarissa, and it was the younger of the sisters who spoke. "I want to go to London too, Aunt Marianne."

"Of course you do," Marianne said understandingly, "but I do not see what you think I can do about it." Clarissa and Dana must have heard everything last night when they listened in the hallway as Arthur humiliated Marianne. It must be obvious to them exactly how little influence Marianne had.

"If you weren't here, Mama and Papa would have to take us all." Diana leaned forward. "If you went to visit Lady Havers, and then joined us in London. Or maybe stayed with the Havers there and just met up with us sometimes."

"I know you both overheard the scene last night, Diana, so you already know it's not a possibility."

"What if you had the money to go, though?" Diana took something from the pocket of her dress. "We both think Papa is very mean to you, and after last night, it's obvious he just wants to keep you here to be, well, a governess, and he's too much of a skinflint even to pay you."

Marianne bit her lip. She would not speak ill of Arthur to his daughters, but it seemed they saw him quite clearly all the same.

"Mama is generous with our allowance, however, and we are not in the habit of spending it. I told Papa this morning I wanted to go to Durham tomorrow and purchase some trinkets before we go to London, and he said we could take the carriage and even gave me some more money." Diana extended the purse she held. "It's not nearly as much as you should have been paid, but we think it should be enough to buy tickets on stagecoaches and rooms at inns to sleep in along the way to Herefordshire."

Marianne hesitated. "Whose idea was this?"

"Mine," Clarissa said firmly. Though she was the younger of the two, she was definitely the leader. "But we are both in agreement this is the right thing to do."

Diana nodded in agreement and tried to press the purse into Marianne's hand. "Please take it. Papa will not think twice of your accompanying us to Durham tomorrow to go shopping, and though you cannot take more than one bag..."

"I could not carry more than one anyway." Coming to a decision, Marianne accepted the purse. "Thank you," she said sincerely. "Come with me, if you will?"

Diana and Clarissa followed her up the narrow stairs to her bedroom and the second, smaller room beyond it which was meant for a maid. Without a maid of her own, however, Marianne used it for her wardrobe - all the beautiful dresses she no longer had occasion to wear were stored there.

"Oh," Diana whispered, amazement on her face as she gazed at the colourful spectacle before her. "Oh, how spectacular!"

"Most of these are not suitable for a debutante, I'm afraid," Marianne said regretfully, brushing her fingers over a wine-red silk gown with a gold lace overdress. "However, there are a few here in lighter colours, and you are very much the same size as me, Diana. They would require minimal alterations for you to wear." Moving confidently among the hanging gowns, she selected one in palest rose, another in spring green with a tiny pink silk flower print, and a silver satin gown which she had never cared for but would look stunning with Diana's dark brown hair and eyes.

"Here," she heaped them into Diana's arms before opening drawers in a dresser and gesturing to Clarissa. "You are not out yet, so I'm afraid none of the gowns would be suitable for you, but there are ribbons and lace aplenty here. Take whatever you wish; it is yours."

"We can't take your lovely things, Aunt Marianne," Clarissa protested.

"Call it an exchange." Marianne hefted the purse in her hands.

"What we gave you wouldn't buy a single one of these gowns!" Diana exclaimed, trying to hand them back, but Marianne refused to accept.

"You are incorrect, my dear girls. You have given me my freedom. I cannot take these with me, and I would far rather have you wear them than let them moulder away here. Everything I leave behind is yours; I give it to you freely."

Overcome, both girls pressed close to embrace her and thank her profusely, but Marianne knew they had given her the greater gift.

CHAPTER FOUR

Havers Hall, Herefordshire, Mid December, 1819

Five days later, Marianne walked slowly up the long tree-lined carriageway to Havers Hall, her bag weighing heavily on her weary arm. It had been a long, cold, exhausting trip from Creighton, and the last leg had been the worst; she had paid a farmer returning from Worcester to Haverford to give her a ride, but he had dropped her at the end of the carriageway with a remark in an accent so thick she hadn't understood more than one word in two.

Two of the words had been 'Havers Hall,' though, and combined with his pointing finger and cheerful smile, she had taken it to mean the end of her journey was finally approaching.

A half-mile walk was the last thing she wanted, but she had little choice. Summoning the last of her internal fortitude, and praying Ellen and Thomas were at home, she trudged up the long gravelled way, almost too weary to appreciate the beautiful house coming into view.

Havers Hall was a large building of golden stone, which would have likely glowed in the sunshine on a summer's day, but still managed to look magnificent even on a grey December day with rain clouds threatening. The closer she got, the more intimidating the house looked, and Marianne found herself nervous of her reception as she climbed the wide, shallow steps to the huge double doors at the main entryway.

Maybe they'll tell me to go around the back, to the servants' entrance, she thought with a small giggle to herself. She was wearing one of her plainest gowns, a dark grey wool practical for travelling but hardly glamorous.

The door opened promptly to her knock, and an imperious-looking butler inspected her from head to toe before saying, "May I assist you, madam?"

"Marianne, Lady Creighton." She tried for her best imperious tone in return and must have achieved it in some measure at least, because the butler looked slightly surprised and immediately stepped aside to welcome her into the house.

"I do beg your pardon, my lady. I understood you were not expected for another week or so, but Lord and Lady Havers will undoubtedly be delighted to welcome you."

"Thank you," Marianne murmured, relieved.

"I am Allsopp, the butler. May I take your bag? The, ah, rest of your luggage?"

"Later, Allsopp," she murmured, allowing him to slip the bag from her frozen fingers with a sense of relief.

He stepped aside with it and tugged on a bell cord, and moments later a footman entered the grand hallway. "Matthew, please advise her ladyship that her guest, Lady Creighton, has arrived ahead of schedule."

The order became redundant a moment later, as Ellen, Lady Havers, descended the stairs, dressed in a blue gown one would think far too simple for a lady of her rank if one was not acquainted with Ellen herself. A smile came to Marianne's weary face at the sight of her friend; it seemed Ellen had not changed in essentials even though she was now a countess.

"Marianne?" Ellen said disbelievingly.

I must look a fright, Marianne thought, *pale, weary and dirty with road-dust*. Ellen's delight at seeing her was genuine, however, and she found herself drawn into a close embrace.

"Dear Marianne, you didn't send word you'd be arriving early! In fact, we haven't received any letter from you at all; I hoped you would accept the invitation... why, you're shaking with cold! Come into the library, it's lovely and warm in there. Have some hot tea sent in immediately, Allsopp, and whatever Cook can rustle up quickly to warm Lady Creighton, please."

"At once, my lady," Allsopp said to their backs as Ellen put her arm around Marianne and led her through a door into a beautiful library, light and airy, quite unlike the dark-panelled, musty room at Creighton Hall. A fire crackled merrily in the grate. Marianne soon found herself pressed to sit down in a comfortable chair, Ellen scooping up a shawl from the back of another chair close by and settling it around her shoulders.

"There, we'll soon have you warm. I'm so glad to see you."

Marianne felt quite ridiculous for being brought to tears by Ellen's joyous welcome, but she could not prevent the fat drops which threatened to spill.

Perceptive and kind, Ellen saw her distress and immediately pressed a handkerchief into her hands. “Hush, now. You’re tired and overset. We’ll have some hot tea and you can tell me everything later.”

Grateful when Ellen didn’t press her, Marianne slowly regained her composure over tea and scones, warm from the oven and dripping with butter and jam. She took the time to survey her friend, thinking that marriage very clearly suited Ellen. The young countess fairly glowed, and though the cut of her gown was simple, Marianne noticed now the quality of the fabric and the delicate embroidery one shade darker than the fine wool which decorated the bodice. Her dark brown hair was beautifully curled and arranged, braids looping around her head in a coronet, while her kindly brown eyes were bright with happiness.

Envy twisted in Marianne’s gut, and she looked down at her teacup, silently chiding herself. Ellen deserved her happiness. She’d lost her parents, her home, everything. If Thomas hadn’t inherited the earldom almost by sheer luck and fallen in love with his distant cousin, who knew what circumstances Ellen might have been reduced to? At least Marianne had never had to worry about having a roof over her head, even now.

"My housekeeper will have your suite aired and warm by now,” Ellen said as they finished their tea, “so let me take you up and you can refresh yourself. Will you come down to dinner tonight, or take a tray in your room? It is only Thomas and me at present, since our other guests aren’t expected to arrive until next week, but we should be delighted to have your company. And then, perhaps, you might wish to tell us what has you arriving on our doorstep in such a state, alone, with only one small bag?”

Ellen’s words were gentle, but they caused another surge of guilt in Marianne. “Yes,” she agreed, looking up to meet her friend’s kind smile. “Yes, I’d love to join you both for dinner, and I’ll tell you everything then.”

Marianne had brought one nice gown with her, a lavender silk which rolled up surprisingly small. The lady’s maid Ellen had sent to attend her pressed it while Marianne luxuriated in a copper tub filled with steaming water and aromatic soap, soaking off the grime of travel and allowing her strained nerves to unwind. She had barely slept since leaving Creighton, and the feeling of finally being safe and warm had her eyelids drooping with weariness.

"My lady,” the maid said quietly, “shall I rinse your hair, now? Else there will be too little time to dry it before dinner.”

"Yes, thank you," Marianne said, pushing herself to sit forward a little reluctantly. "I'm sorry, I didn't catch your name, earlier?"

"Jean, my lady." She had good hands, gentle as she washed out Marianne's long, wavy auburn hair and combed out the tangles, squeezing it firmly in a thick piece of linen to squeeze out as much water as possible before helping Marianne from the tub and swathing her in a beautiful silk dressing-gown which had certainly not been in Marianne's small bag.

"Come sit by the fire, my lady, and let's dry that hair off," Jean encouraged, and Marianne followed, only too pleased to sink into the comfortably upholstered chair and curl her feet up beneath her, tilting her head towards the flames.

She must have drowsed off while Jean went back to pressing her gown and dealing with her other clothes, all of which needed laundering, because the next thing she knew, Jean was gently waking her and her hair was quite dry.

"You do seem very tired, my lady. Are you sure you wouldn't like a tray here and to go straight to bed? I'm sure the Earl and the Countess wouldn't mind..."

"No, no," Marianne waved off Jean's concern. "I thank you, but I feel much refreshed after that little rest, and I am looking forward to seeing Lord Havers again." Her stomach chose that moment to let out a loud rumble, and she chuckled. "I admit to feeling rather famished, too!"

"As you wish, my lady," Jean said with a small laugh. "How would you like me to do your hair?"

Not wanting to put Jean to too much trouble, Marianne settled for a simple coil of braids at the nape of her neck, a few curls hanging loose at the side of her face. Not for the first time, she was grateful for her naturally wavy hair; it took a curl very easily and needed little work to be arranged into any fashionable style she pleased.

Very soon, she was following the same young footman who had taken her bag on her arrival along the twisting hallways of the grand old manor house, admiring the paintings on the walls, the beautifully polished wooden floors and thick carpets, the immaculate cleanliness of everything. "It must take an army of servants to keep the Hall in this condition," Marianne mused aloud.

"Lord and Lady Havers turn away no one who needs employment," the footman answered her, a little to her surprise. "They have begun a programme of training young men and women who wish to enter service, and servants trained at Havers Hall are now in high demand throughout the county. A school in the village has been opened, too, and all the local boys and girls are learning to read and write."

The footman sounded quite incredulous, and Marianne supposed it was quite unheard-of to teach common-born children their letters. Especially the girls. It sounded very much like the thoughtful Ellen she knew and her egalitarian American husband, though. "How wonderful," she said encouragingly as they descended the grand staircase. "And are you one of these trainees?"

"Yes, my lady. Is it so obvious?" He looked quite dismayed, and she tried not to laugh.

"Not at all, I should never have guessed. I was merely curious," she said kindly, though in truth most footmen would not have spoken to her unless she asked them a direct question. Undoubtedly, the young man would learn that rule as he completed his training, though she found his relaxed, informative attitude quite refreshing.

Allsopp, the butler, was in the hall at the foot of the stairs, and he bowed low to her as she descended the last step. "Good evening, Lady Creighton. Lord and Lady Havers await you in the parlour." He gestured for her to follow him.

Thomas and Ellen stood by the fire, deep in conversation, but they at once broke off with welcoming smiles as Allsopp conducted Marianne into the parlour and formally announced her.

"Lady Creighton, it is delightful to see you again." Thomas bowed formally over her hand. "Ellen is overjoyed you were able to come so soon."

Marianne smiled at him. "I am overjoyed to be here... and please, call me Marianne. Since I am imposing on your hospitality without notice, it seems rather ridiculous to insist on the formalities."

Thomas chuckled and nodded. "I'm sure you know formal address doesn't come easily to me anyway," he said frankly, "so I'm very happy to hear you say that, Marianne. You must call me Thomas, of course."

"Of course," she echoed, and let Ellen take her hand and draw her closer to the fire while Thomas poured her a glass of sherry to savour before dinner.

With the warmth of their welcome and an excellent dinner set before her, Marianne felt comfortable and safe enough to slowly reveal what had led her to depart Creighton with such haste and secrecy. Ellen was vocally outraged on her behalf, proclaiming herself disgusted with Arthur and Lavinia for attempting to ban Marianne from London.

"Your nieces sound like dear girls, though!" Ellen declared as Marianne explained how Diana and Clarissa had made her escape possible. "I look forward to meeting them in London, and of course you must accompany us there, and remain with us for the Season. You are welcome to stay with us for as long as you wish, dearest, for life if need be. And please believe me when I say that I certainly do not expect you to act as an unpaid governess or companion! In fact, if you would be interested," she cast a glance at Thomas, who nodded benignly, "there are a number of young women in Haverford who would definitely benefit from exposure to a lady of your quality and talents. I have no doubt we could find some paying work for you, if you wished it."

"I would very much appreciate that," Marianne said stoutly, though she had never worked a day in her life.

Thomas gave her a perceptive look, but said nothing as Ellen went on.

"In fact, if you would be willing, I would greatly appreciate your advice myself. I have never hosted a house party, and there are a thousand and one ways I could make a spectacular social misstep. Your assistance would be invaluable... Thomas, dear, could you find out the going rate for a paid companion? I want to make sure I am not taking advantage of Marianne..."

"Certainly not," Marianne said at the same time as Thomas said;

"Of course, my love."

"I could not accept payment for helping you, Ellen," Marianne continued. "Please consider it my thanks for your most generous hospitality. Anything I can do to assist you, please, you need only ask."

"I most certainly will." Ellen's smile was a little cheeky. "You may regret such a generous offer!"

"Never." Grateful beyond measure for Ellen's kindness and understanding, Marianne reached out to clasp her hand. "Thank you," she said softly, glancing from Ellen to Thomas and back again. "Thank you both so much."

"You're very welcome," Thomas spoke for both of them, and Ellen squeezed Marianne's hand in return. "What are friends for, after all?"

CHAPTER FIVE

I AM LUCKY BEYOND belief to have such friends, Marianne mused as she let Jean dress her hair the following morning. Though she had only a plain gown to wear, it had been freshly washed, pressed, and returned to her that morning looking like new. She thanked Jean profusely, but the maid merely looked surprised before advising her Havers Hall had a positive surfeit of laundry maids who were more than happy to assist her.

"Will the rest of your wardrobe be arriving soon, my lady?" Jean enquired delicately as she inserted the last hairpin to support the arrangement of braids she had deftly woven from Marianne's thick auburn hair.

"I'm afraid not," Marianne admitted.

Jean pursed her lips thoughtfully. "You're taller than Lady Havers, but more of a size with Lady Louisa, the last Earl's daughter," she said. "Caused a dreadful scandal last year, she did, running off with a footman from the London house. Left quite a wardrobe behind. Perhaps you might speak to Lady Havers about adjusting some of the things for your use?"

"I couldn't possibly," Marianne disclaimed, but she thought wistfully of the stunning gowns Lady Louisa Havers had been wont to wear. Thomas' cousin, Louisa had hoped to become the next Countess of Havers by marriage to Thomas, but he had chosen Ellen instead and Louisa had disappeared in a scandal which had been the talk of London... at least until Marianne's husband dropped dead the day after Thomas and Ellen's wedding.

Jean looked thoughtful rather than accepting of Marianne's refusal, and Marianne suspected the maid intended to approach the topic through a roundabout method, quite possibly via Ellen's personal maid. Well, so be it. Marianne certainly could not ask herself, even though she would like something more elegant to wear.

Another young footman waited outside her door to escort her to the breakfast room, a completely different room from the one where they had eaten dinner last night, which Marianne learned now was called the Oak Dining Room, on account of the oak-panelled walls. There was also the Grand Dining Room, for when more than twenty were expected to dine.

"And are more than twenty expected at the house party?" Marianne enquired of the chatty young man. She had not attended such a large gathering since leaving London last year in the wake of her husband's death.

"Not to stay at the Hall, no, my lady, but there are several occasions planned where more will be invited. Local gentry, you understand."

"Indeed," Marianne agreed, finding herself looking forward to the house party with enthusiasm. She had always enjoyed social events, though her pleasure had usually been curtailed by her husband's severe restrictions. To have the freedom to dance and talk with whomever she pleased, male or female, was a much-longed-for treat.

Ellen was alone in the breakfast room, eating muffins spread with blackberry jam, when Marianne entered.

"Good morning!" Ellen exclaimed, pushing aside the newspaper she had been perusing. "Do sit down." She waved at the seat beside her. "Would you like tea, coffee, or chocolate? Hugh will bring you some fresh. And please let Jacob know what you would like for breakfast."

Two different footmen stood ready to leap to her command, Marianne noted with amusement. Ellen must spend her days thinking up tasks to keep all her staff busy. No wonder everything in the Hall looked so perfect.

"Tea would be delightful, thank you," she told Hugh then turned to the other footman, "and I have a weakness for coddled eggs with buttered toast, if that wouldn't be too much trouble for your cook?"

"Not at all, my lady." Jacob bowed, and Ellen and Marianne were left briefly alone as the two footmen left hastily to fetch her breakfast.

Ellen smiled warmly at her as Marianne settled into her chair, and then to Marianne's utmost surprise she said, "What would you like to do today?"

Marianne stared at her, mouth dropping open. She stared so long Ellen began to fidget, obviously becoming a little uncomfortable.

"Is something wrong, Marianne?"

"I was trying to remember the last time I was asked that question," Marianne said with some difficulty, feeling tears welling, "and do you know, I don't think anyone has *ever* asked me that."

"Oh!" Ellen's hand flew to her mouth. In her eyes, brimming with sympathy, Marianne saw her friend comprehended the depth of what her question meant. A choice, given freely to someone who had never had any.

The return of Hugh with Marianne's tea put paid to the moment of emotion, though Marianne still had to take several sips and some deep breaths before she felt able to speak again. "What do you suggest?" she asked Ellen. "I should love a tour of the Hall, but if you have any other ideas, I am all agog to hear them."

"A tour sounds just the thing," Ellen said encouragingly, "particularly since it is set to rain all day today. After a year living here, I think I have my way around all figured out, at least. Or at last, I should say. I cannot tell you how many times I have got lost; Allsopp has had to send out more than one search party for me!"

Marianne laughed, as Ellen had obviously intended her to. "These huge old houses are the devil, aren't they? Creighton Hall is much the same. While the front elevation looks both coherent and elegant, behind there is often a hodgepodge of alterations and additions which make the house into an absolute muddle."

"Indeed," Ellen nodded, "and despite having all the money in the world, the old Earl was an utter miser. He closed off half the Hall, didn't employ enough servants to keep the rooms in good condition, and let them fall into disrepair. Thomas and I have been opening them up, redecorating, and commissioning new furniture, carpets, and curtains from local makers. With everything finally complete, we thought a house party a nice way to celebrate having the Hall fully open again."

"Very nice," Marianne agreed.

"But I do need your advice. Thomas hasn't a clue, of course, and I... well, precedence is a bit of a mystery to me, still. It's always been everyone else above, then me definitely at the bottom." Ellen smiled wistfully. "I have no idea who should get the best guest suite: a dowager duchess or a marquis? Does the widowed sister of an impoverished earl come above the wealthy heir to a viscountcy?"

"The duchess, and yes, she would, because ladies always come before gentlemen," Marianne said, laughing when Ellen looked dismayed.

"Thank God you did come early! I have it all wrong!"

"We'll soon have it all sorted out," Marianne promised as her breakfast was set before her with great ceremony. "As soon as I've done justice to this marvellous breakfast, you can go fetch whatever notes you have, and we'll get to work."

With Marianne's experienced assistance and an army of servants only too willing to jump to her slightest request, Ellen soon had a plan for accommodating her incoming guests she was much more confident about. They spent the entire morning touring the house, examining the bedrooms and the linen, before discovering themselves quite famished when Allsopp appeared to delicately suggest they might wish to take a break for a light nuncheon which Cook had prepared for them.

"Is it near noon already?" Ellen asked, startled.

"I think it must be, for my stomach has been rumbling this last half-hour at least," Marianne admitted.

Tucking her arm through Marianne's, Ellen smiled. "I am an abominable hostess, as you see. Here less than a day, and already I am overworking and starving you!"

"Nonsense." Marianne laughed at Ellen's teasing. "I am delighted to be of use, I promise, and I find myself looking forward to meeting your guests."

"Well, we will be an eclectic gathering." Ellen led her back through the confusing maze of corridors to the central part of the house, and to the pretty parlour where they had taken breakfast. "I hope to make it something of a tradition, to gather at Havers Hall for a Christmas house party."

"A charming idea, and you may count on my future attendance. If I am invited, that is," Marianne added.

"Of course you are, and in future I will be instructing Thomas to send the coach for you, too, so that any further issues with transportation will be avoided!" Ellen was quite indignant on Marianne's behalf, outraged that Arthur and Lavinia had denied her request to travel and effectively tried to turn her into an unpaid companion to their children.

"Thank you, my dear," Marianne said, squeezing Ellen's arm gratefully before letting go and taking her seat at the table.

Thomas came in to join them, and Ellen jumped to her feet to greet him, her face aglow. They shared a discreet kiss before taking their seats.

"How have you spent the morning, ladies?" Thomas asked as the footmen served them soup and bread, pouring cups of a cloudy apple cider which, served warm, was absolutely delicious. Marianne was unaccustomed to eating a proper meal at this time of day, but it was a pleasant idea, she found, and she was hungry from their exertions that morning.

Marianne sipped at her cup while Ellen expounded on their activities and Thomas listened with every appearance of interest, adding a few remarks now and then. He had apparently spent the morning with one of the tenant farmers, discussing that year's crop yields and what seeds would be planted at the next harvest.

Marianne could not remember her husband ever concerning himself with anything so mundane, so workmanlike. He had left all such decisions to his land steward, content merely to count the profits and apportion some of them to his investment advisers. Another portion had been assigned to Marianne, with new gowns produced for her by London's finest modistes every week. She had been nothing more to him than an ornament, something beautiful and expensive which nobody else could have. He had never encouraged her to take any part in the running of the household, though she was a viscount's daughter and had been well-trained in the management of a great house.

Helping Ellen today was the most fulfilling thing Marianne had been permitted to do in years, and she found herself hoping Ellen would keep wanting her input and advice throughout the house party.

This must be what it's like to have a brother and sister, Marianne thought as the meal went on and Thomas and Ellen included her happily in their chatter. Her brother had died fighting Napoleon when she was only thirteen, and he had been five years older, so she remembered him but little. Perhaps if he had lived, they could have been friends, at least.

She felt so very comfortable with Thomas and Ellen, confident she could tell them anything or ask for their help and have it freely given, without expectation of repayment. When Thomas offhandedly advised her he had sent two servants and a coach to collect her wardrobe from Cumbria and they should return before the house party began in earnest; Marianne was hard put to keep the tears from flowing.

It turned out you didn't need to ask, sometimes.

CHAPTER SIX

A WEEK LATER, MARIANNE felt as though she had been living at Havers Hall for half her life. On first name terms with every member of the (very extensive) staff, she now knew her way around the beautiful old house as well as Thomas and Ellen did. If she didn't quite recall the name of every Havers ancestor in the portrait gallery, well, they weren't *her* ancestors.

Marianne sat with Ellen in the large, beautifully-appointed front parlour where guests were usually received. The first guests for the house party were expected today, but at the moment since Thomas was out and about the estate it was just the two of them waiting, both settled in comfortable chairs by the fire with books in hand.

Reading was another joy Marianne had rediscovered. Creighton had all but forbidden it to her, not permitting her to purchase any books or join a lending library and refusing her access to his own library. Ellen, however, was a dedicated bookworm, as was Thomas, and they both liked to spend at least an hour or two a day comfortably ensconced with a book. Ellen had encouraged her to select anything she fancied from their eclectic collection, and Marianne had soon found herself enjoying that quiet hour spent between the pages, discovering the wondrous worlds which lived within the imagination.

The sound of hooves and carriage wheels caused both women to look up, and Marianne slipped a ribbon between the pages and closed her book regretfully.

"You can finish it later," Ellen said with a smile, obviously seeing her regret.

"I'm enjoying it very much, I must admit. Turning down two suitors! Elizabeth Bennet was lucky indeed to have a supportive father who did not make her marry Mr. Collins, but I do hope her mother does not find out she turned Mr. Darcy down as well."

Ellen laughed. "I will not spoil the plot for you, but I'm very glad you are enjoying it. I thought you would appreciate a story where the heroine gets the opportunity to say no - and to tell her unsuitable suitors precisely what she thinks of them!"

"Indeed, I do." Marianne sighed happily. "I shall be honest - the greatest pleasure I am deriving from it is the certain knowledge that Creighton would have flown into a rage at the mere suggestion I should be permitted to read it."

Ellen snickered. Over the last few days, they had become close enough that Marianne felt safe confiding in Ellen how much she had hated her husband, despised and feared him. There were some things about her marriage she doubted she would ever be able to talk about, but in a way, telling Ellen what she could had been cathartic. As they walked down the stairs to the front hall Marianne thought again how glad she was that Ellen had sat down beside her in the wallflowers' corner where Marianne had been hiding from her husband at the ball where they'd first met.

Allsopp was opening the doors, with two footmen at the ready to hurry down the steps and assist the guests from the carriage drawing to a stop. Four handsome bay horses drew a carriage of superior quality, obviously very new, but with no family crest upon the doors. *New money*, Marianne assessed. Not that she cared. Creighton's money was very old, and she despised every adult male member of that bloodline.

"The Alleynes," Ellen murmured as a footman opened the carriage door and a handsome woman in late middle age, wearing a serviceable gown under a heavy woollen cloak, stepped down with a welcoming smile.

"I don't think I know them." Marianne watched as a gentleman with a balding pate and a kindly face stepped down next.

"Sir Tobias and Lady Alleyne - Isabelle. Their daughter Leonora made her debut this autumn. She's a confirmed wallflower, but has the most beautiful singing voice; I will be begging her to entertain us in the evenings."

Leonora was obviously the young lady stepping down with a shy smile and a word of thanks for the footman assisting her. With mouse-brown hair, a round pink face, and a figure a little too plump for fashion, Marianne could see why the girl was a wallflower. She would be no competition for the beauties of the Ton.

"She looks sweet. I shall be glad to know her and her parents."

Ellen shot her a grateful look as the family ascended the steps to join them. They had been joined by a young man of about twenty years of age. Tall and thin, he had the same mouse-brown hair as Leonora.

"Welcome to Havers Hall," Ellen said.

"Lady Havers," Lady Alleyne said. "It is so good to see you again. Havers Hall is even more beautiful than I imagined. Please allow me to present our son, Joseph."

"A pleasure to meet you, Mr. Alleyne." Ellen offered her hand and Joseph bowed quite correctly over it. Marianne was very proud of Ellen then as her friend remembered the proper way to introduce persons of a lower rank to her; she turned to Marianne and said, "Lady Creighton, please allow me to introduce my friends Sir Tobias and Lady Alleyne, and their children Mr. and Miss Alleyne. Marianne, Lady Creighton," she turned back to the Alleynes, who bowed and curtseyed.

"It is a pleasure to meet any friend of Ellen's," Marianne said with a warm smile, offering her hand to Lady Alleyne, who looked a little overawed as she touched Marianne's fingers lightly. "I am delighted to make your acquaintances."

"Oh, we are most honoured to make your acquaintance, Lady Creighton!" Lady Alleyne gushed, her eyes taking in every detail of Marianne's appearance. "Leonora, do make your bows, girl. And Joseph!" She looked to her son, who was staring at Marianne as though he had suddenly glimpsed Paradise. "Oh... I believe I have forgot something in the carriage. Joseph!" Succeeding in obtaining his attention, she sent him back for a handkerchief, even though Marianne could clearly see one peeking from her sleeve, and carried on talking without missing a beat, commenting on everything from the state of the roads to the charms of the rustic inn where they had stayed the night before.

Introductions made and Lady Alleyne finally running out of steam on her commentary, Ellen ushered the Alleynes inside and directed waiting maids to escort her newly arrived guests to the suites she had allotted them.

"We should be delighted if you would join us for a light nuncheon at one o'clock?" Ellen invited, and Lady Alleyne accepted for the family, declaring they would wash up and be down directly.

"They seem nice," Marianne remarked as she and Ellen returned to the parlour.

"They are; I requested an introduction to Leonora after I heard her sing and was delighted with her. She looks a mousy little thing, but is very witty and clever. Sir Tobias invented a new type of ammunition during the war, for which he received his knighthood, and has invented any number of other clever things. I am always utterly fascinated by his conversation, when you can get him to talk."

Which might be a little bit trying when Lady Alleyne is present, Marianne surmised. The woman seemed rather on the chatty side, though nice enough.

They were just reaching for their books when the sound of another carriage's wheels had Ellen rising to her feet again.

"You need not come down, if you wish," she said. "I would not drag you up and down stairs all day, every time another guest arrives!"

"I will accompany you until Thomas gets back from his visit with the tenant," Marianne compromised. "After that, he can climb all those stairs with you!"

Ellen laughed. "I am always glad of your company," she said warmly, and they set off again.

The change in sound disturbed Alex, and he looked up from his book. The carriage wheels were crunching on gravel now, rather than the packed dirt of the road. The horses slowed, which told him they were likely arriving at Havers Hall.

Setting the book down on the seat, he peered out of the window, admiring the handsome larch trees lining the broad avenue leading up to a beautiful house built of golden Cotswold stone. Even on a dull, grey December day, the house had a warm and welcoming look.

"A pretty prospect," Alex murmured to himself, startling his valet awake from his snooze.

"Beg your pardon, m'lord?"

"I believe we are arrived, Simons."

"So soon? Why, we left Worcester just a little while ago!"

Alex hid a smile. Simons was in his late sixties and definitely nearing retirement. He was also fanatically loyal to Alex and extremely protective of his master's privacy, which was why Alex would never dream of going anywhere without him.

"It is nearing noon, Simons," Alex said when he had recovered his countenance. "We have made good time, though. The roads in this part of the country are certainly better maintained than those in the far north."

"Indeed." Simons peered out of the other window. "Very handsome grounds," he approved. "I count no less than four gardeners attending to that shrubbery yonder - in the depth of winter, too! Let us hope the house is equally well-cared for."

"And the stables." Alex turned his head to check on his horse, following behind the carriage, its lead line held by one of his grooms aside another horse. "Else Julius will likely wreak havoc."

"Don't know why you keep that animal," Simons grumbled. "Troublesome beast."

"He saved my life too many times to count on the Continent. I'll not abandon him now."

Simons humphed as the carriage finally drew to a halt. Two footmen immediately approached the door and opened it, placing a step for them to disembark. "Attentive, at least," Simons mumbled from his corner. "Go ahead, m'lord. I'll see to your things."

"Don't be lifting anything yourself," Alex said, receiving a narrow-eyed glare in return. Turning away to cover another smile, he stepped down from the carriage with a nod of thanks to the footmen and started up the steps to the Hall. Three steps up, he raised his gaze to the two women standing at the door and promptly stubbed his toe on the next step.

His only consolation, as he bit back a yelp of pain, was that Marianne looked far more shocked to see him than he was surprised to see her standing arm-in-arm with Ellen Havers. He had, after all, known she was going to be there, and from her expression she had not put together the Marquis of Glenkellie with Alexander Rotherhithe. When he had known her, he was only a distant relation, never expected to ascend to the title.

"My lord." The Countess of Havers curtseyed gracefully as he arrived at the top of the steps, and Marianne perforce followed suit, though she had blanched pale.

"Lady Havers." Alex bowed deep in return. "Lady Creighton."

"Oh, you are acquainted with Marianne? How silly of me; of course you are! With you not in London this year, I forgot you lived there for several years and know everyone." Ellen turned to Marianne with a friendly smile, placing her hand on Marianne's arm.

"It has been many years since Lady Creighton and I last met," Alex said after a full minute of awkward silence. "Indeed, she was then merely Miss Abingdon, daughter of a viscount, and I... nobody of consequence at all."

He had not thought it possible Marianne could turn any paler, but her skin took on the hue of ash, and she swayed a little. Kind, thoughtful Ellen noticed at once, of course, and urged her friend inside, back into the warmth.

Alex found himself delegated to the care of a very proper butler, who promptly escorted him to a handsome guest suite on the second floor with sweeping views across a valley to the west of the house, a winding river at the bottom, and thick woods on the hill beyond.

It was quite lovely, and he was still standing at the window admiring the vista when Simons arrived with four sturdy footmen carrying Alex's trunks. Simons looked quite in his element as he directed the men, and a moment later extended his sway to two more who arrived bearing jugs of hot water for Alex to wash.

"A nuncheon will be served at noon, my lord," one of the footmen advised, "and Lord Havers is expected back in time for it."

"Indeed," Alex murmured, "I believe I see him now." A horse had entered the picturesque view outside, cantering along the river to a crossing point. The rider was still a little too far away to make out his identity, but his coat and hat were clearly those of a gentleman. Perhaps a half-mile distant, the horse and rider would reach the house in no time at all, and therefore Alex should also waste little time in changing his clothes and washing off the dust of travel.

He wondered if Marianne would attend the nuncheon, or if she would cry off after obviously having been surprised by his arrival. Perhaps she would plead illness.

His jaw tightened as he turned away from the prospect beyond the window. She could not avoid him indefinitely, not at a house party expected to last a full fortnight.

Sooner rather than later, they would have the conversation which had been postponed for too many years - and he would have his answer as to why she had lied to his face and broken his youthful heart.

CHAPTER SEVEN

Claiming a sudden sick headache, Marianne retreated immediately to her rooms, grateful for Ellen's kindly disposition. She was quite certain Ellen suspected her illness coming upon her at the same time as the Marquis of Glenkellie's arrival was no coincidence, but Marianne was in no way ready to explain her prior connection with Alexander Rotherhithe.

Lying down, she allowed Jean to place a damp cloth over her brow and then pleaded to be left alone. She needed to think.

Jean retreated only as far as her dressing room, leaving the door cracked open so she would hear if Marianne called for her, but that was far enough. In silence and blissful solitude, Marianne tried to come up with a method by which she might somehow avoid being in a room with Alexander Rotherhithe for the next two weeks.

A headache was coming on in earnest as she tried to find a way out of her dilemma. If only she still had access to the Creighton fortune! But even if she wrote a letter to Arthur, she doubted he would send for her. And she could not possibly ask Ellen and Thomas to convey her back to Cumbria.

She had friends who would take her in - at least she hoped she did - but getting to them without funds was another matter. Running away was not an option open to her, even if her pride would permit it. Ellen would be convinced something dreadful had happened to her, besides, and that was no way for Marianne to repay Ellen's kindness.

Somehow, she was going to have to face Alexander and live with his contempt. She'd seen the disgust in his eyes as he looked at her. So far as he knew, she'd broken their secret engagement a mere three weeks after he sailed for Spain to marry another man: a much older, much wealthier, titled man.

It was a cruel twist of fate that Alexander was now both wealthier and better titled than her husband had ever been. If only her father had known! He might have let her 'throw herself away on a mere Mister' after all.

If the last eight years had taught her anything, it was that there was no use crying over spilt milk. Lying still and silent, Marianne reconciled herself to facing Alexander and being civil to him. She was no longer the naive girl he had cared for; she was a grown woman, married and widowed. She would not be intimidated by contemptuous stares, even though Alexander Rotherhithe had grown up into a very impressive man indeed.

Tall and slender as a young man, maturity and his years as a soldier had added muscle and breadth to that long frame. And the scar on his cheek only added to his dark, wickedly handsome looks as far as she was concerned.

Unconsciously, Marianne lifted her hand to her own cheek, wondering how exactly Alex had received the scar. Though it had faded to pink now, it must have been a terrible wound when he'd first received it, flaying his cheek open to the bone and barely missing his eye. It was hardly something she could ask him, especially as she planned to avoid being in his company as much as she could possibly manage!

The sound of carriage wheels outside again brought a smile to her face. With more than twenty guests to stay at the Hall and more coming from the local area each day for activities and dinners, surely there would be enough people around that she need never find herself alone with Alexander. She could hide behind a shield of politeness and sociability, much as she had hidden her feelings behind a polished social facade when Creighton paraded her around London as his trophy bride.

She could do this.

What choice did she have, after all?

The Earl of Havers grinned as Alex entered the drawing room. "Glenkellie. Glad you decided to come."

"So am I," Alex said honestly, shaking Thomas' offered hand. "Havers Hall is beautiful; my compliments on your home. My valet is in heaven with such facilities at his disposal."

"You can thank my predecessor for most of the Hall's amenities," Thomas admitted. "He liked his luxuries."

"It's not your predecessor who employs a veritable army of staff though, is it?" Alex raised his brows. As the owner of a large estate of his own, he knew the Hall was definitely overstaffed.

"I wanted to talk to you about that, actually. I'm thinking of starting a proper training academy, staffed by experienced mentors who are getting a little long in the tooth for heavy work but have a wealth of knowledge to pass on."

"For house servants?"

"For all kinds of skilled tradespersons. The current system of one apprentice per tradesman - and that's if they're willing to take one on - doesn't increase the supply of skilled workers, does it?"

"I suppose not," Alex conceded. "Where do I come in?"

"I'm looking for investors, of course." Thomas grinned irrepressibly.

"Naturally. Well, if you have a proposal, I'll take a look at it." Alex had no problem with the idea of going into business with Thomas; there were few people he could say that about, but the American earl had proved himself both financially astute and compassionate towards those of lesser consequence to himself.

"Do not start talking business now, Thomas." Ellen came up beside them, resting a hand on her husband's arm.

He placed his own hand over her fingers and gave her an apologetic smile. "Sorry, my love."

"You must let me introduce Lord Glenkellie to our other guests," she reproved gently. "Or are you already acquainted with the Alleynes, my lord?"

"I am not, but I should be honoured to meet any friends of yours, Lady Havers," Alex said gallantly. "I already know Lady Creighton, of course. Where is she, by the way?"

Ellen's glance was sharp. "Resting," she said a little curtly. "She was feeling unwell. Should she be recovered enough, she may rejoin us at dinner."

"I didn't know you were acquainted with Lady Creighton, Glenkellie," Thomas said, his expression surprised.

"It was a long time ago," Alex demurred. "I daresay I don't know the person she is now at all."

Had he ever known her? He had to wonder, even as one part of his mind remained focused on remaining polite as Ellen introduced him to the Alleyne family. Miss Alleyne looked quite overawed and said not a word, which at least meant she was unlikely to pursue him, though her mother positively fawned over him. He was used to that and tuned it out by thinking of Marianne, of the look on her face as she'd recognised him. He'd changed from the young boy she'd known when they were children playing together before he was sent away to school, even from the stripling lad she'd led on that fatal summer. He was grown up now, hardened by war and life.

Of course, she'd changed too. She'd been a lovely child, but at eighteen, she was the prettiest girl he'd ever seen -- fresh and beautiful as a sunrise. Every head had turned when Marianne Abingdon entered a room; she'd had every man in London panting after her.

Alex, a lowly lieutenant with no honorifics before his name, had never got close enough to speak a word to the perfect Miss Abingdon, despite their prior acquaintance. Not until the night when he'd stepped out of an overcrowded ballroom, head spinning from heat and one too many glasses of champagne, and walked through a garden in the darkness looking for somewhere to take a rest. On a stone bench beneath a weeping willow, Marianne Abingdon had been seated, her hands braced behind her, leaning back to gaze up at the sky.

Alex froze, shocked, a few steps away, wondering whether he should back away. Was she waiting for someone?

"I can't see the stars," she said after a few moments, making him jump.

"It's the smoke from the manufactories," Alex replied finally when she said nothing more, and she turned her head to look at him. Realising he stood in shadow beneath the trees, he moved forward, into the bright path of moonlight which stopped just short of her bench. "My apologies. I didn't mean to intrude on your privacy."

"That's quite all right. I was about to go back in anyway." Swinging her feet to the ground, she rose gracefully, the sway of her willowy body making his mouth grow dry. Miss Abingdon never wore fancy frills or lace or even strong patterns; she favoured simple white gowns which contrasted spectacularly with her chestnut-red hair and did little to conceal her lissome figure.

"Have we met?" she asked him quite directly.

He bowed, finding it difficult to speak in the face of her incredible beauty. "Not in many years, Miss Abingdon; you were a child when last I saw you and I daresay you do not remember me. Alexander Rotherhithe, at your service."

She tilted her head, examining his uniform, one long curl bobbing against her neck as she did so. "*Lieutenant* Rotherhithe?"

"Yes, my lady."

"And are you lately returned from the Continent or yet to be deployed?"

"Yet to be deployed, my lady," he answered, startled by the question. She seemed intelligent and informed, unlike the other debutantes - and older ladies - he'd met in London. "My regiment does not yet have orders."

"And do you look forward to the fighting, Mr. Rotherhithe?" She began to walk back towards the house, and he fell into step beside her without thinking.

"No."

"No?" She shot a sideways glance at him. "No dreams of glory on the battlefield, of winning the war for England?"

"Several of my friends have already perished on battlefields far from England's shores," he answered her frankly. "I'll consider myself fortunate if I live to see my home again."

"*Finally,*" she sighed, stopping and turning to look him fully in the face. "A young man with something more than sawdust between his ears!"

Alex couldn't help himself; he grinned. "My apologies, my lady, but I was just thinking something very similar about you."

Her laugh was softly musical. "You are forgiven, Lieutenant... if you will dance with me when we return to the ballroom. I am heartily tired of hearing endless plaudits and paeans to my beauty. Some sensible conversation would be most welcome."

He could not wish for anything more. Gallantly, he insisted she re-enter the house first and go to the ladies' retiring rooms to be seen before returning to the ballroom, while he went back in by a different door. The half-hour until he was face to face with her again, taking her hand to lead her into the dance, seemed the longest of his life. Somehow, he'd convinced himself she was merely amusing herself with him in the garden and had no interest in him at all.

So, when Marianne smiled up at him and said in a confidential tone, "How this last half-hour has dragged!" he felt an overwhelming relief.

"It always does, I find, when there is something one is desperately looking forward to. Conversely, I am sure the next ten minutes will pass in the merest winking of an eye."

She made a little moue and wrinkled her nose, nodding in agreement. "No doubt there is some department of mathematicians at Cambridge studying exactly that. Or philosophers, perhaps?"

"Possibly both, being Cambridge," Alex said dryly. "Though in my experience, there is more drinking and socialising done than actual studying."

"What a waste. I wish women were permitted to study at university." Marianne looked at him almost defiantly; he had the distinct impression she was testing him, watching to see what his reaction to such an inflammatory suggestion might be.

"I have no doubt that one day they will be able to," he said. "Though for the sake of my own gender, I hope they either have their own universities or segregated classes. There were distractions enough without the presence of the fairer sex for foolish young men to lose their common sense over."

Marianne laughed, and Alex thought he had passed her test. "I agree," she said. "Though the foolishness would not be entirely on the part of the young men, I think. Young ladies are equally susceptible to being distracted by a handsome face on a tall young man. Especially in a red coat."

Her eyes twinkled up at him, and he laughed, utterly enchanted by her. "May I call upon you?" he asked impulsively.

"Oh, please do," she answered enthusiastically, and his heart was lost.

CHAPTER EIGHT

Marianne wished, quite desperately, for the armour of a fine gown in which to clad herself to face Alex, but the servants Thomas had sent to Cumbria had not yet returned with her wardrobe. She had to content herself with the lavender silk gown she had worn every evening since her arrival at Havers Hall. At least Jean was doing a wonderful job in keeping it clean and pressed, ready for her to dress in each evening, but she was definitely coming to despise the colour.

Apparently divining that her mistress was self-conscious about only having the one evening gown, Jean had been producing different accessories every night to dress it up from some store of things somewhere in the Hall. Tonight she had a wide sash of golden silk, some gold ribbons for Marianne's hair, and a long string of creamy pearls.

"They're fakes, m'lady," Jean said the moment Marianne opened her mouth to protest she couldn't borrow valuable pearls from Ellen. "See, they don't even have a proper catch."

"Where did you find them?" Marianne inspected the pearls with interest. She'd never seen fake jewels before.

"Lady Havers has been cleaning out the attics," Jean admitted. "There's all sorts of things up there in old trunks: gowns which must be a hundred years old, bits and pieces of rusty armour, children's sewing samplers, and broken old toys. I don't think anything's been thrown away in the Hall since it was built."

"Quite likely," Marianne conceded, seating herself to let Jean put up her hair. "Is Lady Havers throwing it away, though?"

"Oh no; she don't believe in throwing things away much. Finds a use for near everything, she does. I asked if I could take a few bits and pieces to dress up your things a touch and she said I could take whatever I wanted." Jean beamed proudly. "These gold ribbons will look very well in your hair, m'lady, and the sash brightens the dress up a treat."

"They do," Marianne said warmly. "Thank you, Jean. You've been so thoughtful."

"Oh, I'm just doing my job, m'lady," the maid disclaimed, but she beamed brightly, and Marianne determined then and there she would give Jean at least one or two gowns once her wardrobe arrived. She did not have much in the way of money or trinkets, but the maid would be able to sell the gowns or pick them apart as she pleased. It was small enough repayment for the confidence the maid's ministrations gave her, enough to get her all the way to the foot of the grand stairs, where Allsopp bowed correctly to her before opening the door to the Oriental Parlour.

While Marianne had seen the room, they had not used it before. She assumed Ellen and Thomas had made the decision to remove here due to the increase in numbers. More guests had arrived, she saw as she entered, and this time she was familiar with the new arrivals.

"Lady Creighton!" Mrs. Pembroke almost fell over herself scurrying to Marianne's side, smiling widely. "It is so very good to see you again!"

"Amelia!" Marianne was genuinely delighted in her turn. Amelia Temple had made her debut at the same time as Marianne, and, as a notable heiress, had been a target for fortune hunters. Since Marianne had been targeted by rakes, the pair of them had discovered themselves hiding out in more than one retiring room together.

Amelia had been lucky enough to marry for love, however. While her parents had wanted her to catch a title, she had instead married a mere Mister: a country squire with a small but charming estate in Hampshire and a passion for horses. A passion Amelia shared.

Mr. Pembroke stood behind Amelia now, smiling broadly. Marianne felt unexpected tears prick at the back of her eyes. Creighton had not approved of her friendship with the Pembrokes and had forbidden her any contact beyond the briefest of polite interactions at social events they were all attending. Being able to express her delight at seeing Amelia again without fear of reprimand was a true pleasure.

"It is wonderful to see you." Impulsively, Marianne embraced her friend. "It has been an age since last I saw you. How do you know the Havers?"

"The earl purchased some horses from us. The sweetest mare for Lady Havers, and a top-grade stallion to improve the bloodlines of his tenants' plough horses. When he told Mr. Pembroke he did not plan to charge his tenants stud fees for the stallion's services, we knew he was someone we should very much like to know better." Amelia beamed. "And Lady Havers is just *delightful*."

"She most certainly is," Thomas agreed, joining them and making Amelia laugh. "I am glad you are already acquainted; it saves me the probable embarrassment of making a mess of the introductions."

Pembroke and Marianne joined in the laughter, and an atmosphere of general gaiety ensued as they began a lovely conversation. The Alleynes entered the room a few minutes later and were persuaded to join them, and then Ellen herself came in accompanied by a young man and woman Marianne did not know. Ellen introduced them as Viscount Thorpington and his sister, Lady Serena Thorpe.

The viscount was a plain-faced man of around thirty, with a stutter he concealed by speaking as little as possible. Lady Serena was around two and twenty by Marianne's estimation and handsome rather than conventionally pretty, tall and sturdy with a thick mane of black hair barely constrained by her pins. With an unfashionable tan, she looked to be the outdoorsy sort who would have no patience with the languid pace of high society life.

Marianne liked Lady Serena immediately, but she could see why she hadn't been a success in London. The Ton matrons wouldn't have approved of her at all, and her brother's speech issues would have made it difficult for him to make many friends too.

"The Marquis of Glenkellie," Allsopp announced from the door, and a hush fell over the room. Miss Leonora Alleyne squealed a little, hand over her mouth and her eyes wide.

Until her brother nudged her with a frown. "Hush, you goose."

"But a *marquis*!" Leonora whispered back.

Marianne gave her an indulgent smile. "I'll tell you a secret about marquises and dukes," she whispered to the younger girl. "They have to use the chamber pot just like the rest of us!"

Leonora promptly developed the giggles, and Lady Serena Thorpe, who was also close enough to overhear, gave a rather horselike snort before muffling her face in a handkerchief. Blue eyes sparkled as she glanced sideways at Marianne, and Marianne gave her a conspiratorial grin, inwardly thankful for the distraction which meant she didn't have to look at Alexander.

Of course, her reprieve was short-lived, as Ellen escorted Alexander around the room to make introductions. Leonora had edged closer to Marianne, obviously reassured by her apparent nonchalance, and she could hardly flee and leave the debutante alone.

"You are, of course, acquainted with Lady Creighton," Ellen said. Alexander nodded, his eyes cold as they met Marianne's. Instinctively, she looked down at the floor, even as she silently chastised herself for cowardice.

Marianne couldn't even meet his eyes, intently examining the pattern woven into the Turkish rug beneath their feet. Gritting his teeth and ordering himself to be patient, Alex forced a smile as Lady Havers presented a blushing debutante.

"Miss Alleyne." Bowing correctly over the girl's hand, Alex resigned himself to social niceties for the time being. He was acquainted with only one other of the guests -- Viscount Thorpington -- and for Thomas and Ellen's sake he must at least try to be agreeable. He would not for the world spoil their first house party, no matter how much he wanted to shake the truth out of Marianne.

He watched her from the corner of his eye all evening. As the highest-ranking lady present, she went into dinner on Thomas' arm and was seated at his right hand, at the other end of the table from where Alex, as the highest-ranking *gentleman* present, was seated at Ellen's right.

Young Mr. Alleyne was seated on Marianne's other side and watched her in wide-eyed awe, the kind which could well turn into infatuated puppy love, Alex thought grimly, determined to nip that in the bud if Marianne should take it into her head to break another young man's heart for her amusement. At least Thomas Havers was infatuated with his own wife and not likely to be susceptible to Marianne's charms, laugh and smile though she might.

Reluctantly, Alex had to admit Marianne was even lovelier now than she had been at eighteen; maturity had only refined her beauty. If he didn't already know how heartless she could be, he'd likely be crawling after her himself. As it was, he found it difficult to look away. Dressed in a muted lavender gown trimmed with gold ribbon, her auburn hair shone like fire, the perfection of her features outlined by the candlelight. Again and again her softly musical laugh came to his ear, and he only realised he was staring at her in utter absorption when Ellen Havers touched his hand lightly, making him start.

"My apologies, Lord Glenkellie. I was wondering if the soup is not to your liking?" Her brow was creased.

Looking down, Alexander saw he'd taken up his soup spoon in his hand and then failed to even taste from the dish in front of him. "I beg your pardon, my lady," he said contritely. "I was distracted."

"So I see," Ellen murmured, and her eyes flickered as she glanced to the other end of the table. "I do hope you will try it, but if there is anything you particularly wish to have prepared, I pray you will let us know."

Ashamed of his poor manners, Alexander tasted the soup and pronounced it excellent and resolved to pay closer attention to both his dinner and his dinner companions. Ellen had been carrying the entire conversation, with quiet Thorpington on her other side, and he should speak as well with Mrs. Pembroke on his other side. Turning to that lady now, he offered a smile, only to be met with an uncomfortably appraising stare.

"I daresay you do not remember me, my lord," Mrs. Pembroke said almost immediately, "but we have met before, though it was many years ago. Just before you went to the Continent with the army, I believe."

"Indeed?" Alex said, guarded. Mrs. Pembroke looked to be almost exactly Marianne's age, but had none of her mesmerising beauty. Instead, she was positively ordinary, with mid-brown hair, brown eyes, a slightly snub nose, and a round face. A quirky smile lent her expression character, however.

"Why, yes, though I was Miss Temple then, and you merely Lieutenant Rotherhithe. I think we were introduced at Lady Smithfield's garden party."

He still didn't recall the introduction, though he did remember with awful clarity sneaking off from that garden party for a clandestine meeting in a glade of trees with Marianne. A meeting where he'd kissed her for the first time and sworn his undying devotion.

"Ah," Alex said, feeling sweat break out under his collar.

"Yes, I think Lady Creighton, Miss Abingdon as she was then of course, introduced us." Mrs. Pembroke was watching him like a hawk.

She knows, Alex thought, his anger resurfacing. She and Marianne had been friends back then, had probably laughed over his infatuation. Had she egged Marianne on, urged her to agree to a secret engagement only to marry the wealthy Earl of Creighton a few weeks later?

"And have you and Lady Creighton remained close since?" he clipped out, reaching for his wine and draining it.

"Sadly, no. Her husband did not permit her to have friends."

Alex paused in the act of setting his glass down. "I beg your pardon?" he said, confused. "I never met the late Earl, but I heard stories of how he spoiled his wife, buying her more fashionable gowns and costly trinkets than any woman could want."

"If all a woman wanted were expensive baubles, indeed, Marianne was the luckiest woman in England," Mrs. Pembroke replied, and he heard the sarcasm in her voice. "Should she desire affection, respect, and the comfort of friendships, however, she was the veriest pauper."

That's what you get when you marry for mercenary motives, Alex wanted to snap back but forced himself to bite his tongue. Mrs. Pembroke was Marianne's partisan, which was useful information. He would ensure neither she nor her husband were available to intervene when he sought his private audience.

"I daresay being a rich widow will suit her a great deal better, in that case," he said caustically and nodded for the footman to top up his wine.

CHAPTER NINE

MARIANNE WAS ACUTELY AWARE of Alexander watching her. Her hand shook as she tried to eat, and her voice sounded high and thin to her ears -- her laugh forced and artificial. Thomas looked quizzically at her once or twice, obviously picking up on her distress, but she refused to acknowledge his silent query, instead picking up her wine and drinking.

By the end of the meal, she realised what a mistake that was, however, since an attentive footman had kept her glass filled and she was more than a little tipsy. When Ellen invited the ladies to the parlour, it was more than enough reason to make her excuses and retire to bed.

"I have become unaccustomed to wine," she said quite truthfully, "and it has brought on my headache again. Please forgive me for retiring early; I promise I shall be more sociable tomorrow."

"You are forgiven already, though we shall miss your company. Sleep well and feel better, dearest, and please do not hesitate to have Jean or another maid bring you anything you might wish for your relief."

Marianne felt guilty about deceiving Ellen, but she lost no time in hurrying up the stairs, nervous all the while that Alexander might choose to leave the other men to their brandy and port and come looking for her. What he might have to say to her after all this time she could not imagine, but she knew she did not want to hear whatever it was. Merely looking on his face, only grown more handsome with the passage of years, was painful, especially since she'd had to listen to Lady Alleyne eagerly quizzing Lord Havers about Alexander's marriage prospects. He would need to marry, and soon; marquisates required heirs, and undoubtedly he would be choosing from among London's latest crop of debutantes.

Perhaps he even had someone in mind already. Miss Alleyne was a sweet creature with a hefty dowry; perhaps she might suit him. Or Lady Serena Thorpe; she would look very well on Alexander's arm, and she had a strong character and a sense of humour too.

Marianne did not realise she was crying until she tripped, blinded by the tears in her eyes, and almost fell. Catching herself with a hand against the wall, she stumbled on until she found her room at last, pushing the door open with a sob of frustration when the knob stuck briefly.

"My lady!" Jean rose from where she had been seated by the fire mending a stocking, an expression of shock on her face as the sewing fell to the floor. "Are you unwell?"

"I feel sick," Marianne choked out, and Jean managed to get a pot under her nose just in time.

"That will teach me to drink too much wine," Marianne groaned a few minutes later, as Jean helped her to lie down and placed a cool, damp cloth over her brow. "Maybe my husband was right to insist I should only ever be permitted one glass."

"Well, it can be powerful stuff if you're not used to it," Jean agreed. "Especially if you don't eat nothin'."

Marianne's guilty silence made the maid sigh. But she hadn't been able to choke down more than a couple of spoonfuls of soup, not with the anger in Alexander's gaze scorching her from the other end of the table.

"I daresay you won't make the same mistake again, m'lady," Jean said, removing Marianne's slippers. "Let's get you comfortable for bed now, and I'll make a herbal tisane up for your head. A good night's sleep, and you'll be right as rain in the morning."

Privately, Marianne doubted she would sleep at all, but the tea Jean persuaded her to sip after helping her change into her night rail must have had some soothing herbs in it. Her eyelids soon began to feel heavy and she lay back against her pillows without complaint, allowing her eyes to close.

"That's it, m'lady," Jean encouraged softly, and Marianne heard her moving quietly about the room, setting things to rights and putting the noxious pot out for someone to take away and wash. "Sleep. You'll feel better in the morning."

Rejoining the ladies to discover Marianne had already retired infuriated Alexander to the point where he pleaded weariness from travelling and retired himself, ignoring Thomas' expression of disbelief. He was in no mood to be polite to anyone, and with no possible opportunity to corner Marianne tonight, he might as well retire rather than manage to offend one of the Havers' guests with his ill temper.

At the top of the stairs, he paused, considering briefly whether it might be worth trying to locate Marianne's room. His valet Simons would probably know exactly where everyone had been accommodated by now, and have opinions on whether Lady Havers had correctly placed them according to precedence, too. But asking Simons where he might find Lady Creighton's rooms and then going to look for the lady would create a scandal.

Alex did not care in the slightest if a scandal affected him, and Marianne deserved no consideration, but he would not see the Havers' first ever house party marred in such a way if he could help it. No, far better to bide his time and confront Marianne privately. One way or another, he would manage it.

And while he might not feel like company tonight, he had a good book to read, and undoubtedly Simons would be able to procure some of Havers' excellent brandy for him to drink while he did so.

Perhaps Simons might have some interesting gossip from belowstairs he could be convinced to share, as well. Marianne appeared to be well-settled here at Havers Hall; knowing how long she had been in residence and who was attending her could be useful information.

Making his way to the comfortable room he had been allotted on the second floor, Alex nodded to Simons as he entered. "I'm going to retire early, Simons; I'm in no mood for company."

"When are you ever, sir?" Simons rejoined smartly. "I took the liberty of obtaining some brandy for you." He indicated a decanter and glass sitting ready on the mantelpiece.

"In that case, you are forgiven for the snide remark on my social ineptitude." Alex threw himself into a seat by the fire.

"It's not your fault, sir," Simons said kindly. "The army didn't exactly provide you with many opportunities for civilised social interactions."

"Remind me again why I keep you around?" Alex asked dryly. For answer, Simons placed a glass of brandy into his hand, waved at his book placed ready for him on a table at his elbow, and indicated for him to lift his foot so Simons could start removing his boots. "Ah, yes. Of course. Because I couldn't do without you."

Simons gave a small smile and nodded before tugging his first boot off. "Did you enjoy your dinner, sir? I must say, the servants eat well here. I have rarely dined so heartily."

Embarrassed to admit he couldn't recall a single dish served that evening, Alex seized his opportunity gratefully. "Speaking of servants, Simons, who is attending Lady Creighton? I'm assuming she brought her own lady's maid, at least..."

"No, sir." Removing the other boot, Simons straightened up. "A maid named Jean has been assigned to her. A nice young woman and one not inclined to gossip about her mistress, even if it is only a temporary post for her. She was quite repressive when two of the other maids began to gossip about the unconventional manner in which the lady arrived."

"What unconventional manner?" Alex looked up.

"That I have not yet been able to discern, sir. So far, all I know is that she arrived a full week earlier than expected." Simons hesitated. "May I enquire as to your interest in Lady Creighton, sir?"

"No."

"Very good, sir. I shall see what further information I may glean tomorrow." Simons knew better than to press when Alex spoke in that flat tone; the valet removed himself, taking Alex's boots through to his adjoining chamber where he would polish them to a high shine.

Left alone, Alex brooded over his brandy, staring into the glowing coals of the fire. Why had Marianne come a week early, and under what 'unconventional' circumstances? Perhaps she had been escorted by a man, he thought suddenly; that would certainly be unconventional. She was a very beautiful widow, after all. Perhaps a lover had brought her here - cast her off? That would explain her arrival a week early, too.

By the time he'd finished the second glass of brandy, Alex had convinced himself his theory was correct. Which meant Marianne would be looking for a new lover.

A wolfish smile curved his lips as he drained the glass and set it down.

That was a role he'd gladly fulfil for her.

Waking early the following morning, Alex could not remember the last time he'd slept so well. He could not recall the last time he retired so early, either; perhaps that had something to do with getting a good night's sleep, he acknowledged with a grin at his own foolishness.

Simons bustled about importantly, bringing him riding clothes and suggesting he might wish to go for an early ride, as rain was expected later in the day.

"Julius will want a run," Alex agreed, accepting his gloves from the valet. "And I daresay breakfast will be served throughout the morning, at the convenience of guests?"

"Indeed, sir. There is a morning room in the east wing where a buffet will be kept ready until noon, I understand. Any of the house servants can escort you there."

Perhaps I'll catch Marianne there. Or perhaps she will be out riding herself, Alex thought as he headed downstairs and out to the stables, spying a lady by the mounting-block being assisted up onto a pretty dappled grey mare. As he drew closer, however, he recognised Ellen, Thomas waiting to one side, already mounted on a leggy chestnut gelding.

"Good morning!" Ellen called to him in delight as she saw him approaching. "It is a lovely morning for a ride; would you care to accompany us?"

Alex acknowledged it was indeed a fine morning, especially for December; the air was crisp and clear, frost riming the grass, a light breeze blowing. He could hardly decline the invitation, either, though he remarked that his horse would want a good gallop.

"We can certainly accommodate that," Thomas said cheerfully. "I saw your stallion; he's a fine fellow. John Pembroke will want to talk with you about maybe taking him down to Hampshire to visit with some of his mares, I daresay."

"No doubt Julius would enjoy the holiday." Alex winked cheekily at Ellen. "Especially with eager ladies waiting for him at the end of the trip!"

Ellen blushed a little. "Outrageous, Glenkellie," she reproved. "Apparently you have forgotten, in your years in the army, that *true* ladies do not appreciate bawdy talk." Her eyes twinkled, though, and Alex knew she'd already forgiven him.

"Forgive me, Lady Havers." He executed a bow to her. "I shall endeavour to remember my manners."

Julius was led out then by a groom; Alex greeted the stallion fondly. The former warhorse nickered and pushed his head against Alex's chest, sending him back an involuntary step with the force of the shove.

"Behave, you great fool," Alex said in amusement, fishing an apple from his pocket.

"He truly is beautiful," Ellen commented as Alex mounted up and rode up alongside her. "What colour is that called? His body looks almost blue, though his head and legs are black."

"That's what it's called, blue roan. It's a trick of the light; the individual hairs are black and white, evenly mixed." Alex patted Julius' thickly muscled neck affectionately. "He carried me through many a battle in Belgium and France. Frankly, he's earned a quiet retirement and as many lady friends as he wishes."

"If only all England's valiant soldiers could have the same," Ellen said sincerely.

Touched, Alex bowed to her again. Julius frisked a few steps as his weight shifted, and Alex reined him in firmly. "Not yet, boy. Not yet."

"Not so fast as a thoroughbred, I daresay, but unstoppable once you get him up to speed?" Thomas asked, reining in his chestnut on Ellen's other side.

"Quite so," Alex agreed. "Thoroughbreds are all very well for racing a mile or so, but for long campaigns and cavalry charges, a stronger and more durable mount is needed. Your mount might win a short race, but over the course of a day, Julius would run him into the ground." He patted the charger's proudly arched neck.

"Well, we haven't a day," Thomas said, "so we can only challenge you to a short race, I'm afraid."

"We?" Alex queried.

"Watch out for Lady Havers. She races to win," Thomas said with a grin, and was proved right a moment later as Ellen urged her mare to a gallop, shouting over her shoulder;

"Last one to the split oak is a rotten egg!"

Laughing, Alex gave Julius his head, and in the stallion's joyous gallop of freedom forgot for a little while all the concerns which plagued his restless mind.

CHAPTER TEN

FROM THE WINDOWS OF the morning room, Marianne watched the three riders as they crossed the landscape into the distance. Alexander was unmistakable, tall and straight-backed; he sat his horse with the ease of someone who had lived in his saddle for nearly months on end.

"Lady Creighton."

A voice behind her made her turn, and she smiled as she saw Amelia Pembroke. "Please, call me Marianne," she invited. "I would as soon forget my marriage ever happened, to tell the truth."

They were alone save for a couple of servants bustling about the buffet laid out on a dresser at the other end of the room, and Amelia gave her a sympathetic look. "I can quite understand why you feel that way. I never told you before, but I was so very shocked when your engagement was announced and then you married Creighton so quickly. I thought you'd have eloped with Rotherhithe before marrying a man you didn't love."

"Had he given me the opportunity, I would have done." Marianne looked back to the window. The three horses were galloping now, dwindling to specks before fading from sight entirely, swallowed up by a fold of the landscape. "He had already taken ship for the Peninsula, though. The marriage had no doubt already taken place by the time he could even have heard of the engagement, but I still hoped he would do something - come back and challenge Creighton, shoot him dead, and take me away."

Amelia said nothing, but her look spoke volumes of understanding.

"I was very young."

"Do you hold any hopes in Rotherhithe - excuse me, he's Glenkellie now, of course - any hopes in his direction?"

"Good Lord, no." Marianne willed her hand not to shake as she cut her toast into small, delicate triangles. "It's long in the past, Amelia. We've both moved on.

He needs a wealthy, well-connected young bride to produce the next generation of Rotherhithes, not a barren, penniless widow who is all but cast-off from her family!"

"I beg your pardon." Amelia blinked.

Marianne realised the other woman did not know of her full situation. "I'm afraid Creighton was as callous in death as in life," she said ruefully, before quietly explaining the terms of her dower and her falling-out with Arthur and Lavinia.

"How *appalling*," Amelia said with her usual forthrightness once Marianne had finished speaking. "I don't know which I find worse; that Creighton treated you so shabbily, or that his heir seeks to compound the insult!"

Marianne smiled wryly but said nothing as a footman set a steaming teapot and a polished wooden tea caddy down on the table between them. Opening the caddy, she spooned some of the fragrant leaves into the hot water.

"Considering my husband's character, I should have expected no less," she said finally.

"Well, I think it's disgraceful," Amelia said hotly, "and I should like to extend an invitation to you to come to Hampshire and live with us, as my dear friend, once you are weary of London. You need only send a note and I will have Pembroke come himself with a carriage to collect you." She smiled a little shyly and leaned close. "I shall want a friend close by in a few months," she confided. "I am enceinte, at last."

"That is wonderful news and a most generous offer," Marianne said warmly. "I thank you for it most gratefully. I daresay I will spend the rest of my days imposing on all of my friends in turn until they are all heartily sick of me darkening their doors!"

"Never," Amelia disclaimed loyally.

They were joined then by the Alleyne family, who came in en masse, exclaiming excitedly over how well they had slept, how comfortable the beds were, and how attentive the servants of Havers Hall. Marianne was not displeased to end her conversation with Amelia; discussing her future prospects was a depressing topic indeed, though it warmed her heart to know she still had Amelia's friendship.

They were still at table when the riders returned; Amelia's husband had met up with the others out in the countryside somewhere and the four entered the morning room with broad smiles and hearty appetites. Tempted to excuse herself immediately, Marianne realised it would be rather rude as Mr. Pembroke took a seat by his wife and leaned across her to bid Marianne a cheerful good morning.

"It is indeed, sir. Did you enjoy your ride?"

"Very much so; it is a fine morning for a hearty gallop!" He turned to his wife. "I am sorry you were not feeling well enough to join me, my heart," he said in an undertone, picking up Amelia's hand and kissing it. "Are you quite recovered?"

"I am." Amelia smiled fondly at him. "I have invited Marianne to come stay with us, perhaps in early May or so."

"Ah." Mr. Pembroke glanced at Marianne before looking back at his wife, who nodded at him. "Lady Creighton would be most welcome at any time, but if you would like her with you then, I shall move heaven and earth to find some way to persuade her."

"Such efforts will not be required, I promise." Marianne gave him a warm smile. "I am delighted to accept the invitation and may only need to impose on you for some transport, probably from London."

"It is not the slightest imposition, my lady." Pembroke dismissed her concerns with a wave of his hand.

Boots on the polished wooden floorboards heralded another arrival, and Marianne glanced up, only to meet Alexander's eyes as he entered the room.

All the breath seemed to rush out of her body, and she clenched her hands tightly in her lap, digging her nails into her palms.

Steady. Steady, she ordered herself. *It was all a long time ago. Alexander is nothing to you now.*

The pounding of her heart told her she was a liar - and the look of scorn on Alexander's face told her there was nothing she could do to turn back the clock, anyway. Lowering her eyes, she tried to take slow, calming breaths and regain her composure.

Breakfast seemed to last an unconscionably long time, with everyone chatting sociably about their plans for the day. Though he'd worked up a hearty appetite on the ride, the food tasted like ashes to Alexander.

Look at her, sitting among decent folk, acting as though she hasn't a care in the world.

Every smile Marianne offered someone else was like a dagger to his chest. Viscount Thorpington -- seated directly opposite her -- kept missing his mouth with his fork as he gazed at her, utterly entranced, and young Joseph Alleyne was no better. Alexander's hand clenched around his knife until his knuckles turned white; he didn't notice how tight his grip was until his fingers began to cramp painfully.

"Is your beefsteak not to your liking, Glenkellie?" Thomas enquired politely as Alex dropped the knife with a clatter.

"It's fine, thank you," Alex muttered, massaging his stiff fingers. "A sudden cramp, that's all."

Thomas gave him a sceptical look before his gaze moved to where Marianne sat. "Is that what you call it?"

A dull flush suffused Alex's cheeks, and he looked away, picking his knife up and cutting into his steak again. Fortunately, Sir Tobias Alleyne leaned over to speak to Thomas, saving Alex from having to think up a response to the awkward question.

The ladies began to drift away from the table first, Ellen announcing they would be gathering in the front parlour to converse. "I regret I have no particular activities planned for the day, but with the rest of the guests due to arrive I must be here to welcome them," she said, and at once the other ladies were declaring they should like nothing better than a relaxing morning sitting in a comfortable parlour with a warm fire.

"Don't forget your embroidery, dear," Lady Alleyne told her daughter, who sighed.

Marianne sympathised. She had always found embroidery deadly dull, too.

"Or, should you prefer, Havers Hall has a wonderful library," she said confidingly to Miss Alleyne, "which they are most obliging about letting one browse. Would you like to come and look for something to read with me?"

"Very much!" Miss Alleyne said quickly before her mother could object, and Lady Serena promptly asked if she might come with them too.

Marianne led the two young women off to the library, smiling with pleasure as they both exclaimed over the collection. Leaving them considering the choices from a shelf of novels, she browsed deeper into the stacks, recalling she had spied some travelogues last time she'd visited the room. Stories of exotic lands and adventurous (if probably highly fictionalised) derring-do might be just the thing to keep her mind occupied.

Sitting down by a window to leaf through a book about an intrepid Englishwoman's travels in the Orient, Marianne lost track of time. She did not hear the two younger women come to the end of the row of shelves where she sat, did not see the amused glance they traded before they stole away quietly, leaving her quite alone.

She almost jumped out of her skin, however, when a deep voice said, "So *this* is where you're hiding."

Marianne clenched her hands on the book, trying to hide their trembling, and took a moment to compose herself before she looked up. "Hiding? Hardly," she said, trying to keep her tone light and amused. "I'm sure I was quite clear in declaring my intentions to come here. After all, it wasn't difficult for you to find me, was it, Lord Glenkellie?"

Alexander stared down at her, his eyes hard and cold like chips of ice. A tic made the scar on his cheek jump like a living thing as he clenched his jaw. Then he surprised her again by taking a seat on the window seat next to her. Too close! His thigh, muscled and hard beneath tight nankeen breeches, was pressed against hers through the woollen fabric of her skirt. Marianne tried to shift away, but she'd used the wall at her side to lean on when she took her seat and there was little room to move.

"We need to talk," he said finally.

"About what?" She genuinely couldn't imagine what he might have to say to her after all these years.

"I know what you're up to."

Marianne blinked, confused, and stopped trying to avoid Alexander's eyes. "I beg your pardon?"

"Leave Thorpington and Alleyne out of your schemes. They're nice young men who deserve better than to have their hearts broken just because you're bored."

"I *beg* your pardon!" Her mouth fell open with shock.

"You're repeating yourself, and you understand me quite well, I believe. Don't encourage those two boys - or you'll answer to me."

Marianne's cheeks flushed with sudden fury. "I do not care for your insinuations, and allow me to make it clear that I do not answer to you on any matter, Lord Glenkellie!" She made to rise, but a powerful hand closed around her wrist, holding her firmly in place.

"Not so fast, *my lady*." His deep voice put a mocking inflection on her title.

"Unhand me at once!" Her gaze spat daggers as she looked at him, her voice cold and brittle as ice. She was still surprised when he let go, his large fingers opening quickly.

"Your pardon," he mumbled, flushing darkly. "I did not intend - I have never laid hand to a woman in anger before."

"Then what in heaven's name possessed you to do so now?" Marianne demanded, her anger fuelling her tongue. "What have I ever done to you, that you should raise your hand to *me*?"

Alexander stared at her in silence.

Disgusted, she rose and tried to leave, but as she reached the end of the row of shelves, four quiet words stopped her in her tracks.

"You broke my heart."

CHAPTER ELEVEN

Alexander didn't know what made him confess it. Perhaps it had been Marianne's righteous fury after he grabbed her arm, tried to force her to listen. He was still shocked at himself for behaving that way; he had been raised to believe violence against women was utterly beyond the bounds of civilised behaviour.

Marianne's face, as she turned slowly back to face him, was hard to read. She had paled from her flushed rage, but he realised when she spoke that she was no less furious.

"Do you think I *willingly* married a man more than three times my age?"

Opening his mouth to answer in the affirmative, Alex saw the glint of fury in her eyes and closed it again.

"Oh, I see." Her voice softened and she looked truly disappointed. "You never knew me at all, did you? What did you think, that I led you on for my own amusement and then married the richest man I could catch?"

He couldn't remember feeling so small since he was six years old and summoned to meet his grandfather for the first time. The old man's piercing gaze had stripped him to the bone, and he felt just as flayed by the beautiful woman standing in front of him now, shaking her head slowly over his arrogant assumptions.

To his surprise, Marianne returned to sit down, though she moved to the other side of the window seat, leaving a full foot of space between them.

"For the sake of the affection we once held each other in," she said, "and because I believe you when you say I broke your heart, I pray you will allow me to tell you the truth about my marriage to Creighton."

Childishly, he didn't want to hear it. If she was telling the truth, it meant his resentment of her, his unkind thoughts about her, were wrong. That *he* was wrong. It was an unpalatable truth for any man to bear, but particularly one of his rank and his military experience. In all those years on the battlefield, his instincts had never led him astray.

Yet now...

"I hated him." Marianne's voice made him look up at her and meet her eyes despite the guilt which made him want to study his shoes. If she was willing to speak of something which must have been deeply unpleasant, at the very least he owed her the courtesy of listening.

"From the moment I first laid eyes on Creighton, I disliked him. He licked his lips when he spoke to me and looked on me as though I was a possession to be owned -- a *thing* he coveted. My father's gambling debts made it an easy transaction; I was bought and sold with the handing over of a bank draft. Like a piece of livestock, or an ornamental vase."

Alex felt vaguely sick. Marianne showed no emotion as she spoke, merely reciting the facts in a flat tone, despite the ugliness of the circumstances she related.

"Though I objected vociferously when the engagement announcement appeared in the newspapers, my opinion was not sought and my consent not required. Indeed, when I was summoned to my father's study one morning, I had not the slightest idea I was going to my own wedding. With a special licence in hand and a vicar who did not care in the slightest about my protestations, Creighton made me his countess."

"Marianne," Alex said, his voice choked, "please... don't."

"Don't what?" Her tone hardened, her fists clenching against her skirts. "Don't tell you about the way two of his footmen forced me upstairs to a guest suite *in my own home* where my husband of but half an hour raped me with my father's full approval? Of the many indignities I suffered at Creighton's hands -- most particularly every month when my courses came and he would beat me for not conceiving an heir?" There were tears in her eyes, and Alexander hated himself for making her relive the memories which obviously caused her such pain.

"Christ!" Alex couldn't sit still any longer. Erupting to his feet, he ran his hands through his hair, tugging at the strands in frustration. If Creighton was still alive, he'd challenge and shoot the bastard himself, but there was no one to take his anger out on. "Marianne... I'm sorry. I'm sorry that happened to you, and I'm sorry I thought the worst of you. *I'm sorry.*"

She sat with her hands folded primly in her lap now, gazing up at him from her blue eyes, looking like a perfect porcelain doll. Finally she inclined her head a fraction. "We have both been at war," she said, her voice softer now. One delicate hand lifted, gesturing towards his face. "You merely have a more visible scar than I, that is all."

An hour ago, he would have become enraged hearing anyone claim any experience might compare to the battles he had endured, the awful things he had seen in the war. Now, after hearing Marianne's unemotional recital, he knew better. "At least I had days and even weeks where there was quiet and peace," he said. "Your battles were fought every night."

"And every day," she corrected with a twisted little smile. "I was constantly on display as Creighton's most prized possession, you see, and God help me if I allowed so much as a hair to stray out of place."

His voice shook as he asked "Did he beat you?" He had no right to the answer and said so immediately after he asked the question, wishing he could take it back. He'd made her suffer enough reliving the memories she'd already shared with him.

"Yes," she answered him anyway. "Until his arm grew too weak to inflict enough pain to make me cry out, that is. Or perhaps, I just became inured to it." She paused a moment, looking down at her hands. Her fingers clenched again, knuckles showing white, before she deliberately relaxed them to smooth at her skirt. "At any rate, then he had one of his footmen take over, a burly fellow named Stokes who seemed to take a good deal of pleasure in making me scream."

Alex's fists clenched. He could at least hunt down Stokes and make him see the error of his ways - but Marianne leaned forward and placed her hand on one of his.

"Revenge should have no bounds, as the Bard said, and I took mine. Perhaps making a false accusation is a sin, but I took a good deal of pleasure in accusing Stokes of stealing some of Creighton's belongings a few days after his death. The Earl of Havers was of much assistance to me in having him taken up for theft. He has been transported to Botany Bay, I understand."

"That's not enough punishment," Alex growled.

"It is enough for me." Marianne looked surprisingly serene as she lifted her hand from his and sat back against the window. "Creighton is dead. He no longer has the power to harm me."

"Yet you still bear his name; does that not grieve you?"

"Of course it does." She smiled wryly. "It is why I encourage my friends to call me Marianne, and why I seek to make friends with new people as quickly as possible. I would far rather throw out propriety and go only by my first name; if I could, I would never hear the name of Creighton again."

"You could remarry?" Alex suggested, suddenly wondering what her opinion was on the subject.

She laughed, throaty and full. "You jest! Willingly put myself once again under the power of a man who can do whatever he wishes to me and never suffer the slightest consequence for it? No thank you." Standing, she smoothed her skirts.

"Thank you for hearing me out, Lord Glenkellie. I once held you in a good deal of affection, and though you had every right to despise me for jilting you without warning, it grieved me to discover you held such a low opinion of me. I hope you understand me a little better now."

"You have held up a mirror and shown me the ugliness in my own soul," Alex said, "and I hope you will call me Alexander or merely Glenkellie, and permit me the use of your given name should we again have occasion to converse privately. In any case, I vow the name your husband inflicted on you against your will shall never pass my lips again in your hearing; henceforth in public you shall be *Lady Marianne* to me."

"I am not entitled to that, I'm afraid. I am only a viscount's daughter, after all."

Alex found a small smile despite his inner turmoil, hoping to amuse her with his next remark. "One benefit of being a marquis, I have found, is that very few people dare to correct you. I need only declare I am confusing you with the current Countess and you will soon find half London is giving you the honorary elevation."

Her lips twitched, and he thought she might, indeed, be slightly amused. "As you please, Glenkellie. I learned well the advantages of high rank in setting trends among the *Ton*. If you wish to use yours to my benefit, I shall not protest."

"It's the least I can do." He executed a deep bow, far deeper than mere courtesy called for. "If I may be of service in any other way, I hope you will not hesitate to call on me."

"Thank you." She curtseyed in return, and then said, "It is possible I may take you up on that offer, Glenkellie."

"It would be my honour to assist, Lady Marianne."

Inclining her head, she turned and walked away, leaving Alex pacing, furious with himself. What a pig he'd been, making assumptions of the basest kind with not the slightest evidence to support them! And what poor Marianne had suffered! Watching her leave, the skirts of her plain dark grey woollen gown swaying slightly as she moved, he realised she was almost certainly wearing such a plain garment to avoid attracting the attention of men. Perhaps, because of the way Creighton had demanded she display herself, garbed in the finest gowns and jewels -- always a perfect fashion plate -- wearing such a dowdy dress now was a form of rebellion.

Eventually, his anger at himself cooled somewhat, Alex left the library and proceeded downstairs.

"Lord Glenkellie." The butler, Allsopp, intercepted him in the front hall. "May I direct you anywhere? The other gentlemen are in the billiard room."

"Thank you, Allsopp," he said gruffly, "but I am in no mood for company. I might take a walk down to the stables, see that my horse is behaving himself for the grooms here."

"Very good, my lord," Allsopp said, unruffled. "Allow me to fetch your hat and greatcoat."

Impatient with the delay, Alex nonetheless stayed long enough to don the coat and hat which were swiftly produced. It was getting cold outside, and he thought the forecasted rain was likely to begin soon. Walking briskly to the stables, the chill air helped to cool the rage still boiling in his blood. By the time he found Julius settled in a large, comfortable stable with knee-deep straw to lie down in, a manger full of hay, and a bucket full of fresh water, he felt almost normal again. Rubbing the stallion's ears, he murmured nonsense to him and was glad the sensitive horse did not pick up on his mood.

The Havers stable is exceptional, Alex noted as he looked around at contented horses in their stalls and stable lads busily polishing tack or scrubbing out used feed buckets. He need have no concerns for his horses here.

A coach rolled into the yard as he exited the stable, and he sighed.

"More new arrivals? Who are these?" he asked the head stableman, who came out to look.

"Oh no, not this coach, my lord. This is the one m'lord Havers sent to Cumbria to collect the Lady Creighton's belongings."

"I beg your pardon?" Alex said, startled, but the man had already hurried away, going to take the heads of the lead pair.

That made no sense. *Why hadn't Marianne travelled with her belongings? Why would Thomas have had to send for them?* Perhaps this was the 'odd circumstances' surrounding her arrival Simons had heard about. Alex determined immediately to set his valet to further investigation. He'd learned his lesson; he would make no further assumptions about Marianne without being in full possession of the facts, he was determined.

CHAPTER TWELVE

Heart still beating fast as she hurried away from the library, Marianne paused at the parlour door for only a moment before turning away and stealing up the stairs. Allsopp pretended not to see her as she scurried past him, and she shot the butler a grateful look, knowing the apparently crusty exterior hid a kindly heart. He would disclaim knowledge of her to anyone who enquired, she was sure, though she would hardly be difficult to find.

Her rooms were empty when she entered, Jean obviously gone on some errand; not that Marianne cared. Right now, she wanted nothing more than quiet and solitude to think over the astonishing conversation she'd just had with Alexander. He'd obviously thought the worst of her, which was truly disheartening. But then, if she really had broken his heart all those years ago, she supposed he had a right to feel angry. *The most surprising thing*, Marianne mused as she curled up in the comfortable chair by the fire, kicked off her slippers, and tucked her feet under her, *was Alexander's evident fury when I told him of my ill-treatment at Creighton's hands. It's almost as though he still had feelings for me.* She had more than half-expected him not to believe her, to accuse her of making it up. Yet he had listened without interruption, and shown a deepening expression of commingled horror and rage. He really had believed her.

Marianne could not quite comprehend what on earth had made her tell Alexander so much. She had never spoken the whole sordid truth of her marriage to anyone, had never planned to do so. But when she'd discovered he'd thought she had married Creighton willingly, the words had just exploded out of her, and once she started she could not seem to stop until she had told him the worst of it, though not all -- that would have taken days to tell, and she did not care to dwell on all she had suffered. Now she felt curiously light, as though by sharing the truth with Alexander she had purged a dark weight from herself.

Knowing Alexander condemned Creighton's actions was pleasing, too, even if his suggestion she should marry again was laughable. Men who showed a kindly face to the outside world could be monsters behind closed doors. Creighton had publicly played a devoted husband who enjoyed showering his beautiful young wife with gifts, after all. How many ladies had expressed their envy, declared their wishes their husbands would be so generous?

Shuddering at the memory of the price she had paid for Creighton's generosity, Marianne's attention was caught by the sound of hooves on the avenue's gravel-strewn path. Peering from her window, she saw a plain dark coach rolling towards the house, drawn by four horses, unmatched in colour but sturdy-looking. Wondering if she should go down to join Ellen and the others to greet new arrivals, she frowned curiously as the coach did not pull up at the front door but rolled around the side of the house beyond her view. *Perhaps some servants arriving ahead of their employers*, she finally guessed, and returned to her own musings.

Alexander's offer of help if she should ever require it had been most unexpected, but not unwelcome. Indeed, she honestly believed he meant it - and considering the uncertainty of her future, it was very possible she might one day need to ask for his aid in some manner. She would never ask for financial assistance, of course, but as a marquis there were many things he could accomplish with a mere snap of his fingers which would be utterly impossible for her to achieve.

Hasty footsteps outside her room made her look up, and then the door opened.

"Oh, my lady!" Startled, Jean dropped a curtsey. "I do beg your pardon; I thought you were downstairs with the other ladies!"

"It's quite all right, Jean. I just wanted a little solitude, that's all. No, no, it's fine; do come on in." Slipping her feet from under her, Marianne rose.

"It's just that your things have arrived, my lady!" Jean exclaimed. "All the way from Cumbria!"

"Oh!" Startled, Marianne watched as Jean moved aside to let a small procession of footmen enter the room, carrying an apparently unending stream of trunks and packages. "Did they bring my *whole* wardrobe?" she asked, startled.

"M'lord earl sent his steward with instructions that anything which belonged to you must be packed," one of the footmen said with a bow in her direction. "Sent all Lady Havers' trunks for them to be packed in, too."

"Oh, how very kind!" It would have been of no consequence to Thomas, she knew, but it made all the difference to her to have all her own gowns and belongings. Two more maids arrived to help Jean unpack as the footmen filed out. Marianne joined her maids, exclaiming with pleasure as the trunks were thrown open to reveal silks and satins in every colour of the rainbow.

"There's a letter in this one, m'lady," one of the maids said, holding out a folded paper.

Marianne accepted it, moving out of the way as the maids continued unpacking efficiently. *Aunt Marianne* was written on the outside in a neat, precise hand, and she smiled as she returned to her chair to open it. Either Diana or Clarissa, she guessed, had written the note.

Dear Aunt Marianne, I kept the two dresses you gave to me, and Clarissa entirely filled her work box with ribbons and lace, but we helped the maids pack everything else from your wardrobe. Papa did not want to open his strongbox to hand over the jewels the previous Earl bought you, but Lord Havers' steward was quite insistent. We hope you are well and enjoying your stay with your friends, and anticipate eagerly seeing you in London in the New Year, as Mama and Papa are now quite resigned the whole family must go. With love, Diana.

A knock on the door startled Marianne, and Jean left the unpacking to scurry over and open it. "M'lord Havers for you, my lady," she advised Marianne.

"Thank you." Tucking the note into her pocket, Marianne pushed her feet into her slippers and went to the door.

"My lady." Thomas tipped his head respectfully. "I wonder if you would grant me a few minutes of your time, in my study perhaps?"

"Certainly." Nodding to Jean to continue her work, Marianne left her room and fell into step beside Thomas. He offered his arm gallantly, and she accepted with a smile.

"Jean is taking care of you to your satisfaction, I hope?" he enquired.

"She is by far the most obliging maid I have ever had," Marianne said honestly, "and I would be delighted to write her an excellent reference at any time in the future, should she require one."

"I think she was rather hoping you might offer her a permanent post in your service, actually," Thomas remarked.

"I only wish I could. Without a fixed income, though, I fear I could not guarantee her long-term employment, and it would be quite unfair to Jean."

"As to that," Thomas said as they turned to descend the stairs together, "I have some ideas which could provide quite a nice little income for you, with a small initial investment."

"Yet I have no money to invest, Thomas!" She cast a despairing look up at him. "Have you forgotten already how I arrived on your doorstep? Surely not, since your men have just returned from collecting the belongings I was unable to bring with me, for which I cannot thank you enough!"

Thomas made a negating gesture. “Do not think on it. You befriended Ellen in London when she was a wallflower, and I can never sufficiently express to you my gratitude for that kindness.”

"I have never been more glad of the impulse which drove me to speak to her that night,” Marianne insisted, “for I have found the sister I always wished I had.”

"She says the same of you, and I consider you my own sister as well,” Thomas said, “which is why I am happy to perform any service within my power.”

They had arrived at the study, and Thomas opened the door to usher Marianne inside. A large wooden box was sitting in the middle of the desk, a sheaf of paper beside it.

"Please.” Thomas showed Marianne to a chair, and she sat down, looking curiously at Thomas as he gathered the papers up. “Apparently, your late husband kept records of all the jewellery pieces he purchased for you.”

"Well, yes, but I understood they were all estate property and had now passed to the new Lady Creighton,” Marianne said, startled.

"Had he recorded the purchases differently, perhaps they might have, but when his solicitors visited the bank while probating the estate, the jewels were each stored with the purchase receipts, copies of which you see here.” Thomas offered her the sheaf of papers. “Each of them has a handwritten note at the bottom which reads, ‘Purchased for Marianne’.”

Even the sight of her former husband’s handwriting, large and spiky, the pen almost stabbing through the page, sent a shiver down Marianne’s spine. She glanced only at the top sheet before asking, “I don’t understand what that means, I’m sorry. Surely if they were purchased with Creighton money, they still belong to the estate?”

"Under the law, they belong to you. I suspected such was the case; on the last occasion I spoke with the former Earl, he showed me a pearl brooch he had ordered for you, and I saw the receipt with that exact note on it. When I wrote to the current Earl requesting he send your belongings back with my men, I noted it would be simpler for him to send the jewels with my steward rather than me having to contact his solicitors to request their return on your behalf.”

She remembered that pearl brooch. Creighton had given it to her the day before Thomas and Ellen’s wedding and all but commanded her to wear it. An ugly, gaudy thing guaranteed to draw the eye, she had done her best to conceal it by pinning it at her waist rather than to her bosom. She half-thought it had been Creighton’s anger over her defiance, small as it had been, which had led to his fatal apoplexy, though it could have been any number of small transgressions on her part. She’d been enjoying herself that day, after all.

"I don't want it," she said instinctively as Thomas handed her a small iron key and nodded towards the chest.

"The brooch?"

"Any of it." Putting the key down on the desk, Marianne shook her head. "This is the only jewellery I have ever cared to wear." She reached to her throat, where a simple silver cross hung on a fine chain. "It was my mother's, the only thing I have left of her. My father sold her other jewels to fund his gambling, but this wasn't worth enough for him to bother with. Creighton never permitted me to wear it; now that I have the choice, I would as soon not wear anything else."

"Quite understandable," Thomas said kindly. "In which case, why not consider selling them? Some of these pieces are worth a considerable sum, you know."

"They are?" Marianne had never thought on it. Creighton had never permitted her to see bills or receipts for anything; her accounts were all sent directly to him.

"Certainly according to these. Three hundred and seventy-five pounds for a ruby necklace and ear bobs, for example."

Marianne frowned. "A ruby necklace? I never had a ruby necklace."

"Purchased from Garrard's a few days before his passing. It's possible he never got the chance to present it to you." Picking up the key she had rejected, Thomas opened the box, checked a number on one of the papers, and took out a flat jewel case with a number written in chalk on the lid.

"Ugh," Marianne grumbled when Thomas opened the box. The necklace was gaudy in the extreme, the ear bobs heavy-looking. "I would have hated to wear that."

"Well, if I were going to spend several hundred pounds at Garrard's, I don't think that's what I'd have chosen," Thomas said diplomatically.

Reaching out to close the box, Marianne shook her head. "Even if he had better taste, I should still not wish to wear jewels he chose for me. At least I was permitted to choose my own gowns, even if they always had to be in the first stare of fashion. These... were a demonstration of his power over me, nothing more. I don't want them."

"So let us arrange to sell them," Thomas said practically. "If we are able to achieve prices even half what Creighton paid, you will have a nice little nest egg. Look on it as a proper widow's jointure, if you will."

"I shall indeed," she decided, pleased at the notion of disposing of the jewels and gaining a measure of financial independence at the same time. "Would you assist me with the sale, Thomas? I would not know where to begin."

"Neither do I, but I will investigate on your behalf how to achieve the best prices, I promise you."

"Perhaps Lord Glenkellie might assist?" she offered tentatively, knowing Alexander knew far more people in London than Thomas.

Thomas gave her a curious look. "I was under the impression you and Glenkellie weren't on the best of terms," he said cautiously.

"A misunderstanding," Marianne prevaricated, "and one which is now in the past. I believe he would be amenable to providing some contacts, at least."

"Then I shall ask his assistance. In the meantime, would you like me to have the box placed in your room?"

"No," she said immediately. "Just... lock it up somewhere safe, if you please."

"Whatever you wish."

She blessed Thomas for not asking any more questions. He had a very good idea how miserable her marriage had been, she suspected, though she had shared far fewer details with him and Ellen than with Alexander.

Instead, he only replaced the ruby necklace in the box, locked it up again, and handed her a single sheet of paper, saying that was the complete inventory of the box's contents. Written by his steward, it had been countersigned by Arthur, certifying all the jewels belonged to her, Marianne, and were not the property of the Creighton estate. There were far more than she'd realised, and the total at the bottom of the sheet made her eyes pop. Thomas was quite right; if they were able to achieve prices even half the new sale value of the jewels, financial independence truly would be within her grasp.

CHAPTER THIRTEEN

THE JEWELS COULD BE the answer to my money problems, Marianne thought as she folded the paper and put it in her pocket alongside Diana's note. Climbing the stairs to return to her room, she mused on the possibilities. She would be able to offer Jean a position. She could buy a cottage somewhere for the two of them, but retiring to a country cottage didn't appeal. Better to invest the money, with Thomas' advice, and stick with her original plan of spending most of the year staying with friends. At least she would be able to pay her own way now without being entirely dependent on the generosity of others, which was a huge relief.

"My lady." Jean turned to her, face aglow, when Marianne re-entered her room. "I have never seen such gowns!"

The maid was holding a gown in her hands, one Marianne vaguely recalled ordering and not yet wearing. Made of a dark emerald silk, it had delicate gold embroidery all over the bodice and around the hem and cuffs.

"Such *fabric*," Jean said almost reverently. "It isn't even crushed!"

"That's good silk for you," Marianne said with a nod. "I'd forgotten how beautiful this was." Fingering the sleeve, she asked, "Shall I wear it tonight, do you think?"

"Oh, yes!" Jean cried enthusiastically. "I cannot imagine any colour better suited to you, my lady; you will be the focus of all eyes!"

"You flatter me, but I am also convinced." Marianne hesitated before saying, "I know you already helped me dress once today, Jean, but now that my better gowns are here I believe I should like to change out of the one I am wearing. I've been rotating the same two gowns for almost a fortnight now."

"Of course, my lady." Reverently laying the emerald silk on the bed, Jean hurried into the dressing room, where the other two maids were still unpacking trunks and hanging gowns. "How about this one, my lady?"

The gown was wool instead of silk, but a fine, soft lambswool dyed to a lovely shade of gentian blue-violet. Beautifully cut, Marianne recalled it to be both warm and comfortable to wear.

"Perfect," she said, pleased by Jean's choice, and stood still to let her maid help with her buttons.

Changed into a fine gown, Marianne began to feel a little of her old confidence returning. She had always moved with ease among the highest of high society, she recalled, uncaring of what any of them thought of her. Their opinions had no power to harm her, after all, and facing very real threats every day of her marriage had inured her to petty insult. Her apparent fearlessness had made her surprisingly popular among the highest sticklers, including the patronesses at Almack's.

Recalling how she had faced down a Russian princess and any number of duchesses, countesses, and more without fear made Marianne smile as she smoothed her hands over her skirts. Her fine gowns were just as much armour as any medieval knight's plate and shield.

"Oh, you've something in your pocket, my lady." Jean held out the folded sheets of paper she'd discovered in the pocket of the discarded gown. "Would you like them with you, or should I put them in the writing-desk?"

Thinking she should write a letter to Diana thanking her and telling her the expected date of the Havers party's arrival in London, Marianne nodded. "In the writing-desk, thank you, Jean."

"Very good, my lady. What shoes will you wear?"

"Oh, these slippers will be fine." Marianne glanced down at the tan kidskin slippers she had been wearing all morning. Jean looked a little disapproving, but Marianne was unmoved. She'd brought those slippers with her because they were her favourites, snug and comfortable on her feet. It wasn't as though anyone would see more than the tips of her toes below her gown's long skirt.

Garbed in a fresh, high-quality gown, Marianne studied herself in the mirror. *No more hiding out in my room*, she decided. Now that she had made her peace with Alexander, there was nobody else whose opinion she cared for - save Thomas and Ellen, of course, but she already knew she had their loyal support.

"I'm going down to join the rest of the company, Jean," she advised the maid, who was putting her letters in the pretty little writing-desk by one of the windows.

"Very good, my lady. I'll make sure Anne and Polly put all your things away just so." Jean puffed up a little with pride. "We'll spend the afternoon pressing wrinkles out of everything."

"You needn't do it all in one day," Marianne said, amused and touched by Jean's dedication. "Have the emerald silk ready for tonight and select another day dress for tomorrow, and the rest can wait."

"Never put off until tomorrow what you can do today, my ma always says," Jean answered with a smile. "You just leave it all to me, my lady."

Shaking her head, Marianne left Jean to her work and headed back downstairs. Arriving in the front hall as Ellen came out of the front parlour, she smiled at her friend. "I do apologise for abandoning you!"

"No apologies are needed; I heard your wardrobe had arrived! And indeed, I see it. What a beautiful dress!"

Preening a little, feeling happy to be wearing colours again, Marianne swished her skirts a little. "Isn't it pretty? Madame Fallou made it for me; do you know her shop?"

"I'm afraid not."

"I shall have to take you there when we get to London. She would love to dress you."

"Oh, but I have enough gowns already," Ellen disclaimed.

Laughing, Marianne linked her arm through her friend's. "Ellen, my dearest girl. You can *never* have too many gowns!"

Three more groups of guests arrived during the day, completing the roster of those who were to stay at Havers Hall for the house party. They crowded into the house, despite its large size, disturbing the equilibrium and Alexander's peace of mind. Unable to avoid company as he might have in his own home, he forced himself to be sociable with the other gentlemen Thomas had invited, and was agreeably surprised. To a man, they were sensible and intelligent, with conversation which did not bore him to tears. For the first time since leaving the army, Alex found himself among company which did not irritate him.

At least, when he was among the gentlemen. While the ladies were obviously intelligent too, almost all of them seemed to be inspecting him rather as though he were a horse they planned to put to stud; more than once he overheard comments about his fine legs and excellent teeth. Lady Alleyne was all but throwing Miss Alleyne at his head, and though Lady Serena Thorpe was too well-bred to make a spectacle of herself, she still made sure to put herself in situations where he was unable to avoid her entirely.

The one woman he would actually have liked to spend time with was no longer avoiding him, but she did not seem to have a particular desire for his company, either. Wearing the brightly coloured, beautifully tailored gowns from her newly delivered wardrobe, Marianne drew the eye everywhere she went.

Including his.

Especially his.

Alexander almost swallowed his tongue when she sailed into the drawing room that evening wearing the most beautiful green gown, her hair a mass of auburn curls atop her head. From the corner of his eye, he saw Viscount Thorpington drop his glass of sherry, gaping open-mouthed at the vision before him.

Mr. Alleyne was a little less gauche and quick to hurry to Marianne's side, but her glance at the younger man was nothing more than tolerant and amused, Alex saw now. His jealousy had blinded him before, but an evening spent watching Marianne gently fend off both Alleyne and Thorpington made it clear his accusation of her leading them on had been both unfounded and insulting. She gave neither of them the slightest encouragement; indeed, Alexander had cause to be grateful to her when she steered Thorpington in Miss Alleyne's direction, encouraging him to escort her into dinner.

Hoping to be seated beside Marianne at dinner, Alex was disappointed to find himself between Mrs. Pembroke and one of the new arrivals, a Miss Florence Wilson, who had arrived today with her twin sister Miss Fiona and their parents. A pleasant-looking girl if no great beauty, she was apparently too overwhelmed to speak at all, to him or even to kindly Sir Tobias Alleyne, seated on her other side.

Mrs. Pembroke was friendly enough, though she watched him with wary eyes, and his knowledge that she and Marianne were close kept him from paying too much attention to Marianne during the meal. He was still very aware of her at every moment. Seated on the other side of the table and two places down, it was easy enough for him to watch her surreptitiously, admire the way the candlelight gleamed on her fiery curls, drink in her low, musical laugh as she conversed comfortably with Mr. Wilson and Mr. Pembroke.

Even telling himself he was wasting his time, that Marianne had no interest in marrying again and he respected her too much to settle for anything less than marriage, he could not make himself look away. He should be trying to draw Miss Wilson out of her shell, discover what Ellen had seen in the girl, or maybe responding to Lady Serena's frequent smiles, or taking the many opportunities Lady Alleyne offered to get to know her daughter.

None of them appealed to him in the slightest. Marianne drew him to her like gravity: a force as inexorable as it was invisible.

"I believe you have an admirer in Lord Glenkellie," Mr. Pembroke murmured to Marianne as the dessert course was served. "But then, if I were not quite so in love with Amelia, I am sure I should join the ranks of your admirers as well," he added when she said nothing. "I do not doubt she has already pressed you to share the secret of your modiste."

Marianne smiled and chose to respond only to his latter remarks. "I hope Amelia will not put too much strain on your pocketbook."

"At least you've only your wife to spend on, Pembroke," Mr. Wilson grunted. "With twin daughters out at the same time, I swear my banker flinches every time I come to call! Ribbons and bonnets and new dancing slippers every week and I don't know what all."

"You will miss them when they are no longer in your house, I think," Marianne said wisely. Mr. Wilson was a crusty type with a heart of gold, she could already tell. His gaze softened whenever he looked on his wife or either of his daughters.

"Hm," Mr. Wilson muttered, but he nodded. "Have to be a special young man to win either of my girls. Shouldn't like them to be too far apart too. Very close, they are."

"They are quite identical. Tell me, do you insist they wear different colours so you can tell them apart?" Marianne teased gently.

"Oh, Mrs. Wilson and I always know. We make them do it to save other folks from embarrassment." Mr. Wilson give her a sly smile.

She laughed. Across the table, she caught Alexander's eye for the twentieth time and looked away hastily, a slight flush rising to her cheeks. Why *was* he looking at her so much? She had thought all was settled between them after their conversation that morning!

Though some of the men chose to linger in the dining room after dinner, the younger ones of the party chose to accompany the ladies back to the drawing room, where Mrs. Wilson pressed her daughters to perform for the company.

Alexander had chosen to accompany the ladies to Marianne's surprise; the previous evening he had lingered over port and cigars for quite some time. Tonight, he took a seat and accepted a cup of tea with every appearance of delight.

The Misses Wilson expressed reluctance, and Marianne sighed inwardly as their mother insisted. Why did some mothers press their daughters to exhibit in public constantly? She hoped the girls were not too uncomfortable. Finally they exchanged glances and moved to the pianoforte together, where they made a pretty picture in their pastel gowns, Florence in peach and Fiona in pale green.

Expecting an average performance, Marianne shot straight upright in her seat as Florence began to play. She was an exceptionally accomplished musician, true feeling showing through in her playing. Then Fiona began to sing, and all conversation in the room stopped as her voice soared.

Alexander appeared quite spellbound by the music, and Marianne found sudden envy welling in her breast. She had never shown any particular aptitude for music, plunking her way through required lessons in the pianoforte until her father decided to save the expense. It was the rare one of his economies she had not resented.

Now, watching Alexander's rapt face, she wished she had persevered. Perhaps if she had only practised harder - but no, her music teacher had only ever damned her with faint praise. Alexander would never have looked at her like that.

The enjoyment she had taken in the evening gone, Marianne sat back in her chair and sipped her tea. *It should not matter in the slightest if Alexander took pleasure in the playing and singing of two nice young ladies*, she tried to tell herself.

"You must get up next, Leonora!" a voice hissed behind her. Lady Alleyne, Marianne surmised. "'Tis obvious Lord Glenkellie has a fondness for music!"

"After this performance, I should sound like a cat caterwauling," Miss Alleyne replied softly.

Marianne hid her smile in her teacup. Miss Alleyne was no fool.

"I tell you, he is looking for a wife. If you do not put yourself in front of him, some other girl will be his marchioness!" Lady Alleyne snapped. Though she kept her voice low, Marianne's hearing was excellent and she heard every word quite clearly.

Miss Alleyne made no reply, and Marianne found herself examining Alexander's expression again as the Wilson sisters' spectacular performance drew to a close. He rose to applaud with the rest of the gentlemen, the reception a little more raucous than would be considered proper in London salons. But with an earl and a marquis leading the applause, who would reproach them?

Florence Wilson retreated back into her shell after the performance, taking a seat close to her mother, but Fiona preened as praise was heaped on her for her singing. Marianne added her compliments to the general praise, but a tiny ember of jealousy burned in her chest as Alexander kissed the girl's hand and declared she had the voice of an angel.

It is wrong for me to be envious, Marianne tried to tell herself firmly. She should be pleased Alexander planned to marry; he deserved happiness, after all. And he could do far worse than choosing one of the young ladies at Havers Hall; Ellen was an excellent judge of character.

So why did she feel absolutely miserable watching Miss Fiona Wilson smiling up at Alexander?

CHAPTER FOURTEEN

"A VERY PLEASANT WAY to spend an evening, wasn't it, Glenkellie?"

"Excuse me?" Jolted from his thoughts, Alexander turned to find Viscount Thorpington addressing him.

"Yesterday evening. I very much enjoyed it."

"So did I," Alex agreed. He'd been happily surprised, in truth; he couldn't recall the last time he'd enjoyed himself so much. The only small cloud had been Marianne's quiet mood; she had contributed little to the conversation after dinner and he had missed the bright wit and pertinent observations she always brought to any gathering. He could only assume it was his presence which had inhibited her; several times he had glanced up to find her eyes on him and her delicate brows creased in a frown.

"Miss Alleyne is rather lovely," Thorpington said, his tone almost questioning.

"A nice young lady," Alex agreed, his thoughts full of Marianne, but then he spotted the way the younger man's face fell. *Ah, so that was the way the wind blew.* "Very sweet," he added. "I understand her dowry is quite substantial, if you are considering her, Thorpington. Unexceptionable family, all things considered. Sir Tobias is very well thought of at the War Office, even if his wife is a little... well, I hesitate to say encroaching, but she is certainly ambitious."

Thorpington's smile was wry. "Lady Alleyne has nothing on my mother."

"Mine either." Alex smiled back, and companionable silence fell between them as they walked on. Thomas had organised a pheasant shoot for this morning, but Alex and Thorpington had so far not found a single bird, although they kept hearing shots in the distance. Perhaps the others were having better luck.

"So, uh," Thorpington said hesitantly after a while. "Leonora... Miss Alleyne, I mean..."

"The field is yours, Thorpington. Better jump in quick before the lady has her head turned by all the swains who will undoubtedly fall at her feet in London, though." Alexander gave him a nod, though the viscount certainly didn't need his permission.

"Thank you for your advice," Thorpington said with a grin. "But you're really not interested...?"

"As I said, she's a lovely girl. The important word being *girl*. No offence, but girls of Miss Alleyne's age seem very young to me."

"You're hardly in your dotage!"

Alex thumbed the scar on his cheek. "War ages a man," he said finally. "I spent too many years fighting, and sometimes it feels as though I aged five years for every one I was away from England. Miss Alleyne is scarcely out of the schoolroom - as is your sister, no offence intended."

"None taken. She has no ambitions in your direction, I assure you. Rather attached to an old school chum of mine, you see."

"Ah." Alex nodded sagely. "Thanks for the warning. Appreciate it. I'm sure I could fall violently in love with her if given the opportunity."

Thorpington laughed at his obviously disingenuous remark, then pointed. "Look there!"

They were both far too late raising their guns to get the bird, and Alex sighed as he lowered his. "Pathetic. It's a good thing I'm not dependent on my marksmanship for my dinner any more."

"Any more?" Thorpington asked.

"Spain," Alex said, without offering any further explanation, and thankfully the younger man didn't press.

Giving up, they turned and walked back towards the Hall. The house was in sight when Thorpington spoke again. "Are the gossips wrong, then? You aren't looking for a wife?"

"No, I am," Alex admitted. "I wasn't expected to come into the title, but now that I have... well, the next heir after me isn't someone you'd want in charge of anything, much less a marquisate responsible for the livelihoods of thousands. He'd gamble the estate bankrupt within a month."

"So you need a wife to get an heir, but the debutantes are all too young for your tastes?" Thorpington summed up.

"Precisely."

"It's Lady Creighton, then?"

Alex tripped over his feet and almost measured his length on the grass, would have if not for Thorpington's hand thrust quickly under his elbow. "*What* did you say?" he stuttered, regaining his balance.

"Lady Creighton?" Thorpington's brow furrowed. "I mean... everyone's talking about the way you look at her. And her marriage was notoriously unhappy, but she's widowed now and perfectly respectable, unless you have doubts because she didn't give Creighton any children..."

"Oh dear God, please stop talking. And to think, I thought you were quiet!" Alex pressed a hand to his brow.

Thorpington flushed. "Only in the presence of ladies," he muttered. "They make me feel foolish."

"Ladies make fools of us all," Alex said dryly. "Especially if we are foolish enough to repeat gossip associated with them." He gave Thorpington a stern look. "Please don't mention Lady Creighton's name in any such gossip again."

"Yes, my lord." Thorpington had turned bright red with embarrassment. "I do beg your pardon, my lord."

Too much in turmoil to do more than nod acknowledgement, Alex strode back up the steps into the house, handing off his gun to Simons, who was waiting in the hall for him. "No luck today," he said shortly in response to the valet's querying expression.

"A shame, m'lord. If you would come into the boot room?"

He'd been about to storm off up the stairs but stopped in his tracks at the question. This wasn't his house, and it would be unpardonably rude to leave mud all over Havers Hall's pristine floors. Even if Thomas did employ an army of servants to keep them that way.

The other gentlemen had returned to the house - carrying quite a few birds between them, confound it - by the time Alex had his boots off. Unfortunately, he could not think of a graceful way to evade Thomas' invitation to join the others in the billiard room once he had cleaned up. Simons had wash water and a change of clothes ready in his room, and he was soon ready to proceed downstairs.

"Excuse me, Lord Glenkellie," Allsopp intercepted him in the front hall. "A letter just arrived for you." A silver tray was presented.

Alex frowned as he picked up the sealed letter. "Oh God, it's from my mother," he said in dismay, inspecting the impression in the wax seal.

"That bad?" Thomas asked, descending the stairs behind him.

Breaking the seal, Alex grimaced. "Probably."

"Step into my study to read it, if you like." Thomas gestured.

Alex accepted the invitation, sinking into a chair by the window to peer at his mother's script, so flamboyantly looped and embellished it was barely readable.

My Dear Alexander,

I am quite downcast not to find you in London.

"Christ, she's in London!"

Thomas, flicking through some papers on his desk, suppressed a snort at Alex's dismayed tone. Alex ignored him and kept reading.

I planned to spend some time with you before I depart for Italy in April. When you return to Town, we can begin your hunt for a bride. There seems quite a promising crop of debutantes this year; even though some of them are spending Christmas in the country, I have already seen a couple who would suit you. Do write to let me know when to expect you,

Your loving

Mother

"Damn!" Alex said, and then decided that was not nearly strong enough an exclamation. He let loose a stream of curses which made Thomas' eyes widen.

"Glenkellie! What in heaven's name has happened?"

"I'm going to have to go to London." Tossing the letter onto the fire in disgust, Alex shook his head. "My mother will have an announcement of my engagement in the newspapers by week's end otherwise."

"Engagement to *whom*?" Thomas asked in complete confusion.

"Whoever she decides will suit me best." Alex grimaced. "My mother is a force of nature, I'm afraid. Leaving her unsupervised in London is asking for trouble. She didn't have nearly such a wide circle of acquaintance at Glenkellie to aid and abet her mischief, you see, and she's quite capable of selecting a bride for me and telling me about it after she's already arranged things with the girl's family. I'm afraid I will have to go, if only to avoid being sued for breach of a promise she might make on my behalf."

"Of course, but we shall miss your company. Stay another night, at least; it's already noon, and by the time you're packed up it will be nearly dark. Leave at first light."

Thomas was right, of course. With a beleaguered sigh, Alex nodded his thanks. "I'm sorry to disrupt your plans - and I truly do regret having to leave your house party. I haven't enjoyed myself so much in a long time."

"That's good to hear, and we will miss your company. I'm glad you are staying tonight, at least; you can make your own apologies to Ellen. She would be most displeased if you skulked out without so much as a goodbye."

"I should not dare." Alex managed a smile. "I'll return to my rooms, if you don't mind, and start Simons on the packing. I'll rejoin you before dinner."

"Of course. Let Allsopp know if there's anything you need?"

"Thank you," Alex said.

Thomas nodded, heading towards the door before pausing as though struck by a sudden thought. "Actually - since you are headed for London, I wonder if I might ask your assistance with something?"

"Whatever I can do for you, you need only ask," Alex answered sincerely.

"Technically, it's not for me. Marianne - Lady Creighton - has some jewellery she wishes to sell, purchased for her by her late husband. I offered to assist her in the disposal of it for a fair price, but I wouldn't know where to start, apart from taking it back to the jewellers where it was purchased. Do you think you might be able to help?"

"My mother certainly would, even if I couldn't," Alex said wryly. "She has ever been fond of baubles."

Thomas laughed, taking a key from his pocket and unlocking a cupboard before removing a good-sized wooden box and placing it on the desk. "They all have provenance, which is how Marianne comes to be in possession of them. Creighton noted that they were hers specifically, rather than property of the Creighton estate. Even so, my agent had to practically wrest them from the new Earl. Tight-fisted type."

Glancing through the sheaf of receipts Thomas handed him, Alex nodded. "I see. And Mari - Lady Creighton doesn't want to keep any of them?"

"I suspect she can't stand the sight of them. Besides, she needs the funds; Creighton left her no dower income at all and the new Earl would apparently prefer to keep her beholden to him. Wants her as an unpaid companion to his wife and daughters."

Disgusted at hearing of this further insult to Marianne's dignity, Alex made a face. "Anything I can do to help, of course. Would you like me to only make enquiries, or to accept sales if I think I've achieved the best price for a piece?"

"Use your discretion. Marianne has barely a penny to her name and won't accept money from me or Ellen - yes, we've both tried. Do you know, her nieces pooled what they had and gave it to her so she could buy a ticket on the stage to get here? She *walked* the last part of the way." Thomas was clearly outraged on Marianne's behalf, and Alexander found his own fury rising again. "I will never understand why people don't treat family decently, especially when they have more than enough wealth to go around! My predecessor was just as bad; refused even to acknowledge Ellen as his distant cousin and turned her out with nowhere to go when her parents passed away!"

"Easy." Alex put a hand out to touch Thomas' arm lightly. "You and Ellen are doing God's work, believe in that. Marianne is lucky to have such supportive friends."

"I note you call her Marianne as well," Thomas said with a canny sideways glance. "Yet you have only known her a few days."

"I knew her much better many years ago. Wanted to marry her, in fact. Her father had other ideas."

"And now?"

"I beg your pardon?" Alex blinked.

"What's stopping you now? She's a respectable widow, and you're looking for a wife."

"She's not looking for a husband, that's what. Stop matchmaking, Thomas. You're dreadful at it."

Thomas laughed. "It was worth a try. I think the two of you would suit, as it happens. She's not intimidated by you, and you... well, you don't need a wealthy wife."

"I admit I have heard worse reasons for matching two people together. Undoubtedly, my mother's choices will be worse, much worse, so thank you for at least considering how the match might benefit both of us." Alex smiled, to show Thomas he was not offended. "Still, I think Marianne would value my friendship far more than the other, so please don't encourage any speculation." Picking up the wooden box and tucking the key Thomas offered into his waistcoat pocket, he vowed, "I will achieve the best prices I can for her jewels. A true friend would do no less."

CHAPTER FIFTEEN

London, Mid-January

"Aunt Marianne!"

Marianne barely held in her laughter as Diana and Clarissa made to throw themselves on her, before remembering at the last minute they were young ladies now and meant to act with decorum. They almost tripped over themselves, clutching at each other for support. The girls stumbled to a halt, straightened up, and made graceful curtseys, though the effect was rather ruined by what had preceded them.

Lavinia, seated by the fire in the drawing room of the Creighton townhouse, rolled her eyes to the heavens. "Girls!" she said in disgust. "Restrain yourselves, please! This is not the country! What if Marianne's friend Lady Havers had accompanied her?"

"She did," Ellen said with a smile, stepping into the room behind Marianne. "Do forgive your butler for not introducing us, Lady Creighton. I'm afraid he was dealing with a matter related to one of your younger daughters. Something about a stray dog?"

Lavinia's mouth tightened, but she rose to her feet. "It is a pleasure to meet you at last, Lady Havers. May I present my daughters, Lady Diana and Lady Clarissa."

"I am delighted to meet you all," Ellen said with one of her disarmingly friendly smiles. "But please, do not let us be formal with each other; Marianne has told me so much about you I feel I know you all already. You must call me Ellen, and I shall call you Lavinia."

"I… well… of course." Lavinia looked rather as though she would prefer it otherwise, but the Havers earldom was a very old and wealthy one even if the current title holder was an American upstart and Ellen only the daughter of a country parson. Ellen Havers was also widely known to be on excellent terms with at least two of the patronesses of Almack's, which made her someone Lavinia dared not offend.

"Wonderful! Let us sit down and have a coze and get to know each other."

Marianne watched with amusement as Ellen took the seat immediately beside Lavinia. The formerly shy parson's daughter had become quite an impressive lady in the last year, confident in her position and her influence.

"Would you ring for tea, Clarissa?" Marianne requested, as Lavinia appeared slightly lost. Clarissa hurried to pull the bell, and then the two girls made a point of drawing Marianne to a sofa rather distant from where Ellen held their mother's attention captive.

"How long have you been in London?" Marianne asked. "We only arrived yesterday, and Ellen sent one of her footmen out directly to determine if the knocker was on your door; I was so pleased to hear it was."

"One week tomorrow," Diana reported. "And we have already visited a museum and a library and spent two whole days on Bond Street being fitted for new gowns."

Clarissa made a face at the latter. "I was never so bored in my life, nor stuck so many times with pins."

"Because you would not stop fidgeting," Diana smirked. Clarissa narrowed her eyes.

Marianne smiled, putting a hand on each girl's wrist to distract them. *They are still so very young*, she thought, and sisterly rivalry sparked between them often even though they were also best friends. They had no idea how lucky they were. What she would have given to have a sister she could confide in!

"So, we are here to ask if you would join our party at the theatre tomorrow night. Ellen insisted we must come in person to extend the invitation, and I was delighted to agree. I do hope your mother will accept."

Both girls immediately forgot their quibble and smiled with delight, falling over themselves to exclaim how gracious Lady Havers was to include them in her invitation.

"Do say we may go, Mama!" Clarissa cried out.

Lavinia pursed her lips. "You are not yet out, Clarissa," she said sternly.

"Why, this is the opera, not a ball," Ellen said serenely. "It is quite unexceptionable for a girl Clarissa's age not yet out to attend *some* social events, you know. I consider it excellent practice for her own Season. Private dinner parties, public events such as the opera or exhibitions, even picnics when the weather improves. Of course, she cannot be courted yet, but I think it very unfair for younger sisters to be entirely excluded from the fun. How old are your younger children, again?"

"Our son Charles is fifteen, Lucinda fourteen and Penelope twelve," Lavinia said a little ungraciously. "I hope you do not suggest we take *them* to the opera!"

"Of course not!" Ellen looked shocked. "Evening events are quite out of the question. Nevertheless, I intend to host a picnic and a few luncheons later in the year, and I do hope you will bring them along."

"I was included in many events from the age of ten or so, when we lived in London," Marianne put in. "With my governess in attendance, of course. Have you found someone suitable yet, Lavinia?" It could not hurt to press the point that she would not be available at Lavinia's convenience. She would not put it past Lavinia to try and fob the younger girls off on her at events, and while she did not mind chaperoning Clarissa and Diana on occasion, she had no intention of sitting at the children's table.

"Arthur and I interviewed candidates this week," Lavinia said sulkily. "We offered a suitable candidate the post, and she begins on Monday."

"Excellent," Marianne said with a nod, holding Lavinia's eyes until the other woman flushed and looked away.

"You intend to remain with the Havers then, Aunt Marianne?" Clarissa murmured as Ellen asked Lavinia another question, ending the awkward silence.

"For the time being, at least. Though I miss you girls, I'm afraid living in your parents' household was not a comfortable situation for me."

Diana squeezed her hand sympathetically. "We quite understand," she said, her voice soft. "Mama and Papa have changed since Papa inherited the earldom. We are no longer permitted to associate with our friends, girls we went to school with, because they are not situated high enough in life. Everyone else is now lesser, just because of an accident of birth."

Marianne shook her head with an impatient sigh. "Foolish," she muttered. "If your mother treats anyone without a title as lesser, she will quickly make enemies of some of the most powerful people in London."

"She's determined Diana must marry an earl at least," Clarissa said. "She has been making lists of all the unmarried peers in London."

"Some of them are older than Papa!" Diana's look of horror was unfeigned.

Marianne clasped her niece's hand, shaken to the core at the thought of history repeating. "I won't let you be forced into marriage to any man not of your choosing. Either of you," she declared passionately. "I swear it."

"How wonderful this is!" Diana whispered, clutching at Marianne's arm as they took their seats in the front row of the Havers box. Lavinia sat on Diana's other side, trying to hide her own wonder as she gazed around the brightly lit theatre and the glittering throng taking their seats. Clarissa sat at the end, hands folded demurely in her lap, but her eyes were bright with interest as she took in everything around her.

Ellen had insisted Marianne and her nieces take the front row, while she sat behind with Thomas and Arthur. Only Marianne realised it was no sacrifice for Ellen to sit beside Thomas and hold his hand throughout the performance, rather than sit in the front row under full scrutiny of the interested audience.

Marianne had already seen any number of friends, a lot of them waving and smiling. Rather too many men - she hesitated to call them gentlemen - of her acquaintance were eyeing her blue dress with a blue and silver cape, smiling invitingly at her. Sighing, she mentally girded herself for the propositions she would no doubt have to waste far too much of her time rejecting, gently and otherwise. At least staying with the Havers would give her protection from the most importunate, who might be inclined to persist if she had her own household.

"Do you know that gentleman, Aunt Marianne?" Diana asked then.

"Don't point, dear." Marianne caught Diana's hand on the way up, pressing it back to her lap. "Just direct with your eyes, and describe him."

"The box across the way," Diana said, blushing at having almost made a gauche mistake. "The tall, handsome gentleman with a scar, in a blue coat in a box directly across the theatre. There is an older lady with him wearing a burgundy dress; she has a lot of feathers in her hair."

"Oh!" Marianne smiled as she saw Alexander, standing in his box looking directly at her. "That is Alexander Rotherhithe, Marquis of Glenkellie, and though I am not acquainted with her that must be his mother with him, the Dowager Marchioness."

"A *marquis*?" Diana looked as though she might faint.

Lavinia immediately leaned across her. "And is there a current Marchioness of Glenkellie, Aunt?"

"No," Marianne said, and honesty compelled her to admit, "I believe he is in the market for a wife, however. He is but lately come to the title; he spent quite a few years in the army and on the Continent."

"A war hero, too?" Lavinia looked delighted. "You must introduce us at the interval, Aunt!"

Marianne was saved from having to answer by Ellen leaning forward and saying "I must stake a prior claim, Lavinia; I want to introduce you to Sarah Child Villiers, Lady Jersey. I spy her here tonight and we must appeal to her for vouchers to Almack's."

"Oh, yes, that is infinitely more important," Marianne said, relieved Ellen had stepped in to distract Lavinia's attention. "You can meet Glenkellie another time, but you will have only one opportunity to make a good first impression on Lady Jersey."

Thankfully, that made Lavinia subside into nervous silence as the curtain opened and the performance began.

At the interval, Ellen lost no time in hurrying Lavinia off to meet Lady Jersey, asking Thomas and Arthur to get some refreshments and Marianne to remain in the box with Diana and Clarissa -- a request Marianne was more than happy to honour.

Beckoning Clarissa to move one seat closer so they could hear each other over the din of the audience, Marianne asked the girls how they were enjoying the play and listened indulgently to their excited chatter.

When the door opened behind her, she glanced around, assuming Thomas and Arthur were returning. The tall figure entering the box, however, accompanied by the lady in the burgundy dress with the mass of feathers in her hair, was Alexander.

CHAPTER SIXTEEN

Spotting Marianne at the theatre was a stroke of luck. Thomas had sent around a note letting Alex know the Havers party had arrived in London, but he had been fully tied up with business and engagements with his mother -- who was utterly determined to see him married before she departed for Italy in April. He hardly dared let her out alone in case she promised him to some bacon-brained chit.

Marianne's jewellery had been remarkably easy to dispose of. Garrard's had been delighted to assist, telling him the former Earl of Creighton had always wanted their most unusual and collectible pieces for his wife, many of which had now increased in value. They suggested an agent who quickly found buyers for almost all the pieces, in some cases achieving a price a good deal in excess of the original purchase price. Alex had engaged Mr. Coutts to open a bank account in Marianne's name, depositing all the monies into it, and was eager to give her the good news.

Therefore, at the interval, he insisted his mother accompany him to the Havers box. Intrigued by the possibility of meeting the American earl she'd heard was busy setting Parliament on its ear with his radical ideas, she agreed.

Despite seeing Thomas in the passageway, Alex nodded and walked straight on past him. It had just occurred to him that his mother, impossible though she could be, might actually be his best ally in convincing Marianne marriage might suit her. Most especially if Alexander were the groom. If the last two weeks of being paraded before every marriageable young woman in London had done anything, it had convinced him Marianne was still the only woman who could possibly make him happy. Whether he could make her so remained to be seen, but he was willing to spend the rest of his life trying.

Marianne's startled expression as she rose to her feet and dipped a curtsey immediately had Alex second-guessing whether he should have waited to introduce his mother to her. "Lady Creighton." He bowed formally. "Mother, please allow me to present Marianne, Lady Creighton to you? Lady Creighton, my mother Lady Helena, the Dowager Marchioness of Glenkellie."

"Lady Glenkellie." Marianne gave a lower, more respectful curtsey.

"Are you the widow or the new one?" Lady Helena Glenkellie asked bluntly.

Marianne's lips twitched slightly, and Alex knew she'd bitten back a laugh. "I'm the widow, my lady. My niece the Countess has just stepped out with Lady Havers to go and meet Lady Jersey, I believe."

"Ah, Sarah." Alex's mother smirked. "Need vouchers, do you? For these two gels, or yourself?"

"Lady Jersey is a friend of mine already, my lady. Pray, allow me to make known to you Lady Diana Creighton and Lady Clarissa Creighton," Marianne said, and the two girls sank into deep curtseys, expressions of awe on their faces. "I call them my nieces; it is easier than explaining the complexities of our actual relationship. Diana, Clarissa; Lord Glenkellie and Lady Helena Glenkellie."

"Both out, are you?" Alex's mother examined the two girls with a critical eye. Alex could have told her the answer from their dress; while Diana was wearing a lovely white gown with a faint silver stripe in it, perfect for a debutante, Clarissa's dark blue gown with tiny white spots was much more plain and demure.

"Lady Diana is making her come-out this Season," Marianne replied. "Clarissa is only just seventeen and will wait until next year, though her parents are permitting her to attend some social events to gain experience."

"Very wise, too." Lady Glenkellie cast one more glance over Clarissa before obviously dismissing her and turning her full attention to Diana. She seemed to like what she saw, because she glanced at Alex and smiled. "Do you attend the Balford ball on Friday, Lady Diana?"

"I don't believe we have been invited, my lady," Diana said in a small voice, looking nervously at Marianne.

"I shall ensure you receive an invitation. The Duchess of Balford is a particular friend of mine." Lady Glenkellie nodded imperiously.

"That is most generous of you, my lady." Marianne curtseyed again, and Diana and Clarissa followed her lead.

The dowager marchioness looked back at Marianne and blinked, almost as though she had forgotten her presence. "Yes. Well. I daresay we shall see you there, shan't we, Alexander?"

"I look forward to it greatly," Alex said, with a smile at Marianne.

"You should ask Lady Diana for a dance now. No doubt she will be swarmed with eager young swains before you get a look in, otherwise."

Alex gaped at his mother in surprise. *She's got entirely the wrong end of the stick*, he thought. "Ah... yes," he said, caught out by the unexpected manoeuvre. "Lady Diana, might I request a dance with you at the Balford ball?"

"The *first* dance," his mother pushed.

Diana looked at Marianne, wide-eyed. Marianne nodded encouragingly.

"I should be honoured, Lord Glenkellie," the girl said shyly, blushing scarlet.

"Excellent. I take it we will not have the pleasure of your company, Lady Clarissa?"

"I regret you are correct." Clarissa smiled at him, apparently a little less shy than her older sister. "Balls are quite out of the question for me this year, I'm afraid."

"It is Society's loss." Alexander bowed his head to her. "In that case, Lady Marianne, might I solicit the honour of your hand for the *second* dance?"

Marianne looked utterly startled. Diana and Clarissa looked quite delighted, and his mother - his mother turned to him with her mouth wide open with shock.

"Alexander, what are you *doing*?" she demanded.

"I am asking a delightful lady, whom I consider to be a good friend, to reserve me a dance at a ball we will both attend," Alex said, trying to sound calm and placid, as though dancing with Marianne wasn't one of the most desirable things he could imagine.

"Well," Marianne said uncertainly. "I had not intended to dance..."

"But Aunt Marianne, you keep telling us how much you miss dancing!" Clarissa said, and Alex shot her a grateful glance. The minx gave him a conspiratorial wink, and he bit back a shout of laughter. She, at least, knew precisely what he was about.

"I do miss dancing." Marianne nibbled on her lower lip briefly before giving a decisive nod. "I am my own woman these days, beholden to nobody else's good opinion of me. Very well, Lord Glenkellie, I should be delighted to give you the second dance at the Balford ball."

Alex couldn't restrain his smile of triumph. With a kiss to Marianne's hand, he followed his mother from the Havers box and back around to the other side of the theatre, knowing once they were away from prying ears, the interrogation would come. The Dowager Marchioness of Glenkellie missed nothing.

"What are you thinking!" his mother hissed as soon as they were once again seated in their own box. "Wasting your time asking that woman for a dance!"

"Why is it a waste of my time?" He raised his eyebrows at her.

"Because you need someone to give you an heir, and in eight years of marriage, she didn't conceive once." Lady Helena pursed her lips and shook her head.

"Mother, Creighton had three wives and *none* of them ever conceived. Does that not suggest perhaps the fault might not be with the wives?" Alexander had taken the time to research the late earl once he arrived back in London, and been horrified by what he found. Both Countesses of Creighton prior to Marianne had not lived into their thirties, their deaths unexplained.

The suggestion gave his mother pause. "Best not to risk it, nevertheless," she said. "You should choose a girl from a family of proven breeders. One of those younger Creighton girls will do nicely, if you want to ally yourself with the family; there's a whole pack of them, I believe, though they're mostly girls."

"They're *children*, Mother."

"You're barely ten years Lady Diana's senior!" Still, she frowned when he just looked back at her. "You are quite set on her, then?"

"If she will have me."

"She's a fool if she won't." The dowager marchioness snorted magnificently, looking back across the theatre to where Marianne sat talking with her nieces, now rejoined by Thomas and Arthur. "She's very beautiful, I suppose," she said, "but how well do you really know her?"

Alex smiled. "Do you remember my letters home, from Portugal and Spain?"

"Indeed I do, infrequent though they were." His mother tapped him on the knee with her fan. "I was constantly trying to convince you to leave the army and come home where it was safe, but your letters were full of how you were making a difference out there."

"And?" he pressed. "Do you recall anything else I said?"

"Oh, there was some nonsense about how you couldn't bear to come back to England because the girl you were in love with had thrown you over and married some wealthy old earl..." the marchioness tapered off, her eyes widening. "*No*. You don't mean *her*?"

"The Honourable Miss Marianne Abingdon," Alex said wistfully. "We were both young and naive, and while she promised to wait for me, her father's gambling debts were such that a valuable asset like a daughter hailed as the most beautiful girl in London wasn't to be wasted on the likes of me, fourth in line with naught but an army commission to my name."

"Oh Alex." Lady Helena's eyes were soft as she laid her hand over his. "She didn't throw you over, did she?"

"No, but until recently I thought she had. Instead it transpires she was basically sold to a man three times her age and spent years in a desperately unhappy, even abusive, marriage."

"The poor girl, how perfectly dreadful!" His mother sounded quite outraged on Marianne's behalf. "I was one of the great beauties in my day, too, and my father was outraged I 'threw myself away' on a younger son, but he would never have forced me to marry someone I did not want!"

Lady Helena was the daughter of a duke, and her dowry had been more than substantial. Even though his father was the younger son, Alexander had always known there would be a substantial inheritance in his future. He'd also always known his parents loved each other. Indeed, he suspected his mother had become more difficult since his father's death mainly because she missed her husband so. Lord Patrick Rotherhithe had always indulged his wife's slightest whim.

"I love her," Alex admitted, knowing his mother was now firmly on his side. "I've always loved her, and I want no one else for my wife. Unfortunately, after her terrible marriage, she has decided she prefers not to remarry."

"Then we will simply have to convince her otherwise, won't we, darling?" Lady Helena patted his hand and smiled. "You just leave it to me."

"I'd really rather not." He winced, thinking of the chaos his mother might engender with her machinations.

She laughed, unfazed by his lack of confidence in her. "Young men do like to do their own wooing, I suppose. Well, I will spend my time filling her ears with tales of how wonderful my marriage was, and how like your father you are."

"That would be very helpful, Mother," Alex said sincerely.

"You are, you know." His mother reached up and touched his cheek gently. "Very much like him. He'd be very proud - and so would your grandfather, if he'd truly had the chance to know you. Don't hold Duncan's dying words against him. He was grieving for both his sons, you must remember. He pored over every newspaper account of the battles you fought in, and every time you were mentioned in dispatches or bestowed with a medal, he would give a toast in your honour at dinner."

"He did?" Startled, Alex blinked. "I didn't know that."

"You never had much chance to know him, being away at school, then university, then the army. I wish you'd known him better." His mother looked back across the theatre at Marianne. "I think he'd have liked her, you know. He'd have said something about her looking like a proper Scot, with that red hair."

Alex took his mother's hand. "Let's see about persuading her to marry into a good Scots family then, shall we?"

CHAPTER SEVENTEEN

Marianne found herself utterly unable to concentrate on the rest of the play. She was far too aware of Alexander and his mother only a short distance away, heads bent towards each other in intense conversation, both of them with eyes fixed firmly on the box where she sat the whole time. The dowager marchioness had clearly been quite keen on Alexander getting to know Diana, and it would certainly be a good match for her niece.

Not only that, but Marianne knew firsthand exactly how decent a man Alexander was. He would surely take good care of Diana, make sure she wanted for nothing. Diana, with her sweet nature, could not help but love him, and would surely be loved in return.

So why did the very idea make Marianne feel sick to her stomach?

She could not stop Diana and Clarissa excitedly telling their mother about meeting a marquis and his mother, and being invited to a duchess' ball, of course. Or Clarissa needling her sister about being asked for the first dance.

Lavinia could hardly contain her excitement, and Marianne was praised to the skies for being the means of introduction to such exalted personages. "Dancing with a marquis at a duchess' ball!" she kept saying, as though she could not quite believe it. "My little girl!"

"Lord Glenkellie asked Aunt Marianne for the second," Diana said innocently.

"Oh, that was just politeness," Marianne said quickly as Lavinia's brows drew down in a frown. "We are old friends, after all. He could hardly *not* ask. And you were quite right, I do miss dancing. Not many gentlemen will request a set with an old widow like me, so I shall enjoy the opportunities when they come my way." Her tone was a little defiant as she met Lavinia's gaze, and the older woman nodded after a moment, shrugging.

"So long as you do not distract Diana's prospects, all will be well." It was Arthur who whispered malevolently into her ear.

Marianne's jaw clenched, but she pretended he had not spoken and stared fixedly at the stage, though in truth she took in little of the rest of the play.

The following morning as Ellen and Marianne took breakfast together, Ellen confided Lady Jersey had not been prepared to offer vouchers without meeting Diana. Thus, Ellen had promised to collect Lavinia and Diana in her carriage and take them to call on Lady Jersey for tea that afternoon.

"Lady Jersey insisted I bring you along as well, of course," she said.

"I should rather keep Clarissa company," Marianne said quickly. "Perhaps we might take a walk in the park."

"Are you avoiding Lady Jersey?" Ellen's gaze was uncomfortably sharp. "It's quite all right if you are, of course. I'll happily assist - though I should like to know why."

With a sense of relief that she need not mislead Ellen, Marianne said, "I think she will try and persuade me to marry again. She fancies herself a matchmaker; only look how many young men she tried to throw in your way, and she barely had any opportunities before Thomas snatched you up!"

"True," Ellen admitted. She gave Marianne another penetrating look. "And you are quite sure you will never marry again?"

"I could never wish to be under any man's control again," Marianne said frankly. "I will fight Arthur to retain what independence I have, and God willing, with good friends like you and Thomas and the Pembrokes, I shall contrive to live well enough to suit me."

"You will have a place with us always, if you wish it," Ellen promised. "As a valued member of the family, not merely a guest."

Tears of emotion choked Marianne's throat, and she reached out to touch Ellen's hand, her expression full of gratitude.

The clatter of hooves and wheels just outside broke the moment, and they both looked to the window to see a carriage drawn up at the front door.

"That's the Glenkellie crest on the door," Ellen noted. "I think perhaps you have a visitor, Marianne."

"It's rather too early for morning calls." Marianne shook her head, regaining her composure. "I am sure he is only here because he has some business with Thomas."

Footsteps in the hallway and the sound of the study door opening and closing seemed to confirm her supposition, and the two ladies returned to their toast and tea.

Only a few moments later, though, Thomas entered the room. "I do beg your pardon," he said, "but Glenkellie is here to discuss some matters of business with Marianne."

"With me?" Marianne looked blank. "What business could he have to discuss with me?"

But Ellen was already getting up and saying she had a hundred jobs to do and she would leave them to it.

Marianne had little choice but to set her teacup aside and follow Thomas to his study, a smaller room than the one at Havers Hall but no less comfortably furnished.

Alex was waiting there, smiling as he saw her enter the room. "Lady Marianne." He bowed as Thomas escorted her to a seat and then both men took their seats as well.

"Whatever is this about?" she asked in confusion.

"Do you recall I advised you that I had commissioned Glenkellie to see what might be done about your jewellery?" Thomas asked.

"Oh." She had tried to forget everything about the hated jewels. "Yes, I suppose so. Are they worth anything?" she asked, turning to face Alexander.

"A good deal, as it turns out. Some four thousand pounds, all told. I've placed the money in an account at Coutts Bank in your name. If you would at some time make an appointment to accompany me there, I can vouch to Mr. Coutts that the money is yours and then you will be able to do with it whatever you wish."

"Four *thousand* pounds?" Marianne said, flabbergasted.

"Indeed, and there are still some small pieces remaining, plus a necklace my mother wishes to purchase as a gift for her sister, who she intends to visit in Italy this year."

Completely stunned, Marianne merely sat and blinked at him, at least until Thomas said, "Marianne, are you feeling quite well? You've turned pale."

"I just," she turned to him and shook her head. "Four thousand pounds - I never expected so much!"

"You are quite an heiress," Thomas said, teasing. "All the fortune hunters will be chasing after you when they learn of it. For it is yours alone, not a widow's portion you would lose should you remarry."

"But what am I to do with so much money?" For all Creighton's wealth, Marianne had never carried more than a few shillings in her own purse. Everything she purchased was sent on account to her husband.

"We both stand ready to advise you, should you wish," Alex said, and she looked back at him. "Or Mr. Coutts could make some recommendations, if you would like to consult with an independent party. Even placed in the four per cents, though, you would get an income of some one hundred and sixty pounds per annum, which would be more than sufficient to rent a house and keep some servants, if you wish."

"Or you can continue to reside with us, and save the money for the future," Thomas said with a frown at Alexander. "I know Ellen wishes you to remain with us, as one of the family, and your being a woman of means does not change that."

"I will have to think about it," Marianne said at last.

"Whatever you decide to do, I stand ready to assist," Alexander said. "In fact, if it is convenient, I am available to convey you to the bank this morning."

"I think that's a good idea," Thomas encouraged, and Marianne was persuaded to go and collect a coat and hat and ask Jean to accompany her.

"To avoid any appearance of impropriety," she told her maid, "though of course there wouldn't be any; Lord Glenkellie is a perfect gentleman."

"Still, you don't want folks gossiping about you bein' alone with a man," Jean said wisely, putting on her own coat. "I don't mind goin' for a ride in a fancy carriage at all, m'lady. Never been out of Herefordshire before, have I? London's full of wonders to see."

With Jean sitting beside her absorbed in the sights passing by outside the carriage window, Marianne found her eyes resting on Alexander. He looked the picture of a fine London gentleman, though he eschewed the bright colours worn by the foppish, his clothes were perfectly tailored to fit him, and she did not doubt the shine on his boots alone was hard-earned by dedicated hours of polishing by some under-servant.

"Thank you for assisting me in this matter, Lord Glenkellie," she said impulsively.

"You're most welcome." Alexander smiled at her. "I admit I was surprised to find the jewels of such value, but pleased on your behalf." He paused a moment before adding, "You paid a high price for them."

She had not considered it that way, but now that she did, she smiled wryly. "Indeed, I was quite expensive, was I not? Five hundred a year... he could have kept several mistresses for that, if he had wished."

Alexander looked horrified at her flippant remark. "Dear God, never say so!" he exclaimed. "Crei - *that man* valued you far too cheaply!"

Appreciative he had recalled she did not like to hear the name Creighton, and touched by his outrage on her behalf, Marianne gave him a rueful shrug. "I admit I do not know what he paid my father. Several thousand at least, I must suppose. I understand his gambling debts were quite substantial."

"A good woman is a pearl beyond price," Alexander said, and then he leaned forward, gazing at her intently. "The *love* of a good woman cannot be purchased, not for money or jewels or any such thing."

Jean let out a tiny sigh beside her, and Marianne had to admit it was a deeply romantic sentiment. Alexander's intense blue gaze was making her feel a little uncomfortable, though, so she only murmured, "Indeed, you are correct," before turning her head and looking out at the streets.

Mr. Coutts was a rather elderly gentleman, Marianne discovered, in his late seventies, but as professional and charming as Marianne could wish. He listened while Alexander verified her identity and then turned his full attention to Marianne.

"My bank is at your disposal, Lady Creighton. Your funds are at the present time lodged in an account which attracts only minimal interest; I would not recommend keeping more than the amount you would require in, say, a twelve-month period there at any one time."

"I am not presently decided on what, if any, investments I wish to make," Marianne admitted.

"When you are, my lady, we stand ready to assist. Do you wish to withdraw any funds for your own use at this time?"

"It's up to you," Alexander said when she hesitated. "You might wish to have some small amount on hand for expenses - a few pounds, perhaps? Remember, there is more to come when the rest of the sales are concluded, and you can return on any day the bank is open to make a further withdrawal if you wish."

"Ten pounds," Marianne decided. "That is a sufficient sum for any small purchases, I believe. If I wish to make a larger purchase than that, it would be as well to meditate on it a day or two anyway."

"A very prudent attitude, my lady," Mr. Coutts approved. "Small notes would be best, I think? A few moments, and I will have one of my tellers complete the transaction."

Within minutes, Marianne was tucking a small roll of pound and ten-shilling notes into her reticule, along with a small pouch containing a pound in coins. Taking their leave of Mr. Coutts, they collected Jean from the anteroom where the maid waited and returned to the carriage.

"Would you like to return directly to Cavendish Square, or may I convey you elsewhere?" Alexander enquired.

It took Marianne a few moments to reply. She was still too accustomed to having her every move dictated by others, she realised; the need to ask permission to go anywhere or do anything had become ingrained.

"I would like to go somewhere, yes," she said finally. "Would you perhaps have time to take a walk with me?"

"I should be delighted," Alexander replied promptly. "Though it is cold today, it is quite dry. St. James's Park isn't far from here, just along The Strand?"

He was asking, not telling, her where they should go, his hand extended to help her up into the carriage and his driver awaited her instruction.

A heady feeling enveloped Marianne, a rush of lightness, almost as though she was floating. "I should love to go to St. James's Park. Could we perhaps make a stop by a baker's shop to buy some bread? I have ever been fond of feeding the ducks there."

"You heard Lady Marianne," Alexander said to his driver as he handed Jean up after her mistress, "a baker's shop and then the park. Hungry ducks await!"

CHAPTER EIGHTEEN

Arriving back at the Havers' townhouse with muddy shoes and cheeks pink from the cold Marianne could not wipe the broad smile from her face as she accompanied Jean upstairs to change.

"You look pleased with yourself," Ellen said as they met on the landing. "Did you enjoy your outing?"

"I fed the ducks!" Marianne said, laughing as she realised she sounded like an excited child.

Ellen's expression was both puzzled and amused as she tilted her head slightly and said, "That does sound like fun. Are you coming with me this afternoon?"

"Oh, why not. Lady Jersey will only turn up here to see me if I do not, and probably bring a selection of potential suitors with her. At least if I go, I can impress on her the need to see Diana well-settled." Still in a good mood, Marianne shrugged off her earlier concerns. "When do you wish to go?"

"Will a half hour be enough time to refresh yourself?"

"Easily!"

Ellen smiled, obviously delighted by Marianne's happy mood. "I'll have Cook send up a little luncheon for you - some soup perhaps?"

"Begging your pardon, m'lady, but I sent the instruction to the kitchen already." Jean bobbed a curtsey.

"Good girl, Jean. I'm glad Marianne has someone so devoted to her comfort." Ellen praised and Jean blushed, ducking her head shyly.

"Jean is wonderful, and I fully intend to steal her from your employ," Marianne said. "Now I have control of some funds of my own, I hope she will accept the position of my personal maid on a permanent basis."

Jean's eyes shone with unshed tears as she curtseyed again, deeper this time. "Oh, m'lady. I'm that honoured. But don't you want one of them proper French lady's maids?"

"A fine English girl is more than good enough for me," Marianne told her.

"Then you should accept Lady Marianne's offer, with my blessing," Ellen declared.

Jean wasn't the type to repeatedly babble thanks, for which Marianne was quite grateful as they proceeded to her rooms. The fire was soon built up, Marianne's muddy boots and damp gown removed, fresh things laid out for her to change into, and a tray arrived from the kitchen with a light snack to sate her hunger.

"I used to take such service for granted, perhaps because of how grudgingly it was offered," Marianne murmured as Jean took a brush and began attending to her hair, "yet now, I am almost overwhelmed with gratitude for Lady Havers' kindness and your good care of me, Jean."

"Lady Havers has naught but good to say about you, m'lady," Jean said, tucking in a stray curl, "and as for me - well, it's a pleasure to look after you and all your lovely things. You've only kind words for everyone. Believe me, servants notice who ain't so sweet-tempered."

"I'm sure you do." Marianne hesitated, then thought she might as well ask. "Did any of the servants at Havers Hall speak much of Lord Glenkellie? I know he was only there a few days, before he had to return to London, and he brought his own manservant with him, so perhaps they didn't have much to do with him."

"Not so much, you're right, my lady, but everyone as did serve him said he was right civil, 'specially for bein' so high a lord, you know. And his man Simons was fair devoted. Said as how Lord Glenkellie is the best master he could ask for, and everyone who serves him thinks the same. Me, I think anyone Lord and Lady Havers choose as a friend must be one of the finest people in England," Jean insisted. "They chose you, didn't they?"

Marianne chuckled. "Well, one could say I rather thrust myself upon them, in fact, but I will accept your compliment at face value, Jean. For I too think Lord and Lady Havers are excellent judges of character."

Lady Jersey received their little group in her fabulously overdecorated Indian parlour. Marianne, who had been there once before, stifled laughter as Ellen and the Creighton ladies looked around agape. Catching Sarah Child Villiers' eye, she had to look away to compose herself.

Ellen finally pulled herself together to present Lavinia, Diana, and Clarissa to Lady Jersey. Though Clarissa had not technically been invited, Lavinia had insisted she come along anyway, and received exactly what she deserved for her presumption. Lady Jersey looked Clarissa up and down once and said, "Should you not be in the schoolroom, child? There are some kittens in the mews, I believe; go with Frost to see them and Cook shall give you a glass of milk after."

Clarissa was quite obviously laughing as she left in the wake of the imperious butler, and Diana's longing expression said she would far rather be going with her sister than sitting down to take tea with one former and three current countesses.

Marianne didn't blame Diana. She would rather be going to the stables too than face another Lady Jersey interrogation, but the arbiter of the Ton was a very perceptive woman who had seen past the aloof face Marianne had been forced to present to the world by her husband, had been kind to her and invited her into her circle of friends. It was a debt of kindness Marianne could never repay, so she settled herself on a chaise, pasted on an attentive expression, and accepted a lemon biscuit.

"So you're Diana." Sarah inspected the quaking debutante with a gimlet eye. "What's your dowry again, girl?"

"Ten thousand pounds," Lavinia said smugly, "and Clarissa will have as much next year."

Lady Jersey turned her gaze on Lavinia. Not a word was said, but Lavinia shrank back into her seat and clamped her lips shut.

"What do you like, Diana?" Lady Jersey asked, and Diana gulped, glancing at her mother. Lavinia nodded.

"I am accomplished on the pianoforte and sing tolerably well," Diana said in a small voice. "I enjoy needlework and drawing with pencils. I speak French and some Italian..."

"Same as every other young woman of your rank this season, if not a little less," Lady Jersey said with a sniff, and Diana looked as though she might cry. Sarah's tone softened. "I mean, what do you *like*? What do you enjoy doing, if you have nobody to please but yourself?"

"Oh," Diana said, obviously surprised. "Well... I really do like drawing. Animals in particular. I drew Father's dogs, Apollo and Ares, and Father liked it so much he had it framed and hung it on the wall of his study."

Lady Jersey nodded encouragingly. "Animals are good. Many young men are very fond of their dogs and horses. If you are able, for example, to draw each of his horses well enough to show its distinguishing features, he will very likely declare himself in love with you on the instant."

Diana let out a laugh before recalling herself and turning it into a ladylike giggle behind her hand. Sarah winked at Marianne, and she let out a sigh of relief. Diana had managed to endear herself to Sarah, and the influential countess would throw her in the path of not only eligible young men, but ones whom she might like and respect.

"Well, I think you'll take very well, my dear," Lady Jersey said, giving her stamp of approval. "I hope you'll take my advice, which is to always let young men know what you're really thinking. Girls who pretend they're hanging on an idiot's every word tend to find themselves married to the idiot in question."

Ellen laughed at that; Lavinia was staring pop-eyed and indignant, but still too intimidated to speak.

"I must agree," Marianne said, drawing Diana's eyes to her. "A man who will not respect your opinions and your wishes is not a man you would want to become more closely acquainted with. Do not wait until you are already committed to let him know who you truly are."

"I will endeavour always to keep that in mind," Diana said. "Thank you for your advice, Lady Jersey. Aunt Marianne."

"Speaking of advice," Lady Jersey said, "I understand you have spent very little time in London, Lady Creighton?"

Lavinia flushed and looked a little angry to be called on so, but she answered. "Yes, my lady, that's so. My parents did not care to travel much from Durham, where our home was, and where I met my husband."

"You should listen carefully to your aunt." Sarah indicated Marianne. "She has successfully navigated the dangerous waters of London's upper society for years now. Allow her to guide your daughters and they will do very well."

Lavinia spluttered. "But - but - Marianne isn't married!"

"You make an excellent point." There was a familiar, wicked glint in Sarah's eye. "Do you have any suitable candidates in mind, Marianne?"

"I think your ladyship knows perfectly well that I do not wish to remarry." Marianne remained cool and composed, her hands folded in her lap.

"You cannot let one bad experience put you off for life. 'Tis rather like riding a horse; you fall off, you must get right back on!"

"Nevertheless," Marianne said levelly.

"Well, we shall see. I shan't press you, not this year, but I think 'twould be a shame if you closed yourself off from the possibility entirely." Sarah's voice was quite gentle. "You have a great capacity to love, my dear. I would not like to see you wasted as a lonely widow forever."

Marianne looked down, tears pricking at the back of her eyelids. "Thank you for your concern, my lady, but I pray you do not trouble yourself over me. I am very content as I am and wish only to focus on seeing my dear nieces well-settled."

There was a long moment of silence, and Marianne finally lifted her eyes to glance at Sarah, finding the other woman studying her with a slight frown. Essaying a small smile, Marianne prayed her friend would accept her decision.

"Very well," Lady Jersey said finally. "Lady Creighton, I am pleased to advise your application for subscription at Almack's is approved for this year." Leaning forward, she slid open a drawer in the small occasional table before her and removed a stack of pasteboard rectangles. "Three vouchers, for yourself, the Earl and the Lady Diana." She counted out three of the tickets and handed them to Lavinia, who gushed her thanks.

"Yes, yes." With an irritated wave of her hand, Sarah cut Lavinia off. "And here are yours, Ellen." She handed three more over.

"Three?" Marianne asked.

"One is yours, of course." Ellen pressed it into her hand.

"Oh... but I did not apply." She did not have the ten guineas for the subscription, or had not until that morning. She would have to visit Coutts again to pay Ellen back.

"I applied on your behalf. I could not possibly do without your company in my first full season trying to fit in with the Ton, Marianne. Besides, I shall quite depend on you to rein in Thomas' Americanisms, lest he offend someone unintentionally!"

Marianne smiled fondly at her friend. "I'm not sure Lord Havers is capable of offending anyone; he is far too nice!"

"Unless you mention the slave trade," Sarah remarked. "I rather thought he and Portland might come to blows when the topic came up at the Fulton dinner party! Portland was convinced he would be anti-emancipation, " she added to Marianne, who almost choked. She'd heard Thomas rage about the inhumanity of the slave trade on more than one occasion.

"Oh, please don't mention that again," Ellen begged. "I had rather hoped everyone forgot it."

"Quite the opposite. Castlereagh has spoken of it often with great admiration. I believe he is rather hoping Lord Havers will speak as eloquently on the topic in the House of Lords this year."

"Have no doubt of it." Ellen acknowledged Lady Jersey's approval.

Sarah nodded before reaching for a bell-pull beside her chair. "I shall have Frost fetch your other daughter, Lady Creighton. Pray excuse me; I am promised to a soiree at the Drummond-Burrells this evening."

"Thank you so much for your time, Lady Jersey." Taking her cue, Lavinia rose and offered a curtsey; Diana quickly followed suit. Ellen and Marianne made their farewells a little more leisurely, confident Lady Jersey's favour was not about to be withdrawn if they made the slightest misstep.

Clarissa met them in the entrance hall, taking her sister's arm and whispering to her. Diana still looked pale and nervous, but managed to respond to Clarissa's questioning with a small smile. Marianne was confident Diana would be fine, though it might take her some time to find her confidence among the London crowd. At least she had plenty of people looking out for her, unlike Marianne herself. There had been no one at all to speak for Marianne when her father had forced her into a hasty marriage, nobody she might have run to for help.

What could anyone have done, anyway? Marianne mused as she sat opposite Ellen in the Havers carriage on their way home. She'd been eighteen and legally under her father's control. If Arthur decided to marry Diana off to some crony of his, there was little anyone could do about it legally. Outside the law - well, Marianne was quite certain she could smuggle herself and Diana onto a ship bound for the Americas, if it came to that. With her newfound wealth, opportunities presented which had never been open to her before.

"You look very thoughtful; what is on your mind?" Ellen asked from the other side of the carriage.

Marianne answered unthinkingly. "Running away to the Americas."

"Good God, not really?" Ellen looked shocked.

"Not really." Marianne gave her a reassuring smile. "Not for myself, at any rate, though should Diana find herself in an untenable situation due to Arthur or Lavinia's machinations, I would not hesitate to take her beyond their reach."

"Good for you," Ellen said. "I was in an untenable situation myself after my parents died and before Thomas took me in as part of the Havers family. Knowing there is a possible escape route would be a great comfort to any young woman,

I think. I hope you will assure Diana, and Clarissa of course, that they may call upon Thomas and me as well as yourself should they need advice or assistance in anything."

"I shall, and thank you," Marianne said. "It's not that I think Arthur would do anything as terrible as what my father did to me, of course, but... well, Lavinia is very socially ambitious. I wouldn't put it past her to arrange a convenient compromise. I intend to take my chaperoning duties very seriously and attend every event to which they are invited."

"I will be right there beside you," Ellen promised. "It will be good practice, after all, for if I have daughters of my own one day!" Her hand slid to her stomach.

Marianne's eyes widened. "Are you expecting?" she gasped, excited for her friend.

"Perhaps." Ellen leaned close and lowered her voice, though they were quite alone. "I feel dreadfully queasy in the mornings. Susan has taken to bringing me tea and dry biscuits while I am still in bed, to stave off the nausea. I've made an appointment for the doctor to come tomorrow morning, while Thomas will be out. Will you attend me?"

"You haven't told him yet?"

"I want to wait until I am quite sure." Ellen looked down at her hands. "I quite understand if you don't want to. It must be a difficult subject for you."

It was at times like this she was forcibly recalled to the fact that while Ellen acted with remarkable maturity, the Countess of Havers was still only just turned one-and-twenty.

"I never, for one instant, wanted to bring a child into my marriage," Marianne stated with some force. Ellen stared at her wide-eyed, and she admitted, "Which does not mean, I never wanted a baby of my own."

Ellen didn't seem to know what to say, and Marianne was grateful the carriage halted just then outside the townhouse. It had been years since she'd dreamed of a child of her own, yet thinking of it now awakened feelings she had thought long dead. Unexpectedly, she found herself longing for a baby, a little boy perhaps with his father's dark hair and blue eyes.

When she realised she was imagining her son as Alexander's, she ran up the stairs as though chased by wolves, leaving a startled Ellen in her wake, hoping she hadn't upset her friend too badly.

CHAPTER NINETEEN

Brooks' Gentlemen's Club

"YOU'LL NEVER BELIEVE WHO I saw at Almack's yestereve," a loud voice announced behind Alexander, making him sigh and frown at his newspaper. He'd taken to spending afternoons at his club to escape the unending stream of guests visiting his mother, most of them accompanied by eligible daughters, sisters, nieces, or friends they hoped to throw at his head. He'd been rather enjoying the peace until the reading room was invaded by a couple of fools intent on rehashing their entire year to date, it seemed.

Now they had been joined by a third, even louder than the original two. Alexander was about to hush them when the newcomer spoke a name which froze him in place.

"Lady Creighton."

"What, the new one? Met her last week, she's got a daughter she's trying to fire off. Drab little thing."

"She has ten thousand, she's not so drab. Probably why the Patronesses gave them vouchers."

"Not the new one or her daughter, though they were both there too. I'm talking about the former one, whose given name is apparently Marianne. Marianne, Lady Creighton." The newcomer sighed it so dreamily Alexander couldn't quite help lowering his newspaper to see which silly youngster was mooning over Marianne.

His eyes widened with shock when he saw neither the newcomer nor the two he had joined were young; they were all men in their thirties, men for whom Alexander held at least some degree of respect. The one just slumping into a seat was Lord Ferry, second son of a duke and a wealthy man in his own right. Married, too, unless Alexander misremembered, but he was sure he'd met Lady Ferry at some event or other in the past year.

"She's more beautiful than ever," Lord Ferry continued. "And without that old fart Creighton around, she's smiling and dancing. I finally got that dance with her I've been begging years for."

Viscount Snowfield laughed, not unkindly. "Bit late now to make a play for her, ain't it? You've a wife and two brats at home."

"That's where you're wrong, my friend. The lady has been telling everyone who will listen she has no intention of marrying again." Ferry's smile was sly. "And you know what *that* means. She plans to be a merry widow."

Sir Edward Mullins, the third of the little party, sat up, suddenly paying attention. "Are you saying she'd accept a slip on the shoulder?"

"I think the lady knows her value and would be very expensive, but yes. I plan to offer her *carte blanche*." Ferry looked smug. "I know the way to her heart, I think. Her jewels all stayed with the Creighton coffers; she wore only a very plain little cross, whereas the new countess was wearing a spectacular diamond and ruby necklace. I'll buy her a diamond bracelet or two and set her up in a nice house wherever she wishes. Not many can match my resources."

"And most of those who can are as old as her first husband; I don't doubt she'll prefer someone who doesn't have one foot in the grave!" Snowfield laughed again, though Mullins looked a little disgruntled. "Well, I wish you luck in your pursuit, my friend. Will your wife object?"

"No, Honoria knows her place. She's breeding again, besides. I sent her back to stay with my parents."

Ferry's smile was so smug Alexander debated getting up just to punch it off his face. How *dare* the bastard talk about Marianne that way? How dare he even *think* it?

Starting a fight in the middle of Brooks' wouldn't help the situation, though. Alex briefly considered challenging Lord Ferry to defend Marianne's honour, but that would only fuel more gossip. All London would be saying that Marianne was already *Alex's* mistress within hours if he did challenge Ferry, which would do nobody any favours.

So instead of losing his temper, he folded his newspaper and laid it down on the table before getting up and leaving, offering a silent nod to the three men as he passed.

It wasn't a long walk to Cavendish Square, where the Havers had their town-house. Alexander strode along briskly, temper simmering just below the surface. *I should have foreseen something like this happening*, he berated himself. He could not blame Marianne; she was only trying to protect herself, but in doing so she had accidentally opened herself to a far more iniquitous type of pursuit from gentlemen with less noble things on their minds than marriage.

"Good afternoon, Lord Glenkellie," the butler greeted him at the door. "Lord Havers is not at home this afternoon, I'm afraid."

"I was hoping to see Lady Havers and Lady Marianne, as it happens."

"Oh, they are but lately returned from shopping on Bond Street, my lord. I will see if Lady Havers will receive you, if you would care to wait?"

Alexander thrust his hat into the obliging man's hands. "Thank you, I will. If you wouldn't mind conveying that the matter is urgent?"

Ellen joined him in the parlour a few minutes later. "Glenkellie, what's so urgent?" she came straight to the point.

Glancing at the door, Alex wondered if he should wait for Marianne, but perhaps it was better she did not hear what he had to say.

"I need you to be very vigilant in keeping Lady Marianne by your side," he kept his voice low.

"Why?" Ellen asked in her usual straightforward way. "I am quite willing to do as you ask, but if there is anything in particular I should look for, I would prefer to know. Forewarned is forearmed."

"Quite so, Lady Havers." Trying to think how best to phrase the truth without being offensive, Alex said carefully, "It has come to my attention that Lady Marianne's public declaration that she does not intend to marry again may have given the wrong impression in certain quarters."

Ellen looked completely blank.

He sighed and tried again. "I overheard some gossip in my club regarding the possibility of Lady Marianne accepting a less than respectable offer."

This time, Ellen understood. Outrage dawned in her expression and she spluttered for a moment before saying, "Good God, some men really are just... just..."

"Horses' behinds?" Alex suggested.

"Exactly!"

"Who's a horse's behind?" Marianne asked as she entered the room.

Alex and Ellen looked at each other.

"If there is anyone specific you could name, I know I'd want to know so I could avoid them," Ellen said.

"Very well." Alex winced, but turned to Marianne. "You're acquainted with Lord Ferry, I understand?"

"Yes, for some years now." Marianne's brows drew down in a frown. "What about him?"

"I'm afraid your declaration that you do not intend to remarry has given Lord Ferry the wrong impression. His intentions towards you are less than honourable."

Dark colour rushed to Marianne's cheeks. "And you know this, how?" she asked after a moment of silence.

"He was gossiping about his intentions in Brooks'. I overheard," Alex said apologetically.

"*Damn* men!" The words exploded from Marianne, her fists clenching with anger as she turned to pace over to the window and glare out.

"If you would excuse me a moment," Ellen said, "I wish to let the staff know Lord Ferry is never to be admitted to this house under any pretext." She left the room, her heels clipping on the polished wooden floor.

In the silence, Alexander wondered if he should leave too, but Marianne was clearly overset. Not wanting to press her, he moved over to the window adjacent to where she stood and sat down on the cushioned window seat, thinking he would just keep her quiet company until Ellen returned. He was quite surprised when she turned from her contemplation of the street outside and sat down beside him.

"Have you ever discovered any disadvantages to being blessed with good looks?" Marianne asked unexpectedly.

Surprised, Alex shook his head. "No, but they are spoiled now." Unconsciously, he fingered the scar on his cheek. He'd already seen distaste from plenty of ladies as their eyes lingered on it.

"Nonsense, it only makes you look more distinguished," Marianne said with a sniff. "I wonder if it would work for me, though? Some sort of disfigurement - perhaps I could cut all my hair off."

"You would still be the most beautiful woman I know, even if you went ahead and did it," Alex answered, trying to concentrate on her words rather than the warm feelings engendered by her compliment.

Marianne eyed him, her expression wary. "You're not going to tell me I must not?"

"Why should I? 'Tis your hair. I would miss your crowning glory," daringly, he reached out to touch a curl which dangled along her neck, "but I have no right to tell you what to do. That is rather the point of you not wishing to marry again, isn't it?"

"Indeed, but there are plenty of men who would still try to tell me what I may or may not do, without any reason to claim authority over me whatsoever."

Alex offered her a sympathetic smile. "Perhaps you should use that as a tactic to weed out those you do not wish to associate with. Tell them you are considering cutting your hair off, and anyone who tries to tell you not to is not truly worthy of your friendship."

"I fear I should be left with only you and Havers as friends." Marianne's answering smile was wry.

"A tragic but honest assessment of my gender," Alex agreed ruefully.

They sat in silence for a moment before Marianne asked him another unexpected question. "If - *when* you take a wife, Glenkellie, would you forbid her to cut her hair off?"

"Certainly not," he said at once, then re-thought. "I might try to *persuade* her not to, but if she was quite set on it, I would ask that she let a maid do it, lest she injure herself with scissors when trying to cut at the back of her head where she cannot see."

Her expression was wistful. "That is an even better answer than your first response. Your wife will be a lucky woman."

"I hope she will think so," was the only response he could think of, aside from falling to his knees and begging her to marry him. It was definitely not the best moment for a proposal.

But dear God, if only he could!

CHAPTER TWENTY

The Duchess of Balford's Ball

MARIANNE WAS STILL ANGRY by the time she arrived at the Balford ball. Determined to stand firm in the face of spiteful gossip, she had taken particular care with her appearance, selecting one of her most beautiful gowns, a silk creation which changed between blue and green depending on the light. Simple in cut, it depended entirely on the quality of the fabric and the beauty of the wearer to carry it off. She knew she'd achieved the desired effect when Lavinia took one look at her and sighed in despair.

"Nobody will even look at Diana, with you here," she said dismally.

"Lavinia." Marianne shook her head. "You do not *want* a man for Diana whose head might be turned by me. Such a man would not suit her at all, and you do want her to be happy, don't you?"

Obviously struck by the argument, Lavinia nodded in agreement. "I daresay you are correct," she conceded.

"And look, here is the Marquis of Glenkellie to claim you for the first dance," Marianne told Diana, who was looking very pretty in a white gown with a silver net overlay, tiny silver stars sparkling in her dark brown hair. "Everyone will be asking who the lovely young lady he could hardly wait to dance with is, believe me."

Diana smiled shyly back at her. "I know he would far rather be dancing with you," she whispered as Lavinia turned away for a moment to speak to an acquaintance.

"Well, to tell the truth, there isn't anyone else I should like to dance with," Marianne admitted. Ever since Alexander had revealed the gossip to her and Ellen yesterday, she had been thinking about it; if Lord Ferry, a married man, was looking at her with speculation, who could she possibly trust? She would look at every dance partner with caution from now on.

Alexander arrived before them and executed a bow to each of them, greeting them very politely.

"I hope you have not given away my dance, Lady Diana?" he said with a warm twinkle. "The musicians are tuning up now, and I believe we will open with a quadrille."

"The quadrille is quite my favourite," Diana said shyly, placing her hand on his proffered arm. "I am very sensible of the honour you do me, Lord Glenkellie; thank you for asking me to dance."

"It is I who am honoured, Lady Diana." His eyes crinkled at the corners. "That is, so long as you do not step on my toes!"

Diana giggled as Alexander led her away, and Lavinia shook her head. "He's not remotely interested in her, I think, but he does seem very nice."

"Quite the nicest man of my acquaintance," Marianne said a little wistfully.

"Lavinia, who's that tall chap dancing with Diana?" Arthur hurried up to them, rather out of breath. He didn't bother to greet Marianne.

"The Marquis of Glenkellie, dear. You recall, Marianne introduced us to him and the dowager marchioness at the theatre last week, and he requested a dance with Diana."

"A marquis," Arthur puffed up. "Well, that's a coup! Glenkellie's very rich, I hear."

"Do not get your hopes up." Lavinia shook her head. "He only asked as a favour to Marianne, I think."

"Why should he owe *you* favours?"

Arthur looks rather like a carp, Marianne thought, his eyes bulging and his mouth open as he turned to her.

"Lord Glenkellie owes me nothing," she said, "but we are old friends."

"Indeed!" Arthur's brows shot up, and then he leaned forward. "You may have made a cuckold out of my uncle," he said viciously, "but you're still a Creighton, and I'll not have you bringing the name into disrepute. There are already rumours circulating about you!"

"Arthur!" Lavinia sounded genuinely shocked. Grasping her husband's arm, she shot Marianne an apologetic look. "Pray excuse us."

Marianne was more than happy to turn on her heel and hurry away. *How could anyone ever believe she had cuckolded her husband?* He had never tolerated her so much as *speaking* to another man unless he was present, had punished *her* if gentlemen tried to approach, claiming she must have enticed them with her smile, her manner. She would not have the slightest idea *how* to encourage a suitor!

Blinded by tears of rage and hurt, Marianne pushed her way through the crowd, finally escaping the ballroom and hurrying to a retiring room.

Alexander witnessed Marianne's flight and Lady Havers going in hasty pursuit. Caught in the middle of the dance floor, he could only bite his lip and watch, hoping Ellen could help with whatever had obviously upset Marianne.

"Are you in love with my aunt?"

The blunt question from Lady Diana as the pattern of the dance brought them back together made him miss a step.

"I beg your pardon?" he stuttered.

"Because I think she's in love with you." Diana's brown eyes were clear and guileless as she looked up at him.

"She claims she doesn't want to marry."

"She doesn't want to marry someone who would treat her as appallingly as my great-uncle did, she means. Would you treat her badly?"

"I would treat her like a queen," Alexander said, heartfelt.

Diana smiled. "I thought so. Your eyes give you away when you see her, you know."

"And to think, I thought you were shy," he marvelled.

"I am, rather." She blushed prettily. "But sometimes, direct action is called for, and I can be brave if I must. Clarissa and I talked and she said I absolutely had to talk to you. Especially since Mama thinks, er..." she trailed off.

"Thinks I should marry you?" Alexander asked.

"Well, yes. I should never want a husband in love with someone else, though, so I should take it as a very great favour if you do *not* pay me too much attention."

"Noted," he said gravely. "And thank you."

"What for?"

"Helping me come to a decision I have been pondering for some time: what exactly I should say to Lady Marianne. You are correct that I am in love with her, and marrying someone else wouldn't be fair to anyone involved."

Diana is really quite beautiful when she smiles like that, Alexander thought as the dance ended and everyone applauded the musicians. Offering his arm, he led Diana back to her mother and thanked her for the dance. Young men were already flocking around, jostling for introductions, and he paused to say to Diana, quietly so that nobody else would overhear, "Should you ever require any assistance, I pray you will not hesitate to call upon me."

"Thank you, Lord Glenkellie." She sank into a curtsey. "I am sure your partner for the next dance is eagerly awaiting you."

He hoped so. With a final bow in the Countess' direction, he turned and headed for the ballroom doors, hoping Marianne might have returned to the room. He could not see her or Ellen Havers anywhere.

Lady Jersey was close by the door, and he paused to offer his respects and ask whether she had seen Marianne. "She promised me the second dance," he said, trying to make his voice sound casual. "I've waited almost a decade to dance with her, you know."

"I do know, as a matter of fact. Not just a dance you've been waiting for either, is it?" Lady Jersey's eyes were uncomfortably sharp. "Don't waste any more time, Glenkellie."

"I'm trying, my lady."

"She's skittish, and rightfully so, but I believe she trusts you. Don't let her down."

"I won't."

Behind Lady Jersey, Alex saw Marianne re-entering the ballroom, Lady Havers by her side. Her colour was a little high, but she was holding her chin up defiantly, her eyes flashing fire.

Alex approached quickly, making a low bow. "Lady Marianne," he said. "The second dance is about to begin, if you are still willing to grant me the honour?"

She hesitated, and then said, "Would you mind if we danced the third instead of this one? I would like a little fresh air."

The French doors leading to the terrace were thrown wide open to allow cool air into the room, so Alex led her in that direction. Outside, he was careful to lead her to the balustrade well in view of everyone in the ballroom, so nobody could say any impropriety might be occurring.

"I saw you leave the room in something of a hurry a little while ago. Did your nephew say something to upset you?" Alex asked, trying to be tactful. He wanted to demand answers -- maybe punch Arthur a few times for putting that look on her face -- but he had no right to demand anything from Marianne.

"He seems to manage it on a regular basis," Marianne said, her mouth twisting as though she tasted something bad. "Pray, do not concern yourself."

"But I do concern myself," Alex let a little of the intense emotion he felt spill over into his words, "I find myself very concerned for you, Marianne. If gossip has reached your nephew, he could make your life very uncomfortable."

Her face tightened a little, but she met his eyes steadily. "I hope my friends know who I truly am... Alexander."

"I know who you are. You are not only the most beautiful woman I know, you are also the bravest person I've ever met, man *or* woman."

Startled at his description of her, Marianne blinked. "I'm not brave."

"How can you say that? You survived a living hell of a marriage for eight years, never letting anyone else know your true feelings. You carry scars to the soul as deep as any soldier, and yet you concern yourself more with the happiness of others than your soul. Your courage both awes and humbles me."

They stood a decorous foot apart, staring at each other, yet Marianne felt almost as though he enfolded her in a warm, comforting embrace. There was no doubting the sincerity of Alexander's words... or the depth of his regard for her.

"I cannot bear to see you insulted and degraded," he said at last, when she could not find words to speak. "I cannot. I know you do not wish to marry, and I would never press you, though my heart's desire is... well, I said I would not, and I will not." His jaw clenched as though he was struggling with himself, and she saw his fists were opening and closing at his sides. "Instead, I wish to offer you something else, with no expectations. My mother plans to travel to Italy to visit with her sister this year; she will remain at least a twelvemonth. She has taken a liking to you and pressed me to ask if you would like to accompany her."

Marianne's mouth fell open. "Your mother wants me to go to Italy with her?" she said at last, incredulously.

"Indeed. My aunt lives in Florence; she is a *contessa* and very well respected. You might wish to remain with her there, if you wish."

"Because here, there will always be gossip and innuendo," Marianne said quietly. "You're offering me an *escape*."

Her hand rested on the stone balustrade at the edge of the terrace, and he reached out to put his own over it. "I would offer you everything I have, everything I am, if only you would accept," Alexander said.

She could see it in his eyes, his love as intense and unchanging as the day he had been forced to leave her to go to war. "I promised I'd wait for you, and I couldn't," she whispered.

"I promised I would come back for you, and I failed you. I can never make up for what you suffered, but please, Marianne. Allow me to be of service, in this or any other way you wish."

His fingers were warm on hers, and she wanted more. Wanted his arms around her, wanted the *safety* of him, the sure and certain knowledge that he sought only to make her happy.

"Ask me." She could barely get the words out, her voice a thin croak, and she had to repeat herself before Alexander's eyes widened in comprehension.

Slowly, he lifted her hand and brought it to his lips, his eyes never leaving hers.

"Lady Marianne," he said, and she loved him all the more for his choice to be formal while avoiding the hated name of Creighton, "would you do me the very great honour of granting me your hand in marriage?"

She had to take a deep breath to answer, but he had called her the bravest person he knew, and his belief in her courage made it easier to believe in herself.

"Only if you promise we can go to Italy on our honeymoon. I've always wanted to see Florence."

CHAPTER TWENTY-ONE

ALEXANDER COULD HARDLY BELIEVE what he was hearing as Marianne spoke, her words making all his dreams come true. “Anything,” he promised fervently. “Anywhere you wish.”

"Only, perhaps we could wait until later in the year? I did promise to go to Amelia Pembroke when she is brought to bed with her child, and I think Ellen Havers may need me in August for the same reason.” Marianne gave him an appealing look, one he knew he would always struggle to resist.

"Wait until August to get married?” Alexander’s distress at the thought of waiting so long must have been quite obvious, because Marianne chuckled and squeezed his fingers gently between her gloved ones.

"No, no. Just to go to Italy. I should like to get married as soon as it can be arranged, actually. I think we have waited quite long enough.”

"Far too long,” he agreed, lifting her hand to kiss it again. A loud cough nearby recalled him to their situation and the distinct lack of privacy, and he lowered her hand with a grimace.

"This is a poor time and place for this conversation, but I hope you will allow me to say that you have made me the happiest man in England.”

"Perhaps you might call for me tomorrow and you can tell me then,” Marianne teased him.

"A drive in Hyde Park?” Alexander suggested, and she inclined her head in acceptance.

"So long as you remember to bring the bread.”

"Oh, I will not forget, I promise. I cannot ever recall seeing you so happy as when you fed the ducks the other day!” Her laughter had been a balm to his wounded soul; he had sent his driver to get more bread so they might stay longer.

If Marianne wanted to hand-feed every duck on London on a daily basis, he would buy a bakery to provide her with an endless supply of bread.

Marianne giggled, her eyes bright with mischief. "I can only think of one other time I *have* ever been so happy, Alexander... and that is right at this very moment."

"You have truly made me the happiest man in the world," he said through a thick lump of emotion in his throat. "I can only strive in every way I can conceive of to give you equal joy in return."

They returned to the ballroom in time for the third dance. Alexander felt lighter than he had in many years as they moved together through the patterns of the dance, Marianne's happy countenance buoying his spirits. Spotting his mother standing near the edge of the dance floor, he sent her a joyous grin. This was not the appropriate venue to announce their engagement, but tomorrow he would send a notice to the newspapers and perhaps his mother would host a dinner party in the next week or so.

Since Marianne was a widow, there was nobody Alex need apply to for her hand, though he supposed he should do her nephew the courtesy of advising him privately of their engagement. Perhaps he'd stop by the Creighton townhouse after he returned Marianne home tomorrow.

"September would be a good time to leave for Italy," he remarked to Marianne as the dance brought them together. "The seas will not be too rough then, and winter is much milder in the southern climes. We could spend much of the summer at Glenkellie if you like, before going to Havers Hall in August, and then taking ship once you are happy to leave Lady Havers."

"I think that sounds a wonderful plan," Marianne agreed. "Shall we see Rome as well as Florence?"

"Indeed, and Venice too, and anywhere else you might wish. Do you wish to see only Italy, or have you a hankering to visit other places in the Mediterranean?"

"You truly will take me anywhere I wish to go, won't you?" Marianne said in wondering tones as the dance ended.

Alexander offered his arm to lead her from the floor. "Of course I will. Anything you wish for, you need only name it. The throne of England might be slightly beyond my resources, but any lesser goal, I will do anything within my power to attain for you."

"Now just a minute," a loud voice interrupted, and Alex looked around to see Lord Ferry scowling pugnaciously at him. "Are you trying to cut me out, Glenkellie? Damn it, I knew you overheard in Brooks'. Lady Creighton," he turned to

Marianne, "I can assure you, my resources are beyond anything Glenkellie can muster from his Scottish hillsides. You may name your price."

Gasps of shock rippled around them, and Alex tensed. *What the hell was Ferry thinking?* He'd just propositioned Marianne in *public*!

"Lord Ferry," Marianne said in a very clear, cold voice, "I am not for sale at *any* price."

"Come now..." Ferry blustered.

But Alex had heard more than enough. "Ferry," he said, in a low, dangerous voice, "you are speaking to the future Marchioness of Glenkellie. You may apologise now, or you'll meet me at dawn."

Ferry froze, mouth wide open as he took in Alexander's murderous expression, before he gulped audibly. "I, ah," he said, "Ah, ah, do beg your pardon, Glenkellie."

"Not apologise to *me*," Alexander said in disgust, "to the *lady*." God, the man was a complete craven. It would have been satisfying as hell to run him through for the insult. Instead, he had to stand and watch Ferry's panicked, fawning apology to a tight-lipped Marianne.

"Go away, you repulsive little man," Marianne said at last, and everyone with earshot, all of whom had been hanging on every word of the confrontation, burst out laughing.

Crimson-faced, Lord Ferry fled.

"His *poor* wife," Marianne said with a sigh, turning back to Alex. He was fighting down his own laughter and couldn't speak.

"Well done, dearest," another voice said, and Alex turned to see his mother approaching. She drew Marianne into a fond embrace. "What a marchioness you will be! You must let me introduce you to my very dear friend, the Duchess of Balford. Alexander? Do get us some champagne, there's a dear." She pressed an empty glass into his hand and drew Marianne away into a crowd of elegantly dressed ladies.

Alexander could hardly get near Marianne for the rest of the ball. Ladies who had twitched their skirts aside earlier in the evening fawned over her now, and word spread fast of her magnificent set-down of Lord Ferry... faster than news of their engagement, as they were soon to discover.

"A high-perch phaeton!" Marianne clapped her hands with glee as she descended the steps of the Havers townhouse on Alexander's arm the following morning. "I have always wanted to ride in one of these!"

"I know. You mentioned it once to me, long ago. I said one day I would have one and take you driving in it, do you remember?"

"I do, though I had not thought on it until this moment. I'm surprised *you* remember!" She turned luminous eyes up to him as he handed her carefully up into the seat and accepted the reins from his tiger.

"The dream of riding with you proudly sitting at my side kept me going through some of the darkest times during the war," he said quietly, drawing a thick blanket placed on the seat over her lap and tucking it in to keep her warm.

Laying one hand on his arm, Marianne tilted her head deliberately to show off her pretty hat and said, "Then let us to Hyde Park, my lord. You shall have your fill of riding with me today. We might even need to stop for fresh horses!"

Alex's laugh lingered behind them as the horses set off at a brisk trot.

Talking and laughing and having to stop every few minutes to greet someone who wished to congratulate them, they had been parading through Hyde Park for over an hour when Marianne spied her family. "Look, in that open landau there! We must stop, Alexander."

Lavinia was smiling, Diana beside her waving excitedly until her mother placed a gentle restraining hand on her arm. Marianne smiled back. She and Lavinia would never be close, but at least she was reasonably confident Lavinia wouldn't try to force any of her daughters into marriages they did not want. Hopefully she would check the worst of Arthur's ambitions and be an advocate for her daughters if they needed it.

Arthur did not look pleased to see them. "A word, Glenkellie?" he said crisply once polite greetings had been exchanged.

"Since I suspect this concerns you, would you care to accompany me?" Alexander asked Marianne. "I will gladly deal with it if you would rather not."

"I think I would prefer to be involved in discussions about my own future," Marianne decided. "Pray excuse me."

"Go home," Arthur instructed Lavinia. "I will walk back; it's not far."

Lavinia looked at Marianne, her expression concerned, but Marianne gestured she should go. After all, what could Arthur do to her with Alexander present? She was quite safe.

They left Alexander's tiger holding the horses and followed Arthur across the grass towards the Serpentine, a glassy, reflective silver under the winter-grey sky. A pair of mute swans floated serenely by, a stark contrast to the churning in Marianne's stomach. Even though she tried to tell herself Arthur had no power over her, the prospect of a confrontation brought back old terrors.

Alexander's arm under her hand was strong and rock-steady; she drew strength from his calm assurance. *This was her choice*, she reminded herself. She didn't want to let Alexander handle all her problems, though she was confident he could do so. She was taking control of her own life and doing what she wanted, with his support.

Finally Arthur seemed to judge they were far enough from others to speak privately, and he whirled to face them. "What in God's name were you *thinking*?" he half-shouted. "A confrontation in the middle of a Society ball over *her*?"

Marianne blinked.

Alexander looked startled. "I beg your pardon?" he snapped, not sounding apologetic in the least. "Would you have me allow Lady Marianne's good name to be publicly sullied by a disrespectful arse of a man? Not while I breathe."

Arthur didn't even seem to hear him, puffed up with his own rage. "And you!" Turning on Marianne, he jabbed a finger at her. "Two paramours almost coming to blows over you, in public! You *whore*!" Spittle flew as he shouted, and she instinctively took several steps back. Arthur looked only too much like his uncle, her dead husband, in one of his rages.

Alexander moved in front of her at once, letting out a sound a great deal like a snarl, but salvation came suddenly from a far less likely source.

One of the swans which a moment earlier was floating so peacefully on the water obviously took exception to Arthur's threatening gestures and shouts. In a swirling storm of white wings and enraged hissing, the swan attacked, thrashing at Arthur's face with beak and wings.

Cursing as he tried to beat the swan back, Arthur stumbled backwards, toppling into the shallow water behind him with a gigantic splash and a high-pitched shriek.

"Well," Alexander said with a deep chuckle as the swan continued to harass Arthur, "that saves me from planting him a facer, I suppose. Do you think your friends the ducks set that swan on him on purpose?"

Marianne could not hold it in; she burst out laughing, a release of tension like a spring uncoiling inside her bubbling up and out of her mouth in throaty giggles. She could only lean on Alexander and watch as her nephew received a thorough thrashing, quite at the mercy of the furious bird.

The swan finally backed off, retreating to guard its mate, still hissing in Arthur's direction occasionally as the Earl of Creighton climbed out of the water, sobbing with rage and cradling one hand close to his chest in obvious pain.

"If you ever again speak to, or about, my future wife in any kind of derogatory way, I will kill you," Alexander said, his tone cold and dispassionate. "It is only for the sake of your wife and children that I allow the punishment God's creature has meted out to be satisfactory. Let this divine retribution be your final warning!"

They walked away with Marianne still laughing, hoping she would never forget the image of the dripping, spluttering Earl of Creighton casting fearful glances in equal measure at Alexander and the swan.

"Divine retribution indeed," she managed to splutter at last, as they returned to the phaeton and Alexander lifted her carefully up to the seat. "That was *wonderful*!"

"Perhaps we should foster a rumour that God will wreak vengeance on any who offend you." Alexander cast her a teasing grin as he took up the reins. "I daresay it would save both of us a great deal of trouble!"

In the distance, Arthur Creighton began the slow, soggy trudge across the grass away from the Serpentine, moaning at the pain in his injured hand and still keeping a wary eye on the swan.

The sun broke through the clouds just then, thin rays of bright yellow sunshine streaming down on the phaeton as the horses set off once again in a prancing trot. Marianne turned her face upwards, smiling as she thought that not so long ago, she would not have dared for fear of a freckle appearing on her nose. Alexander would likely tell her any emerging freckles were his favourite thing about her, because they were gained while she was enjoying herself. Snuggling closer to him under the thick blanket he tucked over both their laps, she rested her head against his shoulder and sighed with utter contentment.

EPILOGUE

Four weeks later, St. George's Church, Hanover Square

Alexander's heart was full as he watched Marianne walk towards him, wearing a stunning new gown of pale gold silk trimmed with white Brussels lace. While Arthur had issued a suitably grovelling apology the day after the swan incident in Hyde Park, Marianne had declined his offer to walk her down the aisle. Instead, she walked alone, preceded by her youngest niece Penelope, strewing freshly picked snowdrops in her path.

He'd offered to denude every hothouse in London for more expensive flowers for her, of course, but Marianne had told him she'd far rather have snowdrops, that earliest of spring blooms, easily gathered in February.

"The are the first flowers of spring, the season of new beginnings," she'd told him, and Alexander at once had agreed there could be no flower more appropriate.

While he had hoped to obtain a special licence and wed Marianne within a week of her acceptance, his mother and Marianne had persuaded him that waiting for the banns to be called and throwing a grand wedding with the cream of the Ton on the guest list would forever silence any gossip.

Since he was entirely at Marianne's mercy, he'd agreed to whatever they wanted, though he'd privately bemoaned to her his reluctance to wait even a day more than he had to for her.

"We've waited this long," she'd told him tenderly, placing her soft hand against his cheek. "I want - no, I *need* - this wedding to be as different from my first as it is possible to be, Alexander."

Understanding, he'd kicked himself for his insensitivity. "Only tell me what I need do to make it so, beloved."

"Be patient with me - and be yourself," she'd told him, reaching up to kiss him lovingly.

Marianne's hand trembled a little in her white silk glove as she placed it in Alexander's, and he looked a query at her, brow furrowing with concern. She smiled back at him determinedly. The ghosts of her past were not going to cloud this, the wedding day she'd always wanted.

Instead of her father and two bored servants as witnesses in a dusty parlour, there was a church filled with her and Alexander's friends and family. The vicar was a kindly, serious gentleman who had insisted on speaking to them both privately before the ceremony, intent on being certain they were both happy before proceeding. And last but certainly not least, instead of a leering old man, there was her beloved Alexander, tall and handsome, his eyes filled with love for her as he spoke his vows.

"Yes," she said it loud and clear as the vicar asked if she accepted Alexander as her husband. "I do."

His smile was filled with both joy and relief as he squeezed her hands, and Marianne gazed lovingly back at him as the ceremony concluded and they emerged from the church to the rousing cheers of their friends.

Thomas and Ellen Havers had insisted on throwing a wedding party for them after the ceremony, and afterwards they planned to return to Alexander's townhouse and remain in London for another month before travelling to Hampshire to visit with the Pembrokes -- the only friends who were unable to attend their wedding. Too close to her confinement, Amelia had instead sent many excited letters and a promise of a gentle mare from their famous stables as a wedding gift for Marianne.

Once Amelia's child was born, they would go to Portsmouth and take ship there for Scotland, cutting several days off the journey to Glenkellie. Marianne was looking forward very much to seeing Alexander's childhood home, which he described as 'an ancient pile' but his mother had told her was one of the most beautiful castles in Scotland.

Lady Helena was sailing for Italy in late March, and they would join her in September after Marianne saw Ellen through her confinement as well. She had already cornered Lavinia, who as the mother of five children was the most experienced source on childbirth she knew, and quizzed her for so much detail Lavinia turned quite pale.

Their conversations had taught Marianne about a great deal more than just childbirth, however. Despite a great deal of blushing, Lavinia had imparted quite a lot of knowledge about what happened in the marriage bed when the wife wasn't unwilling.

Knowing happy couples like the Havers and the Pembrokes, Marianne had slowly become aware there could be true and genuine affection between husband and wife. More than once while staying with Thomas and Ellen she had accidentally come across them in a passionate embrace, and the thought of sharing such embraces with Alexander made her feel quite warm and flushed.

Far from fearing her second wedding night, she was rather looking forward to it.

"Do you think anyone would notice if we sneaked away?" she whispered to Alexander after they had dined and danced and talked for what felt like hours.

"To go where? Are you feeling quite well?" He looked at her with concern.

"Oh, I'm fine." Sliding her hand into his, she squeezed. "I would like to be alone with my husband, that's all."

"Really?" A wide grin broke across his face. "Then let us not waste another minute, my darling marchioness!"

They slipped out and ran down the stairs, jumping into the waiting Glenkellie coach, where Alexander lost no time pulling Marianne into his arms.

"I love you," he whispered, raining kisses across her face. "I have always, always loved you."

"I love you, too," Marianne said, nestling close against him and resting her head against his strong shoulder, safe in his arms and secure in the knowledge that she was finally right where she had always longed to be.

~ THE END ~

Read on to enjoy the next book in the series, *A Duke For Diana.* Poor Diana's first meeting with her Duke does not go how she always dreamed it might... but when she and her sister Clarissa are invited to join their aunt on her wedding trip to Italy, Diana has a second chance to impress, just by being herself.

A Duke for Diana

CATHERINE BILSON

CONTENTS

CHAPTER ONE

In all her eighteen years, Diana Creighton had never imagined anything one-half so glamorous as the Duchess of Balford's ball. She stood beside her mother in slightly terrified awe, trying not to stare goggle-eyed at the ladies surrounding her, each one dressed more opulently than the last, in silks and satins every colour of the rainbow and gems of incalculable value.

A year ago, Diana was living a quietly respectable life as the daughter of a gentleman lawyer in the city of Durham, her expectations limited to perhaps finding a suitor among her father's acquaintance. Then her great-uncle died before managing to father an heir, her father inherited a wealthy and influential earldom, and Diana was suddenly a titled lady, with a dowry of ten thousand pounds and a whole new set of expectations - and limitations - on her shoulders.

"Try not to gape, Diana," her mother said under her breath, and Diana clamped her lips together tightly before realising her mouth hadn't even been open.

There was no point protesting her innocence, though; Lavinia, Lady Creighton, had already moved on.

"Stand up straighter, and smile, for heaven's sakes. You're positively Friday-faced; what's the matter?"

"Nothing," Diana began, wanting to explain that she was merely a little overwhelmed by the glittering throng.

They hadn't even entered the ball proper yet; were waiting in the receiving line. Diana's aunt-by-marriage - well, sort of - Marianne was immediately in front of them, greeting their hostess quite warmly.

Seeing Marianne again was by far the best thing about this visit to London so far, Diana thought, keeping her back straight and her head high, pasting a smile on her lips. The Dowager Countess of Creighton was not only the most beautiful woman Diana had ever seen, she was also one of the kindest. Diana was thoroughly ashamed of the way her parents had treated Marianne, to the point Marianne had actually fled to her friend Lady Havers with nothing more than the clothes on her back and the small amount of money Diana and her sister Clarissa had managed to raise in her pocket.

"Lady Creighton," Marianne introduced them to the duchess, "and her daughter Lady Diana."

A tall woman with an imperious air, the duchess looked them over with bright dark eyes. She seemed to consider Diana for quite a while before giving her a little nod. "You must allow me to introduce you to my stepson, Lady Diana."

"Oh, your grace," Lavinia gushed. "That would be a great honour!"

"I shall find you a little later. William will dance with Lady Diana." The duchess gave them a dismissive nod, and Lavinia tugged on Diana's arm, pulling her on into the ballroom.

"A real duke!" Lavinia started nattering immediately. "That will be a coup for you, if she does indeed introduce you! Balford's easily the most eligible gentleman on the marriage mart this year, though, so you mustn't get your hopes up..."

Diana had no hopes whatsoever. Yes, her father might be an earl now, but dukes married princesses and the daughters of other dukes. An earl's daughter would have to be blindingly well-dowered, or an absolute diamond, or probably both, even to be considered, and she was neither. Ten thousand was a drop in the ocean compared to the vast Balford wealth, and Diana was self-honest enough to accept her own attractions as merely a sort of bland prettiness. Compared to Marianne, for example, a tall, auburn-haired beauty who drew stares wherever she went, Diana was of medium height, with medium brown hair, plain brown eyes, a slightly snub nose and unspectacular abilities in music, art, languages and every other skill in which young ladies were expected to demonstrate accomplishment.

Lavinia, though, was bound and determined to thrust Diana in the path of every eligible, titled gentleman she could manage, starting with the Marquis of Glenkellie. Which wouldn't have been unacceptable at all, considering that Alexander Rutherford was tall, handsome despite a scar on his face, rich and not even too many years older than Diana. He would have been a marvellous suitor, indeed, were he not completely and hopelessly in love with Marianne.

Glenkellie was both kind and well-mannered, however, and took Diana onto the floor for a dance when declining would have been embarrassing. He even told her that he hoped she would call on him if she ever needed any assistance, a courtesy she thanked him for with genuine appreciation, because she thought he actually meant it. She just hoped Marianne could bring herself to accept him; her first marriage, to Diana's great-uncle, was the stuff of nightmares.

Alex returned Diana to her mother at the end of the set, and Diana winced to see Lavinia waiting with a tall, fair-haired man in his middle years, a man with a thin nose and piercing blue eyes who looked her up and down, his lip curling.

"This is your daughter, Lady Creighton?" he said with a pronounced German accent.

"Indeed, your Highness. Diana, this is Prince Stefan Mondenbosch."

Diana curtsied, a sense of unreality washing over her. A prince? She was being introduced to a real, live prince?

The prince actually sighed, and then gave a stiff little bow. "You will favour me with a dance, Lady Diana."

She didn't think it was a question, which was rather rude of him, but it was quite out of the question for her to decline anyway, so she accepted his offered hand. He said nothing for the first few minutes of the set, barely looking at her, and Diana felt her awe receding until it was suppressed entirely by a wave of indignation at his rudeness. Prince or not, ignoring her while he was actually dancing with her was the height of bad manners.

"Have you been in England long?" she asked, wondering if perhaps she could at least get him talking about himself. The young men she'd interacted with at social events in Durham were always happiest when talking about their own interests, she'd noticed.

"A few months."

"And are you enjoying it?" she tried again when he fell immediately silent after the brief reply.

"Not especially." He looked her full in the face. "The ladies are not as attractive, or such good dancers, as those at home in Germany."

Diana flushed with shock at the insult. A retort hovered on the tip of her tongue, but she swallowed it, knowing that creating a scene here at one of Society's premier balls would be the death knell for any chance of her making a successful match. Instead, she clamped the tip of her tongue between her teeth and concentrated on taking every step in the complicated measure with complete accuracy.

The prince didn't even return her to her mother at the end of the dance, just escorted her to the side of the floor and walked away, leaving her fuming, almost light-headed with rage.

"I see you've met the Petulant Prince," an amused voice said, and Diana turned to see Lady Jersey, one of the influential patronesses of Almacks, watching her. They had met just the once, when Marianne took Lavinia and Diana to meet Lady

Jersey to request vouchers, and Diana had the hopeful feeling the formidable countess might have quite liked her.

She sank a low, respectful curtsy. "Good evening, Lady Jersey."

"Good evening, Lady Diana. I won't ask if you're enjoying yourself, as from the look on your face, you'd rather be almost anywhere else."

"Despite my last partner, I'm quite enjoying myself, I promise." With a glance at the prince's retreating back, Diana asked quietly "Why *is* he so petulant?"

"Doesn't want to be here," Lady Jersey replied promptly. "He's a fourth son, and of no particular use to his father. Something of an embarrassment, if the gossip I've heard is correct, and I can't imagine why it wouldn't be. Sent over here to make himself useful to the ambassador and perhaps find himself a wealthy, well-connected English family to marry into."

"Obviously the Creightons aren't wealthy or well-connected enough for his consideration," Diana said dryly, but Lady Jersey shook her head.

"Don't take it personally, my dear. Prince Stefan is under orders, but he doesn't care for them. Like many young men his age, he'd rather be gambling and whor-, ah, having a good time, than settling down to marriage."

"I see."

"Don't be downcast. There are a few good ones. I heard Julianne say she'd like you to meet William, and I spy him over there now. Come, let me present you."

"Who are Julianne and William?" Diana asked, helplessly drawn along in the countess's imperious wake.

"Oh... the duchess, and her stepson. Balford." The last word wasn't addressed to Diana, but to the back of a tall man, who turned around and smiled wryly upon seeing Lady Jersey.

"My lady." He bowed politely, before his gaze skimmed past her to Diana. Shoulders heaved in a visible sigh, and Diana debated fleeing before she could even be introduced. Lady Jersey's hand locked around her wrist like a manacle.

"Balford, you should meet Lady Diana Creighton, the new earl's daughter."

The duke couldn't be many years older than she was, and he was really very handsome, Diana thought. Or would be, without the irritated look he was clearly not trying very hard to suppress.

"Lady Diana." He bowed, not an inch lower than was suitable for a duke to an earl's daughter. She curtsied the minimum in return, annoyed by his rudeness.

If he didn't want to be here, why had he come in the first place? But then, the party was in his own house, she supposed; it would look a little strange if he didn't attend his own stepmother's ball.

"Your Grace," she murmured.

"Lady Diana has my permission to dance the waltz," Lady Jersey said pointedly.

"Of course she does. Well then, Lady Diana, are you engaged for the next dance?"

She really did think about saying no. Dancing with the Petulant Prince had soured her on dancing for the evening, but the thought of having to sit out the rest of the night because she'd declined an arrogant duke in a fit of pique was even more unpalatable. So she smiled and tilted her head graciously, laid her hand on his offered arm and pretended not to notice Lady Jersey's smug smile.

All the guests had arrived at the ball now, it would undoubtedly be celebrated as a wonderful 'crush' but to Diana it just seemed too crowded and too hot. The duke walked with long strides, making no allowance for her shorter legs or the narrow skirt of her gown which forced her to take small, mincing steps. She had to almost run to keep up with him, was sweating in a most unladylike manner when they reached the end of the lines on the dance floor and he spun her around to face him, expression grim.

The room swayed around her, everything going cloudy and dim. Puzzled by what was happening, Diana frowned.

The duke frowned back at her.

And then everything faded out and she collapsed in a senseless heap at his feet.

CHAPTER TWO

"AND HE JUST *WALKED away*?" Diana's younger sister, Lady Clarissa Creighton, sat cross-legged on the end of Diana's bed and stared at her, agog.

"Well, I didn't see it." Diana sighed, leaning back against her pillows. "But yes, apparently he did, after rolling his eyes and saying 'Not another one!' loudly enough for half the room to hear him."

"What an absolute donkey's behind!" Clarissa said.

Diana managed a small giggle, though the humiliation of the evening still burned hot in her chest. "He's a duke, Clarry. You can't call him a donkey's anything."

"I'll call him what I want, since he left my unconscious sister in the middle of the dance floor! If I ever get to meet him, I shall give him a piece of my mind!" Clarissa swished her hands in front of her, almost as though pretending to slap the offensive aristocrat in question across the face.

"I hope you never do. Undoubtedly, he'd be rude and dismissive to you as well." Pulling her knees up to her chest, Diana wrapped her arms around them, hugging herself tightly. She had no idea what tonight's events would mean for her Season, but she had the sneaking suspicion that the answer was nothing good. She'd come around from her faint to find herself in a retiring room being fussed over by her mother and the Duchess of Balford. There were other ladies present, peering over at them and whispering behind gloved hands, and Diana caught Marianne's name being whispered. Something had happened with her aunt, something shocking enough to distract them from Diana fainting at the duke's feet. Lavinia went white around the lips when Diana tried to ask, though, hushing her sharply.

The duchess was very kind, but Diana had the feeling the other woman was silently laughing at her. She tried to explain she had just been overcome by the heat, but it was apparent nobody was listening, even her mother. With hot tears of frustration stinging at the back of her eyes, she said quietly that she wanted to go home.

"I think that would probably be best, dear," the duchess said kindly. "I shall have your carriage brought around directly. Do you think you will be able to walk, or shall I call a footman to carry you?"

"She'll walk, thank you," Lavinia said hastily. "It was only a momentary swoon. Diana is in very rude health, generally."

"I've never swooned in my life." Diana couldn't quite believe it had happened, still. "I didn't know what was happening."

"Perhaps you're sickening for something," the duchess said. "Or perhaps it's just all the excitement." She gave them a polite smile and left, obviously dismissing them from her attention.

Lavinia didn't say a single word on the carriage ride back to their townhouse, just stared in silence out of the window. As they entered the house, she told Diana to go straight to bed before going herself into the parlour, where Diana was fairly sure her mother headed straight for the sherry decanter.

"As debuts go, I don't think it could have been much worse," Diana told her sister.

"But it wasn't your fault!"

"I'm fairly sure that's not going to matter." Diana twirled a long curl around her finger, tugged on it as she contemplated her dreams of a glittering, successful Season where her ordinary self was somehow transformed into the belle of every ball.

"It's not fair." Clarissa's jaw jutted stubbornly in a way Diana knew all too well, and she let go of the curl and reached out to embrace her sister.

"It's all right, Clarry. It doesn't matter."

Clarissa gave her a doubtful look, but Diana made herself smile in response, even though the heaviness in her chest gave the lie to her words. She suspected it was actually going to matter quite a lot.

When their father broke his arm in some never-quite-explained incident involving a swan in the park the following day, Diana took it as an excellent excuse to avoid going into company for a few days, hoping against hope that everyone would have forgotten about her little faint by the time she re-engaged. A few days was definitely not enough, as she soon discovered, when Marianne (now happily engaged to Alexander) introduced her to a smiling young man at a dinner party about a week after the Balford's ball. The young man had been glancing down the table at Diana throughout dinner, a smile and an expression of apparent interest on his face, and then approached Marianne once the ladies and gentlemen had regrouped after the meal with the obvious intention of garnering an introduction to Diana. Rather flattered by his interest, Diana curtsied as Marianne introduced Lord Amberle, a baronet from the island of Guernsey.

"My niece, Lady Diana Creighton," Marianne concluded the introduction, and the appreciative smile on Amberle's face faded. He took a step backward.

"The Fainting Flower?" he said.

"I *beg* your pardon?" Marianne's beautiful face hardened.

"Do beg your pardon, Lady Creighton, but I've just remembered a prior arrangement. Must be off." He sketched a hasty bow and retreated with all speed, pausing only briefly to speak with their hostess before departing.

"Honestly, he looked more likely to swoon than me," Diana said when Marianne appeared quite lost for words.

"You jest, but I know how nicknames can stick." Marianne recovered herself, took Diana's arm. "Young men can be cruel and thoughtless. I'd have Alex speak to him, but..."

"Lord Glenkellie would end up taking half London to task, I expect." Diana shrugged, trying to give the impression it didn't matter, even though internally she wanted to cry and scream that it wasn't fair, it wasn't her fault. "I highly doubt Lord Amberle was the originator of the nickname." *That was almost certainly Balford*, she thought, fury welling anew at the rude, thoughtless duke. His behaviour was beyond ungentlemanly. Failing to catch her when she fainted was one thing - she supposed it possible he'd just been caught by surprise - but to walk away and leave her literally lying in a swoon on the floor was quite another, and now to discover she had a nickname which she'd almost certainly never live down placed him quite simply beyond the pale.

I hate him. If she ever happened to meet the arrogant young duke again, Diana determined then and there she would give him a piece of her mind. Considering the nickname, she was fairly sure her prospects for finding a husband in London had shrunk to nothing, so she really had nothing to lose with such a confrontation. In fact, she was quite looking forward to it. She'd already written several choice phrases in her journal she'd like to share with him, with some rather pithy language suggested by Clarissa. Just the act of writing them down had felt cathartic, but she was still determined to say them to his face, should she ever be afforded the opportunity.

It wasn't until much later that evening, settled into her own bed with Clarissa sitting beside her as was their custom as Diana recounted the day's events for her sister's edification, that the reality of her situation hit home and hot tears began to spill down Diana's cheeks. Her season was an utter failure, she was stuck with a nickname she'd never live down, the only suitors she would attract now would be those desperate for her dowry, and it was all the fault of one selfish, thoughtless, uncaring duke.

"I hate him," she sobbed into Clarissa's shoulder. "I *hate* him."

"He's a monster," Clarissa said fiercely, enraged on her sister's behalf. "A demon. The Demonic Duke."

Diana sniffled a faint chuckle. "If only *that* nickname would stick."

They both knew it wouldn't. Nobody short of the Prince Regent would dare offend someone as powerful as a duke of the realm with such a nickname. The daughter of a newly-raised earl was fair game; a duke wasn't, even if he was young and had only held his title a year.

"Maybe I could tell it to Lady Jersey. She might laugh." Even if she did, her next remark would be to tell Diana never to repeat the nickname to anyone else, lest it come to the ears of the duke, or worse, the duchess. Diana's own reputation might be in shreds, but Clarissa would have her own come-out in a year, their sister Penelope in three years' time. Diana wouldn't risk the family's good name any more than she already had. Annoying the powerful Balfords would be the death of all their hopes.

Lavinia had heard the nickname too, Diana could tell, even though her mother didn't mention it. She was decidedly white-lipped and wild-eyed when she entered Diana's bedroom the following morning and told her to get up, they were paying calls that day.

"What's the point?" Clarissa said, sitting up and frowning. "Nobody's going to pay court to her, nobody she wants, anyway. We might as well just go home to Durham."

"Durham isn't home any longer, when will you get that through your silly head!" Lavinia threw up her hands before gesturing around the opulently decorated room. "*This* is our world now. We need to fit into it."

"That's not going so well," Diana muttered into her pillow, before sighing and rolling over, touching Clarissa's arm gently as her sister opened her mouth again, obviously about to antagonise their mother further. "Yes, Mama. Where are we going today, and what should I wear?"

"We're going to visit Lady Treeve, and then Mrs. Timms-Lacey, and I've told Anne to put out the pink spotted satin for you."

Diana suppressed a groan. Clarissa let it out for her. "That dress is ghastly, Mama; far too many frills and bows. Diana looks a fright in it, no matter how fashionable the *Ladies' Magazine* proclaims the style to be!"

"It's the most expensive of your new gowns, and you *will* wear it. Lady Treeve's son is in line to inherit his grandfather's marquessate, and Mrs. Timms-Lacey is the older sister of the Earl of Porthcarrick. Both very eligible gentlemen who've let it be known they intend to seek a wife this season."

"Neither of whom will want the Fainting Flower," Diana muttered under her breath, but she knew her mother would not be gainsaid, not in this mood. Lavinia seemed determined to try and brush the whole disaster under the carpet, as though by insisting nothing had happened, everyone would forget all about it.

As she sat in Lady Treeve's parlour wearing the despised pink satin gown, the fabric slippery and sweaty everywhere it touched her skin, listening to the lady give polite excuses as to why her son wouldn't be able to make their acquaintance that day, Diana tried desperately to think up some reason why she couldn't participate in the rest of the Season. Perhaps she could fake an illness? Claim her faint had been merely the first indication of something more serious? Clarissa would cover for her, but a doctor would probably see through the ruse in an instant, she reflected gloomily. She had never had any skill at dissembling.

"Well, we must be off," Lavinia said, rising to her feet, drawing Diana up with her perforce since she had a strong grip on Diana's wrist. "Lord Porthcarrick's sister has invited us to call, you know. Diana is very much in demand."

"I'm sure." Lady Treeve hid a smile behind her hand, and Diana died a thousand deaths at the older woman's glance of condescending amusement.

"Thank you for receiving us, my lady," she said, somehow keeping her voice steady by sheer effort of will, and a little sympathy softened Lady Treeve's expression.

"Perhaps a visit to Bath might be in order," the lady said, as they turned towards the door. "For your health, you know. The climate might suit you better than London."

There might be some people there who haven't heard about the Fainting Flower, Diana interpreted the remark, but she thought it was kindly meant. She curtsied.

Lavinia, however, was clearly fuming as they left the Treeve townhouse and climbed back into their waiting carriage. "Bath, indeed! The only husband you'd find there is some elderly, infirm type who wants a nursemaid, not a wife!"

"I think she was trying to help," Diana murmured.

"She could help by introducing you to her son, as she said she would!" Lavinia's nostrils pinched together.

"It's not as though she signed a legal contract, Mama," Diana attempted to soothe her mother's ruffled feathers. "You're too used to dealing with Papa's clients from his legal practice."

"I cannot abide people who don't keep their word." Expression tight, Lavinia nodded to their coachman. "I begin to realise why your father had very little use for the aristocracy, when he had to deal with them on legal matters. They think nothing of lying to your face."

"So we're going home now?" Diana asked hopefully.

"Certainly not. I sent a note to Mrs. Timms-Lacey, telling her we would call today. *We* will keep our promises. And tonight, we are engaged for a dinner at Lady Danforth's house; she has *two* sons both of an age to marry, the viscount and his younger brother, both very personable, I'm given to understand..."

Diana leaned back against the squabs and let her mind drift, let her mother's natter become vague, meaningless sounds in the background of the scene she conjured in her imagination. She'd always been happier in her own company than anyone else's, save perhaps Clarissa, because she was always able to retreat into a happier place inside her own mind.

The scene she imagined now was a peaceful walk in the woods, giant oak and beech trees towering around her in an ancient forest. Sunlight filtered through the leafy canopy, splashing in bright, random patterns on the forest floor. Birdsong filled the air, lifting her spirits. A light, warm breeze kissed her cheeks, and she breathed in slowly.

And coughed, her eyes flying open. London air was a far cry from the sweet, clean air of the countryside, even in late January when the cold kept the worst scents from lingering in the air. The sheer number of coal fires burning gave the air an acrid, smoky scent which burned her lungs.

"We're here," Lavinia said, as the carriage drew to a halt once again. "Enough daydreaming, Diana."

"Yes, Mama," she said dutifully, though everything in her yearned to shout at the coachman to keep driving, to take her right out of London, to somewhere the air was clear and the grass green.

Instead, she allowed the footman to hand her down, straightened the skirts of the hated pink satin, and lifted her chin, preparing once again to face down those who would laugh at her behind her back.

CHAPTER THREE

Almack's was supposed to be the highlight of any debutante's season, and considering the effort Marianne had expended to ensure Diana and her mother received vouchers, Lavinia was not about to let the opportunity pass by. She ordered a new and exceedingly expensive gown for Diana, convinced Arthur that he must attend to support his daughter, and threw herself into preparations with gusto.

Things had settled slightly in the two weeks since the Balford ball; people no longer snickered behind their hands whenever they saw Diana, and she was even beginning to believe Lavinia might be right, that they might be able to brazen it out. Everyone was talking about Marianne's triumph in securing Lord Glenkellie, and a certain amount of glory reflected onto Diana, easing her path slightly.

Everything fell apart within the first ten minutes within Almack's hallowed halls, however, when she came unexpectedly face to face with the Duke of Balford. Startled, she stopped dead. Several of the retorts she had painstakingly written out in her journal sprang to mind, and she was just mentally sorting through and selecting the most cutting when he obviously recognised her and *laughed*.

Rage flooded through her, her cheeks flushed scarlet, and she opened her mouth to say she knew not what, though it would probably have been exceptionally rude and possibly reputation-destroying. She never got the chance, though, because he turned on his heel and practically fled, his long strides carrying him away at a pace she would have to sprint to try and match.

Tears of frustration filling her eyes, Diana turned to flee herself, to find some private place if she could, before the dam broke and everyone saw her crying. She ran straight into her father, who grunted with pain as she crashed against the sling binding up his splinted arm and put out his other hand to steady her.

"Diana! What are you doing, child… wait, you're crying. Are you all right?"

She looked up at him from eyes glazed over with tears, and told him the only truth she could find at that moment.

"I want to go home."

To his credit, Arthur didn't hesitate for even a moment. Putting his good arm around Diana's shoulders, he steered her straight for the doors, pausing only briefly to ask a footman to find Lady Creighton and send her directly to the foyer.

"Our daughter is unwell. If our carriage is brought around before Lady Creighton meets us, I will take Diana home and send the carriage back for my wife."

Diana wasn't sure how she held the tears in until they were safely in the carriage, away from prying eyes. Lavinia arrived just as Arthur climbed in, demanding shrilly that they stop at once, Diana hadn't even danced with anyone yet!

"Get in the damned carriage, Lavinia," Arthur instructed. "Diana's done in."

"Done in; we only just arrived!"

"She was done in a week ago. Can't you see how unhappy the gel is? Look at her! She's thin and wan; she's wasting away in front of our eyes!"

Her father's unexpected defence was the last straw for Diana. She burst into noisy tears, and Arthur at once put his good arm around her, pulling her face against his shoulder. "Get in, Lavinia," he ordered curtly, and Lavinia, shocked into silence by Diana's tears, obeyed him meekly.

"Whatever is the matter?" she asked. "Sir David Reed had just asked to be introduced to you, and he's a very respectable gentleman with a lovely estate in Buckinghamshire, I'm told. You'll have to meet him at the Hallams' ball on Friday..."

"No more balls!" Diana cried out in desperation.

"Diana, you can't mean that!"

"Leave her alone," Arthur said gruffly. "Can't you see she hates every bit of this? She was raised expecting to marry some quietly respectable gentleman in Durham and live out her whole life without ever even seeing London and what the *Ton* get up to. Let the girl be. She doesn't want to go to another damnable ball."

"Is this about that silly nickname? Because nobody is talking about it any more. Another week or two and it will all be forgot."

"It won't be forgotten as long as the Duke of Balford laughs every time he sees me," Diana sniffled. "I can't do this, Mama. I'm sorry, but I just can't. I want to go *home*."

"London doesn't suit you any better than it does me," Arthur murmured, hugging her closer. "It's all right, my girl. We'll attend Marianne's wedding, to show family support, and then we're leaving London. I can't wait to get home either."

Lavinia protested vehemently, but her husband's mind was made up. He'd had enough of London and the *Ton*; the most he would concede was that they might return in September or October for a few weeks of the Little Season.

Diana could not have been more relieved. Her father wasn't entirely correct about her hating all of London; she had been swept up for a little while by the glittering fantasy of it all, the beauty of the gowns and the sheer romance of being whirled around a ballroom by a handsome, titled gentleman, but the reality of one small incident leading to her complete ridicule had destroyed her enjoyment of it all. She could no longer look at the gathered throngs as anything other than a murder of crows, avid to feast on the carcass of whichever unfortunate would be next to fall afoul of the gossips.

Returning to Creighton Hall, even in the teeth of a bitterly cold winter, Diana felt as though a great weight was lifted from her. The Hall had been home for a scant year, and yet she felt an immense relief as she stepped over the threshold and the butler took her coat with a quiet murmur of "Welcome home, Lady Diana."

She breathed out, feeling the tense pain which had cramped her belly for weeks now finally leave her, and smiled in response. "It's good to be home."

"Amen to that," her father muttered, stumping past her and heading for his study. "If I never have to go to London again, it'll be too soon." He gave Diana a nod and a wink, and she smiled back at him.

"You are a pair of killjoys, and how you expect me to find a husband for Clarissa next season with Diana still unwed, I can't imagine!" Lavinia's voice rose shrilly.

"Maybe you could let her find her own husband. If she even wants one." Arthur nodded to his daughters before firmly closing the study door in his fuming wife's face.

"Papa is an unexpected ally, though a very welcome one," Clarissa murmured to Diana as the sisters made their way up the stairs, doing their best to escape before Lavinia noted their hasty departure. "Having seen what happened to you, I think London is the last place I should go to display myself. I have none of your tact and charm; I should say something regrettable in the first five minutes to precisely the wrong person and the family's reputation would be sealed."

Diana did not disagree. Clarissa was fearless, for which Diana often envied her, but she rarely thought before she spoke and was honest to a fault. Containing her tendency to acerbic commentary was likely to be quite beyond her, especially given her generalised anger at how the *Ton* had treated her beloved sister.

"We shall have to settle for marriages to quiet country squires, if any will have us," Diana said, linking her arm through Clarissa's.

Clarissa made a face. "You would hate it almost as much as I," she said. "You'd be bored in a month. It's a shame Balford was so dastardly, because you'd be a perfect duchess."

Diana had to laugh. "You are viewing me through a loving sister's rose-tinted spectacles, dearest."

"You'll see," Clarissa said, determinedly optimistic. "There must be lots of young men hereabouts who would just love a chance to court you; I know Mama put off entertaining much company until you were officially brought out in London, but that will surely change now."

Now that her hopes for me are dashed and she must somehow get me married off before next season, Diana thought gloomily. She held little hope for a decent marriage prospect miraculously turning up at Creighton Hall and falling at her feet. They weren't in Durham, with a reasonable-sized population of people of all stations of life. Creighton was situated in the midst of wild, remote country, nothing but small villages within five miles of the Hall. Even if some tradesman or farmer should take it into their head to try and court Diana, Lavinia would never let them over the threshold. And in Durham, the nearest town, she already knew everyone... and knew there was no man there she cared to wed.

Maybe Diana should have tried convincing Lavinia to take Lady Treeve's kindly meant advice. Bath was a long way away, but there were spa towns in the north of England. Buxton, Harrogate, Scarborough; they were all magnets for small gatherings of the upper class.

Perhaps in the spring, Diana thought. Lavinia would be going mad with frustration long before then. She might be open to a suggestion of visiting one of the spa towns for a week or two, and Diana might have a chance to meet some new gentlemen who wouldn't have heard of the Fainting Flower.

As things turned out, Diana didn't have to put her plan into action. A few weeks after arriving home, her father called her into his study one morning.

"You sent for me, Papa?" Diana stopped just inside the door.

Arthur looked up from the stack of papers on his desk, brow furrowed. His expression cleared when he saw her, though, and he rose to his feet and gestured her to approach, pointing to a chair set close by the desk.

"I've received a letter from Lady Glenkellie," Arthur said, when Diana had seated herself. "I've been writing to her. I... owed her something of a debt." Though his arm had healed, and the splints and sling long since been removed, he cradled his wrist for a moment, lips twisting with pain. "She and Glenkellie have been gracious enough to forgive my mistakes, and your aunt was quite distressed over the circumstances which caused us to leave London far earlier than we intended."

Over Diana's disastrous debut, Diana surmised, and winced. Kindhearted Marianne didn't need to be worrying over her niece, in the early days of her new marriage. "Did you reassure her I'm not downcast at all?" she asked hopefully.

"I told her the truth, which is that you're putting a brave face on things, and she has a suggestion, indeed a most generous offer, for you and Clarissa both. I would not let Clarissa go without you, I must note, which is why I'm speaking to you alone. If you decline, that refusal will be for both of you."

"I don't understand, Papa; what offer can you mean?"

"Glenkellie and Marianne plan to take a honeymoon to Italy, where Glenkellie's mother is visiting with her sister, who's married to some nobleman from," Arthur paused to consult the letter on his desk, "Florence. Marianne requests that you and Clarissa accompany them on the trip. They will be travelling from Glenkellie's estates in Scotland to visit Lord and Lady Havers in Herefordshire in May, before taking ship on a privately chartered vessel at Bristol, sailing directly to Florence."

Diana stared at him in utter bemusement, not comprehending until Arthur handed her the letter.

"Here. Read it for yourself."

The writing was clearly Marianne's, a looping, feminine hand. Diana read the words several times before they truly sank in.

"They expect to be away from England for eight months at least," she said.

"Indeed they do. Clarissa wouldn't have her come-out in London next autumn, which will no doubt distress your mother, but all things considered it might be for the best. If you decide to go with your aunt, I'll permit Clarissa the choice of going with you or letting your mother take her to London."

Diana had no doubt whatsoever what choice Clarissa would make. A trip to Italy was an adventure beyond their wildest dreams; Clarissa would never be able to resist such a singular opportunity. And though until that moment Diana had never so much as imagined she might be offered the chance to travel so far, suddenly there was nothing she wanted more.

"I want to go," she said.

"I rather thought you might." Arthur's smile was wry. "Would you like to call for your sister, so you may discuss the matter together? I will handle the task of telling your mother."

Diana did not envy her father that conversation. Impulsively, she jumped to her feet, leaned over and put her arms about his neck, kissing his cheek. "Thank you," she said.

"Don't thank me," Arthur said gruffly. "It was all your aunt's idea."

"And your decision to let us go."

"Well, well." Arthur looked vaguely sheepish. "I wronged Marianne badly. Her judgement is a good deal better than my own, it seems, so I trust her and Glenkellie with your welfare. All things considered, I think it's for the best; a chance for you girls to see something of the world." A twinkle appeared in his eye. "And if you should happen to find a husband on your travels, your mother will forgive all."

"I cannot promise that, Papa," Diana said gaily, "but I can promise I won't dismiss any eligible gentlemen out of hand."

"With that, your mother will have to be content. Run along, now; I can see you're itching to tell Clarry everything. Yes, you may take the letter with you. If you should like to write a response to enclose with my return letter to your aunt, please let me have it before you retire tonight. I should like to send my response in the morning."

The door opened as Diana reached it to reveal her mother standing there: Lavinia frowned at her. "Why are you here? You're supposed to be practicing the pianoforte at this hour..."

"I sent for her, Lavinia; come in, please," Arthur said before Diana could speak. "Run along, Diana. Perhaps you should be practicing your Italian." One eye closed in a wink before he urged her out, rescuing her from Lavinia's annoyance. Laughing and hugging herself, Diana hurried to find her sister, desperate to share the incredible good fortune which was about to befall them courtesy of their loving aunt.

CHAPTER FOUR

THE SALT SPRAY STUNG at Diana's cheeks, whipped up from the waves by the freshening breeze, but she did not move from her position at the prow of the ship until she heard her name being called. Turning at the sound, she saw her sister waving from the quarter-deck, the door behind her which led to the cabins their party had occupied for the voyage standing open.

Diana sighed and took one last look at the coastline passing by on the ship's left side; they had been sailing within sight of the Italian coast for the last two days, ever since putting into Florence to discover Alex's mother and aunt had decided to go to Venice, to visit Alex's cousin who was married to a Venetian nobleman. Alex made the snap decision to follow on, before letting the sloop he had chartered to convey them to Italy go on its way. They had made good time from England and the captain was not unhappy to have paying customers so far as Venice, anyway.

Making her way back to join Clarissa, Diana had no trouble keeping her balance as the ship rolled slowly with the waves. They had suffered an unpleasant Channel crossing and a ghastly passage of the Bay of Biscay, with even Alexander, who had crossed the Channel several times in his time as a soldier, succumbing to the *mal de mer*. As they sailed along the coast of Portugal the weather improved, however, and Diana began to find her sea legs. No sooner had they turned into the Mediterranean and passed the watchful fort at Gibraltar than the sea smoothed out, becoming glassy and reflective as a millpond, and she discovered she was rather enjoying the voyage.

"I saw the dolphins again," Diana said as she reached Clarissa. "They like to ride the ship's bow wave."

"Oh, I missed them." Clarissa made a little pout. "Aunt Marianne sent me to get you, I'm afraid. The captain says we'll be entering the lagoon shortly and at the dock within the hour, so you need to finish packing your things."

She had little left to do; the cabin she and Clarissa shared was small enough they had to be neat, taking from their trunks only the things they needed for each day. Still, Diana followed her sister inside.

The ship did indeed dock within the hour, but it was another three before their party was able to disembark. Local customs officials came aboard to examine the papers Alex presented; fortunately he had a letter from some high official in the British government which seemed to satisfy them, and though they gave him some strict instructions about who to see in the next few days to have their stay approved, they also gave them permission to leave the ship.

Alex went straight away to discover how they were to get to the address his aunt had left; Marianne, Diana and Clarissa remained on the ship, leaning on the rail and watching the goings-on in the lagoon with fascination. The gondolas were like nothing Diana had ever seen, long and slender with their high prow and stern, men in striped jerseys using long poles to move the boats to and fro.

When Alex returned, it was with the news that they would take a gondola to their destination, a second one following with their luggage. Excited at the opportunity to ride on one of the exotic craft, Diana and Clarissa hurried down to the quay and jostled each other in their impatience, Clarissa almost falling into the lagoon when she jumped forward in an effort to be first aboard.

“Settle down, girls.” Marianne was obviously struggling to contain her laughter. “I’m eager to reach the end of our journey too, but I assure you I’ve no desire to take in any sea-bathing en route.”

A little chastened by the near miss, Clarissa settled onto the narrow bench seat sedately, smiling sheepishly up at Diana and offering her hand to help Diana steady herself. “Sorry,” she said.

“No harm done.” Diana understood perfectly; the excitement at having finally reached the end of their journey was too much to contain. She stared avidly around them as Marianne and Alex settled onto the other bench and the gondolier pushed away from the dock.

“How far is it, to where we’re going?” Diana asked Alex.

“He told me not very far.” Alex nodded towards the gondolier. “Which, in Italian terms, could be ten minutes or two hours.” He grinned, the long, livid scar up one side of his face pulling his smile askew. “I recommend just enjoying the journey.”

It was hot, the summer sun beating down on them. Diana was grateful for the wide brim of her bonnet and wished for a lighter dress; even though the one she wore was only thin cotton, it was already sticking to her in the humid air. She gazed around as the gondola glided smoothly through the water of the lagoon, making for the wide mouth of a canal.

The gondolier said something in rapid Italian, and Diana listened carefully, wishing she’d had more opportunity to hear the language spoken by Italian natives before now. They spoke faster than she would have expected; she thought she knew the words but the man seemed to run them all together.

"I think he said that's the Grand Canal," she said, and Clarissa nodded in agreement.

"And then something about Saint Mark?"

"The Piazza San Marco," Alex said.

"Oh, I read about that in the guidebook!" Diana had read the little book she'd found in the Creighton Hall library at least a dozen times, and though it was fifty years out of date, she supposed the major landmarks would not have changed significantly. "That's where the Doge's Palace is."

"Shall we visit it?" Clarissa asked eagerly. "Does the Doge still live there?"

"The last Doge was deposed by Napoleon," Alex advised her. "The Austrian administrator of the city lives there now, but we will certainly seek permission to visit and view any rooms which might be open to the public."

The gondolier said something in even more rapid Italian and then laughed. Alex frowned, fired back a question in return.

"No need to visit the Doge's Palace," the gondolier said in slower Italian, slow enough that Diana could follow his words. "Palazzo Franchetti is only a little smaller, and even more magnificent inside."

Diana and Clarissa looked at each other in wordless speculation before turning their gazes on Alex. He shrugged, turning his palms upwards. "I haven't the faintest idea. My cousin Marietta is fifteen years older than I; she married the Duca di Franchetti and moved to Venice when I was only a child. She has a son, I believe, who would be around twenty years old by now, and has inherited the title since his father's passing. My aunt's note said the young duc is getting married, which is why my aunt and my mother decided to make the trip to Venice."

They were passing under a bridge now, the gondolier pausing in his poling to point ahead. "Palazzo Franchetti," he said, and Diana turned on the bench to look.

"Oh, my," she breathed, heard Clarissa echo the sentiment beside her. The palazzo probably wasn't all that much bigger than Creighton Hall, but was infinitely more ornate. Five stories high and rising directly out of the canal, it appeared to take up an entire city block, such as they were in Venice, with the streets replaced by canals.

There was a sort of landing stage at the front, before some imposing doors, and the gondolier pulled them alongside. He chuckled as Alex handed him some coins, nodding cheerfully. Servants came hurrying out of the palazzo and hands reached out to help them from the boat; Diana accepted a footman's steadying hand and stepped up onto the landing, looking about her in fascination. The servants, all male, wore a bright livery of orange and turquoise blue, with long trousers rather than knee-breeches and flat black shoes open at the heel.

"Marchese di Glenkellie?" one of the footmen inquired of Alex, who nodded.

"É la marchesa," he indicated Marianne, "é Lady Diana Creighton, Lady Clarissa Creighton."

A wave of bows followed the announcement, deeper even than Diana was accustomed to seeing from English servants, and they were escorted inside, through a wide hallway with columns on either side, and into an elegantly appointed receiving room. Diana stared around, trying to take everything in; though some things were familiar, others were subtly different, subtly *alien* to English eyes. She took a seat on a sofa with elaborate curlicued, gilded legs, upholstered in rich dark green velvet with gold thread decoration. Clarissa sat down beside her, eyes just as wide as Diana was sure her own were.

A woman swept in, small and slight but exceptionally well dressed in a gown of shimmering emerald silk. Her hair was silvery-white, her eyes bright blue in a face which didn't look old enough to match that hair. Diana wondered if this was Alex's aunt; she'd already met his mother briefly during her ill-fated few weeks in London.

Alex rose with a polite smile and bowed, but there was no recognition on his face. He offered a polite greeting in Italian, and the woman laughed.

"No need to make the effort," she said in English which wasn't merely fluent, it was native. She was an Englishwoman, for certain. "It's a pleasure to make your acquaintance, Lord Glenkellie; your aunt Elizabeth has become a close friend of mine and I was delighted to make your mother's acquaintance too."

Alex nodded.

"But where are my manners! I am Elspeth Franchetti, the dowager duchess... well, the senior dowager duchess. Your cousin Marietta was married to my son."

"Your Grace." Alex bowed again. "Please, allow me to present my wife, Lady Glenkellie, and her nieces Lady Diana and Lady Clarissa Creighton."

"I am delighted to have you all here at Palazzo Franchetti, and I hope you'll accept my welcome on behalf of my grandson the duc." She offered warm smiles all around. "Everyone is out at the present time visiting with friends, but they will all be back for dinner and I hope you will join us to dine *en famille*."

"We should be honoured, Your Grace," Marianne said.

The dowager waved a slender hand, a huge diamond on her finger flashing in the light. "We've three Franchetti duchesses in this house now, and have decided all of us are sick and tired of the confusion engendered. Please call me Lady Elspeth, and I shall call you Lady Marianne, if I may. Since we *also* have two Lady Glenkellies."

Marianne laughed and agreed, and Lady Elspeth beckoned in several footmen. "We have been holding chambers in readiness for you, since your mother was quite sure you would come to join us, Glenkellie. Your trunks have already been taken up. Am I correct that you brought only the two servants with you?"

"That's right, my maid Jean and the valet Simons," Marianne agreed. "We planned to engage some local servants..."

Lady Elspeth dismissed her suggestion with a wave. "We have a houseful here, several of whom speak excellent English. I will put a footman at your family's disposal, a girl to assist your maid, and a maid each for your nieces."

Marianne tried to disclaim the necessity, but Lady Elspeth would not be gainsaid. She snapped out orders in rapid Italian and the footmen stepped forward, bowing deeply.

They were escorted to a quite magnificent suite of rooms on the third floor, a dozen interconnected chambers arranged around a central sitting-room as large as anything Diana had seen in the townhouses of the elite in London, and even more richly decorated. She and Clarissa had a bedchamber each, with a connecting door between them, something she appreciated as she was quite sure they would be sneaking into each others' rooms for late night chats.

Two maids were already in Diana's chamber, unpacking her gowns and shaking them out. They both curtsied deeply as Diana came in, and one stepped forward.

"Good day, my lady," she said in very good, though strongly accented, English. "I am Gianna and will serve you on your stay at Palazzo Franchetti. This is Piera, who will take care of your laundry. She does not have good English like me."

"Your English is indeed excellent," Diana agreed, and then switched to Italian to add "and perhaps Piera will not mind if I practice my very bad Italian on her?"

Piera giggled, hand over her mouth, and Gianna smiled. "If you wish to speak better Italian, we shall be honoured to help you practice, my lady," she said, diplomatically not commenting on Diana's current level of skill. "May I take your hat?"

Diana was pleased to remove her bonnet and gloves; the humidity and heat was making her feel unpleasantly sticky. Gianna sent Piera off to tell footmen to bring in water, and showed Diana the large copper tub concealed behind a screen at one side of the room.

A bath sounded heavenly, though she hoped it wouldn't be too hot. While the men brought in jugs of water to fill the tub, she selected the cleanest of her day gowns and set it aside to wear in the morning, telling Piera in her stilted Italian that all the others should be washed.

"What of your evening gowns, my lady?" Gianna asked, looking at what remained once Piera had taken the mound of laundry away.

She had only brought three, and had worn none of them aboard ship. The pale green velvet was the least crushed, but would also be the hottest, an unpalatable thought. The overly-embellished hated pink satin Lavinia had forced her to pack was equally unappealing, which left the simplest of the gowns, a fine teal silk with a silvery lace overdress. "If you can get some of the creases out, I will wear that one this evening."

Gianna insisted she could have the dress looking as good as new before Diana had even finished her bath, and with that, the last of the footmen were ushered out and the door closed behind them. Five minutes after that, Diana was luxuriating in orange-blossom scented water, just warm enough to be relaxing, a cup of pressed apple juice and a plate of small, delicious sweet pastries on a table at her elbow.

Gianna worked what Diana thought almost amounted to magic on the teal and silver gown, somehow removing every crease it had picked up in weeks of being packed in a trunk. She combed Diana's thick brown hair out gently and put it up in an arrangement of braids which looked subtly foreign to Diana's eyes when she looked in the mirror, but extremely pleasing. Donning the gown and tucking her feet into her favourite evening slippers, she felt refreshed and eager to meet the rest of the Franchetti clan.

"You look lovely," Clarissa poked her head around the connecting door between their rooms.

"So do you!"

Clarissa smiled and swished her skirts. The pale apricot silk suited her very well, and was a more grown-up style than anything she'd worn in England. In a very real sense, tonight was Clarissa's first entry into adult society. Wondering if she was nervous, Diana crossed the room to tuck her hand into her sister's arm.

"Come, we shall go down together. Lady Elspeth said it's just the family tonight, and considering she's the matriarch, I suspect they'll all speak excellent English. No need to strain our minds with Italian just yet!"

"Which is a relief, because I struggle enough when I have to avoid saying something inappropriate in English. Adding a whole other language to the mix is surely a recipe for disaster!" Clarissa laughed, though. "I'm hoping they'll all just decide I'm an eccentric Englishwoman."

"Everyone will be charmed by your beauty," Diana said loyally. "And who knows, perhaps you'll meet some handsome Italian nobleman and he'll sweep you off your feet."

Clarissa scoffed. "I'm not ready for that yet. I want some adventure first. If I meet any handsome men looking for a lady to sweep off her feet, I'll be pushing them in your direction."

The two sisters proceeded down the stairs arm in arm, directed by a footman who led them to a pair of double doors opening into a very grand salon, all white marble and gold and white furniture.

Faces turned to them as they entered, Lady Elspeth's smile a welcome sight in a room more full of strangers than Diana had expected. There were at least thirty people in the salon. She spied another familiar face in Lady Glenkellie, and then, casting her gaze around the room looking hopefully for someone else she knew, was arrested by a tall man just arising from his seat.

"You!" she cried in horror as she came, once again, face to face with her nemesis.

"*You*," the Duke of Balford echoed, his tone and expression making it very plain he was no more pleased to see her than she was to see him.

CHAPTER FIVE

What was he even *doing* here? Dizzy with shock, Diana clung to Clarissa's arm. Alex and Marianne entered the salon on their heels, and somehow she found herself steered away from the duke and pressed to sit down, a glass of sherry placed in her hand.

"Is that him?" Clarissa whispered in her ear. "The Demonic Duke himself?"

Diana gulped the sherry a lot faster than was wise and nodded. Clarissa's lips firmed, and suddenly terrified her sister would say or do something wildly inappropriate, Diana reached out to grab her wrist. "Don't you dare try and confront him, Clarry."

"But..."

"No!" The duke was watching her from across the room, staring at her actually, as he spoke in low tones with Alex. "Leave it. I'll fight my own battles." Almost slamming the empty glass down on the small side table, Diana rose to her feet. "Stay here," she hissed at Clarissa, before crossing the room and offering a low curtsy.

The duke bowed in return, his expression a complex mix of emotions she couldn't quite decipher.

"What an unexpected surprise to see you here, Your Grace," Diana said, doing her best to keep her tone light and airy. "It's quite all right, Uncle," she addressed Alex. "Balford and I are already acquainted."

"So I understand," Alex said dryly, looking from one to the other of them. "If you'll excuse me. I need to greet my aunt and my cousins. I'll return in a moment to collect you for introductions, Diana."

It was clear notice that she'd be quickly rescued, so she felt entirely safe turning to Balford and hissing "What are you *doing* here?" as soon as Alex had walked out of immediate earshot.

"I say," Balford said in response, "you've turned quite white. You're not going to faint again, are you?"

And just like that, the anger flooded back into her, her cheeks going from white to scarlet almost instantly. "No, I'm not going to faint. Which is good, since your skills apparently don't include catching young ladies when they do."

He had the grace to look a little shamefaced. "That was… not my finest moment. I owe you an apology."

Surprised by his words, Diana paused for a moment, lips parted as she considered what to say next. He looked down at her from deep blue eyes and surprised her again by saying; "I think we got off to a bad start, Lady Diana. Perhaps we could begin again? William Penhaligon, at your service." His bow was a little deeper and more flamboyant than technically correct for her status, and she recognised a sense of humour she never expected to find in him.

"Your Grace," she acknowledged, and from the corner of her eye spotted Clarissa approaching. With a wince, she turned to her sister, glaring, but Clarissa was impervious to filthy looks from her sister.

"So this is your demonic duke?" Clarissa said cheerfully, and Diana strongly considered pushing her sister into a canal. Balford, however, burst out laughing, his blue eyes twinkling with what appeared to be genuine mirth.

"Your sister?" he asked Diana through his chortles.

"Lady Clarissa Creighton," Diana said ungraciously, "the Duke of Balford."

Clarissa curtsied, but she did it with her eyes narrowed and lips pursed, her expression showing she was not in the least impressed by his status. For his part, the duke seemed highly entertained by her reaction; Diana supposed it might be quite refreshing, for someone who was probably used to being fawned over by every young lady he met.

"Enchanted, Lady Clarissa," Balford said.

"I see you've met my nephew already," Lady Elspeth said behind them, and Diana turned to give the dowager duchess a respectful curtsy.

"I met His Grace in London some few months past, my lady, but had no idea he was related to you. Your nephew?"

"Technically, step-great-nephew," Balford put in, lips twisting in that slightly sardonic way he had. "Lady Elspeth is my stepmother's aunt."

"Julianne is the only mother you remember, you ungrateful imp, and she was ever my favourite niece." Lady Elspeth nudged him gently, a fond smile on her lips. "You are a part of this family even without a blood tie to bind us."

"Same as Aunt Marianne and I," Diana said impulsively. "She's not really my aunt, she was just married to my great-uncle for a while, but... even though she's remarried now, we're keeping her."

"I'm firmly of the belief that you can't have too many family members." Lady Elspeth glanced around the room, smiling. "As you can see, I'm fond of gathering them all together, too. You must come and meet everyone. William?" She glanced at the duke. "You will take Lady Diana in to dinner."

He looked startled, but bowed his head in acquiescence to the forceful little dowager duchess' command. "As you wish, Aunt Elspeth."

Diana fully expected him to make an excuse, to allow one of the lovely Italian cousins to monopolise his attention, but when the major-domo entered to announce dinner, Balford came at once to her side and offered his arm.

"It's all right, you know," she attempted to excuse herself. "I shan't mind if you don't wish to sit with me."

"Lady Diana." His voice was low and warm, and she looked up instinctively to meet his eyes. "I thought you had agreed we should start again, as though we are strangers meeting for the first time?"

"I don't know if I can," she admitted honestly.

They were in the dining-room now, Balford drawing out a chair for her to be seated before taking his own beside her. He kept his attention on her all the while, his expression tightening as she spoke.

"I understand. You have no reason to trust or even respect me."

Startled by his understanding, she stared at him as he nodded to the footman waiting to fill his wine glass. He seemed a lot less arrogant, more human and approachable. She might not be able to forget, not when he was the reason she was here right now rather than dancing at some *Ton* event in London, but she could at least try to get to know the person he really was.

"So, I know why I'm here," she made a tentative overture, "but what brings you to Venice?"

Balford darted a sideways glance at her, smiled a little crookedly. "Indirectly... you did."

"Me!" Her eyes flew wide.

"Not you specifically, I hasten to add. I'm sorry to say you were a pawn in my stepmother's game; she is quite determined to marry me off as quickly as possible, and has spent the last several months thrusting eligible young ladies under my nose."

Diana thought that didn't sound so terrible. As a man, he had far more freedoms to walk away than the young ladies in question. Her cynical expression must have warned him she had little sympathy for his position, because he hastened to explain himself further.

"Please don't misunderstand me; I love my stepmother. Lady Elspeth was quite correct that Julianne is the only mother I remember. She married my father when I was six and she has never treated me with anything other than a mother's loving care. I accept that she wants me to be happy and she's trying to help, but." He looked down, fiddled with a fork. "My father only died just over a year ago."

"I'm sorry for your loss," Diana said quietly, a little shocked he was baring his soul to her in such a way, but perhaps he felt he owed her a debt, was offering up his own secrets to show her that he was worthy of her trust.

"One of my half-sisters will make her debut next year. Julianne says she thinks I should be married by then, and I admit that the thought of marrying a girl the same age as Regina fills me with horror. So I told Julianne I would try to choose someone this year, and she, well, she rather threw herself into the project. It's been a continuous parade of pretty, well-bred young ladies for the last six months."

"So why didn't you choose one?" Diana asked, unable to help herself. As a duke, he'd have had his pick, and she'd met some of the debutantes who were feted as the Diamonds of that season. Beautiful, titled, wealthy, clever, accomplished; any one of them would have made a magnificent duchess.

Balford took a gulp of his wine before shaking his head. "Look, they were all lovely, yourself included. But how can you get to know someone in the middle of a dance floor, with every eye upon you, speculating whether *this* girl will be the one? When she is on her best behaviour and desperate to impress, frightened to put a foot wrong lest she suddenly become a pariah?"

Diana winced as the comment hit close to home.

"How can I respect a young lady who pretends to swoon, just so that I will catch her?"

"I didn't *pretend* to swoon!" Indignant, Diana sat bolt upright.

"*You* didn't, no," he agreed, and she realised he wasn't talking about her at all.

"Exactly how many young ladies have swooned on you?" she asked, suddenly wondering. Would a lady truly go to such lengths?

Balford's eyes looked far too old for his youthful face when he answered her. "You were the tenth."

Diana gaped.

"In your defence, I think you were the only one who actually swooned. You were the second that *night*, though."

"No *wonder* you didn't catch me."

He had the grace to look sheepish. "I should have done. Julianne was furious with me afterwards; apparently you were out cold for almost half an hour. On the other hand… word got around that it's not a tactic which will work on me. Nobody has swooned on me since."

"I'm so glad I could provide you with such a valuable service," Diana said tartly.

"So I owe you an apology and my thanks. I am greatly in your debt, it seems."

She was beginning to like him, albeit reluctantly. "We can discuss terms of payment at a later date," she said as the footmen cleared away the soup plates and set down the next course. "What is it?" Tilting her head to one side, she peered at the thick green wedge on her plate, topped with a small rolled piece of shaved ham and a preserved cherry.

"Rockmelon. Very light and refreshing." He used a sharp knife to cut the flesh of the fruit away from the rind, then slice it into smaller pieces, before reaching over to exchange her plate with his own. "Here. Try a piece."

She speared a small piece with her fork and tasted it, finding the fruit less tart than she'd expected, cool and rather watery. It reminded her faintly of a pear. She tried another piece.

"Good?" Balford asked, slicing up the other piece of melon.

"Quite pleasant," Diana allowed. "You still didn't explain why you're in Venice."

"You're direct, aren't you?" He smiled sideways at her. "Well, I stuck it out in London until May, even though I was thoroughly sick of the social whirl. Retreating to Balford Priory for the summer months was the escape on the horizon, but when the time came, I discovered how wrong I was. Julianne had decided to throw a months-long house party with a rolling parade of eligible young ladies. If I felt it was too difficult to get to know them in London, she'd bring them to me in my home, give me more time."

"It didn't help?"

"It made everything worse. The Priory is my sanctuary. Every one of them felt like invaders." He shuddered. "Maybe I was imagining things, but all I could see in every one of them was avarice. I couldn't take any more. When the letter came telling us Andrea had married," he nodded to the other end of the table, where the young duc held court, his even younger duchesa at his side, "I jumped at the excuse to come visit and offer my congratulations in person. The Franchettis are Julianne's family, but they've always welcomed me as one of their own. I'm ashamed to admit it, but I sneaked out of the Priory in the dead of night and only sent my stepmother a letter when I was about to board ship."

"A daring escape," Diana remarked.

"A cowardly midnight flit, I'd call it. Fleeing the terrifying prospect of being forced to spend hours in the company of pretty, charming young ladies desperate to make themselves agreeable to me." His smile was self-deprecating.

"I don't think you're a coward," Diana said thoughtfully, re-examining her assessment of his character once again. "It's not cowardly to feel you're not ready to step into your father's shoes, especially since he's only been gone such a short time. Taking a wife and going about the business of getting an heir - well, that would mean he's really gone, wouldn't it?"

Balford looked quite shocked, and Diana realised she'd overstepped. Hastily, she stammered out an apology, flushing red with mortification, but he held up a hand to stop her.

"No, please. You just put into words what I have been struggling to explain to my stepmother for months, Lady Diana. You're quite correct. I'm not ready to let go of my father, not ready to take his place." He glanced up the table at Andrea and Valentina. "And though my cousin seems happy with his arranged match, it's not for me. I'll marry when I'm ready, when I find the right woman to be the next duchess of Balford."

He didn't say anything about love, Diana observed, but then, she rather thought he was aiming for mutual respect rather than actual affection in his marriage. Respect seemed to be the best one might hope for in marriages among the *Ton*, after all.

"When you're ready," she said, "I hope you find the lady who will be everything you're looking for."

They were interrupted by the lady on Balford's other side loudly demanding his attention, but he took a moment to murmur a thanks for her well wishes.

Diana was left alone with her thoughts, since the seat on her other side was occupied by Alex's mother, who was busy gossiping with her sister across the table. *I've misjudged Balford*, she thought, trying the dish which had been set in front of her, some sort of small game bird served with crisp stalks of asparagus. *He's not the arrogant dilettante I'd assumed. He's grieving his father still, and I suspect he was even more uncomfortable in the ballrooms of the Ton than I was.* He'd shown unexpected flashes of humour during their conversation, mostly of the black sort directed at himself, but also he'd showed clear regret that she'd been caught up in the situation. She was beginning to feel almost charitably inclined towards him.

Several courses of delicious, if rather unfamiliar, food later and Lady Elspeth rose from the table, beckoning the ladies to follow her. They returned to the salon and a maid brought in coffee and tea.

Diana eyed the coffee several of the ladies were drinking doubtfully; the Italians drank it in tiny cups which held scarcely more than a thimbleful, and it appeared thick and black, the scent strong and bitter. She was glad to accept a cup of tea from Lady Elspeth instead, the dowager remarking that she never drank coffee in the evenings since it rendered her unable to sleep.

Diana found herself sharing a couch with the new duchess, Lady Valentina, who it transpired was just seventeen years old. Her English was at about the same level as Diana's Italian, stilted and with a strong accent, but she seemed determined to try.

"Andrea is half-English, with two English grandmothers. He says he shall take me to London so I must practice my English and become very good."

"You are already very good," Diana said, recalling that Balford had said Andrea and Valentina's marriage was arranged. The young couple seemed quite besotted with each other, even so, and she rather tentatively asked if they had known each other well before the wedding.

Valentina appeared to think about the question before answering. "The marriage was arranged when I was small," she said. "I have always known I should marry Andrea. Our fathers were good friends. When my father died and my brother became *conte*, Andrea came to see him, to agree that the marriage should take place when I was old enough. We met then and I thought he was very kind."

"How old were you then?" Diana asked, curious.

"Fourteen." Valentina blushed, cast her eyes down demurely. "I thought he was very handsome. I was pleased my father had arranged such a good match. I should not like to have to choose among many suitors, I think, like you must in your London seasons."

"That's not quite how it works," Diana said dryly, but then perhaps it was if you were someone like Valentina. She was exceptionally beautiful and had obviously been raised in an extremely wealthy household; her dress was of the finest silk

Diana had ever seen, stitched with tiny crystals and seed pearls, and a pair of diamond bracelets adorned her wrists. In London, she'd probably have hordes of lovesick swains composing poetry to her eyes and her glossy, silken black hair.

Valentina's face lit up, and even before the rumble of masculine voices reached Diana's ears, she knew the gentlemen must be rejoining the company. She watched with a certain degree of envy as Valentina rose to her feet and hurried to Andrea's side, the young duc welcoming his bride with a kiss to her cheek and his arm slipped about her waist.

"They're so in love," Clarissa whispered, taking the seat Valentina had just vacated.

"Did you know it was an arranged marriage?" Diana kept her voice quiet.

Clarissa's brows rose. "Well, it does still happen among the highest families in England too," she said. "I suppose they must consider themselves very fortunate, then. That they've fallen in love despite not getting to choose each other."

Balford had entered the salon with Alex, in deep conversation with him. He looked around the room, his eyes catching Diana's briefly. He offered her a smile and, instinctively, she smiled back.

I can't hate him any more. Not now I know what he's going through.

CHAPTER SIX

WILL WASN'T ENTIRELY SURE why his gaze seemed to be drawn inevitably back to Lady Diana Creighton. He'd met many prettier girls - some of them were in this very room! - but he found himself dwelling on her face, studying the animation of her features as she talked with her sister, the way her smile seemed to light up her eyes.

He'd behaved appallingly towards her in London and absolutely did not deserve even the slightest degree of her attention. Though he hadn't coined the awful Fainting Flower nickname, he'd done nothing to stop it when he heard it bandied about. He should have done, should have ruthlessly squashed it, but... if he did so, then he would have invited censure upon himself for his ungentlemanly conduct in failing to catch her, and worse yet, walking away as she lay insensible on the floor.

Lady Diana would be well within her rights to give him the cut direct and never speak to him again, yet she'd listened as he clumsily attempted to apologise. Not only that, but she'd seen right to the heart of him with that insightful comment about not being ready to step into his father's shoes.

Will owed Diana Creighton a debt, and Penhaligons always paid their debts. He didn't know yet how he would repay her graciousness in hearing him out, especially since it seemed apparent her family had left London to get away from the gossip and sideways glances Diana had endured.

"Yes, I've visited Venice several times over the years," he absent-mindedly answered a question Glenkellie asked him. "My stepmother took every opportunity to escape English winters."

"So I daresay you've already seen all of the tourist sites? What would you recommend as your favourite?" It was Lady Glenkellie who asked the question, the beautiful redhead's eyes trained on his. She was quite the most strikingly lovely lady he had ever met, and yet... his gaze slid again to the merely pretty brunette sitting on the couch, head bent towards her sister as the two of them spoke quietly together.

"I should be pleased to show your party around some of the best sites, if you like," he said, dragging his gaze from Diana with some difficulty, wondering even as he said the words what on earth he was doing. Spending time with people he did not know well wasn't something he found pleasant, indeed it was normally a chore to be avoided as strenuously as he could manage. "My Franchetti relations have a great deal of influence in Venice, and invocation of Andrea's name will enable me to get you in to see a number of normally private locations. I know of a remarkable da Vinci painting in the private chapel of a palazzo not far from here, for example."

"That would be marvellous!" Lady Glenkellie's smile was blinding. "How very generous of you, Your Grace, but we shouldn't like to impose on your time."

"It is no imposition." Once again, he sneaked a look at Diana. "I should be pleased to. What are your plans for the next few days? Are you aware that the household plans to remove from Venice soon, to escape the summer heat? Lady Elspeth has a villa at Schio, in the foothills of the Dolomites, to which she likes to retire in the height of summer."

"Indeed, she has invited my mother and aunt to accompany her there, and extended the invitation to our party as well." Glenkellie nodded. "We shall certainly consider it; the heat here is wearying."

Will was pretty sure that Glenkellie wasn't feeling the heat at all. The man had been a cavalry officer, had campaigned across the Peninsula in heat equally as extreme if not worse, but his expression as he looked at his wife showed exactly what motivated his concern.

"The villa at Schio is more than large enough to accommodate you," Will agreed. "However, you might consider an alternative; Andrea wishes to take Valentina to visit her brother, the Conte di Bardolino. Their principal seat is at Bardolino, on the shores of Lake Garda, a place I have not visited but I understand to be of outstanding natural beauty. We plan to travel with Lady Elspeth's party as far as Vicenza but then continue west to Lake Garda, if you would consider accompanying us. I have no doubt the Conte would be delighted to have you join us."

Lord and Lady Glenkellie looked at each other, communicating without words, before Lady Glenkellie flashed him another one of those dazzling smiles, thanked him for the invitation and said they would discuss the matter.

"When does everyone leave Venice?" Lord Glenkellie asked.

"Ten days or so, I understand. So there is really no time to lose on your sightseeing. Shall we say nine o'clock tomorrow morning?"

Lady Glenkellie wafted her fan, and he had the definite impression she was hiding a smile behind it. "That sounds very agreeable, but I do hope you will not ask us to do anything too strenuous on our first day."

"I thought we might begin with a stroll along the Rialto and a visit to one of my favourite coffee shops." Will bowed to her with a grin. "Perhaps a visit to a church I know which has a most beautiful painting of the Madonna by Titian, afterwards?"

"That sounds delightful." Lady Glenkellie hid a smile again before saying "My niece Diana has a keen interest in art. She will particularly enjoy the outing, I am sure."

The Glenkellies were both well aware he'd spent the last quarter-hour trying very hard not to stare at Lady Diana, he realised sickly. Lord Glenkellie was giving him raised eyebrows and a look somewhere between cynicism and warning; Lady Glenkellie merely seemed amused.

"Venice has something for everyone," he said finally, "but anyone who appreciates fine art will surely fall in love with the city and her treasures."

He was looking at Lady Diana again; he couldn't seem to help himself. She yawned behind her hand, and apparently Lady Glenkellie noticed that too, because she turned to her husband and laid a hand on his arm.

"The girls are tired, Alex, and so am I, it's been a long day. I think we shall excuse ourselves and retire."

"I shall come with you," Glenkellie said immediately, offering a polite tip of his head to Will. "A pleasure talking with you, Balford, and we'll look forward to seeing you in the morning."

"I'll be in the breakfast-parlour, or if you prefer to have breakfast brought to your rooms, I'll meet you at the dock at nine," Will offered. "I wish you a good night, Lady Glenkellie."

She favoured him with another of those dazzling smiles, and he watched as the couple crossed the room to the settee. Diana and Clarissa looked up, and seemed glad to be invited to retire, rising at once to follow Marianne across to where Lady Elspeth held court with some of the older ladies.

She has a pretty figure. Diana's gown showed her small waist and high bosom to advantage, and she moved with a smooth, quick step which made him think she liked to walk, was accustomed to striding out and moving with purpose.

"The little English miss has caught your eye." Andrea, the young duc, came up beside him and spoke in rapid Italian, his tone amused.

"No," Will denied, too quickly. "I met her before, in London," he attempted to explain himself. "She... I thought she was boring, then. Like every other marriage minded miss with her eye on a title. I was unforgivably rude."

"And yet," Andrea mused as Diana glanced across the room at them, smiling and bending her knees in a slight curtsy before following her aunt out, "she seems to have forgiven you."

"Not yet, I believe," Will said. "I still have some way to go to make amends, but perhaps now she thinks I'm not a totally unredeemable horse's arse."

Andrea burst out laughing, placed a hand on Will's shoulder. "I'm sure you will win her over if you want to, cousin!"

He did want to, Will discovered as he allowed Andrea to steer him over to where two of their younger male cousins were conversing. Lady Diana Creighton had demonstrated an uncommon depth of insight during their short conversation, and he wanted to know her better.

The fact she wasn't at all hard on the eyes was neither here nor there, he was sure.

"Good morning, Your Grace."

Diana curtsied gracefully, and he stopped one step into the foyer and stared at her. She was entirely alone, and wariness crawled up his spine, made him look around.

"Don't worry, you aren't expected to take me out alone." She looked amused, and he winced, realising she had accurately divined his thoughts. "My aunt broke a boot lace and returned to our suite to replace it, and my sister is actually just outside looking at the dock. She is rather fascinated by the gondolas... all things nautical, in fact. I do believe had she been born a man, she would have joined the Navy."

"I beg your pardon." Embarrassed, he bowed slightly to Diana. "I should not have doubted you."

"You're very gun-shy." She cocked her head and considered him, unabashed. "I'd felt envious of some of the rich, beautiful debutantes - Lady Mary Gordon, for example - but it must be wearying to be swarmed with suitors who are desperate to impress, and even those who will resort to less than honourable tactics to get your attention. I feel rather sorry for her now, and I can see it's not all that much different if you're a man, even if you do have rather more freedom to be rude without risking social ostracism."

Once again, Will was struck speechless by this young woman, by her insight and astute observations. Swallowing, he stepped forward and offered his arm, gesturing towards the exterior doors.

"Shall we see if we can find your sister? I asked the house boatman to be at our disposal this morning, so undoubtedly she is bombarding him with questions, and I do know his English is non-existent."

"Both Clarry and I have some Italian," Diana said a little tartly as she laid her hand on his arm, but then she smiled impishly. "Not nearly as good as we thought it was, however. Italians do speak very fast."

"They do." Leading her outside, they indeed found Clarissa standing on the dock peering at the glossy, brightly-painted gondola awaiting them. The gondolier was keeping his distance, eyeing the young Englishwoman a little warily.

"Your Italian is superb, though." Diana eyed him. "How often did you say you'd visited?"

"This is my fifth visit to Venice, but I should also note that during the early years of the war, the entire Franchetti clan spent two years in England, and for most of it we hosted them at Balford Priory. I have four years in age on Andrea, but we get on very well; we practised each other's languages until we were fluent enough to pass for native in them."

"What an excellent way to learn a language," Diana approved. "I learned Italian from a very strict governess, by rote, from books, with no expectation of ever visiting. It was merely another accomplishment I was expected to master."

"I felt very much the same about Greek and Latin," Will admitted, and was rewarded by the brightest smile she'd yet bestowed on him. Her mouth was just a little too wide, an analytical part of his brain noted, for her face to be considered truly beautiful, yet what that meant was that when she smiled, the radiance of it felt like being bathed in pure sunlight.

"Good morning, Your Grace." Clarissa looked away from the gondola long enough to spot him standing there, bent her knees in a perfunctory curtsy, and then looked back at the boat. "Do you know anything about these? Why are they so high at the prow and stern? And how do the poles work to propel them? Why not oars? I can understand why not a sail, there isn't much wind in between the buildings..."

"See what I mean?" Diana whispered, *sotto voce*, and Will laughed.

"I do, indeed. I do beg your pardon, Lady Clarissa, but I have to confess I've never been curious about the design of the gondolas. I'll be happy to relay your questions to the gondolier, though."

"I did try to ask, but I'm not sure if he didn't understand or he just didn't know the answers." Clarissa frowned at the man, standing as far away from her as he could manage in the gondola's stern, looking determinedly in the opposite direction.

Will thought she'd probably just intimidated the poor man into silence, but didn't say so. The younger Creighton sister was definitely the more forceful of the pair, even if he was discovering that Diana wasn't afraid to speak her mind when given the opportunity.

The Glenkellies stepped out of the palazzo to join them then, and greeted Will with friendly smiles. Lord Glenkellie assisted his wife into the boat, and Will turned to help the two girls down. Clarissa barely touched his hand before jumping down, but Diana's fingers folded around his and she leaned on him for balance, tentative as the boat rocked under her feet.

"You won't fall in," Will felt compelled to reassure her. "I've scarcely ever seen anyone fall into one of the canals; it would be more than Gianluigi's life is worth to let you!"

"Oh, no doubt." She took a seat beside her sister. "I don't think I quite have my land legs back after so many days at sea, though. Everything still feels a little unsteady, so when the ground actually is rocking, I'm convinced I will topple head-first into that slightly unsavoury-looking water!"

"I should never allow it," he promised gallantly, before taking his own seat behind her and nodding to Gianluigi. "Let us be off about your first Venetian adventure then, my friends!"

CHAPTER SEVEN

THE DUKE OF BALFORD seemed quite a different man to the arrogant lordling she'd first met on a London dance floor, Diana mused as she relaxed and watched the beautiful architecture of Venice slide slowly by. He was kind and thoughtful; there was no advantage for him in giving up his time to show people he barely knew around Venice, and yet he had offered without hesitation. He leaned forward now, putting his arm between her shoulder and Clarissa's to point at a large building coming up on their right and tell them to look just past it, because there was a beautiful bronze statue to be seen in a courtyard there.

"Oh, look at that lovely bridge coming up ahead!" Diana exclaimed a few minutes later, admiring the fine white bridge topped by multiple arches spanning the canal.

"That is the Rialto bridge." Balford called something to the gondolier, and a moment later, the gondola angled over to the side of the canal and drifted to a stop at some stone steps beside a large white palace. "We'll disembark here."

Accepting his hand, Diana looked about in fascination as he helped her out of the gondola and up the steps, murmuring a warning to be careful as it was low tide and the steps were slippery with seaweed and slime. She was glad she was wearing sturdy half-boots in anticipation of walking a good deal.

"This is a handsome building," Alex said, looking up at the palace they now stood beside.

"The Palazzo dei Camerlenghi. Built by the same architects as the Palazzo Franchetti, incidentally, though this one is now a government building. I'm not sure precisely what function it serves now, to be honest." Balford shook his head sadly. "There used to be quite a spectacular art collection here, but when the French occupied the city, it was all dispersed. Some has been returned to Venice, but it's mostly in the Accademia di Belle Arte now, I understand. Which you absolutely must visit, of course. It's not far from here, around another bend in the Grand Canal, but I'd say leave it for another day. Today, I want to show you one of Venice's hidden treasures." He led them around the palace and along a narrow way with shops on either side, before stopping at a narrow door standing slightly open. "In here."

They followed him in, looking around in amazement as they realised they were inside a church. The arched ceiling held up by white marble columns was almost as high as the church was long; there was only space for half a dozen wooden pews, but all any of them could look at was the spectacular art painted on the walls. And the ceiling, as Diana discovered when Clarissa nudged her and pointed up at the cupola, a circle of angels around a heavenly deity arranged on an ethereally pale blue background.

"What is this place?" Diana whispered in sheer awe.

"The church of San Giovanni Elemosinario, the alms-giver," Balford supplied, offering her his arm for support as she leaned back and tried to crane her neck to look at the incredible detail in the cupola's painted angels. "What you're looking at is a work known as *Eternal God and the Glory of Angels*, by Giovanni Antonio de'Sacchis, better known as *Il Pordenone*."

"I don't know that word, what does it mean?" Diana frowned.

"It's just the name of the town he came from, I'm afraid. Nothing poetic. Come look in this side chapel; there is a beautiful altarpiece there by the same artist, of Saints Catherine, Sebastian and Rocco."

She admired the painting, thought it actually better than the altarpiece in the main church, and said so.

"I agree, though some would have it that Il Pordenone is an inferior artist to Tiziano, I don't think that particular painting is one of Titian's best works."

"Titian!" She looked at the painting of the grey-haired saint again. "Do you know, I had no idea he painted religious works. I saw two of his paintings at Bridgewater House in London; *Diana and Actaeon* and *Diana and Callisto*. For some reason, I had imagined he painted only mythological scenes."

Balford laughed, and she tensed, thinking he was mocking her ignorance. He was shaking his head, though, smiling kindly at her. "Venice will teach you better. For many years, Titian was the premier artist here, employed to create hundreds of works in churches and palazzos all over the city." He pointed back at the side chapel they had just left. "He and Il Pordenone were great rivals."

"And yet, I don't think we should ever have imagined this church was here, if you had not shown us," Diana marvelled.

"As I said; one of Venice's hidden treasures. I do not by any means pretend to know all of her secrets, but I confess this little church is one of my favourites."

"Thank you for sharing it with us." Impulsively, she squeezed his arm. "You may now consider yourself forgiven, Your Grace."

He did not pretend to misunderstand, but he did shake his head. "You are too generous, Lady Diana, and you are also not going to be rid of me so easily."

She laughed, and then covered her mouth as a priest at the altar turned around at the loud noise. "I'm not trying to get rid of you!" she hissed, avoiding the priest's glare.

"No, but I think he is. Come." He gathered Clarissa on his other arm as they passed her, and they met Alex and Marianne at the door.

"That was quite remarkable," Alex said as they left the quiet church and returned to the bustling, busy Rialto market streets.

"Isn't it? And I must tell you, there are dozens of churches in Venice with artistic treasures just as remarkable... and yet Venice is nothing to Rome or Florence. Italy truly is an artist's paradise." With a broad smile, he gestured to a coffee shop a few steps further along the street. "And a gourmand's paradise, as well. This place serves the finest *sfogliatelle* in Venice, or so my aunt always claims. She has several times attempted to hire the proprietor to work at the palazzo, but he will not give up his shop."

They took seats at a table under a striped awning, and a waiter came out to greet them. Balford gave orders in that rapid-fire Italian Diana was still struggling to understand; she gave him a bemused look as he took a seat beside her and he smiled.

"I ordered *cappucino*, which is a milky, frothy coffee, for you all to try, and some of the *sfogliatelle*, which are sweet pastries stuffed with a creamy filling. I asked for a bag of those to take home for Aunt Elspeth, too. She will be most displeased if she discovers I came here and didn't buy any for her."

His fondness for the dowager was evident, Diana thought, and laudable, too. Once again, she thought how very different he was from her first impression of an arrogant, thoughtless man who cared nothing for anyone but himself. It was a mask, she suspected, which he donned in social situations where he felt uncomfortable.

The waiter came to the table with a flagon and some cups, setting them down, and then returning a moment later with a platter piled with small pastries.

"This is pressed grape juice," Balford said, reaching for the flagon. "I asked for it in case you didn't care for coffee. Unfortunately, they don't have tea; while it is drunk here, not every cafe serves it."

"I haven't cared much for the coffee we've been served here so far," Marianne admitted, and Diana nodded in agreement. "It's very strong. I don't understand why they serve it so, in such tiny cups; wouldn't it be better to put it in a larger cup and make it weaker?"

"That depends on your point of view," Balford said with an easy chuckle. "Some Italians would prefer it strong enough that your spoon stand upright in it!"

They all laughed, as he'd obviously intended, and he continued, "But *cappucino* is quite different, I promise. You might find you don't care for it, but you cannot come to Italy and not at least try it."

Diana was uncertain; even in England she had always preferred tea. She only drank coffee with a great deal of cream and more sugar than her mother usually permitted her to take. One sip of the syrupy black liquid the Italians called *espresso* had been enough to make her purse her lips at the bitter, strong taste.

The contents of the cup set before her looked promising, though. Milk whipped to a thick pale froth floated atop the coffee. She peered at it thoughtfully.

"Sip the coffee through the froth," Balford advised, and then leaned a little closer. "Just try a sip. If you really don't care for it, please, don't force yourself to drink it on my account. I know not everyone likes coffee; indeed, my stepmother calls it a vile brew, in any form!"

She smiled, and took a small sip. Her brows flew up in surprise, and she took another.

"That is very pleasant, actually."

Encouraged by her enjoyment of the drink, she accepted one of the pastries from the platter Balford had ordered, and was even more delighted. The pastry was flaky and sweet, the creamy filling delicately citrus-flavoured, melting on her tongue.

Marianne sighed with bliss as she too discovered how delightful the pastries were, and promptly reached over to take another. "I quite understand now Lady Elspeth's attitude; I too should wish to hire this baker!"

They all laughed, and very shortly the platter was empty and Alex got up to go inside, returning a few minutes later with another paper bag full of pastries.

"To have with your tea this afternoon, ladies," he said with a grin. "Since I doubt Lady Elspeth will wish to share hers."

"Perhaps I should simply send someone down every morning to collect a bag for us to have at the breakfast table," Balford mused.

"Yes, please," Diana said enthusiastically, and he glanced at her and smiled, offering a little bow.

"Consider it done, Lady Diana. Now, shall we take a walk? The Rialto is rightly famous for its shopping; I am sure you ladies can find something you wish to take a closer look at."

Diana had never seen such an eclectic mixture of shops, all crammed in cheek by jowl alongside each other in the narrow streets. There were no horses and carts, which seemed strange after London; men moved their goods in small handcarts or carried them in crates or barrels from boats which pulled up to the canalsides.

The fish market was smelly but fascinating, with kinds of fish she had never seen before laid out on stalls, housewives haggling with the vendors for the prime specimens before their selections were wrapped up in paper packages.

"Is that an *octopus*?" Clarissa gasped, and Diana craned her neck to look, shuddering at the sight of the large purple-red creature with far too many legs lying on damp seaweed on the wooden counter.

"Surely that's not for eating?"

The two sisters looked at each other in horror. Balford, seeing what their gazes rested, chuckled.

"A delicacy here. I prefer the small ones, myself." He pointed at a large bowl, and, fascinated and revolted, the girls leaned over to look.

"They're tiny!" Barely larger than the last joint of her thumb, the baby octopi were white and a great deal less alarming-looking than their larger cousin. Diana still didn't think she'd care to eat one. "And you *like* eating these?" She looked up at Balford.

"I didn't say that, exactly. Just that I prefer them to the big ones." He laughed at her expression. "*Polpo* is what you have to watch out for if you happen to be in a restaurant with a menu. Don't worry that it'll be served at the palazzo; Lady Elspeth happens to despise it."

He was teasing, but it wasn't unkind, and Diana found herself giggling. Balford winked before leading them out of the Pescheria and into the Ebaria, which smelled a great deal sweeter, selling herbs, spices and a huge array of fresh fruit and vegetables. Diana had never seen oranges or lemons so large and juicy-looking, nor such tomatoes. Even the apples were vastly larger and seemed more brightly coloured than the ones she'd eaten back home in England. Her head swivelled this way and that, her mouth agape as she stared all about.

“Look at those grapes,” Clarissa pointed, and Diana’s mouth began to water as she stared at the vast piles of deep purple-red and bright grassy-green globes, larger and plumper than any she’d ever seen.

“They look amazing,” she agreed. “Italy is famous for its wine, it stands to reason their grapes would be excellent. Shall we buy some? I’d like to try them.”

“Don’t touch them,” Balford warned as they approached the vendor. “It’s a point of honour that they will choose the very best they have for you.”

Diana was glad that he stood back instead of stepping in to order for her, letting her try out her schoolgirl Italian on the vendor, an old man who listened intently and nodded, giving her a toothless grin before selecting two bunches of grapes for her, one green and one red. Alex had given both her and Clarissa some *lire* and *scudo* to carry in their reticules; she fished out a few coins and puzzled over them. The old man laughed, took the smallest coin - a silver half-lira - and gave her back a quarter-lira and a couple of copper coins.

“A five-centesimi and a three-centesimi. He gave you a good price on the grapes,” Balford said, amused, as the vendor even found a ragged cloth bag for Diana to take the grapes in, since she had no basket.

She thanked the old man prettily, rewarded with another toothless smile and a blast of Italian far too rapid for her to follow. Balford laughed, shaking his head, and said something quick in return.

“Did you just tell him I was your cousin?” Diana checked as they walked away.

“He thought you were my wife.”

“Oh!” Startled, she jerked back slightly, her hand falling from his arm. He reached down, picked her hand up and tucked it back into the crook of his elbow again.

“He would have been shocked if I had told him we aren’t related. In Italy, you’ll soon discover that unmarried young women of rank are usually highly sequestered. Arranged marriages like Andrea and Valentina’s are the norm.” He smiled slightly. “And since our families are indeed connected, if in a very convoluted way... *cousin* is as good a description as any, wouldn’t you agree?”

”I suppose,” she said doubtfully.

“Diana!” Marianne called to her from a small shop a few steps away. “Come over here and look at this wonderful jewellery!”

“Yes, Aunt Marianne,” she said dutifully, disengaging her hand from Balford’s arm.

"Please, allow me to carry your grapes." He smiled warmly at her. "The jewellers of Venice are rightly famous and deserve your full attention."

He's really very nice, she found herself thinking as she joined Marianne and Clarissa in the tiny jeweller's shop, the three of them barely squeezing into the tight space, and then she firmly told herself to stop thinking about him. The Duke of Balford was very handsome and yes, he did seem far nicer than her original impression of him, but allowing herself to moon over him could only lead to heartbreak. He'd already told her that he really wasn't in the market for a wife, and even if he was, she quite simply wasn't the kind of girl he'd marry. She wasn't rich enough, pretty enough or connected to nearly enough noble families.

CHAPTER EIGHT

A WEEK LATER, DIANA walked through the Rialto again, arm linked through her sister's, enjoying the sights and sounds all around her. On Diana's other side was Valentina, the young duchesa, who in the last week had become a firm friend to the sisters. Getting to know Valentina had brought home to Diana that what Balford had said about young Italian women of rank was quite true; they were extremely sheltered until after their marriages.

Valentina looked at almost everything outside the walls of the Franchetti palazzo with wide-eyed wonder. She'd also confided to the sisters that she was quite shocked by the talk she was exposed to now she was married; some of the married Franchetti ladies said the most scandalous things and even Lady Elspeth didn't bat an eyelid.

"This vendor over here is where I bought those beautiful grapes," Diana said, leading Valentina over. The old man smiled his toothless grin at her, recognition sparking in his eyes, and spoke deliberately slowly as he greeted her, for which she gave him a grateful smile.

"More of your wonderful grapes, good sir," she said in her slow, careful Italian. "I shared some with my good friend the Duchess of Franchetti and she thought them very fine."

The old man's eyes widened, and he bowed very low indeed to Valentina as Diana indicated her. "I am honoured by your notice, noble lady," he said. "Please. Allow me to make a gift of the finest of my wares."

"No gift," Valentina refused. "Not with how much I want to purchase! We will have grapes, and your cherries look excellent too."

Diana had thought to bring a basket this time, and handed it over for the vendor to fill. He tried again to refuse payment, but she placed two silver lire in his hand.

"You didn't charge me enough last time," she insisted. "We leave Venice tomorrow and I won't be back, so please take it."

"I will be back in a few months, however," Valentina said. "We go to visit my brother, and plan to enjoy your delicious fruit as we travel."

The old man bowed to her again, his hand closing around the coins. "This one is far beneath Your Grace's notice. The honour is too much."

"Does all the bowing and scraping get to be too much, eventually?" Diana asked as they walked away, their basket heaped high with fruit.

Valentina gave her a bemused look. "I don't understand."

Valentina's English was better than Diana's Italian, but she still tried again in Valentina's own language. The young duchesa still didn't understand, though, and Diana eventually realised it wasn't the communication problem which was the issue. Valentina had been raised to expect such deference as her due. Marrying a duke might have increased the degree of it slightly, but it was still completely normal in Valentina's world.

Even though she was *Lady* Diana now, daughter of an earl, Diana didn't think she would ever become accustomed to being on the receiving end of such attitudes. She wondered if Valentina was even aware of her own influence, if she had even noticed that the vendor was telling his next customers that the Duchess of Franchetti herself said his fruit was the finest in Venice.

Patronage was the name of the game. Diana glanced back over her shoulder to where two dukes walked side by side, heads bent together in conversation. How much power such men wielded, and more knowingly than women.

Balford caught her eye and tilted his head, a questioning look on his face; she offered a slight smile and looked away again, before he approached to ask if there was anything she might need. He had been quite startlingly attentive over the last week, acting the tour guide on numerous occasions for their party; showing them not just the sights of Venice every tourist was advised to take in, but also several of his personal favourites. Like the church of San Giovanni Elemosinario on their first day, a hidden wonder they would otherwise surely have overlooked.

Clarissa had teased Diana quite mercilessly for the first couple of days Balford took them about, but even she had to concede he showed no marked preference for either sister. Lady Elspeth had also made clear, by some fairly unsubtle hints, that she hoped Balford would marry her granddaughter Chiara, Andrea's younger sister. And though Chiara was as yet only fourteen years of age, well, Balford had said himself he wasn't ready to marry. Waiting four years for Chiara to come of age was nothing when the end result would be the cementing of alliances between the powerful English and Italian duchies.

Chiara was sweet, if very shy; Diana had met her once, though it was true what Balford had said about young Italian girls being highly sequestered. Andrea was nice enough, but he also seemed mildly concerned that his sister might somehow be corrupted by being exposed to the 'independent English way of thinking'. Diana was pretty sure steps had been taken to ensure Chiara was kept well away from her and Clarissa.

Certainly, it had originally been planned that Chiara should accompany Andrea and Valentina on their visit to Lake Garda to visit Valentina's brother - a trip on which Balford was also scheduled - but once the Glenkellies had decided they would accept the invitation to go along, Lady Elspeth had suddenly decided it would be best for Chiara to accompany her to her villa at Schio, instead.

Both parties of travellers intended to depart Venice the following day. Sad to be leaving - she had fallen rather in love with *La Serenissima*, the City of Bridges, and was sure there were many wonders she had not had the chance to discover - still Diana was sure there were many more adventures yet to be had in Italy. Why, they would see the cities of Padua, Vicenza and Verona just on their way to Lake Garda; Padua, the city with a university which *women* had been permitted to attend! Verona, immortalised in the Bard's play! Never in her wildest dreams had Diana imagined *she* might get to visit such places, so she would not for a single moment express her regret for their departure from Venice.

On this, their last day in Venice, they had a particular expedition planned after their visit to the Rialto. They were to visit the islands of Murano, a settlement just to the north of Venice, where the famous Venetian glass was made. Andrea had explained that all the glassmakers of Venice were forced to move to Murano centuries ago because the city fathers had feared the risks of fire were too great. Napoleon had closed many of the factories when he ruled the city, and the industry had not yet recovered, but the Franchettis patronised several small families of glassblowers who were yet practicing their trade.

They took a rowboat across the lagoon rather than the gondola, the trip taking about an hour; the ladies leaned back against cushions with their parasols held up to shade them against the hot sun and nibbled on the grapes they'd bought from the toothless old market seller. Diana tried in vain to keep her gaze on the rippling waters around them, the other boats passing by; anything but the handsome, smiling face of the Duke of Balford as he sat at the boat's bow, leaning over to trail his fingers in the water and laughing as he chatted with Andrea.

Valentina was deeply involved in a conversation with Clarissa, but Marianne, sitting beside Diana, clearly noticed the direction of her gaze.

"They want him to marry the Lady Chiara, you know," Marianne murmured quietly, her words pitched for Diana's ears alone.

"I'm sure it would be an excellent match," Diana said evenly. "In a few years, of course. Balford will be ready by then to take a wife, and Chiara's birth must make her an unexceptionable choice for his duchess. Even her English is perfect."

Indeed, the Italian girl had been groomed all her life for the position of Duchess of Balford. Small wonder Balford hadn't wished to engage in the marriage mart in England... although Diana had to wonder why his stepmother had pressured him to participate, since she was the one with the connection to the Franchettis. Did she not want Balford to marry into the family for some reason? Diana could not imagine why not. Some noble Venetian families had lost much of their fortunes under Napoleon's rule, and were not faring well under Austrian governance either, but the Franchettis weren't among them. Lady Elspeth and her husband had raised eleven children apart from Andrea's father, children who had married into noble families all over Italy and cemented trading alliances which profited all of them.

Marianne took Diana's hand, a little to her surprise, and squeezed it. "I'm glad you're looking at the situation with clear eyes, dearest. I wouldn't like to see your heart broken."

"Are you telling me not to fall for him, Aunt? The man whose ungallant actions caused me to be named The Fainting Flower?" Diana laughed a little, trying to indicate with her light tone how ridiculous the mere idea was. "Never fear, my heart is in no danger."

Marianne's level gaze was a little too knowing, and Diana looked away, fixing her gaze on the island they were now fast approaching. "I hope I can find something for Mama within my budget," she said, her voice a little too loud. "I should love to take a piece of Venetian glass home for her."

Marianne squeezed her hand again, and allowed the change of subject, saying kindly that if Diana needed a little extra, she would be happy to contribute towards the cost of purchasing a gift for Lavinia. "She, after all, gave me a gift beyond price; your company on this trip!"

Diana rather thought she and Clarissa were the ones getting something of incalculable value, for which she would be eternally grateful. She had no opportunity to say so, though, since the boat had now pulled up to the dock and it was time for them to disembark.

Andrea wanted to show off to Valentina, it soon became obvious as the young duke escorted them around the glassmaking manufactories, and Valentina was delighted to be impressed by the skills of the artisans under the Franchetti patronage. Each artisan had a gift prepared for the new duchess, as well as being eager to show off their skills and their wares to her friends. Diana marvelled at the delicate beauty of the pieces, and hardly dared to ask the price of a small soda glass vase which she thought her mother might like.

The woman showing the pieces checked with her husband before quoting a price Diana couldn't imagine would be correct.

"Seventeen lire? Are you sure?" she said doubtfully, doing a mental calculation. The piece would sell for the equivalent of ten times that in London, she thought.

"Fifteen, then, but not a centesimi less!" The woman shook her finger.

"Oh no, I... yes. Fifteen lire, absolutely. I'm taking it home to England. Can you pack it for me?" Digging in her reticule, she found her coin purse and fished out the coins, handing them over. The woman beamed, accepting the money, and reached under the counter to pull out a small wooden box. Diana watched as the vase was filled with sawdust, and then packed in more sawdust, the box filled with it until the lid was placed on, and then twine bound firmly around it until the lid was secure.

"Diana, come look at these beads," Marianne called to her, and the woman waved Diana away, intent on finishing off the packing properly. Crossing the room, Diana found Marianne studying some delicate, blown-glass beads, dangling from fine wires and attached to earbob screws.

"Oh, how pretty," Diana admired. "You should get those green ones, Aunt Marianne. They'll look magnificent against your red hair." The emerald-coloured beads glimmered with flecks of gold, shimmering in the sunlight pouring in through the window.

"That's what I said, only I think she should get the sapphire-blue and gold ones too," Clarissa agreed.

"Those ones are on hooks, and my ears aren't pierced," Marianne pointed out.

"Mine, either." Diana touched her earlobes. Valentina had pierced ears, she'd noticed; favoured some large pearls dangling from golden hoops which she wore much of the time. They looked very pretty, but still, she shivered at the thought of a needle stabbing through the sensitive flesh of her lobes.

"I'm sure they can change the fittings over for ear screws, if you want that particular pair," a low voice murmured, and Diana glanced around to find Balford had come up behind her. He nodded to Marianne, lifting a finger to beckon over a young man, who listened as Balford spoke in his fluent, colloquial Italian and nodded eagerly.

"Yes, of course, we can change the fittings. A matter of a few minutes, my lady." The young man bowed to Marianne.

"Well, in that case, I shall take both pairs. What about you girls, would you like to choose a pair each? My gift to you."

Both Diana and Clarissa tried to cry that she was too generous, but Marianne was insistent. She held up a pretty pink and white pair of beads, holding them to Clarissa's ears, and Diana smiled, knowing her sister wouldn't be able to resist.

Clarissa loved that particular shade of deep pink, even though their mother had decreed it was too risqué a colour for debutantes to wear.

"You should get these ones," Balford murmured, and she looked down at where he pointed to a pair of beads in a stunning teal shade, flecked with silver. "They would go well with that pretty evening gown of yours."

She stared at him in absolute shock. She would never for a moment have thought that he would notice the colour of her favourite dress, much less remember it well enough to match quite precisely the shade from this array of earrings in every colour of the rainbow.

"Diana?" Marianne spoke her name, and Diana shook off her surprise.

"Yes," she said. "Those ones; I like them very well, and they will indeed match that gown. How clever of you to notice, Your Grace."

Although, perhaps he wasn't *that* observant. She'd worn that gown on four evenings of the seven they'd spent in Venice, alternating it with the pink frilly one she despised. The pale green velvet one was just too hot in the climate, but she hoped perhaps the weather might be cooler once they reached Lake Garda and she could wear it there. Still, she felt frumpy and shabby when comparing herself to Valentina, who wore a different gown every evening, each more stunning than the last.

CHAPTER NINE

WILL WATCHED AS THE shop owner carefully packed the earrings in wadded cotton before placing them in a small box and handing it to Diana, along with the larger box containing the vase she'd purchased for her mother. He was glad her aunt had bought her the earrings; he'd had a most inappropriate urge to buy them for her himself, an instinct he had to ruthlessly suppress. Even the suggestion of it would be a shocking impropriety.

Still, he was glad she had them. And he couldn't quite keep from pointing to a glass dolphin sculpted from the same teal and silver glass as Diana's earrings, and asking the shop owner to wrap it for him.

Right now, he couldn't figure out a way in which he might give it to her without disastrous consequences for her reputation. But he had some time, weeks in her company hopefully, to work something out. All he knew was that he wanted her to have it.

They went to a second glassworks, this one larger, with a row of apprentices working to make glass rods of different colours and thicknesses, which the masters then melted and twisted together to make the fascinating, colourful pieces known as *millefiori*. They were allowed to get quite close, to stand and peer over the shoulders of the apprentices and see the glass glowing red as it was melted and formed.

The heat was intense, and from the corner of his eye, Will spotted Diana swaying slightly. Instinctively, he reached out to put a hand under her elbow and steady her.

"I shan't faint, Your Grace." She glanced back at him and smiled. "Never fear."

"Perhaps not." He smiled back. "But know that if you do, I will catch you."

She laughed, her brown eyes twinkling. "It is terribly hot in here," she admitted, backing away from the proximity to the heat. "Perhaps we could go outside?"

"Of course." He offered his arm and walked her to the door, and outside. They stood on the narrow bridge crossing the canal right outside the shop door, where a slight breeze stirred the hot, humid air. Diana turned her face to the breeze and breathed deeply.

"The canals smell a little better here in Murano than in Venice proper," Will said a little inanely.

"They do. Perhaps because there are so many more people in the city." She wrinkled her nose a little, glancing at him. "Truly, the smell isn't so bad. One can ignore it, for Venice's beauties."

"Did you get time to explore Florence?" he asked. "I know you visited there before coming here."

"Sadly, no. As soon as we discovered Lord Glenkellie's relatives had travelled for Venice, we set sail again. I didn't even get to leave the ship." She made a little face. "But I think the plan is for us to travel overland back to Florence once we leave Lake Garda, which I am very much looking forward to."

"Indeed, that will be something of an adventure," he agreed. "You will cross the Apennines, and though they are nothing to an alpine crossing, still the scenery is magnificent."

"Have you spent much time in Florence?" she asked.

"I have never been there," he admitted. "I've visited Rome, twice, and Milan, but somehow Florence has never quite made it onto my itinerary."

"That seems quite an omission, considering your otherwise encyclopedic knowledge of Italy!"

He was fairly sure she was laughing at him, but he took it with good humour. "Perhaps I shall ask Lord Glenkellie if I may join your party, when you depart Lake Garda." He said it on impulse, the thought striking him that it would be a way to prolong his time in her company.

Colour rose to Diana's cheeks and she looked away, breaking their eye contact. "I am sure Glenkellie would welcome your company," she murmured distantly.

Will wanted to ask if she would welcome his company too. Sternly, he suppressed the urge. She was an earl's daughter, and not to be trifled with. Glenkellie seemed very fond of her, too, and he had no wish to incur the marquis' anger. Glenkellie was a former soldier, and reputedly had been a very good one. Will had been trained by masters, but he did not for a moment think his skill with sword or pistol could match up to a man who had killed for a living.

"There you are," a deep voice said dryly, and Will looked around to see Glenkellie standing in the shop's doorway, arms folded as he leaned on the door jamb. Wondering how long the marquis had been watching them, Will was glad he had maintained a respectable distance from Diana on the bridge.

"It's terribly hot in there, Uncle Alex. His Grace was kind enough to escort me out for a breath of fresh air, such as it is." Diana turned an untroubled face towards Glenkellie, who nodded.

"Quite understandable. I believe we're ready to leave now." He held his hand out in a clear gesture for her to return to his side, and she moved away from Will, walking down the bridge's curved side. She slipped on the damp timber, and Will lunged instinctively, catching her with a strong hand around her upper arm and keeping her on her feet.

"Steady, my lady!"

"Oh, my goodness!" Diana grasped at him, regaining her balance.

"Careful," he said, letting go of her as Glenkellie stepped forward to take her hand, guiding her down the last few steps off the bridge. "These bridges can be slippery."

"It's good to know you can be quick to catch a lady, when she really needs it." Diana cast him a sparkling look, and he laughed, helpless against her wit.

"I am at your service, my lady."

Andrea glanced around when Will came back into the shop, looked from him to Diana with raised eyebrows. "I thought the English miss wasn't of interest?"

He hesitated, perhaps a beat too long for a convincing denial, and Andrea nodded slowly. "I see."

Andrea had never pressed him regarding a potential match with his sister Chiara, for which Will was grateful; it was Lady Elspeth and Andrea's mother Lady Marietta who had been pushing for the match. Will could not be less interested; he had known Chiara since she was a baby, had indeed rocked her in his arms. She was a sweet child and he doubted he could ever think of her as a man would want to think of his wife, even with a few more years of maturity.

"Chiara is a child," he offered, and Andrea nodded in understanding.

"Yes, I had rather thought you felt that way about her. I am actually grateful my father kept me from meeting Valentina for so many years, despite the long-standing arrangement for us to wed. I didn't meet her as a child, but as the beautiful woman she is now." Andrea smiled fondly as he looked across to where his wife stood with Clarissa Creighton, admiring a delicate glass sculpture being shown off by an artisan. "Valentina likes your English miss. She is… not like the women I know, but if she suits you, then the family will welcome her."

"You're getting ahead of yourself," Will insisted. "I like her, but… I still don't think I'm ready for marriage. And Lady Diana does not think much of me, I'm afraid, after our bad start. She tolerates my presence, but little more."

"For a duchess' tiara, a lady would do a lot more than *tolerate* you," Andrea said dryly, but Will shook his head, everything in him rebelling at the idea. How he was to manage it, he had no idea, but he wanted the woman he eventually married to choose him for himself, not his wealth and position.

Venice at dawn was a mystical, almost magical place. The eastern sky over the Adriatic sea was tinged a pale peach at the horizon, darkening to a warm orange as the sun began to rise, the waters of the lagoon glassy-smooth as their boats cut through the water. The city's marble palaces glowed, reflecting the rising sun's rays; but Will didn't even notice them. His gaze was fixed on the pale countenance of the young woman sitting in the stern of the boat, her expression pure wonder as she gazed back at the shining city on the water.

All too soon, they arrived at the village of Campalto on the mainland, and disembarked to find transport awaiting them, in the form of two fine carriages and horses for the gentlemen if they so chose. Baggage carts had departed the day before with most of their belongings and such servants as would travel with them, and would already be in Padua awaiting them. The Franchettis knew how to travel in style.

They spent two full days in Padua, seeing the sights, before going on to Vicenza, where they bade farewell to Lady Elspeth and her party. From Vicenza, Valentina excitedly told them all it was only about thirty miles to Verona, but the mountainous country meant they would take two full days to traverse the distance, and from Verona one more day to her brother's castle at Bardolino, on the shores of Lake Garda.

Will hadn't visited this part of Italy before, and found it incredibly beautiful, with the Alps looming ever-present to the north and glorious countryside all around. Vineyards and olive groves were everywhere, and every rest stop on the journey was in a village which had a hotel serving the most wonderful food and wine.

On their last day of travel, he stepped outside the inn where they had paused to partake of a luncheon and change the carriage horses, and found Diana sitting on a tree stump outside, sketch book in hand, pencil sweeping rapidly over the page as she attempted to capture the view before them.

Or at least, that was what he assumed she was doing, until he walked close enough to see that she was actually creating a charming little sketch of the innkeeper's two children playing in the dirt with a puppy.

"That is delightful," he said without thinking, and obviously startled her, because she dropped her pencil with a cry of shock. "I do beg your pardon; I didn't mean to startle you. Here." Scooping the pencil up, he handed it back.

"Thank you," she mumbled, cheeks red. She didn't meet his eyes, but returned to her sketch.

"You're very good," he observed.

Diana laughed, still not looking at him. "We are in Italy, the home of the great masters. Even in this small town, the church is decorated with frescoes more spectacular than anything I might ever dream of creating."

"And yet, your sketch is everything delightful. In just a few strokes, you have captured the essence of it; two children, happy in their dirt and with their pet."

"It is a scribble." She tore the page from her sketchbook, and for a horrified moment he thought she was going to crumple it up and toss it away, but she stood and presented it with a smile to the innkeeper's wife, who had come out to retrieve her children and was chiding them for dirtying their clothes. The woman accepted the sketch with cries of delight, running to show her husband, who came out to praise it and thank Diana volubly.

"A scribble which made two loving parents very happy," Will observed as the drawing was passed around to admire.

"The heights to which I aspire with my art," Diana said with a shrug. "It is an amusement."

"You are very down on yourself." He wondered why. Looking down at the book she had left abandoned on the tree stump, he pointed to the sketch left topmost, now the picture of the children and puppy was gone. "Look at this. We passed that house yesterday; I recall seeing it, admiring the aesthetic of the ruin on the hilltop. You could have had it in your view for no more than five minutes, and yet I recognise it instantly, at a single glance."

She looked at him uncomprehendingly, and he gestured towards the happy family now hurrying inside, looking for a place of honour to hang her sketch. "Those children and their puppy didn't sit still for two seconds together, and yet you drew their likenesses unerringly, unmistakably. Please believe me when I say that is unusual; I have had my portrait done twice, by two of the finest painters of the age, and the conniptions they both descended into when I twitched so much as a muscle had to be seen to be believed."

Diana laughed at that, her stiff posture softening a little. "I have heard that. Father wanted to commission a portrait when he inherited the earldom, and was horrified when he heard how long the painter would expect him to sit still. Not about the cost, mind you." Her glance was wry. "He asked me to paint him instead. I completed it before we left for Italy."

"And did he pay you what he would have paid the portrait artist?"

She laughed again, picked up her sketchbook and folded it closed without answering. Her laughter had been answer enough, he supposed, watching her walk away back towards the inn.

Riding away from the inn a short time later, Will wasn't particularly surprised to find Lord Glenkellie falling in beside him. He was a little taken aback by the former soldier's blunt words, however.

"Lady Diana is under my protection. I'll not have her trifled with."

"I would never offer Lady Diana the slightest insult!" Indignant, Will drew himself up, before wincing. "More than I already have," he said sheepishly. "I mean, I find her charming..."

Too late, he saw the other man's sly grin, stumbled over his words, and closed his mouth with a snap.

"I believe you, when you say you mean no insult to her, but I must still query your intentions."

"I'm not looking for a wife at this time." The words were automatic, but even as he said them, he wondered if they were still the immutable truth they'd been when he left England just a few short weeks ago.

"I see." Glenkellie's tone indicated more disbelief than acceptance. "Well, you know your own mind, of course, Balford. But I must request that you have a care for Diana's reputation. My wife is very fond of Diana and Clarissa, and I have come to rather like you. I should hate to have to call you out."

"I should hate to have to face you across a field of honour," Will said honestly. "Indeed, I should quake in my boots if I had to, so I give you my word I will do everything in my power to avoid even the slightest appearance of impropriety."

Glenkellie inclined his head. "I will accept your word of honour, Balford." That sly grin crossed his face again, tugging at the scar slashing down across his cheek, marring his handsome good looks. "But should you change your position as regards matrimony, I hope you'll do me the courtesy of advising me."

It was obvious to Will that pursuing the topic could only lead to pitfalls he'd much rather avoid, so he merely murmured his agreement and hastily changed the subject.

CHAPTER TEN

After several days of travel, Diana was eager to reach their destination. The blue waters of the lake shimmered out the window on the left side of the coach, mountains rising steeply on their right. The scenery seemed to grow more spectacular with every bend in the road, and she leaned close to the window, staring out in delight and wonder. How Clarissa and Valentina could sleep when there were such sights to be seen, she could not imagine, but sleep they did, leaning against each other on the opposite seat, heads nodding with the rocking of the coach.

"Diana," Marianne's voice said softly, and Diana looked away from the view to meet her aunt's gaze. Marianne seemed to hesitate, but then she reached out to touch Diana's wrist and said gently "Is there anything you want to tell me?"

Diana's brow furrowed. A small smile curved Marianne's lips as she saw her evident confusion.

"I'm talking about the Duke of Balford," Marianne clarified.

"Oh." Diana felt her cheeks flush, took a few deep breaths to calm herself. "There is nothing to tell, Aunt Marianne. We have made up our differences. He is a much better man than I understood from my initial poor impression of him; indeed, I think him a very good man indeed."

"I rather thought you had that opinion," Marianne said delicately. "And I rather suspect he thinks quite a lot of you."

The blush was crawling down Diana's neck. She considered letting down the window, but they were traversing a rather dry and rocky part of the road, a great deal of dust kicked up. She stared out of the window and said nothing.

"I will not press you," Marianne said, "but I wanted you to know that I am always here if you would like to talk."

"There is nothing to talk about," Diana mumbled, still unable to look at her aunt.

"Very well, but if that should change, I promise I will neither judge nor press you. Your happiness is my first concern." Marianne squeezed her fingers gently. "Whatever your hopes and desires are, or may come to be, I will always do my best to see them come to pass for you."

Hot tears pricked at Diana's eyes, and she blinked them back, turning to Marianne at last and enveloping her in a fierce hug. Marianne's loving concern and calm trust was such an intense contrast to her parents' smothering overprotectiveness, even though she knew her parents were also motivated by love.

"Don't break your heart, dear one," Marianne whispered into her ear as she returned Diana's embrace.

"My heart is in no danger," Diana replied stoutly, wondering even as she spoke the words if she was telling the truth. Her heart gave a treacherous pang as she thought about the mere possibility of Balford holding her in any regard.

"If you say so." Marianne drew back, giving her a somewhat disbelieving look, but she was kind enough not to press further, for which Diana felt exceptionally grateful.

The carriage jolted, and Clarissa and Valentina both woke, looking about. Valentina leaned forward to peer out of the window, clapping her hands together with delight, her face suffused with joy.

"We are almost at Bardolino! Look, there on the hill above the lake, my brother's *castello*!"

The others looked where she pointed, and let out cries of delight as they saw the castle, made of white marble, shimmering in the late afternoon sun.

"I thought it would be like our English castles, all battlements and grim grey stone," Diana whispered to Clarissa as they climbed out of the carriage a quarter-hour later.

"Me too," Clarissa admitted with a giggle, "but then, the palazzos of Venice are very unlike St. James or Kensington Palace; we should have expected that their castles are quite different too!"

Valentina had disembarked ahead of them, as befitted her higher rank, and flung herself into the arms of a man who stood in the courtyard awaiting them, laughing as he embraced her.

"I daresay that must be her brother," Clarissa murmured, and with a nudge to Diana's ribs, added "Gosh, he's rather good-looking."

Mario Maccarone, *Conte* di Bardolino, was indeed very good-looking. Classically handsome after the Italian fashion, he wasn't particularly tall, but was blessed with a mop of curly black hair, flashing black eyes, and cheekbones which could have been sculpted by Michaelangelo himself. He was possessed of an overly-dramatic disposition and a tendency to exaggeration, or so Diana assumed when he took one look at her, threw his hands up in the air and declared he had been struck by Cupid's arrow.

She was also fairly sure he was no older than she was. His thin, scraggly moustache looked like a rather desperate attempt to appear less boyish and more mature. So she kindly didn't laugh at his dramatics, merely smiled distantly and allowed him to seize her hand and bestow a flamboyant kiss on her fingertips. Stepping back and nudging Clarissa forward, Diana was surprised to catch Balford with an expression on his face she could only interpret as black rage. She tilted her head and raised an eyebrow at him curiously; he caught her watching him and looked away quickly, his expression smoothing into blandness.

What was that about? she wondered, but there was little time to think about it, as Valentina was seizing her arm and leading her towards the *castello's* main entrance, chattering excitedly on about the guest chambers she had written to her brother to have prepared for their English guests.

Diana had thought the rooms they occupied in the Franchetti palazzo in Venice were extraordinary, and indeed in opulence they were unrivalled, but the view from their rooms at Castello Bardolino was utterly spectacular. Spellbound, she stared as Valentina flung open French doors leading out onto a balcony - her own private balcony! - with a view out over the shimmering blue waters of Lake Garda to the soaring mountains of the Alps to the north.

"Good Lord," she breathed, stepping out onto the balcony beside Valentina. "But... this is too much! Is this the best guest suite? You should not have!"

Valentina laughed, and swept her hands out to the left and right. "Look, my friend. Every room on this floor, and the one above, has exactly the same view, and a private balcony. Lord and Lady Glenkellie are next door to you in the corner suite, which is much larger and finer, I promise."

"Will you mind very much if I just spend my entire stay right here?" Diana asked, quite in earnest. There was even a chair on the balcony, a comfortable-looking armchair of woven cane with a thick cushion on the seat. She was quite sure that she could sit there for hours upon end and never weary of the view.

Valentina laughed and squeezed her hand. "If that is what you wish, our staff will keep you well supplied with food and drink, but I hope you will soon begin to wish for our company. I know my brother is already enthusiastic for more of yours!" She went away with a giggle and a wink Diana tried to ignore.

"The *conte* did seem very taken with you," Clarissa said from the next-door balcony, making Diana jump. "Oh, I'm sorry! Didn't you hear me come out?"

Hand pressed over her pounding heart, Diana shook her head. "No. And I don't want to talk about the *conte*, Clarry. I think he's younger than I am, for goodness' sake."

"He's younger than *I* am." Clarissa folded her arms and leaned on the balcony's stone railing, grinning wickedly at her sister. "He's Valentina's twin. Didn't you know?"

Seventeen. With a small laugh, Diana plopped down in her cane balcony chair and leaned back. "But of course he is. The only man who's ever really showed any interest in me, is younger than I am."

"The *only* man? I think not." Clarissa threw herself into her own chair, and in a very unladylike gesture, swung her feet up to rest them on the edge of the balcony wall. Seeing Diana's glance of reproof, she sighed and lowered them again. "Seriously, Di, you might fool Aunt Marianne but I know better. Balford..."

"Firstly, I don't want to talk about it, and secondly, even if I did," Diana cut her sister off quickly, "this is definitely not the place. Anyone on any of the balconies could overhear." She pointed up, indicating the floor above and the balconies there. "And we might not be able to see them."

A sound behind her made her glance around, to see several burly footmen entering her suite carrying her trunks and an empty copper bathtub, accompanied by a pair of maids who bobbed curtsies as they caught sight of her. Undoubtedly, she was to be just as thoroughly spoiled and waited upon hand and foot as she had been in Venice. With a warning glance at Clarissa, she rose and walked back inside the suite to greet the maids, grateful she had taken every opportunity to improve her Italian when they proved not to have a single word of English between them.

The footmen brought in pails of hot water to fill the bathtub and, once the maids had chivvied the men out, Diana was encouraged to remove her dusty travelling gown and settle into the hot water, scented with orange oil and wonderfully relaxing.

One of the maids had slipped out when Diana got into the bath, and returned a few minutes later with her arms piled high with brightly coloured bundles of fabric. The other maid scurried over to help and soon they were shaking out dresses and laying them out on the bed.

"Where did those come from?" Diana asked, pausing and wracking her brain before repeating herself in Italian when they stared at her blankly. The dresses certainly weren't hers.

"Lady Valentina sent them," one of the maids explained, speaking slowly so that Diana could understand her Italian. "When she married, she chose all new gowns, suitable for a married woman. These are her gowns from before, left here. She said if you could use them, they are for you, and your sister."

"How incredibly kind and thoughtful!" Diana exclaimed in delight. The maids shared a smile, probably not understanding her words but certainly appreciating her delighted tone. They were very loyal to the family, Diana guessed, and considering Valentina's sweet nature, probably quite devoted to her.

The gowns they held up for her inspection were beautiful; modestly cut, as befitted an unmarried maiden, but of superb quality fabrics and exceptionally well made. Diana eyed them covetously, especially delighted by the strong colours and jewel tones, so much more striking than anything an English debutante was permitted to wear.

The two maids soon had her out of the bath and standing in her shift, measuring one of the gowns up against her and chattering quickly to each other about alterations which would need to be made.

"Choose which gown you would like to wear tonight, my lady," she was instructed.

Diana hesitated only a moment before pointing to the gown which had caught her eye first, a rich creation of silk in a deep amethyst purple. Beams of approval greeted her choice before she was urged into the gown and they set about her with needle and thread, making adjustments to the bodice where Valentina was obviously rather fuller in the bosom than she. Luckily they were close to the same height, Diana just a little taller, so the hemline could be left alone.

A tap on the door heralded Clarissa joining her as the maids were making the final adjustments. Wearing a lovely gown in emerald-green, Clarissa twirled about, grinning.

"Isn't this a pleasant surprise!"

"You look beautiful," Diana said sincerely. "Very grown-up." With a twinkle in her eye, she teased "Perhaps the *conte* will transfer his admiration for me, onto you."

"I doubt it, considering the look I gave him when he kissed my hand," Clarissa noted dryly. "I prefer *men*, not boys."

Diana had to laugh. "You should give him a chance. Wouldn't you like to be mistress of this beautiful *castello*?"

"If all I wanted in a husband was an impressive house, I'd ask Pa to arrange a marriage for me." Clarissa swished the skirts of her gown. "Like you, I want something more."

With arms linked, the sisters made their way downstairs, guided by smiling servants who gestured them to a large, airy salon with huge French windows opening out to a stunning terrace overlooking the lake where a long table was set with gleaming crystal glasses and polished silverware on a shimmering white linen cloth.

The young conte rose from a chair close to the window, smiling broadly as he strode towards them. "Lady Diana, Lady Clarissa. Welcome, again, to my home. We will dine shortly, but may I offer you some sherry?"

His English was excellent, if heavily accented; Diana complimented him on it politely and he beamed at her.

"I had an Englishman as a private tutor for three years, in my youth."

She had to bite on her lips to avoid laughing, or saying something sarcastic like "Oh, so many years ago, then?"

Clarissa, less tactful, let out a faint snort, and then detached her arm from Diana's and walked away towards the French doors, shoulders shaking slightly as she stared out at the view of the sun setting over the lake.

"Your home is magnificent, my lord," Diana said as the conte handed her a glass of sherry.

He beamed at her, joining her as she too drifted to the doors, drawn in by that astonishing view. "Thank you! And please - you must consider it as your home too, while you are here. My sister tells me how fond she is of you already, that she is delighted to call you family, even if the connection is so distant she could not exactly explain it to me."

He was really very charming despite his youth, and Diana returned his smile. "Valentina is a delight. She has been far kinder and more welcoming than we might possibly have hoped."

"Oh, she is an angel. And since you call her by her first name, you must call me by mine; I am Mario."

"I don't know..." she moved slightly, putting a little more space in between them. "We did just meet. I don't want to be overly familiar."

"As you please." Unabashed, he shrugged. "Perhaps when you know me a little better."

The door of the salon opened again to admit Alex and Marianne, Balford following them in, and the conte strode forward again, declaring his great pleasure and the honour done to his house by the presence of such distinguished guests.

CHAPTER ELEVEN

WILL DIDN'T EVEN NOTICE the young conte's effusive greetings; he was too busy staring in awe at the vision of beauty gowned in purple, silhouetted by the setting sun on the far side of the lake.

Diana Creighton was a pretty girl. He'd noticed that on their very first meeting, before she fainted at his feet, and every moment he'd spent with her in Italy only had him appreciating more and more of her fine qualities. In a purple silk gown of the very finest cut, her hair elaborately curled and braided, she was lovely enough to rival any diamond of the *Ton*... something the Conte di Bardolino had certainly noticed. It didn't take long for the stripling to hurry back to her side, his gaze fixed on her serene countenance as she gazed on the glorious colours the sunset painted into the sky.

Will had never thought of himself as having any tendencies towards violence, but his fists clenched at his sides and he took an instinctive step forward, a thought that he should toss the foolish young sprig in the lake for looking at Diana that way forming in his head.

Glenkellie stepped smoothly into his path, the movement so casual-seeming nobody looking on would have remarked it, but Will found himself brought up short as a solid shoulder glanced his own, knocking him back a half-step.

"Do beg your pardon, Balford." Glenkellie glanced at him, an unspoken warning in his eyes, and Will took a deep breath, gathering his composure again.

"Not at all, my fault entirely. I wasn't paying attention," he murmured.

"I rather think you were, actually," Glenkellie said, and Will flushed.

Saved by the arrival of Andrea and Valentina, Will turned gratefully to his cousin. "You did not tell us how magnificent this place was, Andrea! And what a place to grow up, Valentina!"

The young duchesa laughed softly. "We do not always appreciate what is right in front of us until it is gone, do we? Venice is beautiful, of course." She squeezed her husband's arm. "But a part of my heart will always reside beside the shores of Lake Garda."

"Which is why we shall always journey here every year." Andrea patted her hand fondly. "So let that be a criteria when you look for a wife, Will... choose one whose childhood home is a place where it is no hardship to spend time!"

"Provided she cares to return there," Lady Glenkellie put in dryly.

Uncertain what she meant, Will stared at her. Her expression tightened, her beautiful face as still and cold as marble, before she murmured;

"My father saw me as an asset to be traded for his own advantage. My childhood was not a happy one."

"I'm sorry," Will said, knowing the sentiment was inadequate. He knew a little something of the lady's history; her first husband had been much older than she and notoriously possessive, not even permitting her to speak with other men. Her eyecatching beauty meant she was pursued as soon as her mourning period was over, but she accepted Glenkellie's suit almost immediately. They had become engaged the very night Will had first met Diana.

During the last week, Will had discovered the affection between Glenkellie and his new wife was actually of long standing, but Marianne had been forced to accept the Earl of Creighton when Glenkellie went away to war. The couple were very much in love, Will thought. Even more so than Andrea and Valentina, who were obviously besotted with each other in the first throes of youthful adoration, the Glenkellies were more mature, knowing of their own minds, and certain in their faith in each other's hearts.

The conte had finally torn his gaze from Diana long enough to notice his sister's arrival, and came over now to kiss her fondly on both cheeks. Mario seemed quite a likeable lad, Will thought grudgingly, who obviously thought the world of his sister and was overjoyed she was happy in her marriage to Andrea.

They were soon being invited out to the terrace, taking seats at the table, and a procession of footmen began carrying out dishes topped with domed silver lids, setting them on the tables with great flourishes as they removed the lids.

Diana cried out with pleasure and applauded, and something hot and tight curled painfully in Will's belly as she turned a radiant smile on Mario.

I'm not jealous, he tried to tell himself. *I have nothing to be jealous about. I'm not looking for a wife, but she is looking for a husband. I should be happy for her; Mario is a fine young man with a title, a handsome estate, and a bright future. He'd be a good match for her.*

So why do I want to vomit at the thought of them together?

"You must try the *polenta taragna* and the *osso bucco,*" Valentina told him, gesturing to Andrea to pass the dishes to Will. "They are Lombardy local delicacies. Is there *torrone* for dessert, brother?" she called down to Mario.

"Would I dare serve a dinner for you without it?" he answered with a laugh, before explaining for the edification of the other guests, "*Torrone* is a kind of sweet, a nougat I think the word is in English? Flavoured with honey and almonds, it has always been one of Valentina's favourites."

"It sounds delicious," Diana enthused. "But then, everything looks wonderful! What is that dish with the yellow rice - and how do they make it yellow?"

"*Risotto alla Milanese*, and the colour comes from the saffron threads it is cooked with." Mario beamed at her interest.

Will took a gulp of wine, his appetite non-existent. At least the wine was good. Excellent, in fact. And of course it was from vineyards owned by the Maccarone family, as Valentina proceeded to tell him with great pride. Within moments Mario was declaring his intention to take his guests on a tour of the vineyards on the morrow, and Diana was expressing great delight in the idea.

And Will thought about crawling deep enough into the bottle that he wouldn't be in a fit state to join the party in the morning, but in the end he held his hand over his glass when an attentive footman moved forward to refill it for the third time. Because it might feel like torture watching Mario flirt and laugh with Diana, but given the opportunity to spend more time in her company, he would take it no matter the circumstances.

He just didn't particularly care to think too hard about why he might feel that way.

Will was a little surprised when Diana fell into step beside him as they walked through the vineyard the following morning. The ladies had ridden up from the castello in an open landaulet, the men on horseback, and no sooner had they left the carriage and horses in a yard beside the large barn housing the winery operations than Mario was hurrying to Diana's side, offering his arm and monopolising her attention.

Looking around, Will saw Mario now deep in conversation with the Glenkellies, as Alex pointed to some vines and asked questions. Marianne was watching him and Diana, a curiously knowing look on her face; Will looked away hastily and offered Diana his arm as she picked her way daintily along the rough ground. She smiled sweetly, switched the parasol she was holding to her other hand, and curled her fingers lightly around his forearm.

"Are you not feeling quite the thing, Balford?" she inquired. "You look... well, I should almost say dyspeptic. Rather like my father used to after losing a case before the magistrate. Did you drink a little too much of that rather excellent wine, last eve?"

"You are very direct today." He glanced down at her.

"Well." She shrugged. "We are friends, aren't we? Am I not allowed to be concerned for your health?"

"Of course, we are, and I appreciate your concern." He debated what to say, eventually shrugged. "Perhaps I did overindulge a little. It was very good wine."

"As the conte is eager to show off." Diana rolled her eyes. "He is a very obliging host."

"He admires you." The words spilled from Will's lips. He wanted to take them back at once, immediately wondering if perhaps he was serving the other man's cause by making Diana aware that she had a genuine suitor.

"Oh, he is at that puppy-love stage where he will fancy himself in love with every girl he meets." Diana shook her head. "To him, I am an exotic novelty, that is all. He will soon realise I am as dull as dishwater and would not suit his flamboyant nature at all as a wife."

"You are far from dull!"

"You are kind to say so," she said, but he could tell she disregarded his opinion. Why did she think so little of herself?

A dog barked, and a moment later two huge hounds came galloping down the rows of vines towards them. Instinctively, Will put himself in front of Diana, but she stepped around him with a laugh and bent down to greet the dogs, who immediately leaped up to lick her face.

"Jupiter, Minerva, behave yourselves!"

"How do you know them?" Will asked in bemusement.

"Oh, I woke early today and went for a walk down to the lake front. I met Mario - the conte - out exercising his dogs. They're terribly sweet. The white one with the red ears is Jupiter, and the brown one is Minerva."

Both dogs were wriggling with sheer delight as Diana patted them, obviously her devoted slaves already, though Minerva curled a lip and rumbled in her chest when Will reached to rub her ears. He made a strategic retreat and put his hands behind his back.

"Are they bothering you, my lady?" Mario came striding up, smiling broadly. He chided his dogs gently in rapid-fire Italian; Minerva abandoned Diana for her master, but Jupiter remained leaning against Diana's legs, tongue lolling happily.

"Traitor," Mario laughed, "but I quite understand. Lady Diana won me over immediately as well."

"Oh, I have that effect on most people," Diana said airily, laughing, before casting a sly sideways glance at Will. "Except for his grace of Balford, though. My native charm failed me disastrously at our first meeting."

"I would say rather that my own lack of perception was to blame for me not being instantly bowled over by you," Will said, after a moment of surprise that she was teasing him. "After further acquaintance, I am of course entirely in your thrall by now."

Mario's smile slipped away as he watched the two of them bantering lightly with each other, and Will felt a momentary satisfaction. It didn't take the young conte long to recover his composure, though, and Mario snapped his fingers for his dogs before offering his arm to Diana.

"Please, allow me to show you the treading vats. In October the grapes will be ready to harvest, and we celebrate with a festival when all the townspeople come to the winery... perhaps you will still be my guests, can attend the festival with me..." His voice trailed away as he led Diana away through the vines, the dogs trailing at their heels, Will left alone to follow them down the hillside.

October, he thought. He was supposed to be back in England by then, having promised his stepmother in the letter he had left he would return when the House of Lords sat again in the autumn. Yet, the thought of leaving Diana in Italy, here where Mario Maccarone would undoubtedly be doing his best to woo her, was utterly unpalatable.

Kicking moodily at a clump of soil in his path, he followed the couple down the hill. His hand found its way into his pocket and he fingered the gold pocket watch there, the watch which had been his father's.

"I think you'd have liked her, Pa," he murmured, as Diana's laugh drifted back to him on the breeze, a delightful, honest giggle, so different to the artificial chimes the young ladies of the *Ton* tended to affect. "I think you'd have liked her a lot."

CHAPTER TWELVE

Life at Castello Bardolino settled into a comfortable pattern; every morning, her maid would bring a tray of delicious pastries and hot chocolate to Diana's room, and Clarissa would come to share them with her, sitting on the balcony overlooking the lake, shimmering blue in the morning sun. Once they had broken their fast, they would choose from the multitude of lovely gowns Valentina insisted she no longer wanted, now she was married, and drift downstairs to find the rest of the party. Which had now expanded significantly with the addition of some dozen local Italian gentry, young men and women Mario and Valentina had known all their lives.

There were plenty of activities they could take part in, playing games on the lawn, riding some of the fine horses from Mario's stables, or taking a boat out on the lake, going to visit several ancient castles and beautiful churches scattered in the little villages spread along the lake shore. One day, they took a boat to a secluded, sandy cove and the ladies all swam in their shifts, the gentlemen sitting on the shore with their backs politely turned.

Today, some two weeks after their arrival, a special outing was planned; they were to travel by boat some three miles southward down the lake to visit a peninsula on which Mario assured them they would see something special, though he and Valentina both laughingly refused to disclose exactly what.

Dressing in one of the lightest gowns from Valentina's recycled wardrobe, a pale yellow cotton Diana rather thought might have once been one of the other girl's favourites, from the soft, worn feel of the fabric, Diana crammed a bonnet on her head to protect herself from the fierce Italian summer sun. Already, she had gained quite a spray of freckles across her nose and cheeks, and was grateful her mother wasn't here to see them. Lavinia would have thrown up her hands in horror and forbidden Diana to go outside until the freckles faded.

"So what is the surprise?" Diana begged Mario to tell them once they were all settled on the boats, two good-sized sailing vessels the family kept as pleasure crafts. "Oh, good morning, Balford," she greeted Will as he stepped into the boat and took a seat beside her. He smiled a little tightly and looked away, leaving her to wonder why he looked so moody. She had no opportunity to ask, though, because Mario finally relented and began to explain that they would be visiting the Grotte di Catullo, the ruins of an ancient Roman villa.

"Did Catullus actually live there?" she asked, eyes wide.

"Nobody knows for sure," Mario told her, "though he certainly did visit the area. His family was from Verona and he holidayed at Sirmione, the peninsula where the grotto is located."

Diana soon realised she had seen the grotto's walls from the castello; she had assumed it was another castle, but as the boat approached, she recognised now that it was more a ruin than it had appeared from across the lake. It was even larger than the magnificent Castello Bardolino, and she could not help but be impressed by the skills of the Romans, building almost two thousand years earlier. An actual castle rose just behind it, Castello Sirmione, she was informed, but it did not overpower the stunning site of the villa.

"It isn't actually a grotto," Will muttered in her ear, falling into step beside her as they walked between high arches. "It's just the vines overgrowing everything which make it feel like it's underground."

"It's quite vast. And to think, one family lived here!" She looked about the sprawling site.

Will shoved his hands in his pockets. "It looks about the same size as Balford Priory," he said. "Which isn't in ruins, of course."

"And also isn't quite so old, I should think?" She teased gently, hoping to see him smile. They had all been having such a pleasant time staying at the lake, except for Will, who seemed to have become more withdrawn and grumpy by the day.

"Parts of it date to the twelfth century." Will paused to look through an archway into a darkened, cavelike space. "Look; this must be where one of the hot springs comes to the surface."

A thin steam hung in the air over a pool of dark water with a crumbling brick surround. Despite the heat of the day, a chill suddenly crawled up Diana's spine; she took a hasty step back and stumbled on the uneven ground, falling backwards with a cry.

Will's reaction was lightning-quick; he whirled around and grabbed for her, one strong hand snapping around her wrist, the other around her back, he hauled her back upright and she lurched forward, crashing against him and grabbing onto the front of his waistcoat.

"Are you all right?" he asked urgently, and she could only stare up at him, shocked and trembling.

"Yes... I... I just tripped."

"I have you." He had released her wrist, but kept his other arm around her, strong and steadying, holding her pressed against his body.

Never in her life had she stood so close to a man, close enough to see the flecks of gold in the deep blue of his eyes, feel the heat of his body through his clothes. The fine silk of his waistcoat crumpled between her fingers as she clutched him, and dimly she became aware that she should let go, should step back, put a decorous distance between them.

She didn't move, and neither did Will. He stared down at her, his lips slightly parted as though he was about to speak, though he said nothing.

Diana licked dry lips, whispered "Will?"

Still he did not speak, but his eyes darkened, hooding slightly, and he leaned down towards her, bending his head.

Is he... going to kiss me?

"There you are!" a voice cried close by, and Will let go of Diana and stepped back rapidly, putting his hands behind his back and swinging around to face away from her, moving so fast she swayed, briefly unsteady without his support.

"Did you get lost?" It was Valentina and Andrea who had come to find them, Valentina looking curiously from Diana to Will before disengaging her arm from her husband and coming forward to take Diana's. "We were looking for you everywhere! Mario wants to show you his favourite spot!"

Diana looked back over her shoulder at Will as Valentina half-dragged her away. He wasn't moving, standing with his shoulders hunched staring into the darkened room with the pool in it. She felt entirely strange, almost disconnected from her body, and yet every nerve hummed with intensity, every part of her intensely aware that only a few moments ago she had been pressed up against his tall, strong body.

He can't really have almost kissed me. The thought was so ridiculous she forced herself to dismiss it. He'd merely caught her after she stumbled, had probably been about to make some pointed quip about her clumsiness. There had been nothing in it; why, Valentina hadn't even noted their closeness, and surely she would have!

"I found her!" Valentina called to her brother, and Mario turned to greet them with a broad smile, offering his hand to help Diana climb up a steep flight of crumbling stone steps.

Assuring her that the steps were safe and he would not let her fall, he led her to the top and pointed out the view he wanted to show her, a beautiful prospect of his castle back across the lake.

Murmuring appropriately enthusiastic praise for the view, Diana held onto Mario's arm because she had no choice. As they started back down the steps again, she spotted Will near the bottom, watching them with his arms folded and brow furrowed. She offered him a tentative smile, but he turned away and stalked off, alone.

"Come, my servants have prepared a picnic for us," Mario announced, and Diana really had no option but to walk with him to where blankets had been laid beneath the shade of some large olive trees, picnic baskets opened to reveal bottles of wine and loaves of bread.

Will did not join the party who sat down to the picnic, continuing to explore the ruins alone, and despite the merry atmosphere among the young people sitting beneath the olive trees, talking and laughing as they ate and drank, Diana wished she was walking with Will instead. She found herself watching him, his tall form straight and strong as he moved along an ancient, overgrown wall.

"You seem distracted," Valentina said, moving over to sit beside Diana, and she blinked and mustered a smile for her friend.

"Just soaking in the atmosphere," she said vaguely, and Valentina nodded, accepting the explanation.

"We must start back soon. My brother thinks an afternoon storm may blow in down the lake, and we don't want to be caught out on the water if it does."

"Of course," Diana said, her eyes sliding back to Will again.

Valentina pursed her lips, and then said slyly, "Balford, he looks very high for his marriage prospects, I think. He turned down Chiara, after all, and she is a duke's sister. Lady Elspeth says he looks to ally with a royal family, perhaps the Austrians."

Suddenly finding it difficult to take a breath, Diana had to swallow several times before she was confident her voice would sound normal when she spoke. "He is a duke, and there are very few of them in England who are eligible. It's quite possible the English Crown would ask him to marry a foreign princess to cement an alliance."

Valentina nodded, a look of sympathy on her face. "I was lucky Andrea's father chose me for him."

"And luckier still that you love him, and he you," Diana pointed out.

"Indeed," Valentina agreed, turning a lovesick smile in her husband's direction. "You know... I did not love him at once, though. At first I liked him, and respected him. Love came later."

"Yes," Diana said softly, making herself look away from Will, her heart aching. "I think that's usually how it works."

Diana fitted in here, Will thought as he watched her from the corner of his eye. Sitting in between Valentina and Mario, she conversed with the siblings in Italian which was almost fluent now, her delicate hands moving expressively in the air in front of her as she talked. Mario couldn't tear his gaze from her, which was only indicative that the young count had excellent taste, Will supposed. Mario had seen Diana's sterling qualities from the very first moment. He would appreciate her as she deserved to be appreciated, treat her like a queen.

Will kicked moodily at a small rock, for no particular reason other than that it was in his path. He quite recognised it was his own stupid fault Diana had a poor opinion of him. He had been intolerable at their first meeting, for reasons which seemed stupid and petty now, looking back at them. There was quite simply no excuse for such ungentlemanly conduct. He was lucky she even deigned to speak to him, though he supposed it would have been rather awkward if she did not, considering how much they were thrown into each other's company here in Italy. His higher rank meant giving him the cut direct wasn't exactly an option for her anyway.

He sighed and kicked at another rock, twitched slightly as someone fell into step on his other side. Glancing across, he raised his eyebrows at Clarissa, automatically offered his arm for her. She didn't take it, waving him away with a smile.

"Thank you, I am quite sure-footed."

She was, too. He watched as she danced up a flight of shallow, crumbling steps, agile and graceful, and wondered why nothing about her made his heart beat fast. Clarissa looked so much like her sister, and there was only a little more than a year between them in age, yet it was Diana for whom he yearned. Diana who would probably have tripped up halfway up those steps, and he'd have had to catch her. The memory of how she'd felt in his arms scalded his cheeks scarlet. He'd almost kissed her; what in heaven's name had he been thinking? Thank God Valentina had called out at that moment, or Will would have done something unutterably stupid and probably had his face justifiably smacked for it.

"Come and look," Clarissa called down to him. "There's a lovely view from here."

"Castello Bardolino again?" Will asked sourly, but he started to ascend the steps.

"No." Clarissa looked as though she was about to laugh, but she held it in. "We're on the wrong side of the villa for that, I think. No, there's a beautiful little church, just across the water."

Reaching the top of the steps, he saw she was correct. He also saw something that alarmed him; black storm clouds massing to the north, over the mountains at the far end of the lake.

"I don't like the look of those clouds," he muttered, just as a shout reached them from below.

"It's Uncle Alex," Clarissa said unnecessarily, as Will could now see Glenkellie standing at the foot of the wall.

"There's a storm coming. Mario says we can beat it back to the castello, but we need to go, now." Alex pointed towards the boats.

"On our way," Clarissa called, and she did accept Will's offered arm this time, as they descended and joined the others hurrying back to the boat. Mario was assisting Diana, and Will's urge to go and help her himself was strong, but he held back. Until she stumbled and fell, full-length on the ground, and then Will almost flung himself forward, scooping her up in his arms.

"Are you all right?" he asked gruffly. "You should have caught her!" he cast an accusatory glare at Mario, who looked sheepish.

"I'm fine," Diana tried to insist, but he could see a bleeding scrape on the palm of her hand. Refusing to set her down, he strode swiftly to the first boat and lifted her in, climbing in beside her and plucking his handkerchief from his pocket.

"You're bleeding," he said succinctly when she tried to pull her hand from his grasp, and she gasped and looked down. Her face went quite white when she saw the blood seeping from her palm and dripping to stain her dress.

"Oh… I… I don't like to see blood…"

"It's all right if you need to faint," Will said gruffly, quickly covering her hand with his handkerchief. "I'll catch you."

"Well, that is quite a change of attitude," an amused voice said, and he glanced up to see Marianne settling down on the other side of Diana. She had cloth napkins in hand, obviously from the picnic basket, and reached to lift his handkerchief, quickly checking Diana's hand. "Not too bad, but I should like to clean this and wrap it. Don't look if you don't like blood, Diana. Talk to her, Balford. And yes, if she faints, please do catch her. I promise I won't make you marry her."

The look in the marchioness's eyes said she was well aware he wouldn't require any such coercion to request Diana's hand.

"Don't be ridiculous, Aunt Marianne!" Diana's voice was high-pitched, and she refused to meet Will's eyes. "I am surely the last woman in the world His Grace could be prevailed upon to marry!"

The boat was moving now, Mario and two of his friends rapidly raising the sails and adjusting them to catch the freshening breeze. Will cast another look at the storm clouds, wondering if they really would make it back to the castle before the storm hit. Perhaps, he judged, and hoped Mario was a good sailor.

Marianne used Will's handkerchief to clean dirt and grime from Diana's hand before wrapping it carefully in one of the napkins, and then asking to see her other hand.

"It's fine," Diana said, showing her. "I think that one landed in some grass."

"What about your knees?"

Diana blushed, peeping at Will. "I'm sure they're fine."

"I think perhaps I should take a look. If you'd give us your back, Balford, but just stay there - make sure nobody else gets a peek."

Will was fairly sure Marianne was laughing in her sleeve at him, but he turned his back gallantly, narrowing his gaze at Mario when the count cast a glance in their direction. Mario turned away hastily, tugging on a rope to adjust the sails, and Will humphed under his breath.

"All fine," Marianne said, and Will politely waited a moment or two before turning back around. Diana was still blushing and not meeting his gaze as she tucked her skirts tightly around her legs, and he ached for her embarrassment, wishing he knew what to say to make her feel better.

They made it back to the wooden dock below Castello Bardolino in the nick of time, or perhaps not even that, because fat drops of rain were already beginning to fall as they climbed out of the boat and hurried up to the castle's sheltering walls. Will didn't hesitate before putting his hand under Diana's elbow to help her, rather than taking her injured hand onto his arm. She cast him a sideways glance, and then smiled, unexpectedly.

"You were quite heroic today, Will."

"Heroic?" He blinked at her.

"You caught me from falling once, and then rescued me when I did fall. I should have had a great deal more uncomfortable day without your intervention."

He shrugged awkwardly. "It was no more than any gentleman should do."

"Perhaps," she allowed, "but it was you who did it. You, who are entirely sick of young ladies falling at your feet."

"Falling purposely at my feet," he corrected. "Accidental falls are quite different, and I know you well enough by now to be certain you would never shame yourself so much as to throw yourself at anyone's feet on purpose."

"I just regularly do it by accident," she said with a wry smile. "Most particularly at yours, it seems, for which I do heartily apologise."

"Pray, do not. I would hope to always be there to catch you."

The statement, a pure and simple truth, seemed to almost hang in the air between them. Diana's eyes rounded with surprise as she stared up at him... and then Marianne called out to her to come inside and change her gown, and the moment was lost.

CHAPTER THIRTEEN

THE TIME HAD COME when he needed to make a decision, Will recognised. Lord Glenkellie was giving him more and more frequent stares whenever he and Diana were even in a room together, and though the marquis had said nothing as yet, he obviously wondered what Will's intentions were.

Therefore, the morning after the party's trip to the Grotte di Catullo, Will went looking for Alex. A helpful servant told him Lord Glenkellie was in the library, and Will headed up to the large room on the first floor, a room which was filled with almost more paintings than books. Will appreciated the artwork, but he didn't approve of the count's failure to keep a decent library. He hadn't found a single book in it published in the last ten years.

Reaching to push open the door, he froze at the sound of voices inside. Alex's was one, the precise, clipped tones which had commanded men in battle quite distinct even when speaking in Italian rather than his native English. The other, younger and lighter, quicker and more impulsive, was Mario Maccarone, count of Bardolino and the owner of the castle in which they stood.

"I am aware that you stand as guardian to Lady Diana in the absence of her parents," Mario was saying, "and so I appeal to you in my formal request for her hand in marriage."

Will's heart stopped in his chest. Hand on the door handle, he struggled to draw in a breath of air as he waited for Alex's answer. Surely, there was no other answer Alex could make but in the affirmative; Mario was a good match for Diana any way one looked at it, even if he was a couple of years younger than she.

"I see," was all Alex said, and Mario rushed on, as though concerned he might not have made his declaration clear enough.

"From the moment of your party's arrival, I have been enchanted by the Lady Diana's grace and charm. I can no longer imagine this castle without her in it. Even my dogs are besotted by her!"

Alex made a noncommittal sound; Will was intensely tempted to push the door open a little and see if he could spy Alex's expression, but there was far too great a risk one or other of the men would see him.

"Will you give your approval to the marriage, Lord Glenkellie?" Mario asked, sounding a little desperate, after the silence had stretched another minute or so.

"I have no objection," Alex said, "and you are correct that I do have legal guardianship over Diana at the moment. That being said, I have given her my assurance that I will not enforce my will on her, and as such, my opinion matters not at all in this matter. I leave the decision entirely in Diana's hands."

Mario stuttered out his thanks, and Will stepped back from the door, reeling with shock. He had to get to Diana, and now, because nothing was more certain than that Mario would rush straight to her and propose. Whirling on his heel, Will half-ran down the hallway, desperate to get to Diana first.

He knew she liked to take breakfast on her balcony with her sister in the mornings, and hoped she would still be there. Her maid looked startled to see him at the door, but told him to wait while she saw if her mistress would receive him.

"Will?" Diana said as she came to the door, her eyes widening as she saw his face. "Is something the matter?"

"Might I speak with you in private for a moment?" he asked.

She hesitated, but then she closed the door behind her and placed her hand on his arm. "Walk with me."

He would rather be somewhere Mario might not run across them, but he could quite understand Diana's reluctance to invite him into her rooms. Scrubbing his free hand over his face, he tried to find the words he needed, but could only blurt out awkwardly; "Do you want to marry him?"

A frown pinched her brows together. "Who?"

"The conte, Mario. Do you want to marry him?"

She looked faintly incredulous, as though the idea had never even occurred to her. "No, of course not. Why do you ask?"

"Because even now he's asking Lord Glenkellie for your hand. So, uh, you might want to be prepared to be approached."

He was making a shocking mull of this, Will realised. He wanted to tell Diana to turn Mario down and choose him instead, but he couldn't seem to find the words.

Diana stared up at Will, unable to think what to say. How could she possibly explain that she could never even consider Mario when her heart belonged to a stiff English duke who wasn't looking for a wife? That though she loved the rolling hills, sweeping vineyards and alpine meadows of Lombardy, her home was and forever would be England?

"Thank you for the warning," she said finally. "I will prepare myself and find the words to gracefully decline."

"I could warn him off, if you want," he offered, and impulsively, she squeezed his arm.

"That is very kind of you to offer, but if I have managed to somehow accidentally give him the impression I would welcome his addresses, I must be the one to gently disabuse him of the notion."

"I wouldn't mind," he muttered, his eyes meeting hers. "Tell him you're not for the likes of him."

"The likes of him? Do not let Valentina hear you!" Diana shook her head, thinking of her friend's reaction - Valentina had made no secret of her approval of Mario's admiration of Diana. "Mario is a count, a wealthy one at that, and I'm an earl's daughter - it would be an entirely appropriate match!"

"But you could do so much better!"

"Don't be ridiculous." She shook her head. "I embarrassed myself in my one brief outing in London and showed myself far too naive for Venice. I'm not rich enough or beautiful enough to marry well. Becoming Contessa here would be the best I could possibly hope for."

"And yet you'll turn him down?"

He seemed to be arguing for her to marry Mario, and indeed, if her mother caught wind that she had turned down an Italian count Diana would never hear the end of it, but after getting to know Will, Diana knew she could not settle for anything less than love. It was possible, she supposed, that she might one day fall in love with another man, but marrying Mario when she bore nothing more than a mild sisterly affection for him was unthinkable.

"I could not be happy as his wife," she said finally. Trying a weak smile, she attempted to joke. "I am no more ready for marriage than you, it seems."

His expression was entirely serious as he gazed down at her, but he nodded finally. "You have my support in whatever you wish to do, Diana. If you want to leave the castello after declining Mario's proposal, I am at your disposal to see you safely to Venice - or England, if you prefer."

She hadn't even thought of that, but she supposed it would indeed be awkward to remain at Castello Bardolino once she rejected Mario. Confident Alex and Marianne would support her decision, she knew she wouldn't need to call on Will's help, but she was still touched by his offer.

"You cannot know how much I appreciate your thoughtfulness, Will. Your friendship has been by far the greatest treasure I have found in Italy."

He flushed a little, looked away bashfully. "I don't... I... I will always stand your friend, Diana. No matter what."

"Lady Diana!" Mario's enthusiastic cry reached them.

Diana winced, and looked back up at Will.

"Would you have me stay with you?" he asked in an undertone. "Or I could..."

"I must do this." She squeezed his arm once again before releasing it. "Thank you. For everything." Mustering a smile, she left his side and walked towards where Mario waited. "Good morning, my lord. What a beautiful day it is. Shall we walk on the terrace?" That was a nicely public spot, she judged. She gave him no opportunity to suggest an alternative, anyway, as she seized his arm and marched towards the stairs.

"Of course," Mario said obligingly.

There was nobody on the terrace yet, which Diana supposed was a good thing. Mario was likely to be put at least somewhat out of temper by her refusal of his suit, and the last thing she wanted was for him to be embarrassed in front of guests in his own home.

Mario looked around as though wishing there were others there to witness, though, and she wondered if he thought she would be more likely to accept him in front of others. Quite possibly it hadn't entered his head she might decline, she thought wryly. She was extraordinarily lucky that she wouldn't be pressured to accept him.

"I must tell you that from the first moment of your arrival here, I have been entranced by you," Mario began, turning to face her and grasping her hands in his. She opened her mouth in an attempt to cut him off, but he barrelled on, speaking rapidly, the words spilling out. "I cannot imagine my life without you in it, so please, say you will accept me, accept my hand and my heart!"

"Stop," Diana said sharply as he appeared about to continue with his impassioned speech, and he froze with his mouth open. "Mario," she softened her tone. "You are very sweet, and you have been the most gracious and generous host we could possibly have hoped for, but I'm afraid I cannot accept your proposal."

His dark eyes narrowed. "Cannot, or will not?" he asked.

"As far as I'm concerned, there is no difference. I will not accept because I cannot be the wife you deserve. You deserve what your sister has with Andrea; a marriage of mutual affection and admiration." Attempting to soften the blow, she said "I do not doubt you will find a young lady who will love and adore you as you deserve, and soon; but that lady is not me."

He looked quite crushed, but oddly, she thought, not all that surprised, as though he had half-expected her to turn him down. He kissed her hand, declared himself entirely heartbroken in his typically flamboyant way, and then said something she didn't entirely understand.

"I think I knew from the beginning I could not compete. I wish my rival every success, even though I envy him from the bottom of my heart." Tight-lipped, he bowed before turning and hurrying away, his shoulders bowed, leaving Diana staring after him utterly bemused.

"What rival?" she said to his retreating back, but he didn't turn around.

He can only mean Will, but... he has quite the wrong impression of our friendship. A jealous man was not an entirely rational one, she supposed.

Turning to re-enter the castello, she encountered Valentina at the door; the other girl embraced her, asking excitedly;

"Have you seen my brother? Has he spoken to you?"

Of course Mario had told Valentina he planned to propose, Diana realised. She had probably encouraged him to do it. Valuing Valentina's friendship as she did, Diana hated to break the news.

"I did... and Valentina, I am sorry, but I had to decline."

Valentina's mouth fell open, her eyes opening wide. "You turned him down?" she said in tones of pure disbelief. At Diana's slow nod, Valentina clapped her hand over her mouth with a cry of distress, and then rushed past her down the terrace, going in the direction Mario had taken when he left.

"I did try to tell her this would happen," a voice said dryly, and Andrea stepped out of the house, shaking his head. "She was so delighted by the idea of her dear friend marrying her brother and staying here at her home, she did not actually consider whether he suited you at all."

"He is a very nice young man," Diana said diplomatically, and Andrea laughed.

"He is, and in a few years, he will find a lady who does suit him and they will doubtless be very happy."

"I didn't realise his intentions to propose," Diana admitted, "or else I should have taken steps to more firmly discourage him before it got to this point. I would never for a moment wish for him to be hurt."

Andrea waved a hand, dismissing her concern. "It was at least half Valentina's idea," he noted, "and it will do her no harm at all to have one of her schemes not turn out exactly as she pleases. I love her, but I recognise she has been given her own way perhaps a little too much."

That was a nice way of saying Valentina was a bit spoilt, Diana supposed. She said nothing, and Andrea smiled slightly.

"Our families are connected, Diana, and though I would have been glad to see a closer connection with your marriage to Mario, you have acted with great integrity in following your heart and refusing him. I think you will both be happier for it, even if he does not understand that just yet."

"Thank you for your support, especially since we're not really family," Diana felt compelled to point out.

"Alex is my family, and he considers you *his* family. That's good enough for me." Andrea shrugged, a twinkle coming to his eye. "Do not regret refusing Mario. I will make sure Valentina does not pout about it for too long."

She reached up to impulsively kiss his cheek, and Andrea chuckled.

"Perhaps we may yet become more closely connected, eh? Will is part of my family too, after all."

"Oh!" Diana felt her cheeks redden. She shook her head fiercely. "Everyone seems to have quite the wrong impression; there is nothing but friendship between Balford and I, I do assure you!"

"Is that so?" Andrea raised a dark brow.

"Yes! We would not suit at all," she insisted. "I am entirely unsuited to be a duchess, for one thing."

He looked quite cynical, but bowed in his usual mannerly way and said "If you say so."

"I pray you will excuse me." Diana decided it was time to make her escape, before she said something she didn't intend. "I must find my aunt."

Andrea nodded. “You might wish to advise her that I have made a decision as regards our departure for Venice,” he noted. “We will be leaving in one week, and you are of course welcome to travel with us.”

“I think Lord Glenkellie rather intends to travel directly to Florence, rather than return to Venice,” Diana said, privately feeling very grateful their future path was already determined. Returning to Venice with Andrea and Valentina would be very awkward now she had turned Mario down.

CHAPTER FOURTEEN

Marianne's reaction to Diana's sheepish admission she had declined Mario's proposal was everything Diana could have hoped for; Marianne rose from her chair, seized Diana in a tight embrace and hugged her soundly.

"Good for you," Marianne said. "If you had decided to accept him, I should have done my best to talk you out of it."

"Really?"

"Really! Oh, he's pleasant enough and would undoubtedly treat you well, but anyone can see he doesn't exactly make your heart beat fast. I was trapped in a loveless marriage the first time around, Diana; having found my heart's joy now with Alex, I would not wish for anything less for you." With a final squeeze, Marianne let her go.

Diana found herself blinking back tears. "Thank you," she whispered huskily, and Marianne kissed her cheeks, smiling warmly.

"None of that, my dear. You have done exactly the right thing, although I must strongly suggest we all make a pact never to mention it to your mother. Lavinia might refuse ever to see me again if she discovered I not only permitted, but encouraged you in declining his suit!"

That was rather too close to the truth to be a joke, but Diana laughed anyway. "I certainly have no intention of ever letting her find out I turned down the opportunity to be a countess!"

"Perish the thought!" Marianne laughed along with her.

Diana sobered quickly, though, admitting "I feel so guilty about Valentina. She was upset, and she has been so very kind, giving Clarry and me her gowns."

"And this should obligate you to marry her brother?" Marianne raised a brow.

"Well, no, but..."

"No buts, my dear. Mario had a fair chance to win your heart, and he did not do so. You were disposed to look kindly upon him, even, by your friendship with Valentina and her obvious enthusiasm for a potential match. You cannot take blame upon yourself because things didn't turn out the way Valentina wanted. If I have learned anything in my life, it is this; do not make significant decisions about your future with any consideration for the happiness and convenience of anyone but yourself. Insofar as you have the power to set your own course, do not allow anyone else's wishes to direct your path."

That was excellent advice, Diana thought, and felt doubly grateful that Alex and Marianne had allowed her the freedom to make her own choices without seeking to influence her in any way.

"Alex and I have already discussed our planned departure," Marianne went on. "In fact, Alex said we should stay a little longer to allow you to make your mind up about Mario, but now your decision is made, I think we will prepare to leave in the next few days. His mother sent a letter we received just yesterday; she was preparing to return to Venice, thence to take ship to sail around to Florence, when it was sent. She will be back in Florence before we get there, since we intend to travel overland."

Relieved she would not have to stay long in the awkward situation which would surely ensue here at Castello Bardolino, Diana thanked Marianne profusely again before returning to her room. Best to lay low for a day or so at least, she judged.

Clarissa joined her, but to Diana's relief, her sister neither asked her to go over everything again or teased her. Instead, Clarissa just put her arm around Diana's waist and settled in to sit beside her on the chaise, announcing that she was looking forward to spending the day in her sister's company.

Valentina came by to visit in the afternoon, and Diana stiffened in anticipation of a deeply awkward meeting, but Valentina was quite subdued. Andrea had spoken to his wife, Diana surmised, and Valentina only briefly expressed her disappointment before once again professing her deep affection for Diana and wishing her every happiness.

"Andrea wishes to return to Venice as he has business to attend to, so we will accompany you as far as Verona. Andrea will assist Lord Glenkellie to obtain all the necessary papers and permits for your travel by boat."

"Oh, we're not going by boat," Diana said, "we're going overland."

Valentina smiled at that. "Part of the way, but Italy does have excellent navigable rivers. You will save a few days and be more comfortable taking a boat from Verona as far as Rovigo."

"I need to look at a map," Diana realised, and Valentina at once sent a servant to get one.

The distances were not so great as Diana had expected; as the crow would fly she thought Rovigo looked a good deal out of their way, but Valentina was insistent it would be much more comfortable to travel from Verona to Rovigo by riverboat on the Adige and then take a carriage south to Ferrara, thence to Bologna, and finally cross the Apennines to Florence.

"You will need to overnight somewhere on the journey from Bologna to Florence," Valentina said wisely. "Twice, most likely. I have never travelled that way, but Andrea will know where you should stay. He is writing letters for Lord Glenkellie to carry, to present to officials along your journey as you cross from one district to the next. The Franchettis have family in important positions all over Italy; you should have no troubles."

"Let us hope not." Diana pored over the map, looking at the towns they would visit along the route Valentina described. "Have you ever been to Bologna? What is there to see there?"

They passed a pleasant hour discussing travels Valentina had undertaken with her father some years past, and when the other woman left, Diana felt at least somewhat more comfortable that their friendship was not irretrievably broken.

A week after Diana declined Mario's proposal, they left Castello Bardolino. It was early October now and the weather was beginning to turn cool, grey clouds constantly scudding over the mountains in the near distance. If they waited much longer, the weather would make crossing the Apennines an unpleasant and risky matter indeed, Andrea warned them during the two days they stayed in Verona to arrange permits and travel documents for their journey.

Thankfully, Mario had not chosen to leave his castle to accompany them, despite Valentina's pleas for her brother to winter with them in Venice. He had not importuned Diana again, to her intense relief, graciously accepting her denial at face value, though he did follow her with sad eyes whenever they occupied the same room. She had bid farewell to him with fondness, but without the slightest twinge of regret at her decision, riding away from Bardolino without a backward glance.

Will had avoided her ever since that morning when he intercepted her and warned her to prepare herself for Mario's proposal. She wasn't sure why, but feared he might think she intended to set her cap for him. It had become increasingly obvious that Valentina, at least, thought that was exactly what she planned to do, no matter how many times Diana protested Will was just a friend.

The riverboats on the Adige were larger than the gondolas of Venice, but fashioned in almost identical style. Diana was entirely charmed by them, finding it extremely pleasant to float along slowly with the current and watch the charming scenery go by. She thought it likely they could have gone faster on horseback but Valentina was correct; this was a much nicer way to travel.

The party separated at Rovigo, with Andrea and Valentina continuing on down the river whence they would eventually reach the sea and return to Venice by boat, whereas the English component of the group went ashore to join the horses and carriage Alex had sent word ahead to have ready for them.

Diana bade farewell to Valentina, who wailed histrionically and clung to her neck. Diana felt a little teary herself; she had not expected to make such a close friend in Italy and Valentina, for all her manipulations as she attempted to match Diana with her brother, had truly become dear to her.

"We will meet again, I hope, dear one," she told the sobbing duchess. "Next summer, coax Andrea to bring you to England. You will be the toast of London."

"I shall practice my English all winter," Valentina vowed through her tears, and Diana kissed her cheeks fondly before accepting Alex's hand and stepping off the riverboat onto the dock.

Will was the last to disembark, embracing Valentina and sharing a brotherly hug with Andrea before stepping up onto the dock beside Diana. She smiled tentatively at him, but he looked away and headed for where two horses waited beside a pair of carriages, one carriage for the ladies and the other for their baggage and the two servants who accompanied them, Marianne's faithful maid Jean and Alex's man Simons, both of whom had travelled with the party all the way from England.

Taking a seat beside Clarissa, Diana stared unseeingly out of the window as the carriage set off, wondering miserably if there was any way to regain the easy friendship she had finally found with Will. Perhaps he thought she should have accepted Mario? By any measure, it would have been a good match. Yet Will was the one who had warned her to prepare herself for Mario's proposal, had even offered to warn him off. Had commented that she could do better. Did he think she had taken that remark as encouragement to set her sights on Will himself? Had Andrea or Valentina said something to him?

She heaved an unhappy sigh, her eyes fixed on Will's tall, straight-backed form as he rode alongside Alex, conversing with him. She missed conversing with him, missed their friendship.

"That is quite a sigh, Diana," Marianne noted, not unkindly. "I'm sure you will see Valentina again, you know. She seemed quite enthused about the idea of visiting England. And you will be able to write to her."

"Indeed," Diana agreed, pulling herself together and pasting a smile on her face. "She has become a dear friend and I will miss her company." At least their parting provided an excuse for her melancholy and she need not pretend to be entirely delighted to be travelling again.

The party stopped at a hotel just to the south of Rovigo which Andrea had recommended to them before pressing on to Ferrara the following day, crossing the mighty Po river on a bridge which had stood since Roman times. They stayed two days in Ferrara, taking the time to tour the Este Castle, the moated medieval fortress at the city's heart.

And for every minute of every day, Will was agonisingly, excruciatingly aware of Diana. Of the wonder on her countenance as she admired the architecture of Ferrara's glorious cathedral. Of the way her eyes drifted closed and she sighed with delighted bliss when she first tasted the local delicacy of *panpepato*, a dense fruit and nut cake spiced with pepper and cinnamon and rolled in chocolate. On impulse, he paid a chef handsomely to write out the recipe for him, and then spent two days agonising over how he might somehow ensure it was delivered regularly to Diana in England before reluctantly accepting he could do no such thing.

Every time he looked at Diana he heard those fateful words again, the words she had spoken when he warned her of Mario's impending proposal.

"I am no more ready for marriage than you, it seems."

How could he tell her that his feelings on marriage had entirely changed since meeting her again in Venice? That he had left England entirely resolved on avoiding getting leg-shackled for as long as he possibly could, but now all he could think of was how much he wanted to be married... so long as Diana was his bride?

He had tried to hint at his fondness for her the day they visited the Grotte di Catullo, but he had been clumsy with his words as usual and she had only looked at him wide-eyed and puzzled, obviously not understanding his meaning, or interpreting it only as friendship.

His horse whinnied and sidled under him, and Will realised he was holding onto the reins with a white-knuckled grip, his legs clamped to the poor beast's sides. Breathing out a sigh, he made himself relax, patted the horse's neck. They were almost to Bologna, the vast walls of the city rising up before them, where they would spend three or four days exploring before setting out to cross the Apennines.

"You all right there, Balford?" Alex, riding alongside him, asked.

"Of course. A little cold, is all." Will pretended a slight shudder. "The weather is definitely turning for autumn, even so far south as we are."

Alex was the last person he dared speak to about his feelings. Though Alex and Marianne had permitted Diana to decline Mario's suit, there was a world of difference between an Italian count and an English duke, and Will knew it. Hell, Alex had already nigh on given him permission to propose to Diana! If Will indicated he was even considering it, Diana would definitely be put under a certain amount of pressure to accept him, and that was the last thing he wanted.

He sighed, mustered up a slight smile for Alex, and fished in his coat for his packet of identity documents as they approached the busy city gate. The guards were allowing most people to pass unmolested, but they straightened up at the sight of a group of travellers on good horses with quality coaches.

Alex and Will traded cynical glances. They had already learnt a few coins in the right palms made everything go a great deal smoother, even though their papers were all perfectly in order. If they wanted to get into the city, find their hotel and have their party safely settled in warm rooms before dark fell, it was time to put their hands into their pockets, or sit about for hours while their baggage was searched for 'contraband' that could not be precisely defined when they asked what, exactly, the guards might be looking for.

Within the hour, they were drawing up to the very grand-looking Hotel Grande Albergo Imperiale on the Piazza del Nettuno, though one look at the magnificent statue of Neptune standing high above a fountain in the square and all of them at once forgot their weariness and eagerness to be inside.

"Why, Neptune must be more than twelve feet tall!" Diana marvelled, walking towards the statue with her face tilted upwards, eyes wide with wonder. Will instinctively grabbed her arm, drawing her to a halt, and a horse and cart clattered by, just missing running over her feet.

"Oh!" Shocked, Diana drew back, collided with Will's chest. He drew her against him protectively before recalling himself and stepping back to put a respectable distance between them.

"Here, allow me to escort you over."

"Thank you!" She looked a little shocked, holding tightly to his arm as he led her more cautiously across to the fountain. "I should have been more cautious, but

I was quite taken by surprise with the statue. How old do you think it is?" She tilted her head back again to gaze up at the bronze titan.

"About two hundred and fifty-seven years," Will said, straight-faced.

"That is oddly precise!" She turned her head to look at him, and he failed to suppress his laughter as he pointed to the Roman numerals inscribed into the marble tank at the base of the statue.

"Oh, you are a dreadful tease!" She laughed, though, before a sudden blush came to her cheeks. "Goodness. It is quite a *shocking* sculpture, to be out in a public square in a Catholic country, don't you think?"

Following her gaze, Will saw what she was looking at; the bronze water nymphs surrounding the base of the statue were depicted cupping their own breasts, water spouting forth from their nipples. Neptune himself was nude, he could see from this angle, though his private parts were moderately sized compared to some art he had seen.

"For a Catholic sculpture, it's positively pagan," he agreed, choosing to comment on that fact rather than the rather erotic nature of the sculptures. "But then, mythology has always been a popular subject for artists of all kinds."

Alex had by now noticed the rather explicit poses of the nymphs and hastily declared it was getting far too cold for the ladies to be outside, putting a firm hand on each of Diana and Clarissa's shoulders and marching them towards the hotel. Grinning with amusement, Will offered his arm to Marianne, who was quite obviously stifling her laughter, and followed them into the hotel's warmly welcoming interior.

CHAPTER FIFTEEN

THE FOLLOWING MORNING, THEY set out as a group to explore Bologna. A fine rain had begun to fall overnight, but they shortly discovered the weather need scarcely affect them at all, because every street in the city seemed to be lined with porticoes. Mile upon mile of them they walked, admiring the fine shops, visiting churches and stepping into the Art Academy, which Diana was disappointed to find not overly endowed with fine art.

Making their way back to the hotel later in the afternoon, the two men were keen to visit the tallest sights in the city, two square brick towers, at least one of which was visible from almost any point in the city.

"It's around three hundred and twenty feet high, I understand," Will said as they finally approached the base of the taller tower. "The tallest tower in Italy, though not the tallest building - the dome at St. Peter's reaches higher."

"It's not straight." Diana tilted her head slightly, squinting. "Neither of them are!" Though the smaller tower was only one-third the height, she thought it actually leaned more severely, the top tilting vertiginously above their heads as they stood at its base.

There was a shoemaker's stall just inside the entrance to the taller tower; the man explained he had the care of the building, called the Tower of Asinelli. They were startled to learn it was some seven hundred years old, though looking at the rickety-appearing wooden staircase which wound up inside the building, Diana could well believe it.

The shoemaker told Will there was a small fee to climb the tower, and Will put his hand into his pocket, fishing out some coins. Looking down at them, he made to select some, obviously to pay the man, and without thought, Diana reached out to touch his arm.

"Oh Will, don't," she said. "Not only is the tower leaning, but that staircase does not look in the least safe. Please." Putting her free hand to her chest in a vain attempt to still her heart, beginning to pound far too rapidly with fear at the thought of him ascending the ramshackle steps, she peered up into the dim, dusty darkness. "Don't climb up there. I should worry about you every step until you were safely down again."

No sooner had she finished speaking than she realised she had overstepped, that she had no right to ask him not to do anything. Fully expecting him to laugh and brush off her concerns, she was surprised when he paused, studying her a moment from those striking deep blue eyes of his. And then he finished selecting a few coins, dropped the others back into his pocket and paid the shoemaker.

"Thank you for the information, sir. I shan't be climbing today, however."

"There is a very fine view from the top," the man claimed, pocketing the coins swiftly.

"Undoubtedly, but in a few days we shall ascend the Apennines, which are higher yet, and have fine views aplenty to be had." With one last glance upward, Will gave Diana his arm and escorted her out.

She wasn't quite sure what to say to him. They had scarcely spoken in days, yet she was quite sure he had discarded his plan to climb the tower solely because she had asked it of him. She felt guilty now for depriving him of the pleasure he would undoubtedly have gained from the adventure, though at least the sick feeling in her belly at the thought of him ascending those derelict stairs was abating.

"Do you not care much for heights?" Will asked as they moved out of the tower's doorway, stepping aside as a group of young men came to enter, jostling each other and talking loudly.

"I only mind heights if I think there is a real danger of falling. Admit it; those stairs looked quite decrepit!"

"They did. Surprising in a country with an abundance of marble and stone with which to build, and considering the age of the tower; one would have thought the stairs would have been replaced by now with something more substantial." He placed his hand over hers where it rested on his sleeve, and even though both of them were wearing gloves, she felt the warmth of his touch. "I should not have thought anything of climbing them, to be honest, but I would not for a moment make you worry on my account."

"I was being missish, and now I feel guilty for having made you miss out on an interesting experience," Diana admitted.

Will laughed gently and shook his head. "It is hardly something I have been looking forward to all trip, merely a whim when I heard it was possible to climb it! You have probably saved me from sore legs tomorrow, besides. Five hundred steps up and down again would be quite exhausting."

Accepting his decision as made, she allowed herself a small smile in return. Clarissa came up on Will's other side then and claimed his other arm, chattering excitedly about all they had seen that day, and he turned his attention to her indulgently, leaving Diana alone with her thoughts.

At least he was talking to her again, indeed had seemed to take note of her feelings when he changed his mind about climbing the tower. She would have to be satisfied with that. Her feelings were a hopeless tangle where he was concerned, but the distance he had put between them since she declined Mario's proposal had pained her greatly.

As they walked back along yet another of Bologna's long porticoed streets to the hotel, glad of the cover since rain had begun gently to fall, Diana allowed herself to hope that her friendship with Will might perhaps be rekindled. If she were to assure him he was in no danger of her setting her cap for him, he need no longer concern himself with maintaining a proper distance and they might be at ease with each other as they had been before.

"I am greatly looking forward to reaching Florence, aren't you, Clarissa?" She looked across Will at her sister and spoke cheerfully as they approached the hotel. "Uncle Alex says his aunt fancies herself as a matchmaker and will no doubt know any number of eligible young men she is keen to present to us."

Will stiffened, and she said quickly, "Although of course, she does not even know you are accompanying us, Will, so you need not fear she will have a procession of young ladies ready to throw at your head."

"I'm not concerned for that," he said, "but I had thought you had resolved against marrying an Italian?"

"When did I say that? Just because Mario did not suit me, that is quite a conclusion to leap to." She gave him a pert glance. "He was younger than me, and in no wise ready to settle down. He would have made an appalling husband."

Will just stared at her for a moment, apparently nonplussed, before saying slowly; "So... you are eager to find a husband in Florence?"

"Well, if I do, at least I am assured I will be permitted to make my own choice," Diana said. "If I return to England unwed, my fate is far less certain. My father is keen to cement relations with any number of prominent lords; two daughters of marriageable age are far too useful to be wasted."

"I see," Will said quietly, and then they were at the hotel, a footman opening the door for them, and Will released her arm.

Diana felt a curious sense of loss as he stepped back and made her and Clarissa a polite little bow.

"Why did you say that?" Clarissa hissed at her as the two of them walked up the stairs, proceeding to their shared room.

"Say what?" Diana pretended ignorance.

"Why did you tell Balford that you plan to allow Alex's aunt to matchmake you with some Florentian lordling?"

"Because I have no objection if she does."

"Except for the fact that your heart is already engaged with a very *English* lord!"

"Who is not seeking a wife!" Diana turned on her sister, her own hurt making her lash out. "Every word I said was the truth, Clarry! You know if we go home unwed, Father and Mother will not permit me, at least, the slightest amount of choice in the matter. And you will have to talk fast to convince them to allow you a Season, too!"

Clarissa froze, her lips slightly parted. "You really think that," she said slowly.

"Mother made it quite clear before we left." Diana sank down onto the bed. "She told me to find a husband, or one would be found for me."

After a moment, Clarissa sat down beside her. "Balford thinks a good deal of you," she said.

"We are friends, that is all. He's made it quite clear he isn't looking for a wife, and as a duke, he has certain obligations. Lady Elspeth hinted he might marry an Austrian princess, for goodness' sake; I am entirely unsuitable!"

Clarissa didn't say anything more, but she did put her arm around Diana's shoulders and hug her closer, offering comfort and sisterly solidarity. With a sigh, Diana rested her head against her sister's.

"I wish it were otherwise," she voiced the truth in a soft whisper. "I wish he loved me as I do him. That he would ignore those obligations to marry well and choose me."

"Duchess of Balford," Clarissa kissed her cheek. "Just imagine it!"

"Oh, no." Diana laughed. "No. He would be wise not to choose me, actually. I'd be a terrible duchess."

"You would be quite magnificent," Clarissa insisted loyally, "and Balford is a fool if he doesn't choose you."

"You must not speak to him of it, Clarry!" Knowing her outspoken sister all too well, Diana seized Clarissa's hand in hers and squeezed it tightly. "You *must* not. Promise me!"

Clarissa sighed. "You're making a mistake."

"Promise me."

"Very well, I promise."

Diana kept glaring until Clarissa sighed again and elaborated. "I promise I won't speak to Balford about the fact I think you would be the perfect duchess for him, and I think he should marry you as soon as he can possibly contrive it."

"Clarry!"

"I promise I won't mention anything about you being head over heels in love with him, either."

"God save me from interfering sisters!" Diana couldn't help but smile. "Everything will be fine, Clarry. Things will all work out. I'm sure of it."

Clarissa didn't look so sure, but she leaned back against Diana. "If nothing else, this trip will be an adventure we remember all our lives, won't it?"

"That, it certainly will." Diana looked out of the window of their room, the room which faced right out onto the piazza outside, with the gigantic statue of Neptune and his risque nymphs. "Let's not tell Mother about that particular view, hmm?"

Clarissa dissolved into giggles, and Diana smiled, satisfied her sister had abandoned the topic. For now, at least.

CHAPTER SIXTEEN

Two days later, their party was once again on the move, departing Bologna on the last leg of their journey to Florence. On flat roads it might have been possible to make the distance in a single day, but the roads were far from flat as they began to ascend the Apennines, oxen being added to the carriage horses to help them up the steep ascent.

They stopped at the first summit to gaze in awe at the view, the plains laid out before them shimmering in the morning sunlight, the walled city of Bologna looking almost like a child's toy from their great elevation. The wind was bitterly cold, and Diana shivered as she stood beside the carriage; a gentle touch on her shoulder made her glance around, to find Will there, putting a blanket around her.

"You should not stand in the wind too long," he said. "You will take a chill."

"Oh, for heaven's sake," Clarissa muttered impatiently and not at all under her breath. Even though she stood not ten feet distant, neither Will nor Diana heard her, both far too busy gazing wistfully at each other. "Why doesn't one of them just say something?"

"They'll get there in time," Marianne said on her other side, and Clarissa startled. She hadn't heard Marianne move up beside her, her steps soft. "Don't interfere, Clarissa. I know it's tempting to try and help things along, but you could do more harm than good."

"They're both being stupid." Clarissa scowled. "And now Diana's lying to him."

Marianne's brows arched. "About what?"

"She told him she plans to find a husband in Florence, else our parents will probably have lined up someone for her to marry when we go home!"

Sighing, Marianne linked her arm through Clarissa's. "I hate to break it to you, my dear," she said, "but it is highly likely your parents will have done precisely that.

Why shouldn't Diana make her own choice, if she finds an amiable gentleman in Florence?"

"Because she's in love with Balford!" Clarissa stamped her foot.

"A man who has made it clear he is not ready to marry," Marianne pointed out gently.

"He would change his mind, if she would only give him some encouragement," Clarissa insisted stubbornly. "You must see the way he looks at her!"

"I have seen it, and Alex has spoken to him about it, and his answer was that he is not ready to marry."

"It was?" Clarissa's step faltered.

"You must trust that we have your best interests at heart, darling." Marianne squeezed her arm, and urged her to climb back into the coach. "And you must also accept that we are not always free to follow our hearts."

"That's not fair!"

"What isn't?" Diana asked, climbing back in from the opposite side.

Not wanting to admit to her sister that she had been talking with Marianne about Diana's romance with Balford - or rather, the complete failure of it - Clarissa quickly made up a complaint about not being permitted to attend balls once they reached Florence, because she had still not turned eighteen.

Diana at once agreed it wasn't fair, and turned her best persuasive arguments on Marianne, who fixed Clarissa with a hard stare. Clarissa offered her best innocent expression in return, knowing her aunt wasn't truly angry with her.

They overnighted at a tiny village called Pietramala, where they were obliged to stop anyway since it was the location of the frontier customs-house for Tuscany. Alex had made enquiries and discovered it was by far the most recommended place to make an overnight stop, since there was a very comfortable inn there. They were pleased to discover the reports were true, the inn sufficiently supplied with well appointed rooms and soft beds, and the innkeeper's wife an excellent cook.

As with everywhere they had been in Italy, the wine was both excellent and plentiful, and after dinner Diana realised she had perhaps over-imbibed a little, when she rose from her chair and swayed slightly.

"I think I would like to take a little turn outside before retiring," she admitted, "else I shall feel dizzy when I lie down."

"Please, allow me to escort you," Will said immediately, surprising her.

"Oh, I am sure I will be fine on my own, please, do not put yourself out," she said, but he was already taking her hand to place it on his arm.

"I would be remiss in my duty as a gentleman if I let you go out alone into the night," he said, quite gently. "Though we were assured brigands no longer haunt this route, a beautiful young woman wandering about alone is a temptation to any man who might not be over-troubled by morals or conscience. And regrettably, such men are to be found everywhere."

"Fifteen minutes, Balford," Alex said, "and I will have to come looking for you."

"It is too cold to be outside for longer than that anyway." Will took Diana's cloak off the hook by the door and held it out for her before shrugging into his own greatcoat. She tied her bonnet ribbons under her chin, thinking with amusement that she hardly needed to shelter her face from the sun, but the head covering might keep her warm.

"You are smiling," Will noted as he opened the door and led her outside, "what has amused you?"

She gasped as a blast of chilly wind struck her cheeks. "Oh, nothing of consequence. Goodness, that is icy!"

"Indeed." He closed the door behind them and took her arm again, moving in close. The way he stood, she suspected he was trying to shield her from the wind, but the chill was making her feel better already, counteracting the overheating, soporific effects of the wine.

"Let us walk toward the church." She pointed up the narrow, cobbled street. "It is only a few steps; we can walk there and back within the quarter-hour, easily."

Though it was dark, the way was clear enough, golden light from candles and fires spilling through the windows of the houses lining the street. Arm in arm, they walked up the steep hillside to the church and stood in the square before it.

"Do you think it might snow?" Diana said, breaking the silence.

Will looked up, and then shook his head. "It's cold enough, but look up."

She did, and gasped at the sight of the sky, not a single cloud in sight, the stars so clear and thick in the blackness it almost seemed the whole sky was afire in white light.

"I've never seen the stars so bright," she whispered, almost reverent.

“Me, either.” Will turned slightly, still gazing up, and somehow they were chest to chest, Will’s hands cupping her elbows as they both stared into the dizzying array of lights above them.

Diana felt as though she was drowning in the starlight, falling into the endlessness of it, Will’s hands the only anchor holding her to the earth. She leaned forward instinctively, seeking more contact, pressing against him, and he tilted his head down to look at her.

“Diana,” he said softly, his voice a low, husky rumble, and then he let go of her elbows.

For a moment she swayed, bereft of his support, but it was only for the briefest instant, because he had only let go in order to wrap his arms around her, holding her as close as she had ever been to another human being. She could hardly breathe from the closeness of it, and then she forgot how to breathe entirely, because Will was dipping his head and pressing his lips against hers.

His mouth felt hot, almost searingly so against her chilled lips, and she froze in complete shock. He pulled back instantly, his arms falling from about her so suddenly she staggered.

“Oh God,” he said, his voice husky and raw with emotion, “I’m so sorry. I didn’t mean to do that, Diana... I hope you can forgive me.”

She took a deep breath, trying to steady herself. Telling herself sternly that it had meant nothing. He was a young man who had found himself alone under the starlight with a young woman. A kiss was perfectly natural, under the circumstances. He was obviously regretting it even now, distraught with himself for taking advantage, possibly raising expectations in her he had no intention of fulfilling.

“Of course you are forgiven.” She worked hard to keep her tone level, light and amused. “We have both had a little too much wine; indeed, I feel almost drunk on the starlight! Let us walk back, though. Lest my uncle come looking and gain quite the wrong impression.”

“Of course,” Will said, his tone curiously flat, and then he was taking her arm, turning back towards the inn.

The kiss, brief as it was, had rocked Will to the core. Drunk on starlight, Diana had said, and that was indeed how he had felt, but it was drunk on her presence, on the way she had leaned so trustingly into him as she gazed up into the shimmering sky.

Helplessly under her thrall, he'd gazed on the delicate perfection of her features and lost his head entirely.

Her lips had been so soft under his, her body yielding as he drew her close, for that brief instant before she went rigid and he came to his senses. One more second and she would doubtless have slapped his face for his audacity in stealing a kiss. All he could think to do was apologise.

The tone in which she'd accepted his apology and dismissed the kiss crushed him entirely. It was obvious she thought nothing of it; doubtless he was hardly the first fool to try and steal a kiss from her under the stars. Why, Mario had probably done exactly the same thing!

The inn's door opened just as they reached it, and Alex stood there, obviously just coming out to look for them. He smiled and nodded approvingly as he saw them there.

"Good. Marianne and Clarissa have made their way upstairs, Diana, if you are ready to go join them."

"Yes," she said, and let go of Will's arm. She walked away without a good night, without so much as a backward glance, and he wanted to reach out and pull her back, draw her into his arms and taste her soft lips again, properly this time. Even though to do so in front of her uncle could lead to only one conclusion.

"I think I'll walk a little longer," Will told Alex, ignoring the other man's quizzical glance. "I'm not yet tired."

"I'll walk with you," Alex said, to his horror. "Seems a shame to have put my hat and coat on for nothing."

Sure he was about to get quizzed again, Will couldn't relax as the pair of them walked back up the cobbled street to the church again. Alex said nothing until they reached the square, and then he spoke seemingly at random, not looking at Will, but gazing up at the stars.

"I did some research, while we were in Venice. With Italy being a Catholic country, I was curious as to how two English citizens who happened to be Protestants might be wed in a legally recognised ceremony. Should a situation arise where two such people might wish to, of course."

Will was glad of the darkness. It meant Alex couldn't see the fiery red colour which had flooded his face. He didn't say anything, unable to trust his voice.

"It turns out that all such a couple need do is find an Anglican chaplain - there being one attached to every embassy His Majesty maintains, of course - to marry them, and have the chaplain provide them with a certificate to file once they return to England, in the International Memoranda held at Doctors' Commons, which is a registry of births, marriages and deaths of British subjects abroad."

"I see," Will said when Alex paused significantly, obviously waiting for his response. His voice came out annoyingly squeaky, and he clamped his lips shut.

"The cost to register such a document is one pound. Which might well be beyond the means of some sailors with the Royal Navy or a merchant fleet who have taken wives overseas, of course, but is certainly well within the means of a nobleman whose heir must be unquestionably legitimate."

Will made a noncommittal noise in his throat.

Alex sighed, turned to face him and spoke more bluntly. "I can't make you marry her, Balford. But if you cannot see that Diana Creighton is a fine young woman who would make you an exceptional wife, you are much more of a fool than I took you for."

"I *do* see that," Will cried, unable to keep silent a moment longer. "Of course I do! But I would not for the world have her *obliged* to accept me."

"Ah." Alex's tone conveyed deep understanding, and then he said "Yet, if you do not offer at all, she cannot accept, can she? Let me make something clear. My wife and I would never press Diana to accept anyone she did not want with her whole heart to wed. As you undoubtedly understand, the same cannot be said for her parents."

Will nodded. "Yes, she made as much clear when she explained she intends to seek a husband in Florence."

"She said...? Of course she did. She doesn't want you to feel obliged to make an offer."

Will's mouth dropped open at Alex's dry observation. *Could that possibly be true?*

Alex was watching him keenly. "We have no intention of telling Diana's parents about the Count of Bardolino's declined offer. Or about any other offer Diana might receive, unless and until she chooses to accept a suitor."

Will stood dumb, trying to think through the ramifications of what Alex had just told him. The marquis watched him a moment longer before clapping a strong hand on Will's shoulder.

"I don't entirely understand why you haven't already pressed your suit, but in case you were waiting for my explicit permission, you have it. All I would ask is that if you do not intend to make an offer, that once we reach Florence, you gracefully remove yourself from our party."

Shock at the request, along with instinctive rejection, flooded Will. He understood why Alex was asking, of course - a single duke hanging around Diana would likely scare off any number of potential suitors - but the mere idea of making himself scarce to leave a clear field for a swarm of Florentian swains to pursue Diana made him feel quite nauseous.

In that moment, everything became quite clear to Will. He must declare himself, and as soon as possible, making it clear to Diana that there would be no consequences if she should choose to reject his suit. And if she did reject him, well, he would do as Alex had requested and make himself scarce. With a broken heart, he doubted he would be able to spend another hour in her company anyway.

"Well, with my lovely wife waiting for me, I am for bed." Alex let go of his shoulder. "Don't freeze to death out here while you make up your mind."

CHAPTER SEVENTEEN

WILL SLEPT BADLY, BUT not because he was still struggling with his decision, or owing to any deficiency in comfort of the inn's beds. No, he lay awake half the night staring out of the tiny window at the bright stars planning how exactly he might gain complete privacy with Diana to plead his case, and rehearsing precisely what he would say when he did.

It was the early hours of the morning when he finally fell asleep. When Alex's man came in to stir him in time for their planned departure, though, he rose invigorated, excited for the day ahead. One thing he had certainly resolved; he would propose to Diana before they reached Florence on the following day.

Of course, he realised at breakfast that the first thing he would have to do would be to overcome the extreme awkwardness engendered by his reckless stealing of a kiss the previous night. Diana wouldn't even look at him, huddling in a corner and sticking like glue to Clarissa. Best not to push, Will decided, when his cheerful morning greeting met only a mumbled response and downcast eyes. He would find an opportunity later in the day to speak with her privately.

The way through the mountains continued steep and rocky, though Will thought the roads quite well maintained. While they could have covered the rest of the distance to Florence in a day, they had been informed that there was an interesting sight to see called the Monte di Fò, an actual volcano it was possible to walk right up to. Though only a mile or so from the road, there was no path accessible even by horseback, and it was quite a scramble through the rocks to reach the site. The innkeeper from Pietramala had sent his teenage nephew with them as a guide, and the boy hopped and leapt about the rocks with the agility of a mountain goat.

Will kept a close eye on Diana, almost hoping she would decide she required his assistance, but she and Clarissa seemed quite comfortable helping each other through the rocks and stones of the path until finally, they reached the summit of the hill and looked into the gaping vent at the top.

"Oh," Diana said in disappointed tones, "I expected to see burning orange lava... my goodness! Did you see that?"

Will had indeed, a belch of flaming gas bursting up from the vent so close they could feel its heat. He lunged forward instinctively, wanting to pull Diana clear, but she had already stepped back, pulling Clarissa with her.

"Phew, it stinks like rotten eggs!" Clarissa cried, retreating rapidly. The two sisters laughed, moving back to a safer (and less malodorous) distance.

Relieved Diana was no longer standing so close to the vent, Will gave in to his own curiosity, moving a little closer. The local boy was standing almost on the lip of the vent, and seemed to think he was in no danger, so Will moved forward to look as well. At least, until he happened to glance up at Diana and saw her staring at him with that look on her face he'd seen at the foot of the tower in Bologna, when she'd begged him not to climb the dilapidated staircase.

She's afraid for me, Will thought, and then with a blinding flash of insight, realised, *she's afraid because she cares about me.*

Without a moment's hesitation, he moved away from the vent, sending Diana a reassuring grin. Her answering smile was one of relief, before she looked hastily away, avoiding his eyes again.

She cares about me. He hugged the knowledge to him all the way back to the road. It might not be the desperate love he felt for her, but he was confident they could build a marriage based on friendship and mutual respect, and one much better than most of the peerage would ever have.

The weather worsened as they journeyed on, and by the time they reached the inn at Le Maschere where they planned to overnight, it was raining heavily. Soaked and irritated, Will climbed down from his wet and weary horse and gladly handed it over to a groom, before heading inside, hoping hot baths were among the comforts the inn might offer.

A hot bath was indeed quickly made available, followed by an excellent dinner of onion soup topped with melted cheese, rabbit pie, braised olives, and a delicious pasta dish with a spicy sauce of beans and tomatoes, all served with yet more excellent Italian wine. Hungry from the day's exertions, Will ate ravenously, clearing his plate and gladly accepting second helpings.

Diana sat at the far end of the table from him, and the room was lit with only a few candles, so it wasn't until after he had finally set aside his cutlery that he noticed she had barely touched the food in front of her, merely pushing it around the plate with her fork.

"Diana," he said, "are you feeling quite well?" She normally ate quite heartily, expressing enjoyment in trying local delicacies.

When she raised her eyes to his, he noticed they were glassy. She was pale, and her hand shook as she raised it to her brow.

"I… I don't quite…" she said, and then her eyes fluttered closed and she slid bonelessly from her chair to land in a graceless heap on the floor.

Once again, Will was too slow to catch her, though as he leapt from his chair and scrambled to her side, he vowed he would never fail her again. Scooping her in his arms, he pressed a hand to her brow, horrified to find her burning with fever.

Marianne's hand was right beside his, the marchioness' eyes meeting his with shared knowledge. "Bring her to her room," Marianne instructed, and Will nodded, rising to his feet, holding Diana close to his chest.

Alex stepped forward, making a gesture as though to take Diana himself, and Will's arms tightened. "I have her," he said, trying to keep his voice steady. "Please," he added.

Alex moved back without a word, going to open the door for him, preceding him up the stairs and opening another door to admit Will to Diana's chamber. Marianne had called for her maid and Jean was already there, turning down the bed for him to lay Diana down before shooing him firmly out.

"Find out if there is a doctor here," Marianne said as she brushed past him, and then the door closed in his face and he was left standing alone outside.

Alex was comforting a distraught Clarissa in the parlour where they'd eaten; Will glanced in on them briefly before going in search of the innkeeper.

"A doctor?" The man shook his head, looking almost amused. "Not in Le Maschere. In Florence."

"How far is it?" Will was perfectly willing to get on his horse and fetch a doctor.

"Ten miles, but you will not easily find a doctor from the city willing to come all the way out here. But there are the nuns at the convent of Bosco ai Frati; it is but two miles from here. They will come, in the morning."

"If we send the carriage, would they come tonight? Lady Diana is very ill."

The innkeeper shrugged. "Perhaps. For a donation to their order."

Will didn't think twice before reaching inside his coat and pulling out his purse. Opening it up, he dumped the entire contents on the counter; a hefty pile of gold and some silver clinked as the coins chimed together. "Would that be enough?"

The innkeeper's eyes bulged. "I think that would be sufficient, my lord," he said in a slightly strangled tone.

"Good." Will shovelled the money back into the purse and stuffed it into the man's hand. "You're coming with me, to convince them. Let's go."

The coachman wasn't too pleased to be rousted out of the comfortable room above the stables he'd settled into, but the promise of extra pay finally had him up and grumbling, snapping orders at the grooms as they put the horses back into the traces. The horses looked, if anything, even less impressed than the coachman to be going back out into the rain, coupled now with darkness. The innkeeper produced several extra carriage lamps, though, and they were soon bowling through the night towards the convent, Will whispering silent prayers that his 'donation' would be enough to convince the nuns to come.

He need not have worried. Obviously his anxious expression and stuttered pleas were sufficient, because the Mother Superior didn't even look inside the purse he handed her, just turned to gesture to a pair of acolytes who rushed away without a word needing to be spoken.

Within the half-hour they were on the road back to the inn again, this time with two nuns sitting on the forward seat, a large basket of medical supplies braced on the floor between their feet.

There was no chance Will would be admitted to Diana's room, but equally no possible way he could sleep until he had some news of her condition. He asked for a bottle of wine and sat in the taproom alone, sipping at the wine and failing to concentrate on the book he held on his lap.

At some point after midnight, he heard movement upstairs, doors opening and closing before everything quieted again. Then, a few minutes later, footsteps descended the stairs and Marianne slipped into the taproom.

"Alex said he thought you were still awake down here." Looking at the wine bottle in front of him, she collected another cup from the counter, poured herself some and took a healthy swig. "I was already quite sure before the sisters arrived that Diana is suffering from influenza, but I'm grateful to you for bringing them. They are skilled nurses and will take good care of her."

"I shouldn't have kept her out in the cold last night," Will fretted, but Marianne shook her head at him, taking a seat at the table facing him.

"Oh, I am confident she did not catch it last night. The maid who cleaned the rooms at the hotel in Bologna was coughing and sneezing quite dreadfully the day we left, and Diana insisted on giving her some coins; I daresay she caught it then and is just now showing the signs. Do not for a moment blame yourself, Balford."

Her tone was so matter-of-fact Will could not help but believe her. "She fell ill so quickly," he said. "She seemed fine this morning, when we stopped to look at the volcano."

"That's the influenza for you." Marianne drank some more wine. "She did sleep much of the afternoon in the carriage."

"How ill is she?" Will couldn't voice the question he really wanted to ask; if he spoke the words aloud, that made them seem more of a possibility. Still, he felt the words hang in the air between them. *Is she going to die?*

"I will not mince words with you, or give you false hope," Marianne said, meeting his eyes levelly. "She is very ill, and we both know the influenza can kill. While this is a comfortable enough inn, it is no place to nurse her, so tomorrow morning we will make her as comfortable as we can in the carriage and press on."

"It is ten more miles to Florence, ten miles on these mountain roads, which will take hours!"

"I am reliably informed the road is excellent from here. We will be there in under three hours, and Alex will go ahead of us to have the staff prepare a sickroom for our arrival."

There was little Will could say; Marianne had obviously made her decision and he had no influence over it. He determined immediately that he would be there to escort the ladies in the morning and said so, for which Marianne thanked him.

"You'd best get some rest, in that case," she said, draining the last of her wine and setting the cup down. "We'll be off as early as we can."

Will nodded, knowing she was correct. He should go to bed and try to sleep.

He also knew he would do nothing but stare at the ceiling until morning came.

CHAPTER EIGHTEEN

THEY DIDN'T DEPART SO early as Marianne would have wanted, but a couple of hours after dawn she called Will upstairs to carry Diana down to the coach. Wrapped in a blanket, she looked pale, but fever flags burned scarlet on her cheeks and her eyes were dull.

"This is such a bother," she said as Will lifted her up in his arms. "I'm sure I shall be fine in a day or so."

"I certainly hope so." She felt small and light as Will carried her carefully down the stairs and out to the waiting coach. Her head lolled against his shoulder as though she was fighting sleep, her eyelids drifting closed.

Clambering into the coach with her was awkward, but the maid Jean was waiting inside and helped to get Diana situated on the front-facing seat, pillows and cushions piled high to make her comfortable.

Marianne and Clarissa both looked as though they had slept little, but they both found smiles for Will as he handed them up into the coach. The two nuns from the convent stood to one side, watching; Will took a moment to go over and thank them profusely for their aid before mounting his horse and following after the coach as it trundled out of the inn yard.

Will was very relieved to discover that Marianne's information about the road to Florence was correct: within a very short time of departing Le Maschere the mountainous road became a much gentler one winding through low hills before opening out into the beautiful Arno valley, fertile fields, olive groves and vineyards all around, magnificent palaces and villas everywhere to be seen.

They did not enter Florence itself, but circled around it on the northern side to reach the Villa Ginori, where Alex's aunt resided. Set on a thickly wooded hillside, it was an unspectacular, long building of three stories, which turned out to be a great deal larger than it looked from a direct approach when they discovered it was built on a square, thus being four times bigger than it appeared on first impression.

Alex's aunt Elizabeth, the Contessa Ginori, was waiting for them along with Alex's mother Lady Glenkellie and a veritable army of servants. Will had no opportunity to offer to carry Diana inside; she had been swept away before he even dismounted his horse, and he was left to follow the party inside. A quiet, grey-haired man in a very nice suit greeted him and turned out to be the Conte Ginori, owner of the house.

"Lord Glenkellie went with one of my servants to fetch the doctor," the conte explained, showing Will into a handsomely furnished library. "We have set aside the north wing of the house for your party's use. It is a nasty influenza which has been raging this autumn; I hope the young lady will recover quickly."

"Thank you," Will said, nodding as the conte lifted a glass and decanter in his direction with a querying brow. It was not yet noon, but he still accepted the glass of brandy and gulped it down, savouring the burn on the back of his throat. "I am - Lady Diana is very dear to me. Anything which can be done..."

The conte nodded, an expression of comprehension coming to his face. "I see. Please, be assured she will receive all the care and attention we can supply."

"Thank you." To his shame, Will felt tears prick at the backs of his eyes. "Thank you very much."

"You look worn out." A kindly hand was placed on his shoulder. "I'll have a servant show you to your room... and show you where Lady Diana's room is. Do not worry about socialising with us; take your meals in your room if you wish until she is better."

The older man's kindness and understanding brought a lump to Will's throat. Unable to speak without resorting to a very unmanly display of emotion, he simply nodded and made a humming sound, but he was fairly sure the conte knew what he meant. With another gentle smile, Ginori moved to the door and called in a footman waiting outside.

Diana had never felt so ill in her life. She had felt tired and vaguely queasy as they journeyed to the inn at Le Maschere, but it wasn't until they sat down to dine and she had no appetite for even the delicious-looking spread laid before them, that she realised she might actually be unwell. She had thought to retire early but the room spun most disconcertingly when she tried to rise, and the next thing she knew, she was dimly aware of Will laying her down on a bed and saying something about getting help.

The world dissolved into a hot blur of discomfort. Her skin felt tight and flushed, her head ached and her throat was sore. She began to cough and couldn't stop.

Vaguely aware of Marianne, Clarissa and Jean fussing about, getting her undressed and into a nightgown, Clarissa crying as she applied cool cloths to Diana's brow, Diana thought she was dreaming when two nuns appeared clad in dark habits and white wimples. One of them peered into her eyes while the other talked in Italian far too quick for her to follow, somehow getting her meaning across to Jean who set to and helped prepare a tea.

The tea was sweet, thick with honey, tasting of lemons and ginger, though even that could not disguise the underlying bitterness of willow bark. The nuns helped Diana to sit up and made her drink it all. By the time the cup was empty, she couldn't keep her eyes open and they let her lay down and sleep.

She actually felt a little better when morning came, especially after the nuns gave her another cup of their healing tea. Marianne explained that they planned to press on to the Villa Ginori where they could get a doctor to see Diana and make her more comfortable; she was in no position to object even if she had wished to.

Will looked pale and anxious when he came in to carry her downstairs. She was suddenly conscious that she was still wearing her nightgown, although she also wore a robe and was wrapped snugly in a blanket, her bare feet poked out the bottom and she felt oddly vulnerable as he held her close to his chest. She was fairly sure he wasn't aware that he touched her face with his hand in a tender gesture as he set her on the seat in the carriage, but she held that touch close to her heart for a long time afterwards, dwelling on it even in the depths of the fever which raged over the next few days. Holding tight to the hope that maybe he did care for her.

The carriage ride to the Villa Ginori was miserable, every bump in the road exacerbating the aches in her body and the pain in her head, but it didn't last too long and soon she was lying in a blissfully comfortable feather bed in a light, airy room, servants fussing about her. Marianne pressed her to drink some more of the nuns' tea, and she gulped it down obediently, even though her sore throat made it hard to swallow.

Clarissa told her afterwards that she slept for almost the whole of five days, though Diana remembered little of it. One day, though, she woke and found herself in an unfamiliar place, Clarissa curled up asleep on a cot beside her bed, a maid sewing in a chair by the window.

Her throat still felt scratchy and sore, but her head was clear. Looking about, Diana took in the room, the yellow brocade curtains tied back at the sash windows, a view of a green hillside beyond. Olive groves, she thought, grey-green under a dull, cloudy sky.

Inside the room it was warm, a fire crackling in the grate. Diana wondered what time of day it was; there was no sun to be seen, but she didn't even know what direction her windows faced. She tried an experimental clearing of her throat; the maid jumped and dropped her sewing, scurrying over to the bed and unleashing a burst of Italian a little too rapid for Diana to process at that moment.

The maid's babble woke Clarissa, though, who jumped up at once and gave a cry of relief to see Diana awake, falling on her to embrace her closely.

Diana was horrified to discover that Marianne had fallen sick some two days after she had and taken to her bed; though she had, fortunately, not been as ill as Diana she was still resting under Alex's strict supervision.

"And Balford has been at your door every day begging for an update on your condition," Clarissa said slyly, watching Diana's expression as she sipped slowly at a cup of chicken broth. "He has been quite beside himself."

Diana considered and discarded any number of responses to her sister's teasing comment before deciding to save her breath. It wasn't as though Clarissa had actually asked her a question, after all.

"He's only left the villa once since we arrived, I believe," Clarissa went on, still watching her closely. "He went into Florence to find a bank and cash a banker's draft."

Diana could not see why that information was remotely of interest, and shrugged.

"It turns out he spent every last penny he had on him at Le Maschere. Made a donation to the convent where he found the nuns who came to care for you. They were quite stunned. It was as much money as they would normally get in half a year."

That made Diana's eyes widen, and she wondered if she could blame the telltale blush creeping up her cheeks on a return of the fever. She hid as much of her face as she could manage by taking another sip of the broth.

The maid jumped up to answer a knock at the door. She held it close so whoever was outside could not see into the room.

Clarissa scrambled up quickly too, grabbing a shawl draped across the back of a chair and wrapping it around Diana's shoulders. She smoothed Diana's hair, but Diana could see from the dissatisfied twist to Clarissa's mouth that there wasn't much to be done with it; if she had been abed for five days there would not be the slightest trace of a curl left in her naturally stick-straight hair.

"Leave it, Clarry. And don't you dare pinch my cheeks!" she hissed.

"You're as pale as your linens! Oh, very well." Clarissa smirked at her. "I'm quite sure he won't care."

"You're not going to let him in!" Diana put a hand over her mouth to suppress a small shriek as Clarissa went to join the maid at the door, saying a few words to the woman before swinging it wide and admitting Will into the room.

He took three quick steps towards the bed before catching himself and stopping dead. His hands clenched at his sides, fingers flexing, his upper body leaning forward as though he desperately wanted to continue on to her side. To take her in his arms? Diana told herself she was being fanciful.

"Balford," she said, conscious of the staring maid standing by the door. "I understand I have you to thank for fetching the good sisters to take care of me that first night."

He shook his head. "It was nothing. I am... it is good to see you awake and looking so much better. You gave us quite a fright."

"It was quite unintentional," she attempted to say, but a cough overtook her in the middle of the sentence.

Clarissa sprang back to her side anxiously, but Diana waved her away.

"You must rest," Will said as she was trying to get her breath back, to speak again. "I apologise for intruding, my concern... well. I'm sorry. Undoubtedly I will see you once you are on your feet again." He bowed, very correctly, and backed away before she could think of anything to say to get him to stay.

There was, of course, nothing she could have said anyway, Diana realised once he had gone and she was lying back against her pillows, even having sat up for that short time making her feel unaccountably weary. Clarissa allowing him into her room for even that brief moment was well outside the bounds of propriety, something Will must have known. If Clarissa told anyone - even if the maid gossiped! - Will could find himself obliged to offer for Diana to avoid her reputation being irreparably damaged, something she was sure he would do, having come to know how deeply honourable he was as their friendship progressed.

Diana was honest enough to admit, even if only to herself, that she would not be too distraught if Will found himself obliged to offer for her. She would, however, she thought as she snuggled back down into the warm bed and closed her heavy eyelids, infinitely prefer he offered for her because he wanted to. Because his feelings for her were intense enough that he could not contemplate marrying anyone else.

Because he loved her as she loved him, in other words.

CHAPTER NINETEEN

Although Diana felt herself much better from that first day of waking up, she soon discovered she was not so strong as she thought. Clarissa would not hear of her getting out of bed until the next day at the earliest and even then, she flatly refused to have the maid bring a dress for Diana to don.

“If you can walk to that chair by the window by yourself, I will be very surprised,” Clarissa said, pointing.

It could not be ten steps to the indicated chair, and Diana scoffed, swinging her feet off the bed and taking the first step.

She was only halfway there when her legs began to feel very strange, buckling beneath her quite alarmingly. Fortunately, Clarissa was ready for it, and looped a steadying arm around her waist to support her as she tottered to the chair and collapsed into it.

“Please don’t say I told you so,” Diana said once she managed to find enough breath to get the words out.

“Very well.” Clarissa smirked as she swathed a thick blanket across Diana’s knees. “The Contessa Ginori warned me, I admit. She said you would be very weak and tired for some days yet.”

“I have rarely felt so perfectly dreadful,” Diana admitted. She rested her head against the cushioned back of the chair. “Though at least I don’t feel as though I am liable to fall asleep at any moment. What a pretty view this is! Have you had an opportunity to explore, Clarry? Please tell me you haven’t been at my bedside the whole time?”

“Of course not,” Clarissa said. “I’ve been in my own bed next door quite regularly.” She laughed as Diana frowned at her. “I should not wish to explore without you anyway, Di. You’ll be better soon and we shall go together. With Balford, who is eager to escort us, since Uncle Alex is busy with Aunt Marianne.” She leaned in, her attitude confidential. “I think Aunt Marianne might be increasing. I heard the doctor talking to Uncle Alex and he gave some quite different instructions for her care, than for yours."

"I thought you said she was not as unwell as I've been?"

"She isn't, but Uncle Alex is still determined to swaddle her in lambswool!" Clarissa grinned. "We shall let them tell us in their own time, hm?"

It didn't take long for boredom to set in for Diana; she was manifestly not strong enough to get dressed and go downstairs, but being confined to her room chafed at her. Even when Clarissa fetched her drawing materials and encouraged her to draw the pretty view from the window, it could not hold her attention for long.

At last, the doctor pronounced her fully recovered on one of his daily visits to the villa, and Diana was permitted to put on a gown and proceed downstairs, where she finally met their host, a genial, grandfatherly man who patted her hand and told her not to regard it for a moment when she apologised for the inconvenience of descending on his house when gravely ill.

Lady Ginori and the dowager Lady Glenkellie welcomed her with open arms, declaring that they had been making plans for any number of entertainments for Diana and Clarissa to meet 'all their charming young friends!' and were so delighted they could now proceed.

Protesting would have been entirely useless, so Diana smiled, thanked them prettily and said she hoped they did not plan anything too vigorous just yet, as she rather thought she might tire more quickly than she would like.

The door to the salon where the older ladies were holding court swung open to admit a tall figure moving a little too hastily for grace; Will entered the room and stopped dead as all eyes turned to him. He paused, obviously collecting himself, and then bowed.

"Your pardon for barging in, my ladies. I heard a rumour that Lady Diana was up and about and had to see for myself."

"How diverting," Lady Glenkellie murmured, and both older ladies swivelled to look at Diana, who was once again having to fight down her blush.

"As you see, Your Grace, I am quite myself again. I do thank you for your concern."

"Indeed." Will stood still for a moment, apparently indecisive, before stepping forward and pulling up a chair beside her. "Well, I am very glad to see it. I have missed your company. And yours too, of course, Lady Clarissa," he added, an obvious afterthought which had Clarissa snickering behind her hand.

"Have you seen much of Florence yet?" Diana asked brightly, attempting to lead the conversation onto more innocent lines and head off the speculation she could see growing on the older ladies' faces. "I am most eager to see the Gallery of the Academy, and Michaelangelo Buonaroti's statue of David; even the artists who have made sketches say they cannot do justice to its beauty with pen and ink."

"I have confined my explorations thus far to walks around the Villa Ginori." Will bowed slightly in the contessa's direction. "Though the conte has provided me with quite a list of sights to visit, and also set a carriage and driver at our disposal. Once you feel well enough to go out, we shall visit the Galleria and you may peruse David to your heart's content."

"Perhaps a less ambitious outing would suffice to start with," Lady Ginori suggested, "why don't you escort Lady Diana for a short walk in the gardens, Balford? You stay here, miss," she addressed Clarissa. "I have a few questions for you, about what exactly your parents were thinking, letting a girl your age gallivant around Europe! If you were my daughter, you'd still be in the schoolroom!"

Diana rather thought Lady Ginori didn't mean a word she was saying to Clarissa, who smiled back at the older woman, unabashed. Indeed, it seemed very obvious they were setting up an opportunity for her to be alone with Will. She hesitated, but he did not, rising at once to his feet.

"Shall I send a maid to fetch your cloak and bonnet, Lady Diana?"

Since she had not the faintest idea where her cloak and bonnet might be stored, she nodded, and accompanied him out to the hallway, where the items were soon procured, along with Will's caped greatcoat and top hat.

"You must tell me as soon as you begin to grow fatigued," Will said as they left the villa, walking down four broad steps to a raked gravel path.

"I will," Diana said, not mentioning that she was already quite tired. She could go a little way, she reasoned, and Will seemed inclined to walk slowly. Leaning on his arm, she breathed in the cool, fresh autumnal air and smiled, turning her face up to the sun.

She was too pale, Will thought, and she had lost significant weight; her gown seemed loose on her form. The freckles she had gained in the hot Italian summer stood out starkly on her white face, but her brown eyes shone bright, at least, and the smile on her face was a relief to see. He had been sick with worry over her; Diana falling ill just as he acknowledged his feelings for her had brought home to him just how very much he loved her.

Will had spent the last week rehearsing several different versions of impassioned speeches in which he declared himself to Diana and begged her to marry him, but as they walked together in the Villa Ginori's gardens, he couldn't for the life of him recall a single word of any of them.

Instead, he found himself mouthing inane platitudes about the weather and the gardens. Diana nodded along, saying little until they emerged between some high hedges into a small clearing. A fountain in the centre emitted a soft tinkle of water.

"Oh, how charming," Diana said softly, and spotting a bench, Will asked if perhaps she would care to sit for a few minutes.

"I would, thank you. Not because I'm tired," she added, he thought rather too hastily. "But this is a very pretty spot. Look at the fountain; who do you think that goddess is supposed to be?"

"With a bow and arrow?" The water poured forth from the arrow's tip, as well as spouting in delicate jets about the feet of the white marble goddess. "She can be none other than your namesake, Diana, of course."

She blushed a little. "It could be the Greek goddess, Artemis."

"In Italy?" He raised his eyebrows. "Do not deny the lady her due."

Diana laughed, looked away and back to the statue. "It is a lovely sculpture, actually. Worthy of being in a museum or gallery. It seems almost a shame for her to be here in a private garden; I wonder how many people have ever seen her? Look at her bow and arrows, too; bronze, do you think?"

"Indeed," he agreed, and thought that the metal was well-polished despite the water continually spilling over it. He suspected there was at least one member of the grounds staff whose job included thoroughly cleaning and polishing the statue on a weekly basis at least.

"It does seem that at every turn in Italy, there is a wondrous new piece of art to appreciate. And that is when the scenery itself is not stunning to the eye." She waved a hand, encompassing the hillside rising beyond the gardens, the Apennines looming grey in the distance. "I must bring my sketchbook out here," she murmured, almost under her breath, and Will wondered if she had forgotten he was even present.

"It's all in the way you look at it," he said, and Diana turned to face him, her brow wrinkling.

"What do you mean?"

"Somebody else might look at this and think it's rather ordinary, just another fountain in a garden, but you take the time to look a little longer, and your eyes find something special."

"Exactly!" She beamed at him.

"It reminds me of you, actually."

She frowned at him again, obviously puzzled.

"I think perhaps I'm being tactless again," Will said, knowing he was, since every word of his rehearsed pretty speeches had entirely escaped him and he was making this up as he went along, "but how often have you told me that you think you're ordinary, nothing special about you?"

"Well, but I am," Diana said with a little laugh, "that's not tactless of you at all, merely observant."

He shook his head. "I disagree absolutely. In these last few months in your company, I have come to realise that you are by far the most extraordinary lady of my acquaintance."

She looked startled, and then blushed, casting her eyes down. "How kind of you to say so. I value our friendship very dearly, Will; truly, I could never have imagined when I saw you in Venice and was so horrified to recognise you, just how close we would become."

"I have never had a female friend before," Will admitted, "but I, too, value our friendship."

"It is a shame we cannot continue as we have been once we return to England." She gave him a rueful little smile. "We will be far more constrained; you by the requirements of your rank and me by everything expected of an unmarried young lady who has yet to make a good match. If I do more than acknowledge you as an acquaintance, I will be labelled fast, or criticised for chasing you, setting my sights far higher than an earl's daughter should dare to look."

"I thought you didn't plan to return to England?" Will said, momentarily distracted from his line of thought by her speech. "I thought you planned to find a husband here in Florence?"

Diana looked away, back at the statue of the goddess. "Diana the huntress," she said softly. "Perhaps she could go out and hunt down a husband, but I don't think I have it in me. Perhaps I should just go home to England and let my parents choose, after all. They do love me, I am sure of it; they will choose carefully and take my wishes into account."

"Don't," he said, horrified.

"Don't go home?" She smiled wistfully. "I can hardly remain in Italy forever, imposing on tenuous relations until I wear out my welcome."

"That's not what I meant." Reaching out, he took her gloved hand in his, laced their fingers together. "Come with me."

She looked at him curiously, delicate brows arched. "Where? Do you have plans to travel further afield?"

"No, I have been away long enough," Will admitted. "There were letters awaiting me when I arrived in Florence, from my stepmother, making it clear I need to return home, and soon. In fact, there is a Royal Navy ship in the harbour even now, captained by a cousin of mine who is urging me to be aboard when he sails at the end of the week."

"Oh." She lowered her eyes. "And there would be berths available for our party too?"

"I'm sure there would, but I'm talking about just you, Diana." He squeezed her fingers gently. "I'm making a terrible mull of this, but the truth is... I cannot bear the thought of leaving you behind. We can be married at the Embassy before we leave, host a reception once we arrive in London..."

He trailed off, because her mouth had dropped open and she was staring at him in what was clearly utter surprise. Before she could speak, he found his voice and finally managed to say what he was thinking, tell her the truth he'd been holding in for weeks.

"I don't want to go home without you. I can't imagine my life without you in it, Diana; say you'll marry me."

CHAPTER TWENTY

Diana could not persuade the slightest sound to pass her lips. Shock held her immobile, staring at Will, who cradled her hand gently between his, gazing at her earnestly as he waited for her response.

"I see I've done an even poorer job of letting you know the depths of my regard than I'd realised," he said finally, a rueful smile twisting his lips, "because it is quite apparent from your reaction that you had not the slightest expectation of my proposal."

"I never dared to dream," she managed to whisper finally, shaking her head.

"I think I fell in love with you before we even left Venice," Will admitted.

Diana lifted a shaking hand to her mouth, tears beginning to well in her eyes. "Oh, *Will*," she gasped, and he groaned aloud, leaned in to pluck her hand away from her mouth, and kissed her.

A blissful eternity passed, or perhaps it was only a minute or two, before Will lifted his head and gazed down at her. Diana clung to him, eyes still closed, not wanting to let go lest the wondrous dream come to an end.

"Did you say yes?" he asked, voice low and a little hoarse.

She laughed, opening her eyes at last. "Not yet, but I rather thought that kiss rendered it a moot point? Yes, though, if you need to hear me say it. We will have to ask my uncle's permission, though..."

"I already have it," Will admitted.

Diana felt her eyebrows shoot up. "You asked him?"

"Actually, no, but I rather think everyone but you has a fairly accurate understanding of my feelings for you. Long before even I myself did. Lord Glenkellie made it clear to me some days ago that he would not object, should I ask for your hand and you choose to accept." He cupped her cheek tenderly in one large hand.

"He also told me the choice would be yours; that neither he nor Lady Glenkellie had any intention of putting any pressure on you to accept me. Or even, should you decline my suit, allowing anyone outside our party ever to know the offer had been made."

Diana blinked back tears, realising just how much faith Alex and Marianne were placing in her judgement. "I think they had a pretty accurate idea of just how I felt about you, too," she admitted, "even though I have tried to suppress it. I wanted to keep disliking you; it would have been so much easier if you were truly the thoughtless, arrogant cad I first believed you to be!"

"I was thoughtless and arrogant," he admitted, "at least until you showed me the error of my ways."

She shook her head, threading her hand through the crook of his arm and tugging gently, encouraging him to walk with her back towards the house. "You were grieving your father and trying to avoid being thrust into a situation you weren't ready for, and I was the literal embodiment of your fears. I have long since forgiven you your actions."

"You are too good." He lifted her hand, pressed a kiss against her gloved fingertips. The loving warmth in his eyes made her tremble a little, the evidence of his regard a shock when she had harboured her own emotions close for so long.

"What now?" she asked as they ascended the steps to re-enter the villa again.

"Who should we tell first, do you mean? I daresay the older ladies watched every minute of our interaction from the salon windows."

Diana blushed at the mere idea of their kiss having been witnessed, her steps faltering. A moment later and a door crashed open close by, followed by the quick patter of feet, Clarissa racing around the corner at a most unladylike pace before flinging herself at Diana and embracing her.

"I knew it, I knew he would ask! Took you long enough," she threw a reproachful look at Will before hugging Diana tightly again. "Are you happy?"

"Happy is far too mild a word for the way I feel," Diana chuckled, accepting Clarissa's enthusiastic embrace. "I am overjoyed, ecstatic, in transports of delight."

"We must go up and tell Aunt Marianne," Clarissa clutched at her hand and tugged at her. "Hurry! No, wait, don't, you don't want to get tired too quickly. Balford, why don't you carry her upstairs?"

"Certainly," he said good-naturedly, and scooped Diana easily off her feet. "And since we are to be brother and sister, you'd best start calling me Will, I think."

"Then you must call me Clarry." Clarissa beamed at him before starting to ascend the stairs before them. "I shall run up and see if Aunt Marianne is receiving!"

"She won't be receiving me, so I shall have a quiet word with your uncle," Will noted quietly as he followed Clarissa upwards. "He was the one who looked into how we might legally get married here, incidentally. Though I admit, I have taken the time since we arrived here in Florence to discover the name of the chaplain attached to the British Embassy and write to him. I received a response yesterday that he is quite happy to perform marriages for English citizens and provide a certificate for us to take to Doctors' Commons on our return to London."

"You really have thought all this through," Diana said wonderingly.

"Diana, I have been trying to work out a way to ask you to marry me since before we reached Bardolino. Watching Mario try to court you was nothing short of torture, especially when I thought you might actually welcome his attentions!"

"Oh, no." She laughed quietly and laid her head against his shoulder. "I could not possibly have accepted him... not when my heart already belonged to you."

"If we weren't halfway up a flight of stairs, I should kiss you again for that," he noted, making her giggle.

They reached the door of the suite the Glenkellies were using, which stood open; Alex was just inside, arms folded, a grin on his face.

"You took long enough," he said to Will, who groaned as he set Diana gently on her feet.

"Not you, too! I could hardly barge in on her when she lay in her sickbed and propose!"

"Leave him be, Uncle Alex," Diana chided. "He came to the point eventually, even if he has just admitted to me it has been almost two months since he decided he must."

Will threw up his hands with a laugh. "I confess it; I am a slowtop who should have listened to you all sooner!"

"So long as you recognise it," Diana said pertly, before squeezing his arm and slipping away through the other door into the bedroom at Alex's gesture.

Marianne was out of bed, Diana was glad to see, sitting in a chair by the fire with a blanket on her lap. Her red hair was in a loose braid hanging over her shoulder and she was a little pale, but her smile as Diana entered was bright. She held her hand out to Diana, saying in a slightly hoarse voice;

"Darling girl... I confess Alex saw you and Will from the window, so I have some inkling already of why you are here."

"Oh, no." Sinking to sit on a footstool by Marianne's chair, Diana covered her blushing face with her hands. "Did *everyone* see us?"

"I suspect you were sent to that particular part of the gardens for a reason."

Diana made a miserable squawking sound into her hands, making Marianne chuckle and pet her hair lightly. "It would only be a problem if you didn't want to marry Balford, my dear..."

"But I do!" Diana cried at once, lifting her face to gaze up at her aunt. "I love him most desperately."

"Watching the pair of you fall in love with each other has been quite the highlight of this trip." Marianne touched Diana's cheek tenderly. "He is everything I could have wished for you, and I think he will make you very happy."

Diana found tears trickling down her cheeks. Fishing her handkerchief from her pocket, she wiped them away. "He's a good man," she whispered. "I was wrong about him at first."

"Anyone can have misunderstandings, especially after a first meeting which went as disastrously as yours. It is a testament to both your characters that you were willing to listen and understand each other when you were thrown into company again; it would have been easy to hold onto your grudges like petulant children, but you didn't. I'm very proud of the way you acted, Diana. You will be a magnificent duchess."

"That's the one thing I haven't quite come to terms with yet," Diana admitted. "The duchess part."

Marianne, formerly a countess and now a marchioness, smiled at her. "I'm not concerned at all. From everything I have observed about being a duchess, you simply do whatever you please and nobody dares criticise you anyway."

"That will be nice, if true!" Diana considered it. The only duchesses she'd met, she realised, were Will's stepmother - very briefly, at that disastrous ball where she'd fainted at Will's feet - and here in Italy, the three generations of Franchetti duchesses, of whom only Valentina had a living duke. And yes, Diana thought, all those duchesses did exactly as they pleased, without apparent care for what anyone around them might think of their actions. Even Valentina, who was a very new duchess, was entirely unconcerned about the opinions of others.

"Certainly, I don't think anyone has dared to say anything critical about me since I became a marchioness," Marianne noted. "Although, that may have something to do with Alex looking fearsome at anyone who might dare!"

"Or perhaps the rumours that you really did wreak divine vengeance on my father by dint of having a swan attack him after he was rude to you," Diana said, straight-faced, and Marianne looked shocked for an instant before going off into peals of laughter.

"People don't really say that, do they? Oh, my goodness!"

Diana decided not to mention that she had heard the rumour repeated in with-drawing-rooms on at least three occasions before her family abandoned London. Instead, she chuckled along with Marianne... and considered how rank conferred privileges which a smart woman could use to her advantage.

Marianne's laughter was eventually interrupted by a fit of coughing, settled with a few sips of water. "You should go downstairs," she told Diana when she was able to speak again. "Else you may discover my mother-in-law and Lady Ginori have arranged your wedding to their liking and you will have no say in things at all."

"I don't really mind," Diana admitted, finding to her surprise that it was the truth. Like most young women, she'd always had nebulous dreams of a grand wedding with a beautiful gown and an admiring crowd, but now the groom was determined, she realised none of the rest mattered. Yes, she would like a pretty new gown and Clarissa to stand beside her, but if necessary, she'd marry Will dressed in rags, on the dock before the ship which would take them back to England.

"I'm glad to hear that," Marianne said with a sharp glance. "In my experience, young women who get caught up in the details of the wedding usually haven't thought too much about the actual marriage, which lasts a great deal longer."

"I've thought a lot about what being married to Will would be like," Diana admitted.

"Have you, indeed?" Marianne arched her brows. "Well, one day quite soon, we shall have a discussion about married life."

Diana blushed a little, understanding that her aunt was talking about the marriage bed. "I'd appreciate that," she said. "My mother didn't tell me a lot. Just what to watch out for in terms of avoiding rakes!"

"Useful knowledge, but not all you need to know." Marianne stroked her cheek again. "There's nothing for you really to worry about, my dear. Will loves you, and I have every confidence he will treat you with the loving respect you deserve."

CHAPTER TWENTY-ONE

When Diana adjourned downstairs, she found Lady Ginori and the elder Lady Glenkellie indeed busily planning the wedding, aided and abetted by Clarissa. Will sat by looking slightly bemused but not dissatisfied; he rose to his feet as Diana entered the room and came towards her with such an expression of delight at seeing her on his face she felt warm all the way through.

"There you are. Is your aunt happy for us?"

"Overjoyed." Accepting his offered hands, she squeezed them lightly, gazing up into his handsome face. It was such a relief to be able to show her feelings, not to have to hide them behind a purely friendly facade.

The major-domo entered to announce a visitor, which turned out to be Captain Fordham of His Majesty's ship *Swiftsure*. Will's cousin, Diana soon discovered as Will introduced her as his fiancée and Fordham looked briefly shocked before bowing deferentially over her hand.

Diana saw Captain Fordham looking surreptitiously at her as he conversed with Will a little later, his brow creased with apparent confusion. She had the dreadful feeling he was quizzing Will about what, exactly, made Diana suitable to be the next Duchess of Balford, and it seemed apparent from the captain's expression that he certainly wasn't impressed by her physical appearance.

The euphoria she had felt after the proposal was fading, to be replaced by a vague feeling of panic. Captain Fordham was just the first of Will's lofty relations who would look at her in that confused way, wondering just what exactly Will saw in her, why he would choose her when he could marry literally any lady he wanted.

A chill raced through Diana and she rubbed at her arms; within moments Will was at her side, scooping a shawl from the back of a chaise and settling it about her shoulders. "You must not take another chill," he murmured quietly. "Today has been a great deal for you, considering you are only just out of your sickbed. I have asked too much of you."

Clarissa was making her way over, looking concerned, and Diana allowed herself to be convinced to go upstairs and rest before dinner. She was determined to return to the company for the meal, though, and insisted Clarissa help her into a pretty gown and put her hair up.

Will returned to her side immediately she entered the salon, smiling broadly. He was carrying something in his hands, she saw; a wooden box, prettily inlaid.

"This is for you," he said. "A betrothal gift, though I admit I purchased it in Venice with you in mind... perhaps this will help you to believe you have been in my heart all this time."

Accepting the box from his hands, she opened it and gaped to see what was nestled in strips of finely shredded paper inside; a teal and silver glass dolphin. A precise match in colour to the earrings she was even then wearing, it could only have come from the glass factory in Murano they had visited, that day they had stood on the bridge over the canal and he had suggested travelling with their company.

"Oh, Will," she whispered, awed. "You truly have admired me... since then?"

"Longer." He grazed a finger against her cheek tenderly, the tip of his finger just bumping her earring. "If your aunt had not bought these for you, I would have done so, and figured out some way to give them to you."

"So you bought this for me, instead?" She looked up at him curiously. "What would you have done with it if I had married Mario?"

"Smashed it in a fit of rage, I daresay," he said with a rueful grin.

Instinctively, Diana held the box closer to her. "Well, I am very glad you did not!"

"What do you have there, Diana?" Alex rumbled, coming over and leaning to look over her shoulder. "Why, that is very pretty!" By the glint in his eye, he did not miss that the delicate sculpture was a perfect match to her earrings. "You have carried that a long way, Balford."

Will looked abashed, but met Alex's eyes steadily. "Some part of me knew, even in Venice," he said, "that my heart was inevitably hers."

"If only you had written to her grace the duchess to let her know that," Captain Fordham said dryly, coming up beside them. "She has been busy whetting the appetite of the Ton, telling everyone that this upcoming Season is the one where you will select a bride. Every lady with a daughter making her debut is plotting your capture; they will be fuming when you return to England already married."

Will merely shrugged, expressing perfect indifference. Diana winced, thinking of her likely reception in London; all those disappointed mamas would make a very unfriendly welcoming committee.

Captain Fordham appeared interested in getting to know her, or rather quizzing her about her family background. She held her own, she hoped, but then being an earl's daughter was certainly nothing to be ashamed of, even if her father was only lately come into the title after his uncle's passing.

"I have not met the new earl," Fordham noted. "Was your father raised as the heir, then, since the previous earl had no son?"

"No; the previous earl was until his passing still hoping to sire a son." Diana sneaked an apologetic look at Alex, who smiled at her encouragingly. "My father was educated at Cambridge and studied the law, before practising as a barrister in Durham. He had no expectations of the title."

"I see." Fordham pursed his lips. She could almost hear him thinking; *a barrister's daughter, raised to be a duchess?*

"But you know how it is," Diana said, smiling quizzically. "Only a direct heir can be afforded the luxury of a life without needing to forge his own path. *Captain.*"

Fordham's eyes widened, and then he bowed slightly to her, acknowledging the hit. From the corner of her eye, Diana saw Will's proud smile. She appreciated too that he had not intervened, allowing her to deal with Fordham's probing herself. Having successfully done so significantly increased her confidence.

The captain stayed for dinner, and afterwards came to sit by Diana in the salon. He was rather nicer this evening, she thought, unbending a little to talk about his ship when she asked him about it.

"And when must you sail for England?" she asked.

"No later than the end of the week." He gave her a serious look. "I believe my cousin hopes you and he, at least, will be aboard, if he is able to find a chaplain to conduct the marriage ceremony for you before that."

"Oh, we have already resolved that matter," Lady Ginori interrupted them. "The ambassador is a good friend of ours; Ginori already sent him a note to request the chaplain's services. We are advised that Friday morning will be entirely suitable for us all to attend the chapel and see dear Balford and Diana married. If you have no objection, of course, my dear," she said to Diana, obviously as an afterthought.

"I am grateful for your assistance and influence in the matter, my lady, and Friday morning suits me very well," Diana said with perfect truth.

Lady Ginori beamed on her happily. "I am *distraite* that we have no time to organise you a trousseau, but Lady Glenkellie and I will visit a silk warehouse or two and find some lengths of silk for you to take back to England with you, so you may have some new things made up when you arrive. No, no, I will not hear any objections," she held up a hand when Diana began to protest. "I have no doubt Balford will be delighted to spoil you, but you must have at least a few things which nobody else in London will be able to match!"

Diana had little choice but to accept graciously, even while she came to terms with the timeframe for her wedding; just three days away. And then she and Will would be boarding the *Swiftsure* to return to England. Realising she didn't even know if Marianne and Alex planned to return along with them, Diana excused herself and moved to the other side of the room to sit by her aunt.

Marianne, in conversation with the Count, reached out to take Diana's hand and squeezed her fingers. The kindly older gentleman, seeing that Diana was obviously eager to ask her aunt something, took only a moment to end the conversation and move on, leaving them alone.

"The wedding is set for Friday, it seems," Diana confided.

"Indeed? And are you happy with that? It is very soon," Marianne said gently.

"Yes." Of that, she had no doubts at all. "But returning to England so soon... that, I'm finding a little nerve-wracking. And I was wondering... will you be accompanying us?"

Marianne hummed to herself a little, glancing across the room to where Clarissa sat at the pianoforte, playing a delicate air to entertain the company. "Alex and I discussed it, but... no. Not at this time. I believe I may be increasing," she kept her voice very low, "and am feeling quite dreadfully sick. I am assured it should pass off in a few weeks, but the thought of a sea-voyage at the present time is quite unbearable. We will remain in Florence for a few weeks, go to Rome for a visit, and perhaps see about returning to England in the spring."

"And Clarissa?" Diana said, but she already knew the answer. Marianne would leave the choice up to Clarissa, and Diana could not imagine her sister choosing to return to England any sooner than she had to. The freedom they enjoyed in Italy was too great to willingly give up for anything less than the kind of love Diana had found with Will.

The following morning, a clatter of hooves and wheels outside her window heralded a carriage being brought round, and within minutes Clarissa was hurrying into Diana's room, a broad smile on her face.

"Hurry and get dressed! Will says since you are to leave soon, there is no time to lose!"

"Time to lose?" Diana asked, reaching for the nearest gown hanging in the closet.

"To see Florence, of course. We are to visit the Uffizi Gallery today!"

Of course Will would take her to the Uffizi. He knew how very much she had looked forward to seeing the legendary art collection contained within. She looked up into his face as he handed her up into the carriage and smiled, and his loving smile in return communicated that he knew exactly what she was thinking.

With Clarissa accompanying them as chaperone, the three of them spent a wonderful day wandering the Uffizi's magnificent collection, Will even paying the curator to permit them into the Vasari Corridor to view any number of artworks rarely seen by the general public, and cross above the Ponte Vecchio to the Palazzo Pitti. Tired and hungry, they made their way back down to the lower level and went in search of somewhere to eat, which they found in a charming trattoria near the bridge.

Feasting on ravioli filled with spinach and soft cheese drizzled in a butter sauce, and a delicious bread toasted and topped with grilled tomatoes, basil and olive oil, Diana thought she had never enjoyed a meal more, as she laughed and chatted with Will and Clarissa, utterly comfortable in their company. She was already regretting the parting with her sister to come, but knowing how excited Clarissa was at being permitted to remain in Italy, refused to let her sister know how much she would miss her.

They walked back across the Ponte Vecchio to meet back up with their carriage, pausing to peer into the tiny goldsmiths' shops, filled with dazzling jewellery. Will paused at one window, looking at a display of rings, before reaching for Diana's hand.

"Would you like a ring? A token of my affection for you. The whole Balford jewel box will be yours once we reach home, of course, but... this is from *me*."

A personal gift, rather than just an heirloom which went along with the title of duchess and all the duties it entailed, Diana understood. Smiling up at him, she said honestly "I should very much like that."

The jeweller was delighted to assist them, of course. He attempted to direct Diana's attention to some of the gaudier pieces, but after looking over his selection, she pointed instead to a simpler ring, with a rich blue cabochon sapphire at its heart, surrounded by flower petals of tiny diamonds.

"An excellent choice," the jeweller said, hiding his disappointment poorly, but he perked up when Will pointed to a stack of heavy gold bangles and said he would take two. Diana was startled when, in the carriage, he took the bangles out and handed them to Clarissa.

"I will no longer be with you to look out for you," he said, "and though I am confident Lord Glenkellie will do an excellent job of it, as he has been for months now, you will be my dear sister and I would have you bear a tangible reminder of that - and be also confident in the knowledge that you will have something of value about your person, should you need it."

Diana could not have loved him any more, as Clarissa gulped and slid the bangles onto her wrists, admiring their soft gleam before lunging across the carriage to give Will a hug.

"Thank you for that," Diana whispered to Will as Clarissa settled back into her seat.

Will squeezed her hand and brushed his lips lightly across her hair. "I know how much you will miss her," he said softly, "and I wish I was not taking you away from her. This is the least I can do, to perhaps set your mind at ease that she will always have resources about her if she should ever need them."

"I love you *very* much," Diana said fiercely, uncaring that Clarissa could hear them, and Will's eyes kindled brightly.

"I shall buy her some more jewellery each day until we leave, then," he said, his tone lightly teasing, though his expression was anything but.

Diana found herself thinking she really must have that conversation with her aunt about the marriage bed. And soon.

CHAPTER TWENTY-TWO

Four weeks later

If she were of a mind to believe that poor weather at the beginning of something was a bad omen, Diana thought, she might well be demanding the ship turn around right now and take them back to Italy.

No sooner had the cry gone up that land had been sighted by the lookout in *Swiftsure's* crows' nest, heralding the end of their journey back to England, than the skies had opened and the rain begun to pour down. It had not stopped in the two days and nights since, either, as they sailed up the Channel making for their awaiting berth at Portsmouth.

It had not been an uncomfortable journey. While the *Swiftsure* was a naval ship rather than one configured for passenger comforts, she had previously been used as a fleet flagship and was possessed of quarters fitted for an admiral, quarters Captain Fordham had been pleased to place at her and Will's disposal. Four weeks in close quarters with her new husband had only confirmed Diana's certainty that she was an exceptionally lucky woman.

"We are tying up at the pier now," Will said from his perch on the window seat, where he had been watching with great eagerness as the ship navigated into the harbour and to her assigned dock. "My cousin said he would send a man directly to the George Hotel to arrange rooms for us, so once he returns, we can disembark."

"It will be nice to be on ground that does not move beneath my feet," Diana admitted, laying the book she had been reading down on the table.

"And be able to draw without a sudden lurch sending your pencil shooting across the page?" Will teased gently.

"You know it to be true! 'Tis no wonder seascapes almost all appear to be painted from the viewpoint of somebody standing on land!" Diana laughed, but she truly had missed being able to draw, and Will knew it. He reached for her now, fingers gently encircling her wrist, and pulled her to sit with him.

Already, the ship felt strange, the rocking which had been constant for so long stilled. Nerves welled up inside her. Now that they were back in England, her new life as the Duchess of Balford would really begin. Or in a few days it would, at least, when they reached Balford Priory, the duchy's Devonshire seat. With just four weeks remaining to Christmas, Will believed his stepmother would already have removed to the Priory for the holidays, and if they went to London, they were likely to miss her - or have to set off again almost immediately anyway. Thus, they would stay a day or two at the George Hotel until Will had managed to arrange a suitable conveyance for them.

The pier outside was a hive of activity, men marching this way and that. A carriage rumbled into view and pulled up as close as possible to the timber pier.

"That will be for us." Leaning in, Will pressed a kiss against her temple. "See, there are your trunks being carried to it. Are you ready?"

The book she had been reading belonged to Captain Fordham, and there was nothing else left in the cabin belonging to either of them, so she nodded.

The captain himself met them as Will led Diana up on deck, offering an umbrella with a smile. He had been extremely pleasant throughout the voyage, but while Diana felt he and she now had something of a friendship established, she suspected he still harboured reservations about her as a duchess.

"All is arranged for you at the George," Fordham said. "I am for London in the morning to report to the Admiralty; I will call by your townhouse and see if the duchess is still there, and advise her that you are headed for the Priory if so."

"And will you be joining us at the Priory for Christmas?" Will asked, accepting the umbrella from his cousin and holding it solicitously to shield Diana from the rain.

"That depends entirely on my lords and masters at the Admiralty, as you well know, but I shall hope to join you." Fordham offered Diana a respectful bow. "Your Grace, it has been an honour to convey you home."

Suppressing the instinctive urge to curtsy, Diana instead inclined her head regally, telling herself it was time to start practising the attitude of a duchess. "It has been a pleasure to sail with you and the *Swiftsure*, Fordham, and I second Will's hopes of seeing you at the Priory soon."

He offered another bow before escorting them off the ship and to the waiting carriage. Moments later they were rolling away from the noise and bustle of the docks, though they travelled for only a few minutes before pulling up again outside a handsome whitewashed building.

Will made use of the umbrella again to escort Diana inside, where they were obviously expected, as the hotelier and his wife both waited to very obsequiously greet them and escort them abovestairs to the best guest suite, where a separate room was prepared for each of them. Fordham had obviously requested servants be provided for their use as well, for which Diana was grateful. She had definitely missed the services of a maid these last few weeks.

A hot bath was ready for her, scented with lavender, and she sank into it with a very un-duchesslike groan of relief. A maid helped wash her hair, and then wrapped it in a drying cloth as Diana luxuriated in the hot water, eyes closed.

"Is there a gown you'd like pressed for this evening, your grace?" the maid enquired shyly, lifting the lid of Diana's trunk.

"They all need laundering," Diana admitted. "The yellow silk is probably cleanest, I think. It was too cold aboard ship to wear it, but I don't suppose we will be venturing outside this evening."

"Oh no, your grace, the cook is busy preparing a very fine dinner for you and his grace. Best the George can provide. There's a private dining room for you downstairs; right warm it is, with a good fire."

"Then the yellow silk will be fine. I daresay it is sadly crushed, though, you'll find it right at the bottom."

"'Tis beautiful silk though, your grace." The girl had found the gown, held it up, giving it a gentle shake. "I'll run it downstairs to Elsie and she can press it while you finish your bath."

"Thank you," Diana said, but the maid had already hurried out.

I could get used to such devoted service, Diana thought, closing her eyes and breathing in the fragrant steam from her bath. She smiled wryly to herself as it occurred to her that once she reached Balford Priory, she was likely to find herself overwhelmed by attention from servants. No doubt her mother-in-law would consider a single maid vastly under-staffed for the retinue of a duchess, and would likely throw up her hands in horror once she discovered Diana had travelled all the way home from Italy without even that. Indeed, she had been the only woman aboard the *Swiftsure*.

By the time the water began to cool, the maid had returned with her gown beautifully pressed. Hanging it up, she assisted Diana from the bath, wrapped a robe about her, and pressed her to sit by the roaring fire to have her wet hair combed out.

Dry, clean and dressed in her fresh gown, weariness suddenly assailed Diana, and she eyed the comfortable-looking four-poster bed wistfully. A tap on the door heralded Will coming to take her down to dinner, however, and the rumblings of her stomach convinced her to eat before she allowed herself to fall into bed.

"You look magnificent," Will exclaimed as soon as the maid admitted him to the room. "You have not worn that gown since... Bardolino, I think."

"You are very observant," she remarked. "It was too fine to wear while travelling, and too cool once we reached Florence."

"It is beautiful on you." He lightly touched a curl of her hair, swaying against her neck as she turned her head to look up at him. "You are lovely in yellow. Like sunshine. It makes me feel as though we are back in Italy."

She did not say that she wished they were; she already knew how much he regretted their having to leave and return to England. Instead, she smiled and tucked her hand into the crook of his arm. "Let us see if the George can provide a dinner fine enough to make us glad we are home in England instead, then."

Delicious smells wafted up the stairs as they made their way down, and Diana almost followed her nose into the public dining-room, but the hotelier intercepted them and guided them, with a great deal of bowing, into a private dining room, small but very elegantly furnished, with another roaring fire warding off the winter chill.

The table could have seated ten at least, and a place setting at each end of it had Diana eyeing it askance. Surely she was not supposed to sit a full twelve feet from Will and shout at him in order to converse? Will, looking at the place settings, let out a crack of laughter and strode forward.

"Ridiculous. Some people lose all their common sense when they hear 'duke' or 'duchess'." He scooped up knives and forks and redeposited them at the other end, so Diana could sit alongside him.

Relieved, she sat and allowed him to push in her chair. A moment later, the door opened again and the hotelier came in, followed by two footmen and a maid, each carrying a covered tray. Diana noted the momentary hesitation as they saw the relocated place settings, but they all recovered smoothly and set about laying out the various dishes prepared for their dinner.

Fish in a cream sauce, a ragout of mushrooms, veal and ham pie, roasted beef, lamb chops in minted gravy, duchesse potatoes, buttered carrots and peas, baked apples stuffed with raisins and sugar, custard tarts and a cherry crumble with thick yellow cream to pour over were set out, and Diana suppressed the urge to laugh.

"Is all this just to feed us?" she murmured to Will as the staff filed out again.

"In theory, yes, but don't worry." Will cast her a wry grin. "None of it will go to waste. I'm quite sure the staff will be enjoying a late dinner once we have taken what we want from these dishes."

It still seemed ridiculously extravagant to Diana, but she was hungry, and everything looked delicious. She tried the fish - a succulent fresh plaice - and nodded when Will lifted the bottle of wine set for them, offering to pour her a glass.

It was obvious to Will that his wife - and how delightful it was to be able to think of Diana so! - was struggling to stay awake. She almost nodded off spooning cherry crumble into her mouth, and he reached over to ensure she didn't tip over her wine glass more than once during their meal.

"I'm so tired," she mumbled, hiding a prodigious yawn behind her hand as they rose from the table. "Please tell me we need not be off at the crack of dawn tomorrow."

Will had planned exactly that, the hotelier having advised him earlier that a suitable carriage, horses and driver had been procured for his use. With an indulgent smile, however, he changed his plans. "Indeed no, beloved. Sleep in as long as you wish. I will ensure nobody disturbs you until you ring for a maid."

"You will be... sleeping in your own room?" Her great dark eyes turned up to him, she seemed hesitant, and he realised why. There had been no rooms to spare aboard ship, of course, they had slept together every night. Diana was probably wondering if he planned to impose more formal rules - and separate bedrooms - now they were back on English soil.

"Not unless you want me to, beloved," he answered her honestly. "Let's go on up and get ready for bed. I for one am looking forward to falling face-first into those heavenly-looking feather pillows!"

She laughed, obviously pleased, and squeezed his arm. As they approached the foot of the stairs, however, a voice called out from the public dining-room on the other side of the hallway.

"I say, is that you, Balford?"

CHAPTER TWENTY-THREE

WILL PAUSED, HIS HEAD turning. "Amberle?"

"It *is* you!" The man who approached was almost as tall as Will, fair-haired and florid of complexion, he looked about the same age as Will, and he was vaguely familiar, though Diana could not place the precise occasion where she had met him before. "I heard you'd run off to Italy to avoid getting leg-shackled... oh." Seeing Diana on Will's arm, he paused.

"Diana," Will said quickly, "allow me to present Lord Amberle. He and I were at school together. Amberle, my wife, her grace the Duchess of Balford."

Knowing well by now that Will always chose his words carefully, Diana noted that he had not said he and Amberle were friends. She offered a polite smile and a small tilt of her head, hoping she had gauged correctly the degree of recognition a duchess should offer a baronet.

"Your grace," Amberle said after a moment of obviously stunned silence. He made her a creditable bow. "My felicitations on your marriage."

"Thank you." Realising it would be impolite to just walk away, but honestly feeling too tired to make conversation, Diana squeezed Will's arm lightly. "I shall go upstairs and prepare for bed now, I think. Why don't you take a glass of wine and talk with your friend a little?"

Will looked as though he was considering declining and coming upstairs with her, but Amberle broke in.

"Oh, jolly good idea; the hotelier just brought out a bottle of very nice port. Come and keep me company a little while, Balford, and tell me what you have been up to; I am for Guernsey tomorrow and will be deprived of civilised company for a good while, I fear."

"One glass of wine," Will acquiesced, looking at her. She smiled to show him she really did not object. "I will be up shortly," he promised her, and she nodded.

"An honour to meet you, your grace," Amberle said with a bow, and she nodded, favouring him with a smile too.

"No doubt we will have opportunities to become better acquainted in the future, my lord. I look forward to it."

Turning away from them, she ascended the stairs, covering a yawn with her hand as she did so. She really was incredibly weary, looking forward to sinking into bed and falling into a deep, blissful sleep. Her steps dragged as she slowly mounted the stairs, and she supposed it was her own fault for moving so slowly, for Lord Amberle obviously thought she must have moved out of earshot when he said;

"Lud, Balford, you married the Fainting Flower? What happened, did she swoon on you again?" He let out a loud, braying laugh. "Thought you ran away to Italy to avoid getting leg-shackled to one of her ilk! Did she pursue you out there?"

Diana's feet felt frozen in place. She stood at the top of the stairs, clinging to the handrail, waiting with bated breath for Will's reply. Distantly, she thought of the old adage that eavesdroppers never hear good of themselves, but she had to know what Will would say.

Glasses chinked, the door closed, and Diana could have screamed in frustration as the low rumble of Will's voice sounded, the words unintelligible through the closed door.

She could hardly march back down the steps again and listen at the door, or burst into the room and call Amberle a rude oaf, much though the urge took her. The Fainting Flower, indeed! Feeling a little queasy, and no longer sleepy, Diana turned away from the stairs and made her way to her bedroom, wondering if Will was even then laughing about the silly nickname with the other man.

"I'll thank you to keep a respectful tongue in your head when you talk about my wife, Amberle." Will was sure his expression resembled a thundercloud, but Amberle was obviously in his cups and continued, oblivious.

"Oh, no disrespect intended, she's very pretty, indeed, I congratulate you. Quite rich, too. You could do so much worse. Just didn't expect you to come back from Italy leg-shackled when you left to avoid that very thing! Truth t'tell, it's why I'm off to Guernsey, to hide out and rusticate for a while. M'mother's hounding me again; wants me to marry some horse-faced chit with a huge dowry to revive the family fortunes." Amberle shuddered theatrically. "Can't imagine anything worse."

Will stood staring at the drunken buffoon in front of him, wondering how he could ever have had anything in common with Amberle. Though he would not have called the other man a particular friend, they'd always got on well enough, and shared in a number of pranks and scrapes in their schooldays. Will, it seemed, had grown up in the intervening years, though, and Amberle apparently had not.

"Well, I wish you good luck in avoiding the state of matrimony," he said finally, thinking that the young lady Amberle's mother wanted him to marry was getting a lucky escape. "For myself, I'm finding it suits me very well indeed."

"Long as she doesn't faint at the prospect of the marriage bed, eh!" Amberle guffawed again.

Will finished the glass of wine a silent waiter had handed him with a single gulp and set it down on the table before standing again. "For the sake of our long acquaintance, Lord Amberle, I shall pretend you did not make that remark," he said icily, "but as I said, you will be respectful when you speak of my duchess."

Amberle opened his mouth, probably to make another boorish remark, but Will raised a hand to stop him.

"Otherwise, I will make it my business to ensure your mother discovers post-haste which of your many properties you have decided to visit. I'm sure she - and your prospective bride - would be delighted to join you on Guernsey."

Amberle's look of horror was obviously unfeigned, and Will felt a certain savage satisfaction as he turned on his heel and stalked out, hoping Diana would still be awake when he reached their rooms and resenting the few minutes he'd been forced to spend being polite to Amberle. If being a duke was good for anything, surely it was that he could cut people dead if he felt like it and there was nothing whatsoever they could do about it. He had absolutely no interest in spending a moment more than he had to in conversation with a juvenile buffoon like Amberle, not when he could spend that time with Diana instead.

The room was dark and quiet when he slipped inside, lit only by the low light from the fire, banked for the night with a metal screen in front of it. Diana was a motionless lump under the covers.

With a sigh, Will dismissed the servant who had waited outside the door, bolted it, and began to undress as quietly as he could. Slipping into bed beside Diana, he reached across instinctively to put his arm around her waist and draw her close to him, a sleeping position they had no choice but to adopt in the narrow bed they had shared aboard ship and to which he had very quickly and happily become accustomed.

He was startled to find her stiff as a post, and she flinched away from his touch.

"Diana, are you well?" Leaning up on one elbow, Will reached for her face, horrified to find it wet. "Diana! Why are you crying?"

She turned her face against his shoulder, apparently unable to speak. He held her close and rocked her gently against him, murmuring comforting nonsense into her hair, feeling how her shoulders trembled, though her sobs were silent.

"What's happened?" he asked when she stilled, finally. "What has you so distraught?"

"I heard what he said," she mumbled into his shoulder. "Before the door closed."

Will couldn't remember exactly what Amberle had said first, but just about every word out of the fool's mouth had been utterly offensive. He growled under his breath.

"Did you hear me tell him to keep a respectful tongue in his mouth, or I'd remove it for him?"

Her head popped up. "You didn't!"

"I might not have threatened violence quite so explicitly," Will admitted, "but I did make it clear I wouldn't tolerate any disrespect."

"I don't see how you can stop it. I'll always be the... the F-Fainting Flower, to some of them..."

"You will be the Divine Duchess, if I have anything to say about it."

She laughed, as he'd intended her to, even if the sound was a little shaky. Her arms crept about him, and she clung to him tightly.

"Amberle is an obnoxious oaf, and he was drunk," Will told her, "and even he did not dare say such things to your face. There is power in your title you haven't learned yet. Believe me when I say the Fainting Flower will be entirely forgotten in the desperate clamour to be invited to any social event you might choose to host."

"Do you really think so?"

"Considering the outrageous behaviour I have seen my stepmother get away with over the years, I know so," Will said dryly. "She long ago decided she would not care a jot what anyone thought of her, says and does exactly as she wishes without regard to anyone else - and is fêted as one of the Ton's greatest originals."

"I shall make a great study of her, but I don't know that I will ever be able to be so carefree," Diana said a little wistfully.

"The fact that you care so much for the feelings of other people is part of what I love so much about you," he murmured, peppering gentle kisses across her cheeks and nose. He felt her smile against his cheek, some of the stiffness leaving her body as she softened against him.

"I fear I will make a poor showing of being a duchess," she confessed, a soft whisper against his skin.

"You will be magnificent," he told her with complete confidence. "My Divine Duchess, indeed."

She laughed again, properly this time, before her lips sought his, and they spoke no more of it for the rest of the night.

CHAPTER TWENTY-FOUR

Two days after the *Swiftsure* sailed into Portsmouth, the hired carriage Will had procured for them rolled between the twin grey stone lodges which marked the entryway to Balford Priory's grounds.

Diana was snoozing, her head against his shoulder. They had spent a night in Salisbury, after not leaving Portsmouth until noon the previous day, and then risen early and travelled all day to reach the Priory before night fell, something they had not quite managed on this short winter day. They'd stopped five miles ago to light the carriage lamps and now rolled up the Priory's long drive with only a small pool of light surrounding them, since the stars and moon were entirely covered by cloud.

"We're almost there," Will nudged Diana gently as he caught a glimpse of the first lights from the Priory's windows. The house was suspiciously well-lit, and he sighed inwardly, suspecting that his stepmother was probably hosting a houseful of guests. He'd truly hoped she might not have come down yet and he would have a chance to show Diana around her new home without scrutinising eyes watching her every move.

Diana roused, rubbing sleepily at her eyes. "Oh, 'tis dark," she murmured, leaning forward as he pointed out of the window. "Is that the Priory, Will? Goodness - so many windows!"

"And lights in every one of them," he murmured, "making me think my stepmother is likely hosting quite a gathering."

"Oh." She gulped, but smiled bravely when he took her hand in his and squeezed it.

"Courage, my Divine Duchess."

She laughed softly. "Are you planning to persist with that? Shall I call you my Dashing Duke?"

"If you wish it. I am determined, however, that you shall never be identified by any other nickname."

"I do love you so very much," she said, her eyes sparkling with happiness, and he leaned in to steal a kiss before the carriage finally came to a halt at the bottom of the steps.

It was as Diana was stepping out of the carriage, her hand held securely in Will's, that she recognised his own tension.

Of course, she thought. He had, after all, left for Italy to avoid having to step into his father's shoes, take on the entire responsibility of being the Duke of Balford. His return had been both inevitable and necessary, but he was clearly still affected... and just as clearly, doing his best to suppress it for her sake, knowing how nervous she was.

A surge of love overwhelmed her, and she tucked herself in closer to his side and squeezed his arm as they proceeded up the broad stone steps leading up to the Priory's front door. She knew the manor had been renovated and added on to several times over the years since Will's ancestor had been granted it under Henry VIII, but the front door was still from the original building, a great oaken thing studded and bound in iron. It swung open with an ominous creak, a scene straight out of a gothic novel, she thought whimsically.

"Your Grace!" a shocked voice said as a figure was revealed standing inside the foyer, an older man, at least sixty, Diana estimated. "We had no word... welcome home!"

"Jenkins." A smile creased Will's face. "The butler," he murmured in an undertone to Diana as he led her inside.

Jenkins was staring at her, eyes popping. "Your Grace?" he said, querying.

"You are correct, indeed, Jenkins. Her Grace... the Duchess of Balford." Will grinned, obviously delighted at the old retainer's shock.

Jenkins recovered quickly, though, bowing deeply to Diana before he even closed the door.

"A pleasure to meet you, Jenkins, and to finally be at the Priory," she replied to his heartfelt welcome.

"May I take your bonnet and coat, Your Grace?" he requested, and she nodded, tugging at the ribbon under her chin to free her bonnet.

"Whoever is it, Jenkins?" a female voice called. "We aren't expecting anyone else this evening, and we are just about to go into dinner - is it something I need to deal with?"

"Only if you wish to welcome my new wife and I home, Julianne," Will said.

There was a moment of shocked silence before his stepmother, the dowager duchess Diana supposed she was now, stepped into view, coming from a doorway to one side of the vast, marble-tiled hallway.

"William?" Julianne said, her mouth agape, "and your... *wife*?"

Diana remembered the duchess well from the ill-fated ball where she had first met Will - and fainted at his feet - but it seemed Julianne did not remember her at all, as the duchess stared at her without the slightest hint of recognition.

"We have met before, my lady, but you may not recall," she said, offering a shallow curtsy.

"Diana is the Earl of Creighton's daughter," Will offered.

Julianne's eyes widened. "The... oh, I *do* remember you. When... where..."

"Did you say that is Balford, returned?" an excited voice exclaimed behind Julianne, and a lady came out into the hallway, followed by another, and then two gentlemen, and a very pretty girl of about sixteen who Diana suspected was Will's half-sister Regina. She had his dark hair and deep blue eyes, and the same dimple flashed in her chin as she smiled delightedly.

Two very elegantly dressed young ladies joined the growing throng, both immediately preening and edging closer to Will, casting him inviting smiles. Diana winced internally at the contrast between her tired, travel-stained self and their fresh glamour, but Will didn't move a step from her side.

"I think perhaps we should all go back into the salon," he said, "so I can say something to everyone, and then perhaps you and Regina will accompany us to the study - and maybe Rebecca could come down as well, to welcome us home?"

Julianne seemed in a state of shock; she just nodded, and turned to follow Will as he led Diana through into a very grand salon. She looked about, trying to take everything in; the room was panelled in a beautiful golden oak, elegant landscapes in gilt frames hanging on the walls, tasteful furniture upholstered in blue and gold matching the heavy curtains drawn against the darkness outside. Light blazed from at least a dozen candelabra, making it all too easy to see the avid expressions on every face turned towards them.

There were around twenty people in the room, Diana estimated, all dressed in the first stare of fashion and every one of them staring at her, obviously wondering who she was and why she was on Will's arm. She could almost feel the pressure of all those eyes, the weight of their judgement as they assessed her clothing and her person.

"Dear family and friends," Will began as Regina closed the door, "before I greet you all and tell you how happy I am to be home, please allow me to introduce you to my wife, Diana, the Duchess of Balford."

The words were like a stone dropped into a still pond; utter silence and then furious whispers rippling outward. One of the elegant young ladies gave a dramatic little wail and slumped sideways in a swoon. Fortunately she was seated on a couch beside a rather substantial older lady, so had a soft landing in the other woman's lap.

Will's gaze slid sideways to Diana, and he smirked.

Fighting to suppress sudden and wildly inappropriate laughter, she pinched his wrist lightly.

Regina was the first one to reach them, stretching to kiss Will's cheek and reaching out to take Diana's hands with a friendly smile. "I am so very happy for you, dear brother. Congratulations. And welcome to our family, Your Grace."

"Diana, please," she said quickly, grateful for Regina's warm welcome. "I have three sisters already, but I am delighted to gain two more in you and Rebecca. Will has told me so much about you both."

"Sadly, he told us not a thing about you, despite sending regular letters while he has been away," Regina said with a chiding glance at Will. "Did you meet in Italy?"

"We met for the first time in London, actually, but encountered one another again in Venice when we were both guests of your Franchetti cousins," Will answered.

"*You* know the Franchettis?" Julianne exclaimed to Diana. "How?"

"Duchess Marietta is a cousin of my aunt's husband," Diana said, then realising everyone was listening avidly, decided to drop Alex's title. "The Marquis of Glenkellie."

"A familial connection, indeed, and also the new Duchess, Valentina, and Diana have become particular friends," Will put in, obviously deciding to play up the Italian ducal connection too. "Indeed, Valentina hoped to make a match for Diana with her brother, the Conte di Bardolino, but I am afraid I thwarted her plans by wooing Diana for myself."

That was not precisely how it had happened, but Diana had no objection to Will editing the story slightly. Making it sound as though Diana had chosen a duke over a count would certainly please her mother more, if the story should happen to reach her ears, than the truth; that Diana had rejected the count without even the faintest idea that Will cared for her.

"Well." Julianne looked from Will to Diana, and back again, before putting on a rather forced smile and turning around. "Well, now you have all seen my stepson is indeed alive and well - and home again, with his new bride - I'm afraid I must ask you to excuse us, to have a little meeting *en famille*. Dinner is about to be served, and I will rejoin you afterwards. Lady Susan, perhaps you will preside over the table in my stead?"

She gave the other lady no opportunity to either accept or decline, gathering Will, Diana and Regina and ushering them briskly from the room before anyone else even had the chance to speak.

Will took the lead, escorting Diana along the hall and down a side passage until they entered a study, warmly lit and again expensively furnished. A girl of about thirteen was standing by the fire; she too shared Will's dark hair and blue eyes, which lit up as she saw them.

"Will!" She almost leaped forward, her enthusiasm curbed by Julianne's sharp glance, but Will laughed and reached out to grab her up in a hug.

"How tall you are grown, Rebecca! I declare you must be of a height with Regina!"

"She is," Regina said dryly, "and like to overtop me soon, I'm sure." Her smile was fond, though, and Diana deduced there was plenty of affection between the sisters.

Of course, the introductions had to be repeated for Rebecca's benefit.

"Married?" Rebecca exclaimed, "but why? You said you wouldn't get married until you'd seen Reggie and I both safely married off!"

Will winced, glancing at Diana. "Well. That was the plan. But I rather reckoned without falling hopelessly in love, you see."

"Oh!" Regina and Rebecca both clutched at their hearts and looked starry-eyed; Diana noted Julianne looked a good deal more cynical.

"I made a dreadful first impression on Will, I'm afraid," she said, deciding to take the bull by the horns, "fainting on him at our first introduction in London, so we had something of a history to overcome when we met again in Venice."

"I am glad to say it did not take me long to recognise all of your most admirable qualities, although I was abominably slow in owning to myself how I felt," Will admitted, his fingers curling around hers.

"You must be weary," Julianne said finally, "and hungry too, I daresay. Since we are missing dinner, let me arrange for trays in our rooms... oh." She paused. "Will... I am still occupying the mistress's chamber..."

"And you must continue to do so," Diana said quickly. She and Will had already discussed the matter, during the interminable days aboard ship. "Will tells me that there is a delightful suite of rooms adjoining the ones he is currently occupying; they will do perfectly well for me."

Will had actually wanted to tell Julianne not to concern herself, since Diana would simply share his apparently quite palatial suite, but Diana hadn't wanted to shock her new mother-by-law.

"The Emerald Suite?" Julianne pursed her lips. "Lord and Lady Altmere are presently occupying it."

"Then Diana will just have to share with me until they have departed," Will said firmly, putting his arm around Diana's waist. "We have just come from occupying far closer quarters aboard ship, Julianne; we shall be quite comfortable in my suite."

Julianne looked quite appalled, but she darted swift looks at Regina and Rebecca and simply said "We can discuss that later."

Will opened his mouth, perhaps to say something tactless, but Diana spoke first, quickly.

"I confess it's been a long day, and I should very much like a bath and a hot meal. I'm looking forward to getting to know you all better - but we have all the time in the world for that, don't we?" She smiled, in as friendly a way as she could manage. Regina and Rebecca both returned it: Julianne sniffed a little haughtily, but nodded.

"The ladies gather in the Egyptian Room after breakfasting in our rooms," she noted. "Perhaps you will care to join us."

"How kind, I shall be delighted," Diana said.

"You don't need her invitation to anything here," Will grumbled quietly in her ear as they ascended the stairs together a few minutes later. "It's your house, now."

"Will, you're being tactless," she reproved gently. "Give her time. She has been mistress here for how long? Yes, she has been pressing you to take a wife, but she expected not only to help you choose that wife, but to have a set timeframe on bringing her into the household and training her as a replacement, in effect. She certainly didn't expect you to just reappear one day and tell her that her services as hostess were no longer required."

"I didn't!" Will defended himself, but stopped walking and looked sheepish as Diana cast him a cynical look. "I came a little too close to that, didn't I? I'm so glad I have you, Diana, to pull me into line when I start being arrogantly ducal."

She laughed and squeezed his arm. "So long as you continue to listen to me. I need your stepmother's goodwill; I have not the least idea how to be a duchess, you know."

"You are a magnificent duchess," Will said loyally.

"I am a tired, grimy and very hungry duchess, so unless you wish me to become a snappy duchess, you will start moving again and lead me to your rooms. Else I shall attempt to go by myself and no doubt become horribly lost in this vast place." She could already foresee disaster in the long hallways which all seemed to look alike. Balford Priory was significantly larger than Creighton Hall, in which she had managed to become lost any number of times in the first few months after her family moved in.

"Come on, then." Will led her to a suite in, Diana thought, the tower which formed a corner at the western end of the house's front elevation. The bedroom was curiously shaped, like a quarter-circle with one long curved wall making up two sides, tall narrow windows fitted with leaded glass set in it. It was too dark to see the view outside, but she looked forward to seeing it in the morning.

A veritable army of servants awaited them; a maid was quickly stoking the fires, more maids and footmen scurrying about with trunks and bandboxes, an older man Diana supposed must be Will's valet turning down the bed.

"Your Grace." The valet bowed, a smile creasing his face. "May I say what a pleasure it is to finally see you home."

"You may, Taylor." Will smiled, a look of guilt flickering across his face. "And may I proffer my apology for sneaking off in the dead of night and leaving you behind? I've no doubt it would have been you who found my note and had to break my news to the duchess."

"That was a conversation I would prefer to forget, Your Grace," Taylor said with a pained wince.

"Diana, allow me to present Taylor, who does not deserve to have to put up with me, but does so anyway because I pay him exceedingly well," Will said with a fond grin. "Taylor...my wife, Lady Diana, the new duchess."

"Your Grace." Taylor performed an elegant little bow to her. "From all the staff here at the Priory, I hope you will allow me to extend our most heartfelt congratulations and wishes for your future felicity." He paused before enquiring delicately, "Did you bring a maid with you, Your Grace?"

"No," Diana admitted, "I'm afraid not. I was accompanying my aunt and uncle in Italy, and sharing the services of my aunt's maid, you see..."

"You don't need to explain anything, beloved." Will squeezed her hand lightly. "Consult with the housekeeper and ask her to assign a few maids for Her Grace's personal service, please, Taylor. You might wish to advertise for a lady's maid, or seek recommendations - or was there perhaps a maid from your father's household...?"

Diana shook her head, but then something occurred to her. "Lord and Lady Havers were starting a training academy for household servants and skilled tradespeople. I could write to Lady Havers and see if she has anyone to recommend to me? I know Aunt Marianne's maid Jean came from the Havers household originally and she is so wonderful."

"Redoubtable," Will agreed, obviously recalling Jean's efficiency and her dedication to caring for her mistress and the two Creighton sisters. "You should indeed write to Lady Havers, then."

"And in the meantime, I've no doubt there'll be plenty of the maids keen to do for you, Your Grace," Taylor said with a nod. "If you'll excuse me, I'll just see about your baths, and those trays should be here by now... ah, here they are."

Trays were indeed being carried in by a procession of maids, delicious scents wafting to Diana's nose. She almost moaned as her mouth began to water, and allowed Will to lead her to a small table by the window with two chairs set before it. More maids and footmen were scurrying past with pitchers and jugs of steaming water, obviously going to fill a bath, and even as she took the first bite of perfectly cooked roast lamb, Diana found herself thinking that it would be quite easy to get used to the little luxuries which came with her new position.

CHAPTER TWENTY-FIVE

Diana woke alone in the chilly light of a frosty morning, weak sunlight streaming in the windows of Will's chambers. Will's pillow beside her was cool, telling her he'd been gone some time. Risen early to go about the duties of the dukedom, she supposed, and rolled to her back, looking around the room, seeing it fully for the first time in the daylight.

She liked the colour scheme, she thought, stroking her fingers gently along the edge of the covers atop her, fine Irish damask linen which would likely have cost as much as the most expensive gown she had ever owned. The wallpaper was a pale blue with a muted gold pattern, the furniture a dark English oak, but not heavy as many such pieces were. Sturdy, with finely detailed ornamentation which must have taken a great deal of time to carve. The floorboards were the same colour, what little of them could be seen; almost the whole floor was covered with an exceptionally fine carpet all in shades of blue and gold. Aubusson, she suspected, and probably worth more than everything else in the room put together.

A door creaked, and she saw a panel in the wallpaper open just slightly. A hidden door, and was it the only one in the room? An entryway to the servants' passages, obviously, as a small face peeped through, the door opening wider to admit a shyly beaming maid a moment later.

"Yer awake, mum! Yer shud'uv rung the bell for me, loike."

The girl's West Country accent was so thick it took Diana a moment to understand her, but she spied the bellrope hanging beside the bed the girl was gesturing at and nodded.

"I only just woke up. Don't fret."

"Iffen yer sure, mum. Yer Grace, I mean!" The girl looked briefly appalled by her own lapse into informality. "What can I get fer yer breakfast, Yer Grace?"

Diana thought wistfully of the delicious cappucinos and breakfast pastries she had become so accustomed to in Italy, but she had also become very tired of the dull meals aboard ship since then. "Tea, please," she requested, "and toast, and whatever jam is made locally. Blackberry, perhaps?"

Four different pots of jam were shortly delivered alongside what Diana judged to be almost half a loaf of perfectly browned toast and some very fine tea. The staff were eager to please, she suspected, or perhaps terrified of Julianne's wrath should they in any way fall short of perfection in impressing the new duchess. By the time she had finished eating, a small bevy of maids had efficiently remade the bed, rebuilt the fire, laid out fresh clothing for her and stood ready to spring into action to serve her slightest whim.

Determined to start off on the right foot, Diana smiled at all the maids and enquired, "Now, who is good with hair? Mine has not been dressed properly in weeks, and though it was washed last night, I fear you may have some sad tangles to sort out!"

Two of the girls volunteered themselves, and Diana took herself over to the dressing-table in one corner. It took the girls quite some time indeed to carefully comb all the tangles from her hair and put it up nicely, and one of them showed herself very deft with a curling-iron to make some pretty little curls clustered at her temples and cheeks. Diana barely recognised herself when she looked in the mirror. Dressed in a violet silk gown which had been one of Valentina's parting gifts, she actually looked the part of a duchess, she thought. Good enough not to shame Will, at least, though she knew she would need to begin ordering clothing for a new wardrobe immediately.

One of the maids guided her to the Egyptian Room, where Julianne was already holding court to several other ladies. Regina and Rebecca sat at the side of the room, hands folded primly in their laps, obviously there to observe and learn how ladies should comport themselves. Both of them looked exceptionally bored, and Diana immediately resolved to find some way for them to escape sooner rather than later.

Julianne greeted her cordially, and introduced her to the ladies: Lady Altmere, Lady Claire Court, and Lady Susan Macfarlane, who seemed to be a particular friend of Julianne's. All three were of an age with Julianne, around forty or so by Diana's estimate, and all very handsome and superbly attired in the finest of fashions. They eyed her intently, and Diana knew they were assessing everything about her, from her words to her clothing, and judging her.

She allowed them to quiz her for a half-hour or so, describing her travels in Italy - and making sure she mentioned her aunt the Marchioness of Glenkellie as frequently as she could manage - before carefully redirecting the topic onto the next season's fashions and moving over to sit with Regina and Rebecca.

"And how are the two of you this fine morning?" she asked.

"I wish it was fine," Rebecca muttered, "we could have gone riding, but Mother said it's too foggy and grey."

It did not take much pressing to discover that horse-riding was one of Rebecca's great passions. Diana admitted to not being a great rider, but she liked horses very much nevertheless.

"We did not own horses until Papa inherited the earldom, but Mother was determined we should have all the skills of young ladies, including the ability to ride. I confess I enjoy drawing horses more than riding them, though."

"You draw?" It was Regina's turn to brighten. "And paint?"

"Indeed. And you? Watercolours or oils?"

"Oh, watercolours - though I should very much like the opportunity to try oils."

"I said very much the same thing to your brother," Diana confided, "and he at once promised to buy me all the paints and canvas I could wish, and hire an instructor to teach me the techniques. I am sure I could convince him you should share in the bounty, if you would like?"

Regina's expression was pure delight.

"You seem to have won over my daughters," Julianne murmured to Diana as they left the Egyptian Room a couple of hours later, proceeding to yet another room Diana had not yet seen, where a light luncheon was to be served.

"They are charming young women and a credit to you," Diana replied.

"Hm." Julianne gave her a thoughtful glance. "You're not what I expected," she said forthrightly. "I wrote you off as an empty-headed ninny after that fainting episode. But Will would never have married you if you were, no matter how serious the compromise..."

"There was no compromise!" Diana blushed scarlet.

"It is a love match, then?" Julianne didn't look doubtful. Just surprised. "I would not have thought Will the type to fall in love," she admitted. "Certainly in London, he was extremely pragmatic when I presented a list of potential brides for him to consider."

Diana really didn't know what to say to that. "Perhaps he made an effort to appear so, to please you," she suggested finally, "but he also literally fled the country when he could not bring himself to *pragmatically* select one of your candidates, marry, and step into his father's shoes."

"You may well be correct in that." Julianne inclined her head, gave Diana another thoughtful look, and then gestured to the head of the table.

Diana balked. "I'm not ready to step into your shoes," she said, trying to smile politely.

"I'm afraid you should have thought of that before you married Will and arrived here as the Duchess," Julianne returned, dust-dry. "Start as you mean to go on, Diana. There are some very influential ladies here watching how you handle yourself. If I had any inkling Will might return with a bride, I would have spared you this, but we none of us have a choice now. You *are* the Duchess, and you need to start acting like it immediately."

That set Diana back on her heels. She took a deep breath, pressing her hands to her stomach, where a host of butterflies had suddenly taken up residence.

"I'm here for you."

She blinked at Julianne, startled.

"It is hardly in my best interest to see you fall on your face," Julianne pointed out dryly. "Regina will be having her come-out soon enough, and I want to fire her off well."

And if Diana was a disaster as the duchess, Regina and later Rebecca's chances could be severely affected, she understood. She nodded.

"We'll have time for me to help you. To familiarise yourself with all the things you will need to know. Unfortunately," Julianne gave her a wry little smile, "you have arrived at a very awkward moment, and you are going to have to smile and manage as best you can until this house party is over."

Diana let out the breath. "I don't want to let Will down. Or you. I'll do my best."

Julianne's smile was surprisingly warm. "That's all we can ask for." Her fingers touched under Diana's elbow, gently guiding. "Now, Duchess. Take your seat."

Will and several other gentlemen arrived to join them just as the ladies had all taken their seats. Will, of course, had to sit at the far end of the long table to Diana; she eyed him covertly, wishing he was by her side with his calmly reassuring presence. He looked directly at her, smiled, and then lifted his glass to her in a silent toast. She smiled back, and for a moment it was as though the rest of the room faded away and it was just the two of them.

And then Lady Susan Macfarlane, seated on her left, leaned forward and asked a question about her travels in Italy, and Diana was yanked sharply back to reality. Tearing her gaze from Will, she turned her attention to the influential lady.

I can do this.

Luncheon passed with no major blunders - at least so far as Diana could tell - and afterwards, she braced herself to return to the salon with the ladies and some more grilling from the ladies. However, Will intercepted her just outside the dining room, catching her hand in his, pressing a finger to his lips to urge her to stay quiet, and tugging gently.

Grinning, she followed him unquestioningly through a discreetly placed door in the wainscoting which proved to lead into what was obviously the servants' part of the house; the hallway was much darker and narrower.

“Where are we going?” Diana whispered as the door closed behind them.

“Running away.” Will's expression was conspiratorial. “I thought I detected a distinct look of desperation you shot me in there. Or was that not a plea to be saved?”

“It was definitely a plea to be saved.” She squeezed his hand. “Thank you. Julianne has been very kind and your sisters are lovely, but I was feeling rather like a, a piece of art on sale in a gallery. Being critically examined, everyone discussing whether it is quite worth the price being asked.”

“You're worth every penny, my incomparable, Divine Duchess.” He pulled her into his arms for a kiss, and she melted against him.

“While I would not be entirely averse to just hiding out in your suite,” she smiled up at him when he lifted his head, “I think you had something else in mind?”

“Indeed. It is a fine afternoon and I should like to show you one of my favourite places in the whole world.” He claimed her hand again and led her along the passageway, ending in a small mud room where cloaks hung on hooks and boots were lined up on shelves.

Diana found a pair of boots to fit her feet and chose a cloak from a peg, and they slipped out of the side door, cutting across the back of the magnificent manor house towards the stable yard.

“The stables?” Diana asked, half-resigned to it. She knew Will was fond of horses, had several times mentioned the fine stable of hunters and racers he maintained.

“No,” he kept walking, her hand clasped securely in his, and they passed by the stables, proceeding along a track into woodland which rose up around them, thick trees quickly swallowing them up.

Thin autumn sunlight trickled through the canopy of oaks and beeches, fallen leaves a thick carpet of red and gold crunching under their feet as they walked. A tawny flash among the thick trunks made Diana twitch, and then gasp as the doe dashed across the path in front of them before vanishing again.

"I often see them here," Will said softly. "There's a big stag who's been shedding his antlers in a clearing just up ahead for the last few years. Nine prongs on them last year. And no, I'm not about to let anyone shoot him. He's the patriarch of the herd."

CHAPTER TWENTY-SIX

THE CLEARING SOON CAME into view, and along with it a small stone building, constructed of the same pale grey stone as the Priory.

"A cottage?" Diana queried. "Who lives here, Will?"

"Nobody. It's the duke's private retreat." He grinned at her expression. "My grandfather had it built, and my father used it regularly. I was the only person who was ever allowed to interrupt him here."

Diana followed him in as he pushed the door open, looking around to find that the cottage was really only a single room - a comfortably furnished one, to be sure, with a flickering fire in the grate, a large soft-looking couch, wingback armchairs, shelves and shelves of books, a writing desk, and a dresser against one wall with decanters lined up on it, along with a bowl of fruit and some covered dishes.

"An elegant little retreat," she murmured, unable to resist going to look under the covers and finding crusty bread rolls with butter and jam, and two different kinds of cakes. "Were there always cakes here when you were a child?" She cast him an amused glance over her shoulder. "I can see why you like the place so much, if so."

"There were." Casting himself into one of the wing chairs, Will smiled reminiscently. "Though Father used to insist I eat an apple first, and I was not allowed to come here until my tutor was happy with the work I had done on my lessons for the day, besides."

"Were you a diligent student?"

"Exceptionally, with the lure of being permitted to come here!"

Diana moved across to the bookshelves and began to peruse titles, finding an eclectic mixture of novels and reference titles. The books would still reflect his father's tastes rather than his own, she thought, and then something else occurred to her.

"Have you been here since your father passed?" she asked softly.

"Once." He was staring into the fire. "I couldn't bear to be here alone. It was too quiet."

Which was why he had brought her here, Diana knew instantly. Crossing to him, she turned sideways and plopped herself down on his lap, looping her arms around his neck, smiling at his startled expression. "Thank you for bringing me here," she said sincerely. "I promise I won't intrude without your invitation, but I hope you will one day soon be able to follow your father's example and bring your sons here for clandestine cakes. And perhaps your daughters, too? In fact, I see no reason why you should not practice now. Rebecca is certainly still young enough to enjoy an adventure with her brother, perhaps Regina too, and they will be married and gone away soon enough. Enjoy their company while you have it."

Will looked struck by the idea. "I asked Papa once why he didn't invite Regina here... Rebecca would have been too young. He never did answer me. I know he loved them, but they were daughters. I don't think he believed them to be worthy of his time, really."

Diana gave him raised eyebrows.

"I will do better by *our* daughters," Will said hastily, "and I shall seek to remedy some of his errors with my sisters, while they yet reside beneath my roof."

"Good, because they are both delightful girls. You shall not regret spending time with them."

"Are you missing Clarissa?" Will asked perceptively when she snuggled down into his arms, resting her cheek against his shoulder.

"A little," Diana admitted. "We have never been separated for more than a few hours in the whole of our lives. I am used to telling her everything."

"You know you can tell *me* everything, my love."

"I know." She reached up to press a kiss on his cheek. "But I am still getting used to the idea that you are to be my principal confidant now. And there are some things which are just... not things I could ever discuss with a man, not even you, my dearest! Perhaps Regina and I may become close. Even Julianne. She was very kind earlier, actually."

"She puts on a fearsome front, but she truly has a heart of gold. She has always treated me as her own son."

"Oh, it's clear she is very fond of you. She wants the best for you." Diana grimaced slightly. "I don't think she's convinced that's me, but she's decided she will try to make a silk purse out of this sow's ear."

"A sow's ear!" he protested loudly. "Never again compare yourself to any part of a pig, my divine duchess!"

She laughed, making no protest as he continued to insist that she was already perfect, just as she was. Diana knew she was far from perfect. But she also knew that Will believed in her, and that gave her confidence to think that perhaps, one day... she might just be the duchess he already thought she was.

Nestling deeper into his embrace, she sighed in utter contentment. She could never have imagined, when she fainted at his feet on their first meeting, that she might end up not only married to Will but blissfully happy about it.

Yes, there would be obstacles they would have to overcome. Diana's mother was likely to cause a great deal of fuss and bother and quite possibly cause her daughter no little embarrassment as she crowed about Diana's triumph in catching a duke. There were plenty of members of the Ton who might look down their noses at her, and a few young bucks like Lord Amberle who would still snigger and call her the Fainting Flower.

Time, however, had a tendency to make such things fade away, and Diana was wise enough to know that the title of *duchess* would cause all but the most foolish to ensure any whispers of opposition never reached her ears, or Will's. Especially if she did her duty to the dukedom and produced an heir... and though it was early days yet, she already had hopes in that direction.

A secret smile on her lips, she rubbed her cheek against Will's shoulder, closing her eyes.

At least until he said; "So, about those cakes..."

Laughing, she got up, going back to the dresser to collect the plate. "So long as you promise to share," she said, holding it tantalisingly just out of his reach.

"Of course!" Will looked injured. "I shall even give you first choice," he declared magnanimously.

There was more of each type of cake than either of them could possibly eat, so his offer was nonsensical, but Diana still laughed and feigned delight, selecting one of the dainties before passing the plate over. She watched fondly as Will tucked in, imagining him in future years here with their children, sneaking them cakes and ruining their dinner. He would be the despair of their tutors and governesses, for who could reprimand a duke?

"What are you giggling about?" Will asked.

"Just thinking about the future," Diana replied honestly.

"I like that it apparently amuses you so. You are coming around to the view that being a duchess won't be so bad?"

"Being *a* duchess would be awful, I suspect. Being *your* duchess? The most wonderful thing in the world."

And she meant it. She could never have imagined, after their disastrous first encounter, that a scant year later she would be both married to Will and deeply in love with him, but here they were, and Will was looking at her with his heart in his eyes.

There would still be trials to come, Diana knew. But she and Will would face them together; he would manage her embarrassing family, probably by putting on his imperiously ducal attitude and intimidating her mother into silence, and Diana would learn everything she could about being the perfect duchess from Julianne. When Clarissa returned to England, Diana would be ensconced at the peak of London society, able to help her sister avoid their mother's machinations and marry where she chose, rather than being pressured into a match.

"You look pensive, my love." Finished with the cakes, Will leaned over to kiss her. "Does something trouble you?"

"No, I'm only thinking of Clarissa again." Putting her arms about his neck, Diana kissed him back. "But I'm sure you can make me forget about everything outside of this cottage, beloved."

"I shall certainly try, my darling!" Laughing, he scooped her up in his arms and carried her to the chaise. "My divine duchess," he whispered against her throat, and she did indeed forget about everything outside the cottage, for quite some time.

~ The End ~

Follow Clarissa's story in *A Captain For Clarissa*, Book 4 in the Blushing Brides series!

Author Notes - Historical Accuracy and a Mea Culpa

The Grotte di Catullo wasn't excavated fully until later in the 19th century than this story takes place, but considering the height of the walls, at least some part of it must have been visible across Lake Garda as far as Bardolino - where the Castello Bardolino is entirely my own creation, I'm afraid. I hope you will forgive my artistic licence in having my party explore the Roman ruins, a must-see if you ever get to visit Lake Garda.

Most of the sites in Italy which Diana visits are still accessible today, including the stunning church of San Giovanni Elemosinario, which is just as hidden away and difficult to find as I described. If you ever get the chance to visit Venice, do make the time to go and see it. I promise, it's worth the effort of finding it!

The Vasari Corridor (made even more famous by being featured in Dan Brown's *Inferno*) has just reopened to the public after a years-long closure for renovation. Don't miss it if you visit Florence! And though the goldsmiths' shops are still there on the Ponte Vecchio, I really don't recommend making any purchases there - they're insanely overpriced!

I hope you enjoyed reading Will and Diana's story as much as I enjoyed writing it!

A Captain for Clarissa

CATHERINE BILSON

CONTENTS

CHAPTER ONE

THE SUN WAS SETTING over Athens, casting a golden glow over the ancient ruins high above the bustling city. The Parthenon rose from the Acropolis like a crown, looking down on the busy streets below, now settling into their evening routine. Merchants called out to passersby, hawking their wares. Horses and carts rolled through the narrow cobbled streets, dodging children playing games, while bright-clad women bartered for fresh produce from market stalls.

Lady Clarissa Creighton wound her way through the throng, her adventurous spirit invigorated by the lively city. Her eyes sparkled with curiosity at the rich array of history and culture surrounding her. The hot sun had bleached her brown hair pale gold; it hung loose around her shoulders, having slipped free of the simple ribbon which was all she'd used to tie it back. She'd long ago refused to wear a bonnet, preferring to feel the sun's warmth on her face, much to the horror of the more proper elements of the ton who decried her 'unladylike' golden tan and the freckles scattered across her nose and cheekbones.

"Do slow down, dear!" a voice called, breaking into Clarissa's reverie. Turning, she spotted Helena, Dowager Marchioness Glenkellie, and her sister, the Contessa Ginori. The two elderly ladies were the picture of eccentric aristocratic style, close as sisters despite the decades they'd spent separated when Helena went to Scotland to marry. Their laughter rang like silver bells as they approached.

"Isn't it beautiful?" Helena said, pointing towards the Parthenon. Then she gave Clarissa a mischievous smile. "Of course, not so beautiful as the eligible bachelors we've found for you, my dear."

"Indeed," the Contessa agreed, her accent still carrying a hint of Italian even after almost seventy years living in England. "We've made certain your stay in Athens will be most exciting - both culturally and romantically!"

Clarissa stifled a groan, feeling her adventurous soul wilt somewhat at the thought of their meddling. Still, she could never quite bring herself to be annoyed by the pair's matchmaking efforts. They had taken her under their wing after meeting her in Italy last year, and invited her to join them in Greece - a tour she would never have been able to afford otherwise.

“Thank you for your efforts,” she said diplomatically, attempting to keep any trace of sarcasm out of her tone. “I look forward to making the acquaintance of these gentlemen you speak of.”

“That’s the spirit!” Helena clapped her hands together in delight. “You won’t be disappointed, I assure you, dear.”

“Indeed.” The Contessa nodded firmly. “We’ve arranged a small party at our hotel this evening, where you’ll meet them. Only the best suitors have been chosen, naturally.”

As the three women continued their exploration of Athens, Clarissa could only chuckle at the elderly sisters’ matchmaking efforts. She’d gotten very used to them by now, having spent the past year avoiding the many suitors they sought to thrust upon her in Italy. For the moment, though, she was more than happy to immerse herself in the rich history and culture around her, her adventurous soul undaunted by her friends’ well-meaning interference.

The evening party was in full swing, the large ballroom of the grand Athenian hotel alive with colour and movement. The scent of flowers filled the air, mingling with the flickering light of dozens of candles casting dancing shadows on the walls. Musicians played a lively waltz, and Clarissa found herself tapping her foot to the beat of the music.

Helena and the Contessa, however, were both too busy scanning the room for eligible bachelors to notice. Frequently they would lean their heads together to whisper excitedly, nodding towards one gentleman or another.

“There he is!” Helena suddenly exclaimed, pointing towards a tall young man with an immaculately waxed mustache and perfectly oiled hair. She caught Clarissa’s arm, propelling her towards the poor unsuspecting gentleman. “Clarissa, let me introduce you to Mr Montgomery. He comes from a most respectable family, and is heir to a vast estate in Hampshire.” Her voice dropped to what she probably thought was a whisper, but was actually loud enough to be heard by everyone within earshot!

“Charmed, I’m sure,” Clarissa replied through gritted teeth, forcing a smile as she curtseyed before the startled Mr Montgomery. His gaze lingered on her sun-bleached hair and freckled face, and she could almost hear his disapproving thoughts.

"Miss Creighton," he said finally, bowing stiffly in return. As they exchanged pleasantries, Clarissa stifled a yawn behind her fan, wishing she was anywhere other than here. Somewhere like the Parthenon, perhaps, or any number of interesting ruins she had not yet had the opportunity to explore...

"Delightful! Simply delightful!" the Contessa declared, taking Clarissa's arm and steering her away from Mr Montgomery. "Now, allow me to present Mr Abernathy, a dashing naval captain."

Before Clarissa could protest, she was face to face with Captain Abernathy, who looked to be at least twice her age.

"Miss Creighton," Captain Abernathy growled, inclining his head slightly. Stifling a sigh, Clarissa prepared herself for another tedious conversation about the weather or ships.

"Clarissa, my dear!" Helena fortunately saved her a few minutes later, appearing at her side again. "There is someone you simply must meet!"

Another one? Clarissa groaned inwardly, though she forced a polite smile as she turned around. Then her heart skipped a beat.

Edward Dalton stood before her, a slow smile spreading across his handsome face which made her pulse quicken. Edward! She had known him since childhood—her father had handled legal matters for the Daltons for many years prior to inheriting his earldom—and although it had been many years since she'd seen him last, his familiar presence was a welcome relief amidst a sea of new faces.

"Mr Dalton!" she gasped, momentarily forgetting her earlier irritation with matchmakers in general. "What a surprise to see you here in Athens."

"Miss Creighton... but no, of course you are Lady Clarissa now," he said warmly, taking her hand and raising it to his lips. His kiss on her knuckles was gentle, but his touch sent a frisson of awareness up her spine. "The pleasure is all mine. I must say, you have grown even more beautiful since I saw you last."

"Flatterer," she accused, though her lips curved into a genuine smile for the first time that evening. Falling into easy conversation with Edward, she couldn't help but notice the approving looks exchanged between Helena and the Contessa. They appeared very pleased with the apparent result of their matchmaking efforts.

"Would you care to dance, Lady Clarissa?" Edward asked, holding out his hand with a flourish. There was a glint of mischief in his eye, and Clarissa hesitated only a fraction of a second before placing her hand in his.

"Very well, Mr Dalton," she said primly, ignoring the little thrill which went through her as his warm, strong fingers closed around hers.

"Tell me, Clarissa," Edward said quietly, drawing her closer as the music swelled around them, "what brings you to Athens? I never expected to see you here."

"Nor did I expect to see you," she admitted, her eyes dropping to his strong jawline. "I was travelling with my aunt and uncle on their honeymoon in Italy. My aunt had twins a few months ago, though, so they decided to remain in Florence until the children are a little older. However, Lady Glenkellie and Contessa Ginori kindly invited me to join their party for this excursion to Greece."

"Indeed?" He sounded surprised. "Without a male family member to chaperone? You always did have an adventurous spirit." The lightness of his tone did not quite disguise the slight edge to his words, and Clarissa winced.

"Needs must when the Devil drives," she replied, attempting a smile. "Besides, I couldn't resist the opportunity to travel to such a fascinating city."

"No, I don't suppose you could." Edward's smile was knowing. "Athens has much to offer those who are willing to take chances."

They whirled away again, and Clarissa found herself reflecting on Edward's sudden interest in her. It was not at all unwelcome; indeed, she felt rather flattered by it. Yet there was a slight edge to his compliments, a darkness beneath them she couldn't quite put her finger on. She shook the thought away, determined not to let it ruin her enjoyment of the moment.

"Mr Dalton," she said after a moment, trying to keep her voice from shaking, "it is a surprise to see you so far from home. What brings you to Greece?"

"Ah, Lady Clarissa," he said mysteriously, and his eyes darkened for a moment before brightening again, "let us just say that life does have its twists and turns."

The music drew to an end, and they stepped apart, each bowing to the other. Clarissa found herself considering Edward's words and wondering what secrets he might be hiding. For now, though, she would allow him to pay her court... even if that nasty little voice in the back of her head kept asking why his attention made her feel a little like a mouse being eyed by a cat.

Helena and the Contessa exchanged gleeful glances as they watched Edward and Clarissa chatting animatedly. They had both taken a shine to Mr. Dalton, and agreed that he would make a most eligible suitor for Clarissa's hand. Chattering excitedly, they whispered together of grand weddings, neither of them aware of Clarissa's secret anxiety.

"You see, sister," Helena said with a satisfied smile, "I told you our matchmaking efforts would be successful. Look at them! Like they've known each other all their lives."

"Indeed," the Contessa agreed, her eyes sparkling with pleasure. "And what a handsome couple they make! I always knew my Clarissa would capture the heart of some dashing man of the world, and Mr. Dalton certainly fits the bill. Her parents will be overjoyed!"

Despite her misgivings, Clarissa found herself enjoying Edward's company more and more as the evening wore on. He was an excellent conversationalist, full of tales of his travels, as well as being able to speak knowledgeably about politics, literature, art and many other subjects. It was hard to maintain a wary distance in the face of such wit and charm.

"Tell me, Lady Clarissa," Edward said, leaning in close as they strolled together in the moonlit gardens, "have you ever considered writing? Your thoughts are so very insightful, I believe many would be interested in hearing your views."

She blushed at the compliment, her heart fluttering despite her conviction that he must have ulterior motives. "I... I have tried my hand at it, but no one has been interested in reading my scribblings before." She glanced up at him through her lashes; he was regarding her as though she were the most fascinating creature he had ever met.

"Never underestimate the power of your words," he said seriously. "You have a unique viewpoint which deserves to be shared."

"Thank you, Mr. Dalton," she murmured, cheeks pink with pleasure, though she could not quite shake the feeling that Edward Dalton was concealing another side of himself from her.

In the days following, it seemed as though Edward were everywhere Clarissa turned. Whether by accident or design, they kept running into one another as they toured the bustling Athenian markets and marvelled at the ancient ruins. Each encounter left Clarissa more intrigued and yet more uneasy, her initial caution eroded by his constant attentions.

Standing beside him at the Acropolis, gazing out over the city below, Clarissa found herself questioning her own instincts. Perhaps, she thought, she had misjudged him. Perhaps his intentions were entirely honourable after all, and her suspicions unfounded.

"Lady Clarissa," Edward said softly, his voice barely audible over the sound of the wind, "I hope you do not find my attentions intrusive. It is merely that... well, I cannot seem to help myself. Your vivacious spirit and sharp mind draw me like a moth to a flame."

"Mr. Dalton," she replied hesitantly, her heart torn between hope and uncertainty, "I must admit I enjoy your company, unexpected though it is. But I cannot help wondering why, after all these years, we should meet again in such an unlikely place."

"Perhaps," he suggested with a ghost of a smile, "fate has brought us together once more, two kindred souls who would otherwise never have had a chance of reuniting."

Clarissa smiled at the idea. Perhaps it was foolish to believe in fate, but here, where once the gods themselves were said to have walked among mortals, she could almost believe it.

She quite recognised that she *wanted* to believe. Wanted to believe that a worldly, intelligent man like Edward Dalton truly thought her worthy of his attention. For all the eager suitors who had been swarming around her ever since her sister married a duke, not one of them had ever treated Clarissa as though she had a brain in her head, and she was thoroughly weary of it. Edward's respect for her intellect and willingness to listen to her opinions were different, and despite the wariness she could not quite seem to shake, his attentions were beginning to have an effect on her emotions.

Amidst the bustling markets of Athens, Clarissa paused to admire a stall adorned with vibrant silks and intricate lacework.

"Clarissa," Edward's voice broke into her thoughts, "I must say, that shade of blue would complement your eyes exquisitely."

"Thank you, Mr. Dalton," she replied, absently, her mind still lingering on her aunt as she looked at a beautiful christening gown. The birth of the twins in Florence had been an unexpected blessing, but it had also left Clarissa with a new sense of responsibility. She could not burden her aunt with her presence during such a delicate time, so she had ventured to Athens, eager to explore its rich history and culture.

"Are you well, Clarissa?" Edward asked, concern etching his handsome features as he noted her distant expression.

"Quite well, thank you," she assured him, forcing a smile. "I was merely thinking of my Aunt Marianne and the recent additions to the family."

"Ah, yes, the joyous arrival of twins," Edward mused, his eyes flickering with an unreadable emotion. "Such a delightful surprise for all involved, I'm sure."

"Indeed," Clarissa agreed, though her heart ached at the thought of missing the precious moments with her new cousins.

As they continued their stroll through the market, Clarissa found herself observing Edward more closely. His charm and good looks were undeniable, but there was something lurking beneath the surface that she couldn't quite put her finger on. An undercurrent of secrecy that unsettled her.

"Clarissa," Edward began, clearing his throat. "I have been meaning to inquire about your father's new estate at Creighton Hall. It has been quite some time since I last visited home, and I do miss the beauty of the English countryside."

"Ah, yes, Creighton Hall is indeed a lovely place," Clarissa reminisced, her eyes clouding over with nostalgia. "I must confess, though, that my heart has always yearned for more… for adventure and the freedom to explore the world beyond our borders."

"Spoken like a true explorer," Edward praised. "You are indeed a rare gem."

"Thank you," she replied, blushing despite her lingering suspicions.

As they reached the outskirts of the market, Clarissa noticed a man approaching Edward, his face obscured by the shadow of his wide-brimmed hat. Without a word, he handed Edward a small, folded note before disappearing into the throng of people.

"Forgive me," Edward said quietly, slipping the missive from his mysterious correspondent into his coat pocket. "A matter of business."

"Of course." Clarissa nodded, but her curiosity was piqued by the odd encounter and the fact that Edward had apparently been waiting for someone to meet him here in the middle of Athens. She wanted to believe he was a kind man with no evil intentions toward her or anyone else, but there were too many secrets surrounding him.

"Shall we continue our exploration of Athens?" Edward asked, offering his arm with a charming smile that did not quite dispel Clarissa's concerns.

"Yes," she said finally, placing her hand on his arm as they walked further into the old city, her mood dampened by unanswered questions.

Rounding a corner, they came across several young local children playing some sort of tag game, their laughter infectious. Within moments, Clarissa found herself joining in, helping one of the smaller girls escape from 'it,' and chuckling with delight at the little girl's thanks. Glancing over at Edward, she saw him watching her with a wistful smile and wondered again what he was hiding.

"Mr. Dalton…" she began hesitantly. "I know we have only recently renewed our acquaintance, but I cannot shake the feeling that it is not mere chance that you are here. Is there something you are not telling me?"

Edward's smile faded for a moment before he gathered himself. "Clarissa, you always were far more perceptive than most people give you credit for. But I assure you, my reasons for being present in Athens are completely innocent." He smiled charmingly. "A lover of history and culture such as myself could hardly resist visiting such an ancient city, after all."

"I suppose not." Clarissa sighed, his charm working its magic on her suspicions. For now, at least, she would set her questions aside. But she knew she would not be able to ignore them forever.

"Come," Edward said, offering his arm again. "There is so much more of this wondrous city to see."

Feeling a little lighter of heart, Clarissa took his invitation to explore, ready to enjoy the day with an old friend. Though doubts still lingered in her mind, she decided to allow the sunny streets of Athens to chase away her fears - at least for now.

CHAPTER TWO

THE SETTING SUN CAST long shadows on the cobblestone street where Edward Dalton stood, feeling the other man's eyes upon him. An English lord of no more than three and twenty years, the young man's look was haughty and impatient, as if he expected to be obeyed instantly.

"Mr. Dalton," the young lord said with obvious disdain, "you have put me off paying your debts for too long. You lost heavily at cards, and I hold your IOUs."

Edward shifted uncomfortably, feeling a trickle of sweat run down the back of his neck. He could not immediately think of what to say; he had hoped to avoid this meeting altogether but found himself cornered in an alleyway by two armed men and forced to walk several miles in the heat of the day to present himself before his creditor. "I assure you, my lord, I will have the money soon enough," he said finally, attempting to sound confident.

"Indeed?" The lord raised one eyebrow. "And how do you intend to come up with such a sum?"

"Well, I..." Edward looked around nervously, then lowered his voice. "I am in pursuit of an heiress," he confessed. "A lovely young lady with a very large dowry. I believe I shall offer for her hand within the week."

The sun dipped lower, casting an orange glow over Athens. The other man considered his words, eyes narrowing with suspicion. "And why should I believe you, Mr. Dalton? You are a man known for making grand promises and leaving your creditors unpaid. Your presence in Greece tells the story of how you had to flee England because your debts grew too great."

Edward's heart pounded in his chest, but he forced himself to smile and appear calm. "I understand your reticence," he said, putting on his most sincere expression. "But this time is different, I assure you. This young lady is the daughter of a rich earl, her sister married to a duke. Her family is both influential and wealthy beyond belief. I am an old family friend, and I believe she already has some small tendre for me."

He watched the other man's face for any sign that he'd convinced him. Finally, the young lord sighed, looking resigned. "Very well," he said. "You have one week to provide proof of this engagement, Mr. Dalton. If you cannot, I will tell everyone I see that you are unreliable and untrustworthy."

Swallowing hard against the lump in his throat, Edward nodded, smiling weakly. "Of course, my lord. I will not disappoint you."

As the lord turned and walked away, Edward stood alone on the cobbled streets, the last rays of sunlight fading away behind him. The weight of his lies stole the breath from his chest, but he could see no other way ahead. Desperation drove him now; Edward Dalton was a man on the edge of ruin or redemption. Only time would tell which way he fell.

As soon as the young nobleman was out of sight, another man emerged from the shadows. Edward's heart gave a sickening lurch when he saw the Greek money-lender, his gaze fixed on Edward with a cold intensity that made him shiver.

"Mr Dalton," the man said in heavily accented English, his voice low and menacing. "I hear you speak of dowries and future wealth. I want my money now. Your promises mean nothing to me."

Edward struggled for composure, though his heart was pounding and sweat prickled his forehead. He knew better than most that this was a man not to be trifled with, and though he had been patient up until now, Edward could sense his patience was running out.

"Please, sir," he began, cursing himself when his voice shook despite all his efforts to sound confident. "I swear to you, once I marry Lady Clarissa her dowry will be more than enough to pay my debts to you and everyone else! You have my word."

The moneylender sneered in unconcealed contempt. "Your word is worth less than nothing. And how do you plan to get your hands on her money? Travel back to England and never return here, forgetting your debt to me?" He shook his head slowly. "No, Mr Dalton. I want my money now."

Panic tightened Edward's throat. Desperately, he searched for some way to mollify the dangerous man standing before him - and then an idea came, so repulsive it made him feel physically ill even to contemplate. But if it would save him...

"Perhaps there is another way," he said hesitantly, forcing himself to meet the moneylender's eye. "Lady Clarissa is the daughter of a wealthy earl, and her sister is married to a duke. If something were to happen to her..." He swallowed hard. "She might be worth more in ransom than in dowry."

He could hardly believe what he'd just suggested, but it seemed to have the desired effect. The moneylender's eyes narrowed, and for a moment Edward dared to hope his desperate gambit might work.

"Go on," the man said, a dark gleam in his eye.

"Her family would pay anything to see her safely returned," Edward said, although his voice was barely above a whisper. "And if you were to deliver her..."

His implication hung in the air between them. The moneylender was silent, his eyes fixed intently on Edward's face.

A trickle of cold sweat ran down Edward's spine as he awaited the Greek moneylender's decision. The air felt heavy, pregnant with a sense of impending doom.

"Is she pretty?" the moneylender asked at last, breaking the tension.

"Wh-what?" Edward stammered, caught off guard by the question.

"Lady Clarissa," the man said impatiently. "The English girl you are putting forward as collateral. Is she pretty?"

Baffled, Edward hesitated. Why did it matter whether Clarissa was attractive or not? But he dared not refuse to answer. "Yes," he admitted reluctantly. "She is."

"Good." The moneylender smiled, a chilling expression that sent a shiver down Edward's spine. "Then I find your offer acceptable. But remember this, Mr Dalton," he leaned in close, his breath hot on Edward's ear, "if you betray me, you will live to regret it."

With that dire warning, he turned and disappeared into the darkness, leaving Edward to bear alone the weight of his terrible choice. He felt as if he were standing on the edge of a precipice, legs shaking and ready to collapse beneath him. What had he done? Desperate to avoid bankruptcy, he had delivered Clarissa - sweet, innocent Clarissa, who trusted him implicitly - into the hands of an unscrupulous stranger.

Sinking down onto a nearby bench, Edward buried his head in his hands. The cold stone seeped through his britches, but he barely noticed. Wrapping his arms around himself, he tried to still the shivers that ran through his body. It felt as though the darkness that had swallowed the moneylender was closing in on him now, drowning him in guilt and despair.

"God help me," he whispered brokenly. "What have I done?"

The full enormity of what he had just done crashed over him, and Edward doubled up, wrapping his arms around his ribs as fear gripped his heart. He had delivered Clarissa into the hands of the unscrupulous moneylender, ruined her reputation, almost certainly condemned her to death... all to save himself from financial ruin. And now, there was no going back. The decision was made, and all Edward could do now was wait for the consequences to play out.

It was the middle of the night, the hotel cloaked in heavy silence. Flickering light from the lantern cast eerie shadows on the walls as the Greek moneylender led a party of men through the darkened hallways. With every step they took, their looming presence grew more threatening, like a noose tightening around the necks of the unsuspecting guests slumbering behind closed doors.

When they reached Clarissa's door, the moneylender withdrew a key, the metal catching the lantern light. Inserting it into the lock, he turned it with a soft click that echoed in the quiet hallway. Slowly, carefully, he pushed the door inwards, and his men slipped inside, silent as shadows.

Clarissa lay sound asleep in her bed, unbound curls framing her face. Her breaths were slow and even, her dreams undisturbed by the menace creeping ever nearer.

She came awake suddenly, starting up in bed as rough hands grabbed her, a cloth covering her mouth before she could scream. Her eyes went wide with terror as her heart raced, and she struggled against her captors. Their grip was strong, though, and within moments she was bound hand and foot and deposited in a sack like so much livestock.

"Let me go!" she cried, but her voice was muffled by the thick fabric. She kicked out, trying to scream again, but the ropes around her wrists and ankles held her fast.

Her cries for help went unheeded as one of the men slung her over his shoulder and carried her outside. The cool night air made her shiver, but it wasn't just from the cold: she was terrified. Whatever was happening, her life had been turned upside down in an instant.

As they moved away from the house, Clarissa tried to make sense of what was happening, her thoughts racing. How had they gotten into her room? Who were these men, and what did they want with her? But the biggest question of all was: What was going to happen to her now?

As scared as she was, Clarissa knew she couldn't let herself give in to despair. If she gave up, she would be lost; the only chance she had was to keep her wits about her and to watch for an opportunity to escape. If she could get free, she'd be able to find help and get back to safety.

"Think, Clarissa, think," she whispered to herself, the words inaudible over the men's footsteps and heavy breathing. "You need to figure out a way to get out of this."

It seemed impossible, of course, but she had to consider her options. However long the odds, she refused to accept that there was no hope.

They're not Greek, she suddenly realised as the men spoke to each other. She had lived in Athens long enough to recognise the language, even if she didn't understand much of it. These men were speaking a different tongue, though, and while she couldn't identify it, she was certain it wasn't Greek.

The sound underfoot changed from boots on stone to boots on wood, and the man carrying her stopped. Clarissa thrashed against him, and received a hard hand against her leg for her trouble, making her cry out in pain. An angry voice shouted something at her, the words unintelligible but their meaning clear.

Clarissa's heart pounded as the voice continued angrily. She had no idea what was coming next, but she knew it wouldn't be good. She tried to look around, but the thick fabric of the sack over her head blocked out all light, leaving her in complete darkness.

Suddenly she was tossed onto a hard surface. A moment later, the sack was pulled from her head, and she found herself blinking against dim lamplight. After a few seconds she was able to see properly.

She was in a tiny room, she discovered, with nothing in it except the narrow bunk attached to the wall, the same one she was sitting on.

"Who are you?" she demanded, fear and anger making her voice shake. "What do you want with me?"

One of the men who had snatched her from the house sneered at her, looking her up and down in a way which made her feel deeply uncomfortable, especially given that she was still dressed only in her nightgown. She snatched the thin blanket from the bed, wrapping it around herself.

A sharp voice barked an order in that foreign tongue, and the man's eyes widened fearfully, nodding and backing out of the room.

No, the *cabin*, Clarissa realised, feeling stupid that she hadn't recognised it at once. She must be aboard a ship.

"Where are you taking me?" she asked, her voice high-pitched with fear.

Another man stepped into the doorway, tall and burly, scars marring a face which might once have been handsome. He smirked at her and spoke in heavily accented English.

"Your father," he said in a mocking tone, "will pay whatever I ask for your safe return, yes?"

Clarissa swallowed hard, forcing her voice to remain steady despite the terror coursing through her veins. "Yes," she replied, her chin held high with defiance. "He is the Earl of Creighton, and will spare no expense to ensure my safety."

The captain let out a guttural laugh, his eyes narrowing with amusement. "Do you think I would risk sailing anywhere the English Navy holds sway? Your father's gold is of no use to me if I end up with a stretched neck."

He leaned in closer, his breath hot and foul against her face. "No, my dear girl. It's the slave markets of Algiers where you shall fetch a pretty price for me."

Clarissa's stomach churned at his words, bile rising in her throat. She fought to keep her composure, her thoughts racing as she considered her next move.

"Please," she whispered, her voice barely audible. "I beg you to reconsider. There must be another way."

The captain merely smirked at her plea, clearly enjoying her fear and desperation. "Keep your begging for the market, girl," he sneered, before turning away and slamming the door in her face. A key turning in the lock cemented her new reality – a prisoner.

Don't panic. Don't panic, Clarissa tried to order herself. But as she looked around the dingy little cabin, desperate to find something useful which might aid her escape, the sound of creaking timbers and the slow sway told her that even if she could get out of the cabin, it was too late.

The ship had set sail.

CHAPTER THREE

THE SUN WAS SETTING, casting a golden-orange glow across the Mediterranean sea as Captain Rafael de Silva stood on the deck of his ship, the wind blowing through his dark brown hair as he scanned the horizon for any sign of trouble. Born into a noble Portuguese family, he'd fallen on hard times when the Peninsular War had destroyed his ancestral home. Now his vessel was part of a squadron patrolling the seas in search of pirates and corsairs preying on innocent people.

Rafael leaned on the rail, watching a school of flying fish burst out of the water. A seabird swooped down to catch one of them, scattering the remainder in all directions.

"Captain!" One of his crewmen shouted up from the main deck, startling him out of his thoughts. "Sail sighted off the starboard bow!"

Rafael turned to look in the direction indicated, squinting into the distance.

"I know that ship," he said after a moment, recognising the sail plan. "Ghazi Khadra, up to his old tricks." The other vessel was close to the North African coast, probably hoping to avoid the patrols which operated further out to sea. He barked orders to his crew, turning his ship to intercept the corsair.

"Bring us alongside that ship," he commanded. "And train your weapons on her."

"Heave to!" his bosun bellowed, repeating the order in Portuguese, English and Berber when the men aboard the other ship pretended not to understand.

Rafael grinned as the corsairs looked at each other nervously. Flying the Algerian flag, they could hardly pretend not to understand their own language.

"*Qewwed*!" one of them shouted back, with a rude gesture.

"Fire a shot across the bows," Rafael ordered. His gun crews already had the cannon loaded, and there was barely a moment's delay before the deck shook beneath his feet, the boom echoing across the water. The shot skipped across the waves, splashing down barely fifteen feet in front of the corsair's bow.

"Do you think they will return fire, Captain?" his first mate asked.

"Ghazi Khadra isn't stupid," Rafael replied, still watching the other vessel. "He knows we outgun him. I imagine he's below decks right now, hiding his ill-gotten gains and praying we don't find his secret compartments."

"Not throwing it overboard?" the first mate asked, looking at the water behind the corsair.

"No, he's too greedy. If he thinks for one moment he might be able to keep it, he won't throw it away. He does not know who captains this ship; does not know we have met before." Rafael smiled, showing his teeth. "Last time we met, I was aboard a British Navy ship, and we had to break off, let Khadra go, because a French warship hove into view. This time? This time, I'll have that thieving slave-runner in irons."

The corsair was lowering sails now in obedience to the bosun's increasingly irate shouts, and the first mate turned away from Rafael to order their own sails lowered.

In just a few minutes, the two ships lay still in the water, side by side, and Rafael stepped up to the rail.

"Where," he said, in his own language, "is Ghazi Khadra?"

He saw the shock run through the men facing him. Saw the bluster go out of them, as his men sighted down their rifles at the corsairs. There was no pretending they were honest traders if Rafael knew Ghazi Khadra was their captain.

"*Ḥadremt!*" a deep voice bellowed. "Fight, you cowards!" but the corsairs were woefully under-prepared, most of them armed only with pistols and rusty blades. A few of them rushed forward, there was a brief blast of gunfire, and five corsair bodies fell to the deck.

"Would you like to try that again?" Rafael said urbanely, "or shall we just stop wasting time, Khadra?"

The corsair captain sidled out from behind his men, his ugly, scarred face a mask of fury. "Who are you, whelp?" he hissed in bad Portuguese.

"You don't remember me?" Rafael switched smoothly to English. "How about now?"

Khadra's eyes widened, and he looked in puzzlement at Rafael's coat.

"Indeed, the last time we met, I wore the coat of the British Navy," Rafael enlightened him. "Now I sail for my own King and country. Keeping the Mediterranean clean of corsair scum."

Khadra spat on the deck. One of his men spoke to him in a low voice, gesturing to Rafael and his men, obviously trying to reason with Khadra.

"You are outnumbered and outgunned," Rafael said calmly. "Lay down your weapons and you'll live."

Weapons were clattering to the floor before Khadra opened his mouth to give the order, making the corsair captain's expression turn briefly even more murderous, before Rafael's men began crossing to his ship to secure it.

"Search him thoroughly," Rafael warned. "He's probably got more knives on him than you've got fingers. Toss every one of them overboard, secure him, and start searching the ship."

"You have no authority to detain us, or to search my ship!" Khadra blustered angrily as rough hands searched him, pulling knives from his sleeves, boots and even a thin blade from his long beard.

"The letters of instruction I'm carrying from seven different governments would seem to argue otherwise," Rafael returned blandly. "Including the Dey of Algiers, incidentally. Since that's the flag you're flying today… I do indeed have authority over you."

"We are a legal trader," Khadra attempted to claim.

Even his own men looked sideways at him, and Rafael laughed aloud. "Of course, you are. Pure as new snow fall."

"Captain!" His men were already coming up from below, beckoning to him. "We have found something you should see."

A dozen young boys and girls were the sad sight that greeted him in a small room in the ship's hold, each with an iron collar locked about their neck and chains securing them to the wall.

"Greek," the bosun said quietly as Rafael scowled at the sight. "From Athens, taken from their families in the night. Destined to be sold on the block in Algiers."

"Enough to hang Khadra, even without whatever else he's probably smuggling. Get them loose, and over to the Santa Dorotéia." Turning on his heel, Rafael climbed back up the narrow ladder to the upper deck. He paused before exiting the hatch as something on the rough wooden floorboards caught his eye—a scrap of white lace.

Stooping, Rafael picked up the scrap, rubbing it between his fingers. Very fine lace indeed, he thought, and his eyes narrowed. Turning, he looked around. A door stood open to his left.

Looking inside, he saw nothing out of the ordinary—a tiny, empty bunk with a rough blanket on it was the only furniture. The smell of an un-emptied chamber pot assaulted his nose, and he made a face, stepping back.

"Captain?" the bosun came up beside him.

"Someone was imprisoned in here." Rafael pointed at the lock on the door, a rarity on a ship. There were just two aboard his own ship, the Santa Dorotéia, and they were on his own cabin and on the liquor store cupboard. "A high-value prisoner, I think. Maybe a woman." He showed the bosun the scrap of lace. "Perhaps that was what Khadra was taking the time to hide, before showing himself."

"If she's here, we'll find her, Captain," the bosun vowed, before turning to shout orders to search the ship again.

Where would Khadra hide a woman? Rafael rubbed the scrap of lace between his fingers again. In his own quarters, he suspected, and turned his steps towards the captain's cabin.

It was all Clarissa could manage to get enough breath into her lungs to stay conscious. One moment, she was lying on the hard bunk in her prison, the next the door had been slammed open and the corsair captain had stood over her, his eyes wide with panic.

"You will not make a single sound," he vowed.

Immediately wondering if rescue might somehow be at hand, Clarissa promptly opened her mouth and screamed at the top of her lungs.

A powerful backhand across the face made her dizzy for a moment, and then a thick lump of cloth was being shoved into her mouth, the gag secured behind her head, and she was tossed over the corsair's brawny shoulder and carried out. She kicked and screamed, flailing madly; felt her nightgown catch against a splinter of wood and rip as she struggled, but the corsair did not stop. She was carried through the ship, tossed unceremoniously down and her hands and feet tied together, and then stuffed into a trunk, the lid slammed shut.

She could barely move, and barely breathe through the gag. It was utterly dark inside the trunk, and she wasn't sure if the black spots swimming in front of her eyes were in her imagination, or due to a lack of air.

A loud boom close by made her eyes widen. A cannon? Were they under fire? *Please, don't let me die tied up in a trunk!*

Silence.

The rocking of the ship eased, and she sensed they had slowed, perhaps come to a stop. Distant shouts sounded, then a brief volley of gunfire, then booted feet on timber.

Rescue? She tried to shout through the gag, but the effort made her feel dizzy.

Wait, she thought. *They'll search in here. Wait until you hear them.*

Boots clattered nearby, and she tried to scream. Tried to get any sound out at all, but could only manage the faintest of moans. She tried to kick against the side of the chest, but couldn't move more than a few inches in its cramped confines; her bare feet made no sound against the heavy wood.

The booted feet tramped away again and Clarissa couldn't help herself; she began to cry. Tears streamed down her cheeks as the boots of her potential rescuers faded away. She tried to gulp in air, but the blackness closed in around her.

Rafael looked around the cabin with a frown. There was nowhere here large enough to conceal a woman, unless... his gaze fell on the heavy sea-chest beside the bed, half-draped with blankets. Stooping, he flipped open the lid, and gaped down at the beauty within.

Sun-streaked hair tumbled around a pale, tear-stained face and a slender form that was barely half-covered by a torn nightgown trimmed with expensive white lace. Young, beautiful, blonde and well-born from the look of her, no wonder Khadra had kept this prize locked up and tried to conceal her. She would be a worth a fortune in the slave markets of Algiers.

"Where the hell did he find you?" Rafael murmured, leaning down to lift the girl out of the chest. She didn't seem to be conscious, and Rafael swore as he pulled the too-tight gag from her mouth and leaned in to check that she was still breathing. It would be just like Khadra to smother the girl by accident while trying to conceal her. He cut the bonds securing her ankles and wrists together, cursing the corsair under his breath.

The girl's chest rose and fell as she took a deeper breath, and Rafael tore his gaze away from her form, grabbing at one of the blankets to cover her more properly before backing away. Waking up to find a strange man looming over her was likely to terrify her half to death after what she'd doubtless already been through. "Captain?" he turned to find the bosun at the door.

"I found the woman." Rafael gestured to the girl on the bed.

The bosun took one glance and whistled, long and low. "No wonder Khadra tried to hide her!"

"Precisely. I don't want to frighten her any more. I'll stay here and guard her; secure all the corsair crew and get both ships under way for Valletta." They should make Malta before morning, and the Maltese government was one of the signatories to the anti-corsair agreement under which Rafael was operating. They'd take custody of the corsairs and their ship, and arrange for the return of the Greek youngsters to their homes.

What was to be done with the beautiful young woman remained to be seen.

CHAPTER FOUR

THE WORLD SEEMED TO sway gently as Clarissa slowly regained consciousness. Her eyelids fluttered open, revealing the unfamiliar surroundings of the corsair captain's cabin. She blinked, attempting to clear the fog that clouded her mind and dazed her senses. The cabin was dimly lit by a single flickering lantern which cast wavering shadows upon the wooden walls adorned with sea charts and navigational instruments.

The scent of salt and aged timber permeated the air, mingling with the faint aroma of tobacco. Clarissa felt the coarse texture of a blanket beneath her fingertips, wrapped snugly around her shoulders to ward off the chill brought by the ocean air. As her vision sharpened, she noticed a figure standing nearby, his features gradually coming into focus. Not the corsair captain, but a stranger—a tall, hawkishly dark man wearing what looked like a naval uniform, though the cut and colour weren't familiar to her. She huddled the blanket closer around her and peered at him. He was tall and ruggedly handsome, with dark hair framing a strong, sun-kissed face. His eyes were particularly striking: a captivating sea-green that seemed to hold within them the depths of the ocean itself.

The navy officer spoke, apparent concern etched on his brow. Clarissa's brow furrowed as she tried to puzzle out his words. Not Italian, a language in which she was reasonably fluent after more than a year in the country, nor Greek, nor French. She could almost grasp some of the words...

"I'm sorry," she said in English. "I don't understand."

"Rest easy, my lady," he replied in astonishingly unaccented, perfect English, his voice deep and soothing. "You are safe now."

"Thank you," she murmured, struggling to comprehend the situation fully. The memory of her swoon came flooding back, an overwhelming wave that left her feeling vulnerable and exposed.

"Who are you? What happened?"

His steady gaze seemed to offer a lifeline in the tempestuous sea of her emotions. "I am Captain Rafael de Silva, of the Portuguese ship *Santa Dorotéa*," he said calmly. "We conduct anti-corsair patrols in these waters, and have seized this ship. We will be putting in at the port of Valletta in Malta within a few hours."

"Oh." Struggling to comprehend the sudden change in circumstance, Clarissa lay very still.

"Where did Khadra take you from, and when?" Rafael prompted gently.

"Oh... Athens." She struggled to piece together the ordeal she'd been through. "Four—five days ago? I don't know. It was dark all the time in the cabin. He opened the door and gave me food, I think, twice a day." Every time she had cowered back against the wall, terrified of what he might try to do to her. The food had been meagre—stale bread, and a bottle of foul-tasting wine—but she had forced it down, determined to try and keep up her strength for the fight to come.

"I understand." Rafael nodded slowly, his eyes never leaving hers. "Can you tell me your name?" he asked.

"Clarissa Creighton," she said. "You needn't speak to me as though I'm a simpleton. I've had a nasty shock but I'm going to be fine."

A grin bloomed on his hawkish face, making him suddenly a great deal more handsome, and she returned the smile.

"I am glad to see you have your spirit still, at least. Well." He gestured about him. "We must remain aboard this nasty little vessel until we dock in Valleta in the morning. May I attempt to find you something to cover you better, and perhaps something to eat?"

"Yes," Clarissa said, realising that she was starving hungry. "Please." She pushed herself to sit up, clumsily grabbing at the blanket as it fell away.

Rafael kept his eyes averted, Clarissa noted, and despite her lingering confusion and disorientation, she sensed that she could trust this Portuguese captain with the striking sea-green eyes. For now, at least, she would place her faith in him and hope that, together, they could navigate the uncertain waters that lay ahead.

He allowed no one else to enter the cabin, stopping a man at the door and then bringing her a simple meal of bread, cheese, and a wine far better than any she'd tasted in recent days. He remained, standing at the door, until she had finished eating, and then said;

"I will stand guard outside your door until the morning. You need not fear your sleep will be troubled, and tomorrow, we will determine our course."

They entered the harbour at Valletta in the early hours of the morning, met by the authorities who were happy to take custody of the corsairs and undertake to return the Greek captives to Athens.

Rafael had left Clarissa alone to rest, secure in the captain's cabin with two of his most trusted men at the door to keep watch, but returned to ask her what she wanted to do.

"There are English families on Malta who would be glad to take you in," he began.

She immediately shook her head. "I need to get to Florence. Lady Glenkellie and Lady Ginori will have sent word there of my disappearance and my aunt will be beside herself."

Rafael nodded thoughtfully. "It might take some time to find a ship bound for Italy. I will take you myself."

"Oh... but aren't you bound elsewhere?" Clarissa hesitated to ask any more of him. She already owed him her life.

"I am master of my own destiny," he said, somewhat arrogantly. "I determine the disposition of my ship, and where she will go. I shall take you to Livorno, and thence to Florence."

"Well... thank you," she said finally.

Rafael inclined his head. "I will see if some more suitable clothing can be obtained for you before we depart Valletta," he said rather abruptly, before leaving her alone again.

Later that day, a young woman scratched at the door. "I am Ana," she said in accented English, with a smile and a little curtsy. "Captain de Silva, he hire me to be your maid. We go to Florence, yes?"

"Yes," Clarissa said with relief.

"I have dress here for you. More, on other ship. You change, and we go?"

Of course, they would be leaving the corsair ship here, Clarissa realised, and Rafael had sent Ana and the clothes so that Clarissa could look respectable while transferring to the other ship. She had realised, sometime during the dark hours of the night, that she was utterly ruined, despite having been rescued before the worst could befall her.

Her disappearance from Athens could not be explained. Lady Glenkellie and Lady Ginori would have raised a hue and cry, for which she would not fault them; they would have been in a panic at her disappearance. Reappearing again in Italy more than a week later, on a Portuguese ship, with no explanation for what had happened to her… Well, it would be a scandal of the highest order.

But for now, she pushed those thoughts aside and changed into the dress that Ana had brought her. It was a simple, modest gown of pale blue, with a high neckline and long sleeves. Clarissa pulled it on gratefully, relieved to be out of the filthy, torn nightgown she had been wearing for days.

As she emerged from the cabin, Rafael was waiting for her on the deck. He had changed into a fresh uniform, and looked every inch the dashing naval captain.

"Are you ready, my lady?" he asked, offering her his arm.

She took it, feeling a strange fluttering in her stomach. "Yes, Captain," she said, trying to keep her voice steady.

They disembarked from the corsair ship and made their way to the other ship, a sleek, modern vessel flying the Portuguese flag. The crew bustled about, preparing for departure, and Rafael only nodded to them, gesturing them to go below.

Ana confidently led the way to a large, airy cabin at the stern of the ship. "The captain's cabin, miss," she said with a nod. "He say, you safe here. Lock on door, see?" She held up a key. "We lock door and be safe."

Clarissa nodded, feeling a sense of relief wash over her. She was safe, and she was with a man she could trust. Rafael had been kind to her from the moment he had found her on the corsair ship, and she felt a sense of gratitude towards him that she could not quite put into words.

The sway and creak of the ship soon let Clarissa know that the ship had set sail, and she settled down on the low padded bench beside the windows at the stern, enjoying being able to look out at the sea after so many days confined in a small cabin. Perhaps Rafael would even let them out on deck for a breath of fresh air later; she desperately needed one, but understood that on a ship full of men it might not be possible.

From the corner of her eye, Clarissa glimpsed movement on the floor close to her feet. With a small shriek, she jerked her feet off the floor and up underneath her. "Rats!"

Ana whirled from where she was making the bed. After a glance, the maid laughed, however. "No rats here, miss. Look. Not a rat. A cat!"

Clarissa laughed at her own foolishness as the cat slunk out from its hiding spot, looking up at her from bright green eyes. A sleek black creature, the feline looked well-fed and healthy, obviously a welcome member of the crew. "Hello, puss." Leaning down, she reached out towards the cat, who sniffed at her fingers briefly but did not deign to allow her to pat it, drawing back and padding away, before slipping through a small gap cut out of one of the boards of the door.

"Well, he appears to have the run of the ship," Clarissa murmured with a regretful sigh, before returning her gaze to the window, watching as Malta's shore slowly receded into the distance.

The sun was high and Malta long gone from sight when a knock on the door heralded the captain's return. Rafael waited for Ana to open the door to admit him, offering the maid a respectful tip of his head in response to her deep curtsy, before his eyes immediately cut to Clarissa sitting beside the window.

"I thought that you might like to come up on deck and take some fresh air," he suggested, a smile coming to his lips as Clarissa immediately bounded to her feet. "Ah. The idea pleases you?"

"I've been locked up for days. Some sun on my face would be most welcome!" she declared.

Rafael nodded, and gestured for her to precede him, as the passageway would be too narrow for them to walk arm in arm. Ana trailed along behind them.

As Clarissa climbed the narrow stairway to the deck, a black shadow darted between her legs, almost making her trip. Behind her, she heard Rafael say something in Portuguese that she thought might be a curse.

"Are you all right, Miss Creighton? Fernando is careless of whose feet he gets under."

"Fernando, is that the cat's name? He is a handsome beast." Gaining the deck, Clarissa breathed in a great lungful of fresh sea air, sighing with pleasure at the wind lifting her hair off her hot neck.

"We tolerate him because he is the finest rat-catcher on the high seas." Rafael joined her, placing a hand under her elbow and guiding her to the rail, away from where men hurried about tightening ropes and adjusting sails. "Just do not be fooled into touching his belly, no matter how he may tempt you by showing it off lying on his back. It is a vicious trap and your hand will not escape unscathed. His teeth are sharp enough to penetrate even leather gloves."

Clarissa laughed. "I thank you for the warning, sir! I should surely have fallen into that trap, and likely without gloves on, for I have none."

"I am sorry we did not have the time to obtain you a more complete wardrobe," Rafael said, his tone apologetic. "Purchasing any significant quantity of elegant ladies' clothing would likely have drawn more attention than either you or I would have wished, I think."

"Oh, please believe I have no complaints!" Clarissa smoothed her hand over her skirts. "Everything about my present situation is an infinite improvement over my previous one, from the clothes and the scenery to the company."

He inclined his head in a small bow. The ship lurched just then, changing direction to tack with the wind, a vast boom swinging overhead as the sails moved, and Rafael reached out instinctively to steady Clarissa. She had already shifted her weight, however, quite comfortable and confident even as the rail they stood at swooped towards the waves.

"You are an experienced sailor, I think," he murmured. "Obviously, you sailed here from England at some point?"

"Two years ago, close enough." She looked ahead, thinking of their destination. "My aunt Marianne married, and her husband has family in Italy. They planned a honeymoon and invited my sister Diana and I to join them. Diana married last year and returned to England, but I chose to stay." She didn't add that she was in defiance of her parents' wishes at this point; her mother's letters demanding that Clarissa return to England had become both more frequent and more strident in recent months. Clarissa knew all too well what awaited her at home. At best, a London season where she would be expected to make a grand match. At worst, a suitor already chosen for her.

"And your uncle and aunt are still in Italy?"

"In Florence, yes. My aunt had twins a few months ago and was not well after their birth, and they were quite small, as I'm told twins are sometimes wont to be. They elected to remain in Florence for a while, and I was offered the opportunity to travel to Greece when two older lady relatives decided to take a trip to Athens."

"These are the ladies you spoke of?" Rafael was a good listener, Clarissa thought; quiet and watchful, his eyes never leaving her face as she spoke.

"Lady Ginori and Lady Glenkellie." Clarissa nodded. She had not yet revealed the extent of her relationship, nor the fact that she was not merely 'Miss Creighton' but she knew that she must do so now. Taking a deep breath, she said: "Lady Glenkellie is the dowager marchioness, her son is the gentleman my aunt married. Lady Ginori is her sister, the Contessa Ginori."

"Well-connected relatives," Rafael noted, but he did not look fazed.

Clarissa decided not to explain that the relationship was tenuously based on Marianne having once been married to her uncle. It mattered not to how they looked on each other; Marianne considered Clarissa her niece and no aunt could have been more well-loved. "My father is an earl," she admitted.

Rafael only nodded, and Clarissa blinked. She had expected slightly more reaction at such a revelation.

"The ladies will have turned Athens upside down in search of you," Rafael murmured, and Clarissa winced.

"Unfortunately. Yes."

His sea-green eyes were thoughtful as he looked down at her, but he asked no more questions. Only offered his arm and invited her to walk around the deck to stretch her legs for a little while. Clarissa certainly appreciated the opportunity, and gladly accepted.

They remained on deck for a half hour or so, before one of the men called something to Rafael in Portuguese.

"Regrettably, I am called to my duties," he said after replying briefly to the man. "I will escort you back to the cabin. While I have the respect of my men, it would be best if you and Ana remain in the cabin unless I am there to escort you. I will make sure you are able to come on deck twice a day at least, and we should be in Livorno no later than tomorrow evening."

Clarissa thanked him with genuine appreciation for his taking the time, and she and Ana returned to the captain's cabin. The cat Fernando accompanied them, throwing himself on the floor and rolling to show a thin white stripe on his sleek furry belly.

"Don't touch it!" Clarissa exclaimed as Ana cooed and bent to stroke the cat. "The captain warned me off touching his belly, lest he draw blood."

"Ah, a wicked demon to tempt us so," Ana chided the cat. "Be off with you."

Fernando rolled, yawned, and jumped up onto the window seat beside Clarissa. Sitting down, he wrapped his tail neatly around his front paws and gazed at her. Clarissa reached out a cautious hand and this time, the cat deigned to permit her touch, leaning into the caress as she gently stroked his glossy head.

Lost in thought, Clarissa remained where she was for hours, petting the cat and gazing out at the rolling waves, until a tap at the door heralded the arrival of a meal for them, delivered by a shy young boy who couldn't look directly at either woman.

After the awful food she had been given as a prisoner on the corsair ship, and the simple meal the night before, the food delivered now looked like a feast to Clarissa. Fresh flatbreads, thinly sliced meats and cheeses, olives and tiny tomatoes, were accompanied by grapes and peaches and a pitcher of fresh fruit juice Clarissa couldn't immediately identify the flavour of.

"*Rummien*," Ana said in her own language when Clarissa asked, then tried in Italian. "*Melograno*?"

"Pomegranate?" Clarissa thought that was.

"*Iva*, yes!" Ana nodded enthusiastically. "You like?"

"Delicious." Clarissa was starving hungry. She tried not to make a pig of herself, eating in a ladylike way and forcing herself to slow down so Ana could have her share, but when Ana wiped her fingers on a napkin and said she was done, Clarissa finished off every scrap of food on the tray.

"You should rest, miss," Ana suggested as Clarissa sipped the last of the sweet pomegranate juice, and Clarissa nodded. Her eyelids were already beginning to droop. Terror had kept her from proper sleep since being snatched from her bed in the middle of the night in Athens almost a week ago, even when Rafael stood outside her door the previous night. Now she felt warm and safe, and with her belly full, she settled into the surprisingly comfortable bed, closed her eyes, and fell into a sound, deep sleep.

CHAPTER FIVE

THE GOLDEN SUN PEEKED above the horizon, casting a warm glow on Clarissa's fair skin as she stood at the railing of the Santa Dorotéia, near-becalmed on the still Mediterranean Sea in the early morning. The gentle rocking motion of the ship lulled her into a contemplative state as she gazed out upon the shimmering sea. Her hair, bleached by the sun and tossed about by the salty breeze, framed her thoughtful expression.

"Captain de Silva," she called, turning to where Rafael stood nearby, his eyes fixed on the horizon. "May I ask you something rather personal?"

Rafael's sea-green eyes flickered with hesitation, but he nodded. "Of course, my lady."

"Tell me about your family." He interested her, this enigmatic Portuguese captain.

He hesitated, tugging at the cuff of his jacket before replying. "My father and older brothers were killed in the war. It fell upon me to become the head of the family and care for my mother and sister."

Clarissa's gaze softened with sympathy. "How terrible," she murmured. "How old were you?"

"Twelve," Rafael answered, his eyes growing distant as he spoke, his voice tinged with sorrow. "We had to abandon our home."

"Is that why you joined the English Navy?" Clarissa asked, her curiosity piqued.

"Indeed," he said, a small, sad smile playing at the corners of his mouth. "My mother found refuge in England, and I enlisted in their navy so that I might improve my prospects and provide for my family. That is also how I came to speak English so well."

"And now you have your own ship, sailing beneath the Portuguese flag?" she prompted, hoping to learn more about him.

"Once it was finally safe to return to Portugal," he replied, his voice heavy with emotion, "we found our estate in a state of near ruin. The war had taken its toll, and there was little left of the home I once knew. Plying my trade upon the sea was the only way I could raise the funds to even begin restoring our fortunes."

Clarissa's heart ached for him. "I can only imagine how difficult that must have been for you and your family," she murmured.

Rafael smiled faintly, though the sadness still lingered in his eyes. "It was a great challenge," he admitted, "but I knew it was my duty to restore our home and provide for my mother and sister. Their well-being has always been my top priority."

"Your dedication to your family is truly commendable, Captain," Clarissa remarked, her admiration evident. "Many would have buckled beneath such adversity, but you've faced it head-on and remained steadfast in your resolve."

"Thank you, Lady Clarissa," he replied, inclining his head humbly. "But I am merely doing what any honourable man would do in my place."

"Perhaps," she allowed, her eyes never leaving his face. "But I believe it takes a rare and exceptional individual to maintain such strength of character and conviction in the face of overwhelming hardship."

He smiled slightly and inclined his head, but said no more, looking away from her and up towards the sails, still hanging almost limp from the masts.

She was a curious creature, this daughter of an English earl. He had met plenty such during his years in England, but none were so outspoken as Lady Clarissa Creighton. Nor could he imagine any of them bearing up so well under the ordeal she had endured. She spoke of the hardships *he* had endured, but he had never been kidnapped by corsairs and threatened with being sold in a slave auction to a terrible fate!

"Captain, you have spoken of your family and the hardships they endured during the war," Clarissa began again, curiosity sparkling in her blue eyes. "But what of the lands that are now yours to protect? Can you describe to me the beauty of Portugal and your ancestral home?"

Rafael hesitated for a moment, his heart swelling with love and pride. He cast his gaze towards the west in the direction of his homeland, as if trying to will the image of his home into existence before him, and then began to speak.

"Portugal is a land of contrasts, Lady Clarissa," he said, his voice filled with warmth and affection. "From the lush, verdant hills of the north to the rugged, sun-baked cliffs of the south, there is a beauty that is both wild and untamed, yet also deeply serene."

He paused for a moment, recalling the rolling vineyards that surrounded his family's estate, the vibrant green leaves contrasting against the rich, dark soil beneath. "Our lands lie nestled in a valley, bathed in sunlight and blessed with fertile earth that yields an abundance of crops and fine grapes for our winemaking endeavours. A river runs through it, providing sustenance to the fields and a gentle song to accompany the whispering breeze that rustles through the trees."

As he spoke, a wistful smile played at the corners of his mouth, his sea-green eyes shining with the memories of a happier time. "Before the war, our estate was a place of laughter and joy, filled with the voices of family and friends as we gathered to celebrate life's many blessings. The air was rich with the scent of jasmine and orange blossoms, mingling with the earthy aroma of the vineyards, creating a perfume that was both intoxicating and invigorating."

"Your words paint a vivid picture, Captain," Clarissa murmured, her eyes softening with empathy. "It must have been truly heartbreaking to see such a beautiful place ravaged by the horrors of war."

"Indeed it was," Rafael admitted quietly, his features shadowed by sorrow as he remembered that first sight of his home, the vineyards burned, the few people remaining shattered and terrorised. "But I believe that with time, love, and perseverance, we can restore our home to its former glory. For it is not merely the land itself that holds the key to my heart, but the spirit of the people who dwell within it – my family, my friends, and all those who have stood by us through even the darkest times. My mother runs our estate more than capably in my absence, as we are yet in needs of the funds I earn captaining my ship."

"Your family sounds truly remarkable," she said, admiration shining in her eyes. "And if I may say so, Captain de Silva, you have shown great humility in spite of your noble lineage."

"Ah, but Lady Clarissa," Rafael replied with a wry smile, "it is adversity that often teaches us the most valuable lessons in life. I had no choice but to learn from the challenges that fate has thrown my way."

"Indeed," she mused, reflecting on the countless arrogant nobles she had encountered back in England. "And yet, so many people of noble birth seem unable to grasp that simple truth."

"Perhaps they have not yet faced the trials that force them to confront their own humanity," he suggested, his voice tinged with sadness.

"Tell me about your sister, Isabella," Clarissa ventured, her voice gentle and inviting. "You mentioned her earlier, and I cannot help but wonder what kind of person she is."

Rafael's face softened as he thought of his mischievous younger sibling. "Ah, minha irmã," he began, his tone equal parts affection and exasperation. "Isabella is a force to be reckoned with. She has always been full of life and energy, even when our circumstances were at their most dire."

"Indeed?" Clarissa leaned forward, her eyes sparkling with curiosity. "Do tell."

"Isabella once convinced one of our neighbours that she had discovered a magical spring in the woods near our estate," he recounted, a mischievous twinkle lighting up his sea-green eyes. "She swore it could turn back time and restore youth to all who drank from its waters."

"Goodness!" Clarissa gasped, her hand flying to her mouth to stifle a giggle. "And did anyone actually believe her?"

"Alas, yes," Rafael admitted with a wry smile. "Several of our more gullible neighbors eagerly set off in search of this fabled fountain, only to return empty-handed and thoroughly drenched after Isabella led them straight into a rather deep pond."

Clarissa shook her head, her laughter now unrestrained. "How wonderful it must be to have such a spirited and imaginative sibling."

"Indeed, she is a constant source of amusement and delight," Rafael agreed, his own laughter subsiding as he gazed out at the glittering expanse of water before him. The playful memories of his past momentarily gave way to a more sombre reflection, and his brow furrowed with the weight of his responsibilities.

As captain of the Santa Dorotéia, Rafael bore the lives of his crew and the safety of those they protected upon his shoulders. Yet even as he navigated the treacherous waters of the Mediterranean, his thoughts were never far from his family in Portugal and the duty he owed to them.

"Captain?" Clarissa asked softly, concern lacing her voice as she noticed the shift in his demeanour. "Is everything all right?"

"Forgive me," he murmured, offering her a small, reassuring smile. "I was simply thinking of my duties – as a captain, and as a brother."

"Ah," she nodded, understanding dawning in her eyes. "It must be difficult to balance the responsibilities of both roles, especially when they often seem at odds with one another."

"Indeed," he admitted, his gaze turning introspective. "There are times when I question whether I am truly doing what is best for my family by being so far from them, but then I remember that it is also my duty to protect others from the dangers that lurk upon these seas."

"Sometimes, the most difficult choices we make are the ones that truly define us," Clarissa said softly.

"You are astute, for one so young," Rafael said thoughtfully, his gaze dwelling on her. "And if I might say so... quite different from other gently-born English ladies I have met." A gentle breeze tugged at Clarissa's sun-bleached hair, her refusal to wear a bonnet granting her a rebellious allure that captivated Rafael's attention.

She smirked a little and looked away, but he had not asked a question, and she did not volunteer any explanations. They stood together, watching the quiet sea.

"Family is important too," Clarissa said suddenly, breaking the comfortable silence that had fallen between them. "In fact, my sister Diana is the only reason I would ever want to go back to England."

Startled, he looked at her. "Not your parents, or your home?"

"No." Her face was still and calm as she spoke. "They love me, and I love them, but their expectations of me are not ones I can fulfil. Diana, unlike them, accepts me for exactly who I am."

"Your sister must be someone truly special," Rafael replied.

"Indeed, she is," Clarissa agreed, her voice laced with affection. "Diana is the one person I love unconditionally. She has always been a source of kindness and support, and it was no surprise to me that a duke saw her worth and snatched her up for his bride." Clarissa smiled, a dazzling display that set Rafael's heart racing.

"The breeze is coming up," he noted, seeing her curls beginning to blow about. "I had best escort you below and be about my duties."

"Thank you for spending the time with me, Captain." She made him an elegant little curtsy. "I have enjoyed our conversation."

"So have I," he said, surprised to find that he meant it. Conversing with gently bred young ladies was normally a complicated matter, full of pitfalls and hidden codes Rafael had neither the patience nor the inclination to decipher. Talking with Clarissa felt refreshingly straightforward; she said what she thought without cloaking it in pretty language or riddles.

"We should make Livorno by morning," Rafael noted as he escorted Clarissa back to his cabin. "The lull has delayed us somewhat, but hopefully we will now make good headway."

"Thank you once again, for escorting me." She glanced over her shoulder at him as she made her way along the narrow passageway. "I do not know what I should have done without your aid."

"I will try to escort you up on deck again later," he said a little awkwardly, and she flashed him that dazzling smile once again.

"I will be grateful for it, but do not feel obliged. This has been more than enough."

For a smile like that, a man could be persuaded to do a great many things, Rafael reflected as he made his way back up on deck and over to where his first mate had the wheel.

The sun's last rays cast a golden glow on the rippling waves, painting the horizon in shades of pink and orange. A gentle breeze stirred the sails of the Santa Dorotéia, as Rafael and Clarissa again stood side by side at the railing, their eyes drawn to the breathtaking panorama before them.

"Such beauty," Clarissa murmured, her voice soft and reverent. "It reminds me of a line from one of my favorite poets, Lord Byron: 'She walks in beauty, like the night / Of cloudless climes and starry skies.'"

"Ah, you have a taste for poetry, Lady Clarissa?" Rafael asked, looking at her with newfound appreciation.

"Indeed, Captain," she replied, a playful smile gracing her lips. "I find that words have a power all their own, able to capture the essence of a moment or a feeling."

"Then perhaps I can share a verse from one of my own favourite poets, Luís de Camões," Rafael offered, his gaze returning to the sea. "'All hushed the heaven and earth, and wind the same / The waves all spreading o'er the sandy plain / While sleep doth in the sea the fish enchain / Nocturnal silence brooding as a dream.'"

"Beautiful," Clarissa breathed, clearly moved by his recitation. "There is a depth of longing in those words that resonates within my soul."

"Poetry has a way of revealing our deepest desires, even when we are not aware of them ourselves," Rafael mused.

"True," Clarissa agreed, lost in thought. "Sometimes, it takes the right combination of words to help us understand what lies hidden in our hearts."

As the sky darkened, stars began to dot the vast expanse above them, adding to the enchantment of the scene. Rafael could not help but notice how the silvery moonlight danced on Clarissa's hair, and he felt an unfamiliar longing stirring within him.

"Captain," Clarissa ventured hesitantly, her voice barely a whisper. "Have you ever considered that perhaps our lives, like the verses of a poem, are meant to follow a certain rhythm or structure?"

"An intriguing thought, Lady Clarissa," Rafael replied, turning to face her. "But I believe there is always room for unexpected twists and turns, much like the unpredictable currents of the sea."

"Perhaps," she conceded. "And yet, it is in those unforeseen moments that we often find the most meaning and beauty."

"Indeed," he agreed softly, his heart pounding as the space between them seemed to shrink, drawn together by an irresistible force neither could fully comprehend.

A shout from one of his sailors recalled Rafael to where he was, and he stepped back, silently cursing himself for a fool. This - whatever this was - was madness, insanity brought on by moonlight and the close proximity of a beautiful woman. Lady Clarissa Creighton, daughter of an English earl, was not for the likes of him, and the sooner he convinced himself of that, the better.

"I had best escort you below," he said, his tone clipped. "We will be in Livorno by morning, and I will hire a carriage to escort you to Florence."

Clarissa inclined her head slightly. "Thank you," was all she said, but he felt her eyes on him, the puzzlement on her face at his sudden stiff withdrawal evident.

Not for you, Rafael reminded himself silently as he escorted her back to his cabin and left her in Ana's care. *She's not for you.*

CHAPTER SIX

A CACOPHONY OF VOICES and the creaking of rigging filled the air, while the scent of salty sea mingled with the aroma of fresh fish from the nearby market as the Santa Dorotéia glided smoothly into its berth in the port of Livorno. Captain Rafael de Silva stood on the wooden deck, his sea-green eyes surveying the bustling scene before him. He turned to Clarissa, who leaned against the railing, watching the activity around the busy port.

"Allow me to assist you, my lady." Rafael extended a calloused hand, offering support as she stepped onto the gangplank. Clarissa, ever fearless, looked at his offered hand, then up into his eyes, and flashed him a mischievous grin.

"Thank you, Captain, but I think I can manage," she said, deftly stepping onto the plank without assistance. Rafael admired her independence, though he couldn't suppress a worried frown as she navigated the precarious crossing.

"Enrique!" Rafael called out to one of his crew members. "Secure us a carriage, if you please."

"Sim, capitão!" the sailor replied, hurrying off to fulfil the request.

As they waited, Clarissa idly glanced at the ship in the neighbouring berth, preparing to cast off as the last passengers boarded. A tall figure caught her attention, and she squinted; she knew that form!

"Uncle Alex!" she cried out. Startled, Alex spun around, his face a picture of disbelief and relief as he caught sight of his niece standing on the dockside.

"Clarissa!" He rushed toward her, his arms opened wide for an embrace.

Clarissa's heart swelled with happiness as she took in the familiar sight of her beloved uncle, his face etched with shock and joy at seeing her safe and sound.

"Clarissa, my dear!" Alex cried out, his voice thick with emotion. He swept her up into his arms, holding her close as if to reassure himself that she was truly there and not just an apparition borne out of his deepest hopes.

"Uncle Alex," Clarissa murmured, tears pricking the corners of her eyes as she clung to him. "I am so glad to see you."

"Wherever have you been?" He leaned back, grasping her shoulders, looking her up and down. "I cannot tell you how panicked Marianne was when we received my mother's letter that you were missing from Athens!"

Clarissa winced, too well able to imagine how distressed her aunt would have been.

"I was about to board a ship to Greece," Alex gestured to the ship, sighed as the captain came towards him. "One moment, Clarry. I need to get my luggage brought off." He spoke quickly to the captain in rapid, fluent Italian, before turning back to her. For the first time, he looked past her to Rafael, standing patiently waiting, and his eyebrows went up.

"Clarissa Creighton. *Tell* me you didn't run off from Greece with a man!" Fury darkened his face as he stared at Rafael.

"No!" Clarissa caught at his arm as Alex took a step forward, expression threatening. "Uncle Alex, that's not what happened." She glanced around; several people were watching them with apparent interest. "We need to talk somewhere private."

"Back aboard the Santa Dorotéia," Rafael invited quietly. "Captain Rafael de Silva, at your service," he made Alex a polite bow.

"Oh, I'm so sorry... this is my uncle Alex... the Marquis of Glenkellie." She saw the surprise on Rafael's face, realised she hadn't told him just how highly ranked Alex was. "Uncle, you can trust Captain de Silva. I promise. He's the hero in this story."

"Is he, indeed?" Alex said dryly, but he allowed Rafael to lead him and Clarissa back aboard the Santa Dorotéia and to the captain's cabin.

"All right." Alex folded his arms, looking from Rafael to Clarissa. "Tell me the real story."

Clarissa hesitated now, realising that Alex was likely to be extremely angry on her behalf once she explained. Rafael spoke up, filling the silence.

"My lord, this ship is part of an anti-corsair patrol through the southern Mediterranean. Three days ago, we intercepted a known corsair running along the North African coast, flying the Algerian flag. On boarding, I found Lady Clarissa imprisoned."

"On a *corsair* ship?" Alex unfolded his arms, his eyes blazing. "How...?"

"They took me in the middle of the night," Clarissa said quickly. "I woke up and they were in my hotel room. They put a bag over my head and carried me off before I could even scream."

Alex put a hand over his mouth in horror and sank to sit on the single chair at the table, looking as though his legs would not hold him up. "Did... were you..." he didn't seem to be able to ask the question.

"They wanted me in good condition, so no, nobody touched me," Clarissa said quietly. "The corsair captain said I was to be sold in Algiers."

Rafael said something very fast in Italian. Clarissa didn't catch every word, but she was fairly sure of the gist. *Virgins fetch a higher price.*

Alex looked as though he might be about to be ill, but instead he rose to his feet and extended his hand to Rafael. "Captain de Silva, words cannot express my gratitude for your heroism in rescuing and protecting Clarissa."

"Your thanks are welcome, sir, but there is no need for such effusive praise," Rafael responded, his tone modest. "It was no more than my duty."

"Perhaps," Alex conceded, his expression sobering as he considered the dangers Clarissa had faced. "But it was you who braved those perils, and for that, I shall be forever grateful."

Rafael shifted uncomfortably, unused to such commendation. "My duty is to protect those in need on the high seas. Lady Clarissa's safety was paramount, and I am grateful for the opportunity to have been of service."

"Your sense of duty does you credit, Captain." Alex studied Rafael thoughtfully for a moment before continuing. "In light of all you have done for us, I extend an invitation for you to stay with us as an honoured guest in Florence. My wife will certainly want to meet you, and I insist that you allow us the pleasure of expressing our gratitude properly."

Rafael hesitated, glancing at Clarissa, whose face brightened with hope and encouragement. Despite the allure of spending more time in her company, he remained mindful of his station and the incongruity of accepting such a generous offer.

"My lord, your kindness is overwhelming," he finally said, his voice low and sincere. "But I fear it would be an imposition on my part to accept such hospitality."

"Captain de Silva," Alex countered, a trace of amusement in his tone, "I assure you, your presence would be no imposition. Rather, it would bring us great joy and satisfaction to host someone who has demonstrated such exceptional character. We owe you a debt we cannot possibly repay."

Rafael glanced at Clarissa again, her eyes shining with anticipation. The desire to stay by her side warred with his innate sense of propriety, but ultimately, he could no longer deny the connection that had formed between them.

"Very well, my lord," he acquiesced, a hint of a smile tugging at the corners of his mouth. "If you insist, I shall accept your gracious invitation. I did promise to see Lady Clarissa safely to Florence, and I have not yet completed that task."

"Excellent!" Alex clapped his hands together in delight. "I look forward to getting better acquainted with the man who saved my beloved niece."

Rafael's man returned to the docks soon after with a hired carriage ready to take them to Florence. Rafael assisted Clarissa into the plush interior, her cheeks flushed with excitement at the prospect of their journey.

"Thank you, Captain," she whispered, her fingers lingering in his for a moment longer than necessary. He bowed his head, looking away, and handed Ana up to sit beside her in the forward-facing seat, while Rafael and Alex sat with their backs to the driver.

As the carriage began to move, Alex leaned forward, curiosity etched upon his face. "Clarissa, my dear, I still have some questions about your... adventure, if you feel up to talking about it?"

Sensing Clarissa's discomfort, Rafael interjected quickly, "Perhaps it would be best if we allowed Lady Clarissa some time to recover from her ordeal before delving into such matters."

"Of course," Alex conceded, his concern evident. "You are quite right, Rafael. We shall speak no more of it until you are ready, my dear niece."

"Thank you, Uncle," Clarissa murmured, her gratitude palpable.

However, as the day wore on and the rolling Tuscan countryside unfurled around them like an emerald tapestry, Alex's resolve weakened. The questions seemed to tumble from his lips unbidden, like a stream that could not be dammed.

"Who were these pirates? How did they come to abduct you?"

"Truly, Uncle, I –" Clarissa hesitated, her gaze darting to Rafael for support.

"Perhaps we could discuss something else, Lord Glenkellie," Rafael suggested smoothly, his eyes never leaving Clarissa's. "Like the beauty of Tuscany, for example. It has been years since I last visited this region, and I must say, it has only grown more enchanting."

"Ah, yes," Alex agreed, his attention momentarily diverted. "The vineyards, the ancient towns, the art... this land is truly a treasure."

As the conversation turned to more innocuous topics, Clarissa's tension eased, and she began to enjoy the journey anew. With Rafael by her side, she felt as if she could face anything – even the prying questions of a well-meaning, if overly curious, uncle.

"Thank you," she whispered to Rafael, as they passed a picturesque villa nestled among cypress trees, its terracotta roof gleaming in the afternoon sun.

"Always, my lady," he replied, his hand brushing hers with the lightest of touches, sending a shiver down her spine.

The sun dipped below the horizon, casting a warm glow over the ancient streets of Florence as the carriage pulled up to the gates of the Ginori villa, which was so opulent Clarissa had always thought it should be called a palazzo. Clarissa watched through the window as the ornate wrought iron gates creaked open, revealing a lush courtyard filled with fragrant roses and orange trees.

"Enough evasions, Clarissa," Alex began, his voice taking on a tone of concern as they entered the villa grounds. "I must know what transpired during your ordeal."

"Uncle, please," Clarissa whispered, her eyes pleading. But the words caught in her throat, as if held captive by the very memories she sought to escape.

Seeing her struggle, Rafael stepped in. "With your permission, Conte, I will recount the events that led to Lady Clarissa's safety." His voice was steady, reassuring. As he looked into Clarissa's eyes, she found herself nodding, grateful for his intervention.

"Very well," Alex conceded, his gaze fixed on Rafael with an intensity born of love and worry for his niece.

"Upon discovering the corsair ship, we engaged them in battle," Rafael began, tactfully omitting the most harrowing details. "We prevailed, and it was in the aftermath that I came across Lady Clarissa, bound and hidden away. Their intentions were clear –" he paused, searching for the right words, "they planned to sell her to the highest bidder."

"Dear God!" Alex murmured, his face paling at the implication. "Rafael, I cannot thank you enough for rescuing my niece from such a fate."

"Please, sir, it was my duty and honour to protect Lady Clarissa," Rafael replied, humbly deflecting the praise.

As they disembarked from the carriage, Alex turned to Rafael. "You must stay with us, Captain de Silva. We owe you a great debt, and we would be honoured to have you as our guest - I know the Conte will not hear of you refusing, after what you have done for Clarissa."

"My lord, I –" Rafael hesitated, reluctant to impose further upon their gracious hosts.

"Please, Captain," Clarissa encouraged him, her eyes shining with gratitude. "We insist."

"Very well," he conceded. "Thank you for your kindness, Lord Glenkellie."

The great door of the villa swung open, and there framed in the doorway stood a beautiful red-haired woman in an elegant silk gown, an expression of shock on her face.

"Alex? What happened, why are you not... Clarissa!" With a glad cry, the red-haired woman ran down the steps, arms outstretched.

"Aunt Marianne!" Clarissa called in return, rushing forward to embrace her aunt.

"My dear girl," Marianne exclaimed, enfolding Clarissa within her gentle touch. "I am so grateful to have you back, safe and sound."

"Thank you, dear Aunt," Clarissa responded, her voice wavering with genuine emotion. "I am glad to be with you again, truly."

"Inside, inside; I must know what happened." Marianne - the Marchioness of Glenkellie, Rafael supposed, reminding himself to address her as Lady Glenkellie - cast him a curious look as she led Clarissa back up the steps. "And who is that extremely handsome man you have brought with you?"

Her tone was not quite quiet enough, and Rafael caught every word. He felt his cheeks flush, had to fight against the inclination to turn tail and flee, back to his ship and its familiar comforts.

Instead, he allowed Alex to lead him up the steps and inside the palazzo.

Clarissa was giving Marianne the brief, highly edited version of her adventure. Marianne clutched a hand to her throat, face turning ghostly white, before she pulled Clarissa back into her embrace again, holding her tightly.

As the two women shared their tender moment, Rafael could not help but feel like a stranger in this unfamiliar world. The opulent surroundings of the palazzo were a stark contrast from the sea-worn confines of his ship, leaving him feeling out of place among the rich tapestries and marbled floors.

"Captain de Silva," Marianne said, turning her attention to him. "We cannot thank you enough for returning our dear Clarissa to us."

"Please, Marchioness," Rafael replied, his tone earnest yet humble, "it was my duty and honour to protect Lady Clarissa. I would do it again without hesitation."

"Your modesty only serves to make us more grateful, Captain," she replied, her eyes shining with sincerity. "You are a true gentleman."

"What is this I hear?" a new voice cried, and an older gentleman came striding into the room. "Do my eyes deceive me, it is little Clarissa, safe and well!"

Clarissa accepted an embrace from the older man, who was introduced to Rafael moments later as the Conte Ginori, related to the Glenkellies by virtue of having married Alex's aunt. The Conte immediately reiterated Alex's insistence that Rafael should be their honoured guest, and called a footman to show him to a guest chamber.

As the evening progressed, Rafael found himself at odds with the grandiosity of the palazzo. The meal served for their dinner was more extravagant than anything ever placed before him, yet it was also apparent that the huge variety of exotic dishes were nothing out of the ordinary for the Ginori household. He admired the exquisite art adorning the walls, but his heart longed for the simplicity of his ship and the ocean that had been his home for so many years. He could not deny, however, that Clarissa's company provided a sense of belonging amidst this foreign landscape.

She sat opposite him at dinner, her lovely face animated as she talked of the sights she had seen in Athens, all the while deftly avoiding any question which tended towards the topic of her departure from that city.

After dinner, Rafael felt stifled, and excused himself to step outside. Standing on the terrace breathing in the air fragrant with orange blossom, he was somehow not surprised to hear soft footsteps behind him.

"Captain," Clarissa said softly, coming to join him where he stood on the terrace overlooking the moonlit gardens. "I hope you don't find all this too overwhelming. We may live differently, but we share the same values and love for adventure."

"Thank you, my lady," he replied, touched by her perceptive words. "While I may feel out of place among these magnificent surroundings, your presence makes me feel welcome and at ease. I am content knowing that I have found a friend in you, Lady Clarissa."

"Indeed," she replied, her voice warm and sincere. "I am please to have found a true friend in you as well."

He hesitated, and then asked "It has been many years since I was last in Florence, and I had little time to explore it then. Would you do me the honour of accompanying me on an exploration of the city tomorrow? You have lived here for some months, I understand."

"Indeed, and I have seen all of the major tourist sites at least twice, I think." Clarissa laughed. "But I should be delighted to see them again, with you. I'll ask the Count to place a carriage at our disposal, in the morning."

He bowed, and she dipped a little curtsy in response before turning away. Watching her go back inside, Rafael marvelled at her resilience; it was only a few days since she had been barely rescued from a ghastly fate, and she was apparently none the worse for the experience. Any other well-born young lady would have gone into a permanent swoon, he suspected, but not Lady Clarissa.

The morning sun cast a golden glow over the city of Florence, as Rafael and Clarissa stepped out into the bustling streets. They stood for a moment, drinking in the vibrant energy that seemed to pulse through the very air around them.

"Are you ready to explore, my lady?" Rafael asked, his sea-green eyes sparkling with anticipation.

"Indeed, Captain de Silva," Clarissa replied, her laughter ringing like a bell. "Lead the way."

They wound through the narrow cobblestone streets, past bustling markets and quiet courtyards filled with fragrant flowers. Each new sight seemed to delight Rafael, from the imposing Palazzo Vecchio to the graceful arches of the Ponte Vecchio spanning the Arno River.

As Clarissa and Rafael turned a corner, the morning sun illuminated the grand façade of Santa Maria del Fiore, casting an ethereal glow on its intricate marble carvings. The sight took their breath away, and for a moment, all conversation ceased as they stood in awe of the magnificent cathedral.

"Truly, there is no place quite like Florence," Rafael murmured, breaking the silence that had fallen between them.

"Indeed," Clarissa agreed, her eyes still fixed on the majestic structure before them. "And I am grateful to be able to share its beauty with you."

Their reverie was interrupted by the approach of a group of finely dressed young nobles, who sauntered towards them with an air of self-importance. Their sneers were evident as they appraised Rafael's uniform, which, while impeccably neat, lacked the ostentatious embellishments that adorned their own garments.

"Ah, Lady Clarissa, you have returned from your trip!" one of the men drawled, his voice dripping with condescension. "Fancy finding you here in the company of... a sailor."

"Captain de Silva is more than just a sailor," Clarissa retorted, her tone icy. "He is a man of honour and courage." Her tone implied that the qualities were not shared by any of the young fops before her.

"Your words wound us, my lady," another noble quipped, smirking at his companions. "Surely, you cannot expect us to believe that this common seafarer could offer you anything beyond tales of fish and saltwater?"

Rafael's jaw clenched, but he held his tongue, not wishing to provoke a scene. However, Clarissa would not let such insults pass unanswered.

"Perhaps," she said, her voice laced with disdain, "if you spent less time preening yourselves and more time learning from those you so arrogantly dismiss, you might discover that there is much to be gained from the wisdom of others."

"Indeed," Rafael added quietly, his gaze steady upon the group. "The world is vast and full of wonder, and one need not wear a silken cravat to appreciate its beauty or understand its complexities."

"Come, Rafael," Clarissa said, taking his arm. "I have no desire to waste any more of our time on those who cannot see beyond their own vanity."

As they walked away, Rafael felt a swell of admiration for Clarissa and her steadfast integrity. Despite her highborn status, she refused to tolerate such boorish behaviour, even from those in her own social circle.

"Forgive me if I spoke out of turn, my lady," Rafael said. "I did not wish to overstep."

"Not at all," Clarissa replied, giving his arm a reassuring squeeze. "I'm grateful you stood with me against their thoughtless words. A true friend does not abandon another to face scorn alone."

Her simple statement resonated deeply with Rafael. In her, he had found not just a captivating woman, but a kindred spirit who saw beyond appearances to the heart within.

Clarissa led them down a quiet side street, leaving the unpleasant encounter behind. Soon they were immersed in the sights and sounds of local life once more. As Rafael took in the hanging flower baskets and quaint cafes around them, he realised Clarissa had deliberately brought them somewhere peaceful.

Her sensitivity to his feelings after the confrontation with the nobles touched him.

When they came upon a little bookshop tucked away in a courtyard, Clarissa steered them inside. "I think you'll like this place," she said with a playful smile.

The shop was cosy and inviting, with shelves bursting with books and curious trinkets. Rafael's eyes lit up as he perused the eclectic selection, and before long they were both lost in lively discussion about favourite authors and obscure titles they had unearthed.

In that moment, ensconced among the books with Clarissa, Rafael felt a sense of belonging he had rarely known. Though from different worlds, their shared passions bridged the divide. A deep understanding flowed between them, along with something more - an emotion he did not yet know how to name, but which felt as natural as the turning of the tide.

CHAPTER SEVEN

As the ornate carriage rattled over the cobblestones, Helena, the Dowager Marchioness Glenkellie, clutched the gilded armrest with white-knuckled anxiety. Beside her sat her equally perturbed sister, Contessa Ginori, whose lips moved in silent prayer. The grand Ginori villa loomed before them, its façade a testament to Florentine grandeur, yet it offered no solace to the women tormented by the calamity that had befallen the young woman placed in their charge.

"Dear heavens, if anything has befallen Clarissa," Helena murmured, the words barely escaping her clenched jaw, "I shall never forgive myself."

"Nor I," agreed the Contessa. "To think that such misfortune could strike under our very noses!"

The carriage lurched to a stop, and without waiting for the footman, Helena sprung from her seat, her urgency defying the proprieties expected of a woman of her station. She swept up the marble steps, the click of her heels an impatient drumbeat against the stone. The Contessa followed in haste, her silk skirts whispering as they billowed behind her.

As the grand doors swung open, revealing the marbled expanse of the entry hall, a vision in pale muslin paused their frantic hearts. There stood Clarissa, remarkably unscathed, her hair kissed by the sun's affectionate rays—a rebellious halo refusing the confinement of a bonnet.

"Clarissa!" Helena exclaimed, rushing forward. Her arms enveloped the girl in an embrace that was part maternal fervour, part incredulous relief. The Contessa, momentarily discomposed, soon gave in to her own concern, joining the embrace with a fervency that belied her usual poise.

"Goodness! What is all this fuss about?" Clarissa asked, her voice a playful rebuke that danced on the edge of propriety.

"Child, we feared you lost, spirited away by bandits or worse," Helena replied, her tone scolding yet lined with residual fear.

"Indeed, you vanish without trace nor word, and expect us not to worry?" the Contessa added, her eyes bright with unshed tears of relief.

"Forgive me," Clarissa said, her smile gently loving. "But as you see, I am quite safe, and quite sound."

Helena studied Clarissa's countenance, searching for any hint of distress that might betray her brave front. Finding none, she allowed herself a measured sigh, the weight of dread lifting.

"Very well," Helena declared, her indomitable spirit reasserting itself. "You must regale us with every detail of your unexpected return, but first, pray allow us a moment to collect ourselves. I daresay my nerves are quite frayed."

"Mine as well," the Contessa concurred, the corners of her mouth tilting upwards despite the ordeal. "I shall ring for tea. A strong brew, I think, is in order." Looking past Clarissa, she raised her eyebrows at the unfamiliar, tall gentleman just descending the staircase. "And, I think, some introductions?"

"Oh!" Clarissa turned, her smile blooming. "Lady Helena, Contessa Ginori, allow me to present Captain Rafael de Silva."

Rafael stepped forward, his bearing confident but devoid of arrogance. He bowed deeply, his dark hair falling slightly forward as he did so.

"An honour to meet you both," he said, his voice carrying the warm timbre of his native Portugal.

"The Captain is the reason I am here," Clarissa said, as the group progressed into the drawing room and a maid went scurrying to fetch the tea. "I had something of an adventure, and he heroically came to my rescue."

Helena was quite sure that Clarissa was drastically understating what exactly had happened in an effort to spare their feelings, but the fact could not be denied that she was indeed here, apparently safe and sound, and with a most intriguing companion.

Rafael spoke up again. "I regret that our introduction comes under such unusual circumstances."

"Indeed," Lady Helena responded, afire with curiosity about him. "One does not often encounter a hero in one's drawing room."

'Hero' was a title that seemed to sit uneasily on Rafael's broad shoulders. He shifted, offering a humble smile. "Merely a man at the right place when I was needed, my lady. Circumstance should not be mistaken for valour."

"Nevertheless," the Contessa interjected, "we are all eager to hear of these circumstances." She gestured gracefully to a settee. "Please, Captain, do regale us with your tale."

With their attentions fixed upon him, Rafael recounted the events that had led to Clarissa's safe return. His narrative was sparing in detail regarding his own actions; it focused instead on the precision of manoeuvres, the cooperation of his crew aboard the Santa Dorotéia, and the fortunate timing that had allowed them to intercept the corsairs' vessel.

"Fortunately, we were able to secure Lady Clarissa's release before harm could befall her," he concluded.

"Captain de Silva, your humility cannot conceal the courage required to confront such villains," the Contessa said, waggling a finger at him.

"Indeed," Lady Helena added, her gaze lingering on Rafael's composed features. "One does not simply stumble upon corsairs and emerge victorious by mere chance. Your skill is apparent, sir, and we are most grateful for it."

"Your gratitude is more than enough reward," Rafael replied, directing a respectful nod towards the two women before allowing his eyes to settle on Clarissa.

"Then we shall ensure our thanks are amply conveyed," Lady Helena said, the sentiment echoed by the Contessa's approving nod. As they settled into conversation, warmed by the tea now steaming in delicate porcelain cups, the ladies found themselves increasingly impressed—not merely by Rafael's deeds, but by the measured grace with which he wore his heroism.

After the conversation had wound down and the evening shadows grew longer within the grandiose walls of the palazzo, Helena, with an impish glint in her eye, motioned for Clarissa to follow her to a private alcove away from the others. The heavy brocade of her gown rustled against the marble floor as she led the younger woman with purpose.

"Come, my dear," Helena began, her voice lowering conspiratorially as they reached the seclusion of velvet-draped windows. "You must indulge an old lady's curiosity. There is more to the tale of your rescue than you've let on, I surmise. Tell me truly—what think you of our dashing Captain de Silva?"

Clarissa felt her cheeks warm under Helena's keen scrutiny. She was not accustomed to concealment, least of all from this woman who flouted convention like she did fashion—boldly and without a care for the whispers that followed.

"Captain de Silva is indeed... remarkable," Clarissa admitted, choosing her words with care, yet unable to hide the admiration lacing her tone. "He possesses both bravery and kindness. And his conversation is as engaging as his actions are commendable."

"Ah, 'engaging'," Helena echoed, her smile broadening. "A word scarcely sufficient for the light I saw dancing in your eyes, child. But come now," she said, softening her teasing with a gentle pat on Clarissa's hand, "you needn't don armour around me. Speak plainly—as you and I are both wont to do."

"Very well," Clarissa conceded, her usual forthrightness bubbling to the surface. "There is a certain... connection, I cannot deny. It is rare to find a gentleman so genuine, so earnest. He speaks to me not as a delicate flower to be sheltered, but as an equal, capable of understanding the perils he faces."

Helena's expression shifted to one of satisfaction, her eyes alight with mischief and warmth. "That is precisely what I hoped to hear. Now, on to more pressing matters," she said with a knowing tilt of her head just as Rafael approached them.

"Forgive the interruption, ladies," Rafael began, his sea-green eyes finding Clarissa's with an ease that spoke of their shared adventure. "Lady Clarissa, might I impose upon you for the pleasure of your company tomorrow morning? I thought perhaps a ride through the countryside would offer us fresh air and respite from recent events."

"An invitation most graciously extended, Captain," Helena interjected before Clarissa could respond, her approval nearly tangible. "And I believe it shall be most graciously accepted, will it not, Clarissa? The Count has any number of fine horses in his stables he shall be glad to provide for your use."

"Indeed," Clarissa replied, meeting Rafael's gaze with a joyous smile. "I should very much like to join you, Captain de Silva."

"Excellent," Rafael said. "I shall look forward to it."

"Then it is settled," Helena concluded, stepping back to allow the two a moment's privacy in their parting. "Enjoy the evening, you two. But not too late, mind you," she added with a wink, leaving no doubt that she expected to hear every detail of their excursion upon their return.

The morning sun was tender in its ascent, casting a soft blush over the rolling hills as Rafael and Clarissa rode side by side. The rhythm of their horses' hooves upon the earth was a steady punctuation to the symphony of birdsong that heralded the dawn. Clarissa's laughter—free and unburdened—rose into the air as they navigated through the lush Tuscan countryside.

"Look there," she pointed towards a grove of olive trees, their silver-green leaves shimmering in the light. "Does it not seem as if the very landscape is welcoming us?"

The rapport between them ebbed and flowed like the tide, an easy banter that spoke of a growing familiarity. As they traversed the path, lined with cypress sentinels standing guard, they found themselves at an ancient stone bridge arching gracefully over a whispering stream.

"Shall we rest awhile?" Rafael suggested, dismounting with agile grace. He extended a hand to assist Clarissa down from her mount, but she leapt to the ground with the spirited independence that marked her character.

"Thank you, Captain, but it seems my legs have not yet forgotten their function," she quipped, brushing down her riding habit with brisk strokes.

They settled beneath the shade of an old oak tree, its limbs stretched wide as if to embrace the wanderers seeking respite beneath its boughs. Clarissa gathered a handful of wildflowers, their petals soft and delicate in her palm.

"Tell me, Rafael," she began, using his given name for the first time, her voice lowering to a more intimate cadence, "what dreams do you harbour within your heart?"

He plucked a blade of grass, twirling it thoughtfully between his fingers. "To restore my family's legacy—to see our vineyards flourish once more." His gaze drifted across the fields, to some distant vision only he could see. "And perhaps, to find someone who shares my love for the unpredictability of the ocean's song."

"And you, Lady Clarissa?" Rafael turned his attention back to her, the intensity of his gaze a gentle challenge.

With a wistful smile, she tucked a stray blonde lock behind her ear. "I dream of adventure, of a life defined not by convention but by passion and purpose. To be seen for who I am, rather than what society expects me to be."

The air between them seemed to thrum with unspoken possibilities, the charged moment stretching out like the horizon before them. Their eyes met, and in that silent exchange, the seeds of something deeper took root, each sensing in the other a kindred spirit.

"Perhaps," Rafael said softly, the word hanging between them like a promise, "we are not so different in our desires."

"Perhaps not," Clarissa agreed, her heart echoing his sentiment even as she sensed the complexities such acknowledgment would bring. For now, though, she allowed herself to simply enjoy the company of the man beside her, whose presence felt as natural and necessary as the sunlight dappling through the leaves above.

Later that evening, the grand salon of the palazzo buzzed with the chatter of Florence's elite, gathered for a soirée hosted by the Contessa. Ladies in silk gowns and gentlemen in tailored coats mingled beneath crystal chandeliers that cast a warm glow over the room.

"Captain de Silva," the Contessa said, her voice rich with the promise of intrigue as she guided him through the throng. "Allow me to introduce you to some of Florence's most eligible ladies." With each introduction, Rafael offered a polite smile and a courteous bow, his words measured and amiable. Yet, it was clear to any discerning observer that his attention wavered, drawn inexorably back to Clarissa.

Her laughter rose above the gentle hum of conversation, and Rafael found himself captivated by the vivacious spirit that seemed to illuminate the room. She was a beacon of sincerity in a sea of artifice, challenging the norms with her wit and candour.

"Thank you, Contessa," Rafael spoke with a practised diplomacy, excusing himself from another circle of admirers. "Your acquaintances are most charming." Yet, as he made his retreat, his gaze sought out Clarissa once more. In her presence, the weight of his humble means and the stark reality of his limited prospects paled in comparison to the undeniable connection that sparked whenever their paths crossed.

The evening wore on, with the clinking of glasses and the soft rustling of silks serving as a backdrop to this subtle dance of glances and half-spoken truths.

The moment arrived when the first chords of a waltz began to resonate through the grand salon, and Rafael felt a pull towards Clarissa that exceeded mere duty or politeness. He navigated the sea of guests until he stood before her, offering his hand with a respectful bow.

"Lady Clarissa, may I have this dance?" he inquired, his voice betraying none of the turmoil that churned within.

With a smile that outshone the candelabras overhead, she placed her hand in his. "It would be my absolute pleasure, Captain de Silva."

As they took their place among the swirl of dancers, the world seemed to narrow to just the two of them. The warmth of Clarissa's hand resting lightly on his shoulder, the subtle fragrance of lavender that escaped from her curls — these small intimacies sent a thrill through Rafael that was both exhilarating and terrifying.

They moved together as if they were part of the same melody, each step and turn a wordless conversation between kindred spirits. Around them, the crowd faded into a blur of colour and light, their laughter mingling with the strains of the waltz.

"Your navigational skills are not limited to the high seas, it seems," Clarissa teased, her eyes alight with mirth.

"Indeed, navigating a ballroom requires its own set of charts," Rafael replied, the corners of his mouth lifting in an involuntary smile. "Though I must confess, the company makes all the difference."

Their chemistry was undeniable, and it did not go unnoticed. From the periphery, admiring glances and whispered conjectures followed their every move. They were an enigma, a pairing that breached the boundaries of expectation, yet fit together with a natural ease that spoke of a deeper understanding.

As the music reached its crescendo, Rafael and Clarissa slowed to a stop, sharing a look that lingered just a breath too long, charged with unspoken emotion. Applause rose around them, breaking the spell, and they parted with a mutual reluctance.

"Thank you for the dance, Captain," Clarissa said, her voice softer now, as if reluctant to break the harmony that had enveloped them.

"The pleasure was entirely mine," Rafael responded, his heart racing with a fervour he dared not name.

The soirée continued its ebb and flow, but Rafael felt adrift, caught in the current of his own conflicted desires. It was then that Alex, his features etched with gravity, approached and gently tugged at his sleeve, drawing him away from the festivities.

"Captain de Silva, might I have a word in private?" Alex's tone left no room for refusal, and Rafael nodded, excusing himself with quiet grace.

They found solace in the relative calm of a secluded antechamber, the noise of the party a distant murmur behind closed doors.

"Something weighs on your mind, Lord Glenkellie," Rafael observed, noting the solemnity that had settled upon the other man's countenance.

"Indeed, it does," Alex admitted, locking eyes with Rafael. "It concerns Clarissa — and the delicate nature of her circumstances." His words hung in the air, heavy with implication, and Rafael felt a tightening in his chest as he braced himself for what was to come.

"Captain, you are a man of the world, and I trust your discretion," Alex began, his gaze unwavering. "What transpired in Athens with Clarissa... it is not yet common knowledge here in Florence. But rumours are insidious creatures; they breed in silence and spread with the swiftness of wildfire."

Rafael's eyes narrowed with concern. He understood all too well the power of reputation, especially for a lady of Clarissa's standing.

"Her disappearance, the circumstances of her return —" Alex continued, "they cannot be concealed for long, considering the hue and cry my mother and aunt quite understandably raised when they found her missing in Athens. Clarissa needs the protection of a respectable marriage, and she needs it soon, before her reputation is irreparably tarnished."

The weight of Alex's words settled over Rafael like a cloak, heavy and suffocating. He sensed the unspoken plea behind them, and his honour warred with a potent mix of emotions. His mind raced with visions of Clarissa — her spirited laugh, the fire in her eyes when she spoke her mind. The thought of her reputation being sullied was intolerable.

"Lord Glenkellie, I am but a humble captain," Rafael said after a moment, his voice betraying the turmoil within him. "I have my post, my duties, but little else to offer. My family's fortunes are not what they once were."

"I think you know as well as I that the worth of a man is measured by far more than the weight of his coffers," Alex replied, his tone firm, yet not without compassion.

"Indeed, but knowing one's worth and proving it in the eyes of society are two very different things," Rafael countered. The memory of his family's semi-ruined castle and the neglected vineyard that once flourished under their care weighed heavily on him. "Clarissa is no ordinary lady, and she deserves a life of comfort and security."

"Think on it, my friend. I ask only that," Alex urged before leaving Rafael alone with the echo of his thoughts.

Silence enveloped Rafael as he stood there, the hum of the soirée beyond the walls a distant reminder of the world he navigated — a world where love and duty sailed on tumultuous seas. His heart whispered Clarissa's name, but his mind echoed with doubt, caught between the fervent desire to court her properly and the gnawing fear that he could never give her the life she so richly deserved.

"Character and feelings," he murmured to himself, repeating Alex's words as if they were a lifeline thrown into the churning waters of his doubt. Clarissa's presence had brought a vibrancy to his life that he hadn't realised was missing. Her fearless candour and lively intellect matched his own unyielding spirit. Would it be enough?

"Can love truly be blind to the stark realities of wealth and position?" Rafael pondered aloud, his voice barely above a whisper. The laughter and music from the soirée seemed to mock his inner conflict, serving as a reminder of the joy that felt just beyond his reach. In the solitude of the dimly lit corridor, Rafael considered the possibility that perhaps he could offer something far greater than riches—a partnership of mutual respect and understanding, the kind that could weather any storm.

"Perhaps the truest form of courage is to face one's fears for the sake of love," he concluded, the idea taking hold like the first light of dawn piercing through the darkness. With a determined exhale, he pushed away from the wall, his resolve hardening with each step as he made his way back to the ballroom, back to Clarissa, and to whatever future might unfold with her by his side.

CHAPTER EIGHT

THE CLEAR BLUE SKY over Florence held the promise of a beautiful day. However, the glorious weather did little to ease Rafael's troubled thoughts as he gazed contemplatively out the window of his opulent suite at the Villa Ginori. His mind was consumed with uncertainty over whether or not to confess his growing feelings for Clarissa. The memory of Alex's meaningful words about her need for a swift and respectable marriage weighed heavily upon him.

Rafael let out a weary sigh, his emotions turbulent. He cared deeply for Clarissa, more than he could have imagined. Yet he continued to question whether he could provide her the life she deserved as the daughter of an earl.

His conflicted musings were interrupted by an urgent pounding at the chamber door. Before Rafael could respond, the door burst open to reveal a breathless messenger wearing the uniform of Rafael's ship.

"Captain de Silva!" the messenger exclaimed. "I come with news of gravest importance."

Rafael's heart clenched with foreboding. "Speak man. Has there been trouble with the Santa Dorotéia?"

"No Captain. I bear tidings regarding your sister." The messenger hesitated only a moment. "Another Portuguese ship, the Santa Luisa, made port in Livorno a few hours ago and the captain relayed news from your family. Your sister, Senhorita Isabella, has fallen desperately ill."

Rafael reeled at the news, steadying himself against the windowsill as a swell of anguish rose within him. Isabella was more than just his sister - she was the gentle heart of his family, a light guiding him home through even the darkest of storms. To imagine her life now hanging precariously in the balance was a blow Rafael could scarcely comprehend.

"Tell me... tell me everything," he managed to rasp out, his own voice sounding foreign to his ears.

The messenger relayed every detail he knew of Isabella's sudden fever and wracking cough. With each word, Rafael's fear and desperation grew. His beloved sister needed him, yet the woman who had captured his heart was here in Florence. He was torn between two impossible choices, neither of which he could bear to make.

But deep down, Rafael knew his course had been charted from the moment he heard Isabella's name. She was his family, his home—he would not fail her now when she needed him most. Steeling himself, he turned to the waiting messenger with new conviction.

"Return to the Santa Dorotéia and prepare to leave immediately," he ordered. "I will follow you as soon as I am able to make my farewells here, and we shall return to Portugal with all speed." A fleeting image of Clarissa arose within his mind's eye—her unbound hair kissed by the sun, her fearless candour that had charmed and challenged him in equal measure. Everything in him protested against merely leaving her now, yet his duty called him home. Clenching his fists, he let out a cry of frustration.

"Rafael?" A voice at the door made him turn, and he saw Alex standing there, looking at him with concern. "Is something amiss?"

"Indeed."

"Is this about what we talked of last eve?" Alex raised a brow, and looked surprised when Rafael shook his head.

"No, I have received grave news from home. My sister is seriously ill, maybe even..." He could not even speak the thoughts. "I must go to her. And yet..." He gestured helplessly. "My duty is also here."

"Clarissa is not a duty, Rafael," Alex disagreed at once, "and I know she would be the first to tell you that you must go to your sister at once, without delay."

Still, Rafael could see the conflict on Alex's face. Alex was Clarissa's guardian here in Italy, and safeguarding her reputation was a duty he took seriously. It could not be long before word spread of her disappearance from Athens, and the scandal would not quiet until she was respectably married.

Rafael hesitated, thinking, before delicately posing a question. "I am aware that you and Lady Glenkellie have remained in Florence so long because of the ardours of the journey back to England with your children so young. But it occurs to me that I might offer a solution to several problems at once, if you were to accompany me back to Portugal and accept my hospitality for a spell, thus breaking up your trip home into gentler stages."

And giving me time to see if Clarissa could potentially be happy at my estate, as my wife, he did not add, but as Alex studied him, he was quite sure the other man astutely comprehended.

"We will need to prepare to leave at once," Alex said thoughtfully.

"A hasty leavetaking, I am sorry... unless you wished to wait for another ship to bring you to Portugal?" Rafael thought to suggest.

Alex shook his head decisively. "No. Honestly, I would rather be gone from Florence before word of Clarissa's escapade in Athens reaches the city. My mother might remain with her sister, but I am more than happy to begin our journey home. If you will excuse me, Rafael, I will find my wife and have our packing done; we will be ready to depart in a few hours at most. If you would find Clarissa and advise her of our plans?"

Rafael opened his mouth to say surely that was not his place, but Alex had already left the room, striding confidently off like the former military officer he was, accustomed to giving orders and having them obeyed.

With a rueful smile, Rafael set to the task Alex had left him with. He had little enough to pack, only the one bag of belongings he had brought with him from his ship, so left that with the servant to manage and set off in search of Clarissa.

He found her in the garden, seated on a bench before a beautiful statue of the goddess Diana, writing in the journal he had learned was rarely far from her hands. She set down her pencil at the sight of him, a welcoming smile coming readily to her face.

"Captain de Silva. Do join me!" The smile slid from her face as she noticed his serious expression. "You look as though something troubles you."

"I have received concerning news, I fear." Taking a seat on the bench beside her, Rafael imparted the ill news of his sister's illness.

Clarissa reacted exactly as her uncle had predicted. "Why are you still here, Rafael? You must go, immediately!"

He could not help the smile which came to his face. "I will be off before nightfall... and you shall come with me."

Her eyes widened with shock, and Rafael hastened to explain. "I have spoken already to your uncle, who came upon me just after I received the news. I have offered Lord and Lady Glenkellie the opportunity to break their journey home to England into stages, by accepting transport aboard the Santa Dorotéia to Portugal, and then the hospitality of my estate for a while. He was pleased to accept."

Clarissa stared at him for a moment before her smile returned, breaking wider than ever across her face. "To Portugal?" she breathed.

"Indeed. I shall be able to show you my home." Right then, he could think of only one thing he wanted more than that, which would be to arrive there with her and find Isabella safe and well.

Clarissa leapt to her feet and threw her arms about his neck, startling him again as she kissed his cheek. "I must go and pack. We shall not delay your departure long, I promise!" she called over her shoulder as she rushed towards the villa.

In the end, Rafael went ahead on horseback to see the Santa Dorotéia prepared to sail as soon as possible. It was not many hours, however, before a carriage rolled up at the dockside and Alex stepped out, turning to assist his wife and Clarissa down, followed by Marianne's faithful maid Jean. Marianne and Jean carefully cradled a babe each as they made their way towards the ship.

"Allow me." Rafael stepped nimbly ashore. "Hello, little one," he greeted the child in Marianne's arms, who blinked at him from wide blue eyes. "Will you let me convey you safely aboard the ship?" He knew the children were not yet a year old and the Glenkellies had remained in Italy so long fearing for their health, but they looked well grown and strong to him.

"My son, Edward," Alex murmured, pride obvious in his tone. "And Jean has our daughter Eleanor."

Both children had their mother's red hair. Little Eleanor was apparently the braver of the two, for she held her arms out to Rafael expectantly.

"Come then, my lady." Rafael chuckled, taking the child in his arms, and carrying her easily up the gangplank. Alex followed with his son, and all three women followed confidently after without waiting for assistance.

Rafael had done the best he could in the limited time he'd had, to make comfortable quarters on his ship for the party. Alex and Marianne would have the captain's cabin, of course, and the two on either side had been swiftly cleared out and refurbished with the finest items which could be procured on such short notice, one made comfortable for Clarissa and one for Jean and the twins. The ship's carpenter had just finished installing a bolt on the inside of Clarissa's door and made a hasty exit, bowing respectfully, as Rafael brought Clarissa to the door.

"To ensure your safety." Rafael indicated the bolt. "I hope you will find it comfortable." He glanced about, seeing the bed topped with a goose-down mattress, the brightly patterned rug on the floor. He grimaced. "I regret we did not have time to obtain more comfortable furnishings for you."

"This is everything delightful," Clarissa said firmly. "Thank you, Captain. I appreciate your, and your crew's, efforts very much."

"Much more comfortable than the ship which brought us from England," Jean agreed from the cabin opposite.

"Captain," a voice called, and Rafael turned to see the bosun at the end of the passageway, expression full of urgency. "The tide."

"Very well." Rafael nodded, before turning back to his guests. "I apologise, but the tide waits for no man, and we must have the Santa Dorotéia beyond the harbour walls before the tide turns."

"Go," Clarissa said with a warm smile, "we shall be quite well here. See to your ship."

He made her a quick bow, barely even hearing the words of encouragement from the others, and made his way back up to the deck, a hive of activity with men rushing every which way, securing barrels and crates and preparing lines to cast off.

"Time to focus," Rafael murmured to himself, trying to shake off the vivid image in his mind's eye, of Clarissa's warm smile and wide blue eyes. He needed to think of a different pair of eyes now, his sister Isabella's, the same sea-green as his own, always laughing and bright with joy whenever he came home. He desperately hoped it would be the case this time.

"Cast off the lines," he ordered, his deep voice cutting through the chaos on the deck. "You there... off, unless you're bound for Portugal with us!" He switched to Italian to bark at one of the local stevedores who was still trying to argue with his quartermaster. The man scowled, but scurried off down the gangplank before it was pulled in.

For the next few minutes the air was filled with the shouts of men and creaking of timbers, the rattle of capstans turning and ropes and sails rustling. To an outsider the activity might look frenzied, but to Rafael's satisfied eye the crew of the Santa Dorotéia were moving like a well-oiled machine, every man in his correct place, performing his assigned task with practised precision.

It didn't take long at all to round the breakwater. Rafael spun the wheel, guiding the bow to the open sea while the bosun roared orders to hoist the mainsail. The sails caught the breeze and the Santa Dorotéia surged forward, cutting through the waves as she picked up speed.

"Hold on, Isabella," Rafael whispered to the wind. "I'm coming."

CHAPTER NINE

Clarissa's fingers trailed along the polished mahogany of the writing desk. A silver bowl atop it held an assortment of fresh fruits. Even curtains had been hung to frame the small porthole, filtering the late afternoon sunlight and casting a warm glow over the cosy cabin. Every detail spoke of a host concerned with his guest's comfort and pleasure.

She sank to sit on the goose-down stuffed mattress, a smile playing about her lips. The accommodations on Captain de Silva's ship were a far cry from the dank cell those dreadful corsairs had kept her in. Leave it to Rafael to see to her every need, even amidst the chaos of their hasty departure from Italy. His gallantry knew no bounds.

A light rap at the door startled her from her musings. "Come in," she called, smoothing the folds of her blue muslin gown.

The door swung open to reveal the handsome captain himself, looking dashing as ever in his crisp white shirt and black trousers. His cravat was slightly askew, no doubt from the work of their departure an hour hence; the Santa Doroteia had settled into a steady sway as she cut through the waves, bound for Rafael's Portuguese home.

"Lady Clarissa." He bowed. "I trust you are finding your quarters to your liking?"

"More than satisfactory, Captain." She smiled up at him. "I daresay you've spoiled me quite thoroughly. However shall I readjust to life on land after such luxury?"

Rafael chuckled, his sea-green eyes twinkling. "It is my sincerest pleasure. After your harrowing ordeal, you deserve nothing but the best."

He gestured to the fruit bowl. "Procured fresh this morning for your pleasure; the best Livorno has to offer."

"How very thoughtful." Clarissa selected a ripe red berry and bit into it, revelling in the burst of sweetness on her tongue. Juice stained her lips and she dabbed at them with a linen napkin. "You think of everything, Captain."

"Nay, not everything." A shadow flickered briefly across his handsome features, but he quickly schooled them into a neutral expression. "I shall leave you to your repose."

With another slight bow, he turned on his heel and exited, pulling the door closed behind him with a soft click.

Clarissa released a slow breath, a little irritated with herself. Every encounter with the dashing captain left her increasingly flustered, though she endeavoured not to show it. He was a perfect gentleman, attentive yet restrained.

But in unguarded moments, an unfathomable sadness seemed to grip him--no doubt worry for his sister Isabella, or perhaps the burdens of keeping his ancestral estate afloat. She longed to unravel the mysteries behind those captivating eyes.

Clarissa shook her head. It wouldn't do to entertain such dangerous thoughts, even if the temptation was proving more difficult to resist with each passing day in his intoxicating presence. She was a lady, after all, and he a mere sea captain, despite his gallant manners. Any match between them would be most unsuitable...wouldn't it?

Sighing, she selected a leather-bound volume of Shakespeare's sonnets from the small pile of books that had been placed on the writing-desk and settled in to read, letting the Bard's familiar words soothe her troubled mind as the ship pressed onward toward Portugal.

The salt-tinged breeze whipped tendrils of hair across Clarissa's face as she emerged onto the sun-drenched deck of the Santa Dorotéia. Squinting against the glare, she spotted Captain Rafael near the helm, his tall form a striking silhouette against the azure sky.

As if sensing her presence, he turned, a warm smile gracing his chiseled features. "Lady Clarissa, a pleasure to see you this morning." He executed a courtly half-bow. "I trust your quarters were comfortable enough for you to achieve a good night's sleep?"

"More than adequate, thank you." She dipped into a shallow curtsy. "Though I confess, I found myself yearning for a breath of fresh air."

"But of course." Rafael gestured at the bustling crew members scurrying about their duties. "You are welcome to take your ease on deck whenever you wish, with or without your aunt or her maid. I assure you, you shall be quite safe among my men; I have spoken with them."

Clarissa inclined her head gratefully, though a small part of her bristled at the implication that she required protection. She was no delicate flower, to wilt at the first hint of adversity. Had she not endured captivity with admirable fortitude?

As if reading her thoughts, Rafael's eyes sparkled with amusement. "I meant no offence, my lady. I merely wish for you to be comfortable during our journey."

"No offence taken, Captain." She favoured him with an arch smile. "I am quite capable of looking after myself. But I appreciate your concern nonetheless."

Rafael chuckled, a rich, melodious sound that sent a curious shiver down her spine. "Of that, I have no doubt." He turned back to the wheel, long fingers deftly adjusting their course. "Do you have an interest in navigation, Lady Clarissa?"

"I must confess, I find it rather fascinating." She stepped closer, observing as he consulted the compass and made minute adjustments to the sails. "The notion that one can chart a path across the vast, unpredictable sea using only the sun and stars and a few instruments...it's quite remarkable."

"Indeed." Rafael's eyes shone with enthusiasm as he launched into an explanation of the various tools and techniques he employed. Clarissa listened raptly, marvelling at the depth of his knowledge.

How different this was from the tedious drawing room conversations she was accustomed to, all idle gossip and superficial pleasantries. With Rafael, she could engage in truly stimulating discourse, their minds sparking off one another like flint against steel.

As the sun began its lazy descent toward the horizon, painting the waves in shades of gold and orange, Clarissa found herself reluctant to return to her cabin. The company was far too agreeable.

Perhaps a few more moments basking in his presence wouldn't be so very improper. After all, it was only natural to seek the companionship of a kindred spirit on such a lengthy voyage. And if her heart fluttered a bit more rapidly in his presence, well...surely that was merely a result of the invigorating sea air.

Yes, that must be it. For what else could it possibly be?

Rafael handed the wheel to his first mate with a nod of thanks, then turned to Clarissa with a warm smile. "Would you care to take a stroll about the deck with me, Lady Clarissa? I have been standing still too long at the wheel and would like to stretch my legs."

Clarissa's heart leapt at the prospect of spending more time in his company, though she endeavoured to maintain a calm exterior. "I would be delighted, Captain. Lead the way."

As they meandered along the deck, the salt-tinged breeze whipping at their hair and clothes, Rafael inquired, "I trust you are finding your accommodations suitable? I apologize that they are not as luxurious as what you are undoubtedly accustomed to."

"Nonsense," Clarissa replied with a dismissive wave of her hand. "After my ordeal on that dreadful corsair ship, this feels positively palatial. And the company is infinitely more agreeable." She favoured him with a playful smile.

Rafael chuckled, his eyes crinkling at the corners in a way that made Clarissa's stomach flutter. "I am glad to hear it. I must confess, I find our conversations most stimulating. It is a rare pleasure to discuss literature with someone as well-read and insightful as yourself."

Clarissa flushed with pleasure at the compliment. "Speaking of literature, I have been meaning to ask you about the poetry you recited for me at the Villa Ginori. The words were so hauntingly beautiful, but I am afraid I am not familiar with the poet. Camões, was it?"

"Ah, yes." Rafael's face lit up with enthusiasm. "Luís de Camões is considered one of the greatest poets in the Portuguese language. His epic work, 'Os Lusíadas,' is a masterpiece of Renaissance literature. It tells the story of Vasco da Gama's voyage to India, intertwined with the history and mythology of Portugal."

"How fascinating," Clarissa murmured, intrigued. "I should very much like to read it someday, but I fear my Portuguese is woefully inadequate - indeed, non-existent!"

Rafael's eyes sparkled with mischief. "Well, we shall have to remedy that, won't we? While I do not have a copy aboard, I know there is an English translation of Os Lusíadas at my home. I shall be happy to lend it to you."

Clarissa's heart swelled with gratitude and something deeper, something she dared not name. "I would like that very much, Captain de Silva. Thank you."

"We could seek to remedy the other issue as well, Lady Clarissa?"

Unsure what he meant, she blinked up at him. "The other issue?"

"Your lack of Portuguese.

She laughed, the sound carried away by the gentle sea breeze. "I am an eager pupil, Captain de Silva. Teach me."

He nodded, his expression growing more serious. "Let's start with something simple. 'Bom dia' means 'good day.'"

"Bom dia," Clarissa repeated, the foreign words feeling strange yet exciting on her tongue.

"Excellent," Rafael praised, his eyes shining with approval. "Now, try 'obrigado.' It means 'thank you.'"

"Obrigado," she echoed, the corners of her mouth tugging upward in a smile.

They continued in this manner, Rafael patiently guiding her through the basics of his native language, Clarissa absorbing every word like a sponge. She delighted in the way the Portuguese phrases rolled off his tongue, the lilting cadence of his voice sending shivers down her spine.

They settled in a quiet spot at the bow, Clarissa seating herself on a large coil of rope with little heed for the state of her gown, Rafael leaning on the railing close by, and continued the lesson, Clarissa's laughter occasionally spilling over as her tongue tangled on the unfamiliar words.

The sun began to set in a blaze of glory, painting the sky in a breathtaking array of oranges and pinks. Clarissa fell silent as she gazed, her eyes wide with wonder.

"It's magnificent, isn't it?" she breathed, her voice barely above a whisper. "I've seen some glorious sunsets in Italy, but I don't think I've ever seen anything quite so beautiful as this."

Rafael hummed in agreement. "Indeed, it is a sight to behold."

Clarissa turned to him with a quick smile, and was startled to find him gazing not at the sky, but at her. Her heart stuttered at the intensity in his eyes. For a moment, she forgot how to breathe, lost in the depths of his stare.

But then, as quickly as it had come, the moment passed, and Rafael looked away, clearing his throat. "We should head inside," he said, his voice gruff. "It's getting late, and your aunt and uncle will be wondering what has become of you."

Alex and Marianne did not seem in the least concerned about where she had been when she made her way below, however, and Clarissa found herself wondering just what exactly Alex and Rafael always found to talk about so seriously. Was it her? Surely, Alex could not possibly be considering... she cut off the thought before she allowed herself even to think it, laughing instead at the serious expression on little Edward's face as he tried to grab hold of Fernando the cat, who was far too clever to allow himself to be captured by a toddler, but seemed to be amused by the game nevertheless.

A knock on the door a little later proved to be the ship's boy, asking in broken English if he might lay the table for their dinner, and if they would permit the captain to join them for it.

"We should be delighted," Alex said firmly, "since we have evicted the captain from his cabin, the least we can do is invite him to dine in it with us!"

Rafael entered with a broad smile; Clarissa flattered herself that it grew even warmer when his eyes rested on her. She stepped forward to greet him, thanking him again for the comforts the Santa Dorotéia provided them.

The conversation flowed as smoothly as the wine Rafael poured, their words dancing between topics with the same effortless grace as the ship cutting through the waves. The laughter and warmth around the table made Clarissa feel at home, in a way she had not truly felt since Diana had returned to England.

As the meal progressed, Rafael introduced a new game, challenging Clarissa to craft a story using only a handful of seemingly unrelated words. She rose to the task, weaving a tale of adventure and intrigue that left them all hanging on her every word.

"You have a gift for storytelling," Rafael praised, his eyes sparkling with admiration as Marianne applauded her niece.

Clarissa ducked her head, a pleased flush colouring her cheeks. "I've always loved the power of words," she confessed. "The way they can transport you to another world, make you feel things you never thought possible."

"You should be a writer, Clarissa," Marianne suggested. "Truly, I have always thought so. The way you can recount a simple incident and have everyone fascinated, or laughing, is remarkable."

Clarissa thought of her journal, of the pages of notes she had written during their travels and the half-formed ideas she had to publish a travel journal when they arrived home. Her expression darkened slightly as the spectre of her father's certain disapproval hovered. Perhaps Marianne and Alex might agree to publish them on her behalf? She did not care about any monies she might earn – they could donate it to a charity for orphans – but to see her words in print would be wonderful, an achievement nobody could ever take away from her.

No matter who her father had picked out for her to marry.

Rafael was watching her, his expression thoughtful. "And yet, there are some things that words alone cannot capture," he said quietly.

Clarissa's breath caught in her throat at the intensity in his gaze, the unspoken emotions swirling between them.

But then, as quickly as it had come, the moment passed, and Rafael was rising from his seat, offering her his arm. "Shall we take a turn about the deck, Lady Clarissa?" he asked, his voice carefully neutral. "The sea is very calm tonight; I do not think we are making any headway, but I should like to check on things and thought you might like a breath of air before you retire.

Clarissa glanced at Alex for permission, glad to see his nod. Her heart was still racing as she placed her hand in the crook of Rafael's elbow. As they stepped out into the cool night air, she couldn't shake the feeling that something had shifted between them, a subtle change that both thrilled and terrified her in equal measure.

As they strolled along the deck, the salty sea breeze whipping at Clarissa's skirts, she couldn't help but marvel at the easy companionship that had blossomed between them. It seemed strange to think that only a few short weeks ago, they had been perfect strangers, brought together by the most unlikely of circumstances.

"I must confess," Rafael said, his voice low and intimate in the darkness, "I find myself quite envious of your adventures, Lady Clarissa. To have seen so much of the world, to have experienced such freedom..."

Clarissa glanced up at him, surprised by the wistful note in his tone. "But surely you have had your own share of adventures, Captain? The Navy must have taken you to all sorts of exotic locales, far more than I have seen."

Rafael chuckled, but there was little humour in the sound. "Ah, but there is a difference between seeing the world through the lens of duty and seeing it through the lens of curiosity. I fear I have had far too much of the former and not nearly enough of the latter."

Clarissa considered this for a moment, her brow furrowed in thought. "Perhaps," she said slowly, "it is not too late to change that. After all, life is nothing if not an endless series of opportunities for reinvention."

Rafael looked down at her. "You make it sound so simple."

"Oh, but it is!" Clarissa exclaimed, her face alight with enthusiasm. "All it takes is a bit of courage and a willingness to embrace the unknown. And from what I have seen of you, Captain Rafael de Silva, you possess both those qualities in spades."

For a long moment, Rafael simply stared at her, his expression unreadable in the moonlight. "You are an extraordinary woman, Lady Clarissa," he murmured, his voice rough with emotion. "I find myself quite in awe of you."

Clarissa's heart stuttered in her chest, her skin prickling with awareness as he reached out to tuck a stray curl behind her ear. The touch was fleeting, barely there, but it sent a shiver of longing through her entire body.

"Rafael," she whispered, his name a plea and a prayer all at once.

But before he could respond, the moment was shattered by the sound of footsteps approaching, and they sprang apart like guilty children, their cheeks flushed and their breathing unsteady.

As the crewman passed by, nodding respectfully to his captain, Clarissa couldn't help but feel a pang of disappointment. But when she glanced back at Rafael, she saw the same emotion reflected in his eyes, and she knew that whatever this thing was between them, it was far from over.

Rafael seemed to gather himself, his spine stiffening, before he spoke more formally. "Lady Clarissa, I wondered if you might be interested in assisting me with charting our course tonight?"

Clarissa's heart skipped a beat at the prospect of spending more time alone with him. "I would be delighted, Captain," she replied, trying to maintain a semblance of composure despite the butterflies fluttering in her stomach.

Rafael led her to the navigational table, where a sprawling map lay illuminated by the soft glow of lanterns. He began to explain the intricacies of nautical navigation, his deep, melodic voice washing over her like a caress.

As he pointed out their current position and the various instruments used to determine their route, Clarissa found herself increasingly distracted by the way the light played across his chiseled features, the way his eyes sparkled with passion as he spoke of the sea.

"It's a delicate balance," Rafael mused, tracing a finger along the map's edge. "One must always be mindful of the winds, the currents, the position of the stars. But when you get it right, there's nothing quite like it."

Clarissa nodded, her gaze locked on his. "It's like a dance, in a way. A partnership between the ship and the sea."

Rafael's eyes widened in surprise, then crinkled at the corners as he smiled. "Exactly so. I must say, Lady Clarissa, you have a remarkable understanding of these things for someone who has spent so little time at sea."

She felt a blush rise to her cheeks at his praise. "I've always been fascinated by the idea of exploration, of discovering new lands and cultures. I suppose I've read every book I could find on the subject."

"I can imagine you at the head of an expedition, leading the way to explore lost cities and unknown civilizations," Rafael murmured, making her laugh a little.

"I cannot imagine any man who would follow a lady in such an undertaking!"

"I can," Rafael said, the implication clear in his tone that he was one such man.

Clarissa smiled, looking up at the stars as he pointed out constellations to her, feeling an entirely unfamiliar warmth at the company of this unusual man, this Portuguese sea captain who had not only saved her life but was offering her so many new experiences, all without the slightest expectations of her in return for his kindness.

"Come," Rafael said suddenly. "The wind is picking up a little and we shall be underway again. You shall steer us through the stars tonight, my lady!" His hand under her elbow guided her gently to stand before the ships spoked wheel, almost as tall as she was.

Clarissa's eyes widened, her heart racing at the prospect. "But I don't know how," she protested, even as her fingers curled around the smooth wood of the wheel.

"Then I shall teach you," Rafael replied, moving to stand behind her, his strong, solid presence sending shivers down her spine.

Gently, he placed his hands over hers, guiding her movements as he pointed out the constellations above. "There, do you see?" he murmured, his breath warm against her ear. "That bright star is Polaris, the North Star. It's our constant guide, always pointing the way home."

Clarissa nodded, her breath catching in her throat as she leaned back into his embrace, savouring the feeling of his arms around her. For a moment, she allowed herself to imagine that this was their life, that they could sail the seas together forever, exploring new lands and new love.

But all too soon, the moment was broken by the sound of laughter from the deck below. Marianne and Alex, arm in arm, strolled into view, their eyes alight with mischief as they caught sight of the couple at the wheel.

"Well, well," Marianne called out, her voice teasing. "What have we here? A lesson in navigation?"

Clarissa felt her cheeks flush, and she stepped away from Rafael, suddenly aware of the impropriety of their embrace. But Rafael merely smiled, his eyes never leaving hers as he replied, "Indeed, Lady Glenkellie."

With a final, lingering look, he escorted her back to her cabin, his hand warm against the small of her back. At the door, he paused, his gaze intense as he reminded her to bolt the door behind her.

“Goodnight, Clarissa,” he whispered, his voice low and full of promise. “Sweet dreams.”

As the days passed, their connection only grew stronger, the seeds of friendship blossoming into something deeper, more profound. But always, there were eyes upon them - the crew, Marianne, Alex - a constant reminder of the world beyond their stolen moments.

Clarissa found herself longing for more, for a chance to explore the depths of her feelings without the weight of society’s expectations bearing down upon them. But for now, she would savour each precious moment, each brush of his hand against hers, each secret smile exchanged across a crowded deck.

For in those moments, she knew that whatever the future held, her heart would forever belong to the man who had shown her the stars.

CHAPTER TEN

Clarissa stood at the ship's railing, her gaze fixed on the horizon as the sun dipped slowly into the sea. The wind whipped at her hair, tugging loose strands from her coiffure, but she paid it no mind. Her thoughts were consumed by Rafael, by the way his presence seemed to fill every corner of the ship, every corner of her heart.

She sensed him before she saw him, his footsteps soft against the deck. "Clarissa," he murmured, coming to stand beside her. "Is everything alright?"

She forced a smile, tearing her gaze away from the endless expanse of blue. "Of course," she lied. "I was just admiring the view."

Rafael studied her for a long moment, his sea-green eyes searching her face. "You seem troubled," he observed softly. "Is there anything I can do to help?"

Clarissa hesitated, the words caught in her throat. How could she tell him of the frustration that gnawed at her, the sense that he was holding back, keeping some part of himself locked away? She knew of his worry for his sister, his desperate need to return home, but still, she longed for more.

"I am just tired," she said at last, the half-truth bitter on her tongue. "It has been a long journey."

Rafael nodded, his gaze softening with understanding. "It will not be much longer now," he assured her. "We are making good time. We will put into Gibraltar tomorrow for a day or two, and with fair winds, we should reach Lisbon within the week."

Clarissa felt a pang at his words, a sudden, sharp ache in her chest. The thought of their journey's end, of the inevitable parting that awaited them, was almost more than she could bear. But she pushed the feeling aside, forcing a lightness into her voice as she replied, "I shall be glad to see land again, I must admit."

Rafael chuckled, the sound warm and rich in the gathering dusk. "As shall I," he agreed. "But I will miss this, miss the freedom of the open sea." He paused, his gaze lingering on her face. "And the company," he added softly.

Clarissa's heart leapt at his words, a flicker of hope igniting in her chest. But she tamped it down, reminding herself of the realities that awaited them on shore. Rafael had his duties, his family to consider, and she...she had a life to return to, a future to navigate.

"We should make the most of the time we have left, then," she said, her voice carefully light. "Before the demands of the real world come crashing down upon us once more."

Rafael smiled, a hint of sadness in his eyes. "Indeed we should," he agreed. He offered her his arm, his touch gentle as he guided her away from the railing. "Shall we take a turn about the deck? The stars are particularly lovely tonight."

Clarissa nodded, allowing him to lead her across the weathered planks. She knew that the coming days would be bittersweet, a tangle of joy and sorrow as their time together drew to a close. But for now, she would savour each moment, each precious second in his company.

For in the end, she knew, that was all they could ever have. Stolen moments beneath the stars, memories to carry with them into the uncertain future that awaited them both. And for now, that would have to be enough.

The Santa Dorotéia glided gracefully into the bustling port of Gibraltar, sails furling smoothly as her crew went about their business with practised precision. The cacophony of the harbour greeted them—vendors hawking their wares, sailors shouting orders, and the distant clatter of horse-drawn carriages navigating the cobblestone streets. A salty breeze carried the mingling scents of fresh fish and exotic spices from lands far away.

"Lady Clarissa," Rafael began, extending a gentlemanly hand to assist her down the gangplank, "I trust you are eager for our little excursion ashore while my crew replenish our stores and take on cargo?"

"Indeed, Captain de Silva," Clarissa replied with a playful sparkle in her eye, accepting his hand. "Despite the Santa Dorotéia's comforts, I confess I have grown weary of the relentless rocking of the waves and seek the firm ground beneath my feet."

"Then let us waste no time," Rafael said, his eyes twinkling with amusement.

As they stepped onto the quay, Clarissa marvelled at the vibrant tapestry of life unfolding before them. Dockworkers unloaded crates of goods, while merchants arranged their colourful stalls under striped awnings. The air buzzed with the melodic hum of various languages intermingling in a symphony of commerce.

"Where shall we begin?" she asked, curiosity piqued by the array of sights and sounds.

"Allow me to be your guide," Rafael replied, offering her his arm. They navigated through the throngs of people, drawing curious glances as they walked—a striking pair indeed, with Clarissa's sun-kissed hair gleaming like spun gold and Rafael's commanding presence unmistakable even in the lively crowd.

Their path took them through narrow alleyways lined with quaint shops, where the scent of freshly baked bread mingled with the aromatic allure of Mediterranean herbs. Clarissa could not resist peering into a window showcasing intricate lacework, her fingers itching to touch the delicate patterns.

"Do you admire such craftsmanship?" Rafael inquired, noting her interest.

"Very much," she replied, eyes sparkling. "Each piece tells a story, woven with care and dedication." She fingered the purse in her pocket, considering how much money she had remaining. "Do you think we might enter and inquire about the prices? I might purchase some - a piece for Marianne and one for my mother, perhaps."

Rafael obliged, and Clarissa was sure his commanding presence was of assistance as she haggled with the shopkeeper, who fortunately spoke excellent English. The prices were far lower than she might have expected to pay in England or even Italy, and she ended up purchasing not only lace for Marianne and her mother, but also some for Diana.

Rafael spoke in rapid-fire Spanish as Clarissa finished her transaction, pointing at several more pieces of lace. The shopkeeper bowed obsequiously and made up a second parcel, Clarissa assumed for Rafael's mother and sister, and agreed to send both parcels back to the ship at once while they continued their explorations.

Clarissa adjusted her bonnet, squinting up at the formidable Rock of Gibraltar. The path ahead wound steeply, a challenge she was eager to embrace.

"Are you certain you are prepared for this climb?" Rafael inquired with a teasing glint in his eye.

"Assuredly," Clarissa replied with a smile. "I have faced many a social mountain; surely a physical one cannot be more daunting."

"Touché," he said, laughing softly. "Then let us conquer this peak together."

As they ascended, the air grew crisper, tinged with the salty tang of the sea. The calls of gulls echoed around them, mingling with the distant hum of the bustling port below. Clarissa's skirts swished against the rocky path, each step a testament to her determination. The Barbary apes scampered away as they approached, obviously intrigued but too shy to come close, for which Clarissa was more relieved than sorry - they had large teeth!

"Look there," Rafael pointed out, stopping finally as they reached the summit. "The view—it's worth every effort."

They had reached a vantage point, and Clarissa gasped. Below them stretched an expanse of azure sea, dotted with ships like toys floating on a cerulean pond. The land unfolded in a tapestry of greens and browns, bordered by the sparkling coastline.

"Magnificent," she breathed, her eyes wide with wonder.

"Indeed," Rafael agreed, though his gaze remained fixed on her. "A sight to remember."

"Thank you for bringing me here," she said earnestly, turning to face him. "It's—" She faltered, searching for words that could encapsulate her gratitude.

"An adventure," he supplied, his voice warm.

"Precisely," she affirmed, feeling a surge of camaraderie with him. "An adventure."

They lingered a few moments longer, absorbing the panorama before beginning their descent. Clarissa felt lighter, buoyed by the shared experience and the burgeoning connection between them.

The ship would remain in Gibraltar overnight, and Marianne had requested Alex to take rooms for them in a hotel for the night, so that she and Clarissa could bathe properly and have their clothes laundered. Alex, ever acquiescent to his wife's every whim, had promptly booked a suite in the best hotel in Gibraltar and invited Rafael to join them to dine in the hotel's restaurant.

The establishment exuded elegance, its grand facade promising an evening of refined pleasure.

"How was your excursion?" Marianne inquired, her striking red hair catching the candlelight as they were seated.

"Enlightening," Clarissa replied, casting a glance at Rafael. "And invigorating."

"Excellent." Alex raised his glass. "To new horizons."

"To new horizons," they echoed, clinking glasses as the first course was served.

The meal unfolded in a symphony of flavours—delicate soups, succulent meats, and decadent desserts—all accompanied by lively conversation. Rafael and Clarissa exchanged witty repartee, their words flowing as smoothly as the fine wine.

As the evening drew to a close, Clarissa felt a contentment settle over her, a sense of belonging she had not anticipated. The elegant surroundings, the engaging company, and the day's shared experiences combined to create a memory she would cherish.

"Until our next adventure," Rafael murmured as they parted ways for the night, his voice a gentle caress.

"Until then," she replied, her heart light and hopeful.

The room at the hotel was opulently appointed, with heavy drapes of burgundy velvet, a canopy bed adorned in brocade, and an ornate chandelier casting a soft glow. Yet despite the luxurious surroundings, Clarissa found herself restless. She lay atop the plush mattress, staring at the ceiling.

"Why can I not find solace here?" she muttered to herself, turning onto her side. The room's stillness felt oppressive, a far cry from the gentle sway of the Santa Dorotéia that had become oddly comforting. She missed the rhythmic creaks of the timbers, the distant call of the sea birds, and most disconcertingly, she missed Rafael.

"Clarissa, are you awake?" Marianne's voice floated through the adjoining door, a soft interruption to her musings.

"Yes, Marianne," Clarissa replied, sitting up and smoothing her nightgown. "I fear sleep eludes me this evening."

"Come, join me for a moment," Marianne invited. Her tone held a warmth that transcended their complicated relationship. Crossing into Marianne's room, Clarissa found her seated by the window, a steaming cup of tea in hand.

"Where is Uncle Alex?" Clarissa asked.

"Restless too," Marianne admitted. "He went out for a walk. Sit with me." She patted the window seat beside her. Now tell me, is it the ship you miss or its captain?" Marianne's eyes twinkled with knowing mischief.

"Perhaps both," Clarissa admitted, taking the offered seat. "But more than that, I long for the sense of purpose I feel aboard the Santa Dorotéia."

"Ah, the thrill of adventure," Marianne remarked, her gaze drifting out to the moonlit harbour. "It is a powerful lure."

"Indeed," Clarissa agreed, feeling a pang of longing as she imagined the ship rocking gently in the bay. "I do not know how I shall settle back into the constrained life that awaits me at home, Aunt Marianne," she said quietly, and Marianne reached out to take Clarissa's hand.

"I wonder if we did the right thing, bringing you on this trip," Marianne said thoughtfully, and Clarissa's eyes flew to her aunt's face, a shocked denial springing to her lips. Marianne shook her head. "Hear me out. After what happened to you in Athens..."

"That was not your fault!" Clarissa insisted vehemently. "And if it had not happened, I should never have met Rafael... Captain de Silva, I mean!"

"Indeed," Marianne said quietly, looking at her with a curious expression on her face, before she gave a rueful little smile. "Well. There is no sense crying over spilt milk. You have had enough adventures to last several lifetimes, Clarissa!"

They will have to last me the whole of this one, Clarissa thought sadly, turning her head to gaze out of the window. *Once I get back to London, my mother will never allow me out of her sight until I'm safely married to some suitably staid lord who will never let me so much as think of adventure again.*

Morning arrived with the golden hues of dawn creeping through the curtains. Clarissa dressed quickly, eager to return to the Santa Dorotéia. The bustling port of Gibraltar was already alive with activity as the group prepared to leave the hotel.

"Good morning, milady," Jean greeted her with a curt nod, the toddler twins clinging to her skirts like cherubic barnacles.

"Good morning, Jean," Clarissa responded brightly, bending down to scoop one of the children into her arms. "And how are my favourite little sailors today? Ready to go back aboard the ship?"

"Full of energy, as always," Jean replied, her no-nonsense demeanour softened by her affectionate smile.

As the ship set sail for Lisbon, Clarissa found herself delighting in the simple tasks of caring for the twins. Their laughter was infectious, their boundless curiosity a constant source of amusement. Whether chasing after a mischievous child or soothing a scraped knee, she embraced each moment with enthusiasm.

"Hold still, Edward," Clarissa instructed gently, dabbing a damp cloth on the boy's cheek where he had smeared jam. "You mustn't run amok during breakfast, or you'll end up looking like a ragamuffin. And we cannot have that, now can we?" The child squirmed and giggled, before planting a slightly sticky kiss on her cheek and running away to join his sister at play with their toys.

Jean watched the interaction, laughing quietly. "You have a way with them, milady," she observed.

"Thank you, Jean," Clarissa replied, feeling a swell of pride at the compliment. "They are delightful company."

The day passed in a blur of activity, the ship cutting through the azure waters with grace as she passed out of the Straits of Gibraltar and into the wide Atlantic Ocean.

The Santa Dorotéia rocked gently on the moonlit waters, its timbers creaking softly in the night. Clarissa, her skirts rustling faintly with each step, moved deftly about the dimly lit cabin. A small lantern cast a warm glow, illuminating her serene face as she coaxed the twins to settle down.

From his vantage point by the doorway, Rafael watched in silent admiration. The flickering light caught the golden hues in her sun-bleached hair, making it appear as if spun from threads of sunlight. Her hands, gentle yet firm, cradled the children with an ease that seemed innate.

"Shhh, darlings," she crooned, gathering the squirming toddlers into her arms. She began to sway, a rhythmic motion meant to soothe. Her voice, tender and melodious, wove through the air like a delicate thread.

"While the moon her watch is keeping

All through the night

While the weary world is sleeping

All through the night

O'er thy spirit gently stealing

Visions of delight revealing

Breathes a pure and holy feeling

All through the night," she sang, her tones soft and lilting. The lullaby, an old folk tune translated from its original Welsh, floated around them, its gentle cadence filling the room. The twins' cries began to subside, replaced by intermittent whimpers that grew fainter with each passing moment.

"Clarissa, may I assist?" Rafael asked, stepping into the cabin. His voice was low, careful not to startle the already restless toddlers.

"Thank you, Captain," she replied, her eyes meeting his with a grateful smile. "They are both teething, poor mites. I sent Jean to sleep in my cabin; she is exhausted from several sleepless nights. A distracting tale might do wonders."

"Very well," he said, settling himself beside her and reaching out to stroke Eleanor's red cheek; the child quieted a little and eyed him curiously. "Did I ever tell you of the time we outwitted a corsair near Madeira?"

"Do tell," Clarissa urged, her attention divided between Rafael and the twins.

"Well, it began as all good tales do—with a storm," Rafael began, his tone conspiratorially low. He launched into the story, weaving a narrative rich with daring manoeuvres and close calls. As he spoke, Clarissa's laughter rang softly in the enclosed space, mingling with the slowly quieting whimpers of the children.

"Your adventures are always so thrilling," she remarked, her eyes twinkling with amusement.

"Thrilling perhaps, but often fraught with peril," Rafael responded, his gaze lingering on her face. "Unlike your current endeavour, which seems equally challenging."

"Children are far more unpredictable than any storm or corsair," she said with a chuckle. "But infinitely more rewarding."

Rafael nodded thoughtfully, his eyes never leaving her. "I can see that."

At last, the twins' eyelids began to droop, lulled by the combined effect of Clarissa's gentle rocking and Rafael's engrossing tale. Soon, they were nestled peacefully in their beds, their tiny chests rising and falling with each breath.

"Sleep tight, darlings," Clarissa murmured, brushing a stray curl from one child's forehead.

"Your touch has a magic all its own," Rafael observed quietly, his admiration evident.

"Perhaps," she replied, turning to face him fully. "Or perhaps it's simply the love one feels for those in their care."

"Either way, it is a gift," he said earnestly.

"Thank you," Clarissa said, her voice softening, and for a long moment they simply gazed at each other, unspoken words heavy in the space between them.

"Goodnight, Clarissa," Rafael said finally, his voice tinged with reluctance. He made his way to the cabin door, casting one last glance at the serene tableau behind him.

"Goodnight, Captain," she replied, her smile lingering even after he had disappeared into the shadows of the ship.

Clarissa stood at the ship's railing, her fingers gripping the cool, weathered wood as she gazed out over the endless expanse of the sea. The sun had dipped low, painting the western horizon in hues of gold and crimson, casting a shimmering path across the water. A gentle breeze played with the loose tendrils of her sun-bleached hair, carrying with it the salty tang of the ocean.

"Do you ever wonder what lies beyond that line?" Rafael's voice broke the tranquil silence, drawing her attention from the mesmerising view. He stood beside her, his tall frame outlined against the setting sun, his sea-green eyes reflecting the myriad colours of the sky.

"Beyond the horizon?" Clarissa mused, her brow furrowing slightly. "I suppose I do. It seems to promise so much—adventure, opportunity, perhaps even a new beginning."

"Indeed," Rafael agreed, a thoughtful look crossing his rugged features. "The future is as vast and unpredictable as the sea itself. We chart our course, but the winds and waves have their own will."

"Much like life," she added, stealing a glance at him. "We plan and hope, yet we are often swept along by forces beyond our control."

"True," he said softly, considering her words. "Yet it is those very uncertainties that make the journey worthwhile, do they not? The unexpected moments, the uncharted paths—they shape us, mould us into who we are meant to be."

"Speaking of uncharted paths," Clarissa began, her tone tinged with curiosity, "what future do you envision for yourself? Will you return to your family's vineyard?"

Rafael leaned against the railing, his gaze distant. "Our vineyard... It holds many memories, both sweet and bitter. I do wish to restore it, to breathe life back into the land that has sustained my family for generations. But more than that, I long to see my mother and sister thrive, to ensure they know peace and happiness once more."

"Such noble aspirations," Clarissa remarked, genuine admiration in her voice. "You carry a heavy burden, Rafael. Yet you bear it with such grace."

"Thank you, Clarissa," he replied, his eyes meeting hers with an intensity that made her heart quicken. "And what of you? What awaits Lady Clarissa Creighton upon her return to England?"

"Ah, England," she sighed, her expression becoming wistful. "I suppose I shall return to the usual expectations—balls, social engagements, the relentless pursuit of a suitable match. Yet, after all I have seen and experienced, those things seem so trivial now."

"Perhaps because you have discovered a different kind of fulfilment," Rafael suggested, his voice laced with understanding. "One that cannot be found within the confines of society's strictures."

"Yes," she admitted quietly. "This journey has opened my eyes to so much more—to the richness of different cultures, the beauty of the world beyond England's shores. And... to the depth of human connection."

"Connection," Rafael echoed, his gaze softening as it lingered on her. "It is a powerful thing, is it not? It transcends distance, social standing, even the barriers of language."

"Speaking of language," Clarissa said, turning to look at him directly. "Your family—I wish to make a good impression. They've been through so much, and I want to show them proper respect. Would you teach me some more Portuguese phrases? Enough to greet your mother and sister and thank them for their hospitality."

Rafael blinked, momentarily taken aback by her earnest request. Then, a slow smile spread across his face. "Of course, Clarissa. It would be my honour."

"Thank you," she said, relief evident in her voice. "I've learned a few basics, but they sound so awkward coming from me. I fear I may insult them rather than impress."

"Not at all," he reassured her. "Your effort alone will speak volumes. But let us begin with something simple. Repeat after me: 'Muito prazer em conhecê-la'—'Pleased to meet you.'"

"Meu-to pra-zher em con-he-che-la," she attempted, furrowing her brow in concentration.

"Close," he chuckled. "Let's try it once more. Muito prazer em conhecê-la."

"Mui-to praz-er em con-he-ce-la," she repeated, her pronunciation improving.

"Excellent," Rafael said, nodding appreciatively. "You are a quick learner."

"Only because I have an excellent teacher," she quipped, meeting his gaze with determination.

"Then let us continue," he said, leaning closer, their proximity creating an intimate bubble amidst the bustling ship. "This one is important: 'Obrigado pela hospitalidade'—'Thank you for your hospitality.'"

"Obri-gado pela hos-pi-ta-li-da-de," she recited, her voice gaining confidence with each syllable.

"Perfect," Rafael said softly, his admiration for her growing with every word. "You will do wonderfully, Clarissa. My family will be most impressed."

"Thank you, Rafael," she said, her eyes shining with appreciation. "Your faith in me means more than you know."

"Let us try something a bit more challenging," Rafael suggested.

"More challenging than 'Muito prazer em conhecê-la'?" she teased, raising a mischievous eyebrow.

"Indeed," he replied with a grin. "Repeat after me: 'O jardim da minha mãe é muito bonito.' It means, 'My mother's garden is very beautiful.'"

Clarissa took a deep breath, her lips forming the unfamiliar words with deliberate care. "Oh zhar-deem dah mee-nya may eh moo-ee-to bo-nee-to."

"Almost there," Rafael corrected gently, his fingers tapping the rhythm of the sentence on the wooden rail. "Listen closely: 'O jardim da minha mãe é muito bonito.' Pay special attention to the nasal sounds."

"Of course, those tricky nasals," she said, rolling her eyes playfully. She tried again, this time with increased precision. "O jardim da minha mãe é muito bonito."

"Perfect!" Rafael exclaimed, clapping his hands together in genuine delight. "You have an ear for languages, Lady Clarissa."

"Or perhaps just a highly persuasive tutor," she countered, her eyes twinkling with amusement.

"Flattery will get you everywhere," he responded, his tone light but his gaze lingering on hers a moment longer than necessary.

"Then I shall continue to employ it liberally," she said, laughing. "What is next on our list?"

"Try this: 'A comida está deliciosa,' which means, 'The food is delicious.'"

"Ah co-mee-da es-ta de-li-ci-o-sa," she repeated, her accent still tinged with her English roots but improved nonetheless.

"Excellent!" Rafael proclaimed, his pride in her palpable. "With every word, you grow more confident. Your efforts are paying off splendidly."

"Only because you make it so enjoyable," she admitted, her cheeks flushing slightly under his approving gaze.

"That is the best way to learn," he said, his voice warm and encouraging. "When it is more than mere study, when it becomes a shared adventure."

"An adventure indeed," she echoed, smiling up at him as the evening shadows lengthened around them.

CHAPTER ELEVEN

The Santa Dorotéia glided through the morning mist, slipping into the bustling harbour of Lisbon. Clarissa stood at the bow, clinging to the wooden rail with white knuckles, her hands betraying her anticipation. The tang of salt was sharp on her tongue and fresh against her cheeks, already rosy with excitement and the cool sea breeze.

"Lady Clarissa." Rafael's voice cut through the screeching of the seagulls and the shouts of dockworkers. She turned to see him standing beside her, his dark hair tousled by the wind.

"Captain de Silva," she replied, a teasing note in her voice. "It seems my new adventure is about to begin."

"Indeed," Rafael chuckled warmly. "Shall we disembark? I have arranged for a carriage to collect the ladies and children, taking you to my family's estate, and horses for Lord Glenkellie and myself."

"We'll be ready to leave directly," Clarissa said, though she knew Jean had everything packed and ready to go, their trunks only needing to be loaded aboard the waiting carriage.

Within an hour, they stepped off the ship onto the cobblestone dock. The city of Lisbon spread out before them, narrow streets and sunlit squares beckoning, a kaleidoscope of activity and colour. Clarissa could hardly look from one thing to the next, her eyes wide with curiosity as they darted from one scene to another - a group of children chasing an errant dog, a fishmonger shouting about his catch, a woman in a red shawl balancing a basket on her head.

"Lisbon is... lively," she finally said, clearly fascinated.

"One might say it reflects you, my lady," Rafael teased, and Alex, standing nearby, raised his brows and laughed quietly.

"Flattery will get you nowhere, Captain," Clarissa replied, though she couldn't help but smile.

Their conversation was interrupted by the arrival of a carriage, its polished wooden panels gleaming in the sun. The driver doffed his cap to Rafael, who nodded in acknowledgement.

"After you, my lady," Rafael said, offering his hand to help her into the carriage.

"How gallant," Clarissa said, but she put her hand in his anyway. He lifted her up and she sank down with a sigh of pleasure into the well-padded seat, surprised by the unexpected luxury. However impoverished Rafael's family might be, he himself had the manners of a nobleman, as was evidenced again when he assisted Marianne into the carriage after her, then Jean and the twins. Taking both children from Jean, he handed them into Marianne and Clarissa's waiting arms before assisting the maid to climb in.

"He's a proper gentleman, that one," Jean remarked as Rafael closed the carriage door. He and Alex swung up onto their horses, and the little cavalcade started forward.

"Captain de Silva is indeed a very fine gentleman," Marianne agreed. "Don't you think, Clarissa?" She exchanged a knowing smile with Jean.

Not ready to discuss her feelings about Rafael, Clarissa murmured something noncommittal and turned her attention to the twins. It was going to be a long and boring day for them, she knew, and she would do her best to keep them entertained. Rafael had told them that his estate lay several hours' travel north and east of Lisbon, and they should reach it within a day, so there would be no need to find an inn to stay overnight.

A jolt on the rough road brought Clarissa back to her surroundings, and she leaned forward, gripping the window frame, her mouth falling open further and further with each mile they travelled. The Portuguese countryside spread out before her; rolling hills covered in green and gold, dotted with white cottages and olive groves. The air smelled sweetly of jasmine and carried the hum of cicadas, a natural orchestra that moved her deeply.

"What beautiful country," Marianne said softly beside her, and she nodded, unable to tear her eyes from the view.

The coach entered a picturesque village and drew up outside an inn. Rafael was at the door before Clarissa could even reach for it.

"We will change horses here, and take a meal," he said, offering his hand to help her down. "I have stopped here many times and know the innkeeper well."

A smiling man came out to greet them warmly, ushering them inside and, to Clarissa's surprise, through the building and out onto a covered terrace on the other side.

"Oh, what a wonderful view!" she exclaimed, stepping to the low wall which bordered the terrace and looking out over the wide valley beyond.

"See that gap in the hills?" Rafael came to stand beside her and pointed. She squinted to follow his direction before nodding. "That is the way to Torre do Rochedo."

"Your estate?" She turned to look at him. "What does the name mean?"

"Tower on the rock. Cliff." He shrugged. "You'll see; it's an apt name!"

"I look forward to it."

The innkeeper came out again then, with two servants in tow, all of them bearing platters laden with food. Clarissa sat down beside Marianne, her mouth watering as a veritable feast was set before them.

There was a crusty yellow loaf called broa, made with cornmeal, sharp white sheep's cheese, smoked chicken sausages, olives, figs, and a dish of very salty, addictive little yellow dried beans, all served with a light white wine. It was simple fare, but Clarissa found it delicious and told the innkeeper so in her halting Portuguese, which made him grin even wider.

"What did he say?" Clarissa asked Rafael when the man spoke quickly in Portuguese before hurrying back inside.

"He said, the best is yet to come." Rafael chuckled at her expression. "He takes pride in his desserts, and I must agree - his pastéis de nata are some of the best I have ever tasted, and his toucinho do céu - ah!" He kissed his fingertips. "Truly heavenly!"

The pastéis de nata were delectable little egg custard tarts in delicate flaky pastry that melted in her mouth, and the toucinho do céu, which Rafael explained meant 'bacon from heaven', was actually a dense sweet lard cake with a strong almond flavour.

Clarissa had to agree. The desserts were indeed better than the meal. "I think we've been spoiled," she said, looking wistfully at the platter of custard tarts and realising she could not eat another bite. "Considering this was our first meal in Portugal, your home has quite a lot to live up to, Captain de Silva!"

"Your first meal in Portugal," Alex corrected her. She glanced at him, surprised, then remembered he had spent many years in the army fighting the French. His gaze was dark as he stared out over the terrace and she wondered what thoughts occupied his mind; certainly not of the verdant, fertile valley which stretched before them now, she guessed.

Marianne placed a hand on Alex's, giving it a brief squeeze. He seemed to shake himself back into the present and smiled faintly.

"Though I must agree, I've never eaten such an excellent meal in your country before, Rafael. It was superb."

They lingered awhile longer, allowing the food to digest. Clarissa found herself returning to the edge of the terrace, sitting on the low wall this time and admiring the view. After a few minutes, Rafael came to join her.

"Is it time to leave?" Clarissa asked.

"Soon enough. We'll let the horses rest another fifteen minutes or so." He did not seem inclined to conversation, simply taking a seat beside her and gazing out over the valley.

"Tell me," Clarissa said at last, unable to bear the silence any longer, "what awaits us at your home?"

"Memories," Rafael said after a moment, his expression distant. "And perhaps ghosts."

"Ghosts?" Her brows arched curiously.

"Not literal ones," he said with a faint smile. "The war left wounds on the land, but also on its people. My family bears those wounds, as you will see."

"Then we shall face those ghosts together," she declared firmly.

"Together," Rafael agreed, and for the first time since they'd met, she thought she saw a hint of vulnerability in his dark eyes.

They set off again soon after. As they travelled further inland, the lush green scenery was replaced by rocky outcrops and ancient stone walls. Clarissa noted the vineyards, once neatly tended, now choked with weeds. It made her sad; like so many other things she'd seen on this journey, it was a silent testament to war and neglect.

The carriage finally passed through the gap in the hills Rafael had mentioned and climbed up a steep slope to a castle perched on the edge of a sheer cliff. Clarissa caught her breath as she looked out the window at their destination. Torre do Rochedo was a tall, square structure with a central tower that rose five or six storeys high, its stone walls weathered but still strong, turrets reaching for the sky. Yet even from here, she could see the signs of decay; battlements crumbling into piles of rubble, ivy creeping over windows where glass had long since shattered, and parts of the outer wall lying in ruins.

"It's larger than I assumed," Marianne said quietly beside her, leaning forward to look past her out the window. "And in far better condition than most of the castles in Portugal which Napoleon did not destroy completely. The central keep, at least, appears quite intact."

When the carriage drew to a halt, Clarissa had to resist the urge to leap down eagerly. She wanted to make a good impression on Rafael's mother and sister, who were presumably waiting to greet them inside, and thus composed herself. Folding her hands together in her lap to stop them trembling, she waited until Rafael opened the door and offered his hand to help her descend.

"Welcome to Torre do Rochedo," he said proudly as she stepped down from the carriage. "Welcome to my home."

Clarissa placed one slippered foot on the cobblestone paving of the courtyard, feeling almost reverent, and turned slowly to survey the mixture of grandeur and decay. This place spoke of centuries of history, of battles won and lost, of a family clinging to dignity despite loss and impoverishment.

"Your home," she said softly, looking at him. "It is magnificent, Rafael. A monument to endurance."

"Thank you." He inclined his head slightly, though she saw more emotion in his eyes than his words might have suggested.

Together, they walked towards the entrance, and Clarissa could only imagine what tales these walls could tell. Worn by time and history though it might be, Torre do Rochedo was no less majestic for its age. It stood as a symbol of resilience, a fitting home for the man who was guiding her inside. The large wooden door opened as they climbed the steps, and a woman stood there, face alight with joy.

"Mama," Rafael said, and there was a thickness in his tone, an unfamiliar roughness.

Lucia de Silva was a small woman, slight and somewhat stooped with age and hardship, but her presence filled the space. Her eyes, tired and lined though they were, sparkled with happiness, and she hurried forward, eagerness in every step though it seemed to cost her effort, and threw her arms around her son.

"Meu filho," she murmured, her voice thick with emotion.

"Mother." Rafael's voice was equally choked. He embraced her tightly, then pulled back, grasping her shoulders, and said urgently, "Isabella?"

Lucia's smile was all the answer he needed, and Clarissa felt a weight lift from her shoulders. She had feared they would arrive only to discover Rafael's sister had died of some illness.

"She says Isabella was ill with pneumonia but has recovered now," Alex whispered as Lucia spoke rapidly to her son in Portuguese.

"Thank God," Marianne murmured, and Clarissa echoed the sentiment.

Rafael remembered his manners then, and introduced them to his mother. Clarissa already knew Rafael had sent a messenger on ahead; their arrival was no surprise to Lucia. The older woman greeted Alex and Marianne warmly, though, before Rafael turned to introduce Clarissa.

"Lady Clarissa, welcome to our home," Lucia said in accented but clear English, smiling warmly at Clarissa. "It is an honour for us to receive you."

"Thank you so much, Mrs de Silva," Clarissa replied, dipping into a low curtsy. As she straightened, she took in Lucia's plain gown. It was well made, but the fabric was worn and faded; here and there, tiny patches showed where careful repairs had been done. From what she'd seen of the estate so far, it looked much the same. Though the house itself still stood, its former glory had long since faded, and Clarissa suspected Lucia ran a tight budget to keep things running. She admired the older woman very much, even knowing that Rafael's mother had not always approved of him.

"Please, come inside and rest. You must be weary after your journey." Lucia gestured for them to follow her into the house. "Rooms have been prepared for you all, though I hope you will excuse any inadequacies."

Clarissa looked around. The whitewashed walls were hung with tapestries, but they were old and faded, threadbare in places. Once, they must have been glorious, but time had taken its toll. The furniture, too, was simple, plain wood chairs with woven cane backs, a few small tables, a sideboard or two.

"Your hospitality is most generous," Clarissa assured Lucia sincerely, following her into a small sitting room which, while somewhat shabby, was neat and clean, with a fire in the hearth adding welcome warmth to the cool room.

"I must go to Isabella." Rafael excused himself, leaving them in his mother's care as Lucia called over a couple of maids.

Clarissa almost asked if she might go with Rafael, eager to meet his sister, but held her tongue and smiled politely when one of the maids beckoned her to follow.

The guest rooms had clearly been hastily readied, windows thrown open to let fresh air blow through, linens stripped from the beds and replaced with fresh sheets. Though the furniture was simple, Clarissa found her room charming, and realised that though the buildings had survived the French, much of the original furniture might have been taken and burned for firewood, and the estate's restricted finances meant they could not afford to spend much on guest rooms rarely used.

Still, the bed looked comfortable enough, and there was a small table and chair by the window where she could sit and write letters if she wished. She thanked the maid in her halting Portuguese, receiving a shy smile and a deep curtsy in return before the girl hurried off, returning shortly with a tray bearing a plate of sliced fruit, a few pieces of cake, and a pot of coffee.

"Oh, how lovely," Clarissa said, looking to see if there might be a tea pot hiding anywhere. She had never been fond of coffee. Well, there was a good-sized jug of milk on the side; she would simply drink that.

"*Você não gosta de café?*" the maid asked, pointing at the coffee pot when Clarissa poured only milk into her cup.

Clarissa could guess the meaning, even if she didn't understand the exact words. She pointed at the coffee pot, wrinkled her nose, shook her head and smiled apologetically. The maid nodded and disappeared, and Clarissa hoped she hadn't offended her. Trying a bite of the cake, she discovered it was delicious, strongly flavoured with honey, cinnamon and cloves. She could definitely get used to Portuguese desserts!

The maid returned with a large jug of grape juice, and Clarissa smiled happily. She thanked her as best she could. The coffee pot was taken away, and Clarissa enjoyed her afternoon tea in solitary peace, gazing out of the window at the view.

A knock at the door a few minutes later proved to be Rafael, who stayed outside when she opened it.

"Isabella wishes to meet you," he said, smiling broadly. "I am so relieved to have her safe and on the mend, I find myself unable to refuse her anything."

"I'd love to meet her!" Clarissa stood up immediately. "I'm very eager to make her acquaintance."

Rafael offered his arm to escort her, and they ascended another flight of stairs to the next floor of the castle, which was evidently the family quarters. Rafael stopped outside a wooden door, knocked once, then opened it without waiting for any response.

Clarissa moved through the doorway, her eyes adjusting to the dim light filtering through gauzy curtains. The room was sparsely furnished, but a kind of elegant simplicity prevailed. In the centre of the room, propped up against a mountain of pillows, lay Isabella.

"Lady Clarissa." Isabella greeted her in a faint but clear voice, speaking English as perfectly as her brother. Her skin was ghostly pale, almost translucent, and dark shadows framed her eyes, though they were bright and intelligent. "It's an honour to meet you."

"The honour is mine, Isabella," Clarissa said warmly, moving to take a seat beside the bed. "I have heard so much about you, and your great fortitude in this difficult time."

"Fortitude." Isabella gave a weak smile. "Patience would be more accurate, I think."

"Patience is something I often find myself lacking," Clarissa confided, hoping to coax another smile from the girl. "But I think you must have learned it well."

"When one has no choice but to lie abed all day, one learns patience out of necessity rather than virtue," Isabella replied, though her eyes seemed brighter now.

"Perhaps I might offer some distraction?" Clarissa suggested, leaning forward with a conspiratorial air. "Rafael tells me you are quite the scholar, with a keen mind and a love of literature."

"Does he now?" Isabella's expression softened, and she glanced over at her brother, standing quietly by the door. "He always did know how to flatter me."

"Flattery or not, I should love to hear your thoughts on some of my favourite books," Clarissa continued, sensing she had hit upon the right note. "And perhaps tell you some of my own stories."

"That sounds delightful," Isabella said, colour coming into her cheeks. "It has been too long since I could enjoy a good conversation."

"Then we shall make up for lost time," Clarissa said firmly, settling back into her chair. "Tell me, what were your favourite stories growing up?"

"Oh, many," Isabella said, her voice gaining strength as she spoke. "But my favourite memories are of Rafael telling me the legends of our ancestors. He made them come alive, so I felt I stood beside them in battle or rode with them across the plains. This old castle became a living, breathing place when he told me his tales."

"Ah, the power of a good story." Clarissa nodded, understanding. "Words can turn even the dullest days into grand adventures."

"Yes." Isabella smiled, her eyes sparkling. "In this room, they have been my escape."

“Then we shall make new stories together,” Clarissa promised her, feeling a kinship with the younger woman. “Every day is a chance for a new beginning, no matter what life brings us.”

“Thank you, Lady Clarissa,” Isabella said sincerely. “You have already brought brightness into my day.”

“Call me Clarissa, please,” Clarissa insisted, reaching to gently take Isabella’s hand. “We are friends, aren’t we?”

“Yes, Clarissa.” Isabella’s face lit up with a smile. “Friends indeed.”

Standing silently by the door, Rafael smiled too.

CHAPTER TWELVE

SUNLIGHT STREAMED THROUGH THE lace curtains, casting delicate shadows across Isabella as she reclined in bed, propped up with plump pillows. Her cheeks were finally tinged with rose rather than pallid with illness.

Clarissa perched on the edge of her seat, feeling as though she might burst at the seams with questions. During the last few days sitting at Isabella's bedside, she'd learned to temper her natural tendency to chatter and prod, allowing the other girl to rest. But now, seeing strength and vitality beginning to return, Clarissa could scarcely contain her eagerness to truly get to know Rafael's sweet younger sister.

"Oh Bella, you can't imagine how relieved I am to see you on the mend at last," Clarissa said, resisting the urge to throw her arms around the other girl in an exuberant embrace. "I've been so terribly worried."

Isabella smiled softly, reaching out to clasp Clarissa's hand. "Your presence has given me such comfort, Clarissa. Knowing you were here, willing me to recover with your stubborn determination." Her eyes twinkled with mirth.

Clarissa laughed. "Well, I am nothing if not mulishly stubborn when I put my mind to something. Poor Rafael didn't stand a chance once I insisted on staying to help."

"My brother is blessed to have found such a loyal friend in you. I hope you know how deeply grateful we all are."

Friend. The word lodged in Clarissa's throat. Of course Isabella would think of her as a friend, an adopted member of the family. She couldn't possibly guess at the decidedly non-sisterly feelings Clarissa harboured for Rafael.

"It is I who owe Rafael everything, as you well know." Clarissa had long since filled Isabella in on the story of Rafael's rescuing her from the corsair ship. "Keeping you company is the very least of what I can do." Shaking off her wistful longings that Rafael might think of her as more than a friend one day, Clarissa forced a bright smile. "Now, you simply must tell me everything there is to know about growing up here. I'm endlessly fascinated by your home and family."

"It would be my greatest pleasure," Isabella responded warmly, eyes alight with enthusiasm. "But first, I insist you share more of your own stories. Rafael mentioned you spent time in Italy?"

Clarissa nodded, mind already spinning with memories of the sun-drenched hills and lush vineyards. The months she'd spent touring the countryside had been some of the most carefree of her life. "Indeed, I was quite swept away by the beauty of it all..."

As the two young women talked and laughed, swapping stories of cherished moments and dreams for the future, an unshakable bond began to form. Born of shared joys and struggles, an abiding friendship took root.

A few days later, finally recovered enough to emerge from her sickroom for more than an hour or so at a time, Isabella led Clarissa through the sprawling grounds of the de Silva estate, the warm breeze ruffling their hair.

As they rounded a bend in the path, the vineyards came into view. Clarissa's breath caught in her throat. The once-pristine rows of vines were now choked with weeds, their gnarled branches reaching towards the sky like skeletal fingers. It was a stark reminder of the toll the war had taken on the land and its people.

"It breaks my heart to see them like this," Isabella said softly, her voice tinged with sorrow. "Though I have never seen them otherwise, Mama and Rafael have told me stories - these vineyards were once the pride of our family."

Clarissa reached out and gave Isabella's hand a comforting squeeze. "They can be again," she said, her mind already whirring with possibilities. "In Italy, I saw vineyards that had been ravaged by disease and neglect, but with hard work and dedication, they were brought back to life."

Isabella's eyes widened, a flicker of hope igniting within them. "Do you really think it's possible?"

"I do," Clarissa said firmly, her gaze sweeping over the overgrown vines. She could almost picture them heavy with ripe, juicy grapes, the air filled with the heady aroma of fermenting wine. "It won't be easy, but nothing worth having ever is."

Rafael approached them, his brow furrowed with concern. He had overheard their conversation and felt compelled to interject. "I appreciate your enthusiasm, Lady Clarissa," he began, his deep voice tinged with a hint of resignation, "but I fear the task may be more daunting than you realise."

Clarissa turned to face him, her chin lifted in defiance. "Captain de Silva, I understand your reservations, but I firmly believe that with the right approach and dedication, we can revive these vineyards and secure your family's financial future."

Rafael sighed, running a hand through his dark hair. "The war has taken a heavy toll on our land. Most of the vines were burned, and the new growth is young and fragile. It will take years of hard work and significant investment to bring them back to their former glory."

"But it's not impossible," Clarissa countered, her eyes sparkling with determination. "And the potential rewards are immense - not just financially, but for the spirit of your family and the local community."

As Rafael listened to her impassioned words, he couldn't help but feel a flicker of hope ignite in his chest. Perhaps she was right. Perhaps this was the opportunity he had been searching for - a chance to rebuild not just the vineyards, but his own sense of purpose and belonging.

"I admire your spirit," he said at last, a small smile tugging at the corners of his mouth. "And I must admit, your proposal has merit. But we must be realistic about the challenges ahead. It will not be an easy path."

Clarissa met his gaze, her own smile radiant with optimism. "Nothing worth having ever is, Captain. But together, I believe we can overcome any obstacle."

Rafael felt a surge of gratitude towards Clarissa for her unwavering belief in the potential of his family's estate. Her enthusiasm was contagious, and he found himself considering the proposal more seriously.

He glanced at Isabella, who was practically vibrating with excitement. "What do you think, Bella? Could we really bring the vineyards back to life?"

Isabella clasped her hands together, her eyes shining with hope. "Oh, Rafa, imagine it! The vines heavy with grapes, the air filled with the sweet scent of wine... It would be like a dream come true."

Rafael nodded slowly, his mind already racing with the logistics of such an undertaking. It would require significant investments of time, labour, and resources. But if they could pull it off...

He turned back to Clarissa, his expression serious. "This will be no easy feat. We'll need to clear the weeds, prune the vines, and likely replant entire sections. It will take years of hard work before we see any significant yield."

Clarissa met his gaze unflinchingly, her determination evident in the set of her jaw. "I understand the challenges, Captain. But I also see the incredible opportunity before us. Not just for your family, but for the entire community. Imagine the jobs it could create, the economic boost it could provide for your people!"

Rafael felt a flicker of admiration for her vision and her compassion. She wasn't just thinking of herself or even his family - she was considering the wider impact such a project could have. His mind raced as he considered the implications of the scheme. The vineyards had been a part of his family's legacy for generations, but the need to make money quickly had always pulled him away to the sea, to ply the trade he knew with his ship. Now, with Clarissa's encouragement, he could see a different path unfolding before him, returning to his family's deep roots in this land.

"I must admit," he said slowly, his gaze drifting over the sun-drenched hills, "the thought of spending my days on land, tending to the vines and overseeing the estate, is not without its appeal."

"You have a rare opportunity, Captain," Clarissa said softly, her blue eyes fixed on his face with an earnest appeal. "To create something lasting, something that will endure long after we're gone."

Her words struck a chord within him, resonating with a deep longing he'd long suppressed. The sea had been his mistress for so long, demanding his attention and devotion. But the estate, the vineyards... they offered a different kind of challenge, a different kind of fulfillment.

"It would mean giving up my ship," he mused aloud. "Leaving the Santa Dorotéia in someone else's hands."

"But think of what you'd be gaining," Clarissa countered, her eyes shining with conviction. "A chance to rebuild, to create something new and beautiful. And..." She hesitated, a faint blush colouring her cheeks. "You'd be here, with your family. With those who love you."

Rafael's heart stuttered in his chest at her words, at the unspoken promise they held. Could he dare to hope that she might come to care for him as more than just a friend? That she might one day share his life, his dreams?

"Look at this, Rafael," she exclaimed, pointing to a particularly gnarly old vine. "This one has survived so much. Imagine what it could become with a little care and attention."

He smiled at her enthusiasm, marvelling at the way she seemed to find beauty and potential in everything she saw. "It will take a lot of work," he cautioned, even as hope kindled in his chest. "The vines are in poor condition, and the soil will need to be tended."

"But it will be worth it," Clarissa insisted, turning to face him. "Can't you see it, Rafael? The grapes ripening on the vine, the wine flowing freely once more? Your family's legacy, restored to its former glory?"

Her words painted a vivid picture in his mind, and for a moment, he could almost taste the rich, full-bodied wine on his tongue. It was a dream he had never dared to entertain, a future he had never allowed himself to imagine.

But with Clarissa by his side, anything seemed possible.

"I have some savings," he found himself saying, his mind already racing ahead. "Enough to support us while we work on the vineyards. It won't be easy, but..."

"But it will be an adventure," Clarissa finished for him, her smile brighter than the sun overhead.

Rafael gazed at Clarissa, her eyes sparkling with enthusiasm and determination. In that moment, he realised that his life was about to change irrevocably. The call of the sea, which had once been his constant companion, now seemed distant and muted compared to the promise of a future with Clarissa and the revival of his family's legacy.

"I never thought I would say this," Rafael began, his voice low and earnest, "but I am ready to leave my life at sea behind. This vineyard, this land...it is where I belong."

Isabella let out a cry of delight and clapped her hands before throwing herself at him, flinging her arms about his neck. "Oh, brother! Nothing could be more wonderful!"

He met Clarissa's gaze above his sister's head. She too was smiling joyously, her sun-kissed hair golden in the sun, and Rafael knew in his heart that he wanted to see that smile every day of his life. He was up for the challenge of restoring the vineyards, of rebuilding his family's legacy, but he wanted Clarissa by his side, as his wife.

Having watched her these last few weeks, he no longer doubted that she could be happy at Torre do Rochedo. She and Isabella were already fast friends. His mother adored her and had dropped any number of heavy-handed hints to Rafael about marrying and settling down. And after all, Alex had already made it quite clear that his suit would be welcomed, even necessary to safeguard Clarissa's reputation after the corsair incident.

He just needed to find the right time and the right words to ask. Extricating himself from Isabella's enthusiastic embrace, Rafael offered an arm to each of them.

"Come. Let us return to the castle and tell Mamma what we have decided. I think she will be pleased, don't you?"

"I think there is nothing that would make her happier," Clarissa laughed, taking his arm.

"Oh, I can think of one thing," Rafael said cryptically. "But that will have to wait a little longer."

CHAPTER THIRTEEN

Rafael, Clarissa and Isabella walked arm-in-arm back up to the clifftop castle, talking and laughing, joy infusing all three of them. As they reached the courtyard, Isabella excused herself, running into the castle and leaving Rafael and Clarissa alone on the cobblestones.

Rafael looked down at Clarissa, a frown furrowing his brow. "Clarissa... there is something I have been wanting to say to you," he said.

Her heart almost jumped from her chest. Could it be...? "Yes?" she said eagerly, but before he could say another word, they were interrupted by the sound of hoofbeats and the arrival of two horses.

Curious, Clarissa turned to look at the new arrivals, and an unthinkable sight unfolded before her eyes. Two gentlemen, as unexpected as they were familiar, rode through the stone archway and into the de Silva family estate.

Mr. Edward Dalton's rakishly handsome features bore an expression of utter astonishment as his gaze alighted on Clarissa. "Lady Clarissa! I confess I am overjoyed to see you here. When I heard word of your disappearance from Athens, I feared some dreadful fate had befallen you, yet here you are, as radiant as ever."

Before Clarissa could gather her wits to respond, the second gentleman dismounted his horse and swept into a graceful bow. "Clarissa, mia cara, what a delightful surprise," said Mario, Conte de Bardolino, his mellifluous Italian accent caressing her name.

Clarissa just stared, unable to speak, her heart racing. Two men from her past, materialising here in Portugal? It defied belief.

She dipped into a curtsy, grateful for the excuse to compose herself. "Mr. Dalton, Conte de Bardolino, this is indeed an unexpected pleasure. I had no notion either of you planned to visit Portugal."

Edward stepped closer, his blue eyes sweeping over her in frank admiration. "A happy coincidence, to be sure. I encountered Lady Glenkellie in Florence, where she informed me you had been safely recovered from your mysterious disappearance and were en route back to England. But to find you here..." He trailed off, his gaze flickering around the rustic courtyard, settling on Rafael with a look of barely concealed contempt.

Clarissa's mind whirled. Just moments ago, she had been sharing a private moment with Rafael in this very spot, almost certain he had been about to propose marriage. Now, with these two interlopers from her old life, everything felt upended, uncertain.

She forced a smile. "The de Silva family has been kind enough to host me on my journey. Come, let me introduce you. Captain Rafael de Silva, this is the Conte di Bardolino, and Mr Edward Dalton."

Rafael bowed stiffly as Clarissa made the introductions. "Welcome, gentlemen. You are very welcome to Torre do Rochedo, but to what do we owe the pleasure of your company?"

The Conte smiled broadly, seemingly oblivious to the undercurrent of tension. "Ah, Captain de Silva! I was visiting relatives in Florence when Mr Dalton arrived, and I heard that Lady Clarissa was here in Portugal. On a whim, I simply had to come pay my respects."

Mario was very young, no older than Clarissa herself, and seemed boyish compared to Rafael. His excuse was transparently thin. Clarissa sighed inwardly. Mario had set his sights on her sister Diana the previous summer when they visited his beautiful estate on the shores of Lake Garda. Now that Diana had married her duke and was no longer available, it seemed Mario had turned his attentions to Clarissa. She would have to firmly discourage him.

Mr. Dalton, however, fixed Rafael with a cool stare. "Indeed. Quite the coincidence, finding Clarissa here, is it not?"

Clarissa's heart sank at the barely veiled accusation in Edward's tone. She glanced at Rafael, seeing the muscle in his jaw clench.

"Coincidence or not," Rafael replied evenly, "*Lady* Clarissa is an honoured guest in my family's home. I trust you will remember that during your stay."

The two men seemed to size each other up, the air between them crackling with unspoken rivalry. Clarissa's unease grew. How had her life become so complicated so quickly?

She stepped forward, determined to defuse the situation. "I am sure you are weary from your travels. Perhaps, Captain, you could introduce the gentlemen to Senhora de Silva and she could find them accommodations?"

Rafael hesitated a moment, then nodded. "Of course. Please, follow me." As he led the men away, Clarissa caught the briefest glimpse of something raw and vulnerable in his sea-green eyes.

But it was gone in an instant, leaving her to wonder if she had simply imagined it. With a sigh, she turned away and went to find Marianne, her head spinning with questions and her heart heavy with a growing sense of foreboding.

As Clarissa descended the grand staircase later that afternoon, she was surprised to find Edward waiting for her at the bottom, his posture casual yet confident as he leaned against the ornate bannister.

"Ah, Clarissa," he greeted her with a charming smile that once would have made her heart flutter. "I was hoping we might have a moment to chat."

Clarissa forced a smile, trying to ignore the unease that prickled along her spine. "Of course. Shall we take a turn about the gardens?"

He offered his arm and she took it, allowing him to guide her outside. They walked in silence for a few moments, the only sound the crunching of gravel beneath their feet.

Finally, Edward spoke. "I must confess, Clarissa, I find myself quite perplexed by your sudden departure from Athens. One moment we were enjoying each other's company, and the next, you were gone without a word."

Clarissa's stomach twisted. How could she possibly explain the truth of what had happened? "I...I'm sorry. It was all rather sudden."

He stopped walking, turning to face her with a frown. "Sudden? Clarissa, you disappeared in the middle of the night. Your family was frantic with worry. And now, to find you here, in Portugal of all places..."

She bristled at his tone, at the unspoken accusation behind his words. "I hardly think my whereabouts are any of your concern, Mr Dalton!"

His eyes narrowed. "No? And yet, not so long ago, I had hoped they might be. I had thought perhaps you and I..." He trailed off, shaking his head. "But I see now that I was mistaken."

Clarissa's heart sank. Once, his words would have thrilled her, but now, they only filled her with a vague sense of regret. "I...I'm sorry if I gave you the wrong impression. But my feelings...they've changed."

He stared at her for a long moment, his jaw clenched. Then, he let out a humourless laugh. "Changed? Or were they simply never what I believed them to be?"

She looked away, unable to meet his gaze. "Mr Dalton..."

"No, don't trouble yourself," he said coldly. "I understand perfectly. I only hope, for your sake, that your newfound affections are not misplaced."

With that, he turned on his heel and strode away, leaving Clarissa alone in the garden, her heart heavy with the weight of words left unsaid.

As Clarissa watched Edward's retreating figure, she heard the sound of approaching footsteps. Turning, she found herself face to face with the Conte de Bardolino, his handsome features alight with a boyish grin.

"Clarissa, mia cara!" he exclaimed, sweeping into a low bow and pressing a kiss to her hand. "What a delightful surprise to find you here!"

Despite her melancholy mood, Clarissa couldn't help but smile at his exuberance. She remembered the Conte's infatuation with her sister Diana the previous season, how he had followed her about like an eager puppy. Both sisters had been nothing but amused by his attentions.

"Mario," she greeted him warmly, unafraid to use his first name as she had come to view him almost as a brother during their time in Italy. "I must confess, I'm rather surprised to see you here as well. What brings you to Portugal?"

He waved a hand airily. "Oh, you know how it is. A bit of wanderlust, a desire for adventure. And of course, the chance to bask in your radiant presence once more."

Clarissa laughed, shaking her head. "You are incorrigible, Mario. But I'm afraid you'll find me rather poor company at the moment."

His brow furrowed in concern. "Why, whatever is the matter? Has that odious Dalton fellow been bothering you? He insisted on tagging along from Florence with me and I admit I have not taken to him."

She sighed. "It's nothing, really. Just a small disagreement between friends."

Mario clucked his tongue sympathetically. "Ah, the trials and tribulations of the heart. But fear not, mia bella! I shall endeavour to lift your spirits with my charming wit and dashing good looks."

Clarissa couldn't help but be amused by his antics. Compared to Rafael's quiet intensity, Mario seemed almost childlike in his enthusiasm. She found herself wondering how Rafael was faring with the unexpected arrivals.

As if summoned by her thoughts, Lucia and Isabella appeared, their faces wreathed in welcoming smiles.

"Conte! I would like you to meet my daughter, Isabella," Lucia said.

Mario stopped in his tracks, staring at Isabella, who was looking particularly lovely this afternoon in a pale sea-green silk gown, her glossy black curls cascading around her shoulders.

Clarissa laughed silently to herself as Mario stumbled over his words, his gaze never leaving Isabella's face. For her part, Isabella seemed almost equally taken with the young Italian count, blushing and smiling shyly as he bowed over her hand.

Lucia caught Clarissa's eye and smiled, the smug smile of a mother who has found a suitable suitor for their offspring and seen an immediate result. Clarissa beamed back at Lucia, honestly grateful; if Mario transferred his attentions to Isabella, that was one less problem for Clarissa to worry about.

The days passed in a blur of activity, with Isabella and Lucia taking it upon themselves to entertain their guests, obviously enjoying having Torre do Rochedo full of guests once more. Clarissa found herself drawn into their lively conversations, grateful for the distraction from her troubled thoughts. Yet, even as she laughed and jested with the others, she couldn't shake the feeling of unease that had settled in the pit of her stomach.

At least Mario now seemed utterly enchanted by Isabella. His gaze followed the lovely young woman wherever she went, his eyes alight with admiration and wonder.

Clarissa watched the pair as they strolled through the gardens, heads bent close together in intimate conversation. Isabella's silvery laughter rang out across the grounds, and Mario's answering chuckle sent a pang of envy through Clarissa's heart. Not for Mario's affections, but for the easy camaraderie the two seemed to share.

She couldn't help but contrast their lighthearted interactions with Rafael's distant demeanour. Ever since the arrival of the new guests, he had been conspicuously absent, his duties seemingly taking up all of his time. Clarissa tried to tell herself that it was mere coincidence, that his withdrawal had nothing to do with her, but the ache in her chest told a different story.

As the days stretched into a week, Clarissa's doubts and insecurities grew. She found herself wandering the halls of the estate, hoping to catch a glimpse of Rafael, only to be met with disappointment at every turn. The few times she did see him, he was distant and formal, his sea-green eyes shuttered against her searching gaze.

With each passing day, Clarissa's heart broke a little more. She had thought... had hoped... that perhaps there was something special between them. That the connection she felt wasn't just a figment of her imagination. But now, faced with Rafael's cold indifference, she was forced to confront the painful truth.

She had lost him. Before she ever truly had him.

Marianne found Clarissa sitting in the garden, her eyes fixed on the distant horizon. The Marchioness settled herself on the bench beside her niece, her keen gaze taking in Clarissa's melancholy expression.

"What troubles you, my dear?" Marianne asked gently.

Clarissa sighed, her fingers twisting in the folds of her dress. "It's Rafael," she admitted, her voice barely above a whisper. "He's been avoiding me since Mr. Dalton and the Conte arrived. I fear I've done something to offend him."

Marianne's brow furrowed thoughtfully. "I don't believe that's the case," she said slowly. "In fact, I suspect quite the opposite."

Clarissa turned to face her friend, confusion etched across her features. "What do you mean?"

"I think Rafael is jealous," Marianne said simply.

A startled laugh escaped Clarissa's lips. "Jealous? Of whom? Mr. Dalton? The Conte? That's absurd."

Marianne shook her head. "Is it? You have a history with both men. It's not so far-fetched to think that Rafael might feel threatened by their presence."

Clarissa considered this for a moment, her heart fluttering with a tentative hope. Could it be true? Could Rafael's distance be a manifestation of jealousy rather than indifference?

She thought back to their interactions before the arrival of their guests. The stolen glances, the gentle teasing, the undeniable pull between them. It had all felt so real, so promising. But then everything had changed.

"I don't know, Marianne," Clarissa said uncertainly. "He's been so cold. So distant. If he truly cared for me, wouldn't he want to spend time with me, regardless of who else was here?"

Marianne smiled knowingly. "Men can be foolish creatures, my dear. They often let their pride and insecurities cloud their judgement, and jealousy is the very worst of emotions - as Alex could tell you." She reached out and squeezed Clarissa's hand. "If you want answers, you must seek them out yourself."

Clarissa took a deep breath, her resolve hardening. Marianne was right. She couldn't sit idly by, waiting for Rafael to come to her. She had to take action.

Rising to her feet, Clarissa smoothed her skirts and squared her shoulders. "I'm going to find him," she declared. "I'm going to ask him directly if I've done something to offend him."

Marianne nodded approvingly. "Good. Don't let him evade the question. Demand the truth."

With a grateful smile, Clarissa set off in search of Rafael, her heart pounding with a mixture of anticipation and dread. One way or another, she would have her answer.

Rafael stormed into the stables, his mind a tempest of conflicting emotions. The sight of Clarissa with those two men, the easy way she smiled at them, the sparkle in her eyes... it was more than he could bear.

He saddled his horse with jerky, aggressive movements, his jaw clenched tight. He needed to get away, to clear his head. To figure out what in God's name he was going to do about these feelings that threatened to consume him.

"Running away again, my son?"

Rafael spun around to see Lucia leaning against the stable door, her arms crossed and a knowing look on her face.

"I'm not running away," he snapped. "I have work to do."

Lucia raised an eyebrow. "Work that conveniently takes you far away from a certain English lady and her suitors?"

Rafael's hands stilled on the saddle. That was the crux of it, wasn't it? What could he, a penniless Portuguese nobleman with a crumbling castle and a neglected vineyard, offer a woman like Clarissa? Better to keep his distance, leave her free to make her choice between the two suitors who could offer her a life she deserved.

"I don't..." He swallowed hard. "I don't have a chance. That's why I need to stay away."

Lucia's eyes softened. "Oh, Rafael. Don't you see? She cares for you. Anyone with eyes can see it."

Rafael shook his head. "She deserves better than me, Mamma. Better than this life."

"And what about what she wants?" Lucia asked gently. "Have you even asked her?"

Rafael looked away, his jaw working. No, he hadn't asked her. He'd been too afraid of the answer.

"Pride is a funny thing, dear one," Lucia said. "It can make us do foolish things. Like push away the people we love because we don't think we're good enough for them."

Rafael's eyes snapped back to hers. "I don't..."

"Don't you?" Lucia smiled. "Don't let your pride ruin this, Rafael. Talk to her. Tell her how you feel. Before it's too late."

With that, Lucia turned and walked out of the stables, leaving Rafael alone with his thoughts. He leaned his forehead against his horse's neck, closing his eyes.

Could his mother be right? Could Clarissa truly care for him, despite everything? The thought made his heart race and his palms sweat.

But the alternative... the thought of losing her, of watching her fall in love with someone else... that was unbearable.

Rafael sighed and pulled his saddle off, patting his horse's neck in apology before stowing the tack and leaving the stable. No more running away. His decision was made. He would talk to Clarissa. He would lay his heart at her feet and pray that she would accept it.

And if she didn't... well, at least he would know he had tried.

He knew he had been avoiding Clarissa, knew that his behaviour was causing her pain. But he couldn't seem to help himself. Every time he saw her with Dalton or the Conte, laughing at their jokes or listening intently to their stories, a bitter jealousy rose up within him, threatening to choke him.

How could he compete with them? With their wealth and titles and easy charm? He was just a lowly sea captain, struggling to keep his family's estate afloat. What could he possibly offer a woman like Clarissa? A crumbling estate and an uncertain future? The Conte was rich and titled, Dalton an English aristocrat; either would surely be far more acceptable as a suitor than he.

The sound of footsteps behind him pulled him from his thoughts. He turned to see Clarissa herself approaching, her expression determined.

"Rafael," she said, coming to a stop before him. "I need to speak with you."

He swallowed hard, his heart racing at her proximity. "Of course," he managed, his voice rough. "What is it?"

Clarissa took a deep breath, as if steeling herself. "Have I done something to offend you?" she asked bluntly.

Rafael blinked, taken aback by her directness. "No," he said quickly. "No, of course not."

"Then why have you been avoiding me?" Clarissa pressed, her eyes searching his face. "Ever since Mr. Dalton and the Conte arrived, you've barely spoken to me. You've been distant and cold. I don't understand."

Rafael looked away, unable to hold her gaze. How could he explain the tangled web of emotions that had been plaguing him? The fear, the insecurity, the bone-deep longing that he could never seem to escape?

"I've been busy," he said lamely, the excuse sounding hollow even to his own ears. "My duties..."

"Don't lie to me, Rafael," Clarissa interrupted, her voice sharp. "I know there's more to it than that."

He sighed, running a hand through his hair. "What do you want me to say, Clarissa?"

"The truth," she said simply. "I want the truth."

Rafael closed his eyes, his jaw clenching. The truth. The one thing he couldn't give her. Because the truth was that he was in love with her, desperately and irrevocably. And the truth was that he wasn't worthy of her, could never be worthy of her.

But as he stood there, feeling the weight of her gaze upon him, he knew he couldn't keep running from this. From her.

"The truth," he said slowly, opening his eyes to gaze on her beautiful face, etched with determination as she confronted him, "is that I..."

Rafael's voice trailed off as he struggled to find the words. He turned away from Clarissa, his gaze falling upon the sun-drenched vineyards that stretched out before them. The golden light seemed to mock him, a reminder of all the warmth and beauty he couldn't possess.

"I cannot compete with them," he said at last, his voice low and rough. "The Conte, with his title and his wealth. And Dalton, with his respectable English upbringing and his history with your family. They can offer you so much more than I ever could."

Clarissa stepped closer, her brow furrowed in confusion. "Rafael, what are you talking about? I don't care about titles or wealth. I care about you."

He shook his head, a bitter laugh escaping his lips. "You shouldn't. You deserve so much more than a penniless Portuguese captain with a crumbling castle and a failing vineyard."

"Stop it," Clarissa said fiercely, her hand coming up to grip his arm. "Stop talking about yourself like that. You are the most honourable, brave, and kind man I have ever known. Your circumstances do not define you."

Rafael looked down at her, his heart aching at the sincerity in her eyes. He wanted so badly to believe her, to let himself hope that maybe, just maybe, she could love him as he loved her.

But the doubts still lingered, the insecurities that had been bred into him over years of struggle and hardship. He couldn't shake the feeling that he would never be enough for her, that she would eventually realise the truth and leave him behind.

"Clarissa," he said softly, his hand coming up to cup her cheek. "I..."

"Brother!" Isabella's voice rang out across the vineyard, startling them both. Rafael stepped back, the moment broken.

Isabella hurried towards them, her face flushed with excitement. "There you are! I've been looking everywhere for you."

She took in the tension between them, her smile faltering slightly. "Am I interrupting something?"

"No," Rafael said quickly, forcing a smile. "Not at all. What is it, Isabella?"

As his sister began to chatter about some new idea she had for the vineyard, Rafael couldn't help but steal a glance at Clarissa. She was watching him, her eyes filled with a mixture of confusion and hurt.

He looked away, his heart heavy. He knew he couldn't keep running from this forever. Sooner or later, he would have to face the truth of his feelings for her.

But for now, he would do what he always did. He would bury his emotions, focus on his duties, and try to ignore the ache in his chest that only seemed to grow with each passing day.

CHAPTER FOURTEEN

RAFAEL CLENCHED HIS JAW, quelling the urge to snap at Isabella for her untimely interruption. Just as the perfect words had begun to take shape on his tongue, the delicate balance of the moment shattered like fine crystal.

He drew a steadying breath, willing his frustration to ebb away. It would not do to let his sister see him so vexed. With an effort, he turned to face her, a tight smile plastered across his face. "Yes, Isabella? What is it?"

She clutched at his arm, her dark eyes alight with barely contained excitement. "Oh Rafael, I've had the most wonderful idea!" Her voice was breathy, the words tumbling out in an eager rush.

Despite himself, Rafael felt his annoyance begin to soften at the sight of her animated features. Isabella had always possessed an irrepressible zest for life, an innate ability to find joy and wonder in even the bleakest of circumstances. It was a trait he'd often envied, especially in the dark days following their father's death and their exile to England.

"An idea, you say?" He arched a brow, feigning interest. "And what, pray tell, might that be?"

Isabella clasped her hands together, practically vibrating with enthusiasm. "Well, I was just thinking... About the vineyards, I mean. And how we might go about restoring them to their former glory."

Rafael stiffened, a frisson of unease snaking down his spine. He'd been grappling with that very dilemma for weeks now, poring over ledgers and accounts until his vision blurred and his head pounded. The vineyards were the lifeblood of their estate, the key to their family's future. And yet, for all his efforts, he'd made frustratingly little headway.

"Go on," he said cautiously, bracing himself for whatever harebrained scheme his sister had concocted.

Isabella took a deep breath, her expression turning solemn. "I think we should ask the Conte Bardolino for his help."

Rafael blinked, certain he must have misheard. "I beg your pardon?"

"The Conte," Isabella repeated patiently. "He's been telling me all about his vineyards back in Italy. The man's practically a walking encyclopaedia when it comes to viticulture." Her eyes sparkled with admiration. "Just think of the invaluable advice he could offer us!"

A muscle ticked in Rafael's jaw as he fought to contain the sudden surge of jealousy that coursed through him. The mere thought of the suave, silver-tongued Italian nobleman who had followed Clarissa to Portugal made his blood boil. And yet, much as he loathed to admit it, Isabella had a point.

The Conte's sprawling estate was renowned throughout Europe for producing some of the finest wines in all of Italy. If anyone possessed the knowledge and expertise to help revive their ailing vineyards, it was him, despite his youth.

Still, the idea of asking for assistance galled Rafael to his very core. He was a proud man, accustomed to relying on his own wits and resourcefulness to navigate life's challenges. The notion of seeking aid from an outsider - especially one as insufferably charming as the Conte - felt like a bitter pill to swallow.

He drew in a slow, steadying breath, weighing his options. As much as it pained him to concede defeat, he knew he had to put his personal feelings aside for the sake of the estate. For the sake of his family's future.

"Very well," he ground out, the words tasting like ashes on his tongue. "I suppose it wouldn't hurt to hear what the man has to say."

Isabella beamed at him, her face alight with triumph. "Oh, Rafael, thank you! You won't regret this, I promise you."

He managed a tight smile in return, even as a sense of foreboding settled like a leaden weight in the pit of his stomach. Somehow, he had a feeling he would come to rue this decision. But for now, all he could do was grit his teeth and pray that the Conte's advice would prove as invaluable as Isabella seemed to believe.

Rafael approached the Conte with a heavy heart, his footsteps dragging as if weighed down by the sheer force of his reluctance. He found the man lounging in a comfortable chair on the terrace, resplendent in a finely tailored suit of deep burgundy silk that gleamed in the afternoon sun.

"Conte," Rafael began, his voice stiff with formality. "Might I have a word?"

The Conte turned to face him, a genial smile playing across his lips. "But of course, Captain de Silva. How may I be of assistance?"

Rafael swallowed hard, the words sticking in his throat like thorns. "It's about our vineyards," he said at last, the admission wrenching itself from his unwilling lips. "I understand you have some...expertise in this area."

The Conte's eyes lit up with keen interest. "Ah, yes! I have been blessed with the opportunity to cultivate some of the finest vineyards in all of Italy. It would be my great pleasure to share what knowledge I have gleaned with you."

He gestured expansively, his hands sketching shapes in the air as he spoke. "You see, the key to a thriving vineyard lies in understanding the delicate balance between the earth, the sun, and the vines themselves. With proper drainage and irrigation, strategic planting to optimise sun exposure, and the right trellising techniques, you can coax even the most stubborn grapes to yield a bountiful harvest."

As the Conte spoke, Rafael found himself reluctantly drawn in by the man's obvious passion for his craft. Though he was loath to admit it, the advice seemed sound - and more importantly, actionable.

"I see," he said slowly, his brow furrowed in thought. "And you truly believe these methods could help revive our struggling vines?"

The Conte nodded, obviously enthusiastic. "I have every confidence, Captain. With a little hard work and a touch of Italian know-how, your vineyards will be the talk of Portugal in no time at all."

Despite himself, Rafael felt a flicker of hope kindle in his chest. Perhaps, with the Conte's guidance, they could yet salvage the family legacy from the brink of ruin. It was a slim chance, but a chance nonetheless - and for that, he supposed he owed the man his grudging gratitude.

Over the next few weeks, the once-neglected vineyards began to transform under the Conte's expert guidance. Rafael watched with a mixture of amazement and begrudging respect as the Italian gentleman worked tirelessly alongside the estate's labourers, his fine suits exchanged for practical work clothes and his hands stained with the rich, dark earth.

"Careful now, lads," the Conte called out, his voice carrying across the rows of vines. "Remember, each plant is a delicate thing - treat them with the same care you would a lady, and they'll reward you tenfold."

The workers chuckled at the comparison, but Rafael couldn't help but note the truth in the man's words. With each passing day, the vines seemed to stand a little taller, their leaves a little greener, as if they too were eager to prove their worth.

As he surveyed the progress they'd made, Rafael felt a pang of something that might have been gratitude - or perhaps just a lessening of his earlier resentment.

Much as it pained him to admit it, the Conte's presence had been a blessing in disguise. Without his knowledge and tireless efforts, the vineyards might well have been lost for good.

"I must say, Mario," he said gruffly, coming to stand beside the younger man. "Your advice has been... invaluable. I'm not too proud to admit when I've been wrong - and in this case, I was wrong to doubt you."

The Conte turned to him with a warm smile, his eyes glinting with something like understanding. "You are very welcome, my friend. We all have our pride - but sometimes, the greatest strength lies in knowing when to set it aside for the greater good."

Rafael nodded slowly, the words striking a chord within him. Perhaps, he mused, there was a lesson to be learned here - one that went beyond the simple tending of grapes and vines. Perhaps, in the end, it was not weakness to accept help when it was offered, but rather a sign of true wisdom and grace.

His thoughts were interrupted by the sight of Marianne, her vibrant hair gleaming in the sunlight as she knelt among the vines, determinedly pulling weeds. Despite her fine gown, she seemed utterly unconcerned by the dirt and grime, her face alight with a fierce sort of joy as she worked, piling weeds into the basket between her and Clarissa.

Rafael felt a sudden lump in his throat, a wave of emotion threatening to overwhelm him. That these people - his sister, his friends, even the Marchioness herself - would see fit to join in this labour, to work side by side with his own hands... it was a kindness he had never expected, and one he knew he could never fully repay.

Clearing his throat, he raised his voice to address them all. "I... I cannot thank you enough," he said, his words rough with feeling. "All of you. Your help, your support... it means more than I can say."

Marianne looked up at him, her eyes soft with understanding. Rising gracefully to her feet, she brushed off her skirts and came to stand before him, her head tilted back to meet his gaze.

"Nonsense," she said gently, reaching out to lay a hand on his arm. "We're happy to help, Rafael. After all..." She smiled, a glint of mischief in her eye. "That's what family does, isn't it?"

Rafael swallowed hard, feeling a sudden tightness in his chest. Family. The word echoed in his mind, filling him with a warmth he hadn't known in years. Looking around at the faces of those gathered - Lucia and Isabella, Mario, Clarissa, Alex and Marianne, even Mr Dalton - he realised that, perhaps for the first time in his life, he truly understood the meaning of the word.

"Yes," he said softly, his voice rough with emotion. "I suppose it is."

Clarissa wiped the sweat from her brow with the back of her hand, squinting against the bright sun as she surveyed the sprawling vineyards before her. The air was thick with the heady scent of ripening grapes, and the gentle rustling of the leaves in the warm breeze was punctuated by the occasional chirp of a bird.

She had been working alongside the others for hours, pruning and tying the vines, her hands scratched and scraped from the unaccustomed activity. It was hard work, but satisfying in a way she had never known before. There was something deeply fulfilling about tending to the land, nurturing the delicate plants that would one day yield the rich, full-bodied wine for which the region was famous.

As she reached for another vine, her fingers brushed against something unexpected. Frowning, she bent closer, pushing aside the leaves to reveal an unripe bunch of grapes, cut too early from the vine, crushed and oozing against the soil. *Strange*, she thought, her brow furrowing. *How did that happen?*

She straightened up, scanning the nearby rows with a more critical eye. There, a few feet away - a damaged vine, mangled as though rough hands had torn it from its supports and shredded the delicate leaves. And there, near the end of the row, a pile of discarded pruning shears, as if someone had simply tossed them aside in a fit of pique.

"How odd," she murmured aloud, more to herself than anyone else. "I wonder what could have caused this?"

But even as the words left her lips, a niggling sense of unease began to grow in the pit of her stomach. One crushed bunch of grapes, one damaged vine - it could easily be dismissed as a mere accident. But the shears, left so carelessly behind... that spoke of something more deliberate.

She shook her head, trying to brush aside the troubling thoughts. It was probably nothing, she told herself firmly. A clumsy worker, perhaps, or a wild animal that had wandered into the vineyard in search of a snack. There was no need to worry the others, not when they had already been through so much.

But as she picked up the discarded shears and turned back to her work, she couldn't quite shake the feeling that something wasn't right. And as the days passed and the strange incidents continued - a broken trellis here, a missing basket there - that feeling only grew stronger.

Rafael stormed through the vineyard, his boots crushing the fallen leaves beneath his feet. His eyes blazed with fury as he surveyed the destruction before him - entire rows of vines, once lush and thriving, now lay in ruins, their branches twisted and broken beyond repair. The tool that had done the damage lay discarded on the ground, a simple sickle, brutally sharp. But whose hand had wielded it?

"Who could have done this?" Rafael growled, his fists clenched at his sides. "To attack our very livelihood, our family's legacy..."

Clarissa hurried to keep pace with him, her skirts rustling as she moved. "Rafael, please, you must calm yourself. Anger will not solve this."

He whirled to face her, his expression fierce. "And what would you have me do, Clarissa? Stand by and watch as some coward strikes at the very heart of our home?"

She met his gaze steadily, refusing to be cowed by his temper. "Of course not. But we must be strategic in our response. Rushing in blindly will only make matters worse."

Rafael drew in a deep breath, visibly struggling to rein in his emotions. "You're right, of course. Forgive me, I spoke in haste."

Clarissa laid a gentle hand on his arm. "There is nothing to forgive. Your passion for protecting your family does you credit."

A ghost of a smile touched his lips at her words, but it quickly faded as he turned back to the ruined vines. "What do you suggest, then? How can we hope to catch this saboteur?"

Clarissa considered for a moment, her brow furrowed in thought. "Perhaps we could keep watch over the vineyard at night, in shifts. If we catch them in the act..."

Rafael nodded slowly, his eyes gleaming with a new determination. "Yes, that could work. We'll need to be careful, though - whoever is doing this is clearly not afraid to cause harm."

"I'm not afraid," Clarissa declared, lifting her chin. "I'll take the first watch myself."

"Absolutely not," Rafael retorted, his tone brooking no argument. "I won't have you putting yourself in danger, nor any of the other ladies. I'll stand guard tonight, and I'll discuss with the other men in the morning if they are willing to assist me."

Clarissa opened her mouth to protest, but something in his expression stopped her. There was a fierceness there, yes, but also a vulnerability, a desperate need to protect those he loved.

"Very well," she agreed at last, her voice softening. "But promise me you'll be careful, Rafael. I couldn't bear it if anything happened to you."

He reached out to take her hand, his thumb brushing lightly over her knuckles. "I promise, Clarissa. I won't let any harm come to our family - or to you. I swear it on my life."

But despite Rafael's best efforts, the saboteur remained elusive. Each morning, they would return to the house exhausted and discouraged, only to find fresh damage to the vines. It was as if their enemy was a ghost, slipping in and out unseen, leaving only destruction in their wake.

As the days stretched on with no sign of the culprit, Rafael's frustration mounted. Clarissa could see it in the tense set of his jaw, the way his fists clenched at his sides as he surveyed the ruined vines.

"I don't understand it," he growled, raking a hand through his hair. "How can they keep evading us like this? It's as if they know our every move before we make it. How can they know where we will patrol, and when? We make a new plan each evening!"

Clarissa laid a gentle hand on his arm, feeling the coiled tension beneath his skin. "We're doing everything we can, Rafael. Perhaps... perhaps it's time to accept that this may be beyond our control."

He turned to look at her, his sea-green eyes stormy with emotion. "I can't accept that, Clarissa. This land, this vineyard... it's my family's legacy. I won't let it be destroyed by some cowardly saboteur."

"I know," she murmured, her heart aching for him. "But we can't go on like this forever. We need to find another way."

Rafael sighed, his shoulders slumping in defeat. "You're right, of course. I just... I feel so helpless. What kind of man am I if I can't even protect what's mine?"

Clarissa cupped his face in her hands, forcing him to meet her gaze. "You are a good man, Rafael de Silva. A brave, honourable, loving man. And we will find a way through this, together. I promise you that."

He leaned into her touch, his eyes fluttering closed for a moment as he drew strength from her presence. When he opened them again, there was a new resolve there, a glimmer of hope amid the despair.

"Together," he repeated, his voice rough with emotion. "I like the sound of that."

Across the sun-dappled vineyard, Clarissa spotted Isabella and Conte Bardolino deep in conversation. Mario was gesticulating animatedly, no doubt sharing more of his vast knowledge of viticulture. Isabella, her dark hair coming loose from its pins, was listening intently, her eyes bright with keen interest.

Clarissa nudged Rafael gently. "Look at those two. Thick as thieves, aren't they?"

Rafael followed her gaze, a wry smile tugging at the corner of his mouth. "Indeed. I confess, I had my reservations about the Conte at first, but he's proven himself to be a true friend."

"More than a friend, I think," Clarissa murmured, watching as Isabella laid a hand on the Conte's arm, her laughter carrying across the vineyard. "Have you noticed the way they look at each other?"

Rafael's eyebrows shot up. "You don't think...?"

"I do," Clarissa grinned. "I think Mario is quite smitten with your sister. And unless I'm very much mistaken, the feeling is entirely mutual."

"Hm." Rafael looked uncertain. "Isabella is only just seventeen..."

"And Mario is barely twenty," Clarissa pointed out. "I think they are very well suited, Rafael. Don't you? I know your mother agrees with me."

"Does she, indeed!" His brows flew up, and he looked again at Mario and Isabella. "Perhaps I should have a conversation with my mother on the matter. Before things become any more serious."

"You should probably talk to Isabella about it too," Clarissa pointed out teasingly. "She does, after all, have a mind and opinions of her own."

"You are correct, indeed." Rafael bowed over her hand. "If you will excuse me. Isabella!" He called to his sister, who sighed and rolled her eyes, but left the Conte's side obediently to come to him, and the two of them made their way back up to the castle.

"Clarissa." Mario came to her side and offered his arm, and she put her hand on it with a smile.

"Thank you. I'm tired, and it's a steep walk back up there!"

"But worth the view when one arrives."

"Indeed. A different sort of beauty to your home on the lake, but lovely nonetheless, don't you think?"

"A place I am growing to love almost as much as Bardolino," Mario agreed, his eyes fixed on the brother and sister walking ahead of them. "Tell me... do I have a chance, Clarissa?"

"A chance?" she queried.

"Of pressing my suit successfully?"

For one brief instant, Clarissa thought he was hinting at proposing to *her*, but immediately she saw that his lovesick gaze had never strayed from Isabella.

"Of course you do!" she exclaimed. "Any woman would be lucky to have you... but in this specific case, I do believe your affections are returned in full measure."

"You do?"

They had reached the stone archway into the castle courtyard, through which Rafael and Isabella had passed a moment earlier before going out of sight. Clarissa laughed, stopping and turning to look at Mario.

"Yes, indeed I do."

He fell on her neck with cries of delight in Italian, hugging her tightly and exclaiming that he hoped soon to call her his sister, as he had once hoped before, but this way should be so much better, ensuring the happiness of all concerned. Clarissa laughed and hugged him back.

"You are a little precipitate there, I think," she replied.

"We shall see!"

CHAPTER FIFTEEN

Clarissa's heart leapt into her throat as Rafael strode out of the castle's entryway, his boots echoing sharply against the weathered stones. His sea-green eyes flashed with an intensity she had never seen before, brows knitted together in consternation.

He halted abruptly before her, hands clenching at his sides. Clarissa's pulse quickened. From the stormy look clouding Rafael's handsome features, she instantly knew he must have overheard part of their conversation. But which part? Surely not...

"My apologies for interrupting, Lady Clarissa, Conte Ginori," Rafael said tersely, giving a curt nod to each of them. His gaze lingered on Clarissa, something unfathomable lurking in those ocean depths. "I trust I am not intruding on a...private moment?"

Clarissa's stomach flip-flopped. Oh no. He couldn't possibly think... "Not at all, Captain," she replied with a brightness she did not feel, trying to mask her rising unease. "The Conte and I were merely having a friendly chat. Isn't that right, Mario?"

Mario smiled genially, seemingly oblivious to the tension crackling in the air between them. "Indeed, just a most delightful discourse on the charms of the Portuguese countryside. Lady Clarissa is a keen observer of natural beauty." He winked at her conspiratorially.

Clarissa flushed, her cheeks heating. Why did men always have to be so suggestive? She risked a glance at Rafael, saw his jaw tighten almost imperceptibly. Dear Lord, he had gotten entirely the wrong impression! She had to set things straight, and quickly, before this spiralled out of control.

"Actually, Rafael, I was hoping we might have a word?" She widened her eyes at him meaningfully, willing him to understand. "In private?"

A muscle jumped in his jaw as he regarded her inscrutably for a long, tense moment. Finally, he inclined his head. "As you wish, my lady."

Clarissa turned to the Conte with an apologetic smile. "Pray excuse us, Mario. We shan't be long."

"Of course, of course!" The Conte waved a magnanimous hand. "Take all the time you need."

Pulse thrumming, she followed Rafael's broad back as he led them away from the Conte, her mind awhirl. She had to explain, to make him see reason. The very thought of him believing she would accept another man's proposal made her feel quite ill.

Rafael whirled around to face Clarissa once they reached the relative seclusion of the terrace, his sea-green eyes stormy with emotion. "How could you accept his proposal?" he demanded, his voice low and intense. "I thought...I thought we..."

He trailed off, running an agitated hand through his dark hair. Clarissa's heart clenched at the hurt and confusion etched across his handsome features. She reached out instinctively, her fingers grazing his arm.

"Rafael, please, let me explain. It's not what you think-"

But he jerked away from her touch as if burned, his gaze hardening. "And what about Isabella?" he pressed on, relentless. "She's completely smitten with the Conte, and you encouraged him? I never took you for the type to betray a friend so callously."

Clarissa reeled back, stung. How dare he accuse her of such a thing? Anger flared within her, hot and bright. "Now see here, Captain," she snapped, drawing herself up to her full height. "I have done no such thing! If you would just listen-"

"I've heard enough," Rafael cut her off coldly, turning his back on her. "I thought I knew you, Clarissa. But it seems I was mistaken."

His words hit her like a physical blow, knocking the breath from her lungs. Tears pricked at the backs of her eyes, but she blinked them away furiously. She would not cry in front of him, not now.

"Rafael..." His name escaped her lips, plaintive and small.

But he was already striding away, his broad shoulders rigid with tension. Clarissa watched him go, her heart fracturing with every step he took. How had everything gone so wrong, so quickly?

She had to fix this, had to make him understand. But as she stood there, the sun beating down mercilessly and the scent of bougainvillaea thick in the air, Clarissa had never felt more lost. Or more alone.

If only she could make him see the truth in her heart...but what if it was already too late?

The distant rumble of carriage wheels in the castle courtyard jolted Clarissa from her tumultuous thoughts.

"Now who is arriving?" she muttered, walking back around to the courtyard and watching as a rather grand carriage drew to a halt. Neither Lucia nor Rafael had mentioned expecting any more visitors.

The door swung open, and out stepped the Earl and Countess of Creighton, their expressions a mixture of relief and disapproval as they saw her. Shocked, Clarissa swallowed hard, her mouth suddenly dry as parchment.

"Mama, Papa," she managed, dropping into a curtsy. "What...what are you doing here?"

"What are we doing here?" the Countess repeated, her voice rising in pitch. "We've been worried sick about you, Clarissa!"

The Earl's sharp gaze swept over the crumbling facade of the castle, his lips thinning. "And now we find you living in...in this ruin? With a family of strangers? What in heaven's name were you thinking, girl?"

Clarissa felt her cheeks heat with a mixture of shame and defiance. "They're not strangers, Papa. They're...they're friends. And Rafael...Captain de Silva...he saved my life."

"Saved your life?" the Countess echoed, her hand fluttering to her throat. "What on earth happened?"

Clarissa drew in a deep breath, steeling herself. She had to make them understand, had to convince them that this was where she belonged. With Rafael, and his family.

But as she opened her mouth to speak, she caught a glimpse of Rafael over her father's shoulder. He stood in the shadows of the entryway, his face an inscrutable mask.

And in that moment, Clarissa knew that no matter what she said, it wouldn't be enough. Not now, with the weight of her parents' expectations bearing down upon her.

Her shoulders slumped, defeat washing over her like a cold wave. "It's...it's a long story," she said softly, her gaze dropping to the ground. "But I'm fine, truly. And I...I want to stay."

"Absolutely not," the Earl declared, his voice brooking no argument. "You're coming home with us, Clarissa. At once."

Clarissa's head snapped up, her eyes wide with dismay. "But Papa-"

"No buts," he interrupted, his expression stern. "Your reputation is at stake, and I will not have you ruining your prospects with this...this foolishness. Have your things packed, and we will return to Lisbon immediately. I have a ship waiting for us."

Tears blurred Clarissa's vision, hot and stinging. She blinked them back furiously, refusing to let them fall. Not here, not now.

"Please," she whispered, her voice cracking. "Please don't do this."

But even as the words left her lips, she knew it was futile. Her parents had made up their minds, and there was nothing she could do to change them.

"Lavinia!" A calm voice behind Clarissa made sudden hope leap in her chest. Marianne emerged from the castle, smiling welcomingly. "How lovely to see you! Do come in out of the sun, it's dreadfully hot."

Marianne, lovely and gracious, could soften almost anyone. Both Clarissa's parents were swept up in her greeting, finding themselves agreeing that it was indeed terribly hot and a cool drink would be pleasant.

Clarissa trailed along in their wake, fighting back tears. The misunderstanding with Rafael had been distressing enough, but for her parents to arrive at just this moment could spell the death knell for even the hope of reconciliation.

Lucia was waiting in the salon with Isabella, both the picture of propriety as they welcomed the Earl and Countess, and Alex came striding in a moment later, all calm authority.

Marianne extricated herself from the group a little later and slipped away to where Clarissa stood in the shadows near the doorway. Grasping her hand, Marianne led her out into the hallway.

"I must speak to you. I sent a letter to your parents from Gibraltar," Marianne confessed, her words tumbling out in a rush. "I told them about our travels, which is obviously how they knew we were here, but I didn't mention your disappearance in Athens. I thought it would be best if they heard it from you, in person."

Clarissa's eyes widened, a surge of relief washing over her. "You mean they don't know?" she breathed, hardly daring to hope.

Marianne nodded, a small smile tugging at the corners of her mouth. "I had sent a letter from Florence when we first received word you had disappeared, but it seems that letter hadn't arrived by the time they left England. They don't know about the kidnapping, for now."

Clarissa sagged back against the plush velvet seat, her heart racing. It was a small mercy, but a mercy nonetheless.

But even as the thought crossed her mind, Marianne's expression sobered, her eyes searching Clarissa's face.

"You know they can't be kept ignorant forever," she cautioned gently. "Sooner or later, the truth will come out. And then..."

She trailed off, leaving the unspoken words hanging in the air between them.

Clarissa nodded, her throat tight. She knew Marianne was right. She couldn't hide from her past forever, no matter how much she might wish to.

But for now, she would cling to this small shred of hope, this tiny glimmer of light in the darkness.

For now, it was all she had.

Clarissa's reprieve lasted no later than dinner that evening. The Earl and Countess, somewhat mollified by their gracious reception and finding the inside of the castle much less ruined than it looked from the outside, had accepted Lucia's invitation to stay a few days. At dinner, however, Mr Dalton joined them, and almost the very first thing he said was;

"You must have been so concerned when you heard Lady Clarissa went missing from Athens. Such a relief she was retrieved safely before too many days had passed."

Clarissa felt the blood drain from her face, her stomach twisting into knots. No. No, this couldn't be happening.

But her mother's horrified gasp told her it was all too real.

"Missing?" the Countess repeated, her voice rising to a near-shriek. "What do you mean, *missing*?"

She rounded on Alex and Marianne, her eyes flashing with fury.

"How could you let this happen?" she demanded, her voice shaking with anger. "How could you be so irresponsible as to lose track of my daughter? For *days*?"

Marianne flinched, her face paling under the onslaught. "Lavinia, I--"

But the Countess cut her off with a sharp gesture. "I don't want to hear your excuses," she snapped. "You were supposed to be looking after her, and you failed. Utterly and completely."

"Clarissa's reputation is at stake," Clarissa's father declared, his voice loud in the hushed silence which fell over the dinner table. "She must return home immediately."

Clarissa's heart seized in her chest. "No," she blurted out, before she could stop herself. "Papa, please. I don't want to go back."

Her father's gaze snapped to her, his eyes narrowing. "You don't have a choice in the matter," he said, his tone brooking no argument. "Your reputation has been compromised. The only way to salvage it is for you to return to England and marry at once."

Clarissa shook her head, desperation clawing at her throat. "But I'm happy here," she pleaded, her voice cracking. "I've found a place where I belong. Please don't make me leave."

But her parents refused to listen. "You're coming home with us, and that's final," her mother said, her tone sharp and unyielding. "We'll find you a suitable husband, someone who can help restore your good name."

Clarissa felt as though the ground had dropped out from beneath her feet. A suitable husband? The very thought made her stomach churn.

She looked to Marianne, hoping for support, but her aunt could only offer a sympathetic glance. There was nothing she could do, Clarissa realised with a sinking heart. Her parents had made up their minds.

Tears stung her eyes as the reality of the situation sank in. She was going to be taken away from everything she loved, forced into a life she didn't want. And there was nothing she could do to stop it.

The Earl cleared his throat, drawing everyone's attention. "As it happens, I have a friend who has expressed interest in an alliance with our family. Lord Weatherby is a respected member of the ton and would make a fine match for Clarissa."

"Lord Weatherby? You can't be serious. The man is old enough to be Clarissa's grandfather!" It was Alex who spoke, his face twisted with disgust.

The Earl rounded on him, his face flushed with anger. “You have no say in this matter, Glenkellie! Clarissa’s future is not your concern.”

Clarissa watched the exchange with growing despair. She knew Alex meant well, but his intervention would only make things worse. Her father was not a man to be crossed, especially when it came to matters of family and reputation.

She felt a surge of panic rising within her. The thought of being married off to a stranger, an old man, of spending the rest of her life in a loveless union, was too much to bear. She had to do something, anything, to change her parents’ minds.

But even as the thought crossed her mind, she knew it was hopeless. Her father’s word was law, and there was nothing she could do to sway him. She was trapped, a prisoner of her own circumstances, with no way out.

“Clarissa will return to England with us at once,” the Earl said, his gaze fixed on his daughter. “And she will marry Lord Weatherby, as befits her station. There will be no further discussion on the matter.”

She could not stay in that room a moment longer, with pitying and accusing gazes directed at her. Jumping to her feet, she fled the room, running upstairs and into her room, where she threw open the window and gasped for air, feeling as though she couldn’t breathe. Tears blurred her vision, and she swayed on her feet, feeling as though she might faint. But then a pair of strong, gentle arms wrapped around her, and she found herself being drawn into a warm, comforting embrace.

“Shh, it’s all right,” Marianne murmured, her voice soft and soothing. “I’ve got you, my dear. Just let it out.”

And with those words, the dam broke. Clarissa buried her face in Marianne’s shoulder and sobbed, her body shaking with the force of her grief. She clung to the older woman like a drowning sailor to a life raft, desperate for any shred of comfort or solace.

Marianne held her close, stroking her hair and whispering words of reassurance. But even as she did so, Clarissa could sense the helplessness in her aunt’s touch, the knowledge that there was nothing either of them could do to change the situation.

“I can’t marry him, Marianne,” Clarissa choked out between sobs. “I can’t. I’d rather die than spend my life with a horrible old man.”

Marianne’s arms tightened around her. “I know, my dear. I know. But we must have faith. Surely there must be some way to change your father’s mind, to make him see reason.”

Clarissa shook her head, her tears soaking into the fine silk of Marianne's gown. "There's no use. He's determined to see me married, no matter what I want. Oh, Marianne, what am I going to do?"

But even as she asked the question, Clarissa knew there was no answer. She was trapped, caught between the demands of her family and the desires of her own heart. She could only cling to Marianne and weep, her dreams of a happy future shattered beyond repair.

CHAPTER SIXTEEN

RAFAEL SAT FROZEN AT the head of the table, his heart an aching void in his chest as he watched Clarissa flee the dining room after her father's pronouncement. The room was brightly lit with candles and lamps, but Rafael felt only darkness encroaching, suffocating him. If only he had found the courage to tell her how he truly felt! But his damnable pride and baseless jealousy had held his tongue captive. Now it was too late.

Marianne rose from her seat and went after Clarissa, leaving everyone else looking at each other in uncertain silence - everyone except Mr Dalton, Rafael noted, who picked up his knife and fork and began cutting into his meat, as though it was not his careless words which had ignited the Earl's fury and sealed Clarissa's fate.

Dinner concluded in silence. Neither Marianne nor Clarissa returned, and Rafael heard his mother speak quietly to a maid, ordering food to be sent up to their rooms. He wondered if Clarissa would be able to eat. He had not been able to choke anything down, merely pushing the food around his plate.

As soon as possible after the meal, he made his excuses and escaped, going outside to the terrace to pace in silent desperation.

Somehow, it wasn't surprising that Alex came after him.

"You're a fool, you know," Alex said softly, clapping a heavy hand on Rafael's shoulder. "A damned fool not to go after her and declare yourself."

Rafael jerked away, a mirthless laugh escaping his lips. "And say what exactly? That I allowed my own insecurities to poison what grew between us? That I cannot bear the thought of her belonging to another?" He shook his head. "No, better she leave thinking me an irredeemable scoundrel. At least then she may forget me in time."

"Rafael, surely you don't mean that. Clarissa cares for you deeply, anyone can see it. This cannot be how your story ends."

"But it must," Rafael ground out, his throat tight with barely restrained anguish. "Her life is in England, amongst the glittering ton, not wasted on a penniless sea captain with naught to offer but a dilapidated vineyard and a fool's dreams."

He swallowed hard, forcing his next words past the lump in his throat. "I thank you and Lady Glenkellie, for everything. Will you... will you watch over her? See that she is happy?"

"Of course," Alex murmured quietly. "Marianne would not have it otherwise. And don't abandon all hope just yet, old friend. If it's meant to be, you'll find your way back to each other. Amor vincit omnia, and all that."

He knew something of Alex and Marianne's story, how Marianne's father had forced her into an arranged marriage when Alex was sent away to war, and it was not until after Marianne was widowed that they found their way back to each other. Such a distant, nebulous possibility was no comfort whatsoever to Rafael, though. And the mere thought of Clarissa wed to an old man who would surely crush all the vitality from her spirit made him want to scream his rage at the night.

Alex stepped away with a quiet murmur that he must see to the packing, and left Rafael alone.

He turned slowly, each step leaden, and blew out a deep breath as he looked up at the crumbling facade of his home. There was work to be done. Always more work. Perhaps if he threw himself into the business of the vineyard, the repairs to the estate, his duty to his sister and mother, he could forget the gaping wound where his heart used to reside. Where Clarissa used to reside.

But even as he told himself to let her go, Rafael knew forgetting Clarissa would be as impossible as forgetting how to breathe. She was in his very marrow now. All he could do was carry on, rebuild his life from the ashes of today, and pray that someday - if fortune chose to smile upon him - he might have a chance to win her back.

Until then, he would remain Captain Rafael de Silva. Devoted son, brother, and defender of the seas. But never again a lover. For his heart was about to sail away to England, and he knew not if it would ever return.

Rafael entered the castle, his footsteps echoing through the halls. He found Isabella and Lucia in the salon, their faces stricken with sorrow. Isabella rushed to him, her eyes brimming with tears.

"Rafael, surely there must be something we can do! Clarissa loves you, I know it. You cannot let her go so easily," Isabella pleaded, grasping his hands.

Rafael gently disentangled himself from her grip, his expression grave. "It is pointless, Isabella. Her father has already arranged her marriage. I cannot interfere with that."

Lucia approached, her face etched with concern. "But Rafael, my son, if you love her..."

"It matters not," Rafael interrupted, his voice strained. "We must bear this separation. There is nothing to be done."

Isabella shook her head vehemently. "I refuse to believe that! You are the bravest man I know. You cannot simply give up!"

Rafael's jaw clenched, his eyes flashing with barely contained emotion. "I am not giving up, Isabella. I am accepting reality. Clarissa's place is in England, with her family, marrying the lord her father has chosen for her. Our place is here, rebuilding our lives. We must focus on that now."

Lucia placed a comforting hand on Isabella's shoulder. "Your brother is right, my dear. We must be strong, for each other and for Clarissa. She would want us to carry on."

Isabella's shoulders slumped, her fiery spirit momentarily quelled by the weight of their circumstances. Rafael drew both women into a fierce embrace, his voice rough with unshed tears.

"We will endure this, as we have endured so much already. Our love for each other, for this land, will sustain us. And perhaps, if God is kind, fate may yet bring Clarissa back to us someday."

But even as he spoke the words, Rafael could not bring himself to believe them. For how could fate be so cruel as to bring Clarissa into his life, only to rip her away just as he realised the depth of his love for her? No, he thought bitterly, fate was not kind. And he was a fool to ever believe otherwise.

Rafael stood stoically on the steps of the estate, watching as Marianne and Alex helped Clarissa into the waiting carriage. His heart ached with each step she took, each inch of distance that grew between them. He longed to run to her, to gather her in his arms and beg her to stay. But he remained rooted in place, duty and honour forbidding him from acting on his deepest desires.

Marianne turned back, her eyes meeting Rafael's with a mixture of sorrow and understanding. She approached him, her voice soft yet filled with conviction. "Rafael, are you certain about this? It's not too late for you to speak to her."

He swallowed hard, his voice strained as he replied, "I am certain, Marianne. Clarissa deserves a life of comfort and security, one that I cannot provide. I am grateful that she has you and Alex to watch over her."

Alex joined them, placing a firm hand on Rafael's shoulder. "You are a good man, Rafael. Never doubt that. And if you ever change your mind, know that you will always have friends in England."

Rafael nodded, his throat too tight to speak. He watched as the couple returned to the carriage, their final farewell hanging heavily in the air. Clarissa's eyes met his through the carriage window, a world of unspoken emotions passing between them. In that moment, Rafael felt his resolve waver, the urge to go to her nearly overwhelming him.

But then the carriage jolted forward, the horses' hooves clattering against the cobblestones. Rafael stood motionless as the carriage carried Clarissa away, the distance between them growing with each passing second. He wanted to call out to her, to tell her all the things he had been too cowardly to say. But the words died on his lips, their fight left unresolved, their future together nothing more than a dream that could never be.

As the carriage disappeared from view, Rafael felt a profound sense of loss, as though a part of his very soul had been ripped away. He closed his eyes, the image of Clarissa's face burned into his memory, a bittersweet reminder of all that he had found and lost in the span of a few short months.

He loved Clarissa, with every fibre of his being, with a passion that consumed him like a raging inferno. And now, he had lost her, almost certainly forever.

I should have proposed to her weeks ago. In Florence, probably. We would have been married by now.

The realisation hit him like a physical blow, his knees nearly buckling under the weight of his emotions. He braced himself against the stone wall of the courtyard, his breath coming in ragged gasps as he struggled to compose himself. How could he have been so foolish, so blind to his own heart? He had let his pride and his sense of duty come between them, and now he would pay the price for his stubborn foolishness.

But even as his heart shattered into a million pieces, Rafael knew that he could not abandon his responsibilities to chase after Clarissa. His family, the people who depended on him - they all needed him to be strong, to be the leader that they had come to rely on. He could not simply walk away from his duties, no matter how much his soul cried out for Clarissa's touch.

With a heavy sigh, Rafael pushed himself away from the wall, squaring his shoulders as he turned to face the castle. He would have to find a way to carry on, to bury his heartbreak deep within himself and focus on the tasks at hand. But even as he took that first step forward, he knew that a part of him would always belong to Clarissa, that he would carry the memory of their love with him for the rest of his days.

As Rafael entered the castle with dragging steps, he was greeted by the sight of Isabella and the Conte di Bardolino, their faces alight with joy and excitement. The Conte stepped forward, his expression serious as he met Rafael's gaze.

"Rafael," he began, his voice low and earnest. "I come to you today not just as a friend, but as a man deeply in love with your sister. I humbly ask for your blessing to take Isabella's hand in marriage, to cherish and protect her for all of my days."

Rafael blinked, his mind struggling to process the Conte's words. He had been so consumed by his own heartbreak, so lost in his thoughts of Clarissa, that he had almost forgotten about the budding romance between his sister and the young Italian nobleman.

He glanced at Isabella, saw the hopeful expression on her face, the way her eyes sparkled with love and anticipation. How could he deny her this happiness, especially after all that she had suffered?

Swallowing hard, Rafael forced a smile to his lips, his voice rough with emotion as he replied, "Mario, I can think of no man more worthy of my sister's hand than you. You have my blessing, and my deepest congratulations to you both."

Isabella let out a cry of joy, rushing forward to embrace her brother. "Oh, Rafael, thank you!" she exclaimed, her voice muffled against his chest. "I know that this must be difficult for you, so soon after Clarissa's departure, but your support means everything to me."

Rafael held his sister tight, blinking back the tears that threatened to fall. He knew that he should be happy for her, that he should be celebrating this joyous occasion. But all he could think about was Clarissa, and the future that he had let slip through his fingers.

"I am happy for you, truly," he murmured, his voice barely above a whisper. "You deserve all the happiness in the world, Isabella. And I know that Mario will be a loving and devoted husband to you."

As the Conte and Isabella embraced, their faces radiant with love and joy, Rafael felt a pang of envy and regret. He had had that same chance at happiness, that same opportunity to build a life with the woman he loved. But he had let his own fears and doubts get in the way, and now he would have to live with the consequences of his choices.

With a heavy heart, Rafael turned away from the happy couple, his mind already racing with thoughts of the future. He would throw himself into his work, into rebuilding his family's estate and securing his sister's happiness. And perhaps, in time, he would find a way to heal the wound that Clarissa's absence had left in his soul.

Rafael stood on the terrace, watching as the servants hurried to and fro, their arms laden with flowers and ribbons. The air was thick with the scent of roses and jasmine, and the sound of laughter and chatter filled the courtyard below.

He forced a smile onto his face as Isabella approached, her eyes shining with excitement. "Oh, Rafael," she exclaimed, taking his hands in hers. "Can you believe it? In just a few short days, I will be a married woman!"

Rafael swallowed hard, his throat suddenly tight. "I am so happy for you, Isabella," he managed to say, his voice sounding strained even to his own ears. "Mario is a lucky man."

Isabella's smile faltered slightly, and she searched his face with concern. "Rafael, are you all right? You seem troubled."

He shook his head, forcing himself to meet her gaze. "I am fine, Isabella. Just a little tired, that's all. There is much to be done before the wedding, and I want everything to be perfect for you."

Isabella's face softened, and she reached up to touch his cheek. "You are a good brother, Rafael. I know that you have sacrificed so much for our family, and I am grateful for everything that you have done. But you must not forget to live your own life, too. You deserve happiness, just as much as I do."

Rafael felt a surge of emotion rise up within him, and he blinked back the tears that threatened to fall. "Thank you, Isabella," he whispered, his voice hoarse with emotion. "I will try to remember that."

As Isabella hurried off to oversee the preparations, Rafael turned back to the view of the vineyards, his heart heavy with regret. He knew that he should be focusing on his sister's happiness, on the future that lay ahead for his family. But he could not shake the feeling that he had lost something precious, something that he would never be able to regain.

With a sigh, he squared his shoulders and turned back towards the castle, determined to put on a brave face for his sister's sake. There would be time enough for regrets later, he told himself firmly. For now, he had a wedding to prepare for, and a family to protect.

Rafael walked through the halls of the castle, his footsteps echoing on the stone floors. The sound of laughter and excited chatter drifted towards him from the courtyard, where the servants were busy hanging garlands of flowers and setting up tables for the wedding feast. He forced himself to smile, to nod and exchange pleasantries with those he passed, but inside he felt hollow, as if a vital part of him had been torn away.

He found himself in the library, seeking solace among the dusty tomes and faded tapestries. The room was dim and cool, the only light filtering in through the narrow windows. Rafael sank into a worn leather armchair, his head in his hands.

"What have I done?" he whispered to himself, his voice rough with emotion. "I let her go, without even telling her how I felt. And now she is lost to me forever."

He thought of Clarissa, of her fierce intelligence and her infectious laughter, her forthright honesty, of the way her eyes had sparkled when she looked at him. He had been a fool not to tell her how much he loved her, how much he needed her in his life. And now it was too late.

Rafael sat there for a long time, lost in his thoughts, until the sound of footsteps in the hallway roused him from his reverie. He stood up, straightening his jacket and smoothing back his hair. He had a duty to his family, to his sister, and he would not let them down.

"Isabella's happiness must come first," he told himself firmly, pushing aside his own heartache. "I will focus on that, and let the rest take care of itself."

With a deep breath, Rafael left the library and went to find his sister, determined to make her wedding day a joyous occasion, no matter the cost to his own heart.

As Rafael walked through the hallways of the castle, his mind wandered to the future. The once grand castle lay in disrepair, a shadow of its former glory. The vineyards, too, had suffered from years of neglect, the vines overgrown and the soil untended. Clarissa had made him see that it could be otherwise, that if he dedicated himself to rebuilding his estate, he could bring it back to what it once had been. She had seen the possibility, and now, he determined that he would make her vision complete.

"I will rebuild this place," Rafael vowed silently, his jaw set with determination. "I will make it a home worthy of Clarissa's memory, a testament to the love I never had the chance to share with her."

He imagined Clarissa walking beside him, her hand in his as they surveyed the grounds together. In his mind's eye, he could see the vineyards thriving once more, the castle restored to its former grandeur. It was a vision of what might have been, a dream that he would now have to pursue alone.

Rafael paused at a window, looking out over the rolling hills that stretched to the horizon. The sun was setting, painting the sky in shades of orange and pink. It was a sight that Clarissa would have loved, he knew, and the thought brought a fresh wave of pain to his heart.

"I will never forget you, my love," he whispered, his voice carried away on the evening breeze. "And I will never stop fighting for the life we might have had together."

With a final, lingering look at the sunset, Rafael turned away from the window and continued on his way, his steps heavy with the weight of his grief and his resolve. There was work to be done, and he would not rest until it was finished, until he had created a legacy that would honour Clarissa's vision as she deserved.

CHAPTER SEVENTEEN

Clarissa gazed out through the rain-streaked window of her family's London townhouse, her heart as dark and listless as the rainy night. The clink of silver teaspoons on fine china and the idle chatter of the ladies gathered in the drawing-room after the dinner her mother had just hosted faded into the background as her thoughts drifted across the sea to Portugal, to Rafael.

She could still feel the warm caress of the sun on her skin, the sweet tang of port wine on her tongue, and the thrill that raced through her whenever Rafael fixed her with those striking sea-green eyes. In his presence, she had felt truly alive for the first time - challenged, appreciated, and part of something meaningful. Together they had tended to the vineyards and dreamed of a future restoring his family lands.

Now back in England, Clarissa felt the full weight of the structured, superficial society pressing down upon her. The endless teas, balls and social calls felt painfully hollow. She longed for the simple authenticity of life at Rafael's estate, for the invigorating conversations and shared hopes that had bonded them so deeply in such a short time.

"Clarissa dear, whatever is the matter? You've been somewhere else entirely this last half-hour," her mother's voice cut into her thoughts.

Clarissa startled, nearly upsetting her forgotten tea cup. "It's nothing, Mama. I'm a little wearied from the journey still, I suppose."

"Well, I should hope you recover your wits soon. Your father has arranged for Lord Weatherby to take you riding in the park tomorrow afternoon." The Countess gave her a meaningful look. "He's quite a catch, you know."

Glancing around at the other young ladies in their fine silks and perfect curls, Clarissa felt a rising desperation. Was this truly to be her life now - playing the demure maiden, bartering her youth and beauty to the highest titled bidder? They could never understand the wonders she'd experienced, the deep connection she'd forged with Rafael.

"I think I shall retire early tonight. Excuse me" she said abruptly, setting down her cup and rising. Her mother clucked disapprovingly but made no move to stop her.

Once in her room, Clarissa flung herself across the bed, staring up at the canopy. Unbidden, an image of Rafael's handsome face filled her mind - the way he looked at her not as a prize to be won but a partner to stand beside, an equal in courage and spirit.

"Oh Rafael," she whispered to the empty room, "how I wish I was with you now, finding purpose and adventure instead of withering away in this gilded cage."

Silent tears slid down her temples to dampen the pillow.

Clarissa stood rigidly beside her mother, her face a mask of polite indifference as Lord Weatherby leered at her from across the drawing room. Alex had warned her the man was old enough to be her grandfather, and indeed he must be sixty at least, grey-haired and paunchy. She felt ill at the very thought of letting him touch her.

The Earl's booming voice filled the space, extolling the virtues of the match.

"Weatherby is a man of means and influence, Clarissa. He will provide handsomely for you and any children you may have." The Earl fixed his daughter with a stern look, daring her to defy him.

Clarissa's hands clenched into fists at her sides, the urge to scream building in her throat. She glanced at her mother, hoping to find an ally, but the Countess merely nodded in agreement with her husband.

"Lord Weatherby is a fine catch, my dear. You would be wise to accept his attentions." The Countess's tone brooked no argument.

Bile rose in Clarissa's throat as Weatherby approached, his eyes roving over her figure with undisguised lechery. The cloying scent of his cologne assaulted her nostrils, and she fought the urge to recoil.

"My lady," Weatherby said, reaching for her hand. "It would be my greatest pleasure to make you my wife."

Clarissa snatched her hand away before he could touch her, propriety be damned. "I cannot marry you, my lord. I will not." Her voice rang out, clear and defiant.

The Earl's face reddened with anger. "Clarissa, you will do as you're told! Lord Weatherby has graciously offered for you, and you will accept him."

Tears stung Clarissa's eyes as she turned to her mother, desperation clawing at her heart. "Please, Mama, do not make me do this. I cannot bear the thought of being his wife."

The Countess's expression softened for a moment, but she quickly schooled her features into a mask of determination. "It is for the best, Clarissa. Lord Weatherby will provide for you and protect your reputation. You must think of your future."

Clarissa's heart shattered as she realised her parents would not relent. They cared more for her marriageability than her happiness, more for their own social standing than their daughter's dreams.

With a final, anguished look at her mother, Clarissa turned and fled the room, ignoring her father's shouts and Weatherby's startled exclamations. She would not let them control her destiny any longer.

Lavinia, the Countess of Creighton, followed her daughter into the bedchamber, her silk skirts swishing against the polished floorboards. "Clarissa, my dear, you must be reasonable," she implored, her voice tinged with desperation. "Think of the family's reputation. If word of your...indiscretion in Greece were to spread, we would be ruined."

Clarissa whirled to face her mother, her cheeks flushed with anger and unshed tears. "And what of my *life*, Mother? What of my happiness? Am I to be sold off to the highest bidder, regardless of my feelings?"

The Countess sighed, her shoulders sagging beneath the weight of her daughter's accusations. "It is not as simple as that, Clarissa. We have a duty to uphold, a position to maintain. And Mr. Dalton... he made it clear that he will not keep silent forever."

A chill ran down Clarissa's spine at the mention of Dalton's name. The man who had once seemed so charming, so attentive, now held the power to destroy her future with a few well-placed words. "What does he want?" she whispered, dreading the answer.

"He has hinted that he would be willing to marry you himself, to protect your reputation," the Countess admitted, her voice heavy with resignation. "But your father refuses to consider it, at least for now. He is not the match we would want for you, a younger son with no title or fortune of his own - but if you will not have Weatherby, you may have no other choice!"

Clarissa's heart lurched at the thought of being shackled to Dalton for the rest of her days. The man had nearly ruined her life with his loose tongue already, blurting to her parents! She did not trust him in the slightest.

"I will not marry him," she declared, her voice ringing with conviction. "I will not marry either of them! And if that means I am ruined, then so be it."

The Countess's eyes widened in alarm. "Clarissa, you cannot be serious. You have younger sisters, think of them! Your father and I would have no choice but to disown you, to save *their* reputations, and then where would you go? How would you live?"

But Clarissa's mind was already racing ahead, conjuring images of a life with Rafael in Portugal, far from the suffocating expectations of English society. "I will find a way," she vowed, her chin lifted in defiance.

Before the Countess could respond, a knock sounded at the door. "Come in," the Countess called, her voice weary.

The door opened to reveal Marianne, resplendent in a gown of emerald silk that set off her fiery hair. "I hope I'm not interrupting," she said, her eyes darting between Clarissa and her mother.

"Not at all," Clarissa said, relief washing over her at the sight of her aunt. "Please, come in."

Marianne crossed the room to embrace Clarissa, her perfume enveloping them both in a soft cloud of jasmine. "I've been worried about you," she murmured, pulling back to study Clarissa's face. "Alex and I have hardly seen you since we returned to London - we've delayed going to Scotland to ensure that you were all right."

The Countess cleared her throat, drawing their attention. "Marianne, perhaps you can talk some sense into my daughter. She's refusing to consider Lord Weatherby's proposal, and I fear she's entertaining some foolish notions of running away."

Marianne's brows shot up in surprise. "Running away? To where?"

Clarissa hesitated, suddenly unsure of how much to reveal. But the warmth and concern in Marianne's eyes gave her courage. "To Portugal," she admitted, her voice barely above a whisper. "To Rafael."

Marianne's eyes widened, and she glanced at the Countess, who looked positively scandalised. "Clarissa," Marianne said gently, taking her friend's hands in her own, "I understand your feelings for Captain de Silva, but you must think this through. Running away would ruin your reputation, and your family's as well."

Clarissa pulled her hands away, frustration rising in her chest. "And what of my happiness, Marianne? Am I to sacrifice it for the sake of propriety and the opinions of others?"

The Countess stepped forward, her voice stern. "Clarissa, that's enough. You will do your duty as a daughter of this family and accept Lord Weatherby's proposal. There will be no more talk of Portugal or Captain de Silva. Marianne." The Countess nodded towards the door, making it clear she did not intend to leave the two of them alone, probably not trusting Marianne.

Indeed, Clarissa thought, she would have begged Marianne to help her escape if she could.

Marianne cast Clarissa a pained look before reluctantly departing. The Countess followed her, closing the door with a decisive click, and Clarissa sank onto the edge of her bed, her shoulders slumping in defeat.

No, she thought, Marianne would not help her run away. That would be asking too much. But perhaps... perhaps she would send a letter?

"I could write to Rafael," Clarissa said aloud, dashing the tears from her eyes and setting her jaw stubbornly. "I never had the chance to tell him how I feel about him. If he knows... perhaps..." Perhaps he would not care. She had thought, so many times, he was on the verge of asking, but he never had. Well. She squared her shoulders. Nothing ventured, nothing gained.

She crossed to her writing desk and pulled out a sheet of paper and a quill.

My dearest Rafael, she wrote. *I fear I have made a terrible mistake in leaving Portugal, in leaving you. Every day, I find myself dreaming of the life we could have had, of the love we could have shared.*

The words poured out of her, a torrent of longing and despair. She told Rafael of her misery, of the emptiness she felt without him by her side. She confessed her love, her dreams of a future together, far from the constraints of English society.

Clarissa clutched the finished letter to her chest, her heart racing with a mix of fear and anticipation. She knew she was taking a tremendous risk, defying her parents and society's expectations, but the thought of a life without Rafael was too much to bear. She would put it into Marianne's hands as soon as she could, and trust that her aunt would send it for her.

With trembling hands, she opened her dresser drawer and carefully placed the letter inside, hiding it beneath a stack of handkerchiefs. It was her last link to Rafael, a tangible reminder of the love and passion they had shared.

A sudden knock at the door startled Clarissa from her reverie. "Clarissa, you must make ready. We are leaving in one hour!" It was her mother's voice, tinged with impatience.

"Yes, Mama," Clarissa called back, knowing she must maintain a pliable facade for now, at least. She took a deep breath, steeling herself for the evening ahead, and rang the bell for her maid.

The ball was a grand affair, the ballroom glittering with candlelight and filled with the chatter of London's elite. Clarissa moved through the crowd, exchanging polite greetings and forced smiles, but her heart was not in it. Her thoughts were with Rafael, and the letter hidden in her dresser.

"Ah, there you are, my dear." Lord Weatherby's oily voice cut through the din, and Clarissa suppressed a shudder as he took her hand, his clammy fingers enveloping hers. "I've been looking forward to a dance with you all evening."

Clarissa glanced desperately around the room, seeking an escape, but her father's stern gaze caught hers from across the ballroom. She knew what he expected of her, knew the pressure he was under to secure her future.

But as Lord Weatherby led her onto the dance floor, his hand sliding possessively around her waist, Clarissa felt something inside her snap. She couldn't do this, couldn't pretend to be someone she wasn't, couldn't resign herself to a life of misery and regret.

"I'm sorry, I can't," she gasped, wrenching herself free of Lord Weatherby's grasp. Ignoring his sputtered protests and her father's furious glare, she gathered her skirts and fled the ballroom, tears streaming down her face.

She ran blindly through the halls, her heart pounding in her ears, until she found herself in a quiet alcove, hidden from view. She sank to the floor, burying her face in her hands as sobs wracked her body.

"There you are," a soft voice said, and the scent of jasmine enveloped her as Marianne, resplendent in a gown of shimmering emerald silk, crouched at her side. "Come, dearest. Alex has our carriage waiting. Let me take you home."

Home. The only home she wanted was a crumbling castle on a Portuguese cliffside, beside the only man who would ever hold her heart. Despondently, Clarissa let Marianne help her up and lead her outside, where the Glenkellie carriage waited for them.

"I'll let your parents know Marianne's taken you home," Alex said quietly, helping her into the carriage, his face full of sympathy.

Clarissa could only nod, grateful, but understanding this was all the help they could offer her. She stared out of the window in silence, unseeing as the carriage rolled through the darkened streets, unaware of the worry on Marianne's face as her aunt watched her.

As the carriage halted outside the Creighton townhouse, Clarissa turned to her aunt.

"Marianne, I need your help. I must send a letter. Will you post it for me, discreetly?"

Marianne's eyes widened in surprise, but she nodded without hesitation. "Of course, my dear. You know you can always count on me. But what is this letter? And to whom are you sending it?"

Clarissa took a deep breath, steeling herself for the confession. "It's to Rafael, Marianne. I love him, truly and deeply, and I cannot bear the thought of losing him forever. I must tell him how I feel, even if it means defying my father and risking everything."

Marianne's expression softened, and she reached out to clasp Clarissa's hands in her own. "Oh, my darling girl. I understand. Love is a precious thing, and it's worth fighting for. Give me the letter, and I will see that it reaches him safely."

Clarissa felt a rush of gratitude and affection for her aunt. Rushing up to her room, she brought the letter back down and pressed it into Marianne's hands, a single tear sliding down her cheek. "Thank you, Marianne. Thank you for everything."

As Marianne slipped out, the letter hidden in the folds of her skirt, Clarissa felt a glimmer of hope ignite in her heart. She had taken the first step, had dared to reach out for the love she so desperately craved. Now, all she could do was wait and pray that Rafael would answer her call, that he would come for her and sweep her away to a life of passion and adventure, far from the suffocating confines of London society.

In her mind's eye, she could see Rafael's ship, the Santa Dorotéia, cutting through the waves, its sails billowing in the wind. She imagined herself standing on the deck beside him, the salt spray kissing her face, the warm breeze tangling in her hair.

In her dreams, they would sail to Portugal, to the crumbling castle and neglected vineyard that were Rafael's birthright. Together, they would restore the estate to its former glory, pouring their love and dedication into every stone and vine. She could see herself walking hand in hand with Rafael through the sun-drenched vineyards, laughing and talking, sharing their hopes and dreams.

At night, they would retire to their chambers, where Rafael would take her in his arms and love her with a passion that set her soul ablaze. She would give herself to him fully, body and heart, and together they would create a life filled with joy and purpose, far from the shallow intrigues and petty scandals of the English aristocracy.

Clarissa sighed, her heart aching with longing. It was a beautiful dream. But was it truly possible? Could she really abandon everything she had ever known, defy her family and her duty, for the sake of love?

Clarissa closed her eyes, letting the dream wash over her, filling her with a fierce, unshakable resolve. Yes, she thought. Yes, I will come to you, my love. I will brave any storm, face any obstacle, to be with you. And together, we will create a love that will endure through the ages, a love that will never die.

CHAPTER EIGHTEEN

Torre do Rochado had not seen such celebrations in decades. The castle was filled to the brim with flowers and celebrating guests for Isabella's wedding.

The music swelled as Isabella and her new husband, Mario, the Conte di Bardolino, took to the dance floor for their first dance as man and wife. Rafael watched from the sidelines, acutely aware of the empty space beside him where Clarissa should have been.

As the happy couple whirled past, Isabella caught his eye, her radiant smile fading into a sympathetic frown. She leaned close to Mario and whispered something in his ear. He nodded and gracefully led her off the dance floor. It was mere moments before Isabella was marching up to Rafael, hands on her hips, her new husband trailing in her wake with an amused expression on his face.

"What are you doing, fratello mio? Why are you not dancing?"

Rafael sighed and took a sip of his wine. "I am in no mood for dancing, I am afraid. Do not let my ill temper blight your day, dear one."

"He is missing Clarissa, I think," Mario said with a small laugh.

"Oh Rafa," Isabella shook her head. "Can't you see? The poor girl is in love with you! And you let your silly male pride get in the way."

"In love with me?" Rafael scoffed. "I think not. She left!"

"Men! Honestly, you are all so blind sometimes." Isabella grabbed his arm, her grip surprisingly strong for one so slight. "Listen to me, Rafael. That girl looked at you like...like Mama used to look at Papa. She left only because you did not ask her to stay!"

Could it be true? Had he completely misread the situation with Clarissa? The thought filled him with equal parts elation and dread.

If he had ruined things with his rash words and selfish assumptions… Dio mio, he would never forgive himself. He had to make this right, pride be damned. Even if she rejected him, he had to try.

Rafael set down his glass and kissed Isabella on the cheek. "Grazie, sorella. You have given me much to think on."

She smiled and patted his face. "Go to her, Rafa. Fight for the love you deserve."

"Do not worry about the estate," Mario put in. "Isabella and I will oversee things in your absence."

Relief and gratitude washed over Rafael in equal measure. "Thank you, brother. Your support means more than I can say."

With renewed purpose, Rafael set about making preparations for his journey. As he packed his trunk, his mind whirled with possibilities. What if Clarissa refused to see him? What if her feelings had changed? No, he could not afford to think like that. He would win her back, no matter the cost.

As the carriage carried him away from the sun-drenched vineyards of his homeland, Rafael's heart soared with hope and trepidation. He was sailing into uncharted waters, but for Clarissa, he would brave any storm. England, and his heart's desire, awaited.

The carriage jolted to a stop before an elegant London townhouse, its façade a pristine white against the grey, misty sky. Rafael alighted, his heart hammering in his chest as he approached the door. He rapped the brass knocker, the sound echoing through the quiet street.

Moments later, the door swung open, revealing an urbane butler. "May I assist you, sir?" His gaze raked Rafael, a frown lowering his brow as he took in Rafael's worn travelling clothes. "I don't believe…"

"I must speak with the Marquis and Marchioness of Glenkellie immediately," Rafael interrupted, his voice firm with resolve.

"I will see if they are receiving, sir. Your card?"

Rafael blinked. "Ah - I don't have a card. Please tell them Rafael de Silva is here."

"Very well, sir." The butler ushered him inside, leading him to a well-appointed drawing room and leaving him alone with an expression that suggested he rather thought Rafael might put his dirty boots up on the sofa if left unsupervised for too long.

Scarcely a minute had passed before the door burst open, revealing Marianne and Alex, their expressions a mixture of shock and delight.

"Rafael!" Marianne exclaimed, rushing forward to embrace him. "What on earth are you doing here?"

Alex clasped his hand, his eyes twinkling with amusement. "I dare say this is a surprise, my friend. I thought you were tending to your estate in Portugal."

Rafael ran a hand through his hair, suddenly self-conscious. "I was, but I realised... I realised I could not let Clarissa go without a fight."

Marianne's face softened, understanding dawning in her eyes. "Oh, Rafael. I had hoped you would come to your senses."

She gestured for him to sit, her expression turning serious. "I must tell you, Clarissa wrote to you just a few days past. I posted the letter myself."

Rafael's heart leaped, a flicker of hope igniting in his chest. "She wrote to me? What did she say?"

Marianne shook her head, her red curls bouncing. "I am sorry, Rafael. It was not my place to read her correspondence. But I can tell you this - she has been miserable since returning to England. Her father is determined to see her wed, but she refuses every suitor he presents."

Alex leaned forward, his eyes intense. "Rafael, if you truly love her, you must act now. Her father grows more insistent by the day."

Rafael nodded, resolve settling over him like a mantle. "I do love her, with every fibre of my being. And I will not rest until she is mine."

He stood, his posture straight and proud. "I will call on her tomorrow, and pray she will receive me. But first, I must find lodgings and make myself presentable."

Marianne waved a hand, dismissing his concerns. "Nonsense, you will stay with us. We have more than enough room, and I insist upon it. You are our honoured guest - it is the least we can do to repay the wonderful hospitality you showed us in Portugal!"

Gratitude swelled in Rafael's chest, warming him from within. "Thank you, both of you. Your friendship means the world to me."

As he followed the suddenly much more welcoming butler to his chamber, Rafael's mind raced with anticipation. Tomorrow, he would lay his heart at

Clarissa's feet, and hope against hope that she would accept it. For now, he could only pray, and dream of the moment he would hold her in his arms once more.

He had barely stepped over the threshold when Alex's voice behind him made him turn.

"I say, Rafael... we had not planned to attend, but there is to be a ball tonight, and Marianne believes Clarissa will be there. Would you like to attend? Otherwise, you can call at her house tomorrow."

"But I might not be granted admittance to her house," Rafael said, thinking quickly. "The Earl cannot deny me speaking to her in public, however. Yes, Alex, I should very much like to attend, if it will be possible?"

"I'll pen a note to the hostess now advising we'll bring a guest." Alex flashed him a grin. "The advantage of being a marquis is that people find it very hard to say no even if you're making unreasonable requests! Do you have suitable clothing? Otherwise I dare say my suits will fit you well enough..."

"I have suitable clothing," Rafael said. "I am still a commissioned officer in the Portuguese Navy, after all."

"A military uniform is always acceptable." Alex bowed his head. "I'll send my man to help you bathe and shave!"

Rafael's heart raced as he entered the glittering ballroom, his eyes searching the crowd for a glimpse of Clarissa. The sea of unfamiliar faces and the opulent surroundings of the London society ball were a far cry from the deck of his ship, but he navigated this new world with the same determination that had served him well on the high seas.

And then he saw her.

Clarissa stood across the room, resplendent in a gown of pale blue silk that accentuated her delicate features and sun-kissed hair. As if sensing his presence, she turned, their eyes meeting across the crowded ballroom. In that moment, the rest of the world fell away, and there was only her.

Rafael made his way through the throng of people, his eyes never leaving Clarissa's face. As he drew closer, he saw the play of emotions across her features - surprise, joy, and a depth of feeling that took his breath away. In that moment, he knew beyond a shadow of a doubt that she loved him, just as he loved her.

"Clarissa," he breathed, taking her hand in his. "May I have this dance?"

She nodded, seemingly unable to speak, and he led her onto the dance floor. As they moved together in perfect harmony, Rafael marvelled at the feel of her in his arms, the way her hand fit so perfectly in his own. He had never felt as alive as this moment with Clarissa.

"I thought I would never see you again," Clarissa whispered, her voice trembling with emotion.

Rafael tightened his hold on her, his heart aching at the thought of the pain he had caused her. "I am so sorry, my love. I was a fool to let my pride and jealousy come between us. But I am here now, and I will never leave you again."

Clarissa's eyes shone with unshed tears. "Do you truly mean that, Rafael?"

He nodded, his gaze intense and unwavering. "I love you, Clarissa. I have loved you from the moment I first saw you, and I will love you until my last breath. Please, tell me you feel the same."

Her next words set his heart ablaze.

"I do, Rafael. I love you more than I ever thought possible. But..." She hesitated, worry creasing her brow. "My parents will never approve of our match. They have their hearts set on me marrying Lord Weatherby."

Rafael cupped her cheek, his thumb gently brushing away a stray tear. "I will overcome their objections, my love, however I must. I will prove to them that I am worthy of your hand, that my love for you is true and unshakable."

Clarissa leaned into his touch, drawing strength from his conviction. "I believe in you, Rafael. Together, we can face anything."

The Earl of Creighton sat rigidly behind his desk, his eyes narrowed as Rafael entered the study. "Captain de Silva," he said coldly. "To what do I owe this... unexpected visit?"

Rafael met the Earl's gaze unflinchingly, his posture straight and proud. "My lord, I have come to ask for your daughter's hand in marriage."

The Earl's face turned an alarming shade of red, his fists clenching at his sides. "You cannot be serious! Clarissa is meant for far greater things than a penniless Portuguese captain with a crumbling castle and a few measly vineyards to his name."

Rafael's jaw tightened, but he refused to rise to the bait. "I may not have wealth or titles, my lord, but I have something far more valuable - my love for your daughter.

She is the very air I breathe, the light that guides me through the darkness. I would lay down my life for her without a moment's hesitation."

The Earl scoffed, his lip curling in disdain. "Pretty words, Captain, but they mean nothing in the face of cold, hard reality. Clarissa deserves a husband who can provide for her, who can give her the life she was born to lead. And that man is not you."

Rafael's heart pounded in his chest, a mixture of anger and frustration coursing through his veins. He had faced down corsairs and battled raging seas, but nothing could have prepared him for the Earl's scathing dismissal. "You underestimate your daughter, my lord," he said, his voice low and intense. "Clarissa is not some delicate flower to be coddled and sheltered. She is a woman of strength and courage, with a heart as vast as the ocean."

The Earl's eyes flashed with anger. "You presume too much, Captain. I will not stand here and listen to you speak of my daughter as if you know her better than I do. Now, I suggest you take your leave before I have you thrown out."

Rafael's hands clenched into fists at his sides, the urge to lash out nearly overwhelming. But he knew that violence would solve nothing. With a stiff bow, he turned on his heel and strode from the room, his boots echoing on the polished floor.

As he emerged into the crisp London air, Rafael's mind raced with the implications of the Earl's words. How could he possibly convince the man to see reason? To understand that his love for Clarissa was pure and true, untainted by concerns of wealth or status?

Lost in thought, Rafael barely noticed the carriage pulling up to the curb until a familiar voice called out to him. "Rafael?"

He looked up to see Marianne and Alex, their faces etched with concern. "I came to ask for Clarissa's hand," he said, his voice rough with emotion. "But the Earl...he refused me outright. Said I was unworthy of her."

Marianne's eyes widened, her hand flying to her mouth. "Oh, Rafael...I am so sorry. But surely he must see reason! After all, Clarissa owes you her very life."

Alex nodded in agreement, his brow furrowed in thought. "Indeed. And your character is beyond reproach. The Earl cannot possibly object on those grounds."

Rafael shook his head, a bitter laugh escaping his lips. "You underestimate the man's stubbornness. He is determined to see Clarissa married to some wealthy lord, regardless of her own feelings on the matter."

Marianne exchanged a glance with her husband, a determined glint in her eye. "We shall see about that. Come, Alex...we must speak with the Earl ourselves. Surely he will listen to reason if it comes from us."

As they disappeared into the house, Rafael could only pray that their words would be enough to sway the Earl's heart. For without Clarissa by his side, he knew that his own life would be nothing but an empty shell, devoid of all light and joy.

The Earl sat in his study, his expression stony as Marianne and Alex were shown in. He barely glanced up from his papers, his voice cold as he spoke. "I suppose you are here to plead the case of that... foreigner."

Marianne bristled at the disdain in his tone, but kept her voice calm as she replied. "Rafael is a good man, my lord. Surely you must see that. He saved your daughter's life, at great risk to his own. And his character is beyond reproach."

The Earl snorted, finally lifting his gaze to meet hers. "Character? What does character matter, when he has no title, no fortune to speak of? Clarissa deserves better than some penniless nobleman from a foreign land."

Alex stepped forward, his own voice firm. "Rafael may not have wealth or a title, but he has something far more valuable - honour, and a heart that beats only for your daughter. Can you not see how much they love each other?"

But the Earl only shook his head, his jaw set stubbornly. "Love? What does love matter in the face of practicality? Clarissa will marry Lord Weatherby, and that is final. I will not hear any more arguments on the matter."

Marianne exchanged a helpless glance with Alex, her heart sinking. It seemed that the Earl was determined to remain blind to the truth, no matter how plainly it was laid before him.

As they took their leave, Marianne could only hope that somehow, some way, Rafael and Clarissa would find a way to be together. For she knew all too well the pain of a love denied, and she would not wish such a fate on anyone.

CHAPTER NINETEEN

THE HUSHED WHISPERS FOLLOWED Rafael like a swarm of biting flies as he entered Lord Moncrieffe's ballroom. Ornate chandeliers illuminated the sneers on powdered faces, the aristocratic noses turned up at his presence.

"A Portuguese sea captain, in our circles? The nerve!" Lady Dunmore tittered behind her fan.

"Practically a peasant, I hear. With no fortune to speak of," Lord Talbot added with a contemptuous sniff.

Rafael met their scorn with his head held high, though inside he burned with indignation. A peasant? If only they knew the weight of responsibility he bore, the lives that depended on him. But that was not for them to understand. He was here for Clarissa, and her alone.

As if conjured by his thoughts, Clarissa appeared before him, radiant in a gown of shimmering silver. Her smile was strained but her eyes danced with defiance.

"Captain de Silva. I'm so pleased you could attend."

"Lady Clarissa." He bowed deeply, acutely aware of the dozens of eyes tracking his every move. "The pleasure is entirely mine."

She leaned in, her voice lowered to a conspiratorial whisper. "Pay them no mind, Rafael. Their opinions are as insubstantial as sea foam."

He couldn't help but chuckle, marvelling at her spirit. "And just as easily dispersed by the wind. Shall we give them something to really talk about?"

Rafael extended his hand in open invitation. Clarissa's smile bloomed like a sunrise as she placed her gloved fingers in his. Somewhere, a scandalised gasp punctuated the moment.

As he led her towards the dance floor, Rafael caught sight of the Countess, her lips pinched in disapproval. No doubt she had orchestrated this display of disdain.

But even her machinations could not shake his resolve. For Clarissa, he would weather any storm.

The first strains of a waltz drifted through the air. Rafael drew Clarissa close, savouring the warmth of her through the layers of silk and lace. Here, in the circle of his arms, the rest of the world fell away. No wagging tongues or raised eyebrows could touch them.

Let them whisper, he thought as they began to dance. Let them sneer and scoff. His heart knew the truth, and that was enough. Enough to endure a thousand petty humiliations.

As they twirled across the gleaming parquet, Clarissa's eyes sparkled with mischief. "I do believe we've caused quite the stir."

"Indeed. I fear the Countess may faint from the impropriety of it all."

She laughed, the sound like champagne bubbles in his ears. "Oh, Mama will survive. Though I suspect I'm in for a scolding later."

Rafael's brow furrowed. "I hate to be the cause of strife between you."

"Nonsense." Clarissa's fingers tightened on his shoulder. "I won't let anyone dictate my heart. Not even my own mother."

Pride surged through him. This brave, beautiful woman had chosen him, society's scorn be damned. It humbled and exhilarated him in equal measure.

The final notes of the waltz faded away, and reality crashed back in like a cold tide. Reluctantly, Rafael stepped back, already mourning the loss of her touch.

No sooner had they parted than the Countess descended, her face a thundercloud. "Clarissa. A word, if you please."

Clarissa squeezed his hand, a silent promise, before following her mother to a quiet alcove. Rafael watched them go, steeling himself for the battle ahead.

The Countess's voice, though hushed, carried in the stillness. "Have you taken leave of your senses? Cavorting with that... that nobody?"

"He is not a nobody." Clarissa's tone could have cut glass. "He is a good, honourable man."

"He is beneath you!" The Countess's agitation was clear in the rustle of her skirts. "You're throwing away your prospects, your reputation..."

"My reputation is my own to risk."

Rafael's heart swelled to bursting. In that moment, he knew with blinding certainty that he would love this woman until his dying breath.

The Earl of Creighton's footsteps rang out like gunshots as he marched toward Rafael, face mottled with rage. "You there. De Silva."

Rafael turned, squaring his shoulders. "My Lord."

"I'll not mince words." The earl's eyes were flint. "Stay away from my daughter, or I'll see you on the first ship back to Portugal. Permanently."

The threat hung in the air, sharp as a blade. Rafael met it with a steady gaze. "With respect, my Lord, I cannot do that."

"Cannot?" The Earl sputtered. "You forget your place, sir."

"No." Rafael's voice was calm, unwavering. "I know my place. It is by Clarissa's side, for as long as she'll have me."

The earl's fists clenched, his knuckles white. "She'll have you nowhere, once I'm through. I'll not see her ruined by the likes of you."

Rafael's heart hammered, but he stood firm. "I would never ruin her. I love her, more than my own life."

"Love?" the earl scoffed. "What has love to do with anything? You're a penniless foreigner, a nobody. You bring nothing to this union."

Nothing but my heart, Rafael thought. *And my honour, for whatever that's worth in this glittering world of facades.*

Aloud, he said, "I bring my devotion, my loyalty. I will work tirelessly to give Clarissa the life she deserves."

"Pretty words." The earl sneered at him. "They'll mean little when you're starving in the gutter."

Rafael lifted his chin, his resolve hardening. "I will not compromise my values, not for status or approval. If I must prove myself worthy, I'll do so through my actions, not by bending to the whims of fashion."

The Earl's face darkened to puce. "Then prove yourself from Portugal. You set foot near Clarissa again, and I'll have you exiled. That is a promise."

With that, he spun on his heel and stalked away, leaving Rafael alone in the glittering ballroom, his future hanging by a thread.

"Pay no heed to Arthur." He turned to see Marianne smiling up at him. "His bark is far worse than his bite. I shall be reminding him of what happened the last time he attempted to intervene in a love match."

"And what did happen, Lady Glenkellie?" She gestured to him to lead her out on the dance floor, and he obliged, ignoring the disapproving expressions of those who thought him unfit to dance with a marchioness.

"A swan," Marianne said cryptically, giggling at his confused expression. "Let me just say that divine justice was meted out and Arthur has been a better man for it - for the most part. Leave him and Lavinia to me. Alex is going to take you to his club and introduce you to a few influential gentlemen whose good opinion will carry a great deal of weight in the ton."

"Such as?" Rafael asked a little doubtfully.

"Senior military gentlemen who don't bother with this sort of nonsense." Marianne gestured around them, a gesture of disdain for the frippery and gossip being indulged in by those around them. "Men who will understand and respect exactly who you are, what you have been through and the challenges you now face, because many of them fought in the Peninsular Campaign. You'll see."

He did not like having to trust his and Clarissa's fate to others, but Marianne had never been anything but supportive of his suit. He bowed to her at the end of the dance and thanked her sincerely.

"You are most welcome. Now. Here is my friend Lady Havers... Ellen, do let me present Captain de Silva! He most kindly hosted us at his beautiful castle in Portugal, such magnificent countryside!" Marianne's normally soft voice was quite loud, and several nearby ladies and gentlemen looked at each other in confusion, obviously wondering if the stories they had heard were quite accurate, if the Marchioness of Glenkellie was praising this gentleman so strongly.

Lady Havers was a pretty dark-haired woman in her early twenties wearing a stunning blue gown. She smiled up at him warmly. "Any friend of Marianne's is a friend of mine," she said sincerely.

"He and Clarissa are in love and Arthur's being painful," Marianne said in an undertone, so that only Ellen and Rafael heard.

"I see! How very... Arthur of him." Ellen laughed gently. "Let us see what we can do, then. Come and meet my husband, Captain. He's a foreigner too," she confided, linking her arm through his and drawing him through the crowd.

"American. Caused quite a stir in the ton with his new-fangled ideas when he inherited the earldom, I can tell you."

Rafael liked Thomas Havers at once; the American earl gave off an air of steady calm which felt intensely reassuring. He was surrounded by a group of men who proved to be not only impressively titled but influential in the political sphere. With Thomas's immediate acceptance of him at Ellen's introduction and the friendly attitude of the gentlemen with him, Rafael could almost feel the tide of opinion in the room begin to turn in his favour.

Even Lady Belmont, one of the Ton's most notorious gossips, was heard to remark, "Perhaps there's more to that Portuguese fellow than meets the eye."

"He's certainly handsome enough," Lady Jersey replied. "Can't blame the Creighton gel in the slightest. If I was twenty years younger..."

"Try thirty!" Lady Belmont retorted, before both ladies laughed wickedly.

And then, to Rafael's utter astonishment, a matronly lady in a lavish gown approached, a blushing young woman at her side, nudging Ellen to introduce them.

"Lady Partlebury, Miss Partlebury," Ellen said with a small smile, "allow me to introduce Captain Rafael de Silva."

"Captain de Silva," Lady Partlebury twittered eagerly. "My daughter Amelia is most eager to make your acquaintance."

Rafael blinked, scarcely able to believe the sudden change in his fortunes. The once hostile stares had transformed into appraising glances, the sneers replaced by coy smiles.

"It is a pleasure to meet you, Miss Partlebury," he managed, bowing politely over her gloved hand. His mind whirled with the implications of this unexpected development. Could it be that the tide was truly turning? That the Ton was beginning to see him as more than a foreign interloper?

As more ladies began to approach, their eager daughters in tow, Rafael couldn't help but marvel at the power of perception. How quickly opinions could change, how easily prejudice could be swayed by the endorsement of a respected few.

The same happened when Alex took him to his club. The Duke of Wellington himself was present, and with one glance at Rafael's uniform, rose and offered his hand. "An honour to have you join us, Captain," he said in fluent Portuguese, even before Alex had made the introductions.

"The honour is mine, your grace," Rafael returned with a deep bow.

"None of that, now. Some brandy!" The duke gestured to the waiter. "Take a seat and tell me about your ship, young man."

Clarissa's heart sank as her mother's iron grip tightened around her wrist, pulling her inexorably towards the ballroom exit. She craned her neck for one last glimpse of Rafael.

"Come along, Clarissa," the Countess hissed, her voice barely audible above the strains of the orchestra. "We are leaving this instant."

Clarissa stumbled slightly, her silk slippers catching on the polished parquet floor. "But Mother, surely we can stay a little longer? The evening has barely begun."

"I will not have you associating with that... that fortune hunter," her mother snapped, tugging Clarissa along like an errant child.

Clarissa's cheeks burned with indignation. How dare her mother speak of Rafael that way?

As they reached the cloakroom, Clarissa's thoughts whirled in a maelstrom of emotion. The scent of Rafael's sandalwood cologne still clung to her gloves from their brief dance. She inhaled deeply, savouring the memory of his strong arms around her waist, his sea-green eyes gazing into hers with such tender intensity.

"I cannot believe you would embarrass us so, dancing with that Portuguese upstart," her mother muttered as she roughly fastened Clarissa's cloak. "What will people say?"

Clarissa lifted her chin defiantly. "They will say that I danced with a brave and honourable man, Mother. Captain de Silva is no fortune hunter."

The Countess's eyes narrowed dangerously. "You know nothing of the world, foolish girl. Now come, our carriage awaits."

As they swept down the marble steps, the cool night air kissed Clarissa's flushed cheeks. She cast one last longing glance at the glowing windows of the ballroom, wondering if Rafael was searching for her even now.

"This is for your own good, Clarissa," her mother said, her tone softening slightly. "You'll thank me one day when you're safely married to a respectable English gentleman."

Clarissa bit back a retort, knowing it would fall on deaf ears. As she climbed into the carriage, she vowed silently that this would not be the last time she saw Rafael de Silva. Somehow, some way, she would find a way to be with the man who had captured her heart.

CHAPTER TWENTY

The following days passed in a blur of tedious social calls and carefully curated events. Clarissa found herself longing for the vibrant energy of the grand balls, but her mother remained steadfast in her decision.

"Lady Ashbourne's intimate soirée this evening, my dear," the Countess announced one afternoon, adjusting her daughter's lace collar. "A select gathering of only the most refined company."

Clarissa sighed inwardly. "And I suppose Captain de Silva won't be in attendance?"

Her mother's lips thinned. "Certainly not. Lady Ashbourne assured me of it. Really, Clarissa, you must put that man out of your mind. Now, sit down and pen a thank-you note to Lord Pembrook for the flowers he sent you." With a final stern glance, the countess left the room, leaving Clarissa alone, obviously expecting her daughter to meekly obey.

"Lord Pembrook! Flowers!" She did not even know which of the multitude of arrangements decorating the tables around the room the lord had sent, and she did not care. He could whistle for his thank-you note! Clarissa paced the drawing room, her curls bouncing with each agitated step. A knock at the door caused her to spin around, her eyes wide with anticipation. Had Rafael somehow come to her?

The butler opened the door and announced, "Her Grace, the Duchess of Balford."

Not Rafael, but a truly welcome visitor. "Diana!" Clarissa rushed forward and embraced her sister tightly. "I'm so glad you're here."

Diana returned the hug, her gentle eyes filled with warmth. "Of course I came, dearest. How could I not, after receiving your letter? I'm so eager to meet your dashing Captain de Silva!"

Clarissa pulled back, searching her sister's face. "And you don't mind about Rafael? That he's not...not exactly what Father had in mind for me?"

Diana laughed, a tinkling sound that instantly set Clarissa at ease. "Mind? Whyever would I mind? He sounds perfectly lovely from your description. A dashing sea captain, nobly serving his country despite misfortune. It's all delightfully romantic."

Relief washed over Clarissa like a soothing balm. She had been terrified that even Diana might not understand her feelings for Rafael. But she should have known better. Dear, sweet Diana had always supported her, no matter what.

"He is lovely," Clarissa said with a dreamy sigh. "And brave, and honourable, and handsome as sin. Oh Diana, I do love him so. I can scarcely think of anything else."

"Then that's all that matters." Diana took Clarissa's hands in hers, her expression turning earnest. "If you love him, and he loves you in return, then you must follow your heart. Life is too short to let others dictate your happiness."

Tears pricked at the corners of Clarissa's eyes. How had she been so lucky, to have a sister as wonderful as Diana? "Thank you," she whispered. "Your support means the world to me."

Diana smiled, then looped her arm through Clarissa's and began leading her towards the settee. "Now, you must tell me absolutely everything about your dashing captain. I want to know precisely how he swept you off your feet. Leave out no detail, no matter how small. I insist on hearing the whole thrilling tale."

Clarissa giggled, feeling lighter than she had in days as she settled beside Diana. With her sister by her side, she finally dared to hope that somehow, someway, she and Rafael would find a way to be together. No matter what obstacles stood in their path.

As they entered Lady Ashbourne's opulent drawing room, Clarissa plastered on a polite smile. The air was heavy with perfume and the cloying scent of too many bodies in too small a space. She scanned the room, her heart sinking as she recognized the familiar faces of several gentlemen her parents had put forward as potential husbands.

"Lady Clarissa!" Lord Pembrook materialised at her elbow, his florid face beaming. "How delightful to see you. Might I interest you in a game of whist?"

Clarissa suppressed a groan. “How kind of you to offer, my lord, but I’m afraid I’m feeling rather fatigued this evening. Perhaps another time?”

As she gracefully extricated herself, Clarissa’s thoughts drifted to Rafael. Was he attending other events, searching for her in vain? Or had he given up, concluding that her sudden absence meant rejection? Diana had promised to send a note around to Marianne explaining how ghastly Clarissa’s parents were being, but Clarissa hated feeling so powerless.

“This is intolerable,” she muttered under her breath, accepting a glass of tepid lemonade from a passing footman.

“Did you say something, my dear?” her mother inquired sharply.

Clarissa forced a bright smile. “Not at all, Mother. I was merely remarking on how… intimate this gathering is.”

As the evening wore on, Clarissa found herself cornered by one eager suitor after another. She longed for Rafael’s wit and easy conversation, the way his eyes sparkled when he laughed. These men, with their polished manners and empty flattery, paled in comparison.

Desperate for a reprieve, Clarissa excused herself and made her way to a secluded alcove, hoping for a moment’s peace. As she turned the corner, she collided with a tall figure.

“I beg your pardon,” she began, then froze as she recognized the man before her. “Mr. Dalton?”

Edward Dalton’s handsome face broke into a charming smile. “Lady Clarissa! What a delightful surprise.”

Clarissa’s mind whirled. “I… I thought you had returned to Durham. To your family.”

Dalton’s smile faltered for a moment before he recovered. “Ah, yes. Well, you see, my father had other plans. He’s ordered me back to London to find a wife.”

“How… convenient,” Clarissa replied, unable to keep a hint of suspicion from her voice. Something about Dalton’s explanation rang false, though she couldn’t quite put her finger on why.

“Indeed,” Dalton agreed, his tone light. “And how fortuitous to encounter you here. I’ve missed our conversations ,especially our time in Athens.”

Clarissa’s throat tightened at the mention of Athens. The memory of her kidnapping, and Rafael’s daring rescue, flooded her mind. She struggled to maintain her composure.

"Yes, well, much has changed since then," she said coolly.

Dalton's eyes narrowed slightly. "Has it? I had hoped we might rekindle our... friendship. Portugal was... well, we were not able to be quite so *intimate* as we were in Athens, but..."

Clarissa took a step back, her heart racing. "Mr. Dalton, I—"

"Clarissa, darling!" The Countess's voice cut through the tension like a knife. "There you are. And Mr. Dalton, how lovely to see you again."

Clarissa turned to see her mother approaching, a calculating gleam in her eye. She groaned inwardly, recognizing that look all too well.

"Mother," Clarissa said, forcing a smile. "Mr. Dalton was just telling me about his return to London."

"And my father's instructions for me to find myself a wife," Mr. Dalton put in, bowing obsequiously.

"How wonderful," the Countess beamed. "We must have you for dinner soon, Mr. Dalton. Won't we, Clarissa?"

Clarissa's smile felt brittle. "Of course, Mother."

As they bid farewell to Mr. Dalton and made their way back to the main party, the Countess leaned in close to Clarissa's ear.

"Mr. Dalton might not be quite what we hoped for in terms of wealth and position," she murmured, "but he is from a good family. And at least he's younger than some of the suitors your father favours."

Clarissa's temper flared. "Mother, surely you can't be serious! Mr. Dalton was the one who told you about the... incident with the corsairs," she hissed. "He betrayed my confidence and jeopardised my reputation! I cannot trust him."

The Countess waved a dismissive hand. "Men often speak out of turn, dear. It's nothing to hold against him forever."

Clarissa clenched her fists, frustration building within her. "I won't marry him, Mother," she said firmly. "I won't even consider it."

The Countess's eyes hardened. "We shall see about that, Clarissa. We shall see."

It did not take long for Edward Dalton to discover that Captain Rafael de Silva was in London, having apparently pursued Lady Clarissa Creighton there with a firm intention to marry her.

That could not be permitted to happen, of course. Edward had decided, almost as soon as he discovered Clarissa had somehow escaped the fate she had been destined for at the hand of the Algerian corsairs, that she would make him a fine wife after all. She was lovely, well-dowered, and her sister was a duchess. His place at the top of English society would be guaranteed.

First, though, he would need to discredit that troublesome Portuguese captain and send him scurrying back home with his tail between his legs. And tonight, he had determined that de Silva would be at this ball, likely in hopes that Clarissa would be present. Which she would not be, as the countess had been forewarned of de Silva's likely presence... by Edward himself, of course.

Edward stood by the mantelpiece, swirling a glass of brandy as he observed the ballroom with narrowed eyes. His gaze fixed on de Silva, who had just entered the room, cutting a dashing figure in his uniform. He watched as Rafael's sea-green eyes scanned the crowd, clearly searching for Clarissa. Dalton's fingers tightened around his glass, knuckles whitening. Time to put his plan into action.

"Good evening, Captain!" Dalton called out, his voice dripping with false congeniality as he approached Rafael.

Rafael turned, surprise flickering across his features. "Mr. Dalton, good evening. I didn't expect to see you in London."

"Oh, I'm full of surprises," Dalton replied with a smirk. "I hear you've been quite the sensation since your arrival. Tell me, what brings a Portuguese naval officer to English society?"

Rafael hesitated, choosing his words carefully. "I have... personal matters to attend to."

"Personal matters, indeed. I'm sure Lady Clarissa is thrilled to have you here." He noticed Rafael stiffen at the mention of Clarissa's name. *Perfect*, Dalton thought. *This will be easier than I imagined.*

"You seem well-acquainted with Lady Clarissa's affairs," Rafael responded, his tone guarded.

Dalton laughed, the sound hollow and insincere. "Oh, Clarissa and I go way back. Childhood friends, you know. In fact, I've been thinking it's high time I settled down. Perhaps with a familiar face."

He watched Rafael's jaw clench, satisfaction coursing through him. The seeds of doubt had been planted. Now, to nurture them into full-blown rumours that would destroy any chance Rafael had with Clarissa.

Dalton leaned in, lowering his voice conspiratorially. "Between us gentlemen, I've heard whispers about your... intentions. Some say you're quite the fortune hunter."

Rafael's sea-green eyes flashed with anger. "I beg your pardon?"

"Oh, come now," Edward pressed, relishing the captain's discomfort. "A penniless Portuguese nobleman pursuing one of England's most eligible heiresses? It's rather transparent, don't you think?"

Rafael's fists clenched at his sides. "You know nothing of my intentions, Mr. Dalton. I suggest you mind your own affairs."

Edward raised his hands in mock surrender. "No offence meant, Captain. I'm merely repeating what I've heard in certain circles. But I'm sure a man of your... background... understands how quickly rumours can spread in London society."

As Rafael opened his mouth to retort, a striking redhead in a revealing gown sidled up to them. Edward suppressed a smirk, recognizing the actress he'd hired for this very purpose.

"Captain," she purred, pressing herself against Rafael's arm. "I've been longing to speak with you all evening."

Rafael stiffened, clearly uncomfortable. "Madam, I don't believe we've been introduced."

The woman giggled, her fingers trailing down his chest. "Oh, but we have, darling. Don't you remember our passionate encounter last Friday evening?"

Edward watched with satisfaction as nearby partygoers turned to stare, whispering behind their fans. Rafael's face paled as he gently but firmly removed the woman's hand.

"There must be some mistake," Rafael insisted, his voice strained. "I've never met you before."

The actress's lower lip trembled convincingly. "How could you say such a thing? After all your promises..."

As the scene unfolded, Edward slipped away, a triumphant smile playing on his lips. The trap was set, and Rafael's reputation would soon be in tatters. Clarissa would have no choice but to turn to him, Edward, for comfort and security. Everything was going according to plan.

Edward's smug satisfaction was short-lived. As he made his way through the crowded ballroom, a familiar voice cut through the air, causing him to freeze mid-step.

"I can assure you, madam, that Captain de Silva was with me at the time you claim this... encounter occurred," Alex, the Marquis of Glenkellie, declared loudly, his tone brooking no argument.

Edward whirled around, his heart sinking as he saw Alex standing beside Rafael, his hand clasped firmly on the Portuguese captain's shoulder.

"In fact," Alex continued, his gaze sweeping the room, "Captain de Silva has been at my house every evening last week. I can provide multiple witnesses to corroborate this, as my wife the Marchioness and I have been entertaining every night at dinner and the captain is residing with us, an honoured guest in our home."

The actress faltered, her confident demeanour crumbling. "But... I... that is..."

Murmurs rippled through the crowd as the woman's act fell apart.

"I do not even know your name, madam," Rafael said, his deep voice carrying. "I fear I have never laid eyes on you before this moment. Perhaps you have me confused with someone else?"

"I..." the actress looked around, desperately seeking a supportive face, or, failing that, an escape. "Yes... perhaps I have."

"Then I shall bid you a good evening," Rafael said politely.

Edward clenched his fists, watching helplessly as his carefully crafted plan unravelled before his eyes.

Rafael's sea-green eyes met Edward's across the room, a mixture of relief and suspicion in their depths. Edward quickly averted his gaze, his mind racing.

"Blast it all," he muttered under his breath, tugging at his cravat as sweat beaded on his brow. He needed a new strategy, and fast.

A desperate idea began to form in Edward's mind. If he couldn't destroy Rafael's reputation, perhaps he could force Clarissa's hand another way. It was risky, but he was running out of options.

"Very well," he muttered grimly. "If this is how the game must be played, so be it. Clarissa will be mine, one way or another."

With renewed determination, Dalton slipped out of the ballroom, his mind already formulating his next move. He had one last card to play, and he intended to use it to devastating effect.

Another evening, another boring private dinner where there was no chance she would see Rafael. Another collection of dull-as-ditchwater potential suitors. Clarissa wanted to tear at her hair and scream.

Perhaps they'll think I'm mad, she thought irreverently. *That might discourage a few of them, at least.*

At least tonight she had her sister for company. Diana sat further up the table, of course, as a duchess she was one of the most important guests present. Her husband Will, the Duke of Balford, came to Clarissa's rescue more than once during the evening, deflecting some of her more persistent suitors.

"Are you quite all right?" Will asked in an undertone. "You look quite pale."

"I'm hating every moment of this," Clarissa said with blunt honesty, remembering how much she had always liked Will when he gave her a conspiratorial grin.

"Why don't you sneak through that door behind you into the library and hide out for a few minutes by yourself? I'll claim I haven't seen you."

"Bless you, brother." She gave him the first real smile she'd managed that evening, stole his brandy glass from his hand and took an unladylike gulp before handing it back. "I won't be gone too long, I promise."

Will's chuckle was cut off by the door clicking shut behind her.

The library was blissfully quiet, entirely empty, and pleasantly well lit. Well enough for her to be able to read the titles of the books on the shelves, most of which looked as though they had never been touched. Clarissa spent a happy few minutes browsing before the sound of a door opening made her whirl around. Edward Dalton was just entering the library, by a different door to the one she had used, smiling at her and then closing the door behind him.

Clarissa was suddenly acutely aware that they were alone.

"Mr. Dalton," she said, lifting her chin proudly. "If you'll excuse me." She marched towards the other door, fully intending to re-enter the fray. Better that than to be alone with this man.

Dalton's lips curved into a smile that didn't reach his eyes. "If you'll allow me just a moment of privacy, my dear Lady Clarissa, I'm afraid I have some rather distressing news to share with you."

Clarissa's brow furrowed as she turned to look at him suspiciously. "What news might that be?"

He stepped closer, his voice dropping to a conspiratorial whisper. "It concerns your... unfortunate adventure in Athens. Your kidnapping by corsairs, your days in captivity, and your dashing rescue by Captain de Silva. Quite the scandal, wouldn't you agree?"

Clarissa's hands trembled as she fought to maintain her composure. "How dare you," she hissed. "That's a private matter."

"Private for now," Dalton agreed. "But imagine if word were to spread throughout London society. Your reputation would be in tatters."

A cold dread settled in Clarissa's stomach as she realised the full implications of his threat. "What do you want?" she asked, her voice barely above a whisper.

Dalton's eyes gleamed with triumph. "It's quite simple, my dear. Agree to marry me, and I'll ensure this sordid tale never sees the light of day."

Clarissa's mind whirled, torn between outrage and fear. How could she possibly agree to such a demand? And yet, if word of her kidnapping spread, it would destroy not only her reputation but her family's as well. Her younger sisters might never be able to marry. Even Diana might be harmed by the rumours.

"You're despicable," she spat, her hands clenching into fists at her sides.

"Perhaps," Dalton shrugged. "But I'm also your only option. What will it be, Lady Clarissa? Marriage, or scandal?"

CHAPTER TWENTY-ONE

Clarissa's heart skipped a beat as Dalton's words hung in the air. Suddenly, something she should have realised before snapped into place in her mind.

"Wait," she said, her voice barely above a whisper. "How did you know about the corsairs?"

Dalton's easy smile faltered, his blue eyes darting to the side. "I beg your pardon?"

Clarissa's fingers tightened on her skirts, the delicate silk threatening to tear under her grip. "The corsairs, Edward. You mentioned them just now, as well as telling my parents about it in Portugal, but I never told you about that part of my... ordeal."

A bead of sweat trickled down Dalton's temple. He cleared his throat, adjusting his cravat. "Oh, I'm sure you must have mentioned it at some point, my dear."

"No," Clarissa said, her voice gaining strength as certainty settled in her chest like a stone. "I most certainly did not."

She took a step closer, the rustle of her gown seeming unnaturally loud in the sudden silence between them.

"Edward," she said, her tone deceptively light, "is there something you're not telling me?"

Dalton's charming façade cracked further, revealing a glimpse of something darker beneath. "Clarissa, darling, you're imagining things."

Clarissa's thoughts whirled like a dervish. *How could he know? Who could have told him?*

Dalton reached out to her, but she instinctively slapped his hand away, taking a swift step back. "Don't you dare touch me. Tell me the truth. Now."

Dalton's hand fell limply to his side, his former confidence evaporating. He swallowed hard, Adam's apple bobbing nervously.

"I… I…" he stammered, eyes darting around as if searching for an escape. "Lady Helena told me. The dowager Lady Glenkellie, I mean."

Clarissa's eyes narrowed, her fingers curling into fists at her sides. The lie was as transparent as glass. Lady Helena could be forthright, but she would never in a hundred years have said something so indiscreet and damaging to Clarissa's reputation. "You expect me to believe that?" she hissed, taking a step closer to him.

Dalton stumbled back, nearly tripping over a small table. "It's true!" he insisted, his voice rising an octave. "She… she was concerned about you. Wanted me to keep an eye on you."

The absurdity of his claim only fuelled Clarissa's anger. Lady Helena, betray her in such a way? The very thought was an insult. "Edward Dalton," she said, her voice low and dangerous, "you are many things, but I never took you for a fool. Do you truly think I would fall for such an obvious falsehood?"

His handsome face contorted, desperation replacing his usual easy smile. "Clarissa, please," he pleaded, reaching for her again. "You must understand—"

She jerked away, disgust roiling in her stomach. "Understand what? That you've been lying to me? That you know far more about my ordeal than you should?" Her voice rose with each question.

As Dalton floundered for a response, Clarissa's mind raced. How deep did his deception go? And more importantly, what was she going to do about it?

Clarissa's eyes narrowed as she studied Dalton's face, searching for any hint of truth. "You're not denying it," she said, her voice barely above a whisper. "You lied about Lady Helena."

Dalton's shoulders sagged, the fight seemingly draining out of him. "Clarissa, I—"

But she was no longer listening. Her mind whirled, piecing together fragments of conversations, odd glances, and inexplicable coincidences. The horrible realisation crashed over her like a wave.

"The only way you could know…" she began, her voice trembling with a mixture of fury and disbelief. "The only possible explanation is that you were involved somehow."

Dalton paled, confirming her suspicions before he could utter a word.

Clarissa felt as though the ground had fallen away beneath her feet. "Dear God," she whispered, more to herself than to him. "What have you done?"

She straightened her spine, summoning every ounce of strength she possessed. "Tell me the truth, Edward," she demanded, her voice ringing with authority she didn't know she had. "I want to hear every sordid detail of your involvement in my kidnapping. And may God have mercy on your soul if you lie to me again."

As she awaited his response, Clarissa's heart pounded in her chest. How could the man she once thought she might be able to love be capable of such treachery? And what other secrets might he be hiding?

Dalton's face contorted, a mix of shame and desperation etched across his once-handsome features. "I... I owed money," he confessed, his voice cracking. "A Greek moneylender. The debt was astronomical, Clarissa. I was desperate."

Clarissa's stomach churned, the bitter taste of betrayal rising in her throat. "So you *sold* me to *corsairs*?" she spat, her hands trembling with rage.

"No!" Dalton exclaimed. "I swear, I thought they would only hold you for ransom. Your father's wealth... I never imagined they would sell you."

The room seemed to spin around Clarissa as she processed his words. She steadied herself against a nearby chair, her knuckles white as she gripped the ornate wooden back. Another terrible suspicion began to form in her mind.

"The vineyards," she whispered, her eyes widening with dawning horror. "It was you, wasn't it? *You* sabotaged Rafael's vineyards."

Dalton's silence was damning. Clarissa watched as he seemed to crumple before her, no longer the dashing figure she had once admired but a pitiful, cowardly shell of a man.

"How could you?" she breathed, her voice raw with emotion. "I trusted you, Edward. We all did."

As the full weight of his betrayal crashed down upon her, Clarissa's mind raced with the implications. How many lives had he ruined? How much damage had his selfish actions caused?

Her eyes flashing with righteous anger, her voice trembled as she spoke, crushing him with her words. "I would sooner marry a mongrel dog from the streets than a man without honour like you, Edward Dalton."

She watched with grim satisfaction as Dalton flinched away from her, his face contorting with shame.

"Clarissa, please," Dalton pleaded, reaching for her hand. "We can still make this right. Your father—"

She snatched her hand away, her skin crawling at his touch. "Do not speak of my father," she hissed. "You have no right."

Clarissa's mind raced, considering her options. She knew she held the power now, and a part of her relished it. Taking a deep breath, she fixed Dalton with a steely gaze.

"I will ruin you," she declared, her voice low and dangerous. "Every drawing room in London will know of your treachery. And Rafael—" she paused, savouring the way Dalton blanched at the name, "—I will tell him everything."

Dalton's face drained of colour. "You wouldn't," he whispered, terror evident in his eyes.

Clarissa lifted her chin defiantly. "Try me."

"He - he'll kill me!"

Clarissa had absolutely no doubt of that fact. Rafael would not hesitate to call Dalton out for the sabotage to the vineyards alone, never mind for selling her to the corsairs, and he would shoot Dalton dead.

Dalton's eyes darted about the room like a cornered animal. In an instant, he bolted for the door, nearly knocking over a delicate side table in his haste.

Clarissa watched him flee, her heart pounding. "Coward," she muttered under her breath, smoothing her skirts with shaking hands.

"Clarissa?" A voice called her name a few moments later, and she looked around to see Diana entering the library. "Are you quite well? Will said you were hiding out in here, but Mama is looking for you."

"I am well indeed, thank you." Clarissa lifted her chin and smiled. "The better for your company, of course."

Diana laughed and linked her arm through Clarissa's. "I have missed you, dear one." She leaned closer and said confidingly, "I shall miss you more when you reside in Portugal, however, though I do plan to make Will bring me to visit you at least every year or two."

"I may have got rid of Mr. Dalton, but it still brings me no closer to persuading Papa to let me marry Rafael," Clarissa said glumly.

"Got rid of Mr. Dalton?" Diana's delicate brows rose. "How did you manage that, Clarry? He seemed quite persistent."

"Indeed, even going so far as to threaten to blackmail me!" Her hands were still trembling. Clarissa tried to breathe deeply, telling herself that it was over, even as her sister exclaimed in horror and demanded the details.

I faced him down alone. She was proud of that, even though she had resorted to threatening Dalton with Rafael's vengeance at the end. And indeed, she would tell Rafael... about Dalton's sabotage of the vineyards, at least, because he deserved to know. Somehow, she did not think Dalton would ever risk showing his face in the same city as either her or Rafael ever again, though.

Having vanquished Dalton, suddenly she felt more confident about her ability to win over her parents. They would not force her into marriage, of that she was certain. Her father's bark was far worse than his bite. If she was patient, steadfast in her insistence that Rafael was the only man she would marry, they would, eventually, give in.

If only she could see him!

The thought gave her an idea, and she looked at her sister. "Di. Would you do me a favour?"

"Anything, dearest, you have only to name it!"

"Would you give a ball?"

Diana blinked in bemusement. "A ball?"

"Yes. Mama and Papa can hardly refuse to permit me to attend, and you can make sure Rafael is on the guest list."

Understanding dawned, and Diana chuckled. "Of course, Clarry. It might take a little time to arrange, however... two weeks?"

"That would be perfect," Clarissa agreed. Two weeks should give her time to make it very clear to her parents that none of the candidates they kept presenting to her would ever be acceptable... and she supposed, it would also give Edward Dalton time to make himself scarce from any place Rafael might decide to look for him once she told Rafael of Dalton's sabotage.

Two weeks later, Clarissa found herself standing before a gilded mirror in Diana's London townhouse. The candlelight flickered, casting dancing shadows on the emerald silk of her new ball gown.

"You look radiant, dearest," Diana said, adjusting a stray curl that had escaped Clarissa's elaborate coiffure.

Clarissa forced a smile. "Thank you, Di." She swallowed, her mouth dry. "Is he here?"

"Arrived a few minutes ago with Alex and Marianne." Diana linked her arm through Clarissa's. "Are you ready?"

"Yes." Clarissa lifted her chin, determined. Tonight, she was going to see Alex, to talk and dance with him, no matter what her father might say. The earl wasn't going to create a ruckus at Diana's first London ball; his wife would never forgive him.

As the sisters descended the grand staircase, the sounds of laughter and music washed over them. Clarissa's eyes scanned the crowded ballroom, her breath catching as she spotted a familiar tall, dark form.

Rafael.

Even from a distance, she could see how he stood out among the other gentlemen, his practical but well-tailored navy uniform a stark contrast to their ornate waistcoats and brocade jackets.

"Clarissa," her father's stern voice startled her as she reached the bottom of the steps and started towards Rafael. The Earl of Creighton appeared at her elbow, his expression severe. "I must speak with you."

He led her to a quiet corner of the ballroom, away from prying ears. Clarissa's stomach twisted with apprehension.

"I've noticed how you look at that Portuguese captain," her father said in a low, disapproving tone. "I forbid you to go near him tonight. Do you understand?"

Clarissa's cheeks flushed with indignation. "But Father, Captain de Silva is a gentleman and—"

"A penniless foreigner," the Earl interrupted. "He's not suitable company for you. I won't have any gossip about my daughter and a man of his... circumstances."

Clarissa bit her tongue, knowing that arguing would only make matters worse. She nodded stiffly, her mind already racing with ways to circumvent her father's edict.

"Yes, Father," she replied, her voice dripping with barely concealed sarcasm. "I shall endeavour to avoid all men of honour and good character this evening."

The Earl's eyes narrowed. "Mind your tone, young lady. Now, go make yourself agreeable to Lord Ashbury. He's been asking after you."

"Absolutely not." Clarissa lifted her chin defiantly. "If I cannot marry Captain de Silva, I shall not marry anyone!"

Turning on her heel, she stormed away from her father, losing herself among the glittering crowd before he could begin to shout and cause a scene. Half-blinded by tears of rage and frustration, she stumbled on without looking where she was going, ignoring voices that called out to her, until she ran hard into an immovable object and warm, strong arms closed around her.

"Clarissa." His low voice whispered her name, and she looked up to find him gazing down at her with concern written all over his handsome face. "Are you well, meu amor?"

"Dance with me," she begged, and he asked no questions, only whirled her onto the dance floor. They joined a set with Alex and Marianne, and Clarissa tried to lose herself in enjoying the dance, though she almost began to cry again when Marianne squeezed her hand gently in passing. She could see her mother standing at the edge of the dance floor, glaring disapprovingly, and her father too, with Diana and Will beside him probably the only thing keeping the earl from making a scene.

"I have to tell you something," she began, looking up at Rafael.

"That your parents are determined to forbid me from you?" His mouth twisted in a wry smile. "I will persist, nevertheless."

She loved him all the more for it. "And if it becomes necessary, I will leave it all behind and run away with you," she said, her voice low, for his ears alone. "The only thing stopping me from doing it tonight is the thought of my younger sisters and their future prospects. They do not deserve to be embroiled in a scandal."

"I understand." Rafael nodded seriously. "I will wait, meu amor. As long as I must."

Her heart felt full to bursting as he called her *his love* for the second time, and she clung to his hand for the precious seconds permitted by the pattern of the dance. "And I will marry no one but you, no matter what you might hear, please believe it. But it isn't that which I have to tell you, Rafael. I've found out who the saboteur is."

His sea-green eyes flittered dangerously as she told him what she had discovered, not revealing that Dalton's actions had resulted in her being sold to the corsairs, only that Dalton had accidentally let slip his guilt about the sabotage.

"He was trying to ruin me," Rafael muttered, before letting slip a few words in Portuguese which Clarissa didn't recognise – but from Alex's expression of amusement as he passed them, were probably curse words.

"He's a coward," Clarissa said. "I'm fairly sure he has fled London – I told him that I would reveal the truth to you. I doubt either of us will ever lay eyes on him again."

"He had better hope I do not," Rafael growled menacingly.

"I hope that expression doesn't bode ill for your father, Clarissa," Marianne said lightly as the pattern of the dance forced them to switch partners. Clarissa could tell from the look on her aunt's face that she was only half-joking.

"Rafael and I are agreed that we will wait my father out. As long as it takes." Knowing that Rafael was willing to wait gave Clarissa a surge of confidence. She would wear her father down, eventually.

"Arthur is being quite ridiculous. High time I had a word with him." Marianne's jaw set determinedly. "I shall visit tomorrow morning, Clarissa."

Clarissa could not imagine what her aunt might say that could change her father's mind. She would just have to enjoy these few stolen moments with Rafael, because the dance was drawing to a close and she could see her father approaching, his face a thundercloud.

"I can't let him ruin Diana's ball," she told Rafael, and saw the understanding on his face.

"Do whatever you must," Rafael said, and she wanted to fling herself into his arms and kiss him. Instead, she gave an impeccable curtsey at the end of the dance before walking briskly away and latching onto her father's arm.

"Please don't embarrass Diana," she said quickly, before the earl could say a word.

Her father took a deep breath, the mottled colour in his cheeks receding. "You will not leave my side again this evening," was all he said.

Clarissa bowed her head penitently, but as her father led her away, she sneaked a glance back at Rafael. He was watching her, smiling as their eyes met, and the warmth of that smile carried her through the rest of the evening.

CHAPTER TWENTY-TWO

Clarissa was with her mother in the drawing-room the following morning when Marianne arrived. The butler showed her in, but Marianne only made them the briefest courtesies before stating that she was there to visit the earl, and marching off to his study.

"Well," the countess muttered. "Marianne certainly has a bee in her bonnet today. Is this something to do with you, my girl?"

"I'm sure I have no idea what you mean, Mama." Clarissa feigned innocence, though inwardly she was dying to know what her aunt was saying to her father.

"Excuse me, my lady." The housekeeper entered the room with a respectful curtsey. "There is a slight problem in the kitchen, if you might have a few moments to spare?"

"Very well!" The countess sighed and rose to her feet, and Clarissa was left alone. She lost no time in sneaking out into the hall and hurrying along to the study door, crouching to listen at the keyhole.

"...being utterly unreasonable, Arthur," Marianne was saying in clipped tones that signalled her impatience. "The girl is clearly in love. Forbidding the match will only drive her into his arms all the faster. Is that what you want?"

Clarissa held her breath, heart pounding as she awaited her father's reply.

After a tense pause, the earl heaved a heavy sigh. "No, of course not. But dash it all, Marianne, the man's a foreigner. And penniless to boot. How can I endorse such a union? Clarissa deserves better."

"You're quite capable of changing your mind when shown the error of your ways, Arthur," Marianne pressed on relentlessly. "It's one of your finer qualities, loath as I am to admit it."

Clarissa could practically hear her father's bristling indignation from the other side of the door. She imagined him drawing himself up to his full height, his face flushed with outrage at the very notion that he, the Earl of Creighton, could be wrong about anything.

"Error of my ways?" he blustered. "I'm only trying to do what's best for the girl. She's my daughter, for God's sake. I have a duty to see her well settled."

"And you don't think she would be well settled with Captain de Silva?" Marianne asked, her tone softening a fraction. "A man who clearly adores her, who has proven himself honourable and hardworking? A man to whom, I might add, she owes her life? She would not be here without his intervention with the corsairs, Arthur, a fact of which you must be well aware."

"He's Catholic!" the earl protested, but Clarissa wondered if he was beginning to weaken, as his voice was noticeably quieter.

Marianne scoffed. "What is that to you? Buy a special licence and have them marry from Creighton House. Lavinia will survive the disappointment of not being able to see her daughter married at St. George's in Hanover Square, I am sure."

There was a long, weighted pause. Clarissa held her breath, scarcely daring to hope.

Finally, in a voice so low she had to strain to hear it, her father asked plaintively, "Do you really believe I should allow this, Marianne? That I should give my blessing to Clarissa marrying so far beneath her?"

Clarissa's heart leapt into her throat. Everything hinged on Marianne's reply.

"I believe," Marianne said slowly, carefully, "that you should trust your daughter's judgement. And your own eyes. Anyone can see that Clarissa and Rafael are deeply in love. Surely that counts for something?"

The Earl huffed out an impatient breath. "Love! What good is love when the man hasn't a penny to his name? You saw that crumbling castle of his!"

Marianne's voice sharpened. "Arthur, open your eyes and really *look* at your daughter for once in your life. Have you seen how Clarissa glows when Rafael is near? How quick she is to laugh, how eager to share her thoughts and opinions with him?"

There was a rustle of silk skirts, and then the click of the study door opening. Clarissa hastily lurched to her feet and took a couple of steps back.

"Just think about what I've said," Marianne urged, and then she walked out into the hall, pausing only briefly as she saw Clarissa there, before passing her with a smile and heading for the front door.

Clarissa barely had time to whirl around and pretend to be engrossed in a painting on the opposite wall before her father's voice rang out.

"Clarissa, come in here please."

She winced, feeling like a naughty child caught with her hand in the biscuit jar. Schooling her features into a mask of innocence, she slipped into the study. "Yes, Papa?"

Her father was seated behind his massive oak desk, his fingers steepled beneath his chin as he studied her with narrowed eyes. "Sit down," he ordered, nodding to one of the chairs arranged across from him.

Clarissa perched on the edge of the seat, her spine ramrod straight, her hands folded primly in her lap. Inside, her stomach churned with nerves. She met his gaze, determined not to be the first to look away. The silence stretched between them, fraught with unspoken tension.

Clarissa drew in a fortifying breath, gathering her courage. "Papa, may I ask you something?"

Her father's brow furrowed but he inclined his head. "Go on."

"Why is it so important to you that I marry well?" The words tumbled out in a rush. "You're an earl now. Nobody can take that title away. You have money and status. When is enough, enough?"

The earl's eyes widened at her blunt question. He leaned back in his chair, contemplating her as if seeing her clearly for the first time. "I want what's best for you, Clarissa. A secure future. A respected position in society."

"But I would have that with Rafael!" Her voice rose with passion. "He may not be wealthy now, but he has noble blood, a distinguished naval career. We love each other, Papa. Isn't that what truly matters?"

Her father's jaw tightened. "And what of your dowry? What if I choose to withhold it?"

Clarissa lifted her chin, meeting his challenging stare directly. "Then so be it. I never counted on receiving it." She thought of Rafael, of the dilapidated but charming castle that was his birthright. "Rafael and I are perfectly willing to put in the work to restore his estate. We don't need a fortune to be happy."

The earl drummed his fingers on the desk, conflict playing across his face. Clarissa's heart pounded as the silence lengthened.

At last, the earl sighed deeply, his shoulders sagging. "You really do love him, don't you?"

"With all my heart," Clarissa replied without hesitation, her voice ringing with conviction.

Her father's gaze softened, a glimmer of understanding dawning in his eyes. "I suppose I've been too focused on the trappings of status and wealth. But seeing you now, so resolute, so..." He waved a hand, searching for the right word. "...alive with purpose, I realise that perhaps I've been measuring success by the wrong standards."

Clarissa held her breath, hardly daring to hope. Was he truly coming around?

The earl rose from his chair and came to stand before her, placing his hands on her shoulders. "If Captain de Silva is the man who brings such joy and determination to your eyes, then who am I to stand in the way?" A wry smile tugged at his lips. "I suspect you'd find a way to marry him with or without my blessing."

Tears of relief and happiness welled in Clarissa's eyes. "Oh, Papa!" She threw her arms around him, hugging him tightly. "Thank you. Thank you for understanding."

He returned her embrace, patting her back affectionately. "And you'll have your dowry, my dear. Use it to build the life you dream of with your captain."

Clarissa laughed, a sound of pure, unbridled joy. She stepped back, wiping at her damp cheeks. "I can hardly wait to tell Rafael. He'll be thrilled!"

"Then go to him," her father urged, his eyes crinkling at the corners. "And invite him to dinner tonight. I believe it's high time I got to know my future son-in-law properly."

"Arthur!" The screech from the door made them both turn around. "You cannot seriously be countenancing this... this *travesty*!"

"Sit down, Lavinia." The earl patted Clarissa's shoulder, urging her gently towards the door. "Go pen a note to your aunt, telling her and Glenkellie to come to dinner and bring the good captain with them," he said quietly. "Leave your mother to me."

As Clarissa gratefully fled the study, she heard her father firmly saying "Lavinia, my dear, one of our daughters may have married a duke, but it is quite unreasonable to expect them all to have such success..."

Marianne turned out not to have left the house at all; perhaps she had seen Clarissa go into the study and decided to wait in the drawing-room to discover the outcome. One glance at Clarissa's flushed cheeks and joyous smile, and Marianne stepped forward to embrace her.

"Oh, my dear girl! He conceded?"

"He did. Thank you so much for speaking to him." Clarissa hugged her aunt tightly.

"Pshaw." Marianne shrugged off her thanks. "He'd have seen reason eventually, but I am gladdened if I could help speed your happiness even a small amount."

"A very great amount, dearest Aunt! Why, if you had not invited Diana and I on your wedding trip to Italy, I should never have met Rafael in the first place!"

"I suppose that is true," Marianne said, looking a little surprised. "And I daresay Diana would not have married Balford, either. I did do exactly as I hinted to your mother I might – found you both the perfect husbands, although that was never my intention. I just wanted to offer you the opportunity to see some more of the world."

"An opportunity I will be forever grateful for." Clarissa embraced her once again. "You – and Uncle Alex, of course – will always be honoured guests at Torre da Rochedo."

"I shall be delighted to see how the vineyards bloom for their new mistress. Now, why don't you pen a note for me to deliver to Rafael, with your good news?"

The sunlight streaming through the windows of Creighton House's grand ballroom cast a bright golden light across Clarissa's ivory gown as she stood at the entrance, her heart fluttering like a caged bird. She took a deep breath, inhaling the scent of lilies and roses, huge arrangements of which adorned every surface, and tightened her grip on her father's arm.

"Ready, my dear?" the Earl of Creighton asked gruffly, his usual stoic demeanour betrayed by a slight tremor in his voice.

Clarissa nodded, unable to form words as the string quartet began to play. As they took their first steps down the aisle between rows of seated guests, she caught sight of Rafael at the front of the room with the vicar who would perform the ceremony, his sea-green eyes locked on her with an intensity that made her knees weak. In his naval uniform, he cut a dashing figure against the backdrop of white flowers and golden candelabras.

"I never thought I'd see the day," her father muttered as they walked. "My little hellion, all grown up and marrying a Portuguese sea captain."

Clarissa couldn't help but giggle. "Did you ever imagine I'd settle for anything less adventurous, Papa?"

The earl harrumphed, but Clarissa felt his arm tighten around hers. As they reached the front of the room, he turned to face her, his eyes suspiciously bright. "Clarissa, my girl," he said, his voice rough with emotion, "I love you. And no matter where your adventures take you, you'll always have a home here."

Tears pricked at Clarissa's eyes as she embraced her father. "Thank you, Papa," she whispered.

As her father placed her hand in Rafael's, Clarissa felt a thrill of excitement course through her. She gazed up at her soon-to-be husband, marvelling at how fate had brought them together.

"You look radiant, meu amor," Rafael murmured, his accent sending shivers down her spine.

Clarissa grinned mischievously. "And you, my Captain, look positively dashing."

The vicar cleared his throat. "Dearly beloved," he began, "we are gathered here today..."

As the ceremony began, Clarissa's mind wandered to the life that awaited them in Portugal. The challenges of restoring Rafael's family estate seemed less daunting now, with the promise of facing them together. And as they exchanged their vows, Clarissa knew that no matter what the future held, their love would be the compass guiding them home.

As the newly wedded couple turned to face their guests, Clarissa caught sight of her mother dabbing at her eyes with a lace handkerchief. Lady Creighton's shoulders shook with quiet sobs, her face a mixture of joy and sorrow.

"Oh, Mama," Clarissa whispered, her heart clenching. She hadn't expected her mother to be quite so emotional.

Before she could move to comfort her, Diana glided over to their mother's side, her face glowing with a secret joy. Clarissa watched as her sister leaned in close, whispering something that made Lady Creighton's eyes widen in surprise.

"What do you suppose Diana's telling her?" Rafael murmured, his hand warm on the small of Clarissa's back.

Clarissa shook her head, puzzled. "I'm not sure, but whatever it is, it seems to have worked wonders."

Indeed, Lady Creighton's tears had ceased, replaced by a beaming smile as she embraced Diana tightly. Clarissa caught her sister's eye, raising an eyebrow in silent question. Diana merely winked, patting her stomach discreetly.

"Oh!" Clarissa gasped, realisation dawning. "I do believe we're to be aunt and uncle quite soon, my dear husband."

Rafael chuckled. "It seems the Balford line is secure. Will must be overjoyed."

As if summoned by their words, the Duke of Balford appeared at Diana's side, his chest puffed out with pride. Clarissa couldn't help but giggle at the sight.

"I never thought I'd see the day when my sister outshone me at my own wedding," she teased, her eyes sparkling with mirth.

Rafael kissed her cheek. "Impossible, meu amor. You outshine the sun itself."

Their tender moment was interrupted by a familiar laugh. Clarissa turned to see Marianne approaching, her vibrant red hair a stark contrast to her elegant gown.

"Congratulations, you two," Marianne said warmly, embracing Clarissa. "I do hope you'll forgive me for not standing up with you. The twins have quite worn me out."

Clarissa squeezed her friend's hand. "Of course, darling. We're just honoured you could make it at all."

Clarissa's eyes swept the room, taking in the joyous faces of her family and friends. Yet, a pang of sadness tugged at her heart. She turned to Rafael, her voice low and tinged with regret.

"Oh, Rafael, I only wish your mother and Isabella could be here to share this moment with us."

Rafael's eyes softened as he gazed at his bride. He cupped her face gently, his calloused thumb brushing her cheek. "My darling Clarissa, do not let it trouble you. We shall have a grand celebration when we return home. One that will make even the most extravagant Portuguese wedding pale in comparison."

Clarissa leaned into his touch, her lips curving into a small smile. "Promise?"

"On my honour as a de Silva," Rafael vowed, his voice rich with sincerity. "Isabella will be positively giddy with excitement. She's been pestering me about planning a festa since I wrote to her of our engagement."

Clarissa chuckled, picturing Rafael's spirited sister fussing over decorations and guest lists. "I can only imagine. And your mother? Will she approve of her son marrying an impertinent English girl?"

Rafael's laugh was warm and reassuring. "My mother already adores you, meu amor. She's been praying for years that I'd find a woman strong enough to match my stubborn nature. She and Isabella very nearly pushed me out of Torre da Rochedo to sail to England to fetch you home!"

"Well," Clarissa said, her eyes twinkling with mischief, "I suppose I'll have to do my best to live up to her expectations."

Four weeks later

Clarissa stood at the wheel of the Santa Dorotéia, her hands grasping the polished wooden spokes, Rafael a steady presence at her back as she steered the ship through the Atlantic waves. The salty sea breeze whipped her hair, and she could taste the tang of salt on her lips.

"We should discuss our plans when we arrive home," Rafael murmured in her ear. "The vineyard won't restore itself, after all, and Mario will want to take Isabella to his home in Italy sooner rather than later, I think, so we will lose his expertise."

Clarissa nodded, her mind already racing with ideas. "I've been thinking about that. What if we..."

Clarissa's voice trailed off as the Santa Dorotéia gave a sudden lurch. She stumbled, but Rafael's strong arms caught her, steadying her against his chest.

"What if we what, meu amor?" Rafael prompted, brushing warm kisses against her cheek.

Clarissa gathered her thoughts, leaning back against him so she could look up at his face. "What if we diversified? I've been reading about new agricultural techniques. Perhaps we could introduce some different crops alongside the grapes?"

Rafael's eyebrows rose, a mix of surprise and admiration crossing his features. "I'm impressed. You've certainly been putting that lively mind of yours to good use."

"Well," she retorted with a grin, "I couldn't very well let you have all the fun planning our future, could I?"

A shout from the crow's nest made them both look ahead, and within just a few minutes the coast of Portugal began to materialise on the horizon. Clarissa felt a flutter of excitement in her stomach. This was it – the beginning of their new life together.

"It's so beautiful," she breathed, drinking in the sight of the sun-drenched cliffs and sparkling sea.

Rafael's arm tightened around her waist. "Welcome to my home, my love."

Clarissa turned to face him, her heart full. "Our home," she corrected softly.

As their lips met in a tender kiss, Clarissa knew that whatever challenges lay ahead, they would face them together. With Rafael by her side, she was ready for any adventures life might bring.

The End

I hope you've enjoyed *The Blushing Brides* series! Look out for my new series *The Brides of Belle Haven*, coming soon!

ALSO BY CATHERINE BILSON

You can find more information about all Catherine's books at her website, catherinebilson.com

The Blushing Brides Series

An Earl For Ellen

A Marquis For Marianne

A Duke For Diana

A Captain For Clarissa

The Brides of Belle Haven series (beginning 2024)

A Bride For Belle Haven (prequel novella)

Good Golly, Miss Molly

Miss Anna's Mistake

Miss Clara and the Marquess

Miss Eliza Takes Charge

Regency Novellas

Phoebe And The Pea

Kidnapping Lord Blaymire

The Captain's Runaway Bride

The Bride Said No

St. George and the River Horse

Christmas Courting (collection of novellas)

American Pioneer Romance

Coming From California

Returning From Rhode Island

Pride & Prejudice Variations

The Best Of Relations

Infamous Relations

A Christmas Miracle At Longbourn

Mr Bingley's Bride

Grief and Grievances

The Second Mrs. Bennet

A Loss At Longbourn

The Meddling Matlocks

The Secret Diary of Anne de Bourgh (forthcoming)

Lydia and the Colonel (forthcoming)

www.ingramcontent.com/pod-product-compliance
Lightning Source LLC
Chambersburg PA
CBHW030348310726
48979CB00001B/222

* 9 7 8 1 9 2 3 1 9 5 0 8 0 *